I0587716

Summoned

Siren Prophecy 3

by

Tricia Barr, Jesse Booth, Joanna Reeder,
Alessandra Jay & Angel Leya

SHIFTER ACADEMY

Summoned, Siren Prophecy 3, Shifter Academy

Copyright © 2019 by Tricia Barr

All rights reserved. This book or any portion thereof may not be reproduced or used in any manner whatsoever without the express written permission of the publisher except for the use of brief quotations in a book review.

Printed in the United States of America

First Printing, 2019

Any references to historical events, real people, or real places are used fictitiously. Names, characters, and places are of the author's imagination.

Cover image by Kim Cunningham

Published by Tricia Barr
First printed edition 2019

www.theshifteracademy.com

CHAPTER 1

Myreen

Lost.

Myreen had never felt more lost than she did when she allowed Draven to pull her to the surface of Lake Michigan. The battle was lost. All hope was lost. And there seemed to be no chance of any of it being found again.

Getting smaller and smaller down below her was everyone in the world she had left to care about—except Kenzie, of course, who was hopefully safe with her mom and grandmother miles away. Myreen took the smallest bit of comfort in knowing her sacrifice had bought her fellow shifters some time.

But she had no idea what awaited her in Draven's custody. And she dreaded finding out.

The closer they got to the surface, the faster her heart galloped, as if it could race out of her body and escape.

At last they emerged, the frigid Chicago winter air biting her wet cheeks and nose like a vampire—like it too wanted a piece of her. And she was running out of pieces to spare.

The world above was dark, and she could hardly make out the white faces that hovered above the water, looking down on her and her captor. Draven tugged her closer until her wandering hands ran into the outer shell of a boat, and white arms reached down to pull them both out of the water.

Someone wrapped a large towel around Myreen, and another offered her a dry pair of jeans. Even though she couldn't see a thing in this darkness, these creatures of the night could probably see every inch of her with crystal clarity. But she couldn't find it in her to care. She slipped into the jeans and pretended that a dozen or more vampire eyes weren't watching.

At the same time, Draven pulled off his diving mask and disrobed his wetsuit with the aid of at least three of his loyal followers. Once she was again fully clothed, he sat beside her on the bench in the boat.

"Let's go home, shall we?" he said, voice smooth as dark chocolate. His tone assumed far too much familiarity, as did his closeness. As if he really was her father.

What did he want from her? He'd supposedly spent her whole life looking for her. What was he going to do now that he had her? She'd heard stories of what he did to shifters, and right now those stories flashed horrible scenarios inside her mind— images of her on a stretcher, bound and gagged as he experimented on her. Tortured her. Who knew what else?

But she didn't get the sense that he wanted to hurt her. That scared her the most.

The boat engine turned on, and wind whipped at her hair and face as they sped across the lake. No one said a thing. Or made any movements at all. The vampires were all so still and silent, she felt like she was the only person on the lake for miles—like the others were all mannequins. She imagined that they weren't much different, just hollow beings without souls. She caught the eye of one who sat across from her, and his eyes glistened in the shadows, like glass. *Yup, hollow.*

The boat rounded a bend, and suddenly there was light shining at them from the front of a helicopter several yards from the rapidly approaching shore. The boat docked unceremoniously, and more white arms helped her out, guiding her toward the copter. Its spinning blades threw the cold night air back at her.

She allowed them to hoist her up into her seat, and Draven entered right behind her, never allowing more than a foot of distance to spread between him and his new prize. Her mind told her not to let him too close, but her body wouldn't register the threat. She was just too numb, like an emotional switch had been flipped off. Besides, she was surrounded by vampires, creatures who thrived on the blood of humans and killed shifters for sport. The cab of the helicopter was a cramped space, and she had no choice but to be shoulder-to-shoulder with at least one of them. There was no sense in fearing one of them more than the others—or at least her alarm system didn't think so.

The helicopter rocked as it left the ground, but soon stabilized. Myreen hugged her arms against her to keep them from making contact with anyone else.

"I know this will be hard for you to believe, but I've been looking forward to this day for a very long time, Myreen," Draven said.

His voice sent a chill up her spine, but she didn't respond in any other way. She picked a diamond shape in the plating on the floor and stared at it with strict determination.

"That's alright. You don't have to talk to me. But it's a long flight to Washington." Draven crossed his arms and leaned back, making himself comfortable.

Washington? Where is he taking me?

But she didn't say a word. She kept staring at that little metal diamond, clenching her jaw firmly shut the whole way.

Hours passed in this fashion. No one said anything else to her, but Draven made idle conversation with his followers. Words were only spoken when Draven talked first. She got the impression that his followers weren't allowed to talk to or around him unless directly invited to. What manner of leader was he?

She didn't know how long they'd been flying, only that she was getting very tired. But she didn't dare shut her eyes for longer than a blink.

"And there she is," Draven announced, leaning forward to wave his hand toward the windshield. "Your new home. Heritage Prep."

Myreen broke her gaze away from her diamond to look out the window. A towering black castle rose against the lightening pre-dawn sky. Tall pointed towers stretched upwards, giving Myreen the impression of upside-down vampire fangs taking a bite out of the sky. A fitting dwelling for the vampire leader. The building was dark and beautiful, just like he was, and she was sure it held just as much evil behind its façade.

The helicopter landed on the widest part of the roof, surrounded by towers. An attendant outside pulled open the door, and everyone in the cabin squeezed against the walls to allow Draven to exit first. Draven waited outside the door, but Myreen didn't budge, and for a moment, no one else did, either. After a pause, one of the vampires decided to move toward the door.

Draven back-handed him across the face, slamming him into the cabin wall and denting the metal.

"Didn't your mother ever teach you that ladies always go first?" Draven said with a deadly calm. Somehow that made him even more terrifying than if he'd yelled it.

Myreen jumped at the sudden assault. Draven just hurt his own lacky. And for something as innocent as not wanting to wait for a stubborn girl to get out of a vehicle! The vampire doubled over in obvious pain. She didn't know him, but she didn't want more people getting hurt on her behalf. There'd been enough of that tonight.

She hopped to her feet and climbed out of the copter. Draven took her hand and helped her to the rooftop. Though her hands were chilled by the winter air, Draven's were infinitely colder, intensifying their repellence.

"I'm sorry about that," Draven said, keeping hold of her hand and tucking it under his other arm, as if to act as her escort. "Good help is so hard to find. Come, let me show you to your room."

Touching him made her cringe, but try as she might, she couldn't pull her hand out of his grip. He didn't even seem to notice she was trying.

He led her toward what appeared to be the only door on the roof, which another attendant opened as they approached. They went inside, and were it not for the sconces casting their orange glow on the black walls, Myreen would have thought she'd entered night itself. Everything was black—the walls, the floor, the ceiling. It was hugely unsettling. And the white of the skin of those around her was such a striking contrast that they almost seemed to shine like the moon.

They went down a narrow staircase and came out into a wide area. Several staircases were nestled in black cylinders, which at first appeared to be oversized pillars. He led her past an elevator and down another flight of steps.

As Draven tugged her through the halls, vampires stopped and stood with their backs against the walls until he passed, few of them daring to cast their eyes above waist level. *You know someone is bad when even his followers are terrified of him...*

Black banners hung along the walls, bearing some sort of logo—a large red drop symbol in the middle of the words HERITAGE PREP. *What kind of place is this?*

Finally, he paraded her back up a set of stairs, through the large room again—or at least one that looked similar, she couldn't be sure—and up one of the winding staircases. He stopped when they reached a landing with a door and released her hand, which she jerked away.

Draven gave her a black card with the same red drop on it as the banners. "This will be your new room. If you need anything, knock on the door and your attendants will get you whatever you want. They'll be standing outside your door at all times." He gestured to the two bulky, white-faced men on either side of the door.

The thought crossed her mind to refuse the keycard, but the heaviness of her eyelids made a private space too tempting to resist. She took the card with a snap and glared at him straight in the eyes. She wasn't going to show him the same fear everyone else around here did. She wasn't going to give him that kind of power over her.

"So I'm to be your prisoner then?" she asked behind gritted teeth.

Draven smirked, a twinkle in his blue eyes. "You haven't seen your room yet. I'd hardly call your accommodations a prison. Besides, the dungeons are in the basement."

"Accommodations I'm not allowed to leave," she hissed,

narrowing her eyes further.

"On the contrary," he replied with a shrug. "You're allowed to go anywhere within the walls of this school, granted you're accompanied by a chaperone."

School? This place is a school? She snorted, even though this answer surprised her.

"Get some rest. We'll talk first thing at dusk." With that, Draven turned on his heel and was suddenly out of sight.

His preternatural speed was only one of the many disturbing things she'd seen tonight, so rather than dwell on it, she ran the keycard through the scanner and escaped into her new confines, pressing her back tightly against the door as it closed. As if her meager weight could keep a vampire out.

After a deep, cleansing breath, she opened her eyes and took in her surroundings. Draven wasn't lying about the room; it was the most lavishly-furnished birdcage she'd ever seen. There was a huge canopy bed across from the door, elegantly carved in black wood and adorned with dark red sheets, curtains, and more pillows than she could ever want or need. To the left of the bed was a closet that she could see was fully-stocked with colorful clothing, some that appealed to her even from where she stood. There were several matching black dressers, and a bookshelf filled with books. And most of the wall catty-corner to the bed was a giant TV screen, at least five times bigger than any TV she'd ever seen in person. The carpet was plush and the color of fresh blood, and though she wasn't a fan of red, she appreciated the deviation from black.

Slowly, she peeled her back off the door and made her way across the lake of blood that her carpet resembled, to the bed that beckoned her aching body. She sat on it, loving the cush beneath her. The sheets were velvet and begged to be nuzzled.

She didn't trust sleeping in this place, but she was so tired, and if Draven was planning on hurting her, he would have done it already.

Finally, she gave in to her only desire and slipped under the covers, sleep consuming her as soon as she closed her eyes.

***

Bang, bang, bang.

Myreen snapped to consciousness with a fright, hands instantly roaming for anything she could use as a weapon. Her eyes adjusting to the rude awakening. Nothing was amiss in her empty room. She climbed out of bed and crept forward, scanning the shadows in the corners.

"Just let me see her," she heard a voice outside the door say. It sounded familiar, but in her slightly disoriented state, she couldn't place it. After all, how could anyone she knew be here?

"Lord Draven said she is not to be disturbed," responded another voice she assumed belonged to one of the guards.

"Lord Draven has given me special privileges. Or have you forgotten?"

Silence for a moment. Myreen didn't realize that she was on her tiptoes until another set of bangs caused her to trip forward.

"Myreen, please open the door," that same familiar voice insisted.

Her soul knew that voice, but her mind said it wasn't possible. It had to be some trick. Draven playing a sick game. And yet, she found herself edging closer.

She hovered in front of the door, her hand resting on the knob. She told herself not to open it, but her curiosity got the better of her. And she reminded herself that if a vampire really wanted to get in, it wouldn't matter if she opened it or not.

She turned the knob and cracked the door enough to peek

outside.

The handsome, sandy-blond-haired, beach-blue-eyed merman stood on the other side. Myreen gasped, frozen in disbelief as Kendall pushed inside and wrapped his arms around her.

This was no vampire trick. His skin was caramel colored and warm, something she didn't expect to find in this place. But then again, she didn't expect to find him here, either.

The initial shock of his appearance wore off as the memory of his betrayal returned. She shoved him away and took several steps back, hugging herself.

"You really did it," she accused. "You really came *here*? To Draven? What, so you could sell your knowledge of me for protection?"

Kendall pursed his lips bracingly. But as he hesitated, the truth dawned on her.

"You're the reason he attacked the school!" she gasped. "You told him where it is. Dozens of mer died because of you! And hundreds of shifters may still die if the glass gives!" She shoved him again, all her anger and sorrow flooding into the assault as she thrust him against the door.

"Ow," he winced. "Myreen, I'm sorry, but I had no choice." He took a step closer.

"No choice?" she yelled back. "You *had* a choice, and you chose wrong! Do you have any idea what you've done? How many lives you've doomed?"

"They were doomed anyway," he insisted. "Draven was going to find the Dome one way or another. I've foreseen it, remember? And if he attacked the school with you inside and didn't know, you could have died. Don't you see that I'm trying to save you?"

"Oh, don't give me that crap," she snapped. "You saved

yourself and sacrificed everyone else. I can't believe that you actually came here. I had no idea what happened to you after you left. You could've died coming here. Even after what you did, I still..." She bit her tongue, hating that she still cared about him, after all this time, even now. The anger boiling up roused the ursa within, and she didn't know if she could contain it. But then, why would she want to? "And to find you here, safe and sound and bossing vampires around. So, what, you're Draven's pet or something?"

"I'm one of his advisors," Kendall replied with an air of pride. The way he said it made her want to slap him, but she feared she'd scratch his face clean off if she did. "A seer is too valuable a prize to kill."

"That's too bad," she hissed, injecting anger into every word.

He closed his eyes, visibly stung.

"I know you think you hate me for my actions," he said, brows creasing in a way that made him look disgustingly cute. "But I did what I did for you. For *us*."

"Don't give me that crap. You saved yourself and sold everyone else for that safety."

"And what would you rather I have done? Wait around in that fishbowl to die with everyone else? When the vampires attacked, you got out. You saved yourself, too."

Her anger was at a tipping point, and she could feel the fur bristling underneath the goosebumps on her arms. "I didn't save myself! I left to save everyone else! You think I give a flying feather what happens to me? I'd give everything to save the people I love."

"And that's exactly what I did," Kendall declared, stomping his foot as he neared her. "I gave up everything and everyone to ensure that you'd be safe. You may not care what happens to you, but I do."

Red tinged the periphery of her vision, her muscles itching with the prickle of an imminent transformation. "Get out," she growled.

Kendall startled and tripped backward. He squinted at her in confusion and fear, but swiftly recovered and stood tall.

"I'll give you some time," he said, backing toward the door. "But I'm not giving up on you. One day, I hope you know just how much you mean to me." His blue eyes lingered on her with a desperate intensity for a moment before he turned and left.

That look reached something inside her, something that soothed the beast within enough for her to regain control of her breathing, as Mr. Coltar had shown her. She closed her eyes and took several deep breaths, feeling the prickle and the anger subside.

Calm now, she sat on the bed and stared at the red carpet.

Maybe she should've let the ursa out. See how much damage she could inflict before the vamps could take her out.

CHAPTER 2

Kenzie

Kenzie sat at the kitchen table, eating a bowl of Lucky Charms. Her stomach was still in knots from everything, but at least it was accepting food again.

Wes still rested on the couch in the living room, though his sleep wasn't altogether peaceful. He'd had a few thrashing episodes, and each one sent Kenzie into a panic. What if something was wrong? There was no way to know until he woke up, and he'd passed out nearly two days ago.

Meanwhile, Leif was rotting in Heritage Prep. She'd used her magic to contact him once or twice, but conversations were difficult when he was so weak. What the heck were they doing to him? She broke down and cried about it last night, but she knew what she had to do. She just didn't know how she was going to pull it off.

Thankfully, Mom and Gram hadn't missed the grimoire

yet. They'd been too busy tending to Wes.

Mom popped into the kitchen and grabbed a cup of yogurt from the fridge. "I have to go out and deal with Mrs. Parson. It's a bit of a drive, so I'll be gone for a while." She cast a worried glance at Wes, who thankfully was still as a stone. Kenzie followed her gaze a moment longer, making sure his chest still rose and fell in steady motions. "Your grandmother is working on her own stuff, but if you need her for anything, or Wes wakes up, please go get her immediately."

Kenzie smiled briefly and nodded, then continued chewing on her latest spoonful of cereal.

"Kenzie. I'm serious. If Wes wakes up—"

"I know. I know. I go to Gram. I've got it."

Mom stared at Wes as she downed her yogurt, but he continued to look peaceful. She sighed as she put her emptied cup on the counter. "I just need you to be careful. First shifts can be rather... volatile. And he's not staying."

Kenzie rolled her eyes. "I know! Go! Please?"

Mom pursed her lips, but nodded. "I'll be back as soon as I can. And I'll leave my phone on. I love you."

"Love you too," Kenzie said before shoveling another mouthful of marshmallowy goodness in. She'd gotten almost all the cereal bits out and was looking forward to the sugar rush she was about to get.

Her phone beeped from where it rested on the table, and Kenzie pulled it over. The text she saw from Juliet left her feeling numb.

Juliet: Myreen surrendered herself 2 Draven 2 save the Dome. I'm freaking out. We have 2 save her! :-O

What the heck? Kenzie shot back, then dropped her phone on the table like it was hot.

Why in the world would Myreen surrender to the vampires? Kenzie's stomach groaned, but she couldn't bring herself to finish filling the void.

The phone beeped and she snatched it again.

Juliet: I know!!! What do we do?

Kenzie shook her head. Well, now she had *two* very important reasons to go to the vampires. And chances were, they'd take Myreen to the same place they were keeping Leif. At least, she hoped so.

Me: I've got it covered, J. Any idea how to enroll in a vampire school?

Kenzie bit her lower lip. Yeah, that looked as crazy on the screen as it sounded in her head.

Juliet: A vampire school? What are you talking about?

Kenzie frowned at the text. She'd just assumed the shifters knew about the vampire school, but maybe they didn't.

Me: Just trying to find the best way behind enemy lines.

Juliet: Are you insane???

Kenzie laughed.

Me: Yup.

Juliet: I'm coming with you.

Kenzie shook her head.

Me: No way. Just hold down the fort till I get back. I'll make sure I get credits that will transfer. ;-)

Kenzie silenced her phone, her stomach churning. Again. She didn't even want the marshmallows anymore. She threw the rest of her breakfast away and headed for the office. Maybe a little time with the grimoire would calm her nerves. Or help her find a way out of this mess.

She wasn't sure how long she studied, but maybe an hour in, she heard Wes moan from the couch. Kenzie spit out the spell to hide the grimoire and was by his side a moment later. It wasn't like it was the first time he'd made a noise, but that didn't stop her from checking on him.

"Uhn, where am I?" Wes asked, his eyes fluttering open.

Kenzie gave him a half-smile as she let out a long breath. "Yo mamas."

Wes's brows creased, then bent upwards. "No, I— Kenzie. You're still with me."

Kenzie snorted. "Actually, you're still here. Mom and Gram decided not to throw you out on your hunter butt until after your first shift." And she should be running to Gram right now, but Kenzie didn't want to leave him just yet. It was stupid, but she almost felt like if she took her eyes off him, he might fall back asleep and never wake up.

Wes's brows creased again, then he laid back with another groan and closed his eyes. "The mao."

"Yeah. What exactly happened?"

"I was tracking this girl and I got ambushed by more of her kind."

Kenzie smirked. "A girl, huh? That was quick."

"What? No, not like that. Kenzie, you can't—"

Kenzie snickered. "Relax. And they're *your* kind, now. Congrats, by the way."

Wes bolted into a sitting position, and Kenzie scooted back. Wes groaned at the sudden movement, but he still had enough energy to glare. "Really? Congrats? My whole life is ruined because of them."

Kenzie held up her palms. "Hey, sorry. But to be fair, if you hadn't been hunting them, you wouldn't have gotten bit."

Wes snarled. "Yeah, because weres are known for keeping their disease to themselves."

Kenzie's brows rose. "Excuse me? If you're gonna be rude, you can leave."

The anger melted, and Kenzie could have sworn she saw Wes pale. "You're not going to... to kick me out, are you?"

Kenzie shook her head. "Not my call." She stood. "You're probably hungry."

Wes grabbed her hand and gently pulled her until she sat on the couch next to him. His fingers traced Kenzie's jaw, leaving her body tingling with goosebumps. "I missed you, you know?" he said, his voice low.

Kenzie gasped and blinked, trying to bring her brain back into focus. "Who, me? I thought hunters hated everything non-human."

Wes grimaced. "I'm supposed to. But I couldn't, not with you." He pulled her forehead to his and closed his eyes.

Kenzie's lips itched to taste Wes's, but her mom's warning rang in the back of her head. This was his first shift. He'd be emotional. And if she wasn't careful, he might mark her, whatever that meant—there was no way she was having that kind of a conversation with her mom, of all people. And she liked Wes, but she wasn't sure if it was a forever kind of love. Being marked as his mate was out of the question.

Carefully, she pulled back from Wes, willing her racing heart to calm and the rush of longing to simmer. Truth was, she'd missed him too.

She had to change the subject. "You're a hunter. What do you know about the vampire school?"

"The one in Washington?"

Kenzie shrugged. "Is there another?"

Wes shook his head. "Not that I know of. It's nutso. Most people there actually want to become vampires. They're supposed to be brilliant, but I can't believe that's true. I mean, who would want to be a vampire?"

Kenzie thought of Adam, and then of Leif. Adam would make a horrible vampire—and sinfully sexy, to be sure. Leif was probably one of the best people she had ever met. Period. They couldn't be more different, despite both being in the vampire camp, so to speak.

"Like, how brilliant do you have to be to get in?"

Wes narrowed his gaze. "You're not thinking of enrolling, are you?"

Kenzie stood, tugging on a strand of hair. "Sort of?"

Wes shook his head, his eyes glowing a dangerous red color.

Kenzie whirled on him. "I have friends in there, and I'm not going to just let them rot!" She glanced at the thin wall that separated her townhome from Gram's and chewed on her lower lip.

"Kenzie, they'll rip you apart." Wes had his hands in his hair, making the strands stick up at odd angles. She hoped this conversation wouldn't force him to shift early.

Still, Kenzie folded her arms. "I'm a selkie. I have magic."

"They move faster than you can speak your spells."

"Then I'll just have to be smart about it!"

"I don't think—" he said, pointing to his neck.

"Not like that, thank you very much. Ugh!" Kenzie threw her hands in the air. "I'm not asking for your blessing, I'm just asking if you know anything that will make this easier. I should go tell Gram you're up." She turned to leave, but Wes rushed to her and caught her hand again.

"I'm sorry," he said, and she let her head loll as she turned back to him. "I just... I lost you once. I don't think I can do it again."

Kenzie peeled her fingers from his, injecting as much firm

calmness into her voice as she could muster, though she couldn't bring herself to meet his gaze. "You can't lose what you never had."

"Kenzie..."

She looked him in the eyes. "If you really care about me like you think you do, you'll let me go save my friends."

Wes took a deep breath, lacing his fingers with hers. "Then I'll go with you."

"No. It's not exactly subtle, bringing a hunter mao with me."

Wes growled. "Stupid shifters."

"Hey! If it weren't for those shifters, you'd have no idea I was going anywhere."

He examined their twined fingers, then sighed. "I guess. I just hate feeling helpless."

Kenzie snickered. "Welcome to my world. I only recently got enough magic to change that."

"But if you're going in, you need to have something they want. Something they can't get right away."

Kenzie thought again of Leif, and an idea bloomed. "What about daywalking?"

Wes's gaze shot to her face, his brows lifting into his granola hair—which of course looked more adorable than normal. Kinda shaggy. Dang shifters. "You can do that?"

Kenzie shrugged. "I guess. It's in the grimoire." A small smile worked at the corner of her mouth as she considered the selkie who had turned Leif into a daywalker—a selkie she'd just found out she was related to. It was almost no wonder Leif had held onto his love for Gemma all this time.

"You can't! It's not natural. Vampires shouldn't be able to walk during the day. I've already seen one of those." Wes shuddered.

"You have?" She'd suspected he'd seen Leif at some point,

but the thought of the two of them running into each other...
She couldn't face that kind of possibility. Not with everything
else hanging over her head

"Yeah, Kenz. It's not right. They're way too powerful as it
is. Giving them daywalking abilities will all but ensure they
achieve their goal of taking over the world. There's gotta be
something else you could give them."

Kenzie folded her arms. "Like what?"

"Your... your..."

"Look, I'm open to ideas, but I don't see any other way. Do
you?"

Wes was quiet for a few moments. "No." He sighed, closing
his eyes. "Just, don't go turning them all into daywalkers, okay?"

Kenzie snorted. "Yeah, not exactly my dream scenario,
either." *Though, not all vampires are bad.* But she didn't want to
get him riled back up again, so she kept that thought to herself.

"I really should go tell Gram you're up. My mom will kill
me if she finds out I talked to you unsupervised."

Wes's brows scrunched. "Why?"

Kenzie blushed and ducked her head. "I'll let someone else
explain. Just, sit down and pretend like we haven't been talking,
or something." She waved her hand around the room, then
bolted for the front door.

She stopped in her tracks when she saw Gram sitting on the
porch swing. The chill winter air was still too cold for Gram to
be out here for the fun of it.

"How much did you hear?" Kenzie asked.

"Enough."

"Okay. Well, sum it up for me."

"Wes is up, it sounds like he's pretty serious about you,
maybe even the other way around, and you're going to a vampire

school to rescue your friends. Sound about right?"

Kenzie sighed, sitting next to Gram. Her teeth were beginning to chatter, but she didn't want to have this conversation in front of Wes. "Are you gonna tell Mom?"

Gram pursed her lips. "I ought to. Lita will kill me if she ever finds out. How do you know your friends haven't been turned?"

Kenzie hung her head. "One was a vampire when I met him. The other is Myreen, and I have to believe she's still her."

"Myreen I understand, but you're rescuing a vampire from other vampires?"

"He's not like the rest, Gram."

"Oh?"

"And he didn't kill anyone."

"Kenzie, he's a vampire. Anyone who's lived long enough with that kind of thirst has killed someone."

Kenzie pulled her lips in and clamped down on them.

"But occasionally there are vampires worth their salt. It's not often. Becoming a vampire changes a person on the most fundamental of levels."

"He's a good one, Gram. I swear."

"And do you love him, too?"

Kenzie looked down at her lap. "I don't know what he is to me. But if nothing else, he's a good friend. And they're torturing him. Gram, he sounded so weak the last time I talked to him."

Gram sighed. "Then I don't suppose there's any stopping you. You already have the grimoire."

Kenzie's head shot up. "When did you find out?"

Gram laughed. "I found it missing earlier this morning. Don't worry, I haven't told your mom yet."

"Why?" Kenzie whispered, guilt eating at her. She'd done

nothing to deserve her grandmother's help. She'd gone against everything they'd told her not to do, keeping secrets, caring for Wes at such a volatile time, trying to handle everything on her own.

"Because somewhere, your Mom and I forgot what we wanted you to be. We raised you to be strong and ambitious and loving—and you are all of that and more—and then we tried to lock all that in a cage. We wanted to keep you safe."

"But after what happened with Dad—"

"It's no excuse. We've had time to mourn that very tragic mistake and move on, but we didn't. And for that, I'm sorry."

Tears welled in Kenzie's eyes. It was all so backwards, but she couldn't be more grateful for Gram's support than in this moment.

"I'll cover for you here. And I'll need you to contact me—daily, if possible."

Kenzie sniffed, wiping the tears dripping off her chin. "There's a spell for that. Claoigha." She laughed, swiping at her still-leaking eyes. "Just say that and think of who you want to talk to. Better than cell reception."

Gram smiled and pulled Kenzie into a warm hug, and they stayed that way for several long moments.

"When are you planning on leaving?" Gram asked, finally breaking the silence.

"I'm trying to wait for Wes to make his first shift."

"The full moon is tomorrow. That usually pushes them over the edge."

Kenzie smiled. "*I'm* pretty good for pushing people over the edge."

Gram laughed. "Yes, you are, but no need to press your luck with a mao on their first shift. I'm just glad he woke up before the moon waxed full. No telling what would've happened if he woke during his first shift."

Kenzie let out a long breath. "Yeah. Lucky guy."

Gram winked. "He's got you, doesn't he?"

Kenzie blushed. "Sort of."

"Never mind. You just get yourself back safe and we can sort through the rest later. Together."

Kenzie jutted out her bottom lip and gave Gram another hug.

"Now, let's get inside before we freeze our arses off."

Kenzie snickered and shook her head. She definitely took after Gram. And it was nice to know she had the woman in her corner. She had a feeling she'd need it.

Hold on Leif and Myreen. I'm coming for you guys.

Kol

Kol's snout ground through the wet-compacted sand, filling his nose and mouth on impact. A wave washed in a second later, adding salt water to the mix and burning his nostrils and eyes. The deep laceration where his wing connected to his body stung. The damned creature had nearly ripped it clean off.

Krakens didn't fight fair.

And besides, it was tricky to fight one when he was more comfortable in the air. He imagined Myreen would have a better chance.

Myreen...

The image of her blue eyes looking at him as she *willingly* left with that wretched vampire burned into his retinas. The image taunted him. It haunted his dreams. All he thought about day and night was how he could save her.

Even if she did hate him forever because of a hellish curse.

The burning in his chest was suddenly more than the actual fire within, but he didn't care. He finally knew why his mother stayed with his father all these years, despite loving and not being loved in return. Because love made a person do crazy things, even if it meant a lifetime of torture.

He was in love with Myreen. That was for sure.

Taking advantage of Kol's momentary pause, a translucent grayish-pink tentacle wrapped around Kol's ankle, dragging him back to the sea. The color, and thickness, and *sliminess* of it made him want to vomit.

But this time Kol was prepared. Seconds before he and the tentacle submerged and rendered his fire useless, he tucked his chin to his chest and breathed white-hot flames along his chest and abdomen. The fire didn't hurt him, but it charred the flesh gripping his leg instantly. The appendage let go and curled in on itself, making a sickly sizzle when it sunk into the waves.

Of course, it had plenty of limbs to replace that one. Two uninjured tentacles shot out to grip him again, but he twisted and managed to clamp both between his powerful jaws first, piercing them in several places for a sure hold. They wrapped themselves around his snout in defense, but he'd counted on that. He pumped his wings, taking to the air with a massive splash.

Higher and higher he flew, carting the giant *squid*—technically an octopus, but *squid* somehow felt more derogatory, more fitting an enemy—along with him as it twisted, attempting to wrap itself more firmly around him. Being three times Kol's size, he struggled with the weight, but his grip held firm. Still, he found himself again falling closer and closer to the depths with each beat of his wings.

Digging deep, his patience won out, and he managed to reach a height that would ensure instant death when he finally released the kraken. The stain that bloomed against the deep blue below and the sinking of the motionless monster was proof.

He'd barely had a moment's breath—feeling near weightless with the kraken's weight gone—before something appeared in the distance.

His next attacker.

Kol groaned. He thought dispatching a *kraken* would be the last of the tests. He'd beaten a horde of vampires, a dozen hunters, several enemy nagas and a gryphon who looked a lot like Oberon. There had even been a dark-haired mer who very nearly managed to manipulate his blood. The sim wouldn't actually kill him that way, but he nearly failed. *Nearly.*

Certainly he was done by now?

He'd studied the videos, but the tests were never the same, so they didn't help. Even if a student failed a hundred times, the program would give them a new test each attempt. It was all about skill and strength, nothing about algorithms or patterns in the system. And in all the videos, not a single student had been required to do as much in order to pass.

And yet another threat raced toward him.

Instead of racing at it, like he had the others, Kol hovered in the air and took advantage of his momentary reprieve. Catching his breath and watching the blue dot grow closer, he noticed it flew like a dragon, but he was surprised it wasn't another invisible one.

Surely an *invisible* dragon would be the ultimate test. But he'd already beat one—while Myreen watched. Perhaps that had been enough?

As the dragon grew closer, the shade of royal blue seemed very familiar. His large dragon heart skittered as it neared.

"Char?" he asked when he knew without a doubt it could

be no one else. *No, it's just a simulation*, he thought. *She's not really here.*

"Hi, Kol," she said, almost shyly. "Miss me?" she asked, then attacked.

Throwing himself into auto pilot, he barreled and rolled through the air, snapping at claws and wings without once sinking into flesh. She did the same, clipping the tip of his tail once and slashing at his already injured wing.

But it felt different. *She* felt different. Like she was really here and not a part of the sim.

Kol hadn't seen Charlotte Izabella Stern—blonde hair, brown eyes, *royal blue scales*—since she tested out last year and left the Dome to enlist. They'd known each other almost their entire lives, so it was a bit strange that he hadn't thought about her much after she left. Just when Eduard passed along that greeting from her on Christmas day. It was especially weird since they'd been friends most of their lives, and were on the verge of becoming more right before she left. Well... that's what *she* wanted. Kol never viewed her beyond a friend except that one stolen moment that fizzled before it was anything.

Kol rammed into her. The force knocked them both from the sky and they plummeted several feet below the surface of the water, sending millions of tiny bubbles racing to the surface. They both immediately recovered and were back in the air within a handful of seconds.

His parents would have rejoiced if he and Char had become something more. His and hers, actually. When he was ten, and she eleven, their parents had unofficially arranged them to be *married* when they grew up. With the curse, any attachment was bound to be one-sided eventually, and her parents knew that.

Still, arranged marriages were how the Dracul's survived.

"You've improved, Kol," she said, a little breathless.

She's just part of the sim, he reminded himself as he used her momentary pause to swipe at the scales along her side, leaving deep red slashes. Neither of them bothered to use fire, since it was pointless, but it also meant they had to be touching to injure the other. Sim-Char took Kol's closeness as an opportunity to bite down on his shoulder.

He cried out, but she held firm, gripping him with all four claws, keeping him close before releasing her jaw.

"Let's move this to dry ground, shall we?"

Just a sim. She's just part of the sim.

Maybe they were finally reaching the end. "Alright," he said, using the hind leg that was free to grip her calf.

Sim-Char released all but one of her claws, keeping a firm, painful hold on his hip and they flew in an awkward, limping fashion back to the beach.

A thick forest of palm trees and ferns carpeted the tiny island, leaving only a small stretch of white sand around its borders. Just enough room for two or three rows of beach-goers if the island wasn't deserted.

Or fictional.

Just like Char.

Planting their feet in the soft sand, Charlotte immediately shifted back to her human form, revealing her military smart-clothing that somehow made her blonde hair look whiter—and it had been quite a bit longer when he'd last seen her. Now it barely brushed against her jaw.

But her eyes looked the same. Soft brown, and... safe. Char had always been *safe.* Maybe it was because he loved her the way he loved his sister, Tatiana.

Despite suddenly feeling *safe,* Kol's heart sped again, and he braced himself for a continuation of the fight. Who would've guessed the grand finale of his test would be against the sim version of a dear friend in their human form?

She laughed, her smile spreading to her eyes, and crossed her arms over her chest casually.

Kol's eyebrows pinched. "What?" he asked, not relaxing in case it was a trick. "Aren't you gonna fight me?"

Char shook her head again and looked down at her toes, which were partially hidden in the sand. "They know you can fight," she said. "That's not your final test."

She dropped her arms and sauntered toward him. "The vampires, the hunters," she said.

She looks just like her, Kol thought with each step. He reminded himself again that she wasn't actually there.

"The nagas," she continued. "Although I thought the look-alike of Oberon was a little cruel." Her mouth twisted in disgust as she said it in a low voice. Almost like she didn't want the teachers and his father who were watching the test to hear. "You were brilliant with that kraken—I don't think the sim has unleashed that thing on anyone else." She stopped when they were only a few feet apart.

"And yet, you're my final test?" Kol scoffed, falling into the familiar banter he used to have with the real Charlotte. "Who's afraid of a tiny dragon girl?"

She laughed again, and he found himself smiling for the first time since Kenzie had *supposedly* lifted the curse and he thought he could begin a life with Myreen. That had been the best and worst day of his life.

"And that mer... *whew!*" Sim-Char threw her hands in the air. "With that dark hair, she almost looked like..."

Actually, she had looked more like Alessandra than Myreen,

but the intent was obvious.

"It's a good thing the sim can't actually kill you," she added.

"It wouldn't have mattered," Kol said, his tone leveling while his brain calculated just what he needed to do to win. "I beat her anyway."

"She's gone, Kol," Char said, at a near-whisper. "She chose to leave and... join *him.*"

Kol gulped. *Just a sim. Just a sim.* But he'd suddenly forgotten that he wasn't supposed to miss Char. Seeing her here, he *did* miss her.

Char reached up—she had to reach high—to flick the lock of hair that had fallen into his eyes. In the motion, he could smell the salt mixed with the flowery scent of her skin.

He suddenly had the urge to kiss her, to wrap her in his arms and close his eyes and pretend that he was kissing Myreen. He could see in her eyes that she wanted it, too.

Sim-Char wanted it.

And he remembered that he had at least a dozen eyes on him. Tests weren't closed to other students, so it was possible that the entire school was watching this strange final test with the fake version of a person he'd long forgotten.

He wanted to disappear. He wanted to find this fake-island in the real world and wallow on it until he was old and gray. Or until everyone who was watching had forgotten all about Kol's final test.

Of course, that was ridiculous. He wouldn't disappear because he had to find Myreen. Somehow. But the feeling of mortification was potent.

Just disappear, just disappear.

Sim-Char's face suddenly shifted into a confused expression before she took a few steps back.

He watched her closely, waiting for whatever came next.

"Kol?" she asked, looking on either side of her and turning as if he was behind her. "Kol?" She walked past him and toward the tree line.

Kol looked down at his hands—which weren't there. He'd done it. He'd managed to use his invisibility power in *human* form.

"Bravo, Malkolm!" Eduard's voice boomed. He appeared as the sim scene pixelated back into white walls.

Kol stared at him, a little stunned at the last part of the test. But his father couldn't see him, so he evaporated the invisibility.

When Kol was finally visible, Eduard clapped a hand on his shoulder. "I'd heard reports of your skill, but that was magnificent!" Pride rolled from his father. He looked legitimately impressed.

Kol beamed.

"You must join the military at once!"

And just like that, Kol's mood deflated.

"Now son," Eduard frowned. "You knew this was an eventuality. We could really use your skill."

"We really could," a small voice said. It was Char, looking just like she had seconds ago.

Charlotte wasn't part of the sim.

***

He'd done it. Kol tested out of defense class—although many of the students and teachers were confused about the way his had gone. None of them had ever seen a test quite like Kol's. Some suspected Mr. Suzuki made adjustments to the program before he resigned and left with Oberon.

Kol suspected Eduard was the actual reason for the change. After all, he had his own kitsunes at his disposal. And he'd been the one to bring Char in.

After congratulations and handshakes, Kol escaped to his room feeling very much betrayed by someone he once thought a friend. But it wasn't like him to pout long, and at the urging of Nik and Brett, he found Char near the fountains.

Their actual reunion was a mixture of Kol shouting at her for her part in his test, and her shouting at him that he needed to grow up and if it weren't for her, he might never have learned to use his invisible powers as a human. But mostly they were just glad to see each other. Kol left out the part about forgetting her very existence the second she left the school.

She told him about her adventures in the shifter military. And he told her about Myreen... though he left out the part about activating the curse. He wasn't sure he wanted to rehash his stupidity.

But Char acted slightly different after hearing that. He didn't regret it. It felt like he actually had his friend back.

"You really should consider joining," Char said, her voice suddenly soft. "Draven is getting dangerous and we could use someone with your skills." She stared at the ground, picking at the grass.

Kol ran both hands through his hair, gripping tightly. "I know he's dangerous." He heard the edge in his tone—the edge that meant he might snap any second. "Don't you think I know? He took Myreen!"

But his anger didn't scare Charlotte because she yanked his hands away. "Don't do it because Eduard told you to!" she said, her voice injected with confidence and force again. "Look, I agreed to come to help *you*. Not because he ordered me to. I knew you had it in you and I'm sorry it played out the way it did. But we *need* you Kol. All of us." She paused and blew out a breath—perhaps to hold back the threatening tears Kol could see building in her light-brown eyes. She smiled, then shoved him lightly. "*Shifterkind* needs you, Malkolm Torq Dracul."

Kol shook his head and rolled his eyes. "I have to get her back, Charlotte Izabella Stern." He winked at her, but then fell serious. "I have to get her back. I have to find a way."

"Then tell him! Look, I bet you can demand the world right now. You may be his son, but the general *needs* you!"

"What do you mean?"

Char shrugged. "Tell him you'll join on one condition." She paused. Probably for effect or something, but Kol only found it annoying.

"What's my condition?" he asked, not wanting to play this game.

"Tell him you'll enlist in his precious shifter military if he puts you on the team that's going after Myreen." She said it nonchalantly, but her attitude suddenly shifted into bubbling excitement that leaked out in her smile.

Kol's eyes widened. "There's a team going after her? To rescue her?" Hope welled beneath his ribcage. It was a dangerous kind of hope, but he was a glutton for anything that might bring Myreen back.

Even if she hated him forever.

Char brushed her fingernails against her shoulder, then blew on them. "Yep!" she said with a mock-haughty air. "And I'm leading that team."

Juliet

Tossing and turning couldn't quite describe how Juliet spent the last few nights. She couldn't sleep. And it affected her mood immensely, leaving her unstable and prone to clumsiness. Again.

But despite her fury against her dad, her worry because of Myreen, and all the changes Lord Dracul brought to the Dome, glee still filled her heart, all because of Nik. Occasionally, she'd felt guilty for being so selfish, but more often than not, she'd hold onto that happy feeling like a buoy.

The only downside with being back together was that her mind was on overdrive, always spinning in circles. She wished she could talk to her dad about it, but Malachai was on his high horse and wouldn't budge.

She tried to confront Malachai the morning after she heard the news, but he brushed it off—as if Lord Dracul being in charge of the Dome was better for her safety. She tried again the next day. And the next. *Still* he ignored her prying.

So today when she'd awoken, she skipped her first class, fearing that she couldn't control her emotions well enough. Even one more little change could completely set her off—and she didn't want to know how the new director would punish her for losing control.

But not even that little bit of rest had been enough.

Juliet's hands squeezed into fists as she stared at the closed door of her dad's office, trying to find the nerve to knock. It wasn't like talking to him would get her anywhere, but she didn't want to stop trying—no matter how annoying she was being.

She took a deep breath and banged on the door twice.

Malachai's deep voice mumbled, "Enter."

Juliet took another deep breath, straightened her spine, and pulled the letter out of her back pocket. She entered his office and beelined straight to his desk where he sat with his head buried in a pile of papers. When he saw her, his head fell back, and he let out a sigh.

Juliet wanted to blow up. Sure, she'd been annoying, but she didn't think he'd be so cross at the mere sight of her.

"Nice to see you too, *Dad*." She slammed the letter down on top of his pile and paced the space in front of his desk. Malachai unfolded the crumbled paper, but Juliet didn't give him a chance to get through it. There wasn't anything there he hadn't seen before.

"How could you be okay with all of this?" she asked, her voice rising in pitch. "How is cutting time for art and music okay? And now we have an *offensive* training class? Seriously, that's a disaster waiting to happen!" She barely took a breath as she made her speech, but she'd waited so long for this moment with Malachai. Her *father*. "We're learning military strategies and the history of warfare! How do you expect me to be okay with the new expectations of your lame boss?"

"Juliet Quinn, watch the way you speak about General Dracul. There are eyes and ears everywhere." He used his stern voice, but it was laced with concern.

"Oooh, I'm shaking in my boots. Why won't you answer any of my questions? I just don't understand any of this. No one does. And you're my *dad*. Shouldn't you be giving me some words of encouragement or something? Instead of icing me out? I thought we were finally getting somewhere, then you go and join this bully's lackey club." It was borderline disrespectful, and she didn't like it, but she had to get through to him.

"Watch your tone. What I do is none of your business and I don't need your permission. And I absolutely do not have to explain myself. What I *will* tell you is that I have obligations to the school and a contract that I can't just walk away from. You will no longer burden me with interrogations like this. Understood?" Malachai stood, towering over Juliet as he peered at her with hard, stubborn eyes.

"Loud and clear." Juliet grabbed the letter and spun around. She huffed and puffed the whole walk to the door, but stopped with her hand on the knob. "You've lost me once over a decision like this. It looks like you're on that same path. I hope your precious leader is worth pushing me away. Again."

She refused to look back to see the look on his face—or to let him see the look of guilt on hers. The doorknob was heavy as she slammed the door closed, the cool metal the only thing keeping her hands from overheating. She had to get control of her emotions and she had to do it fast.

Usually, she'd stop by her dad's office to let him know when she was having a rough day. And usually he'd let her off the hook for a class or two—or the whole day. But not anymore. Not with them being on non-speaking terms. No, today she'd go AWOL, rather than seeking his permission. Although, hitting the defense room wasn't exactly hiding out. Anyone could find her there. But she needed to let the steam off before she lost control of her powers.

She made a quick stop to her room to change into her workout gear, leaving her phone on her bed. She didn't want to be reached. She wanted to focus on hitting the punching bag over and over and over again without wondering if her dad would apologize through text message. He wouldn't, but still.

Juliet raced to the Defense Room, practically falling over her feet when she saw who was inside. Men wearing the same uniform that looked so handsome on Nik patrolled the defense room, scanning the faces of those inside as if sizing up who to recruit next. Juliet scowled. If she was going to have soldiers breathing down her neck while she tried to ground herself, there was definitely going to be a fire accident.

Pulling her headphones securely over her ears, Juliet roamed the room with eyes of steel. She stared down every guard she passed until she reached the boxing corner. She needed to hit some*thing* before she hit some*one*. So punching bag it was. She hit play on her #GirlBoss playlist—not to spite the guys she'd dated, but to spite the man in charge and all the robots he brought with him. Excluding Nik, of course.

For the next half hour, Juliet focused on the punching bag only. She got lost in the music and let her frustration out through her jabs and hooks. She worked up quite the sweat, but moved on to the treadmill for a two-mile run before heading back to the punching bag.

When she finally felt the anger leave her, she turned off her playlist and headed toward the exit.

But a soldier blocked her path.

And just like that, her fury was back.

"What? Am I not allowed to shower?" she huffed.

"Every student must do a minimum of one sim fight after training." He wore a straight face, but she still couldn't quite believe it.

"Excuse me?" She knew the rules, but this was ridiculous. "That was *extra* practice! I've already completed my *vampire kill* quota." Her heart rate picked back up, and this time it wasn't from the workout rush. Okay, so maybe she hadn't done a sim today, seeing how she'd skipped all her classes, but that really was an extra workout, not her normal training time. "You've got to be kidding me."

"Do I look like a comedian?"

Juliet cringed. Her hands began to sizzle white hot, but a voice from behind the soldier spoke up.

"She can join me for mine. Thanks, buddy." Jesse patted the disturbed guard on his shoulder, then stepped past him and toward Juliet. Surprisingly, the mean man walked away without another word.

"Thanks. I almost just lit him a new one. Seriously, though? Like, what the heck is next? We're gonna work ourselves to death. I hate this." Juliet wished she had the bag next to her again, so she'd have something besides Jesses to hit. But her sore muscles weren't as ready for another round.

Jesse walked with her toward the sim room where another soldier gave them an eyebrow raise before punching in some code.

"It could be worse." Jesse's tone had a sad lilt—hopefully it wasn't because he'd heard that she was back with Nik. Still, he looked calm and collected, even as the walls changed and three vampires appeared before them.

"How are you so zen about this? It's unfair and you know it," Juliet said when they'd finished. It was fun whipping out her fire-rope again in a non-life-threatening situation, but she was so ready to be done. She stumbled a step or two, feeling a bit light-headed. She was probably dehydrated. "And I thought you'd do better with a bunch of sim-vamps." *She'd* killed all of them.

"Well, I'm not *zen*. But personally, I'd like to stay off their radar." He gave her a tight smile, and it ripped her heart in half. "After Kol tested out of defense today, none of us want to fight to our true potential. Afraid of receiving the same offer he got. None of *my* friends want to join up, at least." Jesse shrugged, then picked up some blue boxing gloves hanging on the wall just outside the sim room

"I didn't know about Kol," Juliet said quietly, speaking more to herself.

"A word of advice?" Jesse offered.

She nodded.

"Don't squeeze in any more *extra* practices. One of the recently-turned hounds passed out this morning because the soldiers wouldn't let her have a break."

"Thanks," Juliet said. Her feet felt like lead, her arms like wood, and she just wanted to curl up somewhere dark and warm. She'd *way* overdone it—and not by choice.

Jesse shrugged, then winked. "Thanks for dispatching those vamps for me."

Juliet smiled. It was nice to know that Jesse was still there for her as a friend.

***

Juliet and Nik's secret spot in the library felt like it was theirs again, and it was the perfect retreat from the chaos of Lord

Dracul. Juliet spent the rest of her day there, since she could barely move after her workout. She waited, hoping Nik would join her when he could. She still didn't have her phone to check, but she assumed he would show eventually. Her emotions were so out of whack that she didn't want to be found by anyone that wasn't Nik.

Or Myreen, but that couldn't happen.

Frustrated, Juliet sat cross-legged on the dusty floor. With her hands in front of her, she closed her eyes and welcomed the lingering heat in her body. She felt it collect in her stomach like a group of butterflies coming together. Focusing, she led the heat to her arms, then to her fingers. Usually, she'd feel a single spark with the release of her flames, but this time her fingertips looked like sparklers on the Fourth of July. And her fire didn't come out the red-orange color she was used to, instead blazing a blinding white. It felt bizarre, but more than that, it scared her.

Juliet shook her hands out, but they felt heavy, like she was carrying bricks. Why was she having such a hard time with her power after so much success? The uncertainty from school came to mind, as well as the rest of the emotions that ran through her.

Maybe that's all it was. *I should try again.*

With her eyes tightly closed, Juliet took a few deep breaths. She thought of her fire and the comfort it brought. She thought of the exhilaration it gave her. And she thought of the bond and control she'd had with it. Again, it started in the pit of her stomach and grew and grew until it filled her arms. That amount of fire could be dangerous, but she *needed* her fire to work. She didn't care what damage came from it.

A push of bravery was all she needed, and the thought of Myreen in the hands of vampires was all it took. Heat sparked through her fingers, the orange-red glow coming together in a beautiful, perfect sphere.

But she felt her control begin to fade. Heat turned cold, the fire in her hands turning as blue as the sky on a cloudless day, though it still glowed and flicked like flames. She didn't know what to think and didn't want to panic again, so she stuffed it back into her body. What could be wrong with her?

When Nik finally showed up, he startled her so much that she almost called to her heat. But she stopped herself before she could fail again—this time in front of someone else.

"Hey, you. Are you alright? You seem... distracted."

She knew he was just being nice. She looked like a hot mess with her hair in a haphazard bun and bags under her eyes. But with everything going on, she wanted to keep her little power troubles to herself. She didn't want to add stress on anyone else.

"I'm okay. Just gotta try to get better sleep. How was your day?" She looked away from his intense stare. He always seemed to know when she wasn't telling him everything. But he didn't push.

"It was crazy. The general... I just don't agree with any of this." Nik fell back into the empty chair and a cloud of dust blew around him. "Did you hear a student fainted in defense?"

She nodded. "I heard. A hound." Juliet buried her face in her hands. A moment later Nik wrapped his arms around her. "And yeah, you're preaching to the choir."

"And now Kol's gone," he said, his voice eerily quiet.

"I heard that, too," Juliet said, her volume matching his. "Are you okay?"

Nik sniffed, then kissed her on the head. "I'll be okay. Kol will be okay. What about you?" He rested his forehead on her shoulder.

"You're here. I'm good."

"Me too," Nik said. Juliet clung to Nik's arms, not willing

to let him go just yet. "I have good news, though." He paused, and Juliet nodded to let him know she was still listening, unsure if she could trust her voice not to wobble. "I worked out my duties so I'm positioned near the library. I'll be able to meet you here just about whenever."

Juliet nodded again. That was good. She definitely needed Nik now more than ever. And she'd tell him just how upset she was over all the changes—later.

For now, she would soak in his presence and the love he gave her. For now, she wouldn't freak out about the loss of control over her powers. For now, she'd smile and bottle her worries until there was no room left.

CHAPTER 5

Oberon

"So let me get this straight," Ren Suzuki said, his short black hair disheveled. Heavy bags were under his eyes, and he needed to shave. His patchy facial hair made him look old and worn. Oberon knew that he looked just as bad. Probably shabbier, actually. After all, Ren wasn't the one who'd been marched out of his position at the Dome. He'd left willingly.

The kitsune took a sip of his steaming cup of tea before continuing. They'd been holed up in a small hotel in Chicago, just in case anybody at the Dome reached out for help. They hadn't heard anything yet.

The room was tight, with two queen beds and a small table surrounded by a couple of chairs—where the duo now sat.

"You really have been working with a vampire behind the scenes? We've been away from the school for five days, and now you decide to tell me that bloated dragon general was right?"

Ren's incredulous tone caused Oberon's heart to flare defensively.

"I hope you, my friend, will let me explain things, unlike Eduard did," Oberon replied, his patience teetering on falling apart.

Ren scowled, his fingers turning white from squeezing his ceramic cup. "You better explain. The Oberon Rex I know would *never* have vampire dealings. Ever."

Oberon sucked in a deep breath, held it for a few moments, then released it slowly. A little bit of calmness entered his soul. "You actually met this particular vampire once, back in South Dakota."

"South Dakota?" Ren gave him a questioning look, then snorted. "I met a lot of vampires in South Dakota. I also killed most of the ones I came across."

Thinking of Leif, Oberon chuckled. "Not this one. He's not one for fighting. Although, you *did* encounter him during a fight. Remember the convenience store we visited right before the vampire attack on The Island?"

"With the doofus cashier who'd been bitten the night before?" Ren asked. "Yeah, I remember. But there were two vampires in that store."

Oberon nodded. "The male vampire is who I'm referring to."

A flicker of humor played at Ren's eyes. "The last thing I remember seeing was food and candy flying through the air after he went crashing into a stand. Like fireworks."

Ignoring the visual that came into his mind, Oberon said, "His name is Leif. And he defected a few years after The Island fell."

Ren stared at him, as if waiting to see if Oberon was trying to pull his leg. Realizing that Oberon was dead serious, he said, "Wait. How does a vampire defect? Has that ever happened before? And how in the world do you know he really defected?"

Oberon held up his hand and cast his eyes toward the light

weaving through the white curtain covering the hotel's window.

"Too many questions," he said. "Just... let me relay what happened with Leif Villers. Fifteen years ago, Delphine used her abilities and found a family of harpies in Seattle. The family had a set of triplets dealing with their first shifts all at the same time. I went to recruit them, because I knew the school could help."

"The Lowry girls," Ren said. "Yes, I remember them."

"It turns out Delphine hadn't been the only one to discover them," Oberon confirmed. "I arrived just minutes before a group of vampires converged on the Lowry household."

Ren's eyes sparked with interest.

"I shifted in an attempt to protect the Lowry family from the attackers, but I was caught off guard, and the vampires were quick. I had three on my back, holding me down before I could finish shifting, and they were far too strong for me to throw off. Manipulating the weather would've put the Lowrys at risk. And that's when Leif came."

Ren blinked once, then twice, then three times. "A vampire... turned on his own and took down three vampires?

"The three on me, yes," Oberon said with a nod. "But he killed the three other vampires going for the Lowrys first."

"Why?" Ren asked in confusion. "Don't get me wrong, I'm glad he saved your life. But why would he fight his own kind to save a few shifters?"

Oberon sighed, slumping forward. "Leif Villers is a complex man. He hates what he is. But he hates the vampire cause more. After being a part of the destruction of The Island, Leif cast himself out from among Draven's forces. After having numerous discussions with him, he moved to Chicago to keep an eye on vampire activity. There are many reasons the Dome has remained safe for as long as it has—your technology, for example, has shielded us from evil eyes.

But Leif has ensured that vampire activity has stayed at a minimum here. Until Kendall Green spilled everything to Draven."

"By my ninth tail, Oberon," Ren said. "Why haven't you told me about this before?"

Oberon chuckled. "Because I was afraid. Afraid to tell anybody about my *dealings with a vampire*." The room seemed to darken, but Oberon knew it was only his mind. "It seems I didn't have to tell anybody. Eduard was sharp enough to do the digging himself."

Ren looked into his cup of tea, which was no longer steaming, and muttered to himself.

"What's that?" Oberon asked, looking for some kind of solace from his friend.

Ren shook his head. "Just mumbling a few choice things I'd like to do to a certain fire-breather right about now. He cast you out for *protecting* the school!"

Oberon looked back at the window, hoping the light would brighten his mood. It didn't. "Eduard did what he did because vampire dealings look bad."

Ren slammed a tight fist on the small table, sloshing his tea up and over the lip of his cup, making a mess. "He did what he did because he wanted your position! He wanted Myreen!"

Oberon couldn't argue with Ren's outburst. It was true. But thinking about Eduard's true motives only stirred the boiling pot of aggravation within.

"Where is this Leif dude?" Ren asked. "He sounds like a good fellow to join our little duo of exiles."

Oberon shook his head. "I don't know. I last saw him in Canada. He was the one who supplied me with the gryphon sightings in Yukon. I haven't heard from him since."

"You mean the bad intel?" Ren questioned, raising an eyebrow.

"He was given the bad intel by Draven," Oberon defended. "I'll admit, I accused him of it at first, but he was as surprised as I was by the lack of gryphons in the area."

Ren shrugged, placing a finger in his tea and swirling its contents. "I suppose *a gryphon, a kitsune, and a vampire* is probably more of a first line for a joke, anyway." He used his fingers to make quotation marks as he named them. "Still, you should tell Delphine your story about Leif."

"Even if she knows the truth, what will she be able to do?" asked Oberon. "Eduard's in charge."

His phone, sitting upside-down on the table nearby, buzzed loudly, causing both friends to jump.

"Maybe that's your vampire buddy now," Ren said, licking his tea-covered finger, then took another sip from his cup.

Oberon turned his phone over. "It's Delphine," he mumbled, hardly believing she was actually calling.

"After five days, she realizes how much she misses you," Ren said with a smirk. "You going to answer it or what?"

The phone's vibration seemed to cause Oberon to freeze. Why would Delphine be calling? A simple check-up? Was something going on at the school? Had Myreen discovered *another* shifter form to add to her chimera repertoire?

Ren reached over and snatched the phone. Tapping the screen a few times, Ren said, "Lady Delphine, we are delighted to be graced by your melodious voice."

The funny thing is, Oberon knew there was some truth to his words. The kitsune had been infatuated with the leader of the mer ever since she'd appeared after The Island was destroyed.

"Cut it, Ren," Delphine said with a tone that was anything but melodious. Ren had put the phone on speaker mode. "Where's Oberon?"

"I hope you're doing well, too," Ren said sweetly, winking at Oberon.

Oberon shook his head. "I'm right here. How are things at the Dome?"

"Not so good, actually," Delphine said after a mild pause. "Two nights ago, we were attacked by Draven and his vampires."

Her words felt like a blow to Oberon's chest, the air taken right out of him.

"What?" Ren said, sitting straight up.

"They very nearly cracked through the top of the school," Delphine continued. "But that—that can be fixed and reinforced. The worst news is that Myreen was taken—"

"Taken?" Oberon boomed. "The military leader is directing the school and Myreen got *taken*?" What good was Eduard if he couldn't even protect the shifter world's most valuable asset?

"That's not entirely what happened," Delphine corrected. "Myreen surrendered herself on conditions that the vampire attack would end. She allowed herself to be taken to save the school."

"It's like the vampires knew you were gone," Ren whispered, arching an eyebrow.

Oberon ignored Ren, mostly because he doubted the vampire attack was based around his dismissal. Not even Draven would have known about that.

"Where did they take her?" Oberon asked.

Another pause came. "Oberon, look, I didn't call you to ask you to go after the siren. Lord Dracul has already assembled a team to do just that. It would be inadvisable to go."

Oberon found his heart thudding against his rib cage. "Then why call me? To remind me that there's nothing for me to do? That I'm a waste of space?"

"You're not a waste of space," Delphine shot back. "Right

now, you can be of more help to us outside the Dome than within. Listen. Back at the New Year's Eve Ball, I tried to tell you about a vision I had. Last night, I had the same one, and it involves you finding a flock of gryphons."

Oberon's breathing stopped, and he looked at Ren with wide eyes. "Delphine, you better not be plucking my feathers. I already got burned once based on a similar lead."

"I know that," Delphine replied. "But that info came from a non-seer. I have seen this twice now."

"Don't tell me they're at Mount Logan," Oberon said, desperation flooding his voice. He wasn't about to travel back to Yukon to see if gryphons really were there.

Delphine laughed. "Nope. No more trips to Yukon are in your future. Have you ever been to Calgary, Alberta?"

"Twice," Oberon said. "Both were trips for recruitments."

"I'd tell you to pack your bags, but something tells me they're probably still packed from when you left the Dome," Delphine said. "Your destination is the Canadian Rockies. Upon doing image searches online, I've determined that you'll want to go to the remote location of Mount Joffre."

Like the heat from Ren's cup of tea, hopelessness faded from Oberon's heart. Ever since leaving the school he'd lost his sense of direction. Being purposeless was debilitating. Going after Myreen would've been his preferred purpose, but with the surety of Delphine's vision, finding more gryphons was a worthy alternative.

"Thank you, Delphine," Oberon said. "We'll leave as soon as possible."

"You're more than welcome," replied the mermaid. "I'll keep adding funds to your account as necessary. Traveling won't be cheap, especially for two."

"Again, thank you," Oberon said. "You're likely taking a

risk reaching out to me behind Eduard's back."

"This falls outside of the general's domain," she said with a snarky tone that made Oberon grin. "I don't know your reasons for your vampire dealings, but I do know you, and there isn't anybody in the world I trust more."

"You'll have to let Oberon tell you about his vampire friend sometime," Ren said. "It'll make you appreciate the big bird even more."

"Another time," Delphine said. "But I must be on my way. Classes won't teach themselves."

"We'll keep you posted on our findings," Oberon said. "In the meantime, give the students my best."

"I will," replied Delphine. "Good luck, both of you."

The call ended, and Oberon made eye contact with Ren.

"I don't know, Ren," he sighed. "At this point, the Myreen incident seems far more important than finding a group of gryphons."

"If Lord Dracul has things covered, then let him take care of it," said Ren, sweeping his hand through the air nonchalantly. "We're not exactly military, anyway. Besides, it's always been your dream to find more of your people. This is the perfect opportunity."

"You don't understand," replied Oberon. "Myreen is our only hope to end Draven. And due to my recent history with Eduard, you can imagine I don't exactly trust his capabilities when it comes to Myreen."

"So what, you want to go storm the vampire castle and rescue the damsel in distress?" Ren laughed. "Don't get me wrong—my mind has been pushing me to get more involved in the fight, too, but the two of us charging into the vampire hideout seems like an excellent way to die. Really fast."

Oberon set his jaw and glared at his friend. "Coward." He regretted the word as soon as he said it. Ren flinched as if he'd been slapped. "Hey, I'm sorry. It's just that a few weeks ago, you were begging me to allow you leave of the Dome so you could run off and join the military. Where's that drive now?"

Ren's typically-humored eyes sank.

"Chances are, if Delphine knows about a flock of gryphons, so do the vamps. Something tells me we'll be seeing enough action in our future."

"So we just abandon Myreen?"

Ren shook his head. "Delphine said the general will execute a plan to bring her back. This is a military task. Let the wondrous Lord Dracul try. Tell you what: if he fails, we can talk about our own *mer-aculous* rescue mission. I'll even document it, then upload it to ShifterTube." The kitsune held his hands up, gripping an invisible camera while humming a random theme song.

Oberon grunted, sitting back and folding his arms. Eduard didn't have the scales to pull off the rescue operation. But whatever plans the general *did* have might be foiled worse if Oberon went barreling into the middle of it.

"Fine," he said at last.

They sat there in awkward silence for some time, and Oberon twiddled his thumbs.

"You know, I've never been to Canada," Ren said, breaking the quietness. "I hear it's pretty. But let me tell you this. If we bring a bunch of Canadian gryphons back to the school, they'll be setting the expectations pretty high."

Oberon furrowed his brow. "Why's that?"

"Because they're so used to getting *eh's*."

It was a dumb joke, and Oberon knew it. Still, he found himself laughing. A weight had been lifted off his shoulders. There were still other gryphons in the world, and he was about to find them.

Myreen

"Good evening, Myreen. May I come in?"

Draven.

Though she'd been expecting to hear that voice for hours, it still quickened her heart rate as it resonated from the other side of the door. The fact that a few inches of metal sat between them offered little solace.

She swallowed, attempting to recover, to build courage. "Would it stop you if I say no?"

"Of course. You're the only one with a key. This door won't open without your direct consent, and contrary to what I assume you believe, it's framed with copper and as such is impenetrable to vampires. You can stay in that room by yourself for as long as you desire. However, you are only mortal, so you will eventually starve." He paused. "And I have no intention of leaving until I've spoken to you."

Myreen perched on the edge of her bed, rooted by

indecision. She was pretty convinced by now that he wasn't going to hurt her; he'd had ample opportunities to do so, and he gave her this gorgeous suite. But assuming he did just want to talk, she didn't want to hear what he had to say. He was the notorious vampire villain who was to blame for the attack on the Dome, the attacks that almost killed Alessandra and Kol, and the attack that *did* kill her mother. Whatever words came out of his mouth were guaranteed to be lies—or laced with venom. Either way, she wasn't interested.

But she *was* getting hungry. Would a school for vampires even have food? How long could she hole up in this lavishly-furnished prison cell? Especially since it became clear after Kendall's visit that sleeping here was going to be just about impossible.

Finally, she decided to get it over with. She crossed the room and opened the door just enough to look out. He was alone, dressed in a fancy black suit and shoes that outshined his glossy, marble-like eyes. He smiled at her, the kind of smile that could disarm a high-security vault. Her chest warmed, but she shook it off, reminding herself that charming people was what vampires did, and that she mustn't let her guard down.

She opened the door all the way, planting her hands on her hips as he strode into the room. Closing the door, she kept him in sight the whole time, scowling as he made himself comfortable at the foot of her bed.

"What do you want with me?" she asked, crossing her arms.

With his knees apart, he leaned forward, resting his elbows on his thighs and lacing his fingers together between them. "I know this will be hard for you to believe, but all I want—all I've ever wanted—is to have the father-daughter relationship that was stolen from me."

She snorted loudly and rolled her eyes.

"It's the truth," he said with a shrug. "Your mother no doubt spent your whole life turning you against me, but I've spent your whole life trying to get you back. Both of you." His brows creased, making his expression heartwarmingly vulnerable. She could almost believe that he truly cared.

"Is that why you killed her?" Myreen shot at him with every ounce of snark she could inject.

A red spark of anger flashed in his dark eyes. "*I* did not kill her. The fool I sent to fetch you both did, and I can assure you he has been *fully* dealt with." The look on his face was the epitome of deadly, and for the first time since she'd handed herself over, fear of him flooded her.

She pulled her gaze from his face. She had to, otherwise she'd be paralyzed by that fear. She had to continue playing the rebellious teenager, because if she gave in to the fear she knew Draven had earned a thousand times over, she'd be useless.

"So you think you can force me to abandon everything and everyone I care about and we'll just start fresh and be a happy family?" She kept her eyes down as she spoke, not yet ready to look at him again.

There was a rustle of fabric as he stood, and from the corner of her eye she saw him come toward her. She forced herself not to flinch.

"And what was it that I forced you to leave behind?" he asked, now standing less than two feet from her. "Young Kendall tells me you weren't quite welcome there, that the mer refused to accept you and made your life miserable."

Draven's insight into her life caught her off guard, and she couldn't help but look at him with surprise. He seemed to enjoy that, satisfaction tugging at the corners of his lips underneath those deceptive eyes.

"The mer were less than welcoming, yes, but I still managed to make true friends outside my species." She thought of Juliet and Nik, and even Kol, and a sting pierced her heart. But she kept her expression unwavering. "Because you stole my mother from me, they were the only family I had left, and now you've taken that from me, too."

His hands were on her shoulders in a flash, and she did jump this time. "I *loved* your mother." The sincerity in his voice stunned her. "Zaia was my match. We had the same goal—to create a lasting peace between all species of supernaturals. It broke my heart the day she ran away, and her death wounded me as greatly as it did you."

Myreen swallowed. "If peace with the shifters is what you want, then why did you attack the Dome? Why have you been attacking shifters for decades?"

He released his grip on her shoulders and took a step back. "You think we're the ones who struck the first blow?" He shook his head. "You're so new to the shifter world. How could you know our history? No, it was they who started hunting us. There was a time, centuries ago, that vampires and shifters lived separately, autonomous of each other, yet harmonious in our domains. But the adoration of the mortals over whom we reigned gave us great power, and the shifters felt threatened. The Draculs led an army against us, wiping out thousands of vampires. We've been battling ever since. But I dream of a world where that's no longer necessary."

That wasn't the way she remembered the story. But she only read the shifter version of history, and there were always two sides.

"And how do you plan to bring peace? Your vampires killed dozens of mer today, and if I hadn't come out, they would've flooded the Dome and killed every shifter inside. Tell me how war ever brings peace."

Draven looked down, nodding and pursing his lips. "Yes, that would've been an unfortunate turn of events. I didn't want to kill them, but every war has necessary casualties. And I would've gladly paid that price if it meant getting you back. You see, Myreen, you're the key to the peace I dream of."

His sapphire eyes bored into her, and for a moment she felt like the most important person in the world.

"M– me?" she asked, putting her hand to her chest and taking a step backward. Did he know about the prophecy? Was it his intention to kill her after all? Was all this just some twisted game?

"Yes. Within your blood lies the key to linking vampires and shifters once and for all."

"M– my blood?" And then she remembered what Kendall told her the night he attempted to drag her off to Draven. Myreen was the result of DNA experimentation, the one successful chimera. He thought he could use her blood to create a hybrid: a vampire shifter. He was the reason she was such a freak. "So that's what you're really after? The guinea pig of your experiments? If that's the case, then why this charade?" She waved her hands at the room. "Why not just take my blood and be done be with me?" After the words came out, she bit her tongue so hard she thought it might bleed. *Why not just ask him to kill you, Myreen?*

"Because I meant what I said about wanting to be a family. If your mother hadn't gotten cold feet, we would've been a very happy family all these years. But I've missed out on so much of your life. I want that time back. I want to earn your trust, be the father you never had."

The question of who her father was had always plagued her.

She loved her mom, but she always wondered what life would've been like with a dad. Would they have stayed in one place? Lived a normal life? Would she have siblings? A dad was the longest-held, secret desire of her heart. With her mom gone, the concept of a true family was incredibly tempting. And Draven was terribly convincing. She couldn't see the seam in his façade. Could he really be telling the truth? Could the infamous vampire leader really be a bleeding heart deep down?

"And what about my blood?" she asked, her tone noticeably less hostile.

"I do need it for my plan to work," Draven said bluntly. "But I won't take it from you by force. I want you on my side. I only have one condition: that you never use your powers against me. So long as you abide by this one simple rule, I'll wait until you offer me your blood willingly."

The terms seemed fair enough. "And if I never offer it willingly?"

Draven held her gaze for a moment, and for the first time, she saw whispers of her reflection in his features. He had the same thick black eyebrows, the same hairline framing his face. There was no denying the family resemblance now that she recognized it.

"I have faith that you'll come around. In the meantime, there's someone I'd like you to meet."

He brushed past her and opened the door—being sure to only touch the inside—and stuck his arm out, curling his finger in a come-hither motion. Myreen leaned forward, apprehensive yet curious.

A boy no older than ten walked in. He looked like a miniature version of Draven—same head of shiny black hair, same dark blue eyes, even carrying himself with the same dignified posture, assuming a sense of nobility. The only difference was that he was cute as button and pink-skinned, and he exuded an innocence Draven could never fake.

The boy stood beside Draven, who draped his hand over the boy's shoulder. "This is Tyberius Denholm. He's my son and heir... and your little brother."

Myreen gasped. *I... I have a brother?*

"Hello, Myreen," Tyberius said with a nod of his cute little head. "I've been looking forward to meeting you for a long time." He smiled, and her heart warmed instantly to him. Just as with Draven, the family resemblance was obvious.

"Hello," she felt compelled to say back.

Draven looked at his son. "Tyberius, would you do Myreen the honor of showing her around the castle? She's not yet had a proper tour."

"Of course, Father," Tyberius said with strict obedience.

"When you're finished, report to your chambers for dinner. You'll both need a hearty meal after such an excursion."

"Yes, Father."

Draven patted Tyberius's head, careful not to ruffle his hair. "Well, I leave you both to it." Draven smiled diplomatically and turned for the open door. But then he stopped and looked over his shoulder. "Oh, and Myreen, please don't do anything foolish. The security here is quite extensive, and it would devastate me to see you injured." Then he disappeared without so much as a change in the air, his silent threat hanging like a cloud over her head.

But the door was open, and young Tyberius had taken her hand and was tugging her toward the stairwell beyond. She felt uneasy about leaving the presumed safety of these four walls, but the morbid curiosity of seeing the inside of Draven's secret headquarters pressed her forward.

And despite Draven's warning, an escape attempt was inevitable. She'd need to know every inch of this place if she had any hope of being successful.

They exited the room and proceeded down the stairwell. Myreen was keenly aware of the fact that her two guards followed them. She wasn't sure if she was comforted or uneased by their presence.

"This is my room," Tyberius said, pointing to a door as they passed. "Our rooms are right on top of each other, so you can come visit me any time." His tone was so restrained, which was odd for such a youthful voice. Like he was always holding back any strong emotions he may be feeling. "If you want," he added with a shrug.

Myreen's previously creased brows smoothed. "I'd like that." She offered a small smile, and he smiled back briefly before continuing to guide her forward.

"We're in the tallest tower of the castle," he explained. "Only the Elite live up here."

They came to the large room she remembered going through before, and Tyberius led her to an elevator tucked between some pillars. He tugged her inside as the doors slid open, the guards following behind. The light inside was surprisingly dim, intensifying Myreen's claustrophobia. Tyberius slid his keycard through a slot by the door, then pushed a button as the doors closed, and they descended.

When the elevator stopped, the four of them walked into a central foyer from which it seemed all other rooms branched. It was filled with both vampires and humans bustling about. The sight of so much warm flesh in this place was alarming, like seeing cattle roaming obliviously through a pack of drooling wolves.

"This is the Great Hall," Tyberius said. "Through those

doors are the training rooms and the conference room, and over there is the library. The kitchen is towards the back. And the human's quarters are downstairs. I'm not allowed to go there." He leaned close and whispered, "At dawn, all the vampires start setting up for classes, and I sneak into the kitchen sometimes for a snack."

She wanted to smile at his confiding in her, but she couldn't get over the disturbing mix of living and dead around her.

"Tyberius, why are there so many humans here? Don't they know...?" She stopped, unsure if Tyberius was even capable of understanding the question, or if he was aware that his father was a vampire and he was human.

He nodded with understanding beyond his years. "The humans are here because they want to become vampires. The transformation is the greatest honor anyone can ever receive. They study below until they can prove they deserve the privilege."

Her heart thudded. He was completely brainwashed. Pity stabbed at her gut.

"What happens to the ones who don't make the cut?" she asked, even though she knew the answer.

He shrugged. "They become donors."

"Donors," she repeated. What a clever yet calloused word for it. Her stomach twisted.

Tyberius showed her all the places of leisure in the castle: the library, the game room, the spa where humans were nervously eager to massage and please, the pool—which Myreen's skin and inner tail ached for. But for all the prettiness that she saw, she knew ugliness hid elsewhere. Tyberius said the human's quarters were downstairs. She doubted they were as nice as her room.

After the tour, they went back up the elevator—using a

separate entrance on the top level of the school—and rode it back to the large room with the pillars.

Tyberius hadn't let go of her hand through the entire walk, and holding his little hand gave her more comfort than she ever expected to find in this place. So warm and frail. She held onto him as tightly as he held onto her.

"Father says we're to eat breakfast in my room," he said, leading her there.

At his door, he slid his keycard through the scanner and went inside. His room was nothing like she expected. The décor was all red, like her room, but the space was much bigger. In one corner stood a long, rectangular dining table made of the same black wood as her bed, and a serving table sat against the wall. In the opposite corner was his bed—smaller than hers, the four-poster bed was covered in sheets depicting some popular kid's show—and at the foot of the bed was a round, plush carpet, where a toy chest sat wide open. In the middle of the room was a desk, behind which was a freshly wiped, free-standing dry erase board.

"Tyberius, do you ever get to leave this room?"

"Of course," was all he said.

"Do you... eat all your meals in here?"

"Yes. Father says it's unbecoming of the Heir to eat with humans."

"So you always eat alone?"

He shook his head, his black tufts of hair swaying as he did. "Agnus eats with me. And sometimes Father comes, too. And now, I have you." He smiled so big it made her heart hurt.

"What about school? Do you go to school?"

"He's given the best education money can buy," a dry female voice interrupted from the left corner of the room. Myreen turned to see a middle-aged woman emerge from a hidden door in the wall. She approached Myreen with a cold smile on her stern face. "You must be the Master's daughter, Myreen. I've waited a very long time to meet you. I'm Agnes, Ty's governess."

"Ty?" Myreen asked, looking down at Tyberius.

"Agnes calls me that," he said, bouncing on his heels playfully. "You can, too, if you want. My name *is* kind of long."

Myreen smiled warmly at him. "Alright then, Ty it is."

"Come, let's eat," Agnus said, gesturing toward the table where more human servants who had emerged from the secret door were arranging silverware and plates loaded with food.

Ty ran to the table and dug into a tower of pancakes. Myreen helped herself to the second tallest pancake mountain and began to eat as well, and Agnus joined them and ate slowly, her eyes boring into Myreen the whole time.

"How do you like it here so far, Myreen?" Agnus asked after wiping her lips with a napkin.

I was pretty much kidnapped, sacrificing my freedom for everyone I love. What do you think? That's what she wanted to say. But she didn't want to upset Ty. Regardless of what he'd already been exposed to in this godforsaken place, she wanted to preserve whatever innocence he had left.

"Fine," was what she finally decided to go with, then shoved another fork load of fluffy cake into her mouth.

"Well, I hope you grow to like it," Agnus said. "This is your home now, and we're very glad to have you. Aren't we, Ty?"

"Mm-hmm!" Ty mumbled with stuffed cheeks and syrup-glossed lips.

"Tyberius, what have I told you about speaking with your mouth full?" Agnus chided.

Ty swallowed loudly. "Technically, I didn't speak, I hummed."

Agnus scowled at him. "That's not the point. You must always remember your manners. You're to be the Master one day."

"Yes, ma'am," he said, his tone agreeable even as he privately rolled his eyes.

"Do you always have pancakes for dinner?" Myreen asked, hoping to lighten the mood.

Ty shook his head. "No. But pancakes are my favorite, so we have them for pretty much every special occasion."

Myreen nodded, picking at her food again. She had a thousand questions bouncing around in her mind. Questions about Ty's childhood and upbringing, about Agnus and why on earth a human would choose to knowingly work for a vampire dictator, or why the countless humans below would want to become vampires, themselves. This place was news to her, and she suspected no shifter knew it even existed. That the vampires would have a school of their own like the Dome, but with such a dark and twisted purpose, was just mind-boggling.

But she didn't want to ask any of those questions in front of Ty. She would wait. As everyone had made quite plain to her, she would be at the citadel for a very long time—plenty of time to find answers for herself. At least she had *something* look forward to, however bleak.

Juliet

Extra defense classes.

Added offensive classes.

Required simulations.

Juliet was having nightmares—not about *actual* vampires, but about *simulation* vampires that were somehow becoming stronger and taking over the school. Thank goodness the actual simulation vamps were following the rules.

Too bad *she* wasn't a sim. The new "school rules" and schedule were tempting Juliet's rebellious side.

She'd heard of sim sessions that went into the night because someone wasn't *up to par*. And more than one student had been sent to Miss Heather for exhaustion.

Keeping her worries bottled made it worse.

Her father was definitely right about one thing: there were eyes and ears *everywhere* now. It seemed like every corner held a guard just waiting to narc on someone.

She wanted to tell Nik just how furious and unbalanced she felt. He'd shown disdain toward Lord Dracul and his new rules, too. But it never seemed like the right time to commiserate, and in a way, she was afraid Nik was worse off.

Juliet was tempted to start a riot. They were kids, not the general's good little soldiers. But if she did, her dad would probably never forgive her. So instead, she just daydreamed about causing an uproar. It wasn't like she had the energy for much else these days, anyway. The rules were so strict and the training so rigorous that if she did have extra time, she was too tired to do anything but crash.

Or sneak away to *their* library spot at any and every free chance. Like she was doing right now.

A guard stood just inside the library, in a spot where he could see pretty much everything. Nik was there, too, making her heart flutter. He let the other guard perform his duties, giving Juliet a quick wink behind the other guy's back.

The guard definitely took his job seriously.

After assuring him she'd done her morning training and that she needed to study for a history exam, Juliet had to pick a random book out of a section she'd never been in and act like she was reading it. Something about governing bodies in world history. Ugh. But she had to time her escape perfectly.

Finally, a few students walked in. As Nik leaned in to say something to the other guard, who was busily assessing the students, Juliet took her shot. With one fluid movement, Juliet ducked and ran in the direction of her and Nik's secret place.

When she arrived, out of breath and afraid of getting caught, she almost squealed when Nik slid in behind her. Juliet bent over and tried to catch her breath as Nik put an arm over her shoulders.

"Are you okay, Jules?" Nik whispered.

"Yes, just sick of this." Juliet spoke through her teeth, her voice coming out harsh. Enough for Nik to take a step away. *Not* how she wanted him to know how she really felt. She stood straight and regulated her breathing. "Sorry. I hate sneaking around. And if they catch either one of us in here, they'll never let us come back."

"I know. This is how it was at the base. But we signed up for that. But the Dome?" Nik wrung his hands as he sat in the dusty old chair. "We need Oberon back."

"Yeah, try telling that to your boss. Can't you say something to him?"

"Really? You think it's that easy? I'm replaceable, Juliet. I'm not Kol. And even if I were, he wouldn't listen. You don't know the General. He'd kill me just for a suggestion. And then my dad would revive me just to kill me again." Nik's voice rose, causing Juliet to cringe. But maybe pushing him was a good thing. She wanted them to be on the same page.

And now, it seemed like they were finally getting there.

Juliet kneeled next to where Nik sat, and she grabbed his hands. His palms were sweaty and there was a slight tremble to them. "I'm sorry. I didn't mean to assume that he'd listen. I'm just as frustrated as you are. As are many other students. I— *we*—just want things to go back to the way they used to be."

"I do, too. I really do. Oberon should be here. I don't even... Jules, those younger kids hate me. I can see it in their eyes and I don't blame them." Nik withdrew his hand.

Juliet's stomach churned. Nik had been ordered to run sparring drills with a group of younger students, pushing them farther than he liked. He'd been melancholy ever since. It was a side of Nik she hadn't seen before. But she could still see the fire in his eyes, sense the dragon wanting to come out. Oddly, Juliet thought it was hot. But this wasn't the right time to be flustered, so she stood and spun to face the crowded bookshelf and hide her rising blush.

"Then quit." She knew it was easier said than done, but she needed to get off the swoon train. "Tell him you won't drill sergeant those kids anymore."

"Juliet, please. You know I can't quit." He sounded defeated, and Juliet's fury rose. Yeah, that turned the heart-eyes off instantly.

"Then stay and take orders from the guy that's ruining our school and pushing everyone to *exhaustion*. Before long, all his little toy soldiers will be too tired to even open their eyes, let alone be worth anything in their own defense. And we shouldn't have to do that. We're not the military." Juliet trembled with rage.

Nik stood and began pacing the small space. "I don't *want* to follow orders, I *have* to. But you're right, we need to do something."

"We?" Juliet stood too, worry pulsing through her. She wanted things to change, but she wasn't sure she had the strength to help lead that change.

"Yes Jules, *we*. I mean, think about it. You said it yourself, there are other students who feel the same way. If we play it smart, we might actually be able to do something about this." Nik stopped pacing to hold eye contact.

"Well... there is strength in numbers..." Juliet said, starting to come around. This could work. But like Nik said, they'd have to be smart about it.

"And with me on the inside, we'll have access to the information we need." Nik's eyebrows scrunched in concentration. "But I think we need to get to Delphine first."

"That would be really helpful. What would we do, though?

What could *she* do?"

"For one, she controls the finances, but I'm afraid..."

"What?" Juliet leaned forward, making Nik meet her gaze. "What are you afraid of?"

He took a breath. "I'm afraid Lord Dracul is using his dragon abilities to... *influence* Delphine."

Juliet leaned back, her mouth hanging open. *Would he* do *that?* She knew that dragons could alter a person's emotions by using pheromones. It wasn't exactly compulsion, but emotions were powerful and could easily persuade someone to think or act a certain way. The thought that their new director was using it on Delphine made Juliet sick to her stomach.

"But I think we need to get the support of other students," Nik said as he resumed his pacing.

Juliet shoved her previous thoughts aside. First things first. "Okay, so rally everyone together for... what, a protest? Our new director doesn't seem like the type to give in to a riot. In fact, he seems like the type to have a punishment specially prepared for *just* that scenario."

"No, we need to be more subtle than that. And it's imperative that we don't get caught. I mean it. We *cannot* get caught." He waited for Juliet to acknowledge him. With a nervous nod of her head, he continued. "What can we do to put the General in his place? Some sort of check and balance."

Juliet thought for a moment, then looked at the book she'd brought with her, the one she'd dropped when Nik came in behind her. She picked it up, looking again at the title. *Governments in World History.* "What if we form some sort of governing body? That way Lord Dracul couldn't just act like a king. He'd have a body of shifters that he'd have to answer to."

"Form a council?" he said, his handsome face splitting into a grin. "Of course! A shifter council. Of adults, obviously. But if we get enough students together, maybe we could get the ball rolling."

"And they could oust Dracul," Juliet said, her enthusiasm beginning to match his. "And bring Oberon back."

"Exactly. If we can get some students together who feel the same as us... and maybe your dad...?"

"Um, my dad's a no-go. He cares too much about his duty to *Lord Dracul*. But if we could recruit the right students, ones with influential parents and connections, I think this could work." She took a deep breath as the enormity of it all hit her. It was going to be a lot of work, but if they pulled it off, it could solve all their problems—and if it didn't work, it could ruin them.

"Are you sure this could work? Dracul is kind of intense and I don't think I'm prepared for whatever punishment he has for this kind of betrayal." She didn't want to back out, because it was a good start to a good plan, but doubt was beginning to dampen her enthusiasm. Thankfully, Nik came beside Juliet, taking her hands in his and locking eyes with her.

"I swear that I will always do anything and everything I can to keep you safe. Don't forget how strong you are, Jules. You saved Myreen once. I have no doubt you could do it again." Nik leaned in and placed his soft lips on Juliet's forehead. His words did make her feel better, her worry replaced by defiance.

Nik looked at the entrance, crinkling his brows. "I should get back out there."

"Okay, captain, but where should we tell everyone to meet?"

Nik squinted as he studied the small space they were in.

Juliet shook her head rapidly. "Oh, no. We are *not* bringing anyone here. There wouldn't be enough room." She was right, of course, but mostly, she didn't want to share their secret place with anyone.

"That's true. I have a place in mind. I'll have to check it out before knowing for sure. For now, just get some names. *Carefully.* We'll let everyone know when and where when we know for sure."

A sly grin came over his face, and Nik tapped his cheek.

"Yes sir." Juliet saluted, then gave him a quick peck.

They snuck out of their hidden sanctuary and quietly went their separate ways.

Juliet hoped with all her might that they could pull this off without any hitches. And with Nik on her side, she was crazy enough to think it just might work.

Kenzie

Kenzie watched the full moon rising as she rode the school bus home, her stomach churning.

This was it.

Normally a were had more time from bite to first shift, but Wes hadn't been so lucky. Four days. That's all he got—and only two of them conscious. And while she was grateful to have it over with, she worried for him. What if something went wrong? What if the shift changed him? What if she didn't like who he became? There were already some obvious differences, like the darker, thicker hair, and how his appearance had magically become more rugged. And the mood swings...

But perhaps the most frightening and exciting change was the way he looked at her. It turned her insides into wobbly Jell-O and stifled at least half of her witty quips. That was new. She always relied on her humor when things got awkward. Now, she just kind of went silent. But just with Wes, thank the fates.

And of course, there was still high school to manage, but

that seemed trivial in comparison to everything going on.

Like leaving for the vampire school tonight. Gram had counted on the shift happening and set up a plane ticket for Kenzie to get her to Washington. And though Kenzie was eager to get that over with as well, the thought of walking into the midst of vampires made her skin crawl. It didn't help that the mere thought of blood caused her gag reflexes to act up, though her experience with Kol gave her some hope that she could overcome that particular issue. *Having to smear your blood on someone for a spell will change you.*

Today, though, her thoughts had been consumed with Wes, and she worried all through classes that she might miss his shift. She wasn't sure why she wanted to be there so much. Maybe it was the lure of seeing someone make that first leap from human to... shifted. Maybe.

But for whatever reason, her heart swelled when she barreled off the bus, through her house and into the kitchen to find Wes in the backyard—still human, still glum, and with her mom confirming that he hadn't changed yet.

She stared out the sliding glass doors while Mom sat at the dining table looking over bills. "Do you think he's just not ready to shift?" Kenzie asked.

"I can't imagine he wouldn't be," Mom said. "I'm actually surprised he's held off this long. That happens to be a wolf moon."

"A wolf moon?"

"A Native American naming system," Gram said as she came in and sat next to Mom with a mug in her hand. Kenzie hadn't even noticed Gram was there, but it made sense. She'd probably been in the office doing something, just in case she needed to be on hand for Wes's transformation. "But the wolf moon seems to have more power over weres than the other moons."

Kenzie turned back to watch Wes. He didn't move, despite the deep chill of the day. His breath came out in large puffs of mist, and it looked like he was sweating. Sure, he was wearing a coat, but she didn't think he could be *that* warm.

Why isn't he moving? Gram and Mom had warded the yard to keep out prying eyes, but it wouldn't keep him locked in. He could leave any time, if he wanted. Kenzie wondered what he'd do with himself once he made the shift and Mom and Gram made him leave. How long would he remain a cat? What kind of cat would he be? What if she never saw him again?

"I'd like to go talk to him, if you don't mind."

Gram nodded, but Mom's eyes hardened. "No. I will not have my daughter out there with a young man who could shift at any moment."

Gram placed her hand on Mom's. "Lita."

The two women exchanged a long stare before Mom's shoulders drooped. "Fine. But if he mark's my daughter, so help me—"

"You're not protecting her from anything by keeping her inside. Besides, Kenzie can take care of herself." Gram turned her gaze to Kenzie. "And we'll be here if you need us. Okay Kitten?"

Kenzie swallowed and nodded.

She pulled her coat tighter—she hadn't yet bothered to take it off—as she slid out the door into the backyard. Wes whipped his head in her direction, a sad smile on his lips.

"Aren't you freezing?" Kenzie asked as she approached, her boots crunching in the hard crust of snow half-melted and refrozen.

Wes shrugged. "It's keeping me distracted."

"Distracted from what?"

"Everything."

Kenzie stood beside him, her hands buried in her pockets, shoulders up around her ears. The tension in the air was thicker than the puffs of breath freezing in the winter chill. Kenzie had nothing. She thought she could help, but now that she was out here, with *him*... Yeah, she had nothing.

Kenzie thought about turning around and going back inside, but Wes's voice caught her, keeping her there.

"I keep thinking that if I don't shift, maybe you won't have to leave. Maybe I won't have to leave. But the pull is strong. Has been since I woke up, really."

"You're scared. It's understandable. This is all new—"

"No." Wes shook his head, his eyes trained on the ground. "I'm scared, but not of shifting."

Kenzie's eyes rolled toward the sky. "Wes, you can't think—"

"I know. And I'm sorry. I know you're not... That you don't... It tears me up, knowing just how messed up all of this is." Wes stood and began pacing, and Kenzie swore she could see his eyes beginning to glow red, even if he refused to look at her.

Wes stopped and locked his gaze with Kenzie's. "Forget it," he growled as he started toward her.

Faster than she could think, Wes was crushed up against her, one hand holding her to him, the other cradling her neck. And his lips, hot and soft against hers with the faintest traces of chocolate, made her tremble. She closed her eyes as she savored what might be their last moments together, praying that everything would work out okay—for him, for her, for Leif and Myreen and the world.

But the sound of the sliding door and her mother's yells broke them apart at record speed.

"Kenzie! Get back in here at once."

Wes shook his head, taking a few steps back. He met

Kenzie's eyes once more, an apology without regrets lingering in his steadily reddening irises. He turned and ran for the edge of the yard.

Kenzie stared wide-eyed, wondering if Wes was taking this moment to leave. But the crack of fabric and another growl—this time decidedly feline in nature—signaled that the blur that was Wes had finally found his inner mao.

Kenzie gawked at the granola cat stalking around the perimeter of the yard, seeing Wes's eyes looking back at her. Muscles rippled through his back, his tail whipping back and forth. He walked in a tight circle twice, then curled into a ball and laid his head on his paws. Not once did he stop looking at Kenzie.

"Ohhh, shift," Kenzie breathed.

Mom grabbed Kenzie's hand and hauled her back into the house. "What were you thinking? Letting him kiss you like that. For all you know you're stuck with him now."

Kenzie looked back at Wes, the memory of his lips still burning against her skin as she let her mom drag her along. But the kiss hadn't been what sealed her fate. Somehow she knew that he didn't need mao DNA. Something had clicked a long time ago. The shifter in him just made it a little more tangible.

"I never should've trusted you," Mom continued to rant. "Falling for a hunter was one thing, but now that he's a mao?"

But it was Gram, still sitting at the table that captured Kenzie's attention. She winked. "A cougar, eh?"

"Mom!" Kenzie's mom said. "We need to get Kenzie as far away from here as possible. Right now."

"Relax, Lita. I've got this handled."

"Like you just handled my daughter—your granddaughter—being marked?"

"You don't know if that's what just happened. Besides, now

that he's shifted, he's not your problem anymore."

Mom glared at Gram.

"I have a friend in Washington Kenzie's going to visit," Gram continued. "By the time she gets back, everything will have worked out. You cool, kitten?" Gram raised her brows, as if she was asking for Kenzie's permission, but Kenzie knew what Gram was really doing.

Kenzie shrugged her consent, playing along with the charade. But despite her casual demeanor, her heart had raced ahead of her. Though if she were being totally honest, it had a hard time slowing when it was around Wes these days.

"Go. Go now and pack your things," Mom said, herding Kenzie toward her room.

"Okay, okay! I love you too."

"You'd better!" Mom called after her, then quieter she added, "That girl is going to be the death of me."

Kenzie went into her room and shut the door, then pulled out her suitcase and began throwing things in. Halfway through, she stopped, feeling compelled to look out the window.

Wes lay exactly where she'd last seen him, his gaze still trained on her. Her face flushed as she stared back. His mao form really was magnificent. She might have to stop calling him granola. Maybe mocha or spiced chai would work? She could think about that later. Maybe.

Because right now he was killing her with those pleading eyes of his. Kenzie considered staying. She could get lost in him, maybe for a while. But Leif needed her. Myreen needed her. And she'd made promises she intended to keep.

Tears blurred her vision and she swiped them away, giving Wes a small wave before closing her blinds, erasing him from her view. Would she ever see him again? He wouldn't be here when she returned—*if* she returned. But she didn't think something like that would stop him. Maybe.

There was a light knock on the door, and a moment later Gram popped her head in. Kenzie swiped at her face and nose, trying to clean up the mess.

"Having a rough time, are we?" Gram asked as she eased in and closed the door behind her.

Kenzie shook her head. "Who me?" She sniffed, then laughed to try to keep from crying again. "I'm fine. Never better."

"Do you love him?"

"Hah! Right." Kenzie whispered the reveal spell for the grimoire, and put it in her bag before hiding it with her magic once more.

"Nice trick. You'll have to teach me that when you get back."

"*If* I come back."

Gram frowned. "Are you planning on staying?"

"No. But I'm worried I'll get eaten alive. Literally." Kenzie stuffed a few more things in her suitcase and then leaned on it to zip it up. She had to keep stopping to stuff clothes back in so they didn't jam the zipper, but they kept oozing back out. Kenzie growled at it, yanking harder and harder.

Gram's hand on Kenzie's shoulder stilled her. "Let me." Kenzie reluctantly stood aside, and Gram unzipped the bag. She pulled a few clothes off the top and neatly folded them. "You remember that hound I dated?"

Kenzie nodded, folding her arms.

"He was a real charmer. And a husky when he shifted. Those eyes." She hummed as she neatly zipped the suitcase closed and pushed it back, then turned to Kenzie.

"But like I said, he was a real dog." Gram sighed, then sat

on the bed and patted the space next to her.

Kenzie let her arms loose and lumbered to the bed. Gram put an arm around Kenzie's shoulder and pulled her tight, and Kenzie curled into the warm embrace. "I thought he and I would be forever. But we weren't. I'm not sure if it's because we didn't have that kind of connection that binds people together or if he was just too stupid to realize it. Either way, we were over before too long. No harm, no howl."

Kenzie snorted, shaking her head.

"He's got strong feelings for you, but that doesn't mean you two are destined for forever. Or that you're marked. Only he can tell you that, but if he's of half the caliber I think he is, he won't until you're ready. If that day ever comes."

"And what happens then?" Kenzie asked, pulling back from Gram.

Gram tucked a strand behind Kenzie's ear, then turned to cradle Kenzie's cheek. "You're so young. You've got plenty of time to figure all that out."

"Maybe," Kenzie mumbled.

"You've got your strategy worked out?"

Kenzie nodded.

"And your login information for that online school I signed you up for?"

"Yes, Gram." Gram insisted Kenzie not fall behind while she was out saving people. Good old Gram. At least she wouldn't be bored.

"Good. Call us whenever you get a chance. And bring our girl home."

Kenzie nodded. She cast a worried glance at the now-shuttered window, and Gram caught her gaze.

"He'll be fine."

For now. Would his hunter friends come looking for him? He belonged at the school—the Dome—though Kenzie had a feeling he wouldn't go there. She couldn't blame him, though she hoped he'd at least consider it. It wouldn't be easy, going from enemy to ally, but he'd need help now that he was a mao.

Kenzie huffed a laugh. "You seem so sure of yourself, Gram. What are you? A mermaid seer?"

"No. Just very old." Gram shrugged. "It has its perks. And I'll keep an eye on him for you."

"Thank you," Kenzie whispered, giving Gram a big hug.

This whole thing was nuts, but at least she had her grandmother on her side. It made her believe, if only for a moment, that everything really would turn out okay.

Myreen

Several days passed since Myreen had been brought to Heritage Prep. After coming to terms with the fact that she was absolutely a prisoner here, she was surprised to find that she didn't completely hate it. With her ever-present and apparently mute guards, she had full access to the citadel and its amenities. The vampires she came into contact with never dared speak to her, but didn't look at her like they did the other humans, or even as she'd expect them to look at a shifter. The look in their eyes was one of reverence, like she was some sort of princess.

When Ty wasn't studying with his tutors, Myreen spent her time with him, playing with him and trying to indulge the child in him. She was fairly certain he'd never played with any kids his age, and it was a wonder he was so socially functional, if just a bit too formal for a ten-year-old.

But Ty spent at least half the day with his tutors, so when

sharing his company wasn't an option, she roamed the citadel, feigning idle curiosity when in fact she was carefully committing every inch of the building to memory so she could formulate an escape plan. One fact became obvious right away: there were no windows—or if there were, they sheeted over with metal—and no air ducts anywhere. There were only 2 doors she'd found that led outside—one in the Great Hall on the ground floor, and the one on the roof she'd come in that first night. She couldn't trace her steps back to find the rooftop door, and a pair of guards always flanked the front door. Escaping would not be easy.

In her wanderings, there were some places her guards wouldn't allow her to go, especially anywhere below the ground floor. That's where the humans lived, and she guessed that would be where she'd find a way out. Her only hope was to find some way to ditch them so she could explore unhindered.

Then again, why bother escaping? she thought as she lay on her bed the morning of the fourth day, staring blankly at the underside of the canopy. She had nowhere to go. If she went back to the Dome, Draven would just send his army to get her again, and she didn't think he'd spare the students a second time. She had no other family outside these walls. There was Kenzie, but Myreen knew she'd only be putting Kenzie in danger if she tried to find refuge with her. Maybe things really were better off for everyone if she stayed put.

After all, the prophecy did say the siren would kill Draven. What if she was meant to do that under his own roof?

She remembered how Delphine had ruptured that vampire's heart in the sim. Myreen was nowhere near that level of skill. She could try to drown him with water manipulation, but drowning didn't permanently kill vampires. She could shift into a harpy and fling her weaponized feathers at him, but he was far faster than her and she'd never land a blow. There was her new ursa powers, but she didn't know much about them at all, except that whenever she got mad she pretty much turned into the Hulk.

Myreen smash!

She laughed out loud, certain the guards outside thought she was losing her mind.

If she was meant to kill Draven with any of those powers, though, the prophecy would've been about a mer, harpy or ursa. But it specifically said a siren. She was meant to use her siren voice. She'd forced that poor vampire girl to kill herself under General Dracul's orders. Could the same thing work on Draven? And the question remained: was she capable of killing him? She'd only killed that vampire girl because she believed—*hoped*—it was part of a sim, and she was devastated when she realized it wasn't.

She'd only heard of Draven's cruelty, but she hadn't witnessed it for herself, aside from the fear emanating from his followers. Though maybe that was just respect?

Every night, he'd come to Ty's room to join them for dinner. He didn't eat, of course, but he sat at the table and engaged them in conversation. For all the millions of ways in which she was sure he was a horrible person, he seemed a pretty good dad to Ty, asking him about his day and actually listening to what Ty said. Myreen could swear she saw love in Draven's dark blue eyes whenever they were on his son. If someone was capable of love, did they deserve to die? Did anyone really deserve it?

Knock, knock, knock.

"Good morning, Myreen." *Speak of the devil.* "I have something for you."

She rolled off her bed and slowly went to answer him. "What is it?" she asked after she cracked open the door.

Draven held a thin, square box in his hands. It looked like a jewelry box. "Something that can help you with your current predicament." He held up the box, looking at Myreen imploringly. She sighed and opened the door wider, closing it behind him.

My current predicament is that I'm trapped here. I don't think you're going to give me anything to help with that.

"I do believe I've been smelling ursa pheromones the last few days," he continued. "Your ursa DNA has been triggered, then?"

She crossed her arms. "Yep. Just over a week ago." *And it's your fault I have it in the first place.*

"Ah, what awkward timing," he said with a nod. "And during a full moon, no less. It's amazing you haven't shifted and destroyed half the citadel by now."

"It's been tempting," she said, boldly meeting his gaze.

He hummed a laugh as they stared each other down for a split second. "In any case, I brought you something that will put your were abilities under your full control, so you'll never be a slave to those volatile urges again."

He opened the box and lifted a clunky yet elegant turquoise necklace from it. Without asking for permission, he was behind her in a blink, fastening the necklace around her neck and gently lifting her hair up and over the chain.

"The Navajo believed that turquoise warded off weres, which is the initial reason the stone ended up in so much of their jewelry. But that's not exactly the case. Turquoise merely dulls the intense reactions of the hormones, so weres are able to keep their shifted form reigned in more effectively, without the random outbursts."

As Draven spoke, the coldness of the stone soaked into her skin. The fuzzy anxiety she'd been feeling the last few days dissipated, leaving behind a strange tranquility. She took a deep breath, savoring the absence of the static that had been sizzling across every inch of her skin.

Draven sniffed the air. "Ah, much better. The scent of angry bear really doesn't suit you."

"Thank you," she said, uncertain how to feel about Draven's gift.

"Anything for my daughter," he said, the intensity of his gaze making her blush and turn away. "Only a week, you say? Then you haven't been taught anything about this side of yourself."

She shook her head, blindly fingering her new necklace.

"What have you been taught? Have you discovered your harpy abilities yet?"

She narrowed her eyes at him, remembering why she should be angry at him. "Just how many different species' DNA did you put in me?" If there were any other shifters waiting to jump out of her, she had the right to know.

"Harpy and Ursa."

"No others?" she interrogated, narrowing her eyes further, as if she could force the truth out of him.

"No. I've been splicing shifter genes for several decades, and those were the two that worked best together and were least likely to result in mitosis failure or prenatal death."

Several things about that rubbed her the wrong way. "How many times did you run this experiment on unborn children?"

He brought his hands together in front of his waist. "Three hundred and eighty-seven times. Every single one of them failed. Except for you."

Three hundred and eighty-seven forcefully mutated children died before drawing their first breath.

"Did their mothers volunteer for the experiments?" She had to ask.

"Most." Judging by the wicked twinkle in his eyes, mercy had not been given to those who weren't volunteers.

"And my mother? Did she volunteer to give birth to a monster?" There it was, the question that had been burning inside her since she found out she was Draven's daughter.

His face softened, his lips parting slightly before answering. "It was different with Zaia. The other volunteers were just strangers to me. And, let's just say that the immunization process was purely scientific."

Myreen grimaced at that bit of information, not wanting to envision any part of what that sentence implied.

"But Zaia and I had a true connection. She was a princess of her people, and she'd come to land right before she met me, trying to find a way to bring them up."

"She was a princess?" Myreen blurted, astounded. "Wait, that means I'm..."

"Mer royalty?" Draven finished for her. "Yes. Higher even than your friend Kendall, I'd wager. Your mother's kingdom was the oldest."

"What happened to them? Did Mom succeed?" *Maybe I do have family out there somewhere after all!*

Draven shook his head sadly. "I don't believe she did. After she ran away with you still in her belly, I had scouts scouring every coast in search of her. I don't believe she ever went back to her people after she left me."

Myreen's insides burned with promise and curiosity. A whole civilization of mer were still underwater—mer that were directly connected to her. She *needed* to know what became of them. All the more reason to get out of this prison. But how?

She decided to change her line of questioning. "You said you and my mom had a connection. If that's true, why did she leave?"

He lowered his head, as if his sadness made it heavy. "She got scared. She forgot that wars have casualties. She walked in on an interrogation that went awry, and she started to fear she made the wrong choice. She snuck out that night and I never saw her or our unborn baby girl again."

There was so much information to process. Every time Myreen thought she knew her mother, another skeleton jumped out of the closet. She really didn't know her mother at all. Could Draven be telling the truth? Even Kendall had said her mother fell for Draven. But would her mother have willingly allowed him to experiment on her baby? Myreen couldn't imagine any woman doing that.

"Is Ty like me? I mean, is he a chimera too?"

"No. Ty is completely human."

"Why?" She felt like it was a stupid question, but she couldn't see why the boy would be so important to Draven as just a human.

"He's my Heir."

"But what does that mean?"

Draven's face brightened. "My family is the oldest and noblest vampire line in existence. Every fifty years, the patriarch produces a male heir, and when that heir comes of age, he's turned into a vampire. This compounding of vampire blood produces a stronger vampire each time. I'm more powerful than my father, and he was more powerful than his. Ty will be more powerful than me."

"Wait, so Ty's going to become a vampire?" She was suddenly horrified, struck by an urgency to protect the little brother she hardly knew.

"Yes, when he turns eighteen." Draven was practically glowing with pride.

"Does he know?" Myreen's voice raised a whole octave, but

Draven didn't seem to care.

"He's known all his life that he's being primed to take my place as leader of the vampires."

No, no, no! Not sweet, innocent Ty!

"Why don't we get off this conversation. I can see it's making you upset." He put a hand on her shoulder. "I have something else in mind for today. You don't have any ursa training. Let me show you what you're capable of."

He went around her and opened the door, gesturing for her to follow him out. She didn't want to go with him. As curious as she was to learn about her ursa side, she was disgusted by Draven for what he was doing to Ty. Ty was nothing like his father. The boy may look like a miniature version of his dad, but he was pure and kind. Myreen hated that Ty was destined to become a monster. She would keep that from happening, even if it was the last thing she did.

"Come, Myreen," Draven insisted.

Getting rid of Draven was the only way to ensure that Ty's innocence remained intact, that her friends and all shifters stayed safe, and that she could one day reconnect with her mother's people. If she could use Draven to perfect the monster he'd created her to be, the easier it would be to fulfill her destiny.

***

"What have they taught you at your shifter school about ursas?"

Draven took her down to the main level and into a training room in a section she hadn't previously ventured. He instructed her to change into the smart suit she'd arrived in, and now they stood in a large, empty square room with a mirror lining one wall.

Myreen skimmed through her mental repertoire on bear-shifters before answering. "Ursas, like all weres, have their transformation triggered by full moons. They're bitten, not born. They're the strongest of all the weres, impossible to contain when they're having a fit, and struggle the most with self-control." She'd experienced that last bit first-hand.

"Good," Draven said, pacing in front of her with his hands clasped behind his back. "Basic, but good. What do you know of their powers?"

Myreen pondered. "I thought their strength *was* their power?" she said, her answer coming out more like a question.

"In a manner of speaking, that's true. Ursas have the most physical strength of pretty much all shifters, not just weres. But they're hyper-strong in other areas as well. Some have been known to have very powerful telekinetic abilities, even able to create forcefields at will."

Draven snapped his fingers and a projection began to play on the widest wall in front of them, though Myreen had no idea where the projection was coming from. The video showed a man in shredded clothes being circled by black-clad opponents—vampires, she assumed. The man let out a bestial roar, then every muscle in his body bulged and expanded, making him twice as large as he'd previously been. A coat of thick, brown fur covered his skin as his clothing ripped and fell away, his face mutating from that of a handsome man's to a snarling, nightmarish monster. She wasn't even sure she could call him a bear. Red shame flushed her face at the thought of what she must look like when she lost control.

As she watched, a visible disturbance rippled through the air, radiating outward from him. The ripple sent his opponents flying backward, and he leapt off-screen and out of sight. The projection faded like it was never there, the wall blank once more.

"Wow, I didn't know ursas could do that," she said, still staring at the naked wall.

"Few do," Draven said. "Ursas aren't as aware of themselves when in shifted form, so it's rare they're ever lucid enough to explore their powers. After all, such a thing takes patience, and ursas aren't known for that virtue. But there are some that find a way to manage their emotions and hone their special talents. I would like to help you do this."

"How?" she asked, incredulous. "I think we both know that if I shift, this room won't be safe for you."

A smirk curled Draven's pale, pink lips. He looked down and hooked his thumbs in his pockets as he strolled forward. "That's why I won't be in the room. I'll be in a safe location, instructing you via intercom." And then he was gone, the click of the door's lock the only evidence that he didn't just vanish into thin air.

She took a step toward the door, but a puff of yellow gas assaulted her face, a painful sting forcing her to squeeze her eyes shut. She stumbled, hearing the hiss of the gas filling the room. And before she had time to get angry or worry about what the gas might do to her, an insatiable, agonizing prickle seethed under her flesh—*everywhere!* She struggled to contain it, but it was no use. In several palpitating heartbeats, the beast unleashed, her thoughts, senses, and vision a blur of red and fury.

She slammed against the walls, clawing at the door. The urge to destroy was the only thing she understood.

"It's no use, Myreen." Draven's voice echoed around her. "I've had this room reinforced with a silver-steel alloy specifically for your training. You can't escape."

A guttural roar quaked out of her throat and rattled the mirror wall.

"The only way for you to get out is to concentrate." His voice was muddled and distant, reverberating in her eardrums as if spoken through water. "Hone your breathing, clear your mind, and gain control. Do not be slave to the beast. Be its master."

Every one of her muscles ached with frustration, and the

desire to throw a huge fit nearly overwhelmed her, like an itch that had to be scratched despite knowing that no amount of scratching could make it go away. She wanted to *hurt* someone. Anyone. Draven, especially.

No. She didn't want that. That was the bear talking. She had to resist.

Clenching her oversized teeth, she closed her eyes and stood as still as she could. She tried to ignore the pain of irritation that seized throughout her entire body, tried to drown out the wacky emotions that whispered all manner of angry demands.

Breathe in. Breathe out. Breath in. Breathe out.

She repeated the mantra in her mind over and over, feeling each breath as it entered and exited her lungs. The itch slowly became less intense, the fog that clouded her mind thinning ever so slightly.

"Very good, Myreen," Draven's voice said, and she heard it much more clearly than before. "Now, shatter the glass."

The bear wanted to ram an angry fist at the reflection it detested and savor the satisfying sound of glass crashing, but she had enough clarity to understand his meaning. She was to break the mirror without touching it.

She closed her eyes, took a deep breath, and pushed her will outward from her core. The room shook, and the sound of exploding glass surprised her eyes open in time to see fragments raining to the floor.

Another puff of gas—green this time—sprayed all around, and in seconds she shrank, returning to her normal height, returning to human form.

Wobbling in place and disoriented, she saw Draven enter the room, clapping his hands. "Very well done, and on your first try. You're nothing short of incredible!"

"Wh– what was that stuff you sprayed at me?" she asked, rubbing her aching head. The shifts had both been too quick, and now she felt sore, almost hungover.

"The first one was a toxin to force to you to shift," Draven explained. "And the second, obviously, forced you to shift back to human form. I apologize for using them on you, but they were necessary for this first exercise, don't you agree?"

No. She never wanted to feel anything like that again. It was horrible. She felt violated and nauseous and ashamed—too many things to list. Just about the only good thing she felt was surprise at being able to access such a difficult ursa skill on the first attempt.

"Why was it so easy for me?" she asked, mostly to herself.

"The necklace." Draven touched the center stone on her neck. "Remember I told you it gives you more control? Without the necklace, you would've had little chance of making progress. But even with it, withstanding the ursa toxin takes a great deal of willpower and inner strength, and that's something that can't be manufactured. I'm very proud of you." He rested a hand on her shoulder and squeezed.

She didn't feel the urge to jerk away this time. His methods had been forceful, to say the least, but none of that was meant to hurt her. It really seemed as though everything that Draven did was for her benefit, and his praise felt oddly... good.

She still didn't trust him as far as she could throw him—in human form, anyway—but she was starting to sense that maybe he wasn't all bad.

As much confusion as she felt regarding her mother, she knew that her mother had been a good person with a kind heart. If she had found something to love in Draven, maybe he wasn't the monster she thought he was.

Kol

Kol crouched between some pines. His new, military-issued smart uniform cut the majority of the northern Washington biting wind, but his cheeks and fingertips still burned from the frigid air.

Fortunately, the amount of fire churning inside would've been enough to keep his limbs warm even if he didn't have the protection of the high-tech clothing. Dragons never worried about frostbite.

Entering the shifter military facility that morning was uneventful. Kol had visited his father enough times over the years that he was familiar with the layout of the building. He and Tatiana had been scolded more than once for playing hide-and-seek in the barracks. And since Kol was *destined* to enlist, he went through the motions of his orientation, filling out the forms and being issued his equipment—he suspected his uniform was commissioned months before, since it fit perfectly without a single measurement—practically on autopilot, as if he'd done it a hundred times.

Only once did Kol find himself paying particular attention, as if anticipating the curious questions from a bright, piercingly blue-eyed Myreen, who would want to know every single detail. For instance, she might've been interested to know that the military headquarters mimicked the shape of the Dome, but it lay above ground. From the inside, the world could be seen with perfect clarity through the pristine, smudge and crack-free glass, but from the outside it was camouflaged to blend into the Shawnee hills in southern Illinois. But the moment passed as quickly as it came, and Kol turned back into the robot she always accused him of being.

He was tired of waiting. Char and her insufferable second-in-command, Corporal Modder, were reconning the vampire headquarters at Cle Elum. Kol insisted on joining, but was overruled by the corporal. Apparently even a dragon prince could not be trusted with such a task on his first day.

So he stood back, perhaps sulking a bit, while the rest of the team huddled casually several yards away.

Fortunately, Kol didn't have to wait long before two small dots appeared in the sky. One a bright blue—their leader and commander of this mission, Charlotte—and the other a muddled brown that was close to the color of mire and mud. *Much like Cpl. Modder's personality,* Kol thought bitterly. *Corporal Mudd.*

Kol rolled his eyes and puffed out a visible breath as they drew nearer in broad daylight for anyone to see. Surely, his talent for invisibility would've made the better option for scouting out a tower full of vampires in the middle of the day.

When Char and *Mudd* landed and shifted, the group formed a semi-circle around them.

"It would be suicide to barge through the front doors, day

or night," Char said, a little disheartened. "The fortress is well-protected and fortified, and the number of vampires would have no problem squashing us like pesky flies."

"Yes, we will surely need to find another way," Mudd added in his haughty tone. "I thought that if we—"

"What about your idea, Char?" Kol interrupted. "Let's just tear the citadel apart right now and let those monsters burn."

Mudd shot a nasty look at Kol. His expression remained stoic, but Kol didn't keep eye contact for long. After all, Mudd was his superior, even if Char was in charge. Plus, he would hear it from his father if it got back to him that he was being insubordinate.

"The sun will set soon, Private Dracul," Char said softly, but loud enough that all could hear. "And it's risky. We could lose half, if not all, of our numbers if we aren't careful."

The others glanced back and forth at one another, careful to avoid eye contact with the corporal, who huffed when he realized he'd lost the argument. The team was silently on board.

"We'll do it," said Specialist Torisei, a wiry kitsune who looked physically inept to be part of such a mission. "We have more than brute force at our disposal."

"Yes, we can do it," said Private Gibson, an ursa who looked very much like he would be using said brute force.

Char smiled. "Alright then, but we can't do it tonight. I suggest we all get some rest, then reconvene tomorrow at dawn. You're dismissed."

The group dispersed. Kol reluctantly took the cue to leave—he wanted to storm the castle *now* and rescue Myreen, but he promised Eduard he'd follow orders. Plus, it would be dark soon and the vamps would have the upper hand if they tried to attack after sunset. He headed in the opposite direction while Char huddled with Mudd, probably discussing their plans for attack.

He was mid-shift when Mudd shouted, "Where are you going?"

Kol didn't shift back, but paused. Invisible scales covered his arms and torso—there was no point hiding his little trick anymore. Kol looked into the trees, feeling like he might be in trouble, but unsure why. "Char, *er...* Sergeant Stern said we were excused?"

"Yes, to *rest.*" Mudd said, stomping toward him and pointing in the direction the others had taken. "Not to go scampering about the Cascades." He walked closer. "Or going AWOL to save a certain mer." He narrowed his eyes up at Kol.

"I wasn't going after her," Kol said. "That would be stupid." He glanced over the corporal's head at Char, who watched the pair with a studied glance. Kol didn't know whether to feel grateful or annoyed that she was staying out of this one-sided show of power. He supposed she was well aware that Kol had learned to fight his own battles years ago. He was a Dracul, with Eduard as a father, after all.

Corporal Mudd folded his arms across his chest and widened his stance. Kol felt the man's dislike rolling off him in waves.

"We were dismissed," Kol repeated. "I didn't plan to be gone long, just take a flight down to Vancouver." He resisted the urge to glance at Char again.

"Vancouver?" Mudd frowned. "That's a two-hour flight there and back, at *least, Private* Dracul. Were you planning to come back?"

Kol's blood boiled within seconds. "That *mer* who was taken, *Myreen*?" he said, setting his jaw before speaking again. "I asked to be on this mission to rescue her, not to go *AWOL.*"

Mudd poked Kol in the ribcage. "You will talk to me with respect, Private," he spat. "Just because your father is the general, doesn't give you the authority to do whatever you wish."

"Why do you want to go to Vancouver, Kol?" Char asked, finally stepping in.

The way she asked—as if suddenly stripping her title and becoming *just Char* here in the middle of Washington's frozen forest—caught him off guard. The question didn't hold the weight of Corporal Modder's question. She wasn't demanding respect or chiding him for being insubordinate. She truly wanted to know, and it showed in the softening of her brown eyes.

He stared at her for a few seconds, stunned and not quite sure what to say—especially with Mudd watching and listening.

"Could you give us a minute, Corporal Modder?" she asked without even looking at him.

Kol expected a grunt or noise indicating his disapproval, but the corporal stiffened and nodded before walking the same direction as the others.

"What's his deal?" Kol asked, glowering at the corporal's retreating form.

"Oh, I don't know," she said. "Maybe he has a problem with the fact that you walked into your barracks this morning and onto a private jet an hour later with an elite team headed for a dangerous and sensitive mission?"

Kol glanced down at her.

"Corporal Modder has been in the shifter military ten years, Kol," she said.

"Well he must not be very good if he's only a corporal," Kol scoffed. "Look at you! You're a sergeant and you've only been in a year!"

She narrowed her eyes at him. "He's a talented dragon and an obedient soldier. He doesn't have his eye on ranks."

Clearly, Kol wanted to say. Instead, he steadied himself, forcing himself to cool. There was no point getting worked up over something so trivial. If Corporal *Modder* was essential to bringing Myreen back, Kol wouldn't have an issue with him.

"So why Vancouver?" she asked. "I really can't have you leaving to go so far. Even you, *Malkolm Dracul*, need to follow my orders."

Kol's shoulders dropped in defeat. "I just wanted to kill time. And he's wrong, you know? I could be there in fifty minutes, maybe even forty-five *easy*. I'd be back in three hours, tops."

Char raised an eyebrow, then pushed a lock of her blonde hair away from her face and behind her ear. He was so close to winning her over, he could feel it. They might not have seen each other for a year, but he still knew her tells.

"Come with me?" he asked. "And I'll tell you *why Vancouver*."

"Fine," she said quicker than expected. If he didn't know better, he could've sworn she hid a smile when she pressed her lips together.

Realizing he was still mid-shift, that his arms and torso were invisible, so she'd been essentially talking to a disembodied head—but kudos to Mudd for locating his invisible ribs in his physical show of authority—he quickly shifted completely.

Char shifted quicker and beat him into the air, heading south.

***

Their little mini-competition actually brought them to the outskirts of Vancouver in forty minutes, but that's where Kol found himself lost. He wasn't exactly sure what he was looking for. Finding himself in Washington and with time to spare before he could rescue Myreen had given him only one idea: to find the place where his ancestor, Aline Dracul had lived.

Vancouver, Washington. Where Aline was cursed.

Kol and Char stood along the bank of the Columbia River in silence. They shifted back to their human forms seconds before the rain started. Kol preferred the snow.

"So *why Vancouver*?" Char asked, shouting over the torrents.

Kol scooted closer to her, his arm pressing against her shoulder, so they could better hear each other.

"My ancestor lived here somewhere," he said.

She looked up at him with a cocked head and twisted mouth. "History nerd?" she teased with a nudge. "Or what is it they call it? *Genealogy* nerd?"

"What can I say?" He shrugged, looking back over the river. He didn't want to get into the fact that Aline was the only ancestor he really knew about—well besides his grandparents. Curses were difficult to explain. Especially *activated* curses.

His heart twinged in the same spot Mudd poked him earlier.

"No, it's something else," she said. Char always knew when Kol was holding something back.

He didn't dare look at her.

"You triggered the curse, didn't you?" she said, not looking at him. "You fell in love with that mer-siren girl we're getting ready to rescue and you triggered the curse."

Kol stared down at the top of her now-soaked head. He could see the rivulets falling from her lowered lashes, streaming down her face like tears.

"You know about the curse?" he asked, his voice so low he wasn't sure if she could hear him over the storm.

Finally her eyes lifted to his, blinking rapidly to prevent raindrops from blurring her vision further. Kol could feel the rain plastering his own hair against his forehead and along his neck.

Char's lips were pressed tightly together. Kol wondered if she was holding back some emotion, though he couldn't guess what. It was a look he couldn't remember ever seeing from her.

"Nik told me once," she said with a shrug, as if it would

lessen whatever she was feeling.

"Traitor," he said, a small smile lifting the corners of his lips. He felt the need to lighten the mood somehow. But it didn't seem to work.

"Don't blame him," she said, still serious. She looked back out at the river. "Our parents wanted us to marry..." she paused. "They still do. I think he was just trying to warn me."

Still do? Kol hadn't heard anything from his parents about him and Char in quite a while. But suddenly everything clicked, and a seed of anger blazed to life.

It was all Eduard's doing.

The reason why Char was a part of his final sim test, the reason she led this mission to rescue Myreen. His father *knew* Kol would insist on helping rescue Myreen and was trying to throw him and Charlotte together in hopes that their unofficial marriage alliance would finally come to fruition. Eduard always wanted Kol to end up with a dragon. It was practically expected. And a *Stern* dragon—Charlotte—would help both of their families politically and socially in the shifter world.

Kol could hear it now. *You've already fallen in love with the siren girl and she hates you. Why not form an alliance with someone who cares for and respects you instead? You've always liked Charlotte.*

Kol clenched his fists. He wanted to punch the rain-drenched tree next to him, but resisted. It wasn't Char's fault. He suddenly needed to get back to the mission. He wasn't sure why he'd come to Vancouver or what he thought he'd find, anyway. He was ready to storm the vampire towers tonight and free Myreen—to hell with the danger.

He needed to see her.

But he wasn't stupid. He calmed the white-hot fire that

threatened to destroy something.

"This *Aline Dracul*, she's the one who was cursed in the beginning," Char said. "Wasn't she?"

Kol couldn't tell if she noticed the shift in his mood or not, but he didn't trust his voice and merely nodded.

"Are you hoping to find a way to break it? The curse?"

"I don't know!" he shouted, ripping at his drenched hair. "I don't know why I wanted to come, or what I thought I'd find. The boarding house Aline lived in was destroyed by vampires one hundred years ago, and I'm sure the apple orchard is gone by now too."

After several silent moments, Char said, "We could ask someone. A store owner or something? They might know the spot."

Kol's anger dropped to a simmer as he contemplated just how Char knew so much about his family's curse. He doubted Nik knew the name *Aline Dracul*. Plus, she made it sound like Nik had spilled that information years before. But there was too much going on for him to figure out. He was too wearied with the gut-wrenching dread he'd felt every second since watching Myreen's submerged form—dark hair creating a slow-moving halo, her pink fins paled against the murky water—grow smaller in Lake Michigan's depths before disappearing from sight.

But he doubted asking townsfolk about a *shifter* boarding house would work, since it wasn't likely it would have any importance for humans. Still, he nodded and followed Char into the forest.

As it turned out, Char actually had a *contact* in town. An old phoenix who had family in the area went on and on about the history of the city. Kol was pretty sure most of the story was made up. Three alicorns in one city, let alone one *century* sounded like the makings of a fantasy novel. He thought alicorns had been extinct since the black plague.

The old phoenix knew next to nothing about the boarding house, except its possible location, but Char insisted that they check it out anyway and determine for themselves if their crazy little side mission was a dead end. And yes, she included herself when she called it *their side mission.*

Kol couldn't figure out why she cared so much.

It was fully dark, but the rain had stopped when they found the location, so they easily found the remains of the stable. Three rotted walls of wood were all that remained. It was small and probably only housed one or two animals, even when it was functional. The entire property was overgrown and wild, like the very land had been cursed when it was destroyed by the vampires. Kol wondered if the selkies had something to do with that, though he couldn't fathom why. A development of condominiums to erase any trace seemed more like something a group of selkies would have a mind for.

And Kol felt nothing.

No sense of magic or wonder standing on a plot of ground that his ancestor likely walked. The whole selkie line of thinking was probably his way of grasping at straws. Like if he found some clue or relic...

"Let's go," he said.

Char had been kicking at something in the dirt near the edge of one of the leaning walls and jerked her head in shock. "But we found it!" she said, hands up, and eyebrows raised in confusion. "This is where the house was, and now you want to *go?*" She crouched down, gripping at what looked like a half-buried rock.

Kol shook his head and looked northeast—the direction of Cle Elum. Toward Myreen. "Let's just go," he repeated. He heard the flatness in his tone. "I'm ready to crash."

Char brushed at the rock she'd plucked before tossing it to Kol and walking past him. "It's a dragon scale," she said without looking back, sounding a little deflated.

He barely glanced at the violet scale before throwing it over his shoulder and following her. He knew Aline's scales were a purplish-violet color. But a dragon scale wouldn't make Myreen love him back.

"I hope you're in hell, Aline," he muttered under his breath, then shifted and took flight.

***

Kol was antsy in the morning. He'd slept horribly in anticipation of the attack and was ready to get it underway. The sky was nearly cloudless as the sun peeked over the horizon, proving to be a good day for vampires to die. He shuffled from foot to foot in the snow as Char and Corporal Mudd spoke in hushed, serious tones a few meters away.

Char's arms were folded across her chest as she spoke calmly to an agitated Mudd who flailed his arms and gestured at Specialist Torisei. Apparently the two had a chat about the plan while Kol and Char were slogging through the mud and rain in Vancouver.

Finally, the two officers approached.

Char cleared her throat as soon as the team came to attention. "I've been advised that a full-frontal attack on the vampire school is too reckless and dangerous."

Kol's stomach dropped. "Says who?" he shouted, knowing full well he was speaking out of turn, but he shifted his glare right at Corporal Modder as he spoke.

Char glared at him. "You will show your sergeant respect, private," she shot back. Then she gritted her teeth. "We're formulating a new plan."

"No," Kol said, breaking rank and stalking into the trees, but pausing to look back. "I'm going. *Now.* We have the element of surprise. Specialist Torisei has the tech to tear the towers apart. Let's do it!"

Specialist Torisei's mouth twitched, and he turned his head to the side as if changing his mind again. "Private Dracul is right," he said, looking apologetic. "I had my doubts, but if we attack now..."

Corporal Mudd turned his dagger-glare at the kitsune, who cowered slightly.

Kol didn't wait for another response and continued walking.

"This is against orders, *private*!" Mudd shouted.

"Actually," Char said, cutting him off, "I never ordered anything. I never called off the attack."

Kol turned with a smirk directed at Mudd.

"However," she continued, "It's dangerous. *Very* dangerous." Char stiffened. "If anyone feels it's too risky, I will not order anyone to sacrifice their lives for this."

Kol rolled his eyes. Of course they would all come. He'd seen the respect in every single one of the team's eyes for their leader. This little demonstration of cowardice was merely wasting precious time. Kol folded his arms and leaned back. He knew he'd won.

But Corporal Modder's expression slipped into disappointment—directed at Char. She shrugged a weak retort and mouthed something Kol couldn't see. Corporal Modder shook his head before walking away. The rest, minus Specialist Torisei and Private Gibson, followed the corporal.

Kol's arms dropped, but he kept his expression neutral when Charlotte turned to look at him. He refused to name the emotion he saw there, and pretended that he was still too robotic to notice. Myreen was his only focus.

Even if their numbers had gone from twelve to four in a matter of seconds.

Leif

Rainbow—the vampire cat—leapt from Leif's lap and landed gently on the ground. He stretched his furry limbs, straightened his back, and pointed his gray tail upward, all the while purring a middle C, at perfect-pitch.

"Don't leave," Leif mumbled, his shackles rattling slightly as he moved his arms and extended his fingers. But he didn't mean it. The cat had yet to be discovered by anybody within the black walls of Heritage Prep. Rainbow only left Leif when somebody else was approaching—usually Beatrice. It was the cat's sixth sense.

"Be safe out there," he whispered, watching Rainbow with blurry eyes. The copper injections not only weakened him physically and mentally, it even messed with his vision. Still, he saw the blurry fur-ball leap onto the couch and slip behind a heavy curtain.

Leif had no recollection of how much time passed since

he'd become Beatrice's prisoner. However long-ago Rainbow had torn off the metal plating that used to cover the window, there was now a triple-layered black sheet to replace it. When Beatrice discovered the open window, Leif told her he needed to see the sunlight—that it was the only thing that had brought him comfort. Which wasn't entirely a lie: Rainbow *did* bring him comfort. And amazingly, Rainbow survived the sunlight, indicating that the cat had taken on Leif's daywalking abilities.

Fortunately, the curtain made it easy for Rainbow to get in and out of Beatrice's quarters. Leif watched as his little friend scurried out of sight.

In the loneliness the cat left behind, Leif's muddled thoughts turned to Kenzie. She'd reached out to him several times—or at least he thought she had. But he couldn't remember what she'd said, or what he'd said in response. The conversations seemed like dreams that were trying to disappear without a trace. He just hoped she wasn't making the mistake of coming to the vampire school. If she was... well, hopefully she'd have a plan that could actually get him out.

Only a few moments went by, then a beep sounded at the door, and in walked Beatrice Morton. She'd been his intended over one hundred years ago. Then she'd become the one who bit him, transforming him into the vampire he still was. She'd *then* become his teacher in utilizing his powers. And now, she was his captor. Draven turned him over to Beatrice for whatever purposes she desired.

"Hi Honey, I'm home!" Beatrice said the words in a sing-song voice, and Leif felt like hurtling himself out the window. It was probably a sixty- or seventy-foot fall. He wondered if he could survive such a drop.

Instead, he cast his hopeless gaze to the floor. "Hi Beatrice," he mumbled.

"Hey, cheer up, cheer up!" she said. "I brought a bloodmix for us to share!"

Bloodmix—a vampire cocktail that contained a variety of blood from different humans. Sure enough, Leif spotted the tall glass, filled to just a half-inch from the top, two bendy straws poking out, and found himself licking his lips. He was thirsty.

"You need to keep up your strength," she said, kneeling in front of him while placing her free hand on his cheek. "Besides, what's better than a date with me?"

Anything, Leif thought. The idea of going on a date with Beatrice was so revolting, it almost shoved his desire to drink aside. Almost.

Beatrice's face fell, and she put the bloodmix on the desk next to him. Lifting his chin with her hand, her brown eyes filled his view. "It's the copper, isn't it? It subdues you—alters your thinking."

Leif nodded.

"It doesn't have to be this way, you know," Beatrice said softly. "I can remove these shackles. You and I can still leave Heritage Prep. But you know my demands." She tapped his chest, then hers as she said, "You and I—forever."

Leif didn't blink, staring deeply into her eyes. Into her soul. At last, he said, "I will never meet your demands."

Her jaw tightened, and Leif heard her teeth grinding.

"A date it is, then," she said through clenched teeth.

"Let me go," Leif begged. "Please, just let me go."

"Your freedom will come when I have your heart," Beatrice said. "It will happen sooner or later. And if it happens later... well, I have eternity to wait. I guess I've gotten used to quick results over the years." She snatched the bloodmix and held it between them.

"No vampire date can start without a little drink," she said, shaking the cup ever so slightly, causing a little vortex to spin in the center of the crimson liquid. It was hypnotizing, and Leif had a sudden urge to rip the cup out of her hands and consume the entire glass himself.

Taking a few deep breaths, he forced himself away from such animalistic behavior.

Beatrice eased the cup forward, and as his lips closed over one of the straws, he closed his eyes and began to drink.

A burst of flavor tickled his taste buds, bringing much-needed pleasure to his entire being. The blood was still warm— freshly extracted.

His body tingled, and he found himself unable to pull away from the straw. Right now, the only thing in the word was him and the bloodmix.

And then the flow of heaven stopped, followed by loud slurping sounds. His eyes flashed open, and he pulled away from the tall glass, shocked to see that he drank it all.

Beatrice chuckled as she rose to her feet, placing the empty glass back on the desk. "It's been a while since I've seen anybody chug like that. You must've been thirsty."

Leif's eyes followed the empty cup, wishing it were full again. But his body still tingled, and he felt good. Not cured of the copper slowly poisoning him, but content. Life wasn't so bad.

"Now let me set the mood." Beatrice turned her wrist over, tapping her smartwatch. All the lights in the room went dark, and Leif found himself blinded. It was as if Beatrice had placed a cover over his eyes.

"Wh- what are you d- doing?" he stammered, trying to focus his eyes. Never had any darkness been able to blind him since he'd become a vampire.

Beatrice didn't respond.

Slowly a small light appeared, revealing that he was no longer at Heritage Prep. As the light continued to brighten, he gasped at where he was: Frost Boarding House.

He wasn't shackled anymore. But more shocking was the fact that Beatrice wasn't anywhere to be seen.

Leif found himself sitting in the Frost's wooden chair—the same one that resided at his apartment in Chicago.

A cruel chill crawled down his back. "Beatrice?" he called, hoping she'd enter and explain what was going on. "What trick are you playing on me?"

And then he heard her—not Beatrice, but *her*!

"Gemma?" he whispered, his eyes widening and his heart beating so rapidly it threatened to jump out of his body. Her voice was coming from the dining room, and he leapt to his feet.

And then he heard Camilla's voice, a little louder than Gemma's—just loud enough that Leif could hear what she said.

"Leif is going to propose to you any day now."

"What?" Gemma gasped. "You are sure of this?"

"He told me just today," Camilla replied.

There was a moment's pause, then Gemma said, "What should I do?"

"That is the great puzzle you will have to solve, I am afraid," Camilla said with a laugh.

"Would it be too rude to tell him to try proposing to one the trees in the orchard, since they are all he cares about?"

Again, Camilla laughed. "I would *love* to see his reaction if that was your reply."

This isn't right, Leif thought. Before he met Draven, he'd frequently re-experienced memories from his past. Draven had stopped them from emerging. But while this felt like a memory, it wasn't. He'd never heard Gemma and Camilla talking about his imminent proposal, and he couldn't imagine it would've gone like this.

It wouldn't have, right? The question was posed to the Gemma in his mind, but she didn't respond. Her voice hadn't come to him for quite some time, either.

"What is quite sad," Gemma continued, "is that he does not realize that I have only allowed him to court me out of pity. It is no small wonder that he let Beatrice Morton go without even thinking twice. Can you imagine, dear Camilla? Me falling desperately in love with that poor fool, then getting thrown out to pasture because of his duty to the orchard?" She laughed in a way Leif had never heard. It sounded too... wicked.

"You have to admire his dedication, though," Camilla said. "The orchard would not be as successful as it is without his hard work."

"Again, he really should consider proposing to one of the elegant apple trees that waits on his caressing hands every day," Gemma said.

Both girls must've covered their mouths, for their laughs were muffled. Leif's heart slowed to a dull *thump-thump*. Hearing Gemma's voice behind those words... It sounded so real. He tried to think about other memories that would disprove this conversation, but the effort was broken as Camilla spoke again.

"Please let him down easily," she said quietly. "Deep inside, he can be quite vulnerable."

"I might not have it in my heart to tell him 'no' right away," Gemma replied.

"Actually, that might be the wisest path to take," Camilla replied. "Perhaps accepting his offer now, then allowing a slow rejection to occur would work out for the better."

Leif's throat dried and his sinuses sparked, causing his eyes to water. *You will not cry,* he told himself, as if the command would actually work.

"Quite alarming, isn't it?"

Leif whirled to find Beatrice in a lackadaisical posture in the Frost's chair—her back against one arm while her legs dangled over the other.

"You!" he growled. "You're doing this!"

She shrugged. "All I've done is tapped into your past."

"This *isn't* my past," he said, pointing toward the dining room.

Beatrice swung her legs to the front of the chair, then leaned forward. "This is *your* mind, Leif. I'm just here to watch."

"No," Leif said, shaking his head. "Gemma would never... This isn't how it went."

"Are you *sure*?" Beatrice asked. "If this really did happen, would Camilla or Gemma have told you about it?"

Would they have? The idea that Camilla—a sister in every way but blood—would speak in such a way was heartbreaking. But to think that Gemma had been faking their relationship? It was enough to kill him. He fell to his knees, tears rolling down his face.

"You know what they say, Leif," Beatrice said, bringing her face close to his. "The truth hurts." She raised her hands to the sides as she leaned back. "And this? Sure looks like truth to me."

Leif sniffed, grasping at his emotions, trying to keep them from falling out of control. Closing his eyes, he felt the world shift around him. By the time he opened his wet eyes, he was back in Beatrice's quarters, his wrists still bound and his head still swimming.

"Thanks for the date," Beatrice said, then kissed his cheek.

Leif bit his lip, then let loose a pained groan.

He felt Beatrice's hand rest on his shoulder. "There might be more for us to dig out of that ancient mind of yours."

Leif shook his head. "Please, no. I don't want to know any more."

"For now, you don't," Beatrice consoled. "But maybe later you'll want to check, just in case."

Leif felt empty, like a glove without a hand inside. Gemma was perfect, right? Or had he been blinded by love? Had she been hiding her true feelings? Even with all the effort she'd put into helping him? But she'd called it pity. Had she done nothing but show pity for him?

He'd only known her for three months. Was that really long enough to truly *know* somebody? Their connection made it seem like their souls had known each other forever. But Gemma was a selkie—could she have simply put a spell on him? Was their relationship built on pure magic?

It cannot be! Leif told himself. But the words felt hollow. Since knowing her, his whole life had been dedicated to Gemma. It tore him up to think that something that felt so real to him could've been nothing more than an enchantment—or charity.

Beatrice's hand slid down until it gripped Leif's.

"Hey, I know you don't get much news up here, but I thought I'd inform you about some success we've had."

Welcoming the distraction, Leif sniffed as he looked back into Beatrice's almond eyes.

"We've got Draven's daughter!" she said, a light sparking in her eyes.

"Myreen?" he sputtered. His mind was a mess.

"Yes, Myreen. She came of her own accord. And the best part is that it seems she and Draven are actually getting along."

His mind was muddled. How had Oberon let Myreen get caught? But Beatrice said she came all on her own? Why would she do that? After all Oberon had done to protect her, he just... let her go?

"This is a game-changer," Beatrice said, excitement building in her voice. "With a siren on our side, imagine what we'll be able do. The shifters will obey our every command!"

There was no way he was hearing things right. Beatrice was messing with him. "Why would Myreen... work *with* vampires?"

She laughed. "It's all about the cause. I think Myreen has seen Draven's vision. They've been training together. Her skills are impressive—particularly with Draven's guidance. Father and daughter, joining forces, working toward the same cause. Leif, it really is a sight to behold."

He couldn't process it anymore. Leif's brain overloaded. His peripheral vision faded, as if shadows were at the edges, slowly creeping their way towards the center, until darkness consumed him.

CHAPTER 12

Myreen

Myreen woke in her dark room and looked at the clock. It was nearly seven in the morning, though it felt like it was still the middle of the night. She wondered if her body would ever get used to west coast time, considering she spent her days in a building with no windows. Myreen sighed and turned over, not quite ready to face the day, but sleep had left her.

She got up instead, wondering what she should do with herself. Exploring her ursa powers with Draven had been exhilarating, but she had no real schedule here, no classes to attend or job to perform. And she'd already explored a good portion of the citadel. Maybe she should go to the training room and try something else?

A small voice sounded from outside her door, and Myreen's ears perked.

"Is she up yet?" It was clearly Ty.

A matronly voice—Agnus, obviously—was trying to dissuade Ty, but she wasn't getting very far with him.

Myreen opened the door and peeked her head out. "It's okay. I'm up."

"Do you wanna have breakfast with me?" Ty asked, and Myreen's heart melted once more. Not only was he adorable, but he was so polite. It was hard to think she was speaking to a ten-year-old.

"I'd like that," Myreen said with a smile.

Agnus pursed her lips.

"Let me just go get dressed and I'll be right over," Myreen said, remembering she was still in her pajamas.

Ty nodded, and he and Agnus left while Myreen changed. It still amazed her how much trouble Draven had gone through to make her comfortable. She still thought of her room as a gilded cage, but as she pulled the sky-blue cashmere sweater over her head—perfect for the cold halls of the citadel—it was almost difficult to remember why she hated Draven in the first place.

Of course, at this point, maybe she didn't hate him.

She pushed the thought aside and made her way to the room below door. Her guards barely acknowledged her passing, almost looking bored. Maybe with a few more days they'd relax enough to let her do whatever she wanted without their attention.

The table was already set with waffles covered in strawberries and whipped cream, crispy slabs of bacon on the side. Myreen's mouth watered as she sat beside the little boy waiting patiently for her to start.

"Where's Agnus?" Myreen asked, looking around as she sat across from Ty.

Ty wrinkled his nose. "I told her I didn't need her this morning. I'm spending the day with you."

Myreen smiled as she cut off a bite of waffle. "And you can just do that?"

Ty nodded and smiled, his own mouth full.

She lifted the fork to her mouth and bit down on sweet, creamy, crispy goodness, closing her eyes as she did so. The Dome had great food, but their stuff was more utilitarian, stuff that could be easily cooked and served for a large group. This? Well, this was the stuff of special occasions.

"What? No pancakes today?"

"Nah."

"Do you get waffles for breakfast often?" Myreen asked as she swallowed another bite. "Because I could eat these every day."

Ty smiled and looked down. "No. Not every day. But today kinda counts as a special occasion."

"And why's that?"

Ty looked up at her, his cheeks reddening even as he met her eyes. "Because it's the first day I really get to spend with you." He looked back at his plate and poked the bacon with his fork. They'd had a few days together, but always interrupted by his classes. Apparently today would be different. "I've never had a sister before."

Myreen's lip pouted as her wax heart melted further. "Aww, Ty, I'm so sorry."

Ty shrugged. "It's not so bad most of the time."

"What...?" Myreen paused, unsure how to ask about his mom, especially when the loss of her own hurt so much. She decided to just bite the bullet. "Where's your mom?"

Ty's face clouded, his cherubic features hardening. "Shifters killed her. Father says they would've killed me, too, if he hadn't discovered what was happening."

"Oh. I'm so sorry."

"It's okay. Father says when I'm old enough I'll become a vampire, and then I'll be able to take revenge, if I want."

Myreen felt the color drain from her face. To hear Ty talk like that—as if becoming a vampire was the most natural thing in the world—dispelled her growing comfort. "Do you... want to become a vampire?"

Ty pushed his plate away, glancing at the hidden servant's door. "Wanna go for a walk? I've got something pretty cool I wanted to show you."

Myreen took the last bite of her breakfast and swallowed. "Yes. Lead the way."

Ty led her to the stairs and they made their way to large room filled with the pillars—she'd since figured out there was only one of those.

The guards followed at a distance and Ty soon pulled ahead, Myreen hurrying to keep up. When they reached the elevator, Ty swiped his card. When the door opened, he darted in, hit a button, then tugged on Myreen's hand, leading her toward the far end of the floor, making sure to keep the pillars between them and the guards.

Myreen's brows furrowed as she tried to figure out where Ty was taking her. At the last moment, he took her upstairs— the same ones they'd just come down—to a blank wall. When she squinted, she saw the faint outline of a door, hidden in the same manner as the servant's entrance into Ty's room. It was the entrance to the roof, the one she hadn't been able to find! To think she'd been walking past it all these times, though the seams *were* really well hidden.

And apparently Draven had wanted to parade her around for a moment when they first arrived, because he could've easily brought her up to her room, rather than taking her down and around. Myreen wasn't sure how to feel about that little fact.

Ty pushed on a stone, and the door eased open, revealing a twilight sky, the first blushes of dawn lending color to the horizon.

The guards weren't in sight, but the chime of the elevator sent her heart rate spiking. But it chimed again, and then there was silence. Ty was sending them on a wild goose chase. *Smart boy.*

Myreen wrapped her arms around herself as she stepped outside, the chill winter air poking through the holes in her sweater.

"Oh, hold on," Ty said, and he darted back indoors.

Myreen had a moment of panic as the door closed behind him, and she wondered if maybe he was playing a trick on *her* instead of the guards. But Ty came back a moment later with a couple of blankets, and he handed her one.

"It's almost always cold up here, so I keep some blankets near the door."

"Do they know you come up here?" Myreen asked, gratefully tugging the heavy fabric tighter around her shoulders.

Ty looked at the ground and kicked at a loose stone. "You're the first person I've brought here. You have to promise not to tell anyone."

Myreen nodded. "Cross my heart. A place like this, it's probably nice to have a spot you can call your own."

Ty smiled big, warming Myreen more than the blanket could. "We can talk more out here. The guards will be busy for a while trying to catch up to the elevator. And being vampires, they won't be able to come out now that the sun's rising." He nodded toward the sherbet hues on the horizon, and Myreen smiled.

"What you were asking before," Ty continued, "about wanting to become a vampire?"

Myreen nodded.

Ty stared eastward, and Myreen waited, not wanting to burst the moment.

"I don't know." Ty turned back to Myreen, pulling his own blanket tighter. "In some ways, I do want to be a vampire. I mean, they're so cool! Super-fast and strong and smart. And Father says I'll be the best of them all. I'm the next Denholm heir. I'll get born with like, ten times the power. Or however many Denholms there are."

"That does sound pretty cool... But you're still not sure?"

Ty met Myreen's gaze, the golden glow catching in his blue eyes. "It kind of scares me. And I'm not sure I want to take Father's place as leader of the vampires."

"Big shoes to fill."

Ty nodded. "Don't tell anyone that, either."

"I wouldn't dream of it."

Ty looked back toward the horizon, the cherry pinks and soft peaches chasing the last of the evening from the sky. "I think I'd miss sunrises most of all. Do you think Father misses the sun?"

Myreen shrugged. "I don't know."

"'Cause he's not so mean, you know. He can be really nice."

"Yes, he can."

"Myreen?"

"Yes Ty?"

"I'm glad you're here."

Myreen smiled. "Me too." And she actually meant it.

It was strange. With her harpy wings, she could leave right now, but she didn't feel the pull anymore. Ty needed her, and this place was growing on her. She fingered the turquoise necklace, feeling strangely grateful for this moment.

***

Myreen and Ty spent most of the day exploring the citadel. She half-heartedly looked for another escape route, but wasn't too disappointed when she didn't find one.

The guards caught back up with them, but didn't say anything about Myreen and Ty's excursion. She had a feeling they wouldn't be the first to admit their mistake, and she was still here, so it wasn't like there was anything to get in trouble over. At least she knew what to do if she decided she wanted to leave.

When they made it to the lobby and Myreen spotted Kendall slipping down the stairs to the Initiate quarters, she knew she needed to go further. If she was really going to embrace this life, then she needed answers, and despite the tension between them, she felt Kendall was her best bet at finding the truth.

"Ty, I think I want to head downstairs for a bit."

Ty crinkled his nose. "Really?"

"Yeah. I'm sorry. I know Draven doesn't let you go down there. Do you mind if I leave you alone for a bit?"

Ty brought a finger to his chin and hummed. "I suppose. As long as you're back in time for dinner."

"Six o'clock, right?"

Ty nodded.

That left nearly two hours. It should be enough. "I'll be there."

"Promise?"

"I promise," Myreen said, and was rewarded with another beautiful smile.

Quick as lightning, Ty wrapped his arms around Myreen's waist, then dashed off to whatever he had in mind. Myreen stared after him for a few moments. The boy seemed so starved for affection. Had she been like that when she was his age? She didn't think so. Even though their upbringing was similarly strict, she never felt deprived. But even as she thought that, a little voice whispered that she was lying to herself. *Would a happy, content child have broken her mom's rules?*

Myreen shook the thought aside. She still wasn't ready to deal with that. Somehow, she didn't think she ever would be.

Gathering her courage, she headed downstairs to the Initiate quarters. Her guards hesitated, looking to each other with questions in their eyes, as if wondering what kind of trouble they'd be in for letting her wander through. But there was no way to escape beyond the main level, from what she could tell, and Draven hadn't forbidden it. After all, what harm could letting her mingle with humans do—humans who were just as loyal to Draven as they were? And they still trailed her like pale shadows.

She wasn't sure what she was expecting—maybe students lined up like cattle, waiting to give blood to thirsty vampires—but the room she stepped into was rather normal. Almost mundane. The modest furniture looked comfortable, the common area warm enough, the students lounging around looking relaxed. At least, until they spotted her. Then they buried their heads again, as if by not looking at her, she wouldn't be in their space.

After a few awkward seconds, Myreen decided to speak up. "Does anyone know where Kendall stays?"

A few startled glances met hers, but no one spoke up. Myreen was about to go search on her own when a petite girl whose head barely reached Myreen's chin stepped forward.

"He's the fourth level down," the girl said, not meeting Myreen's eyes.

"Thank you."

The girl merely nodded, dipping into what felt like a small curtsey, and quickly swept back to the chair she'd been in.

Myreen shrugged and followed the stairs down until she reached the fourth level down. It wasn't until she was there that she realized there was still another set of stairs leading deeper. She turned toward it, curious about just how many levels there were when a hand caught her arm.

"I don't recommend going that way." It was Kendall, his voice low, his hand around her arm just tight enough to tell her how serious he was. The guards eyed him, but Myreen waved them away.

"Why not?" Myreen asked, casting another glance toward the stairs.

Kendall looked around the common room, which only had one or two Initiates in it, and at the guards still standing on the stairs leading to the next floor. He nodded his head to the side. "Come on."

Myreen planted her feet. "Not until you let go of my arm."

Kendall let go and held his hands up. "You know I wouldn't do anything to hurt you."

"Do I?" She could feel the tense gaze of everyone in the room, but she didn't care.

Kendall's handsome features crushed, but he nodded. "I understand your hesitation. Can we talk?"

Myreen crossed her arms.

"Alone? You can cut my tail off yourself if I so much as look at you funny."

Myreen sighed, dropping her arms. "Fine."

She followed Kendall into a hallway as necks craned to watch them go. Doors dotted either side of the long hall, and Myreen wondered just how many humans were housed here.

At last, they reached the final room in the corridor, and Kendall opened the door, stepping aside so Myreen could enter. She nodded to the guards, who took up some wall space in the hall as she went in with Kendall.

The furnishings were stark—a bunk bed, a couple of cubbies with drawers underneath, some chairs and a small table. It wasn't much, but then again, the Dome hadn't exactly been a luxury suite. Truth be told, the only real difference here was that the walls were all the same dark obsidian as the rest of the citadel, casting a permanent gloom on pretty much everything.

Kendall closed the door and sat in one chair, and Myreen followed his lead, sitting in the other.

"So what are you doing way down here?" he asked, looking at his fingers.

"I just..." Myreen took a deep breath. "I'm trying to decide..."

"Whether to trust me or not?"

Myreen shook her head. "I've been spending time with Ty—"

"And the little guy has stolen your heart," Kendall said, the corner of his mouth pulled into a half-smile.

"Yeah." Myreen grabbed a strand of hair and gently tugged, curling it around a finger. "I was brought here against my will, but now? I need the whole story. I thought maybe you'd be able to help."

Kendall sighed and leaned back in his chair, running his hands through his hair. "If you're looking for me to badmouth Draven, you're fishing in the wrong pond."

"No. I just... are they happy here?" Myreen asked pointing at the ceiling. "Are *you* happy here?"

"I don't know if I'd call it happy, but they're not *un*happy. And I'm confident I'm where I'm supposed to be."

"But everyone is so scared of Draven. And upstairs, they seemed afraid of me."

Kendall crossed his arms. "Yeah, well you're walking around with a couple of guards. Besides, no one wants to get on Draven's bad side, and since you're his daughter..."

"I get it. I just wish it wasn't like that."

"He's united the vampires, the first time that's ever happened, as far as I've heard. I imagine you have to be at least a little ruthless to keep so many vampires under control."

Myreen nodded. His reasoning made sense, though the whole atmosphere of fear still bothered her.

"Are you afraid of Draven?"

Kendall laughed. "Terrified. But he's kind of charming, too. Like if Draven likes you, everything is right with the world."

Myreen got it. She'd had a taste of that the other day when she saw the pride in his eyes. But there was something else she wanted to know. "Why can't I go downstairs?"

Kendall gave her another small smile. "That's the dungeon."

"So he really does have a dungeon." He'd mentioned it that night she was brought here, but she hadn't seen it, and it had pretty much disappeared from her thoughts. But knowing it was just below her sent a shiver down her spine.

"Draven has a lot of things, but yeah, he has a dungeon. Like I said, you're not going to get a bunch of bloodthirsty vampires to behave by patting them on the head."

"No. I suppose not."

"But hey, it's not like it's full or anything. Most of the time when someone goes down there, it's only for a day or so before being restored."

"Oh." Myreen wasn't sure how she felt about all of it, but at least she was getting the truth—or at least as much of the truth as she could get from Kendall.

Kendall sighed. "Look, my advice is to keep your head down and your ears open. You're smart. And you're Draven's daughter. You'll be fine. Heck, you could probably do something relatively stupid and still be fine. Unlike the rest of us." He smiled at her like it was a joke.

Myreen stood as she smiled back, though it didn't quite meet her eyes. Suddenly she wanted to be alone again. "Thanks. That gives me a lot to think about."

Kendall stood too, grabbing the door for her. "Any time. Really. My door is always open."

"Thanks," she said again. She walked into the hallway, tugging on another strand of hair.

"Myreen?"

She turned to face him. "Yeah, Kendall?"

"For what it's worth, I'm sorry."

"For what happened the other day?"

Kendall shook his head. "For everything."

Myreen nodded once, then continued back the way she'd come, the guards trailing her once more. She wanted to go to her room and just think for a bit.

Hopefully she'd be able to sort through everything by dinner, because there was no way she was going to disappoint her "date."

Oberon

The white noise of the bus let Oberon escape to his thoughts, and he found himself analyzing his situation in the same manner his beloved wife, Serilda, would have. Finding the gryphons in Canada would've been her chosen path. Seri would've left the vampire fight to the shifter military.

He smiled, thinking of her, and allowed his mind to dig through numberless memories until it stopped on one particular recollection.

It was a rainy day, and Oberon had an itch to attempt to blow the storm clouds away and draw out the sunshine. He was new to his abilities, only performing his first successful shift just a few days ago. While shifting was exciting, it was painful. But manipulating the weather? That was *fun*.

Oberon had waited fourteen whole years for his abilities to surface. During that time, he'd witnessed his mother and father control the weather as needed. La Framboise Island was always protected from the harsher elements. While they saw snow in winter, they were never bombarded with blizzards. Tornados and other crazy natural disasters always avoided them.

"Watch this, Ren!" Oberon yelled over the slap of raindrops striking the Missouri River close by. He wouldn't chase the storm away, but that didn't mean he couldn't have *some* fun. Calling upon the roiling clouds above, he summoned the built-up energy to crash together, causing a lightning bolt to spear downward, lighting up the dark sky. The strike of energy hit the ground just ten feet away, and Oberon jutted out his chest, taking pride in his precision.

The eyes of the short, teenage Ren widened, and his long, dark hair stuck out from the static. "That was amazing. Here, do it again!"

Ren's eyes glowed a light purple in anticipation of using his own powers.

Looking up at the sky, raindrops pelting his face, Oberon created another flashing bolt and released it, letting it arc down. Before the bolt could crash into the ground, Ren tapped into his abilities. Oberon watched the streaking light bend at the last minute, shooting past him, then spiraling around Ren like a snake. It sizzled and cracked, and Oberon found it difficult to look directly at it. Still, it was fascinating enough that he stared through squinted eyes.

Like a spring, the manipulated energy flew up, then plummeted, coming to a sudden, hovering stop an inch above Ren's cupped hands. The spiral swirled down, compacting until it was a crackling ball.

Ren's hands glowed, and his dark eyes reflected the magnificent light. But Oberon had to close his eyes and look away—it was as if his friend was holding the sun in his hands. Opening his eyes with his back turned, Oberon could see the top of the plus-sign shaped school nearby. His heart leapt as he heard rushed footsteps approaching through the greenery along the bank of the river.

To his surprise, his mother appeared among the bushes. Her hair was soaked and matted against her head. As soon as she spotted Oberon, she stopped in the mud and placed her hands on her hips.

"Oberon Alexander Rex, what do you think you're doing out here in the middle of a storm?" But her eyes were ripped away as the dazzling sphere of electricity held in Ren's hands filled her view. "What have you two been doing?"

"Hi, Mrs. Rex," Ren said bashfully, looking around nervously, as if trying to find a place to dispose of his lightning creation. "We've just been playing around."

"*Playing around?*" she said in an accusatory voice. "Using your abilities out here in the wild—unsupervised...?" Oberon's mom trailed off, but her face was as red as Director Slegr's nail polish.

"Practicing!" Oberon corrected, throwing Ren a glare. "You and Dad are always trying to get me to practice. And now you're mad—"

She pointed at the crackling ball. "Do you realize how dangerous that much energy is? If Ren accidentally lost control of it, it could do significant damage to something or someone!"

"Come on, Mom," Oberon replied, wiping his hand through the air, as if such an action could erase her emotional outrage. "Nobody else is around. And besides, we've got this."

Whether or not the booming thunder overhead was triggered by his mother's anger, it was loud enough to make him jump. Worse, it was loud enough to make Ren lose control of his ball of lightning.

The blinding sphere shot past Oberon. As it went by, it caused the wet hairs on his arms to stick straight up. Had he been hit with that much concentrated electricity, it would have stopped his heart in a second. Instead, the crackling orb swung back around, zig-zagging through the air as if a selkie was having some fun with it, then crashed into the nearby river. Water leapt into the air where it impacted, like an asteroid creating a crater. The water hummed and hissed as it sloshed back down, dissipating the electric current as it spread along the long river.

It all happened so fast, and Oberon found his small chest heaving with rapid breaths. He winced, then looked slowly at his mother. Her face was stoic, all except her eyes. Her eyes were fuming.

She pointed back toward campus, and with venom in her voice, she said, "Off to the school. Both of you."

Ren didn't hesitate, but set off with as wide of strides as his little legs could muster. Oberon drooped his shoulders and followed.

"Wait till your father hears about this," his mother said as he passed her. "He just returned home and is in great spirits. Hopefully your actions tonight won't put a damper on his mood."

"I'm sorry, Mom," Oberon said quietly.

"You better be," she replied. "What you two did today was unwise. Your father and I expect more from you."

Dejected, Oberon took heavy steps through the foliage. He heard a whooshing sound and looked up just in time to see one of the tree branches Ren had pushed forward swung back and smacked him in the forehead. He yelped in pain, rubbing at it while tears sparked in his eyes.

"Gotcha!" Ren yelled up ahead. He disappeared among the trees and bushes in a hurry.

"Ren!" he yelled, chasing after his friend with intent to

return the favor. "When I get my hands on you—"

Oberon was cut short as he watched Ren phase through the exterior wall of the school.

"That's no fair," Oberon grumbled, still rubbing at his head. No doubt the branch that whipped him had left a mark.

His mother chuckled from behind.

"It's not funny," he said with annoyance. "It hurts."

"I'm not laughing at you, Obe," she said, nodding her head toward the wall of the school.

He took a closer look and discovered a leg sticking out of the wall, wiggling about like a panicked worm. On the other side of the wall, he could hear Ren yelling for help.

"From what I hear," his mother said, "phasing isn't exactly the easiest ability to master. Ren has natural talent, no doubt, but his overconfidence has him a bit stuck, don't you think?"

Oberon laughed, and—thanks to his mother's humor—the edge of his pain wore off.

"We should probably help him," he said. "His pant leg's soaked and his shoe is full of water. It's only going to get worse dangling out here in the rain."

"You're a good friend," his mother said, placing a hand on his shoulder. "Others would let him deal with it after being whipped in the head. But we'll see if he can work things out for himself, at least for a few minutes. It'll be good for Ren. Come along, now. Your father has something to show you."

Something to show him? From Oberon's experience, that wasn't always a good thing, and did little to help motivate him to move faster. Usually it was a piece of boring family history, or something for him to work on or fix.

Oberon let his mother take the lead, and he followed her like a shadow through the wet grass surrounding The Island. At last, they arrived at the entrance. His mom pushed open the heavy, wooden, arched double-door, and to his surprise, his father was standing just inside, waiting for him.

His father held in a laugh. "Miriam, you're soaked! You should have at least taken an umbrella with you. Or you could've pushed the rain aside so you wouldn't get wet at all."

She let loose a fake laugh. "If *you* had seen what your son was doing outside, you wouldn't have been too eager to stop and grab an umbrella, either."

His father's features sank like a rock in the Missouri River. "What trouble have you been causing, Oberon?"

He cast his eyes to the ground, hating the piercing gaze he was receiving. "I'm sorry. I was practicing some lightning manipulation while the storm was out. I didn't want the storm to end without getting a chance to."

Oberon brought his eyes back up to his father and saw confusion on the man's face.

"What's so wrong with Oberon working on his abilities?" he asked, glancing back at Oberon's mother.

"We can talk about it later," she replied, and Oberon sighed with relief as the conversation was swept away for the time being. "Why don't you tell Obe the good news?"

Excitement flashed upon his father's face again. "Right! Oberon, I want you to meet someone. Someone *very* important."

Oberon tried to hide his anxiety. Who was his father talking about? A tutor? Was he doing so poorly in school that he needed one? Or maybe a new teacher had been brought in, one who was specialized enough to help him with his new abilities while his father taught at the school and his mother managed the kitchens?

He was so busy falling into his spiraling thoughts that Oberon gasped as a girl with long, blonde hair poked her head out from behind his father. Her eyes were like the blue of the Missouri River, and her small nose came to a point. She looked to be about his same age.

His father stepped aside, revealing the girl in her entirety. She was gangly, mere skin and bones, and she was wearing a hot-pink t-shirt and baggy corduroy pants, both of which were much too large for her wiry frame. "Oberon, this is Serilda Vogel."

Serilda's lips formed a slight smile and she nodded her head. She didn't take his eyes off him, and he felt his cheeks redden. She was cute, and he didn't know how to react. Oberon froze—everything except his thudding heart.

His father stepped over to Oberon, placing large, strong hands on his shoulders.

"After we heard rumor of a girl who could transform into a lion-like bird in Minnesota, I had to check it out."

Amazement slammed into Oberon harder than a whipping tree branch. "You're a gryphon?"

"Am I talking to a corpse or what?" Ren's voice—old Ren, that is—pulled Oberon out of his memory.

They were on a bus, and Oberon had no idea where they were precisely, geographically. But they were somewhere in Canada at this point. They'd been traveling for three days now. Their destination was Calgary, Alberta. From there, they'd make their way to Mount Joffre.

"Where are we?" Oberon said, looking out the bus window. All he saw were blankets of snow, trees lining the highway here and there.

"We just passed a town called Milk River," Ren replied. "But a better name for it would've been Ice Cream River, or Popsicle River, or something, because it was completely frozen."

Oberon blinked a few times, then rubbed at his eyes.

"So... did you hear anything I've been saying for the past five minutes?" Ren asked.

Oberon shook his head. "I was... thinking."

Ren studied him for a few moments, then nodded his head. "Thinking about how masterfully made the upholstery is on the back of the seat in front of you?"

Oberon looked down at his intertwined fingers. "I was thinking about Seri."

Again, Ren studied him, then sat back in his chair and looked forward. "I suppose finding out that there are more gryphons would lead you down memory lane."

"If Delphine is right, that is," Oberon said.

Ren snorted. "What, you think she's lying?"

Oberon shrugged. "Eduard seems to have her wrapped around his finger. He might have instructed her to send me farther away from Myreen. Just to lessen the likelihood of me getting involved."

Ren blinked a few times. "I suppose that's a possibility. But it doesn't seem like Delphine's style."

"Ren," Oberon chided, "she was right there when I was thrown out of the school. She was standing *with* Eduard."

"You can't start thinking that way. If you start second-guessing your friends, you're going to find yourself miserably alone."

"And what do I do if we find gryphons?" Oberon asked. "Ask them to take *me* in? I've spent my life searching for my people, knowing I could offer them a home at the Dome. Now I can't even do that!"

"And vampire's love sunbathing," Ren said. "The Dome will gladly take in any shifter, gryphon or not. I think the real question is, would *you* want to return after being ousted?"

Oberon set his jaw and thought about that. The Dome was a part of him. The school had become his purpose. Could he just abandon that part of him? Could he forsake twenty years of his life?

"You're Oberon Rex," Ren said. "You have the respect of every shifter in the Dome, whether they admit it or not. And someday, even Eduard will realize that. So don't sit there acting like you've swallowed naga venom. You're nobler than a daydreamer. You're a dreamer. And by my tails, we're going to keep making your dreams happen."

Oberon's heart leapt at Ren's little pep talk. The kitsune was right. He didn't have to live in the shadows that Eduard had thrust upon him. He'd find the gryphons and bring them home.

Looking into the dark eyes of his friend, Oberon said, "You know, you never did tell me how you got your leg out of the wall of The Island all those years ago..."

Kenzie

Kenzie trudged through the snow, cursing under her breath. Whoever had set this school up obviously didn't care if students got there or not. Two miles. That's how far it was from the nearby city. Sure, vampires wouldn't have any problem with the trek, but seriously? They took human recruits, for crying out loud.

And the snowy trail was wreaking havoc on her travel suitcase. Those wheels were meant for pavement and comfort, not four-wheeling through the backwoods.

Of course, she was the only one on the trail at the moment. *Probably because no one else is stupid enough to trek to, or from, the school in this weather.* But Kenzie had a mission, and she couldn't put it off any longer.

Hopefully Leif was still intact. And Myreen.

Her stomach churned at the possibilities, death not even being the worst of them. She wondered how parents could allow their children to go to a school like Heritage Prep—or if they even knew where they were sending their kids.

At least she couldn't get lost. The black towers loomed from the lonely branches of the frozen forest, a crown promising pain and death. Real welcoming.

Kenzie shuddered and pulled her hat lower over her head, then thought better of it and pushed it back up. She didn't want her vision obstructed.

Still, the cold air licked at her bare neck, and Kenzie sighed. Gram had insisted on cutting and coloring her hair before she left. The strands still seemed stiff or hollow or something, even if the outer layer was soft from whatever had been in the after-color conditioner. Red. Gram had chosen Fiery Copper, or something like that. She couldn't deny the hue was perfect for her skin tone, but she thought the red would make her stand out more than anything. And the cut was so short. It irked her. She'd worn her hair at least long-ish for most of her life, particularly fond of the longer locks in the winter. But now? It would be years before her hair grew back out to an acceptable length. Hopefully that sacrifice would be worth it.

The closer she got, the more ominous the towers loomed. She swallowed her doubts and kept trudging forward. She prayed the castle would be warm. Or at least warmer than it was out here. Even hiking, she was having a hard time shaking the chill. *Stupid hair.*

Kenzie groaned when the trees opened up and the front entrance came into view. Stairs. Hadn't she been through enough? She sat down in the snow, not caring that her butt was getting cold. Her legs needed a break, and she wanted to gain her bearings before she entered the dungeon.

The cold sun would keep the vampires indoors, though that

wouldn't prevent them from sending humans out, if they deemed it necessary. She wondered how tight of a guard they kept on the place, and if they'd spotted her already. The school was solemn as a grave, and silent to boot. *Figures.*

Movement in her periphery startled her, and Kenzie whipped around and tried to get up, stumbling on the frozen snow.

"Who are you?" asked a voice in her ear, and Kenzie froze.

She knew that voice. Kenzie pulled off her hat and turned toward Adam, trying to give him the most unimpressed expression she could muster. Her heart beat in her throat, and she was glad he wasn't a vampire. She took a quick glance again just to make sure, but he looked about like he had last time. No way had he turned into a vampire. Yet.

"I'm a new Initiate."

Adam squinted at her. "Do I know you?"

Kenzie stifled a snort. He *should* know her, after all the time they spent sucking face. Looked like the hair had done the trick. *Thank you, Gram.* She shook her head and shrugged. "It's my first time here." She kept her face angled down. Hopefully he'd take it as respect and not recognize the fear coursing through her—or her face.

Adam grunted. "Hey Thomas!" he called as another person approached.

Kenzie let out a breath when the new guy came closer, also looking very human. *Stupid me. Vampires wouldn't be out here during the day.* It was early yet. Leif was the only vampire she'd ever heard of who could daywalk. Still, being this close to the nest made her feel vulnerable, like the snowy white blanket was camouflage for their pale skin.

"Have you heard anything about a new Initiate?" Adam asked Thomas.

Thomas shook his head. "No, but they'd be more likely to tell you than me."

"Leich ín dhaermandah," Kenzie breathed, and both boys froze, getting a glazed look in their eyes. Kenzie's heart fluttered. She wasn't sure if that would work on more than one person at a time. Thank the fates it had.

"You will forget the past five minutes. You just met me and you were expecting me. You're supposed to take me to Draven." She hoped that would do it. "Dhaermandah," she said, finishing the spell.

The look on both boys' faces lost that glossy look, and they smiled at her.

"Let's get you to Draven," Adam said.

Thomas nodded and grabbed Kenzie's bag, making light work of the contraption that had fought her all the way here. Kenzie grimaced. Some days she wished she were something more useful. Magic had its uses, but it took so much effort to access. If she could just pull out strength or warm against the chill like a phoenix or a dragon or a... mao. Kenzie shoved the thought aside. She couldn't think about him. Not now. There was too much at stake.

A few other Initiates wandered around, sending curious looks at the trio. They seemed to defer to Adam, though, and since he seemed confident, they didn't question it. Kenzie was both grateful and terrified that Adam held that much power. She just needed him to not recognize her. But if everything went smoothly, surely she could avoid Adam in such a large structure.

Finally, they reached the colossal stairs, and Kenzie trudged up them between Adam and Thomas. Her legs were screaming at her to stop, but she had to keep going. If she just made it to the top, maybe then she could pass out. Okay, so she had to make it past the lobby, but still. A lobby had to have chairs, right?

But as she entered the enormous doors—which were even bigger than they'd appeared to be—her spirits sank. The interior was just as black as the rest, making the vibrant red accents pop. Banners flanked the room, bearing the Heritage Prep logo, a single drop of blood dripping between the words. Kenzie could almost appreciate the darkness of the whole setup—if she wasn't already so nervous about the vampires this place housed.

There was a loud sniff and a sigh of satisfaction. Kenzie whirled to see a young woman with long golden hair framing a pale face leaning toward Kenzie, her eyes heavily lidded. "Ah, fresh blood. I love new recruits." She sniffed again, and her brows crinkled. "But now's not the time for them. And something about you smells different."

"Hey Ann, what do we have here?" asked another young man, also pale and blond, though nearly a foot taller than Ann. He sniffed the air too. His eyes snapped open and zeroed in on Kenzie. "You're a selkie," he hissed.

Kenzie took a step back, the hair raising on her neck. Of course. That was how Leif had figured her out. He'd been able to sense the magic in her. She'd just walked into a den of creatures that could smell her magic. Great. Maybe she could mask her scent? It might buy her some time.

She muttered under her breath. "Sweeph an bolladhá, sweeph an bol— Ahh!"

Kenzie hit the floor with an "oof," her head spinning. She tried to suck in air, but failed, her lungs burning.

"Don't you say a word, selkie," the young man hissed again.

Kenzie shook her head and held up a hand. "I just want—"

But she was interrupted again, this time by the young man pulling her into the air, pressing her against the cold black stone.

A heartbeat later he was clamped down on her neck, Kenzie kicking and screaming. He placed a hand over her mouth, stifling her cries. Her will was seeping from her. The pull of venom tried to lull her into complacency. Kenzie wanted to give in, but she clung to her purpose. She bit down on the hand over her mouth with all her might, and the hand flinched back in surprise, though the teeth seemed to tighten their latch.

"Daywalk," Kenzie croaked.

There was a clamor in the room, something she hadn't fully noticed in light of the attack. It buzzed and droned, and she knew she was the epicenter of the excitement. But the venom was working, and Kenzie relaxed against the wall and sighed.

"What did she say?" came a shrill voice.

There was a crack, and the teeth braced on her neck unclamped, the body in front of her yanked away.

Kenzie fell to her hands and knees, gasping for air, though it wasn't her lungs that needed replenishment.

"What the hell were you thinking?" It was that voice again, less shrill now, though the feminine tones still held a hardness that exuded authority. "Who is this girl? What's she doing here?"

Kenzie looked up to find herself looking into a face so angelic, she could hardly breathe. The woman's pale skin was offset by blood red lips. Stark white curls framed her petite face.

"She's a selkie," spat the vampire who had bit Kenzie, but her eyes were still locked with the woman in front of her.

"What did you say about daywalking? And no magic, or I'll be forced to let Todd finish the job."

Todd smirked, but Kenzie ignored him. "I have a spell. For daywalking."

"Where? Tell me."

"In my grimoire. Which I've hidden by magic."

"And why bring such a thing here?"

"I want to be admitted to the school," Kenzie said, her eyes dropping to those ruby lips. She had no idea why they were suddenly so attractive, but under the influence of the venom, she meant every word. She needed to be here, with these beautiful people. It was her destiny, her calling, her path.

"And why would a selkie want to go to a vampire school. You could never be turned, not without losing your magic."

"The shifters won't have me," Kenzie said, all the disappointment she'd felt for months coming out in those few words, coloring her voice with bitterness.

The angel in front of her smiled. Her gaze went to Todd, and she snapped a finger. "Get Draven. He'll want to see this."

Todd nodded, though he wore a brooding frown. Kenzie guessed he wasn't happy about this new development, but he didn't voice anything to the woman, just darted off in a blur.

The angel wrinkled her nose and sniffed. "Does anyone have anything to stop the bleeding?"

"I do," volunteered a young woman, who rushed forward and kneeled next to the angel. She had large glasses that made her eyes huge, her tall, spindly frame looking frail next to the woman with the red lips. "I keep a tube of superglue on hand at all times," she said as she dabbed some on Kenzie's neck.

Kenzie sucked in a breath at the sting, and nearly jerked her head away when cold fingers clamped her skin.

"Sorry," the young woman said. "I probably should've warned you it would sting." The pressure on Kenzie's neck stopped, and the young woman put her hands on her lap. "There. That should do it." She stepped back, clasping her hands together and lowering her head, as if she was afraid she might get yelled at for her actions.

"Thank you. Piper, right?"

"Yes, ma'am."

"I thought I recognized you."

Kenzie swallowed, the fuzz in her head beginning to clear. Her heart rate kicked up a notch as she realized how close she'd been to becoming a meal. If not for the woman before her, she'd be dead. "Thank you for saving me," Kenzie said.

The woman smiled, her ruby red lips practically glowing against her pale skin. "We'll see what you say when Draven arrives."

"And what is so important that I must be pulled from spending quality time with my daughter?" a man asked, and Kenzie nearly lost her breath again.

He was beautiful, an angel of death if she ever saw one. His devilishly handsome face was bespeckled by a five-o'clock shadow that she wanted to run her fingers over, his dark hair shiny and silky, swept back in a style that looked both pristine and effortless, like a model in a fashion magazine, perfectly captured for all time.

"Draven, this girl claims she has a spell for daywalkers."

Draven cocked a brow at Kenzie, stepping closer. "Ah, a selkie. I've only heard of one other selkie with such a spell."

Kenzie blinked at Draven. Did he know where the grimoire came from? Would he know her relation to Leif?

"Well? I'd like proof of this spell."

"Um, it's in my bag," Kenzie said, looking around the room. She didn't see her suitcase, or Todd. But Adam was staring at her, his brows drawn. Kenzie looked back to Draven quickly. "And I hid it with magic, which I'll need to use to reveal it."

"And how do I know you're not here to use your magic to try to destroy us? Selkies aren't known for looking out for anyone but themselves."

"I hate the shifters," Kenzie said, channeling that feeling of disappointment that she'd tapped into just moments before. "They wouldn't let me in their school."

Draven laughed. "So you come to a vampire school instead? And what do you hope to accomplish?"

"Revenge."

Draven smiled, wagging a finger at Kenzie. "I have a feeling I'm going to like you. But I'm going to need you to prove yourself, first."

Kenzie's brow shot up. "I thought I just did."

Draven shook his head. "Words, my dear. Those were just words. I want to see action. I want to see that hate light your eyes."

Kenzie took a deep breath to try to steady her racing pulse. "Of course. Whatever you need."

Draven narrowed his eyes at her. "I recognize your face. You know my daughter, Myreen, don't you?"

Kenzie's eyes widened. "Myreen's your *daughter*?"

Draven laughed again. "Don't look so surprised. I should've known her friends would come for her."

"I came to join her."

"We'll see."

"Wait a minute," Adam said, recognition lighting his eyes.

The tower shook, and there was a rumble. Some shouts came from outside, only discernible once the clamor from the lobby died down.

Draven's eyes widened. "There's an attack? On my towers?" His gaze shot to the Initiates. "How many did you leave patrolling?"

Adam stepped forward. "There were still four when we came in."

"Six! It takes at least six to cover all angles of these towers. And the middle of the day, too." Draven scowled. "Cowards.

Initiates, take up the front lines. The shifters will be less likely to kill humans. Vampires, let's take care of any who come through their ranks, shall we?"

The angelic woman threw a glance at Kenzie. "What should we do with her?"

Draven looked at Kenzie thoughtfully. "Take her with you, Beatrice. If she's true to her word, she'll help us in this fight. If not...?" Draven let the words hang in the air as he dashed up the stairs.

"Come," Beatrice said, clamping a hand around Kenzie's shoulder. "We've got work to do."

The pair headed for the stairs, and Kenzie inwardly groaned. Of course there were more stairs.

She peered at the ceiling as they ascended, cringing at the sounds of yelling coming from above. She wondered how Myreen was doing. Hopefully she hadn't been injured in the attack. Maybe they'd rescued her already. That would make Kenzie's job a lot easier.

Kenzie gulped as she considered having to defend the vampires. Maybe the shifters could do a better job than she could, but she wasn't going to give up now. She'd come too far. She just hoped she wouldn't regret this decision.

CHAPTER 15

Kol

The sun neared the top of the sky. It was the perfect time for vampires to die.

Kol was grateful for the weight on his back. It forced his lungs and wings to work twice as hard—effectively pushing the fire and adrenaline throughout his body. Finally, they were going to rescue Myreen.

Kol barely felt the hands of Private Gibson. As far as he could tell, he wasn't holding on at all. He just hoped Gibson could keep his bear inside long enough to get him to the tower. Ursas could be unpredictable, even the trained ones, and Kol would hate to lose a wing before the actual fight.

He glanced at Char beside him. Specialist Torisei gripped the edges of the blue scales at her neck with white knuckles. His eyes were closed tightly, and he looked like a ten-year-old riding his first rollercoaster. It was almost comical, except he also looked as if he might vomit the second Char dropped him off—if he could hold it that long.

The black looming spires grew in size as they drew closer. When Char and Corporal Modder scouted the location the day before, they had to stay hidden and keep below the tree line to avoid detection. With Kol's invisibility skill, Char merely had to position herself above and behind Kol as they approached, adjusting slightly as they flew closer. She was directly above him when they arrived in position, above one of the roofs where the vamps had laid tinted glass.

Kol assumed it was a sort of torture area—darkened skylights in a vampire tower—for disobedient vamps, rather than a strange masochistic fetish.

Private Gibson was up first. He leapt from Kol's back and onto the glass, shifting mid-air and growing three times his already-hulking size seconds before crashing onto the reinforced glass. Of course, the glass never thought a full-grown, monster-sized bear would ever attack it from the sky, and it shattered almost instantly.

Kol didn't stick around to spectate what happened next, because their next target was an obscure shadowed area lower down for Specialist Torisei. Kol and Char were to create chaotic distractions—as if a giant ursa wasn't distraction enough. They would then help plant more of Specialist Torisei's devices.

Kol didn't know the exact details of the devices, mainly because he specifically asked *not* to know, but they were made to change the material on the outer walls from their solid state to either a liquid or gas state without burning. In other words, melting and evaporating the very walls that protected the vampires from the sun.

Kol suspected it had something to do with changing the

molecular structure. Normally he would've insisted on learning every single detail, but his focus was on Myreen and only Myreen. He couldn't allow his own hunger for further knowledge to distract him from the goal. He could study the tech later.

When Specialist Torisei leapt lithely from Char's back onto his target area—and to his credit did *not* vomit—Kol immediately shifted his invisible scales to match Char's perfectly and split from her. He went to the right, she went to the left. The two of them only had one device each, Sergeant Char's orders, so they had to plant their devices where they could make it count. If Kol had any idea where Draven imprisoned Myreen, he would race to her wall and pluck her out before the device evaporated more than a square meter. After all, the sun's rays wouldn't harm a mer. They could be safely back at the Dome by dinner.

But he didn't know where they were holding her, and the place was enormous with its twelve towers, so there was no guessing either.

Kol found a place in the center of one of the larger towers that looked like it might do the most damage. He used his hind claws to grip the wall, but slipped. It was made of some sort of smooth stone, like obsidian. Not some high-tech metal as he'd assumed.

Could obsidian melt? he wondered, but didn't let that line of thinking get far and pumped his wings to steady himself. He'd have to plant the device while hovering. It was only a small setback, and he figured it didn't need to be bullseyed in any one spot. He just made sure to stick it firmly, like the characters did with C-4 in heist movies. Instead of a small explosion, Kol was instantly gratified with the once-solid rock looking very much like black molasses—the gingerbread house protecting the blood suckers melting right before his eyes.

Kol pushed hard against the walls to jettison himself away

from the tower, but it was to give him the space and momentum to hurl himself through the now-open wall and into the room. His brilliant blue form filled almost the entire area.

A large vampire huddled in the corner of the room. His face and arms were a scorched, angry red. But he was alive.

Kol felt a hint of disappointment at that. He'd hoped the sun's effect on a vampire would be instantaneous. As he slowly shifted, he watched the clearly weakened and suddenly non-threatening immortal creature. He waited for it to lunge at him, but since Kol shifted in full sunlight and the hole in the wall grew ever larger, he was safe.

Kol stalked from the room as the entire east-facing wall was completely melted, leaving no corner in shadow. Satisfied that the vampire was certainly a goner now, he didn't even bother to look back to make sure.

The hallway was a different story. Except for the sunlight streaming from the open door, it still had the protective darkness, albeit illuminated from artificial lighting. So he'd need to be careful. He silently cursed himself for not picking a wall with a grand hall or conference type room full of vampires, but how could Kol know the wall he chose was just individual vampire quarters?

Fortunately, the screams in the adjacent rooms both on the same floor, the floor above, and the floor below, told him that the device was creating an ever-increasing hole.

Concentrating hard, trying to remember how he had succeeded before, Kol wished himself to be unseen. To be invisible to the eyes of those who resided in these walls as he searched for the girl he loved. Finding her still seemed an impossible task, but being unseen would allow him to look longer without detection.

And it worked. Kol looked at his arms as he held them out

and saw nothing but the wall in front of him and the floor below.

It made him feel better about disobeying orders. He and Char were to plant the device only, then create a distraction by encircling the towers as if planting more devices to create panic inside while Private Gibson destroyed and killed as many vampires as he could and Specialist Torisei figured out how to get the devices to evaporate and melt more than they were capable of. Kol changed his scales to blue to match Char's, but his instructions were to shift between several different colors to give the illusion of more dragons attacking to give Gibson and Torisei time.

But there were no damned windows except those on top! How could that plan possibly work if Draven's minions couldn't even see them? And besides that, no one was tasked in finding Myreen.

So Kol improvised.

He walked down several floors without detection, hoping to overhear or find some clue about where they were holding Myreen. But the entire tower was in utter chaos, and the hallways soon became crowded with vampires at various stages of *burned to death*, staggering and slumped against the shadowed walls. Both the dead and the dying. He decided to make his way back up. Maybe one of those towers held Myreen?

"What was that?" one tiny girl asked, her tone filled with venom and her hair a mess of pink curls. She looked mostly unscathed.

Kol swore under his breath. In his desperate need to hurry and the ever-thickening crowd, he'd jabbed her shoulder with his elbow by accident. He backed against the wall as if it would help, but his own panic and growing discouragement—that his search would not only be endless, but near impossible even with his new-found skill... he suddenly felt exposed.

And then he was.

Five pairs of narrowed eyes shot to his location, including the small girl who looked years younger than Kol. The other four were clearly weakened or dying, but the girl was barely hurt.

But he was exposed. His invisibility no longer worked, and he was in a hallway full of vampires.

He did the only thing he could think of and explosion-shifted, breaking walls and furniture, and crushing a few bodies underfoot. The girl let out a shrill shriek when he clamped his teeth into her forearm, but she returned in kind with a kick to his front claw with enough force that he heard the bones cracking before they bent at a ninety-degree angle.

Kol released the girl's arm, letting out his own pained shriek, and fled—as best as he could—down the hallway, up the stairs, and away from her. But swift footsteps unimpeded by a *too-big-for-the-hallway* size, gave her the upper hand, and she soon caught up to him.

He shifted back, clutching his broken arm with his good one, and staggered toward the next door he could find, cotton-candy girl-doll on his heels. If she caught up to him, dragon or not, he'd be finished. So he put all his weight into his good shoulder, crashing through the door and into the safety of the blood-red plush carpet and streaming sunlight.

It wasn't planned, but the timing was perfect. She thought she had the upper hand and was on his heels seconds before he busted the door open, seconds before she sank her teeth into his neck as she leapt forward. But the leaping forward and Kol's collapsing to the floor gave the sunlight a straight shot. A full-frontal attack.

She screamed and clawed at her eyes—a bit dramatic in

Kol's opinion—but she was dying. He supposed it was her party. But in the burning, she managed to get behind a piece of furniture, an armoire of sorts that was partly shadowed. Then she slumped to the floor.

Kol stood, his chest heaving as he watched her. There was an open wall behind him. He could escape into the sky right now and away from the murderous vampires. But he still didn't have Myreen, nor did he have any idea where they housed her.

The vamp's breaths were labored, but she was still alive, so Kol took the opportunity to ask her. Maybe a dying vamp would be open to spilling the secrets of their leader?

"Where's the siren girl?" Kol asked, his voice low and slightly trembling.

She spat in his direction right as a voice crackled in his ear.

"Where. Are. You. *Private Dracul?*" It was Char. They'd gone radio silent when the citadel came into view—was it only a handful of minutes ago?—and Kol had forgotten he still had the earpiece in his ear.

"You mean Draven's little trophy from the fishbowl?" the vampire asked, seemingly not bothered by the burns on every inch of her skin, which were beginning to look like a red version of the melted tower walls.

Kol averted his eyes, resisting the urge to gag.

"Her name is Myreen," he said. "Where is he keeping her? One of the towers? Is there a dungeon?"

"Private?" Char hissed. "Private?" Her voice cracked on the second one. She was concerned for his safety.

Covertly, he reached up to respond, clicking the mic on and off in a Morse code response to tell her that he was all right, as well as his location.

"Why would I tell you?" the melted girl asked.

"Because you're probably going to die soon?" Kol said, feeling a little triumphant. "Because my sergeant will be here soon, and we plan to finish you off anyway before continuing our destruction?"

Since Kol had been studiously keeping his gaze away from the ruined face of the cotton candy girl, he nearly missed her eyes dart over his shoulder before a stifled sob sounded behind him.

Kol whipped around and saw *Myreen* huddled on the far side of the large bed—he should have thought it strange that this one had a bed, since the rest didn't because vampires didn't need them.

"Myreen?" he whispered, his heart suddenly stamping out an irregular beat. He felt lightheaded seeing the top of her dark, silky hair. And suddenly he felt the pain radiating from his broken arm with acuity.

He was so close to victory. All he had to do was shift, grab Myreen, and fly right out of the room. They'd done it. They'd rescued Myreen. In the split second where he considered waiting for Char or leaving now, she flew in and shifted before landing next to Kol.

"C'mon," she said. "Torisei and Gibson are out, let's find this girl and go."

With a smug smile Kol motioned with his eyes that Myreen was only a few meters away.

She smiled back. "Then let's go!"

But when Kol took one hurried step toward the beautiful girl still crouched and hidden, the forgotten vampire let out a hideous laugh that seemed to echo along the entire length of the tower.

Instinct told Kol to shift and get out before she could call for help. But suddenly he felt like he was nine years old again. Something that was normally effortless and easy for him was suddenly impossible.

He couldn't shift.

He tried again, focusing on his skin, urging it to turn into invisible scales, willing his shoulder blades to shoot out with his wings. But nothing. He remained human.

The look on Char's face told him that she couldn't shift either.

Melted-cotton-candy-girl's laughter died down a bit, but she still chuckled to herself as a figure gave her a wide berth and entered the room.

A redhead, with suddenly shorter curls, who was definitely *Kenzie*, slowly stepped forward, muttering some sort of spell under her breath. Her arms reached out as she chanted.

"Kenzie?" Kol whispered.

"Kenzie!" Myreen shouted louder. Kol witnessed Myreen finally stand in his peripheral.

Kenzie gave a half-smile to them both, but didn't stop her chanting.

"What are you doing?" Kol asked, hearing the betrayal in his voice.

Char remained silent at his side, but she reached out for his hand. He wanted to jerk away so Myreen wouldn't see, but he couldn't deny his friend that tiny bit of comfort. Char guessed before he did exactly what was happening.

"Instruct them to come this way," Draven's voice called from the shadows of the hallway.

They'd been caught. And Kenzie was helping.

Why was she helping?

Kenzie motioned with her fingers for them to follow, but Kol and Char remained where they stood. Kol because of stubbornness, but he suspected Char was frozen because of fear. Her fingers trembled in his.

"Instruct them to come this way, *now*, or the blonde one doesn't get to live."

That kickstarted Kol's feet, and the two of them scrambled toward the doorway leaving the safety of the sunlight... and Myreen, behind.

One last glance at the now-dead vampire slumped behind the armoire, Kol could see some sort of panic button clutched between her ruined fingers.

And a wicked smile on her face.

Juliet

Anxiety played Juliet like a bad song she couldn't get out of her head.

She looked over her shoulder for the sixth time to make sure no one saw her leave her bedroom. It wasn't like she was going far. And yet, she stuck to the walls like glue as she made her way to the large supply closet by the avian common room. She only had to go a few feet, but it turned her stomach completely upside down. All it would take was one of the night patrol guards to catch her—or any of the other students—and she was done for.

Sneaking around the Dome had her nerves seriously out of whack. Maybe it was because if she was caught, the punishment would come from General Dracul and not her father. She could handle a lecture from Malachai. What she *couldn't* handle was whatever awaited her if she was found gathering students to form some sort of shifter council—a council intended to oust

Eduard Dracul.

The moment Juliet's hand touched the knob, she peeked over her shoulder again, then snuck in with her back still plastered to the wall. She gave herself a second to regulate her breathing before she let her gaze fall to the students huddled inside.

Nik and the four others visibly relaxed when they saw it was only Juliet. She smiled at the group. These were shifters they could trust.

Brett was there, of course, and Alessandra, the mer who used to torture Myreen. Juliet didn't expect Alessandra to be there, but she wasn't surprised by it, either. Her connection with Kendall and her more recent support of Myreen—and hatred of all things that messed up her hair—meant she was a powerful ally for their cause. When Nik suggested Leya, the loud harpy, Juliet had her reservations, but she trusted Nik's judgement. The final student was Jesse, her ex. She was still in awe over Nik's reaction when she suggested Jesse join them.

"I know Jesse didn't agree with the new rules in the defense room," she'd said. "And I know we can trust him, we'll just have to keep that temper of his down. Maybe he knows a few other people, too." She didn't realize how nonchalant she was about her ex until she said it aloud. To her boyfriend. *She hoped it didn't rub Nik the wrong way.*

"Good idea. Ask him next time you see him. But remember to be as quiet as you can about this. I wouldn't even speak about it in front of any other students." Nik didn't even flinch. Juliet guessed there were more important things to worry about.

And Jesse was respectful of Juliet and Nik's relationship, never trying to make a move on Juliet anymore. He treated her like a friend would, and she appreciated it. She could use some friends with everything going on.

"I think we're all here," Nik said, glancing at Juliet, who nodded.

They hadn't asked anyone else. They weren't sure who they could trust.

"Okay," Nik continued. "Thank you for meeting with us."

The four other students looked at Nik expectantly. Leya wore a slightly skeptical expression, but Juliet remembered her loud complaints about being forced to keep up with the training even after healing several other students of their sprains. The harpy could barely keep her eyes open that day, let alone run laps.

"I think we're in agreement that what's happened to our school since General Dracul took over isn't ideal."

"Ha!" Jesse burst out, his tone incredulous. "*Ideal,* Candida? This *military* regiment is torture, especially for the younger students. It's hard on us too, but they're just kids!"

"Exactly," Nik agreed.

"So what do we do?" Leya asked.

Nik glanced at Juliet again. "Juliet and I thought that if a sort of shifter council was formed—of adults, obviously," he added when the other's eyes widened, "Maybe the General could be replaced with someone more... appropriate to lead the school."

"And leave General Dracul to the military," Alessandra said, crossing her arms.

"That's the idea," Juliet agreed. "And maybe even bring Oberon back."

Everyone sat in silence a moment, letting that sink in.

"I'll talk to my dad," Jesse said. "I doubt he'd be on a council, but he has connections."

"Good. This is good," Nik bounced a bit in his excitement.

The conversation then turned to which adults in the shifter community they thought would be good for a council. Delphine's name came up, obviously, but Alessandra also mentioned Queen

Anali, Kendall's grandmother. Kendall might be a traitor, but Queen Anali was definitely not. And she had plenty of influence. Besides, they still weren't sure if Delphine was being manipulated by Lord Dracul or not.

"What about your dad, Juliet?" Nik asked.

"Why are you so concerned about my dad?" she said, her defenses rising. "That's the only thing that I'm not seeing eye-to-eye with you on. He's stubborn, Nik. It'll take time to get through to him, if it doesn't take forever." She wanted to be honest with him.

"I think he could be the key, though."

"My dad?" Juliet scoffed. "You must be thinking of someone else. He wouldn't tarnish the Quinn name for something like this." Juliet was sure of it.

"He would follow you wherever you went. You might not be able to see it, but I do. He really loves you, Jules. And I can tell that he's really trying to mend what you two have. In due time, he'll come over to our side. And in the meantime, we prepare. The better prepared we are, the more he'll consider helping us."

"I'm not bringing my dad into it." Juliet folded her arms, soured by the idea, even as the other students looked hopefully between her and Nik. But something sparked in her mind, something that had been niggling at the edges of her thoughts. Something that sent chills down her back. If Dracul was using his *abilities* to influence Delphine, maybe he was using it on others, as well. Like her dad.

The conversation had moved on to other possibilities, and Juliet gladly tuned in, saving her fears about her dad for later. When they'd finished discussing the heavy stuff, and the topics turned to lighter ones, Juliet felt something she hadn't felt since Oberon left and the general took over.

Hope.

It had a contagious effect, too. Suddenly the thought of Myreen being rescued and everything going back to the way it was didn't seem so impossible.

A lull fell over the group for a brief moment.

"You know," Jesse said, looking around the small space. "Since we're practically banned from watching movies or playing video games in the common rooms, it might boost a bit of morale if we had a *secret* place to relax."

Leya's eyes widened. "I could smuggle my TV in! My parents gave me one for Christmas for my room, but I'd be happy to share it!"

"That sounds heavenly," Juliet said, daydreaming about cuddling next to Nik and falling asleep while watching a rom-com.

The chatter turned into what everyone could donate, and which other shifters they could invite into their club. Nik cautioned them about making sure they were students who could be trusted, even though it was a given. They'd all had encounters with the guards and General Dracul.

"Are you sure this is the best place to meet?" Leya said after some time, looking around the supply closet with that same skeptical look she'd worn earlier.

Nik grimaced. "It's the best we can do for now. There are eyes and ears everywhere, and the further we have to travel, the more likely we are to run into someone who'll report us."

"Maybe Katya could point us to some kitsune invention that would help," Brett suggested. When Nik raised an eyebrow at him, Brett shrugged, but even in the dim light he'd visibly colored. "She helped us before." At Juliet's look, he added, "When we took over the PA system so Kol...?"

Juliet remembered. It was kind of epic the way Kol had

stood up for Myreen in front of the whole school—via video feed—but remembering just reminded her that both Kol and Myreen were in the hands of Draven. "Right. Just don't tell her what it's for," Juliet said. It was the only thing she could think of to break up the awkwardness that had settled over their group.

Brett scoffed. "I can *guarantee* I'm better at sneaking around than your boyfriend, here," he said, hooking a thumb at Nik.

There were a few chuckles, but then the awkwardness returned. *What do we do now?* Juliet wasn't quite ready to leave the comfort and safety of this closet, and she got the sense that the others felt the same.

"Juliet," Jesse said with a warm smile. "You should show these guys that fire-rope move you did the other day when you kicked some serious vampire ass in the sim."

All eyes turned to Juliet, who squirmed under the sudden attention. "In here?" she asked, looking around the small room.

"There's an extinguisher if things get messy," Jesse said, and shrugged as he pointed to one of Mr. Suzuki's special extinguishers sitting in the corner.

Juliet glanced at Nik, but he looked more curious than concerned. And so, with as fierce a look as she could muster, Juliet stood and placed herself at the far end of the closet. She closed her eyes, and with a little bit of reluctance, found her fire. It was ready to obey her, licking at her fingertips, almost bursting to get out.

But she was afraid.

After how her fire had reacted the last time, she wasn't sure what would happen. And this time, she wasn't alone. All eyes looked at her, one pair belonging to the guy she loved.

Juliet inhaled deeply and exhaled, bringing out the fire within. Relief flooded her when the bright red and orange colors danced along her palms. She combined her hands and focused on the rope of fire that she'd created. Her fire twisted and turned at her command, coming together to make one long piece of rope. For a second, an image from the night that they'd first been attacked flashed through her mind. It was enough to keep her fire power strong.

Like a whip, Juliet slung the rope forward, and appreciative oohs and stares from the other students followed her movements. The heat coming off the rope comforted her. Her fire was back! A smile on her face, she brought the rope back behind her for another whip forward.

But this time when it snapped straight, the entire rope transformed into a thick rod of ice. Juliet tried to let go of the frozen rope, hoping to extinguish it—or whatever—but the second her fingers left the ice, it shattered. Thousands of shards crashed loudly on the floor, and it seemed to take the breath right out the room.

"Juliet," Nik said slowly, his skin pale. "What was that?"

"I... I... I don't know." Juliet stared at her hands like they were foreign objects. They'd been with her her whole life, but now they seemed like strangers.

"Okay, guys. Let's meet again in two nights." Nik's deep voice echoed through the supply closet. "Remember to watch your back and don't mention anything about what we're doing here." His gaze cut to Juliet, who still stared forlornly at her hands. "Or about what just happened. Understood?"

There was a general murmur of agreement before the students started leaving one by one—just in case there was a guard patrolling.

When the last person left, Nik grabbed two brooms from the corner. He tried to hand one to Juliet, but she didn't take it. She didn't even move. He bent so he could look her in the eyes, pulling her chin up to meet his gaze.

"Juliet, I know you're freaking out right now. Let's get this cleaned up, then you can get some sleep. That's probably all that was—lack of sleep and overworking yourself. You can skip the next meeting if you need the rest." Nik spoke fast, like he was nervous someone would cut him off. Someone like Juliet.

"No. I'm fine. You're probably right." Numbly, Juliet grabbed a broom and tried to sweep up the ice before it melted completely. "But I'm not missing any meetings," she added when Nik still sent her worried glances.

After they swept everything up, they slid on the floor with towels under their hands and knees. Not even that could bring a smile to her face. She just wanted to get everything done so she could fall apart in the comfort of her own bed.

"Jules, everything's going to be alright."

"I know. I'll meet you for breakfast tomorrow." In her haste to escape his concern, Juliet ran to the door without thinking and slammed it behind her. Her heart raced so fast that it was all she could hear in the silence of the night. When after several tense moments there was no sign of a guard, Juliet booked it to her bedroom, locking the door behind her. She didn't even look back.

Pressing her back against the door, she slid to the floor and again stared at her hands. "What the heck is happening to me?" She buried her face in those traitorous hands and stayed there until her eyelids got heavy.

Her mind spinning and her body tired, Juliet threw herself into bed and hid under the sheets, her eyes squeezed shut. If she stayed that way long enough, maybe sleep would take her.

Nik is right; sleep is all I need, she told herself over and over, though doubt plagued even her dreams.

Kol

Kol had no way to tell how much time had passed since being thrust into this cliché of a cell. It was dark and dreary and damp, just as one would expect. He wanted to laugh at how comically *mundane* it was. But they lined it with lead, so he couldn't shift or use his powers. He couldn't even stave off the stupidly typical cold, because the fire within just wouldn't ignite.

So Kol couldn't laugh. He was too weak and too *miserable* to laugh at their situation—thrown into the dungeon. And what was worse, was having Char huddled next to him, her teeth chattering uncontrollably.

It was a small blessing someone had put them in the same cell, otherwise one or both might've frozen to death. Their smart clothing was malfunctioning for some reason—probably another result of whatever also suppressed their powers—but dragons without their fire were more susceptible to cold than humans.

It's probably *why* they were jailed together. To keep each other alive with only their body heat.

But Char shouldn't have to suffer alongside him. She should've gotten out while she could. It should've been only Kol. Not her. Feeling her trembling frame pressed against him only made Kol more miserable.

He could barely keep his eyes open. Not because he was exhausted and wanted to fall into a restful sleep, but because the lead took so much out of him. It drained him. It was so effective that he had to be careful not to let even a tiny sliver of skin contact the walls or floor.

Which meant he couldn't sleep, because he'd wake up with burns—on hands when they fell to the floor, or a cheek that rested against the wall. His palms and fingers on his good arm were already an angry red from gripping the bars when they were first thrown in.

He should've known.

He should've assumed.

He shouldn't have let his damned emotions get in the way and he should've used his brain to avoid such a stupid injury.

At least the cold took away the biting pain in his broken arm—a different kind of stupid injury. There was the silver lining.

Loud footsteps warned them of someone approaching. Several someones. Char stiffened and sat up straighter, using Kol's good arm instead of the floor to re-adjust herself. Kol didn't bother to do the same. Whoever was coming—and it probably wasn't Myreen or Kenzie—didn't deserve such respect from them.

The lead bloodsucker himself came into their line of sight, marching toward Kol and Char's cell. There was a bright light shining from behind him, making Draven a tall and dark silhouette. But whoever was holding the light angled it away, so it didn't blind Kol and Char.

Kol didn't move. He was certain the vampire leader could have him killed with the snap of his finger, but he also knew if Draven had wanted him dead, it would've happened already.

"Get to your feet, Dracul prince," Draven spat when he was only a few steps away from the cell. With the light turned away, Kol's eyes slowly adjusted so he could see Draven a little clearer.

Kol only moved his eyes to look at his captor. "Lead weakens avians," he said. "Dragons, phoenix's, and harpies. But of course, you knew that because you once pumped me full of it with one of those fancy bombs."

Draven looked impatient. "I've been around since before even your father was out of diapers. I'm quite aware of what weakens *dragons and phoenixes and harpies.*" He whirled his hand as he spoke, and his tone changed at the end.

Kol hoped that meant he'd annoyed Draven and resisted the urge to smile.

"Why do you think I've lined your cell with lead?" Draven asked.

Kol shrugged and pretended not to notice how tightly wound Char was. It terrified her, and she probably didn't like the flippant way Kol was speaking to the vampire king. Kol ignored it, and she didn't say a word, either.

"If you knew, then you would know just how difficult it would be to *get to my feet,*" Kol said. He knew he was pushing the limits, but couldn't help but use a mocking tone when he repeated Draven's words.

Draven merely glared, his eyes briefly flashing red. But without saying another word, he motioned for someone unseen to come closer. A tall, slender vampire—whose cheeks were sunken-in, making him look almost malnourished—swiftly walked forward with a small device in his hand aimed at the cell.

Char let out a tiny squeak, then gripped Kol's arm tighter. Kol inclined his head to hers and whispered one word: *video*. She instantly relaxed her grip. Maybe she assumed it was a torture device. It hurt like hell, but using his broken arm, Kol gave her a reassuring tap on the hand that gripped him. It was a good thing Kol knew Charlotte so well. For being a sergeant in the shifter military, he might've expected more from her.

Maybe it was *because* he was with her, she didn't feel the need to put on a brave façade.

It was fine. Kol could be the strong one. He doubted he'd act much different if he were alone. Eduard was his father, after all. He'd long ago stopped cowering in the presence of that brand of power. The difference was that he respected his father; he had no respect for the leech.

Draven motioned to someone else out of sight, and a short, stocky, spiky-white-haired man—who looked as if he had an addiction to hair gel despite a receding hairline—rounded the corner and made quick work of unlocking the cell.

If it weren't for the weakening lead, Kol could've taken advantage. He'd been trained to defend himself without shifting—and suddenly realized Oberon's foresight and genius for insisting that they were. But he could barely keep himself upright, and he was fairly certain that without his and Char's bodies leaning against each other, they'd both be lying prostrate on the poisoned floor.

Mr. Hair Gel tore Char from Kol and shoved her at the cell's back wall—slightly less poisonous than the bars on every other side—where she crumpled like a pile of laundry, clearly in pain. He yanked Kol to his feet by jerking his good arm—

thankfully. It was quite the feat, since Kol was nearly two feet taller than the man, but the short vampire was strong and had little trouble getting Kol upright.

Draven looked Kol up and down, like he was looking for something.

Kol remained silent, certain that a string of cuss words would escape as a result of the way Mr. Hair Gel had treated Char if he allowed even one word to escape. Plus, he had to focus on staying on his feet. Crashing to the floor with a broken arm was not something on his bucket list.

Without looking at the tall vampire, Draven said, "Steadman, begin broadcasting."

Broadcasting?

Steadman pushed something on top of his recording device. A blue light lit up and pointed at Kol.

Kol's mouth went dry, but he still managed another quip. "Yes, please Steadman," he said. "We must show the other vampires how to bring down a dragon." He waited for the blow or some other show of force from Mr. Hair Gel next to him. A kick, a punch in the gut, or a twist of his broken arm so the other vampires could watch him scream.

But... nothing.

"We're in," Steadman finally said in a high-pitched, nasally voice, and Kol realized Draven had been waiting for that cue.

"Not just the vampires," Draven said, his tone calm and even. "Although they are watching." Draven brought his hands together, interlocking his fingers and dropping them in front of him. "No, your *shifter* friends in their no-longer-secret fishbowl can see you too. As well as your father."

Kol didn't have a retort for that. What purpose would Draven have to broadcast Kol in a cell? For their sakes, he hoped his execution wasn't in the script.

He gulped. "And what are you wanting my father to see?"

"Well, first of all," Draven said, holding his arms wide and entering the shot with his back toward Kol. "I want to greet our viewers, vampire and shifter alike." But he didn't keep his back toward Kol long and turned to stand next to him—on the opposite side of Mr. Hair Gel—before addressing the blue dot again. "I, Draven, have captured one of the famed Dracul line," he said. "This is Malkolm Dracul—the youngest Dracul, if I'm not mistaken." He turned to wink at Kol. "Well... *legitimate* Dracul, that is."

Kol narrowed his eyes at Draven. What was he playing at? Mention of Kol's younger half-brothers was a jab at his mother more than anyone. But he didn't think Draven said it loud enough for the mic to hear, so why mention it?

"Are you aware of your rich history, Malkolm?" Draven asked, speaking loud again for the camera.

Kol's stomach lurched and his first thought sped to Aline and the Dracul curse. But the feeling passed quickly. What could Draven do in relation to the curse that the curse hadn't done already?

"Your ancestor, *Vlad Dracul* specifically?"

Ah, Vlad. The entire world knew about Vlad.

"He was a dragon king who killed a lot of vampires," Kol spouted with no emotion. "Everyone knows that," he added.

Draven reached out and gripped the fingertips of Kol's injured arm and twisted slightly, causing a twinge to radiate all the way to his shoulder. He felt his face flinch, but gave no other indication of the intense pain. He'd had worse. Draven immediately released his fingers, then turned to face him, but made sure the camera could still see his profile.

"If everyone knows the history of Vlad *Dracul*, can you

guess what I plan to mention next?"

Kol stared at him without breaking eye-contact. "That you have a lot of angry vampires who want my head?" Somehow, he kept his tone and volume the same as before, even though he could feel his pulse beating inside his arm.

Draven laughed a throaty laugh, acting as if he had thousands of audience members joining in. After a moment, he made a *tsk* sound directed at Kol, then pointed a finger at his face. "That princely arrogance," he said. "You've had it your entire life, no? You've waved your *title* around like you're the son of a king since you learned to crawl."

Kol was silent. He wasn't sure the reaction Draven was expecting, but whatever his aim was... he didn't seem to be getting what he was looking for.

"But the Dracul's are nobodies, amiright? Just haughty dragons who think they're better than the other shifters." Draven aimed a smirk at the blue light.

Was he trying to start some mutiny? Did he have any idea about the Dracul's at all? Sure, Kol abhorred the deference he often received for being a Dracul, but they'd been instrumental in the safety of shifters for centuries. Was Draven trying to drag the name through the mud?

"*Dracul Royalty* is a delusional title. You aren't *royalty*." He paused for effect. "You're all nothing more than a bunch of fire-breathing lizards."

Kol couldn't help the way his eyebrow arched.

Draven stared at him for a handful of seconds, but didn't allow emotion to give away his thoughts.

"Do the other shifters realize that they've allowed the Dracul's to throw their name around as if they're *gods* for long enough? Someday I hope they wizen up and realize that they don't need the likes of Eduard Dracul dictating them."

Kol refused to comment on that. He could see what Draven was trying to do, and most of it had nothing to do with him, other than being a Dracul himself and the son of Eduard. But Draven clearly didn't know Kol hated being treated like royalty. Perhaps he was attempting to damage Kol's family pride?

Draven stared at Kol again, like his face would somehow reveal the right buttons to injure him. Obviously, the vampire leader didn't know about his history with Myreen, otherwise he might've used her.

He prayed that Draven wouldn't look to Char, and he kept his posture and gaze studiously away from the corner where she cowered. Char remained essentially motionless, which was smart; keep the attention off her.

With clenched teeth, Draven leaned forward and gripped Kol's good hand. "I will make an example of you, *prince*," he said and snapped Kol's other arm at the word.

Kol couldn't help but cry out, causing Char to lurch toward him before realizing what she'd done.

Draven gave her one knowing glance before turning back to his blue light. "I assure you my friends, I will make an example of this *pretender*. Many of you remember the actions of Vlad, and you will finally get your revenge." Without taking a breath, but shifting his expression to one of malice, he continued. "And to the shifters... I would advise you to surrender now. You have lost."

The blue light blinked off. And Kol blacked out.

Myreen

Myreen woke the next day in a room she barely recognized. The same terror she'd felt on the first day welled in her again as she remembered the horror of the attack. How the walls melted to nothingness under the shifter tech. How one of the vampires who had been guarding her ended up dead, sizzled to a crisp by the sunlight that had never before penetrated the towers.

And Kol.

Myreen wasn't sure she ever wanted to see him again. The betrayal still stung, but now he was here, in Draven's custody. He and the other dragon had been taken to the dungeon immediately, thanks to Kenzie's magic—another mind boggler. Who was the other dragon and why had she grabbed Kol's hand like that? Did he have another girl on the side, just waiting for him to be free of his "job" seducing the prophesied siren?

It was awful to consider, but him being in Draven's custody

was worse than anything she'd ever wish on him. Especially after seeing the video of him with Draven. Myreen shuddered to think of what he was going through down there. Did Draven have that gas in the room to keep Kol and the other dragon from shifting?

So she decided to sneak down there and see him for herself. Kendall had warned her to stay away from the dungeon, but if Kol was in there, she had to risk it. And now was the perfect time—the time of day Ty had told her the vampires started teaching classes, leaving much of the school open to curious eyes.

And Myreen pulled a Ty and raced ahead of her guards down the stairs, hopping in the elevator and forcing the doors closed, descending before they had a chance to catch up. That should buy her some time.

But when she reached the lobby, she spotted a shock of red hair, and her jaw clenched. Kenzie. Myreen wasn't sure whether to be excited or angry to see her friend. And the whole Kol matter only further muddied things.

Myreen changed course to pursue, and caught up with Kenzie in the stairwell leading to the classrooms.

Kenzie whirled around, her face flooding with shock, then relief. She launched into a hug that Myreen didn't know how to respond to, so Myreen patted her back and waited for Kenzie's anaconda arms to loosen.

"There you are!" Kenzie said, keeping her voice low despite her excitement.

"Yeah, I'm here. What are you doing here?" Myreen crossed her arms and stepped back.

"What do you think?"

Kenzie scanned the stairs, and Myreen glanced around too. They appeared to be alone, and Kenzie started walking up again, but Myreen went the other way, and once Kenzie realized, she followed. They could talk in the human quarters, and it would get Myreen closer to the dungeons, her original goal.

"What does he want with you?" Kenzie asked when the lobby faded from view.

"Well, for starters, I'm his daughter." Kenzie nodded like she already knew, but Myreen went on, knowing the next part was the clincher. "He says he wants to unite shifters and vampires by creating hybrids—through my blood."

"What?" Kenzie asked, grabbing Myreen's arm as she came to a halt. "You're kidding me."

Myreen shook her head. "He's also got a son. My half-brother. Ty." Myreen smiled. "He's super adorable. You'd love him."

Kenzie eyed the stairs again, then leaned toward Myreen. "I have a hard time believing *he* could spawn anything but the devil."

Myreen half-laughed. "You'll have to meet Ty."

"You're not considering staying, are you?" Kenzie's brows furrowed.

Myreen hooked an arm through Kenzie's elbow as she guided her toward the next flight of stairs. "Let's just say I'm undecided."

"You can't be serious."

"Kenzie, he's my biological father. And I think Ty needs me. He's only ten, and he's the only kid in this castle. I think he's lonely."

"Myreen, he's a vampire."

Myreen shook her head. "Not yet. Draven won't turn him until he turns eighteen."

Kenzie's chin lengthened as she appeared to consider the new information. "Okay. So we break him out. Along with you and Kol and that other dragon chick and..."

Myreen wasn't interested in leaving just yet, but the sentence hung in the air, piquing her curiosity. "Is there someone else?"

Kenzie sighed. "Okay, so you remember there were three guys I was interested in?"

Myreen nodded.

"Well, one's a vampire."

"Kenzie!" Myreen said, then clamped a hand over her mouth.

"But he's not like a normal vampire. He's kind and good and sort of sweet when he's not being a complete dork."

Myreen's brows rose.

"I'm sorry I didn't tell you before. I just thought... with your mom and all—"

"I get it. It's okay. Before this, I probably would've freaked."

"I'm still freaked. One of the other guys is one the Initiates here. Adam. And he's pretty high up."

"Seriously?"

"Yeah, but Adam's a jerk. I think he's part of the reason Leif—the good vampire—is in trouble now. Adam was basically stalking Leif when I got in the way."

Myreen raised a questioning brow. "Anything else you've been hiding?"

Kenzie looked at the floor. "Yeah. I got the family grimoire back. It's the key to unlocking my magic, and now I'm here, using it to give Draven the daywalker ability—"

"Wait. What?"

Kenzie gave a sheepish grin. "Unless you want to come with me before he can get the ingredients needed to perform the spell?"

Myreen shook her head. "You'll have to figure that out on your own. I can't believe you'd do all that just to try to get me back."

Kenzie shrugged one shoulder. "You're my girl. And like I said, I had more than one reason to stage a rescue. And the list keeps growing."

"Yeah." Myreen looked at the floor as they stopped in the

middle of the bottom common room. The final room before the dungeons. "Any chance you can break Kol out of here?"

"I'm going to try. I hate that I had to trap him. And I'm sorry I had to do it in front of you."

"I'm not gonna lie. Part of me felt like he deserved it."

"Why?"

Myreen sighed. "He was only dating me because his father ordered him to."

Kenzie's brows furrowed. "Are you sure?"

"His dad told me. And Kol never denied it."

"Do you... hate him?"

Myreen shrugged. "I don't know. Maybe? I haven't had a lot of time to process."

"Yeah. I get that." But Kenzie was still peering at Myreen, doubt clouding her face. Myreen rubbed her arm, wondering what was going through Kenzie's head.

"Do you feel like you're... in control?" Kenzie asked, still looking at her funny.

"Of course. Why?"

Kenzie shook her head. "It's probably nothing. I should go. You know, people to check on, places to see, school to sludge through."

"Okay." Myreen wasn't sure if it was okay. The way Kenzie had looked at her made her feel like something was off. But she had her own person to check on. "If you do stage a rescue, the only places I've found to get out are the front door and the one to the roof. It's at the top and up the central stairwell."

"Thanks." Kenzie headed for the exit, but stopped when she noticed Myreen wasn't following. "You coming back upstairs?"

Myreen shook her head. "Not yet. I think I want to visit..." She looked over her shoulder, thinking of a reason not to have to go back up, but remembered Kendall lived on this floor. "A friend."

Kenzie snorted. "Made a friend with the lowly humans already?"

"Ha ha," Myreen deadpanned.

Kenzie shrugged. "Alright. See ya."

Myreen waved goodbye, waiting until Kenzie was out of sight before taking one last glance around the room and heading toward the dungeon.

She crept down the stairs slowly, unsure if she was allowed down here after her talk with Kendall. But she needed to see for herself that Kol was okay, that he hadn't been killed because of her.

As she reached the bottom of the stairs, she stiffened. There were two guards a little further in. They couldn't see her yet, and she took a moment to breathe and think. Kendall had warned her to stay out of trouble, and there was a good chance trying to see Kol wouldn't earn her any brownie points. But she had to see him. Despite everything, she couldn't deny there was still a draw there, something pulling her toward Kol.

She had an idea, one that turned her stomach, but she didn't see any way around it. She'd have to use her siren ability. Draven's one rule was that she not use her powers on him. But he didn't say anything about not using her powers on anyone else in the school. It was a flimsy loophole, but it was her only option and she was going to take it.

Myreen held her head high, calling on the burning need inside her and stepped into the room. The guards there froze at the sight of her, both men looking at her like she was the predator, even though they were the vampires.

"I'm to be allowed to see the dragon shifters unhindered and unaccompanied," Myreen said, her voice a melodious tone vibrating with the power of her will. "You will not interfere as long as I'm here, and you will forget I was here once I leave. Do you understand?"

The guards, who had taken on a glassy-eyed look, nodded.

Myreen let go of her hold and proceeded forward. She walked with her head up and her shoulders back, as if she belonged there. The men shook out of their stupor, but let her pass without further glance.

Myreen scanned the cages in this room for any sign of Kol. Instead, she found a human—an Initiate, she assumed—wide-eyed and cowering. Myreen bit her lip and turned her head. She didn't know what the guy had done to deserve such treatment, but she couldn't allow herself to become side-tracked.

Myreen went through the door and found herself among more cages. This room was empty of both guards and prisoners, and Myreen breathed a sigh of relief. She pressed forward again.

Peering into the third room, she saw Kol and the girl he'd been caught with. There were also four vampires standing guard. She almost turned back right then. Myreen didn't know to what extent she could use her siren ability, and the thought of Kol's hand holding tight to that girl's as they were captured threatened to derail her mission. But she'd already come this far.

Myreen gathered what remained of her courage and stepped into the room, commanding these guards the same way she'd commanded the last. And to her surprise, all four of them listened and obeyed. She wondered just how many people she could influence at once.

Thankfully, her influence seemed to be attached to her will, because Kol and the other dragon-shifter remained unaffected. She didn't want to siren them unless absolutely necessary.

The girl huddled in the corner of the cage, but when she spied Myreen, her eyes went wide. She nudged Kol, who lay next to her on the floor like the cold robot he always pretended to be.

Myreen worried for a moment that Kol was dead, but he sat up—with help from the girl, thanks to his two broken arms—and took on the same worried expression. "Myreen! What are you doing here?" he hissed, warily eying the guards. But they didn't even acknowledge Kol or Myreen.

"It's okay. I just wanted to talk." Myreen had the urge to go to him, to try to heal his wounds. But there wasn't enough light down here, and her gaze wandered to the girl sharing Kol's cage, triggering an uncomfortable tightness in Myreen's stomach.

Kol looked baffled. "About what? If you can move freely—"

"I'm not a prisoner, but I'm not exactly free to leave, either. And there are... complications."

"What complications? Never mind. I don't think I want to know." Kol lowered his gaze, and the girl with him put a hand on his shoulder.

Even as dirty and frightened as the other dragon was, she was beautiful. It almost didn't surprise Myreen that Kol would be with her. She looked to be everything Myreen wasn't. And she was a dragon—a great one too, if her brief glimpse during the attack was accurate.

Myreen addressed the blond. "What's your name?"

"Char."

Myreen took a deep breath, then turned, her mind whirling. "This was a mistake. I'm sorry. I just needed to make sure..." Make sure what? Myreen didn't even know anymore. And she worried that the guards would find her any moment now. She fingered the necklace, grateful the ursa in her wasn't in control.

"Myreen, wait." Kol's voice cracked, freezing Myreen to where she stood.

"What?" Myreen didn't like the hard tone in her voice, but if it weren't for that, she'd probably sound pathetic.

"Promise me you'll get out of here."

"No." She whirled back on Kol, venom seeping into her voice. "I don't have to do anything you say. You're. Not. My. Boyfriend."

Kol looked visibly stricken. "I know. I just... Please. If you died..."

Char looked at Myreen with pleading eyes, chewing on her lip as her hand tightened on Kol's shoulder.

"I'm Draven's daughter. He wouldn't kill me. Just don't do anything stupid, okay? Kenzie's working on a way to get you two out of here."

Kol's mouth puckered like he was sucking on a lemon. "I'm not sure her *magic* will be enough."

Myreen rolled her eyes. "Enough or not, she's the best shot you've got right now."

Kol sighed.

"It'll be okay," Char said, though she looked as unsure as Kol.

"And I'll see what I can do," Myreen added, tugging again at her necklace.

"No. Just let Kenzie work her magic," Kol said. There was a thread of panic in those steely eyes of his, and Myreen nearly relented. But Char was still there, still comforting Kol.

"Goodbye." Myreen left in a huff. She wasn't sure who she was angry at—Char for being there for Kol, Kol for letting her, or herself for letting her heart lead her into a world of pain. Again.

Myreen fled from the dungeon, back to the safety of the rest of the citadel, and headed toward the kitchen. The guards could find her there, stuffing her face and feelings with chocolate or ice cream or something—anything—sweet.

CHAPTER 19

Kenzie

Kenzie sat in one of the Initiate common rooms, staring at her thumbs. They spun in circles around each other, accomplishing nothing even while staying perpetually in motion.

Right about now, she hated herself. What was wrong with Kol? He was right there, with Myreen. If he'd been quicker, she wouldn't have been able to use her magic on him, trapping him there. Now he was stuck down in those dungeons with his dragon friend—she knew the girl couldn't be anything more, not to Kol—rotting away. All because of her.

She'd used a fairly simple binding spell, just one of the ones she'd ended up memorizing for fun and a little added protection. It didn't make sense, guarding herself against vampires but not shifters. And so she'd armed herself. Sure, the shifters were supposed to be the good guys, but so was she.

Except now she wasn't.

Playing the villain sounded like fun, but when it hurt her friends—or her best friend's... well, whatever he was—it sucked. Her stomach had tied itself in knots, and she'd barely touched any food since. This whole ordeal sickened her.

And Myreen was Draven's daughter. Talk about complicated. Kenzie had no idea how she was going to convince Myreen to give up her "happy little family." And she had serious doubts about this Ty kid. Would Draven be so cruel as to use someone so young to manipulate Myreen? It certainly seemed possible.

Not to mention she was now questioning the spell she'd done with Mom and Gram to lift Kol's family curse. She'd been so certain. She'd *felt* the magic flowing from her, the warmth as the blood seeped into Kol's skin. But Myreen hated him. Kenzie nearly spilled the story when Myreen confronted her, but her promise to Kol rang through her mind—that she wouldn't tell Myreen until the curse was broken. The silence was killing her. She wanted to scream at something, but she had to keep her cool. She'd sort through this mess, one way or another. Maybe.

"Kenzie!" came a familiar voice, and Kenzie looked up, her eyes wide. Adam ambled over, sitting next to her and snaking an arm across the couch behind her.

Kenzie wasn't sure whether to throw herself at him or flee, anger at what he'd done warring with the attraction she still felt toward him. Instead, she sat still, waiting to see what he'd do next.

"Ha! A selkie. You know, just seeing you and hearing what you are has brought back a lot of memories. Memories I seemed to have forgotten. You wouldn't happen to know anything about that, would you?"

Kenzie bit her lower lip, staring at her thumbs again, which had resumed their pacing, kicking up the speed a notch.

"But you're cute. And if you pass Draven's test, then I'm

willing to forgive all that." He put his lips next to her ear and whispered, "We had so much fun together."

Kenzie broke out in goosebumps, and she pulled her arms over her stomach. "Test? I thought I'd already passed Draven's test."

"That was before he made the connection between you and Leif."

Kenzie blinked several times, then tilted her head to look at Adam. His guy-lined eyes twinkled, and a jagged clump of hair fell in front of his face, begging to be pushed back. Kenzie's breath hitched as Adam brought his face closer to hers. "I've proven myself to be very useful to Draven, and I'm due for a promotion. If I'm lucky enough to earn an Initiate, I want you."

Kenzie's heart beat an erratic tune, longing and repulsion warring within her. There was something almost animalistic about Adam in the way he looked at her, and Kenzie couldn't deny the chemistry between them was strong. But he was a vampire wannabe.

And he's no Wes.

Kenzie shook her head at the errant thought. She needed to put Wes out of her mind.

"I'm flattered you'd think of me," Kenzie said, looking up at Adam through her lashes, her mind racing a thousand miles a minute. She didn't want Adam, not really, but his position with the vampires might prove a useful resource. Kenzie prayed to the fates that she wouldn't end up in over her head, but she was going to do her best to keep on his good side. If he had one.

"Good. Now go show Draven what a gem you are."

Kenzie nodded and stood, wincing as Adam gave her a tap on her rear. She hated that her attraction to him was still so strong, especially after everything he'd done. But if it played in her favor, she'd use it. She didn't feel like she had much choice.

Not with so much at stake.

***

Kenzie made her way back to the lobby—up another flight of steps, which it seemed there was no end of—and to the room that everyone called Draven's trophy room. She knocked tentatively on the door, and when she was told to enter, she did.

The trophy room was more like a horror showcase. Bits and pieces of different shifters lined the room—stingers, wings, tails, fins—each piece well-preserved, many bearing the lacquered gloss of taxidermy specimens. Kenzie's stomach turned as she stared at the mountings with a slack jaw, envisioning the shifters they'd belonged to—shifters like Myreen and Juliet and Kol.

"Ah, the selkie of the hour. Come in, come in." Draven beckoned Kenzie to the seat in front of his desk, and she sat down, giving him as genuine of a smile as she could muster. If she just stared at his face—his flawless, incredibly drool-worthy face—maybe she could forget he was a soulless monster. Maybe.

"So it comes to my attention that you were aiding Leif in his exploits in Chicago. Adam seems to think you were Leif's main food source, but I know how repulsed Leif is by taking blood straight from humans."

Kenzie's face paled, and she looked at her lap, biting on her tongue and breathing hard through her nose. She'd come a long way with the whole blood-phobia, but even the mention of it still made her twitchy. She adjusted in her seat.

"Nervous?" Draven asked, coming to the front of the desk and leaning on it.

Kenzie shook her head. "No, I have hemophobia."

"A fear of—"

"Yes," Kenzie said, then clamped a hand over her mouth. She'd seen the way the other Initiates treated Draven, and she didn't want to make a bad impression by not following protocol. "Sorry."

Draven chuckled. "It's okay. I prefer to know these kinds of things about the people in my employ. It also continues to beg the question: why turn to vampires?"

"I told you. I hate the shifters."

"Because they wouldn't let you in their school?"

Kenzie shrugged. "What can I say? I can be petty."

Draven chuckled. "Not with me, I hope."

Kenzie smiled. "Of course not. I know when I can cross the lines and when I can't."

"Smart girl. And you've chosen wisely. Soon the vampires will rule the world, as nature intended."

Kenzie nodded numbly, wondering if it had anything to do with his plan to create hybrids with Myreen's blood.

"You don't agree?"

"I'm sorry?" Kenzie didn't think he'd asked her a question, but she worried her mind had wandered off.

"That vampires should rule the world. You were rather chatty until I brought that up."

Kenzie snorted. "I don't care who rules the world, so much, as long as I get to use my magic in peace."

Draven nodded. "Then our purposes should align nicely." He pushed off the desk and began walking around the room, admiring the pieces he'd placed there. "So what exactly did you do with Leif?"

Kenzie wrinkled her nose. That was one question she wasn't prepared for. Should she tell him the truth? "He was using me for my magic." She hoped her poker face held. If Leif was being tortured, then he obviously wasn't on the nice list. She didn't want to appear to be an ally of Draven's enemy.

Draven snapped his fingers and turned to her. "His selkie

love. Of course. I should've seen that one coming. He's never quite been able to let go of the past." He peered at Kenzie. "Yes. And you must be a relation, if you have the daywalker spell. MacLugh. Am I right?"

Kenzie bit her lower lip.

"Don't play coy with me. There are no secrets here, Kenzie MacLugh. You were on my radar long before you decided to come. The question is, will you last?"

Kenzie met his steely gaze. "Of course. I don't do things by halves."

"Good. Then you won't have any issue stripping Leif of his daywalking abilities." Kenzie's eyes widened. "He has a gift, one that he's refused to use to its full potential. And while I'm eager to possess such power, I need to know you can be trusted first."

Kenzie nodded. "Of course. My grimoire has a spell for nearly everything." She hoped. Well, sort of. It didn't seem right, taking away Leif's daywalking ability, especially as it was one of the few remaining things Leif had from Gemma.

"Such a good little selkie. I wonder if your mother and grandmother would agree?"

Kenzie adjusted in her seat again, leaning an elbow on the armrest and her cheek on her fist. Somehow she was managing to keep her heartbeat steady. All these years of pretending to be bored had finally paid off. Hopefully. "They do their thing, I do mine."

Draven laughed.

"Are we doing this thing now, or do I have time to prepare?"

"Do you *need* time to prepare?"

Kenzie shrugged.

"You don't know, or you don't care?"

Kenzie smirked. "A little of both. There's not a counter-spell in the grimoire. I'll have to improvise based on what I do have. Enacting the daywalker spell is pretty complicated, but deactivating shouldn't be nearly as hard. I think."

"And why is that, exactly?"

Kenzie shrugged again. "I guess because selkie magic is a funny thing. But if you really think about it, a vampire walking in daylight kinda goes against the rules. It's like putting in a cheat code. It's going to take more work to set that up than it would to reset it to the way it's supposed to be." Not exactly true. Selkies did a lot of magic that went against nature. *Like trying to bring a person back from the dead.* But Draven didn't need to know that. As it was, she hoped her knowledge of the spell would allow her to take away Leif's daywalking ability, but only temporarily. Assuming neither of them caught on fire in the process. Spell manipulation wasn't exactly safe magic.

Draven nodded. "Well then, let's test this theory of yours out and see if we can't make a daywalking vampire just a vampire again."

Kenzie nodded and stood. She tried to think of it as anything but what it was. Anything at all. But she kept envisioning Leif's face as he realized what a monster Kenzie had become.

She followed Draven to the lobby.

Thank the fates this place had an elevator. Her first time to the top of the citadel was on the back of Beatrice, the world a blur as the vampire raced up what seemed like millions of steps. Kenzie hadn't noticed the elevator then, and she'd been too distracted by her role in capturing Kol to really pay attention to the way they got back down.

But an elevator was the last thing she'd expect in a place like this. If she had to guess, the citadel had been around for a very long time. It had the ancient, unchanging quality of Leif, though the school was decidedly darker and more disturbing.

Draven reached the elevator first and slid his keycard through the waiting slot. The silvery door sprang open as if it had been waiting for them. Kenzie took a spot in the corner, leaning against the railing. Her heart was already racing, so it didn't much matter when the door closed, and she realized she was alone with the most dangerous vampire in the world. She was betting on him not wanting to kill her, but that didn't stop her from worrying that no one could hear her scream if he changed his mind.

And the elevator seemed to take forever. Even Draven started tapping his foot. No doubt with his speed, he could've taken the stairs and beat her to the top. But Kenzie was grateful she didn't have to walk those stairs—or ride Draven's back.

"And you don't need your grimoire for this?" Draven asked as a chime sounded and the doors slid open.

Kenzie followed him off the elevator and to one of the large round stairwells—of course there were more stairs, this place was riddled with them—and began the ascent into what she assumed was one of the towers crowning this place. Some of the stairwells had been blocked off by yellow caution tape.

She'd heard three towers were destroyed, the walls stripped away like magic, making them unlivable for vampires. And there had been some additional damaged, though she had no idea what happened there. Why a vampire castle would have a glass window seemed odd, and why the shifters would break through the glass as well as strip away walls was beyond her.

She still couldn't believe Kol had been so stupid. But she'd get them out. What was rescuing one more person, right? *Or two.* The dragon he'd brought with him probably didn't want to stay here, either.

At last they reached a room, and Draven knocked before stepping inside. Kenzie entered, marveling at the silver and purple decorating the space. It was so different from the rest of the citadel, almost soft in its feminine beauty, though with a hint of the hard edge that every vampire seemed to carry.

"Draven, I'm honored," said Beatrice, the woman Kenzie had once thought an angel. Her features were just as beautiful as the last time, though this time Kenzie wasn't fogged by the haze of venom.

Kenzie wanted to say she saw the cruel glint in Beatrice's eyes, but it was the pitiful form of Leif lounging on a couch that really drove that point home. His hands were bound in front of him, caught between shining steel cuffs, his head lolled back. He looked exhausted—quite the feat for a vampire—his eyes sunken in, a haunted look to them.

And the haunted look only grew worse when he noticed Kenzie.

"Gemma?" he said, his voice barely more than a whisper.

Kenzie's breath hitched. If only she *were* Gemma. The woman he loved was practically a legend. *She'd* figured out how to make Leif a daywalker. *She'd* have known what to do. *She* could've pulled a perfect spell from the grimoire to fix all of this.

Kenzie was no Gemma.

Kenzie shook her head, but as Beatrice shot narrowed eyes at Kenzie, the dangerously beautiful woman suddenly smiled.

"Perfect. Yes, Gemma. I hear you have a spell you'd like to show Leif."

Kenzie paled. "You want me to pretend to be—?"

"Yes," Beatrice said.

Draven nodded. "It seems fitting, doesn't it?"

Kenzie swallowed. "Yes. Of course." She gave Leif a small smile—the same one she'd flashed at Kol to try to let him know that she wasn't the enemy, despite her actions.

Leif sat up, fear and hope flashing across his face. What had he been through to elicit this type of reaction? "Your hair..."

"Do you like it?" Kenzie asked, self-consciously touching the short locks.

Leif shook his head.

Kenzie swallowed hard, then turned to look at Draven and Beatrice. Draven had his arms crossed, and Beatrice looked like she wasn't enjoying this interaction at all. Kenzie needed to get it over with.

With a deep breath, Kenzie sat on the lush purple couch beside Leif and took his hands in hers. "Just know that I'm only trying to do what's right."

Closing her eyes, she took a deep breath and began, a slight tremble in her voice. "Vampír, créatúrnal ghealaís, glachadha leissana noíche, bíodha eaglortír ansalágh. Vampír, créatúrnal ghealaís, bhithina chúpúla solaras noíche." She'd memorized the daywalker spell, so she didn't need the grimoire to come up with a deviation. She just hoped leaving off the final phrase would make everything temporary.

She ended the spell strong and sure, letting the magic flow slowly through her, setting every intention for it to do the job only half way. She needed Leif to show a weakness for the sun to convince Draven of her compliance, but she didn't want to completely destroy the magic that had allowed him to walk in light for so long.

And she could almost feel that magic, the protection balling tight within Leif as her spell did its work. It was as if she'd formed a box around Gemma's magic, locking away his daywalking ability. For now.

Kenzie opened her eyes and looked into Leif's. He held a look of awe, one of rapt attention. Guilt swamped her, but she shook it off, slipping out of his hands.

She stood, turning to Beatrice and Draven. "It's done."

Draven lifted a brow. "That remains to be seen. Beatrice?" He gestured to the door.

Beatrice nodded, picking up Leif like a doll and carrying him out of the room. Leif didn't even squeak in protest, his head lolling back.

They made quick work of the stairs, but at the room with the many stairwells, Beatrice headed toward one with caution tape in front and strode through, Draven behind her. Kenzie followed, chewing on her lip. They climbed until they stood in front of a door, bright light seeping under the bottom.

Beatrice put Leif down and nudged him forward, then looked back at Kenzie. "You'll have to do the honors."

Kenzie nodded, her mouth in a firm line. She marched forward and gripped the knob, then slowly turned, easing the door open a crack. Beatrice and Draven were far enough back, though Kenzie saw Beatrice take another step. Leif, however, took a step forward. The smile on his face instantly melted as his arm passed through a shaft of light, and he cried out as he fell to the floor, whimpering like a puppy.

Kenzie slammed the door shut, gagging at the sight of Leif's charred flesh. It curled up in spots like burned paper, an angry, blistering red with black edges. And the smell, like burned hotdogs, filled her nostrils.

Kenzie gazed at the floor as she composed herself, opening her mouth to keep the stench out of her nose. She concentrated on keeping her face neutral, though all she wanted to do was descend in a fit of tears on Leif, to try to apologize, to make everything better. When she felt she was ready, she turned to Draven. "Am I in?"

Draven smiled. "Yes. Excellent. Just as soon as you make me a daywalker."

Kenzie took a deep breath through her mouth and released

it. "I'll need two more things for my spell to work."

Draven's face hardened.

Kenzie plunged ahead. "The petals and roots of a moonflower picked during a full moon, and the seeds of a sunflower. I would've gotten them both myself before I made the journey, but I don't have the means for the moonflower, and I'm sure you'd rather your sunflower seeds were fresh."

"You do realize we just had a full moon."

"I do. And if you're lucky, someone picked a moonflower, roots and all, the other day. The internet has all kinds."

Draven scowled. "And if not?"

Kenzie shrugged. "I guess we have to wait for the next full moon?"

"For your sake, I hope that's not the case. You're lucky I'm a patient man, but my patience has limits."

"Of course." Kenzie nodded and prayed to the fates. Hopefully she'd have Myreen out of here before Draven found the ingredients.

"Why didn't you tell me about this little stipulation from the beginning?"

Kenzie cleared her throat. "Between the attack and getting settled, I didn't really have the time."

Draven gave a noncommittal hum, but didn't press her further. To be honest, she had hoped it wouldn't come up, just in case she needed more time.

She cut another glance at Leif, who was curled on the floor like a child, still whimpering. It was so tempting to just break down. The only thing that kept her going was pretending that it was Draven on the floor instead of Leif.

It almost made her feel better. Almost.

Juliet

Juliet stopped and leaned against the wall to calm her breathing. She tried to think of all things positive in her life. She was back together with Nik. She knew the students weren't on board with the new changes in the school. And... that was it. But it was something.

Think of the good, she repeated to herself as she slipped her headphones on. *Think of the good.* That would be her new mantra. She needed something to stay afloat, especially after seeing that horrible video of Kol at the hands of Draven. Juliet shuddered. Kol had only been in Draven's custody a few days, if the rumor mill was to be trusted, and if he looked like *that* after only a few days, she couldn't even imagine what Myreen was going through. And Kenzie going after her...

Think of the good. She had to get her emotions under control before she lit something on fire. Thinking about the things she couldn't control wasn't helping anything.

"Keep walking. Get to your next class." A large guard with blank eyes poked Juliet's arm.

She hadn't even realized she'd stopped moving.

"Excuse me!" Juliet slung her hand down and brought her fire to the surface of her palms, giving the guard a menacing glare. Still, he met her with a blank stare.

"Juliet, please," Nik said as he came beside her, his voice like a ray of sunshine peeking from a dark and cloudy sky. "Come on, come with me."

Her fire sizzled out, but she didn't drop the stare-off with the guard. "Touch me again and I'll burn your finger off." She was crossing a very dangerous line, but her pent up frustration bubbled over, and in that moment, she didn't care what the repercussions were.

The guard opened his little electronic tablet and entered something, then snapped it shut. He turned to face Nik. "Control her, private."

That. Was. It.

The mantra she'd been repeating melted away. If she didn't shift, like *now*, she might explode. But she couldn't, not without going to the Defense Room and punishing herself with more work. So like an upset toddler, Juliet stomped the whole way to her room, slamming the door behind her.

She threw herself onto her bed and stuffed her face in her pillow so no one could hear her scream. Despite her theatrics, she heard the door softly open and close. She lifted herself off the bed, giving her sheets a final punch. But none of it had helped.

She needed to let her fire out, she just had to.

Juliet saw the look of worry in Nik's eyes, but she was too furious to care. With her head back, she opened both of her fists in front of her and let her power escape. As soon as it did, she felt weightless. Her hands looked like flamethrowers. She smiled, her chest swelling with pride. She felt at one with her fire again.

The deep red color of her flames was almost hypnotic, but ultimately, it was a distraction.

Like a waterfall, the new freeze enveloped her warm comfort, turning her insides cold. Her stomach tightened in response until her breath hitched. But the freeze didn't make her shiver or want to cover up. It felt comfortable, like her heat. It was just so... different.

And then the cold reached her hands. She tried to suck in her heat before it changed, but it was too late.

As if in slow motion, the flames straightened and stilled, no longer dancing like waves. Then, like magic, the redness morphed into a sparkling blue, starting from the bottom where her fire met her palms and ending at the tip top of her rigid flames. Juliet looked at them like they weren't real. If Nik wasn't with her, she would've thought she was dreaming.

"Jules," Nik whispered and walked slowly toward her.

Juliet couldn't move. Couldn't breathe. Couldn't comprehend what was happening. She blinked a few times just to reacquaint herself with her surroundings. *What should I do?* With her fire, she could just put it back in her body. But ice? That seemed impossible. Instead she dashed to her towel and slid the pillars of ice off her hands as gently as she could—she didn't want to clean up another mess.

Nik was right behind her, and as soon as her hands were free, he pulled her into a much-needed hug. She sunk into him as the lump in her throat grew, her eyes burning, and sobbed into his chest.

They stayed that way until Juliet began to hiccup from crying so much.

She pulled away and wiped her eyes. As she looked at the melting ice towers, all she could do was shrug. "I just don't understand. I had my fire under control. Why is this happening?"

Juliet stared at the floor, but Nik lifted her chin.

"I strongly believe that things like this happen only to those who are valiant enough to endure it. Don't let this set you back. These changes will only make you stronger." He sounded like he was reading from a fortune cookie.

Juliet wanted to smile, but she wasn't there yet. Even if his words helped. "Everything is just such a mess."

"And every mess has to get cleaned up. Right now it's up to us to do the cleaning."

Juliet scrunched her nose. "Okay, *zen master.*" She sniffled and rolled her eyes as Nik pulled her in for another hug.

"Sorry if it's too soon, but wow, Juliet, that was just... beautiful. The way your fire turned to ice? It was like magic."

Now she did giggle. "Isn't our whole world magical?" She nudged him in the arm and stood to get a bottle of water.

"Well, sure, but a phoenix that can turn her flames into icicles is unheard of."

"Great, so call me Myreen 2.0." The moment Myreen's name came out, grief crushed her all over again.

Nik shook his head. "I don't think it's a chimera thing. It definitely feels different. But it should stay between us. Well, and maybe your dad. You should probably ask him for a recap of your lineage."

"Why? And no, I'm not speaking to him."

"What do you mean, *why*? Jules, your fire power alone made you incredibly powerful. Add ice to the mix and your power excels... by a lot."

She hadn't thought of it like that. "But I don't want to be more powerful. I was just getting used to my fire. I don't want this." Her eyes brimmed with tears again, but she refused to go there.

"Let's slow down. I know it's going to be hard, but try not

to experiment with your fire until you speak with Malachai. Your dad could be the only person that knows what's going on."

"If my dad wants to apologize, then I'll talk to him. But he's showing no remorse over kicking Oberon out." Juliet paused, looking at the floor as she remembered her thought from their secret meeting. "What if... What if General Dracul is using his dragon abilities on my dad?"

"I wish it were that simple, but no, I don't think so. Your dad signed up for the shifter military. That's not something you do lightly, and you don't oppose leadership without facing severe consequences. And with the General at the school now..." Nik gave Juliet a meaningful gaze.

Juliet sighed. Sure, the idea had occurred to her that Dracul might try to use her to keep her dad in line, but would the leader of the shifter military really be so cruelly manipulative? It seemed the answer was yes... "Fine. Maybe when I'm cooled down, I'll see if I have time to stop by his office. I'm skipping the rest of my classes. I don't want to deal with anyone or anything else today." Juliet kicked off her shoes and sat on her bed burying her feet under the sheets.

Nik didn't look pleased, but he nodded, his lips pulled into a grim line. "Just be sure to stay in here. Keep your phone by you and text me if you need anything. And Jules, please, try to stay off their radar. That means no more talking back to the guards or losing your temper around the Dome. That guard took your name down, which is a reminder for them to keep a closer watch on you. So stay low. Try to stay calm. Do some yoga or make yourself some tea or something."

"Okay, *Yoda*." She laid back, grabbing her phone to scroll through her apps. "Have a great day being a slave to that monster."

"My day is only great when I get to spend it with you." Nik

kissed her on the forehead. "I love you."

Before he could get away, she pulled his head down so their lips could touch. "Love you, too," she whispered.

Juliet watched him leave with so many mixed emotions running through her. But when he closed the door, she ditched her phone and covered herself with her sheets. She stayed in the darkness until her eyes drooped, then succumbed to a much-deserved nap.

But even sleeping, she couldn't escape from the mean old dragon ruining her school, as he filled each dream with nightmares.

CHAPTER 21

Oberon

"We're wasting time," Oberon growled. He and Ren were walking down a street that lined the Bow River. Its rushing waters reminded him of the Missouri River. There were even small islands within, and Oberon couldn't help but think about La Framboise Island and the old shifter school he'd attended as a boy.

"We're searching for your kin," Ren said, bundled up in winter gear from the top of his head down to his thick, warm boots. "Explain to me how *that* is a waste of time?"

Oberon stooped to the ground and picked up a small rock, his gloveless hands feeling its cold, rough surface. Narrowing his eyes at the ice chunks floating in the currents of the river, he targeted one and launched the stone. The rock missed its target and *thoinked* into the water, sending a splash into the air.

Nearby, he noticed a teenage girl standing against the fence that blocked off the way to the river. She was wearing a white beanie, underneath which flowed long, blonde locks. She had a scarf that matched her hat, and was wearing a thick, light-pink parka. She wasn't looking at the river, but down at her hands, deep in thought. He'd seen plenty of students with similar expressions—hopeless expressions. He was immediately reminded of Myreen.

Wrenching his thoughts away, he answered Ren's question. "Searching for gryphons is a wild goose chase," Oberon said. Throwing his kitsune friend a look, he found a smile crawling on Ren's face. "Why the mischievous grin?"

"Oh come on, you can't really expect me not to play off a line like that," Ren replied. "Not with the commonality between geese and gryphons—"

"The commonality between geese and gryphons ends with beaks and wings." Oberon wagged a dangerous finger between them.

"Don't forget the feathers and how easily ruffled they get," Ren added.

Oberon set his jaw. "I'm not in the mood, Ren."

"Of course you're not," his friend replied. "Which is precisely why I crack a joke here and there—to help get you in the mood. Seriously, Oberon. You've always been a grump, but ever since you found Myreen Fairchild, it's like your irritableness has been set to turbo. I'm afraid you're turning into an old man."

If the past few months had done anything to Oberon, they'd made him feel older. The icy river drew his attention again. Distantly, he said, "We've been searching for Delphine's gryphons for four days now. We've been out to Mount Joffre twice. We've walked the streets here in Calgary. There's been no sign of them. Not even the shadow of a scent of my kin."

He could feel Ren's eyes on him, could sense his humored expression deflating.

"I think Delphine really is trying to keep us preoccupied,"

Oberon mumbled.

"Or maybe her vision was wrong," Ren offered.

Oberon shook his head. "She's never been wrong before. I have no reason to believe she'd have a false vision now."

Another splash sounded, and Oberon looked toward the fence where the girl had been standing. She wasn't there anymore. And that splash had sounded bigger than a mere stone.

Movement among the ice in the Bow River caught Oberon's eye, and he saw the girl's pink coat arms flailing in the river.

"She fell in," Oberon said, a jolt of panic striking through his body.

"What?" Ren asked.

Oberon didn't answer, but hopped over the fence and ran down the rocky shore, determining how best to rescue the girl. He could shift into his gryphon form, then easily scoop her out of the water with his strong claws. But he'd be seen in broad daylight by humans. To most of them, he was nothing short of a myth. It would be dangerous. But seeing the girl's head go underwater threw out all thought of self-preservation.

Oberon unzipped his coat and stepped out of his boots, pulling his pants off as quickly as he could. In no time, he was down to his smart clothing, and was already shifting. The momentary cold disappeared as his thick gryphon body formed and his brown feathers sprouted.

Strength flowed through his wings as he flapped them, lifting off the ground and moving forward with the flow of the river.

Swooping down, he managed to catch the girl's only visible gloved hand right as she was about to go under again. Pulling her wet body out of the freezing cold depths, he hugged her against his belly. She coughed and sputtered, but at least she was alive.

With his eagle eyes, Oberon saw witnesses pointing and

exclaiming one to another. A few of them held phones up, and he knew he'd been recorded. No doubt, a gryphon sighting would hit the news. No doubt the vampires would be hot on his tracks. If a flock of gryphons were indeed around, he'd just spoiled their trouble of hiding. He had to get out of sight and land somewhere so he could shift back to human form. Hopefully Ren would be hot on his feathers, carrying his winter gear along. Because it was going to be really cold for both he and the girl when he shifted.

Speaking of cold, the girl shivered in his grasp, and he knew his body heat was only providing so much comfort. He needed to get her somewhere well-heated. Unfortunately, Oberon didn't keep open the window of the hotel room he and Ren had been staying in. There was no way of just flying in.

Suddenly, the girl let loose a piercing scream, and Oberon assumed she had just realized she was flying in the arms of some big beast.

"It's all right," he said softly. "I've got to get you to safety."

His attempt at calming the girl failed. She fidgeted and screamed all the louder, and Oberon knew he was only going to draw more attention. Seeing a patch of trees lining a part of the bank, he angled himself their way.

Once he cleared the welcoming foliage, he slowed until he felt safe enough to let the girl go. She landed with a soft thump, and Oberon grounded beside her. He didn't wait another moment to shift back to human form.

The girl's shrieking ended abruptly as he returned to normal, standing in nothing but his glorified underwear.

"High winds, it's cold," he said, throwing his arms around himself.

The soaked girl was pointing at him, her arm shivering. He could hear her teeth chattering. "You're a... you're a..."

"Hero?" he offered. Oberon shook his head. "I saw somebody who was about to drown and I reacted."

"You're a bird-man!" she finally said, scurrying backward and kicking up powdery snow. She hadn't made it to her feet since landing.

Bird-man?

He held his hands up. "It's okay, I'm not going to hurt you."

Footsteps sounded through the trees, and Oberon whirled about, taking a defensive stance. They weren't consistent: pit-pat-pause, pit-pat-pause, pit-pause, pat-pause.

Please be Ren, he begged to the sky. If it was anybody else, they'd be wondering what an almost-naked man was doing with a teenage girl in the confines of the trees.

Out of one of the trees, Ren phased.

Oberon chuckled. "That explains the randomness of your footsteps. You couldn't even duck around the trees, could you?"

Glancing at the girl, Oberon saw her eyes widen, her finger now pointing at Ren.

"Why go to all that work?" Ren said, winded from his mad dash to catch up. Under his arm was Oberon's winter clothing, and he gladly accepted it.

Getting himself appropriately covered, he indicated to the girl. "Can you see to her? I'm afraid she's going into shock, although, whether it's from freezing water or witnessing us using our abilities, I can't tell."

Ren snapped his fingers. "I have just the thing." Removing his backpack, he undid the drawstring and rummaged around a bit. "Honestly, I thought we'd end up having to use it first."

He pulled a foot-long metal stick, then tapped the top. Blue lights at the top and bottom came on, and the stick suddenly extended and bowed, growing four times its original length.

"What in the world is that?" Oberon asked, slipping his now sock-covered feet into his boots

"A personal dehumidifier, heater mode enabled," Ren said, giving a thumbs up. He held it at its center and walked toward the girl. She'd gotten to her feet and was shaking uncontrollably, steam puffing from her lips in hurried breaths.

"Stay... away!" She backed into a tree and lost her balance. Ren ran to her side, holding the bowed dehumidifier forward. Her scared expression lightened as her clothing visibly dried out.

Oberon raised his eyebrows in surprise. Ren had kept his little contraption a secret. It was an extremely useful device, especially for this part of the world.

"That's amazing," the girl said, her pale lips returning to a pinkish hue.

"Quite a handy tool." Ren twirled the device in his hands like a bow staff. He turned back to Oberon and winked. "I call it the *Hot Rod*."

Oberon shook his head. "I think there are cars that have already claimed that title."

"Which has never made sense to me," Ren said. "Why would a car ever be referred to as a rod?"

Oberon shrugged, then looked past his friend. The girl had her gloved hands held out toward the *Hot Rod*, taking in its warmth.

Zipping up his coat, Oberon made his way over to her. "What's your name?"

She gave him a distrusting look with her deep, dark brown eyes. They slowly softened, though, like ice melting in sunlight. "Kathrine."

"Hi Kathrine," he replied. "My name is Oberon, and this is my friend Ren."

Ren gave her a cheesy smile, then held the device closer to her. She nodded in thanks, but didn't return the smile.

"Kathrine," Oberon said, "might I ask you what happened back there in the river? How did you fall in?"

She threw her glance to the snow-covered ground, and Oberon sensed her attempt to conceal guilt. He'd been around enough teenagers to detect such vibes.

"Nothing," she mumbled.

"Nothing?" he asked. The response was a sure sign that she'd meant quite the opposite. "Look, I know we're strangers, and that you have no real reason to trust me. But I'm a school director..." He cleared his throat. "I'm a principle of a school, and work with boys and girls about your age."

She shrugged quickly. "I fell in. Big deal."

He half-smiled and looked down at his feet, then back up at her. "Before you fell in, I saw you standing on the other side of the fence. You'll forgive me for finding it hard to believe that you merely *fell in*."

Oberon watched her and saw the pain in her eyes—saw the hurt set therein. Her shoulders drooped, and her head bowed.

"It was a spur-of-the-moment thing," she said softly, folding her arms across her chest, her parka fluffing out from the compression. "You don't understand. I can't go back."

Ren gave him a worried look. Oberon walked over and placed his hand on her shoulder.

"I won't claim to know what you're running from, Kathrine," he said. "But I will tell you that I have a special place in my heart for those who have suffered at home."

She looked up into his eyes with sad wonder. "I didn't say anything about... How do you know about what I'm going through?"

He gave her a warm smile. "Your eyes tell the story—at the

very least, pieces."

Kathrine bit her lip, then finally spoke. "My parents died when I was young. I've lived with foster families. And I just can't take it anymore."

Pity coursed through Oberon like water in a river, looking for an outlet. His emotions threatened to take over, his eyes beginning to water. This girl prompted an explosion of memories.

"Mr. Oberon?" she asked.

He sniffed, bringing his eyes and mind back into focus. "Forgive me. Your words—they triggered some thoughts about my wife, Seri. She, like you, grew up in foster care, and when it became very apparent how *different* she was..." Oberon trailed off.

"What happened to her?" asked Kathrine.

"My father found her and brought her to the school I was attending," he said. "It was a place where she felt like she finally fit in."

And then Oberon watched a transformation in Kathrine's brown eyes. Hope. The very thing that drove Oberon to lead a school. Of all the shifts in the world, the magical change from hopelessness to hope was the most wondrous of all.

But this girl was no shifter, and would find no solace at a place like the Dome.

"Is there room at the school for me?" she asked.

Oberon sighed heavily. "Unfortunately, I'm no longer a school director. My career has... changed." He looked at Ren. "But what I do now is go looking for those who are lost. I try to give them guidance."

Her hope began to fade as he spoke, and he held up a hand. "Just because I have no say at the school I used to lead doesn't mean you are without hope. Kathrine, there is a place for you in this world, and I can promise you, it's not in a river. But you must have the courage to find your place and not give up. I promise that if you look hard enough, you'll find it."

Again, Kathrine bit her lip as her eyes went distant. After several moments, she nodded. "You're right. I can feel it." She tapped her chest. "Right here."

Oberon smiled. "I'd be lying if I said it'll be easy. But keep my words in mind. You'll find your way."

She looked back at him. "And what about you? Where will you go?"

"I'm still looking for my way," Oberon said. "I suppose that's life."

Kathrine mulled his words over for a moment. "I hope you find what you're looking for."

Nodding, Oberon said, "Me too. Now run along. Ren and I have some business we must see to."

She nodded, then walked between two trees before looking back. "Will I ever see you guys again?"

Oberon chuckled. "You might, Kathrine. You just might."

She smiled and waved, then turned and walked out of sight.

"You know, Oberon," Ren said, twirling the *Hot Rod*, "You've still got the touch, even without the title."

Oberon grinned at the compliment. "Thank you, my friend. After that experience, my hope seems to have been restored. Now, let's go see if we can find those gryphons."

Kenzie

Kenzie climbed the stairs to the lobby, her footsteps feeling heavier than normal. Sure, the stairs were still bugging her, though her body was starting to get used to them—was the Dome so upwardly inclined? She hoped not, but if so, at least she'd be ready. But this time she traveled the stairs in response to a summons. She wondered what Draven had in mind. She'd been successful at staying under the radar since her arrival, but apparently time was up.

And she hadn't even gotten a chance to check on Leif. He was so out of it last time. That he thought she was Gemma was both frightening and flattering. But she knew her betrayal had to hurt more if he thought it came from Gemma. She wanted to tell him her plan, but she couldn't. She'd tried using her spell to contact him, but he'd been almost incoherent. There was no getting any information through to his mind. And even if she could, she didn't want him blabbing it.

No, for now he'd have to suffer. She just hoped he'd be able to recover. And that he'd be able to forgive her for it.

And there was still the mystery of how to get Kol and the other dragon out. Myreen's request wasn't even necessary. There was no way Kenzie was leaving them here.

Ty, however, was another story. Kenzie had a feeling Draven wouldn't let them just take his son away. But how to break the news to Myreen? And she still hadn't gotten Myreen to agree to leave. That worried her the most. Was Myreen being brainwashed? Sure, Draven was a cutie, but he seemed laced with sinister intentions. Why couldn't Myreen see that?

Kenzie tried to clear her thoughts as she came up to the door to Draven's trophy room. The place totally creeped her out, but she couldn't think about that. She had to stay focused, purposeful. If not? Well, failure wasn't really an option.

She took a breath and knocked on the door, which immediately opened inward.

Draven drank a deep breath, then smiled. "Ah, my favorite selkie has arrived. Thanks for coming."

Kenzie nodded, then stepped in, beelining to a seat before her quaking legs could give her away.

Draven sat behind his desk, steepling his fingers on top of the dark, smooth surface. He almost looked scholarly with his chin stubble. A pair of glasses would complete the picture, though she didn't suppose a vampire would have need for those.

"So, you've asked to attend this school, but I'm afraid we were cut short before we could discuss what that looked like."

"Oh, yeah, I guess you're right." Truth be told, she'd been so preoccupied with her mission she hadn't given much thought to that initial exchange. Sure, she'd floated around the classrooms, trying to stay under the radar and glean as much info as she could, but she'd spent most of her time trying to figure a way to get everyone out—too bad she still didn't have a solid escape plan. Kenzie flashed a grin. "Got any magic classes?"

Draven laughed good-naturedly. "No, I'm afraid not, though I'd be happy to give you room to exercise your skills."

"Thank you," was all Kenzie could come up with. She was both stunned and a bit nervous by the offer, eager to use her powers but anxious to consider how she'd be expected to use them.

"I'll have one of the teachers draw up a schedule for you, with a free period for your magic, of course. Adam has been speaking of you."

Kenzie's face puckered and her brows lifted. "All good things, I hope."

Draven smiled, the look more predatory than friendly. "Of course. I've informed him that he's earned his place in the vampire ranks. He's interested in taking an Initiate, specifically you."

Kenzie's cheeks reddened. "He may have mentioned that."

"I'm a little hesitant to assign you to him. Freshly turned vampires can sometimes be unreliable, and I'd hate for him to do something stupid."

Kenzie pulled her lips in and bit on them, hoping against hope that Draven would see fit to ignore Adam's request.

"But he's particularly taken with you, and he comes from good stock. If I have your permission, I'll arrange the pairing. I assume you have ample magic to take care of yourself in the unlikely event that Adam forgets his manners?"

The way Draven looked at her, Kenzie wasn't sure she really had a choice. If she said no, then what? Would she be assigned to another vampire? She at least knew the devil she'd be working with if she accepted Adam. Now wasn't the best time to gamble.

Kenzie took a deep breath. "Yeah, I guess that would be fine. Adam and I have some... history."

Draven smiled. "Excellent. I have one more request for you before I send you on your way. I'm afraid it involves another trip to the top of the citadel. Do you mind?"

Kenzie shook her head, again sensing that this was more of a command than a request, despite the way it was phrased. "At least this time the school isn't under attack." Kenzie laughed, but Draven didn't join her, and the laughter died on her lips.

"Indeed." He stood up and started toward the door, and Kenzie scrambled to follow, wondering what the heck she was getting herself into.

***

The long elevator ride was again excruciating. Kenzie didn't think she'd ever get used to being in a closed space with someone so dangerous and powerful. Her mind flitted to the Dome, and she wondered if being around the shifters would give her the same sensation. She doubted it, though she knew shifters were just as powerful in their own ways.

She tried very hard not to think of a certain feline shifter, his spiced chai eyes following her every movement.

When they reached the room of stairwells, Draven went to one near the center, yellow caution tape hanging limply to the railing. They traveled upward until they reached a room that had obviously taken damage in the attack. The exterior wall had been replaced with some sort of material, though the color and texture were off. It was more charcoal than obsidian, rougher than the smooth walls predating the repair. Draven sneered at it, but moved to one side where a smooth metal panel stood. Kenzie followed him, wondering if this was another elevator, and if so, just how tall was this tower?

Instead, it opened to another set of stairs shrouded in

darkness. Kenzie groaned inwardly, afraid to voice her reluctance, and again followed Draven. Luckily there was only the one flight of stairs, and Beatrice was already at the top.

Beatrice looked at Draven and smiled. "I've done as you asked. Leif is in the Sunroom."

"Excellent. Kenzie, I'd like you to do the honors."

Kenzie looked back and forth between the two. "I'm sorry, but I don't understand. What would you like me to do?"

Draven pointed to a crank on the wall. "Rotate that a few times and you'll see."

Kenzie stepped forward, for the first time realizing that one of the walls in this narrow space was glass. She could almost see a figure out there, and she figured it must be Leif. Dread pooled in the pits of her arms and stuck her tongue to the roof of her mouth.

She shuffled toward the crank, smiling at Draven and Beatrice who were both watching her closely. Taking a deep breath, she braced for what would come next. A Sunroom sounded like a lovely thing—until you put a sun-allergic vampire inside.

Kenzie pushed on the crank, and it spun easily, much to her dismay. Light began to pour in, first in a sliver, then widening. Leif pushed back to the edge of the room as the beam of light got bigger and bigger. Kenzie looked to Draven, hoping he'd give her a signal to stop, but he didn't, his eyes now focused on Leif. Beatrice stood beside him, her posture rigid.

Kenzie's stomach rolled as she saw the angry red welts standing up on Leif's skin. Part of her was glad his daywalking ability was still gone, otherwise her cover would be blown. But seeing him writhe under the power of the sun made her want to tear out her own heart.

Kenzie wanted out. She could hardly stand to stay here another day. And Leif! How much longer could he last under these conditions? The room obviously had some protection against the sun, but not enough. Not nearly enough.

At last, Draven signaled and Kenzie reversed the crank with more gusto than the first time. The light slowly closed until the room was once again shrouded in darkness. But Leif's cries carried on. She wanted to throw herself on the floor and weep, but Kenzie bottled it up and buried it deep inside. She couldn't show Draven any weakness. Not even a shred.

"Excellent. Thank you, Kenzie, you've done well. The Sunroom seems to be back in working order. Beatrice, I trust you'll have Leif cleared out shortly."

"Yes, Draven. Thank you." Beatrice bowed, but there was a stiffness there. Apparently she didn't enjoy the whole ordeal any more than Kenzie had. But like the good little vampire she was, she didn't question Draven. Kenzie would be screaming at the woman if she wasn't doing the same thing.

Kenzie swallowed as she followed Draven out of the room. He pulled something from his pocket and handed it to Kenzie. It was a watch, small, black, sleek. She tapped a button on the side of it and the screen lit up, several apps depicting everything from the time to messages.

"It's a school watch. You can use this to keep up with your schedule, which will be uploaded to your profile as soon as it's arranged. I request that all Initiates keep their watches on at all times while in the school. It's invaluable, and I would hate for you to lose it."

Kenzie had a feeling that wasn't the whole story, but she nodded as she slipped it around her wrist. She'd seen some of the Initiates checking their smartwatches from time to time, but hadn't thought much about the uniformity of it. "Thank you."

"Of course. And I'll let you break the good news to Adam."

Kenzie smiled as convincingly as she could. "Sounds good."

"The ingredients should arrive in a few days. We'll make a grand show of it, announcing Adam's ascension and your placement in the Initiate program after you complete the spell."

"Okay. Cool." So not cool. Kenzie needed to get out of here by then, but she didn't think there was enough time.

"Until then."

Kenzie caught the dismissal and left without a backward glance. This time, she was grateful for the long elevator ride. It gave her a little space to process, even if most of that process was numbly stuffing every feeling into a tightly-lidded box. She might have let out a good scream, too, just for the fun of it. Maybe.

Adam was waiting for her at the bottom, his face hopeful. Kenzie blinked and nodded.

Adam broke into a wide grin and picked Kenzie up, spinning her in a circle before planting a passionate kiss on her lips. Kenzie fought the urge to vomit, closed her eyes and pretended it was Wes on the other end. It did little to ease her conscience or fool her heart, but with a little practice, she could almost believe she wasn't kissing a snake. Almost.

Leif

Leif's mind was like a bag of puzzle pieces that had been shaken up and sent through a shredder. He could focus on bits and fragments, but he felt so... broken.

Another piece of Gemma was absent. Leif had never considered it as a remnant of his betrothed before, but he did now. It was her daywalking enchantment—something he'd taken for granted all these years. She had gifted it to him so they could spend more time together. It was also what ended up getting her killed.

Now it was completely gone, like dust in the wind.

Gemma had come. Or was it Kenzie? Leif's muddled mind couldn't remember. The new memories that had been injected into his brain by Beatrice had him struggling to differentiate fact from fiction.

So it was that he'd been reduced to a monster once more, incapable of withstanding the sun's rays. Although ever so briefly, his skin had sizzled and burned like meat in a skillet. Twice—*that* he could remember. The copper flowing in his veins made his regenerative abilities slow. Leif didn't know how much time had passed since the enchantment had been stripped, but he could still see sores on his arms from where the light had scorched him. On top of it all, his face throbbed. He probably looked diseased from the mutilation. Draven's Sunroom had never been a cause for fear before. But now, he could still hear the haunted, pained screams of his own voice ringing in his ears.

He'd been granted a bit of freedom since that harrowing experience. Beatrice had left her door open, telling him he was free to walk the citadel if he liked. His shackles contained a GPS unit, so even if he dared to leave Heritage Prep, they'd be able to find him. In his weakened state, he wouldn't be able to get far. Chances were, he'd collapse from exhaustion and become a pile of ash when the sun rose.

Rainbow hadn't shown his fur for some time, and Leif found himself helplessly alone. He hadn't left Beatrice's quarters, although that option was still there. He needed comfort, and the only possibility that came to his fractured mind was feeling the cool keys of his piano under his fingertips. He'd have limited mobility due to his handcuffs, but at least there would be notes to lose himself in.

And so he forced himself from the couch he'd been sitting on. His legs were weak, and he nearly lost his balance.

"What... did I do?" he mumbled, shaking his head in an effort to clear it. The action did little to help, and no answer came to solve his lackluster question. "I don't deserve this."

He placed one foot in front of the other, then did it again. He found that as he continued the process, it got easier. Soon, he was in the hallway.

Looking both ways, he wondered which option to take. His own quarters were in a different tower.

As he stood just outside Beatrice's room, somebody wordlessly passed by him. Leif brought his blurry eyes up to see if he recognized the person, but they were already turning the corner and heading down the dark staircase to his left.

His heart plummeted. How was he going to manage *stairs*?

"Are you okay?"

The sudden voice to his right made him jump, and he had to grasp the doorway to keep from falling over. The effort was almost more than he could bear, and his arms flared from their achy burns.

As Leif struggled to control himself, his eyes rested on the girl who'd spoken. She had blue-black hair and sky-blue eyes. He didn't have to dig too far in his mind to recognize her. "It cannot be," he mumbled. "The siren?"

The girl looked him up and down, a pitying look crawling upon her face. "Kenzie said..." she trailed off. "What are they doing to you?"

He closed his eyes, trying to focus on her words. They seemed so distant, like a voice carried on a wind through a canyon.

"Myreen, you shouldn't be here," he said at last. "Draven..." He knew what he wanted to say, but the words wouldn't form on his lips.

Myreen waited for him to finish what he was saying, but he couldn't.

"What are they doing to you?" she asked again. This time, she came to him and tapped his bonds.

He found himself laughing, and not just a little. It sounded manic in his own ears. When he stopped, he saw that he'd frightened the girl. Holding his shackles up. "This... is what they do to traitors."

"Okay, that's something," Myreen said.

"I helped Oberon... protect the siren," he said, remembering the splintered memory of Oberon in the restaurant, asking him to join Draven and work as a double agent. But yes, Beatrice had told him that Myreen had come to Heritage Prep. She was working with Draven. Everything had been a waste—helping the shifters, giving Kenzie the grimoire. In a matter of months, he'd thrown his life completely away.

"Oberon," Myreen said with wonder. "He was kicked out of the school for working with vampires. But you were the vampire working with him all that time, weren't you?"

He nodded, but didn't have any idea how the girl could possibly know about that. And Oberon had gotten kicked out of the school? The world was moving far too fast for Leif to keep up.

"Kol's dad was wrong about him," Myreen said, her eyes growing distant.

Leif had no idea what Malkolm Dracul's father had to do with anything, but didn't have the focus to think too hard about it.

"You need to get out of here," he said, the words falling lazily from his lips. "Draven... wants to do terrible things with you."

"*I* need to get out of here?" she said. "No offense, but you seem to be a lot worse off than I am."

Shaking his head, Leif said, "You don't understand. Draven is going to use you. Whatever he's promised you, however he's making you think you should spend any time here..." His head swam, and he couldn't finish the sentence. Leif shook his arms in agitation; if only he could rid himself of his shackles.

"What's your name?" Myreen asked, her soft voice helping to iron out his thoughts, if only for a moment.

"Leif," he mumbled. At least he remembered his name. At least somewhere inside he was still an individual. Draven and

Beatrice hadn't stripped that away from him. Not yet.

He met her blue eyes.

Myreen stared at him for a few moments, then checked the passageway for eavesdroppers.

In a whisper, she said, "The same Leif Kenzie mentioned?"

Kenzie. Gemma's relative. The girl who'd reverted him back to an average vampire.

"I thought I knew Kenzie," Leif said, looking down at the burns on his arm. "It turns out she's on Draven's side."

Myreen shook her head. "No, she wants to help me escape. And Kol. And you."

Leif wagged his head back and forth, as if a giant weight were tied around it. "She took the grimoire and used it against me."

"She'd never turn her back on a friend, let alone hurt one," Myreen said, her voice soft.

Lies. More lies. Kenzie had even tricked Myreen.

"You can't trust her, Myreen," Leif cautioned. "She won't hesitate to betray you."

The siren bit her lip and looked to the side. Leif wondered if she was seeing him as a drugged-up, disillusioned freak. And he wasn't getting through to her.

"You *must* find a way to get out of here," he said again. He had no desire for self-preservation. But he'd seen Myreen in action. She was the siren from the prophecy Oberon had told him about. "The shifters are counting on you—no, the world is. You have to get out and find a way to stop Draven before he enslaves everybody."

Myreen's eyes grew wide, and she took another look around before saying, "I'm scared, Leif. This place... I feel like I'm being watched all the time. But leaving Heritage Prep isn't so easy. Did you know I have a brother, here in the school?"

"Lies," Leif said. "All lies. Draven will do anything—say

anything—to keep you here."

She shook her head. "Ty—short for Tyberius. He's my half-brother, and he's only ten years old."

An image of the boy he'd crossed paths with a few times since returning to the citadel popped into his mind. Leif assumed that Draven was using the boy for evil purposes... but was he actually the vampire leader's son? The Denholm Heir?

"Then take him with you and get out of here," Leif said. His mind had become clearer during the conversation—likely a rush of adrenaline, or whatever the vampire equivalent was. "If your brother becomes a vampire, he will be extremely dangerous."

"What if Ty doesn't want to leave?" Myreen asked. "The school is all he's ever known. And Draven—my father—he's really good to Ty."

It seemed so odd, hearing Myreen refer to Draven as her father. In these short moments, he'd discovered just how opposite she was of him.

"When I first arrived, I thought I'd hate it here," Myreen continued. "But the cruelty and evil I thought would be all over this place... it's not."

Leif narrowed his eyes. "Have you seen your father's trophy room yet?"

She gave him a confused look.

"Ask him about it sometime," he said. "It might change your view on just how cruel he can be."

A worried look filled her face, and Leif was relieved to see it. Whatever light Draven had cast himself in, Myreen needed to know it was fake.

"Has Draven told you about his vision for the future?" he asked. "About vampire-shifter hybrids?"

Myreen nodded slowly. "I know about that, yes."

"It's not going to end there," Leif said. "He's going to take your blood and make himself the greatest abomination the world has ever seen."

"So I should just run and hide so he can't use me?" she asked. "Run and hide like my mom did?"

"No," Leif said. "Like I said, you run and find a way to stop Draven. Use your siren abilities and save the world."

As if it were that easy. Leif had no idea how it all worked. He came from a simple time, and had never met a siren before.

She crossed her arms, and her shoulders slumped. Myreen looked so conflicted, and Leif could tell at once that she wasn't one to run when things got hard.

"Running won't work forever. Draven will never stop searching for you. So if you decide to stay, then you will have to figure out how to stop him here, in the heart of his domain."

Myreen brought her eyes back to his. "Can he be stopped?"

He stared at her for a few moments, then nodded. "Oberon believed with all his heart that you are the only one who can. He believes in you." He reached out and pointed both of his index fingers directly at her. "And I believe in you." And he did. He truly believed it. After all his doubting of Oberon's words, Leif believed that Myreen was *the siren*.

Even though she looked so fragile, standing against the wall, hugging her arms closely to herself, he could see it in her eyes. Raw determination. Myreen was full of untapped purpose. And Draven would pay the price for thinking he could bend it to his will.

A half-smile formed on her face. "You and Oberon are a lot alike," she said. "I can almost hear him saying the things you've said."

"I consider that a compliment," Leif said. "Oberon is a good man."

"And so are you," said Myreen. "Leif, I'll do what I can to

help you get away."

He appreciated the sentiment. "I'll accept any help, but don't you dare put yourself in danger because of me. Your life is far more important than mine."

She laughed softly. "I think Oberon would argue that every life is important."

Myreen placed a warm hand on his shoulder, and he nearly lost his balance. Again, he was reminded of his weakened state, and he thought about asking her to help him to his quarters. But the conversation had taken a lot out of him—and had ignited the small embers of hope.

"I've got to go," said Myreen. "I don't think it would go over well if they found me talking to you."

Leif nodded back toward Beatrice's quarters, realizing he hadn't gotten as far as he'd thought. But it still looked like a long way in his weakened state. "Would you mind helping me get back to my prison before you go?"

"Of course." Myreen hesitated before grabbing him—by his better arm, thankfully—and escorting him along the short hallway that felt like a thousand miles to Leif's legs. Upon reaching the purple and silver room, she helped him to the couch.

"Thank you very much," he said. "Maybe someday I won't appear so pitiful."

"You'll be free soon enough," Myreen said. "I promise."

Seconds later, he was alone in Beatrice's room again. But he didn't feel quite so hopeless anymore.

Could the girl help him? Leif believed there was nothing she couldn't do.

A jolt of fiery pain shot through his arms as more copper released into his wrists, slipping him into the gray mistiness of sedation, until all darkened to black again.

CHAPTER 24

Juliet

Nik wanted her to keep a low profile.

Like *that* could happen.

No matter how much sleep she got, or how much she trained or meditated or tried to do anything to calm herself down, as soon as something dumb happened, Juliet's fingers would begin to spark and sizzle. And with what was happening at school and with her friends at the hands of Draven, it seemed like everything was completely out of control. Definitely not helping.

She went her whole life not knowing she was a phoenix, and now, when she'd finally gained control over it, it changed on her again. She felt helpless. If she had to use her power for anything, it would probably fail her. That broke her. She was afraid for herself in more ways than one, and it was showing.

She'd thrown her hair up in a messy bun, but it only brought attention to how pale and drawn her face was. She refused to attend any of her classes looking like this. Besides, she couldn't risk a fiery outburst right now—or in her new case, an icy one.

She might have gone little overboard with Nik's advice to stay low. It was certain to catch up with her at some point. She wasn't sure what would be worse—being punished for not attending her classes, or for simultaneously burning and freezing something or someone.

When she heard loud and forceful knocks on her door, she thought her time was up. She cautiously walked to the door and opened it with wide skittish eyes.

"Juliet. Are you ill? What is the meaning of this?" Malachai stomped into her bedroom, then turned to face her. "You look... terrible."

Juliet let out the breath she didn't know she was holding and closed her door. "No, I'm not ill. I think." She went back to her bed and flopped on it, burying her face in the pillows.

"What does *that* mean? If you're not sick, why are you missing so many classes?" His tone lowered, becoming less tense. The bed sank beside Juliet as her dad sat.

Juliet sat up and wrapped the blankets around her shoulders.

Malachai raised the back of his large hand to her forehead and held it there. It was awkward because it felt like a maternal thing, not something he'd usually do. But then again, lately, she hadn't given him a chance.

"Um, well can I trust you?" She was dead serious, but she wanted it to sound playful. It didn't.

"Of course you can. What kind of a question is that?" Malachai's eyebrows scrunched. He was clearly worried.

She couldn't figure out what to say, how to explain what was happening to her, so she showed him. She slithered her hand from under the blanket and took a reluctant, deep breath. Her fire waited beneath her heart, and it obeyed her call.

Like sparks, the warmth traveled down Juliet's arm to her

fingertips. When the flames escaped, she felt that familiar surge of pride. But like a turned faucet, the warmth switched to cold. It started in her body first, so she knew it would change her flame any second. To get a good look at her father's reaction, Juliet gazed into his eyes.

His eyebrows were still pulled together, but by the way he squinted, he was more studious than confused.

Until her fire turned icy blue.

As his eyes grew wide, Juliet rolled her own. She handed him the flame-shaped ice and threw herself back onto her bed.

"What...? How...? Why...?"

"Yeah, I know. *This* is why I haven't been to class." His silence made her uncomfortable, so she sat back up and wrung her hands underneath the blanket.

"Okay, first I think it's a good idea that you stay out of sight, but that's already rubbed him the wrong way. You're on his watch list. He probably sees you as weak and powerless, which you're not. Clearly."

"Wait, I'm on his watch list?"

Malachai gave Juliet a withering stare. "Let's see. Talking back to an officer, skipping classes, physically threatening an officer..." He ticked each point off a finger, then stopped to look at her.

Juliet hung her head, but she refused to apologize for what she'd done. It wasn't her fault the rules were stupid.

"This isn't the same school, Juliet. Everyone and everything is being watched. I know you're dealing with a lot, but maybe don't cut out of every class. Try to show face in a few of them, and no snapping when you do. I'll put in a word that you're feeling... off. Hopefully that'll get you back off the list. Or at least lower your threat level."

It was Juliet's turn to throw a withering glare, but her dad was so focused on planning that he didn't notice.

"Maybe we should get back to our one-on-one sessions. I'll suggest it. Maybe it'll convince General Dracul that you're still getting the training you need." He looked down at his hands, worry lacing his words.

"Sure. Since you're so buddy-buddy with him, I'm sure he'll approve your request." She said it like a robot, but not even a flat tone could erase the bitterness her words carried.

Malachai stood, his fists clenched. "Juliet, this is serious. I've told you, I have no choice. My rank calls for me to be one hundred percent. And right now?" He ran a hand over his cropped hair. "Right now your safety is my highest priority. If General Dracul finds out about this new ice thing, who knows what he'll do. Nothing good, I imagine. Look what he did to your friend." His voice was low as he said the last part.

"Welcome to my bubble of worry and fear. Trust me, I won't tell a soul. Except..." She'd forgotten Nik already knew and she was afraid of Malachai's reaction.

"Except what? Juliet Quinn, what did you do?" The use of her full name brought chills to her spine.

"Jeez, I didn't *do* anything. But remember that you and I haven't been on speaking terms. I've been spending all my time with Nik, so... obviously he would notice." She didn't want to upset her dad but she also didn't want to lie. Of course there was still the matter of the students who had seen her fire turn to ice at their secret meeting, but they'd all sworn not to tell. And their group—and the purpose for such a group—was the one subject she wasn't ready to bring up with her father yet.

"Okay. That's alright. I understand. And I'm glad you had someone who you could trust to share this with. I can't imagine dealing with this alone." He sighed, covering his eyes with his hands. "But I really need you to keep this hidden." Her dad was being much more understanding than she thought he would.

"I'm glad Nik was with me, too. He also suggested that I keep a low profile. And he thought I should go to you for information. But by the looks of it, you know as much as we do. Which is nothing." Juliet knew she was being pessimistic, but she didn't feel like taking anything back.

"Well, you're right there. I don't have much information to give. But if my memory serves me right, I could swear I used to hear an old crazed aunt of mine ramble on about alicorns. She would always repeat '*Quinns are birds who favor fire, but ice is the secret gift to acquire.*' She wasn't right in the mind, so none of her words were ever taken seriously. But now? It seems to be our answer. If only she was still alive..." He got a faraway look in his eyes.

"Alicorns? They're real? I thought they were a myth... though I guess I haven't really learned about them. I just don't understand." Juliet wasn't entirely disappointed with their conversation. She was finally getting somewhere with him, but she still couldn't completely forgive him for not standing up for Oberon. But that was something she had to push aside. At least until she could get herself back under control.

"Why don't we put a pin in it for now. I'm going to see about getting our sessions back and I'll try to see what I can find out about what dear old Aunt Lidia had going on in her head. Meet me for dinner and we'll talk about this more. I have meetings to get to, but I'll stop by to speak with the general first. I might be able to buy you a few more days, but I can't promise much. Jules, I'm sorry for disappointing you. Again. One day you'll understand, but I don't expect that of you now. Just know that I love you. Always have, always will."

All she could do was nod. Tears built to bursting, but she refused to the let them fall. Just as Malachai went to walk to the door, there was a knock. Juliet could've sworn she saw fear flash in his eyes, but it was gone before she could be sure. Malachai cleared his throat and opened the door.

"Oh, sir, hello." Nik saluted Juliet's dad and stepped out of the way. Malachai exited, returning the salute as he went on his way.

Nik walked in and closed the door. "You told him, didn't you? I could see it all over his face."

"I did. And you're not going to believe what he told me." For dramatic effect, Juliet paused. For a minute too long.

"Well?"

"Alicorns," she said, pausing again as Nik's eyes widened. "He told me he has some distant memory of a crazy aunt that would talk about them."

"Whoa. I wasn't expecting that. Not by a long shot. But it gives us something to do."

"Like what? I never learned anything about them in any of my classes. Ugh. I just don't know." She didn't want to sound so down, because any news was good news, but this seemed impossible.

"The reason why they don't teach about them is because they're so rare that there's really no reason. My mom told me once that they're so uncommon that there hasn't been a known alicorn shifter for decades. *Decades*, Juliet." Nik ran his hand over the back of his neck.

"Why does me maybe being an alicorn make you so nervous?" Juliet took Nik's hand off his neck and laced her fingers through his.

"'Cause I know who my boss is and what he'd do if he found out," Nik said, his tone grim.

"What would he do?" She didn't really want to know but

she couldn't help but ask.

"Exactly what he did to Myreen. He'll use you until you're drained." Nik squeezed her hand.

"Okay. Well then, we have to make sure that doesn't happen. No one else can know. *No one.*" She hoped she sounded as dire as she felt. "We can trust the others in our group not to say anything, right?" She was almost certain they could, but in her current state, she needed Nik's reassurance.

"Yeah. They wouldn't be in the group if I didn't think they'd be able to keep a secret."

Juliet nodded.

"For now, let's do some research. I'm going to leave you to search the net while I run to the library to see if there are any books on the subject. I'll stop for snacks, too. I have a feeling we're going to need them."

"Sure. I'll let my dad know about anything we find out. I'm meeting him for dinner so we can talk more."

"Good." Nik grabbed Juliet's tablet from her desk. He handed it to her, kissing the top of her head. "Be right back."

"Wait. What about your duties?" Juliet asked, her brows pulling down.

Nik grinned. "I've got the rest of the day off. It looks like you're stuck with me." And with that, he left, taking his adorable dimples with him.

The following silence reminded her that she was alone again. Only this time she had a purpose. Something to wrap herself in. Something new to unravel.

She typed *What is an Alicorn?* into the search bar, ready to learn about this whole new world.

***

"Thanks for dinner." Juliet cleaned her mouth with a napkin and sat back.

"Thanks for joining me. Now that our sessions are back on, maybe we could do this regularly again?" Malachai sounded hopeful, and Juliet's nod of agreement was enough to bring a small smile to his usually-tight face.

Juliet stared at her empty plate. "So, Nik and I learned a lot, but it still feels like we're missing something."

"Probably are. You can't expect to get all the answers right away. You'll get everything you need to know in time. I think what I want you to focus on for now is gaining control over your new ice power. We know you have it, let's see what you can do with it."

"*You're* going to train me? You know how to teach fire, Dad, but ice is different. It *feels* different." Juliet looked at her hands. "They think..." She paused to swallow. "They think it was an alicorn who causes some crazy epic ice age. They called it the Arctic Winter or something, and it covered the entire country."

Malachai paused too. "I don't doubt it feels different, but it's all the same in the end. We just have to find the control. You've done it with your fire. I have complete faith that you can do the same with your ice."

He leaned forward, willing her to meet his eyes. "You will not set off another *Arctic Winter.*"

Juliet wanted to believe him, but the look in his eyes told her that he'd at least heard of that epic freeze, so it was possible things could get out of control. And the way she was feeling lately made that fear all too real.

He placed a hand on hers. "It'll be okay. Who knows? Ice could be cool."

She rolled her eyes at the pun, but said, "My ice. So weird." With a deep breath, Juliet stood and paced the space in front of him. "Alicorns had so many amazing gifts, like purification and healing. How am I to be sure that ice is the only one I have? I'm pretty sure I read they have super speed, too, but maybe that's just a myth."

She hadn't wanted Nik to see how overwhelmed she was, so it was all coming out now, in front of her dad. "And why me? If it's a family thing, then why did it skip everyone else? Am I going to grow another pair of wings? A horn?"

"Whoa, whoa, whoa. Slow down. Everything's going to be okay. No, you're not going to grow any new limbs. And you shouldn't be gaining any more powers because you're not a chimera. You simply inherited a gift from an ancestor. We just have to figure out which ancestor you got this ice ability from. Or maybe we don't. But we have to accept and embrace it, Juliet. Do you really want to freeze the Dome the way you lit it up when you were out of sync with your emotions? Oberon isn't here anymore. A lot more is at stake." Malachai was as serious as he was going to get.

"And who participated in that? *You* did. I wish Oberon was still here." She thought she was done playing the blame game, but obviously not.

"I'm learning that was a mistake. But before we can go down that road, let's focus on you. Can we do that?"

"Okay. Sorry, I... It's just so much."

"When is it not? The way you handle it shows the true warrior within. Now let's show them what being a Quinn is all about." Malachai clapped his hands, encouraging Juliet to lift her mood.

She stood and lifted her hand for a high five. Malachai grinned as he slapped her hand. With her dad and her boyfriend behind her, maybe she could be the warrior they saw in her.

CHAPTER 25

Myreen

Myreen rounded what had to be the millionth corner, blindly roaming the citadel as she gathered her thoughts. It was cold, past the floors the humans occupied, but she didn't mind. It helped snap her thoughts into focus, and kept her from dwelling on anything for too long.

Her heart bled for Leif. She'd had no idea he was helping Oberon all this time. Helping her. And now he was being punished for it. Just another person who was suffering because of their allegiance to her. And look at what she was doing with their sacrifices—living with the enemy, sitting across from him at the dinner table every night like it was nothing.

And if Leif, one of Draven's own, was being punished so severely, she couldn't bear to think what Draven had in store for Kol. She hadn't been to see Kol since he'd been captured, poisoned by jealousy over that dragon girl who clung to him so tightly. At first, she told herself that the shifters would come for him. He was General Dracul's son, and she knew first-hand how ruthless that man was when it came to getting what he wanted; she had to believe he wanted his son safely returned to him.

Days had passed, though, and no one had come to anyone's rescue. And Kenzie couldn't possibly get everyone out by herself, either. As much as Myreen claimed to hate Kol for toying with her heart, she couldn't stand by and let him suffer any longer. The purpose of this seemingly-endless walk had been to build up the courage to approach Draven, as her father, and appeal for Kol's release. If he cared for her as much as he claimed to, and if she pulled his strings right, maybe he'd be lenient. She didn't really believe that, but she had to try.

Finally, she turned around and headed for the stairs that would take her down to Draven's office. There was no elevator in this particular tower—the only elevator in the complex was put in place for Ty, leading to the Elite towers which contained his and her bedrooms—but she didn't at all mind the extra time to prepare what she was going to say.

As her feet landed on the ground floor and warmth started to unfreeze her nose and fingers, her heart skittered nervously in her chest. The door to his office was in sight. She froze for an instant as she stared across the Grand Hall at it, until a shoulder nudged hers and shook her out of her stupor.

"Sorry," said an all too familiar voice—the best voice in the world.

"Kenzie?" Myreen asked, turning around to see her newly redheaded friend passing her by.

"Oh, Myreen," Kenzie stammered, looking a bit dazed. "Sorry, I wasn't paying attention. H– how are you holding up?"

Though Kenzie's face was a mask, Myreen could see a struggle blazing in her hazel eyes.

"Fine, but... are you alright?"

Kenzie laughed, and only Myreen could hear the fake note in her laughter. "Me? Of course! Never better." Kenzie's eyes darted to something behind Myreen, and she turned, remembering the guards trailing her. She'd almost forgotten they were there. Myreen looked back at Kenzie, giving her an apologetic smile.

Kenzie shook her head and smiled. "Walk with me to my room and I'll tell you all about it."

Myreen's concern was instantly sparked, and she decided her big talk with dear old dad would have to wait. Kenzie took her arm and they walked together through the human quarters to Kenzie's room. The guards waited in the hall, while Kenzie and Myreen went in, Kenzie quietly bolting the door behind them.

"Aonrúgh," Kenzie said softly, putting her hands flat together in front of her then spreading them out. Myreen watched in bewilderment. Kenzie smirked. "A privacy spell. Now no one outside this room can hear us, not even vamps."

Sometimes Myreen forgot Kenzie was a selkie, so it was still a shock to her any time her best friend used magic. "Okay, spill. What's really going on?"

The brave face Kenzie had been wearing faded away, replaced by a look of sickly white disgust. "I've done something terrible," she all but croaked. "Leif... Draven made me strip away his daywalker abilities to prove my loyalty. I tried to make it temporary, but... Then he put Leif in the Sunroom and made me open the ceiling." Tears welled in Kenzie's eyes, and she clutched her abdomen like she might vomit.

"Oh, Kenzie..." Myreen pulled Kenzie in for a hug, unsure of what else to say. Should she mention that she'd spoken to

Leif? Probably not. Leif had said Kenzie wasn't to be trusted. He'd lost faith in her. Even Myreen didn't exactly understand what Kenzie was doing. It was because of her that Kol and Char got captured in the first place, but Myreen wasn't about to bring that up now, not when Kenzie was one strong wind away from falling to pieces. Myreen knew Kenzie was doing what she thought was right. Still, Myreen could live a thousand years and the image of Leif's charred flesh would never fade.

"I came here to rescue him, and instead I've—" she bit her bottom lip and rolled her eyes upward to keep her tears from falling. "I don't know what I'm doing, Myreen. I don't have much time left. Draven has the ingredients for the daywalker spell. And on top of that, my big *initiation* is tonight, and I'm going to be assigned to Adam, of all the baby bloodsuckers in the world."

"Adam, the guy you had a thing with?" Myreen asked. "I thought he was just an Initiate."

"Well, he's earned his big bite, apparently." She threw her hands in the air. "Now I get to be his plaything." Myreen didn't miss how Kenzie's cheeks reddened. "Sorry I'm dumping this all on you. I just thought I was staging a rescue. Now I feel like I'm becoming a monster."

Myreen hated that Kenzie had gotten herself into this. Kenzie needed to get out of here. Her, Leif, Kol and Char all did.

"I was actually on my way to talk to Draven about letting Kol and Char go," Myreen intimated. "Maybe I can appeal for Leif, too."

Kenzie snorted. "Yeah, good luck with that."

"I'm his daughter," Myreen declared with more conviction than she felt. "Maybe he'll listen to me."

"And maybe he'll throw you in a cell right next to Kol!" Kenzie snapped. Then her brows pinched and her lips puckered.

"I'm sorry, I didn't mean that. I'm just freaking out. I don't want to see you get yourself on the bad side of the most dangerous vampire in the world."

Myreen gripped Kenzie's shoulders comfortingly. "It will be okay. He won't hurt me, I'm pretty sure of that."

"For all our sakes, I hope you're right," Kenzie said shakily. They looked at each other for a moment, savoring each other's company. "Well, I have an initiation to prep for, and you have a maniacal father to persuade."

Myreen nodded and headed for the door. Then she turned back and said, "Kenz, if Leif and Kol do get released, I want you to leave immediately. Don't wait for me. Okay?"

Kenzie didn't answer, but after a brief staring contest, she nodded once. Myreen unbolted the door and left, heading for Draven's office with even more purpose.

***

Myreen knocked on the door, the sound very staccato, very direct.

Draven had never allowed her to enter his office. She'd come knocking twice before, and both times he'd slipped out and closed the door faster than she could peek inside. She hadn't paid much mind to it before, but after Leif warned her about "Draven's Trophy Room," now she was suspicious. Was this it? And what did he have in there that he didn't want her to see?

She heard the lock click, and once again, he exited in the blink of an eye and now stood between her and the closed door.

Draven cocked a brow, ignoring the guards standing behind Myreen. "Hello, Myreen. If you've come to witness the daywalker spell, you're a little early."

Yeah, he definitely doesn't want me to see what's in that room.

"Actually, I was hoping I could talk to you about a delicate matter," she began.

"Oh? And to what does this matter pertain?" He cast scrutinizing eyes down on her while wearing a playful expression on his perfect face.

She looked around the Grand Hall at all the vampires lounging about, and the guards standing behind her. "I was hoping we could speak in private." She nodded toward his office.

"Ah, yes. We can go to the conference room." He put a hand on her upper back and started to lead her away.

"What's wrong with your office?" She couldn't help but pry.

"It's just a little too cluttered at the moment for a private conversation with my daughter," he dismissed. "The conference room is much better."

She let go of the issue, reminding herself that she didn't come to interrogate him about a silly room. She came to try to save Kol, Char, and Leif.

Draven held open the door to the conference room for her and closed it behind them, leaving the guards standing outside. The room was large with a very long, rectangular table taking up the majority of the space. He took the seat at the closest end and offered her the seat catty-corner to it.

"What's on your mind?" he invited.

For a moment, she considered using her siren voice on him to force his cooperation. He trusted her. All she had to do was the say the words and he would never know the decision wasn't his own.

But they were in his conference room—she wouldn't put it past him to have cameras set up in here. In fact, she expected it. And if he found out she had broken his one rule... She wanted to believe this whole father bit was sincere, but she wasn't prepared to face the consequences if it wasn't.

She took a deep breath, mustering all her courage and hoping her heart rate was steady enough to prove her a worthy advocate.

"The Dracul boy. I'd like for you to let him go," she declared. "As well as his female companion."

Draven gave her a blank look for a moment, then burst out laughing, the sound so sharp it rang in her ears. She suddenly felt very small and insignificant.

"Do you have any notion of wartime politics?" he asked, still chuckling. "They attacked us, and they lost. It's then our right to execute or keep them prisoners, as we see fit. I feel I've been rather lenient on the boy. Why do you care what happens to him?"

"I'm not as comfortable with violence as everyone here seems to be." Myreen swallowed. "I'd appeal to you for mercy regardless of who it was, but this particular dragon happens to matter to me." She thought about bringing up Leif in that moment, but decided to wait. If she could secure Kol and Char first, then she'd bring up Draven's own.

Draven cocked his head, studying her. "I noticed you didn't say the dragon *prince* was your friend. Strange choice of words. Could it be that he's something more? Has my daughter fallen in love?"

Anger flared in her chest before she could conceal it, and it was clear by the smirk on his face that he caught that telltale reaction.

"Ah, so that's it," he said with a knowing nod. "The royal pretender has broken your heart."

She kept her expression blank and her breathing still, but sorrow spilled out through the cracks in her heart, spreading through her chest like a poison. The truth hurt.

"If that's the case, then why do you want him to go free? Why do you care what happens to him?"

"Love isn't just something you can wash away when you're done with it," she said, looking at the table. "No matter what he did or didn't do to me, I still don't want to see him suffer."

Draven stood. "I'm sorry to deny your request, but I cannot and will not set him free. It's become quite clear to me that he deserves much *less* mercy from me."

"Wh– what? No, p– please—" she stuttered, reaching for his hand unintentionally. How had this conversation gone so horribly wrong?

"No filthy dragon is going to break my daughter's heart and get away with it," he said, accepting her hand and squeezing it. "You deserve so much better than the likes of him, and maybe when he's gone, you'll understand that."

"Please, don't kill him!" she begged.

He put his other hand on top of the one he was holding. "Oh, don't worry. I can assure you he won't be dying for a long, long time. Now, if you'll excuse me, I have an initiation to prepare for."

Then he released her hand and vanished, leaving her alone in the conference room, trembling all over.

***

Myreen raced to the dungeons after she recovered from the shock of Draven's decision. She felt as though her heart was doubly broken—once by Kol's doing and now by her own. She had to at least warn him of what was to come, even if she had to confess it was her fault. He'd hate her. Not that he ever really cared for her to begin with, but now the fate of their relationship would truly be sealed.

Tears streamed down her face as she practically tripped down the stairs of the lower levels to where he was being held. She used her siren voice on her bodyguards, telling them to stay in the conference room until she returned. Her will was desperate enough that she hardly needed to say anything for them to let her go. And the guards below were the same she'd encountered last time, and apparently needed no further persuasion. Just as well.

She slowed as she neared the room with Kol's cage. Her thumbs were practically glued inside her back pockets, her right one nervously fingering her keycard, as if doing so would give her courage. The heads of Kol and Char snapped in her direction as she came into view, caution plastered all over their faces. Myreen whipped her hands out of her pockets, instinctively hugging herself, and not just because of how inhumanely cold it was down here.

Kol's face had aged in the handful of days he'd been here. A handsome, unshaven shadow darkened his jawline, and the skin under his eyes looked bruised, his eyes dry and bloodshot. The lack of sufficient food and water worked quickly with his fast metabolism, making him look even taller and more gangly. And then there was Char, who still looked gorgeous even with dirt smudged across her face and hair bunched in tangles. Myreen cast her gaze away.

"Myreen? What are you doing here?" Kol yelled at her in a whisper, if such a thing was possible—leave it to Kol to be a walking contradiction.

She crept to the bars, gripping them for support, but hissing and pulling her hands away as the metal seemed to burn her. Understanding dawned. The bars were lead. Even the floor and back wall of the cell were lined in it. Her mind flashed back to the attack in the alley when Kol had been shot with those lead pellets, and she remembered the horrible effect they had on him. Draven knew full-well avians were allergic to lead. This wasn't just war politics to Draven; no, he enjoyed making his enemies suffer. A lesson Myreen would not soon forget.

Myreen took a deep breath. "Kol, I messed up. I tried to talk Draven into letting you two go."

"You did what?" he asked, looking bewildered.

"I thought that as his daughter, I could change his mind," she went on. "I thought he'd do it just to make me happy, to further convince me he was on my side. But, then..."

Kol scooched closer, looking like he desperately wanted to touch her, to comfort her. But he eyed the bars, and kept his broken arms to himself. Myreen covered her mouth, trying to keep the bubbling emotions from spilling over.

Kol looked at her. "I take it he didn't grant your request?"

Myreen shook her head. "Kol, I'm so sorry. He figured out that you... that you weren't just a friend to me and... that it didn't end well. I didn't mean to tell him, he just—"

"And now he wants to punish me for hurting his daughter," Kol guessed. It wasn't an accusation. There didn't even seem to be any anger or resentment in his tone. His expression was smooth, though somewhat defeated.

"Kol, I really am so sorry," Myreen pleaded, tears beginning to spill. "I know you must think I did this on purpose to get back at you, but I would never—"

"It's okay, Myreen," he interrupted. "I know you wouldn't do that. Getting information out of people is what vampires do, and Draven is a master at it. The truth is, he wouldn't have let me go no matter what. He has a particular hatred for my bloodline. But I'm touched that you tried." He offered her a weak smile.

She wiped at her cheeks and under her eyes until she could see clearly again. Then she reached through the bars as far as she could and put her hand on his knee, ignoring the slow burn. "I will get you both out of here, I promise."

Kol huffed a defeated laugh and smiled wider. "No, you won't," he said, shaking his head. "The best you can do is get yourself out. Draven's daughter or not, this isn't where you belong."

Her brows creased as she stared at him. She saw no point in arguing. She had no intention of leaving the citadel, but certainly not without him and Char.

Char. Myreen had nearly forgotten about the other girl, but she'd been so quiet. Myreen stole a glance at the girl, who looked at the floor, her face red.

Myreen began to withdraw her hand, but Kol's fingers brushed hers, and she held her hand in place a moment longer. "For what it's worth, I truly am sorry that I hurt you."

As always, his hand felt so warm and comforting on hers. She tried to draw out that moment, wishing it could last forever.

If Draven was true to his word, he wasn't going to just kill Kol, which meant this wouldn't be the last time she saw him.

She still had time.

This wasn't goodbye.

So she gave him no words of farewell, but slipped her hand out of his and padded silently and quickly down the dungeon hallway.

CHAPTER 26

Kenzie

Kenzie made her way to the trophy room, dread building with every step. The moonflower had arrived, and Kenzie was out of time. She hadn't figured out how to get Leif or Kol out. She hadn't convinced Myreen to leave. She was failing in every way possible.

Not that she hadn't been failing before this moment. She'd stopped taking those online classes Gram had signed her up for, the stress eating away her concentration. Besides, she had vampire classes to attend. Those were... strange. Listening to the teachers, she could almost believe that the vampires were the good guys and the shifters were evil. Almost. But the shifters she knew were good, the only person they wanted dead being Draven. And Kenzie couldn't fault them for that.

She'd also taken to contacting Gram first thing in the mornings. Which meant she was waking Gram in the middle of the night. She hoped the befuddled state of both her and Gram would dampen the despair Kenzie was beginning to sink into. But she didn't want Gram to worry and pull Kenzie too soon.

Not even confessing everything to Myreen had helped. Kenzie really was becoming a monster, and she hated herself for it. This was worse than when she lost her dad. This was rock bottom. She didn't think it was possible to fall any further, to feel any worse than she already did.

Except now she was giving the most evil, most powerful vampire in the world a ticket to freedom. Now, thanks to her, Draven would be a daywalker.

Kenzie wanted to meddle with the spell, try to make it temporary like she'd tried to make Leif's reversal temporary—and she hoped against hope that it really *was* temporary. But she didn't want to risk making things worse. There were notes with the daywalker spell, notes about the dire consequences of not following it precisely. What Leif must have gone through to earn his right to walk in the sun... Kenzie didn't want to even think about it.

But she couldn't risk botching the spell with Draven. She'd never make it out alive if she did. Draven would see to that. And if she wasn't killing the vampire, and her friends weren't out of harm's way, then there was no sense trying to make the spell temporary.

And so she found herself aiding the enemy once more.

And now, Adam was a vampire. If that wasn't frightening enough, knowing that she was his main source of food for the foreseeable future was enough to give her night terrors. She'd stayed away during the transformation process—thankfully, she'd been ordered to, though she wasn't sure she'd have gone even if she was supposed to. Draven didn't want to risk Adam losing control and turning Kenzie or draining her dry. But after today's ceremony, she'd be Adam's, and it made her skin crawl.

Kenzie knocked on the trophy room door and shouldered

her bag as she waited.

Draven opened it with a smile. "Excellent. Time for the fun to begin."

Kenzie smiled as she entered and hoped that Draven wouldn't notice that it didn't meet her eyes.

"Nervous?" Draven asked as he closed the door.

They took their seats at the desk, the moonflower sitting in a cup of water, its roots looking like pale worms, magnified by the curve of the glass.

Kenzie shrugged. "Yeah. I'm nervous. I'm doing a big spell for a big guy."

Draven laughed. "You are. Honesty. I like that. Are you anxious to see Adam?"

Kenzie gave him a demure smile. "I'm curious, but I've been too busy with school and thinking about this"—she waved a hand at the moonflower, as if presenting a prize—"to really have time to think about Adam."

Draven nodded. "I think you'll be pleasantly surprised. He turned quite nicely."

Kenzie nodded, her curiosity officially piqued.

"Shall we begin?"

Kenzie stood and removed the bag from her back, muttering the reveal spell before pulling the book out. She was so afraid she'd lose the ancient tome that she barely took it out, and keeping it hidden by magic was the easiest way to ensure it didn't get stolen. Although if someone ever took her bag, she'd be screwed.

She murmured her name next, then opened the book to the daywalker spell. Just seeing the delicate handwriting—strong but undeniably feminine—always made Kenzie want to be more like the woman who had written the spell. She still hadn't found a way to bring Gemma back from the dead, but her words to Draven were true—she *had* been incredibly preoccupied as of late.

Kenzie cleared her throat and grabbed the flower, tearing off the petals and roots and placing them in one pile. They smelled a bit like lemons, and Kenzie wondered if they'd taste that way, too. Draven handed her a bag of sunflower seeds, and she made a new pile with them. She sat back and eyed the parts, then nodded. They looked about equal to her. Hopefully.

She pushed both piles toward Draven. "You'll need to eat all of this first."

Draven lifted a brow, then shrugged and began consuming everything she'd measured out. The moonflower was poisonous to humans, but Kenzie knew it wouldn't affect Draven. Though apparently the flavor was less than appealing, because he grimaced as he swallowed, not even bothering to chew. When he was done, he sat back.

Kenzie took a deep breath and turned the grimoire to face Draven, then came around the desk. She didn't know if she needed to be in contact with the man for the spell to work, but she figured it couldn't hurt.

Kenzie swallowed as she placed her hand lightly on his shoulder. Draven eyed her. "It's okay. I won't bite you." He smiled, and Kenzie gave a nervous chuckle.

"Sorry. I'm just trying to make sure I don't screw anything up."

"Take your time and do it right. I'm sure you'll do fine."

Kenzie nodded, glancing at the book. She didn't have to read the spell, since she'd memorized it, but the wizened pages provided a sort of comfort that she needed right now.

Kenzie closed her eyes and found that tingle of magic in her chest, then refocused on the book. "Vampír, créatúrnal ghealaís, glachadha leissana noíche, nábíodha eaglortír ansalágh." A gentle breeze lifted Kenzie's hair as she sank deeper into the magic, letting it wash over her. The office and its atrocities fell away, leaving Kenzie in a warm void that glittered with possibilities. "Bhithina chúpúla, deú solaras noíche. Choinanonn echlipsée andúlray tú chábháliteh. B'fhélidira i mbeah séi gcónascí." The words left her lips with a strength she didn't know she possessed, her vision snapping back to the present, the wind ceasing.

A silver glow settled on Draven's skin, sinking in until it faded completely. Draven smiled, looking at his hands, then up to Kenzie. "I feel good. Shall we test your handiwork?"

Kenzie swallowed, the peace that had accompanied the spell tearing away from her like a cockroach in the light. "Sure. Just... be careful."

Draven's smile cocked to the side. "I always take every precaution."

He pulled up his wrist, tapping on the watch face. A few moments later, a beanpole of a man came in, his pale skin making his sunken cheeks look somewhat sickly. He held a small device in his hand. "Are you ready, sir?"

"Let's find out," Draven replied.

Kenzie shoved her book back in her bag and quietly spat out the hiding spell, then dashed to keep up with Draven. Her stomach twisted and turned, underpinned with a sort of excitement that only served to confuse matters further.

Draven went to the front door, cracking it open. Only a sliver of light spilled in, thanks to some ingenious design, but it was enough. Draven didn't even flinch in the warm glow. A slow smile spread across his lips, and he took another step into the gap. Draven began to laugh, stepping all the way out, and Kenzie and *Mr. Bean* followed. Some of the students and vampires milling in the Grand Hall watched with interest, but only those still human dared to venture out behind the trio.

Draven stood a few steps down, his arms upturned, his eyes closed as he faced the midday sun. He looked back at Kenzie with a sly grin, then dashed down the stairs so quickly Kenzie couldn't keep track of his form. Excited murmurs from students sounded behind Kenzie. A sense of pride welled up, knowing what she'd accomplished, even as terror filled her.

She'd just unleashed the most powerful vampire in the world.

As if her thought had summoned him, Draven zipped to the bottom of the stairs. "Start rolling, Steadman!"

Mr. Bean—or Steadman, apparently—pushed a button on his device as he held it in front of him, and a blue light blinked on.

"Vampires, shifters, supernaturals everywhere! I wanted to share the glorious news. Your leader has been liberated from the chains of the night. I can now walk fearlessly through the day. Our greatest dreams are about to be realized, and all thanks to this young selkie."

The camera panned to Kenzie, who froze. She cracked a sheepish smile as she brought her hand halfway up and curled her fingers in a weak attempt to wave. The butterflies in her stomach turned to frightened bats, beating at her insides in a mad attempt to escape. But there *was* no escape.

The camera panned back to Draven, and Kenzie took a deep, shuddering breath. *Fudgsicles.*

Kenzie buried her face in her hands as Draven made his final remarks. She could almost envision the horror on the faces of shifters as they watched—Juliet, Oberon, Delphine. Draven had just put the final nail in her coffin. Steadman lowered the device, the blue light winking off.

Draven climbed the stairs, stopping next to Kenzie and putting a steadying hand on her shoulder. "Excellent work. Soon we'll have an entire army of daywalkers at our disposal. You're a great addition to the team. I trust you won't let me down."

Kenzie swallowed. "Of course not," she croaked.

Draven turned his attention to the students. "As you can see, being a vampire no longer has limitations—*if* you're willing to work hard and prove yourself. And today has another treat in store. One of your own has ascended! Let us go inside so we can all greet Adam."

Kenzie followed Draven, her face numb, her hands trembling. Adam as a human was one thing, but Adam as a vampire? And he'd be feeding off her, his first taste today. It was part of the pageantry Draven was putting on. He wanted everyone to see her loyalty, her commitment to the cause. Though he hadn't told her she was going to be filmed, or her image broadcasted to the shifters. She only hoped they would be able to see her true intentions, though she doubted it.

By the time they reached the lobby, it had been filled. The vampires and Initiates had obviously seen the broadcast, and they chattered excitedly.

A table was pulled out, and Draven hopped on top, patting the air with his hands to get the crowd to quiet. When it was soft enough to hear a pin drop, Draven spoke. "As you all know, I recently reunited with my daughter, Myreen. Her presence gives us all hope of a better, brighter future. Apparently, she's our good luck charm. Her friend, Kenzie, is a selkie who has brought us the ability to walk in daylight. And one of your own, Adam, has proved himself committed to our cause. His ability to spot flaws and holes in our research has allowed us to come closer than ever to creating a vampire-shifter hybrid."

As if summoned by hearing his name, Adam appeared. He spotted Kenzie through the crowd and flashed her a fanged smile. Kenzie lost her breath for the second time that day. Adam wasn't just alluring now, he was heart-stopping. It wasn't fair.

"And I've paired Adam and Kenzie as vampire and Initiate, a power couple to aspire to."

There was applause, and Adam jumped onto the table, next to Draven—at Draven's bidding, of course. Draven held out a hand to Kenzie, and she took it, and was instantly on the table as well, the world spinning, the crowd cheering. Or maybe jeering; Kenzie couldn't tell.

And just like that, Adam was next to her ear. "Ready for your first bite?"

Kenzie gave a nervous laugh. It wasn't exactly her first bite, but it might as well have been. And this was so different from being attacked, at once more sinister and seductive.

Adam took a deep sniff, then gently placed his fangs against the skin of her neck. Kenzie held her breath. Pain lanced through her as Adam sunk in, the world around her wavering. Kenzie closed her eyes as the venom pumped into her system, helping her relax. She didn't fight it. It was easier this way. She could forget about the dangerous game she was playing, forget her failures and disappointments.

When Adam released her, the crowd cheered again. Kenzie didn't open her eyes, basking in the afterglow of Adam's bite. His warmth was still at her back, his hands rubbing her arms. Which was essentially useless, as his cold skin couldn't warm her. But Kenzie didn't mind.

His lips were by her ear again. "I hope that was as good for you as it was for me."

Kenzie hummed and nodded. On some level, she knew this was so messed up, but she ignored the feeling. She'd stay in her happy place a little while longer. There'd be time to clean things up later. Maybe.

Kol

Kol's knee was still warm where Myreen's hand had touched him only minutes ago. The moment was brief and though he knew it didn't mean anything, he still couldn't resist holding it there for few seconds longer, even as his heart crumbled.

And now she was gone.

The second her feet hit the stairs, she'd probably forgotten all about him, the very thought of him fleeing from her mind. But she wasn't gone from his. She would never be gone from his. The image of Myreen—her dark, shining hair, her sparkling blue eyes—would forever be in his mind and heart for as long as Kol lived—which he realized, in his current predicament, might not be much longer.

Char shifted behind him, and a different sort of agony pierced through. She shouldn't be in this cell. Being Draven's prisoner, half-starved and surrounded by poisonous lead, was made worse knowing Charlotte suffered too. And it was likely his fault.

The mission should've been called off. Kol should've kept his damn mouth shut and listened to Corporal Modder. Instead, like the stupid, love-sick dragon he was, he insisted on going anyway, and practically forced Char's hand. When she felt she couldn't cancel the mission, she did the only thing she could by giving her unit an out before they began.

All but four of the team members leaving should've been Kol's second clue.

But he stormed the castle anyway.

And she'd come too.

And she'd been captured and was suffering right alongside him.

Char's teeth chattered. Kol moved toward her as quickly as his severely weakened body could, trying to pull her into his broken arms. The least he could do was try to keep her warm. For the thousandth time he wished their smart clothing was working properly.

"How are you holding up?" he asked, feeling her stiffen, but then relax against him. He felt warmer already, and hoped she did too. "I– I'm sorry I got you into this mess." His voice cracked.

Her shivering stopped, and he thought she might've fallen asleep because she didn't answer right away. But then she cleared her throat. "That was her."

Kol knew it wasn't a question. Char had seen Myreen before. "Yes. That was Myreen," he answered anyway.

"She's pretty."

It was a gross understatement, but he didn't think he should correct her.

"But I don't think you activated the curse," she said, her voice breathless like she'd only spoken half a thought.

The edges of Kol's torn heart burned painfully. It was a new sensation he still wasn't used to. "You're wrong," he said. "I should've stayed away from her, but I couldn't. We became a thing instead." He snorted a humorless laugh. "I even went to her selkie friend to try to lift the curse when I felt myself getting close. But it didn't work. I saw the look in her eyes the instant the curse was triggered." He took in a ragged breath that wasn't entirely from their physical situation. "I felt it, and then saw the change in *her.*"

Charlotte twisted in Kol's arms so she could look at him. He loosened his grip to give them both space. Dark rings circled her eyes, almost looking like bruises. Her blonde hair snarled and tangled in places.

He figured he looked similarly terrible and rubbed some of the dirt from her cheekbone without thinking. "You shouldn't be here," he said, realizing what he rubbed was an actual bruise. He wondered what monster gave it to her.

"Neither should you," she said, suddenly motionless.

He dropped his hand.

"Don't stop," she whispered, but ducked her head the second the words left her lips, like she wanted to take it back. "I know it's not possible because my name and my blood isn't *Dracul,* but sometimes I feel like *I* triggered the curse a long time ago."

Kol wanted to put distance between them. He knew he should, because their proximity was clearly messing with Char's emotions. Or maybe it was the lack of food and too much lead that made her head muddled. He knew it was affecting him, but not in *that* way. He wanted to put distance between them, but they both needed the body heat to survive. So, he went rigid like a statue and racked his brain for the right words. Too bad his brain wasn't working at full capacity. Still, he was pretty sure he'd never be ready for this sort of conversation with her. All neurons firing correctly or not.

"I've always accepted it, you know?" Her eyes lifted to his and she let out a shaky laugh. "And I know... we're young. I'm only eighteen and you're only seventeen, but I've always accepted and looked forward to the eventuality that one day it would be you and me against the world. You know?"

Definitely the symptoms of a muddled-head.

"Char—"

"I'm glad we were so close at school before I left," she interrupted. "At least we'd always have that friendship foundation when either you or I..."

"What? Got married and one of us triggered the curse?" He dropped his arms and scooted a few inches away so they were no longer touching. But his temperature drop at the loss of contact was almost tangible. He knew she felt it too, and hoped they could get over this emotional hurdle before either of them froze to death. "Have you *seen* my parents? Do you think my mom is *happy* to be crazy about my dad when he's so indifferent to her?"

"He respects her," she said, though her argument was weak. Still, she scooted closer to him again, moving quicker than he could have. "Which is a sort of love."

"Char—"

She pressed a finger to his lips. "Do you respect me?" she asked.

He stared unblinkingly at her as confirmation that he did.

"Do you..." she choked. "*Love* me?"

Of course he loved her, and too late he felt the expression on his face shout the truth of it but—

She leaned forward and kissed him. He remained motionless until she'd finished. Kol had been kissed by plenty of girls in the past, and he'd never had an issue with kissing them back, even when he didn't have any feelings for them.

But loving Myreen had changed that.

Even though she hated him now, even though she was probably glad he'd been thrown into this dungeon—although her face and actions didn't exactly advertise that—*focus!* Even with all of that, he couldn't kiss Char back. He didn't *want* to. As much as he loved and respected Char, he could not kiss her back.

Rejection replaced whatever emotion Char had been wearing before the kiss and she shrunk back to escape to her corner. He touched her arm, and she stopped. He wrapped her in his arms again. They both needed the warmth. And she needed a friend.

"I do love you, Char," he said. "Always have."

She shuddered against him, but he suspected it wasn't from the cold.

"But I *love* her." He put emphasis on the word. "I fell in love with *her*... and triggered the curse."

"I hate to interrupt," Draven's booming tone filled the entire dungeon. "But you and I have some *business* to take care of, Malkolm Dracul."

Kol didn't move, though Char gently tried to pry herself from his grasp.

Draven tsked. "Is this hatchling the reason my daughter has a broken heart? Huh?"

Kol's head snapped to Draven and he released Char. *Broken heart?* What did Myreen tell him?

"It's too late now, *Kol.* I witnessed that little embrace you two shared." Draven paced outside the bars. "There's no need to hide it. The question is, should I tell Myreen?"

Kol opened his mouth to speak, but was interrupted before his lips could move.

"I won't. But for her sake, not yours." Draven stopped pacing and crouched so he was at Kol's eye level. "Now, for the reason I've come." He snapped his fingers and Hair Gel arrived with a couple of archaic gas masks that looked like they were stolen from the set of a World War I movie, and what appeared to be a garden hose.

Hair Gel handed one of the masks to Draven before hoisting the hose underneath his arm, ready to put out... a fire, probably.

Kol gave them both a withering look. Whatever was put in his cell prevented even a spark inside him, let alone a blaze large enough that needed extinguishing. He made a point not to think about the purpose of the masks.

Draven ignored the look and paced again, his arms behind his back. "I wonder if you have any insight into that little shifter military and what they're planning?"

Kol knew his look was incredulous, but Draven didn't seem to get the message. "You know I'm in here, right?" he said. "How could I possibly *know* their plans?" He hoped a rescue mission to save himself and Char was underway, but there was no way of knowing that either.

When they'd been captured, Charlotte drilled into Kol's head—as covertly as possible, of course—that they shouldn't assume anything. So far, nothing had connected them to the military. Char wanted to keep it that way, and Kol agreed. Let them think they were driven to rescue a friend and were working of their own accord. If Draven knew they were under orders of the larger body of the shifter military, they could be held for ransom, tortured for information, or killed.

So far, the only thing Draven had deduced was that he'd captured a Dracul dragon and his dragon friend. The longer he believed that and didn't figure out the truth, the better. And if he did somehow figure out their roles in the military, Kol prayed Draven wouldn't learn Char's rank.

Revealing or slipping that information could mean a death sentence for Charlotte.

"You're the son of Eduard Dracul, certainly you must know *something*." Draven gripped one of the bars, his mask still clutched in the other hand.

"You think my father doles out military secrets to me? Just like that?" Kol scoffed. "I assure you, the General is smarter than that."

Draven's carefully crafted expression slipped, but he instantly covered it with the mask. "This will hurt a little," his muffled, inhuman voice warned.

Hair Gel lowered his mask too, before a nod from Draven prompted him to pull a lever on the hose.

A loud *hisss* sounded as yellow smoke poured from the nozzle.

Kol looked back at Char, whose eyes were wide and frightened. He wanted to reach back, to try to take her hand, but worried it would turn Draven's attention to her instead. Still, neither of them were escaping the yellow gas.

Kol's right leg cracked first, bending backward at the knee as it was forced to shift into his dragon leg. Then his left. More bones popped and cracked, both his and Char's, and she let out a yelp. It felt like the first shift, awkward and uncomfortable and *painful*. Actually *more* painful than his first shift, but that was most likely the intended result of the toxic gas.

Blue scales flipped like fingernails, bending back from his and Char's skin, identical in color just as they'd been when they first flew to the towers. Tears streamed down Char's face, but she only gave the occasional whimper. Kol bit his tongue hard enough to taste coppery blood as his spine stretched to form his tail, his shoulder blades breaking from his skin to stretch into enormous wings.

As the dragons grew to their full size, their cell became excruciatingly cramped, until they pressed against each other and the bars with equal force. The burning pain of the lead only slightly trumped the awful smell and sizzling of his and Char's scales. And it mercifully kept his weight off his broken arms.

Draven removed his mask after the gas vanished, a smile plastered to his face. "Now," he said, allowing a painful pause to hover in the air. "What do you know about the shifter military?"

"I. Don't. Know," Kol said, more out of exasperation at the question rather than his current tight situation. "I thought you were smart." And there went his mouth.

Hair Gel pulled out a set of very large pliers and handed them to Draven, who held them precariously, like they could hurt the vampire, too. Kol didn't need to be told what they were for.

"Did you know that the scales of a dragon are not only impenetrable, but they don't decay like the rest of the body?" Draven asked, his eyes on the pliers as he turned them in his hand. "It makes one wonder why a person wouldn't happen upon dead dragons more often."

Char stiffened.

"And why humans are so unaware of them."

Kol didn't feel the need to answer the question. Dragons kept track of each other. If one died in dragon form, the body was taken care of to avoid detection from humans.

"But if one lost only one scale, say in battle or an unfortunate accident..." In one quick motion, Draven ripped one of Kol's stony blue scales from his side, not even bothering to make sure he took the scale from Kol and not Char. The surprise and ripping of his flesh was too much, and Kol let out a roar. Unfortunately, there was still no fire within to retaliate against the bloodsucker.

Draven palmed the brilliant blue scale, though it was much bigger than his hand.

"It's almost like a stone," he said, testing the weight of it. "It'll last forever. Unlike you and your friend."

Kol willed his fire chamber to ignite as he pressed harder against the lead bars in an attempt to break free. But his insides were cold, and the bars didn't even groan with the pressure.

Draven handed the scale to Hair Gel behind him, before turning back to the dragons in the cage. "You might not know about shifter military plans," he continued. "Your father is a smart man. But you've attended that fishbowl of a school for long enough that I'm sure you're in the good graces of the headmaster? Oberon Rex?"

"Oberon?" Kol blurted. "You want to know about Oberon?" He was feeling hysterical, probably the result of the stinging wound where his scale was torn from. "I highly doubt *you* would have any interest in what Oberon Rex is currently doing."

This got Draven's attention. "Oh?"

Char cleared her throat.

"He isn't in charge of the school!" Kol said, feeling like his voice was too high-pitched, even in his dragon growl. "My father is."

"Interesting." Draven rubbed the stubble of his chin. "I'll have to look into the gryphon's whereabouts."

Char shifted uncomfortably next to him before he finally realized what he'd done. What would Draven do with that information? Was Oberon in more danger? Was the school?

Draven snapped his fingers at Hair Gel. "Take one from

her," he said, handing over the pliers. "Then shift them back and cuff him." Draven pointed at Kol before turning to walk away.

"Yes, sir." Hair Gel muttered.

Draven paused. "Also put the belt on him," he said. "The one that shoots out lead barbs whenever the wearer speaks. He's too mouthy for my liking."

"Yes, sir," Hair Gel said, with more enthusiasm than Kol thought necessary.

Draven hadn't even reached the doorway before Char screamed.

CHAPTER 28

Myreen

As Myreen traipsed back toward the steps of the dungeons, inserting her hands into her rear pockets, she realized her keycard was no longer there. Fear instantly spiked through her at the consequences of losing it—in the dungeon, of all places! Draven's daywalker spell would be completed soon, and she had no doubt he'd pay a visit to Kol right after. If Draven found her keycard down here, she'd lose any chance of breaking Kol out.

She raced back down the stairs, scanning every inch of the floor until she saw the shiny white plastic winking at her in the darkness. Flooded with relief, she knelt and picked it up, clutching it to her chest as if it were something precious.

"I don't think you triggered the curse," Char's voice carried from down the hall.

Curse? What are they talking about?

Myreen told herself that curses weren't real. And yet, neither were dragons and mermaids and spells that allowed vampires to walk in the day, but she'd encountered them, nonetheless. What kind of curse could Kol have triggered?

Myreen crept closer, hiding herself in a little shadowed nook in front of the first cell, and listened.

Kol's hollow voice carried toward her, echoing cynicism down the hallway. "I should've stayed away from her, but I couldn't. We became a thing instead. I even went to her selkie friend to try to lift the curse when I felt myself getting close. But it didn't work..."

Kenzie? Kol went to Kenzie to lift a curse? And this curse has something to do with me?

"I saw the look in her eyes the instant the curse was triggered," Kol said before drawing a ragged breath. "I felt it, and then saw the change in *her*."

Myreen hugged her knees, staring into the blackness. What did this all mean? She continued to listen, trying to derive some kind of understanding. Kol and Char talked more, about his parents, how his mom loved his dad but wasn't loved in return. And how Char felt the same way, loving Kol without being loved in return. Was that because of this curse they were talking about?

"Do you... love me?" Char asked, and Myreen held her breath as she waited for Kol's answer.

There was a long silence, and Myreen's eyes were practically bulging from her skull by the time Kol finally answered.

"I do love you, Char. Always have."

And for the hundredth time at Kol's hand, Myreen's heart broke. She squeezed her eyes shut as the stabbing pain of rejection split her chest open.

"But I *love* her."

Myreen's eyes popped open, and for a moment, her heart ceased to beat.

"I fell in love with *her*... and triggered the curse."

Love? He loves me? Could Kol still be lying? He couldn't know she was listening, but maybe he just needed an excuse to reject Char's affections. But she didn't really believe that. Part of her wanted more than anything to believe he was telling the truth. Because a very big part of her still—

"I hate to interrupt, but you and I have some business to take care of, Malkolm Dracul."

Oh no.

Draven was here! He'd sped right past her and she didn't even know it.

She covered her mouth and stifled her breathing. If Draven caught her down here... She didn't even want to imagine what would happen.

After mentioning how Kol had broken Myreen's heart, implanting the idea in Kol's head that what he was about to endure was somehow her wish, Draven drilled Kol about the shifter military. Myreen silently pleaded for this interrogation to end quickly. Kol was the General's son, but Kol hated the military, avoiding dealing with it at all costs, and he couldn't give Draven information he didn't have. Torturing Kol over that kind of intel would be pointless, and possibly endless.

She heard strange sounds, then a familiar yellow fog filled the air.

No!

It was the same gas he'd pumped into the training room to force her to shift. She couldn't transform into an ursa now! She'd expose herself for sure! Her only comfort was that she still wore the necklace. Maybe she'd be able to control herself.

But before she could fully process the thought, agonizing pain splintered across her back and in every bone in her feet. She clenched her jaw tight to keep a scream from slipping out as the transformation rapidly progressed. She squeezed her eyes so tight that her face hurt as her wings bulged under her sweater and eventually burst through the fabric, and her talons shredded through her tennis shoes.

In seconds, the nightmarish mutation was over, and she could once again take a silent, steadying breath.

It wasn't her ursa that came out, but her harpy. Why? Was it because her ursa had been so closely under the surface that first time she'd been exposed to the gas?

She didn't have much time to ponder, because an ear-splitting, pain-filled roar wracked the dungeon walls, and Myreen knew it came from Kol. Tears freely spilled down her face. The torture had begun. It was all she could do to keep herself from bursting in to come to his rescue. But this was a fight she couldn't win. Not here in the heart of Draven's dungeon with hundreds of vampires above that could be at his defense in a heartbeat.

No, she had to keep herself hidden and *hear* every horrible second of it.

"Shift them back and cuff him," Draven finally told his lackey after a bit more interrogation. "Also attach the belt, the one that shoots out lead barbs whenever the wearer speaks. He's too mouthy for my liking." Then Draven sauntered down the hallway, walking at a human pace this time, no doubt so he could savor the screams as his minion tortured them further.

As he walked past her hiding place, he paused. Myreen held her breath. Did he know she was here? Did he smell her harpy scent? Could he hear her heart beating rapidly out of control? She was done for.

But after a moment of standing perfectly still, he continued forward. Myreen didn't release the breath she was holding until she heard his footsteps fade down the hall and ascend the staircase, the door to the dungeon booming closed.

She got to her feet—or talons rather—and hovered in the shadows in indecision. Draven's lackey was going to torture Kol further, using some device that would once again force lead pellets into his body. She couldn't bear the thought. Even though she couldn't use her siren voice on Draven, she might be lucky enough to catch his lackey off-guard and use her voice on him.

But she wasn't ready to help them escape yet. She had no plan. Sure, she could get them out of the cell right now, but not out of the fortress.

There was a hiss, and green vapors rolled around the corner and filled her nostrils. She welcomed the rapid shift back to her human form, though she dreaded it for Kol and Char. At least in their dragon forms, they were more formidable. As humans, they were completely at the vampire's mercy.

Metal clanked, and Kol groaned painfully, weakly.

That's it! Myreen was damned if she was going to just stand here and do nothing while the man she... had confused feelings for... was tortured! She had to do something to stop it.

She spun out of her hiding place, strode up behind the vampire with way too much hair gel, and tapped him on the shoulder. "Stop," she ordered, her voice deep, melodious and resonating.

The vampire froze in the middle of locking the second lead cuff around Kol's still-free wrist.

Those were the first things that had to go.

"Remove those cuffs and slam them on the floor," she commanded. "You will tell your master that the Dracul boy was stronger than you thought and broke them himself."

As instructed, the vampire unshackled Kol's wrists and smashed the cuffs against the hard floor, breaking them beyond repair.

Kol and Char gawked at her as if they'd seen a ghost, their mouths hanging open.

She ignored them and kept her eyes trained on the vampire, not wanting to break her concentration. There was a strange looking object at his feet, a thick metal oval with bolts at both ends. That must be the belt Draven mentioned.

"Now, the belt," she said, her voice still musical and compelling. "Break it in the most believable way possible and tell Draven it was already broken."

Without hesitation, the vampire picked up the large belt and jammed his razor-like thumb nail into the edge of the control panel on the outer wall, making little sparks fly and sputter.

Satisfied with that, Myreen commanded, "Leave and make yourself scarce until Draven calls for you, and only then will you report to him."

The vampire robotically stood up and marched down the hall and up the stairs.

The dungeon was silent after he left, and Kol and Char continued to stare at Myreen like she'd just turned water into wine.

"Myreen," Kol said slowly. His arms still hung awkwardly at his sides, but she didn't have the means to heal him, not with the little amount of light in this place.

"I'll come back for you," she said. "As soon as I can. Kenzie and I will get you both out."

With a newfound determination, she stalked out of the dungeons to find Kenzie.

***

The Grand Hall was a circus of celebration. Vampires and humans were dancing about, rejoicing in the victory of Draven's new status as a daywalker—the only one in existence, now that Leif's ability had been stripped. Scattered throughout the frolic, Myreen could see vampires locked in intimate embraces with their Initiates for a twisted kind of toast. It made her stomach turn, and she wondered if she'd find Kenzie in the arms of Adam.

She scanned the crowd, searching for the two of them. When she did spot Kenzie's unmistakable bright-red bob, she was relieved to see that she was unaccompanied.

Myreen pushed her way through the melee—which wasn't easy to do with vampires, and she was sure she ended up with quite a few bruises.

"Hey, Kenz," she said.

Kenzie turned around, her expression giddy and her eyes glazed. She looked a little intoxicated.

"Myreen, there you are, I was looking all over for you." Her speech was slurred, and she actually looked like she might fall over.

Myreen slipped her arm around Kenzie's waist supportively. "Let's get you to the kitchens. You look like you need something to eat. And maybe some coffee."

Kenzie gave her a playful navy salute and allowed Myreen to escort her through the mob, and around to where the kitchen stood, which was thankfully empty. Myreen sat Kenzie at a table and raided the fridge for any protein-rich food, then brought them back to Kenzie, who promptly dug in.

"Kenzie, are you drunk?" Myreen asked bluntly.

"Who, me?" Kenzie asked with a mouthful. "No. Why would you think that?"

"Well... you can barely walk, for one."

Kenzie swallowed. "Oh, that. Um..." She blinked hard and rubbed her eyes. "Have you ever been bitten before? Not like attacked, but... eaten, I guess? Vampire venom has a kind of... inebriating effect on humans, you could say. Adam doesn't quite know when to stop yet."

Myreen's stomach lurched, and suddenly the food in front of Kenzie looked disgusting. Kenzie must have had the same thought, because she pushed the plate of food away, her face turning a shade of green. *Poor Kenzie.*

Myreen coaxed the plate back toward Kenzie, urging her to fill her belly, making sure she drank plenty of water between bites. Slowly, the color returned to Kenzie's complexion, and the gloss left her eyes. When the loopy demeanor vanished, Myreen was confident the venom had worn off.

"Are you okay?" Myreen finally asked.

Kenzie stared blankly forward. "I just made the most powerful vampire in the world even more powerful, and I'm officially a snack. What do you think?"

Myreen put her hand on Kenzie's back and began to slowly rub up and down. Neither of them said anything for a moment.

"I've decided to go with you," Myreen said softly.

Kenzie's face blossomed with hope as she turned her face to Myreen.

"Draven visited Kol just now, I guess right after you performed the spell, and I had to listen the whole time as he tortured him."

Kenzie cringed, that hopeful blossom wilting.

"We need to leave before Draven decides he's done with Kol."

"I thought you hated Kol," Kenzie said, a knowing look in her eyes.

"Yeah, about that. Before Draven showed up, I overheard Kol and Char talking about something quite interesting... Something that involves you."

Those knowing eyes played dumb as they looked up at the ceiling evasively.

Myreen didn't buy it.

"He said he asked you to break some curse for him?" she continued. "I need to know about it."

Kenzie sighed. "He made me promise not to tell you."

Myreen grabbed Kenzie by the shoulders, albeit a little too roughly. "Well, right now he's inches away from dying. You need to tell me everything you know."

Kenzie's shoulders slumped under Myreen's grasp. "Alright. So a long time ago, some pissed off selkies—my ancestors, if you can believe that—cast a curse on Kol's family. Basically, whenever a Dracul falls in love, the object of their affection will hate them in return. It's why he tried so hard to be Mr. Robot. But then you came along." The corner of Kenzie's mouth twitched, a sad sort-of smile. "He remembered that I was a selkie and tricked me into meeting him to ask me if I could break the curse. For you. So I did. Maybe."

Now everything was starting to make sense. All his hot-and-cold behavior, it was all because he was afraid he'd get too close and trigger the curse.

"Wait, Kol said it didn't work." Myreen shook her head. "He was telling that dragon girl that he triggered the curse."

Kenzie shook her head. "I don't know. I know we did the spell right, but when you said you hated Kol..." Kenzie shrugged. "But now... Well, why don't *you* tell me? Do you hate Kol? Like, cursed to despise him forever, kind of hate?"

Myreen straightened her back and analyzed her feelings. Kol had used her. He lied to get close to her because his daddy told him to. Curse or no curse, anyone would be furious at someone for doing that to them. But did she hate him?

No. She still felt drawn to him, bound to him in some way. And the thought of any harm coming to him made her angry and sad and *crazy*! No, what she felt toward Kol wasn't hatred; it was just the aches of a broken heart, one that yearned to be mended.

"I think that answers our question," Kenzie said quietly. "He loves you, and you... well, I'll let you figure that out."

Which Myreen was still no closer to doing. Kol claimed to love her. They'd had quite a few wonderful moments together, but she couldn't be certain which of those were real and which were an act. And sure, Kol had risked his life, attacking the headquarters of the most dangerous vampire on the planet just to rescue her, but he still spent the first half of their relationship pretending to like her just so he could report back to the general. Did any of this really make up for that? There was still the possibility that his father had sent him here to retrieve his secret weapon, and that it had nothing to do with his feelings for her.

She just didn't know how to feel. But she knew she didn't want to see him die in that cell. That was the last thing she could ever want.

"Either way, we need to start formulating an escape plan," Myreen declared.

Kenzie nodded. "Yes. We do. Any ideas?"

Myreen pursed her lips, pondering. "Well, one. It's gonna be tricky, but it's the best chance we've got."

Kenzie

Kenzie wandered the cold halls of the vampire quarters, pulling her sweater closer around her shoulders. She had a spell to warm herself up, but she didn't deserve it. She deserved to be absolutely miserable. Like everyone else she loved.

She'd sent a message to Gram, letting her know that she'd be attempting to come home soon. Gram's response would've been heartwarming—but Kenzie hadn't told her everything. Not by a long shot.

She'd tried using her magic to contact Leif, to tell him the good news, but he wouldn't listen. Thanks to her new school schedule, Kenzie only had time between and after classes. That meant Ms. Morton kept interrupting her attempts to magically talk to Leif. She could always tell when the woman arrived, because the despair coming through the connection amped up. Leif wasn't gone, but he was losing his will to fight. Kenzie could feel it.

She just needed him to hang on a little longer. Which was why she was skipping classes now, trying to get through to him that she wasn't the enemy.

Kenzie shivered as she remembered the bellowing coming from the dungeon yesterday. On an instinctual level, she knew it was Kol and the other dragon. They were suffering—Kenzie was glad Myreen finally saw that. And thanks to Kenzie's placement in the human dorms, she got to suffer right along with them, although at the hands of her own guilt, rather than the devices of Draven.

Draven told Kenzie that all Initiates started on the bottom floor, and he couldn't change the rules on her account. She had a feeling he just wanted her to remember how easily it would be for him to do to her what he did to anyone who crossed him.

And while his implied threat had the intended effect, she was about to cross him, anyway. Even if the shifters hated her for giving Draven daywalker abilities. Even if Wes hated her for turning to Adam for comfort, for letting him feed off her, for liking it on some twisted level. And Mom and Gram? Well, her homecoming looked bleak.

Kenzie cursed herself. She should've gotten Myreen out on day one. At least Myreen had finally come around. If she hadn't? Well, Kenzie couldn't let everyone else suffer. Not any longer. Not as horribly as everyone was being treated. At least now the suffering was almost over.

She should've gone looking for Leif yesterday, after she talked to Myreen. But she hadn't. She hated herself for even entertaining Adam's company, but he'd been so excited from the ceremony. How could she refuse? She couldn't, not without making him suspicious. And he made her forget how miserable she was, if only for a little while. She could get lost in a feeling stronger than her guilt. So she'd indulged.

But today she was skipping classes to make up for it.

She'd sent a message to her instructors telling them she didn't feel well, which was technically true. And she'd climbed all the way to the top of the citadel—the elevator was useless without an Elite keycard, and she wasn't about to test her magic on it—and into the towers that housed the special few. She'd start with the tower that led to the purple and silver room she'd first seen Leif in. Hopefully he was there.

Hopefully he'd found some way to escape.

Kenzie mounted the stairs with a groan. Her body was adjusting, but she didn't think she'd ever really get used to it. Not that she wanted to. If she never saw a stair again once she got out of this place, she'd be okay with that.

The door came into view, and Kenzie approached quietly, her ears perked. Ms. Morton was one of the instructors, so chances were good she'd be working, but vampires could move fast. Kenzie laughed. It was kind of weird she'd come to think of Beatrice as Ms. Morton. First names were strictly forbidden in the classroom. At least she'd realized that Ms. Morton was no angel, despite appearances. She played a very real part in Leif's torture, although on some level, Ms. Morton suffered while watching Leif suffer.

But it wasn't like she was letting him go, either.

Kenzie gave a tentative knock. There was a moan, and Kenzie softly pushed the door open. Leif was stretched out on the purple couch, looking as awful as last time—maybe even worse. His burns still hadn't healed properly, the rest of his skin ghostly white, almost translucent. Deep, dark circles ringed his eyes, making him look almost dead.

Kenzie's breath caught in her throat. This image would haunt her forever.

Leif cracked an eye and tilted his head her way. "Gemma?" His eyes widened as if seeing a ghost, then narrowed. "Kenzie."

Kenzie nodded and came into the room, shutting the door behind her. "I've been trying to contact you."

"Why bother?" His head lolled back, and he closed his eyes again.

"Because I'm still trying to get you out of here."

"So I can burn? I'm not a daywalker anymore, remember?"

The bitterness in Leif's tone made Kenzie's eyes sting, and she hardened her chin as she swiped at the building moisture. "No. It's supposed to be temporary. I tried to make it temporary."

"And how long is *temporary*?"

"I don't know." Kenzie sighed, walking further into the room.

"You tried to trick me."

"What?" Kenzie stopped moving toward him, her teeth taking up a miserable chatter. Sure, her body would choose this moment to betray her. "Cheás," she said, and the chattering stopped, her body warming. If only she had some spell to ease Leif's pain.

Maybe she shouldn't have warmed herself, but she didn't want Leif's sympathy. She wanted his forgiveness.

"The red hair." He pointed to his head, then dropped his hands back onto his lap. "You tried to make me think you were *her*."

"No." Kenzie shook her head, the movement becoming more and more emphatic. "You can't believe that. I didn't even *know* she had red hair. When did you ever tell me that? How would I have known?"

Leif hated her. Kenzie could tell by the tone of his voice, the look in his glassy eyes. She didn't blame him. She hated herself, right now, too. "I'm going to fix this. I'm going to fix all of this."

Leif waved her away. "Feed your lies to someone who cares."

Kenzie felt like she'd been punched in the gut. He was right. She'd been waiting for the right time, waiting for an easy way out, waiting to make the perfect escape. She should've never settled. She should've never let things go this far.

"I love you, Leif Villers," she whispered, unsure if he could even pick up what she'd said. Hopefully not. Maybe.

At a normal volume, she added, "We're getting you out of here, I promise."

Before he could respond, she was gone. The tears flowed freely, blurring her world, making every step a hazard. She ran down the stairs and away from Leif and his mutilated body. Away from his anger. Away from his complete loss of faith in her.

Need fueled each step as she ran to end the suffering, to right all her wrongs. She should've studied last night, memorized the spells she'd need to escape, rather than making out with Adam. Why was she still being so careless?

She raced, running until she reached her room. Slamming the door closed, she pulled out her backpack and practically spit out the reveal spell between gasps for air. She slammed the book onto her bed and spoke her family name—a name she no longer felt she deserved. How could she, after everything she'd done?

She opened the grimoire, the pages twinkling their welcome. Closing her eyes, she concentrated on the magic, on what she needed to do. She opened her eyes again and flipped to the daywalking spell, wondering if she could figure out how to end Leif's temporary reversal—if it really was temporary.

But as Kenzie scanned the page, she noticed another spell that trailed onto the next leaf. It was the same writing, and Kenzie was surprised she hadn't noticed it before. In fact, she was pretty sure it *hadn't* been there before.

She rubbed her eyes, then peered at the script again. It was...

another spell for vampires? Kenzie's brows lifted as she tried to decipher the notes. But... it was incomplete. Kenzie would have to remedy that.

"Thank you, Gemma," Kenzie said, lifting the book to kiss it, but then deciding that might not be the best idea, seeing how it was magicked. Kenzie wondered what kind of spell Gemma had used to keep her work concealed until now, and what Kenzie had done to unlock it.

There was a knock at her door, and Kenzie started. She went to close the grimoire, but Adam was already inside, sitting on the bed next to her. Dang vampire speed.

"I heard you weren't feeling well and came to see if there was anything I could do."

Kenzie swallowed. "I'll be fine. Thanks."

Her body responded to his nearness, her skin tingling, her tongue licking her lips as his kisses filled her memory. She knew on some level that Adam cared for her, and part of her cared for him in return. But he'd never captured her heart.

Not like Wes. Not like Leif.

Kenzie closed her eyes and sighed. She could feel Adam's smirk. He thought he could own her, body and soul. She wouldn't correct that. Not yet. Maybe not ever, if she could help it.

"What are you working on?" Adam asked, bending to look closer at the grimoire.

Kenzie grabbed the edge of the book and tried again to close it, but Adam stayed her hand.

"Is this what I think it is?"

Kenzie shrugged. "Depends on what you think it is."

"Kenzie, do you realize what you have here? Our weakness to copper is only second to the sun. And you can fix that, too!"

Kenzie shook her head. "The spell is incomplete."

"Not incomplete," Adam said, squinting at the book. "Unfinished. Look." He pointed to the page, then flipped back a few pages. "See here? There's a pattern. If you see this spell"—he flipped forward—"or this one. Or even this. The one you're working on just needs a closing statement."

Kenzie leaned back, looking at Adam for what felt like the first time. "Can you *read* any of this?"

Adam shook his head, laughing. "Most of it, no. But my mind can take in information pretty rapidly and sift through for discrepancies. It's part of the reason we were able to crack the code for making a hybrid."

"Seriously?" Kenzie couldn't help but be impressed, even though the thought of Draven having shifter powers scared the living crap out of her.

Adam beamed, his chest puffing out. "Yeah. It's kind of my super power."

Kenzie frowned. "But didn't you *just* become a vampire?"

"Oh, I've had this ability my whole life. The Beaulieu family prides themselves in breeding smart."

"Beaulieu..." Kenzie tapped her chin. "Where have I heard that name before?"

"Probably vampire history class." Adam ran his fingers down Kenzie's arms, giving her goosebumps.

"Wait a minute. Beaulieu, as in one of the sire lines, Beaulieu?" Kenzie's heart sped a pace. The sire lines were powerful. And if Adam was from a sire line, and now a vampire...

"That's right, babe."

"How does that even work? You weren't turned by your father, were you?"

Adam laughed. "No. The old man lost that right when he sent me to school to earn my fangs, rather than giving me my birthright when I turned eighteen. I had Draven do it, though that was a feat in itself. The master doesn't turn just anyone. So I'm sort of from two sire lines." He brought his mouth to her ear and whispered, "You're one lucky girl."

"Oh." Kenzie shuddered as Adam nibbled at her neck—thankfully, with fangs retracted. She wanted to try to keep her mind clear, which was nearly impossible when he fed on her.

"In fact," Adam went on, pride shining through his voice, "this brilliant mind of mine helped Draven find his long-lost daughter. If it weren't for me, none of this would be happening right now."

Kenzie gaped at him, this time in horror. It was *him*. He'd set these vipers on Myreen's mom. He'd made it possible for Draven to fulfill his dream of becoming a hybrid. Maybe they'd have been able to get it all done without Adam, but chances were it would've taken longer. Suddenly, she had someone to blame, someone besides herself.

All affection for Adam burned away. He was the enemy. He'd ruined her life, and the lives of countless others, with that brilliant mind of his. A brilliant mind bent on aiding the destructive forces in her life—in the world.

If Adam noticed the change, he didn't show it. Maybe he thought she was still marveling, because he bent forward and kissed her. And for a moment, Kenzie let him. She put every emotion swirling through her into that kiss, determined it would be their last. This was goodbye. Forever.

When she felt she'd said all she needed to say, Kenzie pulled back.

Adam's eyes were glossy, a smile on his lips. "There's that magic I so love."

Kenzie caressed Adam's face, then gave a roll of her wrist as she quickly recited the binding spell she'd learned from Gram what felt like an eternity ago. "Fiáscha na olch. Tóggo boggé na folía. Diúltódha darshada."

Adam's eyes widened in surprise, and he staggered back until he hit the wall, as if pulled by a magnet. "What did you do?"

"Leich ín dhaermandah." Kenzie stared into Adam's eyes as they went glassy and distant. "Sorry *babe*, but I'm going to need you to forget this conversation ever happened. I was sick, you comforted me, and then you went on your merry way. Oh, and it might be good if you stay away for a bit. You wouldn't want to *catch* anything." Kenzie put her fist over her mouth and fake-coughed. Time to close the spell and seal his memory loss. "Dhaermandah."

The light came back to Adam's eyes, and he groaned, trying—and failing—to pull himself away from the wall.

"Oh, crap. Ligam'amach." The spell of release lifted Adam's binding, and he fell to his knees.

Adam shook his head as he stood. "See you later." He left the room without looking back, almost robotic in his movements.

Kenzie heaved a sigh and threw herself back on her bed. After a few breaths, she sat up and focused on the grimoire. If she was serious about helping Myreen break everyone out, then she'd need to know everything. Immediately.

And she was dead serious.

Kol

"She saved us," Char said through chattering teeth.

Kol leaned heavily against her. His arms had dropped to the lead-laced floor hours ago, but the skin didn't burn too badly. The floor wasn't as well-coated as the bars, apparently. The pain in his shoulder where *Hair Gel* took the liberty of plucking two more souvenirs—royal blue scales—mixed with his broken arms, ached too much to embrace Char, even if it was for their survival.

She held him, instead.

"Your girl saved us," Char repeated.

"Is that supposed to be a question?" He felt a wheeze in his lungs.

"Just an observation." Her tone was thoughtful.

They'd agreed that it would look bad if a vampire came in and saw them outside the cage, or with the door wide open, so while they waited for Myreen to come to their rescue again, they'd climbed back inside and shut the door. Kol just hoped they weren't making their rescue more difficult.

Kol shifted awkwardly. A nerve in his right thigh felt pinched and the leg had gone partially numb. "You want to argue that I haven't triggered the curse," he said.

"You know me well, private." Her voice cracked.

"Myreen saving us from further torture doesn't prove anything," he said. "She's a kind person. Even if she *hates my guts*, she would never want to see someone suffer if she could help it."

Kol felt Char's shoulders shrug.

He was never good with emotions, expressing them or noticing them in others. But the fact that Char kept insisting the curse wasn't broken could only mean one thing.

"I love her, Char," he said. It was a fact. "For whatever reason you don't think it's happened..." Or maybe she *wished* it didn't happen, but he didn't voice the thought. He sighed instead. "Look, I don't know if we'll get out of here or not, and I don't know what will happen if we do. If Myreen will escape or..." He couldn't finish the thought. "I don't know what my future holds, but I do know that I love Myreen Fairchild and that I have activated the Dracul curse. Just like my mother did years ago. Just like my ancestors have through generations for over a century." There was a chance he'd end up with Charlotte, but he was more likely to end up alone. He wouldn't put someone he cared about through the agony his mother went through every single day of her life. What he was doomed to live with for the rest of his.

But surprisingly? He didn't regret it.

"I'm sorry, Kol," Char's voice was softer than a whisper when she finally spoke several minutes later.

He pretended not to see the glistening tear on her cheek, but at least he reached up to hold her again.

***

Tentative footsteps sounded on the cold floor not long after. A small part of Kol thought he might've drifted off for a second, because the sound jolted him to awareness, but he was in too much pain and discomfort to really get any sleep.

Char shifted next to him and he realized his arms weren't around her anymore. He must've dozed off for at least a minute or two, because he couldn't remember consciously letting go of her.

"Kol!" A voice hissed through the poisoned bars.

"Myreen?" His head cocked to the side. He couldn't be certain if it was actually *her,* or a part of his imagination. A dream.

Dark hair flicked over her shoulder as she looked behind, maybe to see if she was being followed. When she turned back to face them in the dim light, concern lining her face, he knew she was a dream. Not because of the concern—as he'd told Char how kind-hearted she was—but because she looked at him in a way he'd never seen Eduard look at Victoria. So she couldn't be real.

But the look vanished, and he realized she really was there, perfect and beautiful, standing in the shadows.

She was there.

Her eyes fell on his shoulder and she let out a small gasp. Kol didn't bother to look. The smart clothing had been torn when his scales were removed, so she could probably see how macabre the wounds were. Kol had an identical wound in his side from the one Draven took.

Char's hip looked the same. Fortunately, Hair Gel only ripped one from her.

"Come to see dear old dad's handiwork?" he asked, but regretted it the instant it flew from his mouth and he ducked his head.

"I can't believe he did this to you... to her." She pointed at Char, who snuck a glance at Kol.

He kept his eyes lowered.

"Kenzie and I are working on a plan," she whispered, which brought Kol's eyes back to hers. "To get you both out. But I couldn't just stay away and let you suffer."

The memory of the greenhouse and Myreen healing his injured leg with harpy magic intruded his thoughts. It felt like so much time had passed, so much had happened since, yet he felt like it happened only five minutes ago.

"No," Kol said. "You can't risk it."

"I'm Draven's daughter," Myreen said, exuding confidence he wasn't entirely sure she actually had. "I can do what I want. For instance, I stole this from the Initiate's medical wing." She pulled out a white box with a red cross on it. *A first aid kit.* Then she asked, "Can you come closer?" Something flashed across her face, as if she just realized Char was clinging to Kol and he wasn't objecting. But he was certain he imagined it.

Char dropped her arms and Kol scooted toward the toxic bars with great effort. If Myreen did notice their closeness, he hoped she also saw the shiver that attacked both he and Char the instant they broke contact.

Myreen studied him. Like she wanted to ask a question, but wasn't sure how to arrange the words. But the look passed, and she asked, "Any way you could conjure up a fireball for me?"

"I thought you were using good, old-fashioned human first aid?" Kol pointed at the box.

"That's to cover *after*," she said. "I don't know what would happen if they knew I healed you."

"I thought you said you could do whatever you want?" he teased. He didn't realize he had it in him. Her mere presence gave him strength. And stupid humor.

"Draven is the most powerful vampire in the world," she said. "I don't want to take any chances. And thanks to Kenzie, he can daywalk."

"What?" Char practically shouted.

Myreen waved an apologetic hand. "No time to explain. The quicker I do this, the better." She opened the box. "Hopefully he won't be too angry if he sees that I've just cleaned and dressed your wounds. But please... *fire?*"

Kol sighed. "I thought you knew? They took away our abilities." He gestured to himself and Char. "Do you think we'd still be in here if we had our fire power? Do you think we would be freezing to death down here if we could warm ourselves?" The latter he hoped would explain his and Char's earlier embrace. For survival.

Without responding, Myreen rifled through the first aid kit and pulled out a tiny flashlight that was probably put there to look into mouths for sore throats. She flicked it on, emitting a tiny light not much brighter than the dull glow of the sconces around the dungeon.

"This will have to do," she said and captured the light with her fingertips.

Kol scooted back to Char causing confusion to flit across Myreen's face. He prodded his lifelong friend as gingerly as possible back toward Myreen.

"Her first," he said, then thought, *In case there's only enough for one.*

Something passed across Myreen's face briefly, but she didn't seem to want to argue and sent the light through the bars, directing it at Char's wounded side.

Her aim was a little bit off, but as the light swarmed and

swirled, part of the wound closed, leaving pink and healthy skin. The other part still looked red and oozing, but Char let out a gasp of relief.

"Any chance you can come closer?" Myreen asked before inspecting the flashlight to ensure it still worked.

Kol and Char eyed the bars. Kol felt like a magnet with the same polarity as the iron, pushing away at any and all cost to resist touching.

"Never mind. I'll reach through." Myreen threaded both of her arms through the bars until she leaned in to them at her armpits, giving a brief wince. She turned on the flashlight and manipulated it into another tiny light dancing on her palm.

Char scooted closer. Myreen's aim was better because she could nearly touch them. Within seconds, Char's flesh was healed completely.

Myreen reached back for the box and pulled out a roll of gauze and medical tape.

Char took it from her hands slowly. "Thank you," she whispered. "I can do it. Heal him." She seemed to convey something to Myreen with her eyes, but Kol didn't speak *girl* and couldn't translate.

Myreen's eyes lifted to Kol's and his heart jumpstarted. "Your turn," she said.

Kol didn't allow as much distance between himself and the bars as Char did. Because with those delicate healing hands reaching through, the hands attached to the girl he loved, he had to be closer. He *needed* to be closer.

She flicked on the light. Kol leaned his shoulder closer and held his breath as Myreen weaved a brilliant and beautiful light show between her fingers. Like delicate lace, it tethered together in intricate patterns and spun until it landed on Kol's skin. He could only watch from the corner of his eye as the light waltzed to and fro along his jagged and raw flesh, knitting it back together. When the sharp pain finally ceased to exist, he felt the warm pressure of Myreen's hand on his now-healed skin.

She jerked her hand back as if remembering something.

Probably the fact that she now hated him.

Damn curse.

Myreen made quick work healing his side wound, his broken arms, and then expelled as much of the lead from the dragon's bodies as her dwindling harpy magic could—which wasn't much at that point, but at least the awful feeling lessened.

Also, he felt the stirrings of his fire returning. When he tried to access it, it was as fleeting as waking up from a pleasant dream and trying to remember the details. It wasn't quite usable. Not yet.

When the gauze was taped and the remainder packed away into her box, Myreen stood to leave.

"Thank you," Kol whispered, standing as she did because he finally could. He finally had the strength.

She looked at him sternly. "You have to act like you're still weak and injured," she said.

"Right." Chagrined, Kol melted back to the floor. He actually noticed the slow burn on his palms when they made contact with the ground. It wouldn't take long for more lead to seep into his and Char's systems.

"But hey," Myreen said, reaching through the bars again to place a hand on his knee. Like before. "I'm getting you out of here." Her gaze was aglow, staring at him. Clearly the harpy light wasn't completely gone from her eyes. A sly smile played on her lips and he resisted the sudden urge to reach through the bars and kiss them, *damned curse or not.* But he didn't want to create more injuries after everything she'd fixed. "It'll just be easier to break out healthy dragons than sickly ones." She looked at Char, including her silently with her gaze. "And I'll need both of you healthy for the plan to work."

She turned to leave.

"Thanks, Myreen." Kol blurted, stopping her. He wished she'd stay longer.

She turned, her mouth agape as if she wanted to say or ask something. But she closed her mouth again as if thinking better of it.

Then, another sort of look Kol couldn't read crossed her expression and pinched her eyebrows together. "I've heard rumors of a curse," she said. "A *Dracul* curse?"

Kol kept his expression neutral as his insides played pinball. "I think we should talk."

Heavy footsteps sounded on the stairs at the end of the hall.

And she left.

CHAPTER 31

Juliet

The excruciating migraine Juliet woke up with just wouldn't go away. Nik told her she was pushing herself too hard. But between training with her dad, keeping up with her classes, and everything Dracul, there just wasn't enough time in the day.

And it was catching up with her.

Not to mention that without Myreen there, her spark was gone—although she used that to fuel her fire. She didn't know how, but she promised herself that she would get Myreen, Kol, *and* Oberon back. And maybe that was why her temples pounded—the expectations were just too much.

Juliet massaged her temples with as much pressure as possible until her head felt almost numb. But it gave her no relief. She shoved her hand into her bag and took out the two headache pills that she'd stuffed there this morning. After swallowing them, she leaned her head against the wall, her foot tapping as she waited for the medicine to take effect.

She cringed when a guard raised his voice to her, a spike of pain accompanying his voice.

"What did you just take?"

Juliet gave him an incredulous look, her eyebrows raised, her fists clenched at her sides. *Does he* have *to assume the worst?* "I have a headache. I'm done for the day and I'm going to my room." All the warnings her father and boyfriend repeated rang in her mind, so she gritted her teeth and tried to respond as respectfully as she could.

"I'll escort you to the infirmary to make sure that was all you took." His voice was thankfully lower, but it still rumbled with authority.

"Um, no thanks? I swear, I'm clean. Check my record." All she wanted to do was close her eyes so the light couldn't hurt her head.

She thought luck was on her side when the guard gave her a nod and stepped out of the way. But when he opened his tablet, he wrote something down. From what Nik and her dad had told her, that wasn't good.

She shuffled on, looking over her shoulder every other minute until she got to her room. When she was sure no one had followed her, she changed course and tiptoed to the supply closet.

She couldn't help but look around at the deserted common room as she crept through. It was usually boisterous, packed with students hanging out. Now, it was dark and empty. No one dared get caught lounging around. Punishment for such a "crime" was more defense training. And not going straight from class to class? Expect impromptu push-ups, sit ups or wall sits. Juliet sadly turned her back to the silence of the avian common room and entered the closet.

Inside their small, secret sanctuary, Nik, Brett and Jesse sat on the floor with a laptop open, Leya and Alessandra a little further in. Their backs straightened and their eyes widened, but when they saw it was only Juliet, their shoulders relaxed. With guards on constant patrol, there was always the possibility of getting caught.

Juliet joined the guys.

"Hey. Are you okay?" Nik said. She didn't like his tone, but he wrapped his arm around her and she scooted into his chest. "You don't look so good."

"Gee, thanks. No, I'm not okay. I have a killer migraine and a guard just wrote in his tablet about me 'cause he thought I was taking drugs." Juliet sighed, massaging her temples again.

"Well, did you?" Brett teased, but Juliet was in no mood to play along. Even rolling her eyes brought pain to her head.

"Have you *met* my father?" she asked. "Imagine all the wonderful things he would do to me if I was ever stupid enough to take drugs. Out in the open. In front of an armed soldier." She didn't mean to sound sour, but he chose the wrong time to joke around. "I just took some over-the-counter stuff for my head."

Brett lifted his hands in surrender, then turned back to the game on his laptop.

"How did training with your dad go?" Nik asked, thankfully changing the subject.

"It was fine. Making progress, I guess. He wants us to train for another hour a day, but it's not part of the approved time that the *director* agreed to. He thinks the general will know we're up to something if we request more time. But we'll need someone to keep watch." She didn't say that to get an offer, but she was glad when he did.

"I can do that for you. Just let me know what time." Nik kissed her forehead and rubbed her arm.

"Thanks. First one will be after dinner tomorrow." She

leaned her head back to rest on his shoulder.

Brett scoffed. "Dude, we have plans." His ears turned red as he shut his laptop.

"Sorry, I forgot. We'll just reschedule." Nik shrugged and playfully punched Brett's arm.

Brett shook his head and stuffed his computer into his bag, his eyebrows scrunched. "It *is* a big deal. Kol's gone. Don't you get that? Everything just sucks now. I'm over it. I'll see you around."

Without another word, Brett quietly stormed out of the small supply closet. If the circumstances weren't so grim, it would've made Juliet giggle. But with her pounding headache, she didn't have the energy.

Jesse, Leya, and Alessandra packed up their stuff and waved a subtle goodbye to Nik and Juliet as they followed Brett out.

Finally alone, Nik placed his hands on the back of Juliet's neck with his thumbs against her hairline. As he massaged the area, Juliet couldn't help but groan from the relief it gave her.

"Sorry about that, Jules."

"What's his *deal?*"

"He's just... worried. And lonely. With Kol as Draven's prisoner and Lord Dracul taking over, he hasn't been taking things well," Nik said.

"None of us are taking things well," Juliet agreed. "Did you see that new broadcast? The one about Draven being a daywalker and Kenzie being the one to help him?"

Nik's mouth hardened into a straight line. "How could I miss it? Kenzie really screwed us all over with that one."

"If it's real." Juliet had a hard time believing Kenzie would just hand Draven daywalker abilities. And she looked so different with her hair cut short and dyed red. Not to mention the circles under her eyes. Maybe Draven had tortured it out of her?

Juliet sighed. "But I get it. Maybe now that I'm training with my dad again, you can spend some more time with Brett."

Nik stopped massaging, and she immediately regretted saying anything. "I think I will. Thanks!" He gathered his things, then took her hand in his. "So, I'll meet you at the avian training room tomorrow after dinner, right?" Nik walked them to the door, still holding her hand.

"Yes. Right. I'll see you tomorrow," Juliet said, her voice dropping to a whisper.

Nik kissed her forehead, then opened the door for her to sneak out first. "Hope you feel better."

He gave her a light push when she didn't immediately move. Once out the door, she rushed to her bedroom, wanting nothing more than her bed and darkness.

Hopefully she'd wake up *without* the migraine.

***

It would be too obvious if Nik walked her to the avian training room, so their plan was for Juliet to go five minutes ahead of him.

It was a good plan... until Juliet reached the Grand Hall. Her stomach sank. Students lined against one part of the wall, sitting as if on invisible chairs, some of them in tears from the pain in their legs.

A student on the opposite wall was hunched over a trash bin, vomiting his brains out. A group of students were precisely lined, their hands raised in a salute to the soldier standing in front of them. Another soldier yelled in a girl's face because her hair was down instead of in a bun.

Usually the Grand Hall was a place of motion and emotion. Groups of friends would gather to talk, exchanging ideas, teasing and joking, and sometimes even flirting. *That* was normal. Now, everyone was synchronized and dull. Their footsteps marched, happy conversations replaced by silence or canned responses to orders. Everyone looked scared. One wrong step could get anyone into serious trouble, and all the rules were nearly impossible to follow. Juliet's heart broke to see what had become of the school she'd come to love.

"What are you doing?" came Nik's clipped voice as he walked up behind her. "You were supposed to get there before I did."

"I just... Look at what that monster has done to our school." Juliet regretted saying it as soon as it left her mouth. Both she and Nik looked around to see if anyone had heard her.

"Juliet!" Nik hissed. "Just... go meet your dad. I'll find a way to delay myself. *Go.*"

Nik was right. Juliet lowered her head and fell into step with the other students anxiously passing through. She had to fight the sting behind her eyes because she knew she'd get in trouble for it. For *crying.*

Juliet slipped out of the crowd, discreetly heading toward the avian training room.

The second she walked through the door, she burst into tears. Malachai came out of the darkness and wrapped his large arms around her shoulders.

"Are you all right? What happened? Did someone touch you?"

He would *go straight to the worst.* "No. It's just so... unfair," she said through her heaves. "What the general has done to the Dome, to the students..."

"The Grand Hall?"

Juliet nodded. Of course he knew what had upset her. "But not just there. Everywhere." She sniffled, and her dad handed her one of the handkerchiefs he always kept on hand.

"I know, hon, I know. I feel sick knowing I contributed to this. If I had known... But I did it for us. And because the general didn't give me a choice."

"I know." But his words—the general hadn't given him a *choice*... Juliet had to ask. "You don't think...?"

"Think what, Juliet? Spit it out."

Juliet looked at her hands. "You don't think General Dracul is using his abilities, you know, to *influence* your decisions, do you?"

Malachai studied her for a moment, his eyebrows drawn, and then realization lightened his face. "You mean those dragon hormones? No, I don't think so. I'm too bullheaded for that, really. But I signed up for all this a long time ago. I'm contractually obliged, nothing more. Why do you ask?"

Nik walked through the door just then. Juliet cleaned herself up and stood, trying to shake off everything that had happened in the last five minutes.

"Is everything okay?" Nik asked, giving Juliet a once-over.

"Yes," Malachai answered, pulling himself to his full height, his voice exuding authority. "We'll try not to be long—one hour, tops. If you hear someone coming, take this key and lock the door. If worse comes to worse, you were just patrolling the halls and saw this room was unlocked."

Nik took the key, gave Malachai a nod, and exited.

Malachai took a shaky breath, then turned back to Juliet. "Right. Okay, why don't we take the emotions you're feeling right now and put them toward today's lesson. I want to see what you can do using both your powers."

"You mean use them at the same time?"

"Exactly. We know you can kick ass with your fire, and we have a pretty good idea what you can do with your ice. But what we don't know is how they work when they're one. Remember that globe of life you did? Let's try that again, but this time mixing your fire in ice and vice versa. You think that's doable?" He leaned against the wall and crossed his arms.

"Yeah. I can try." It didn't come out as confident as she wanted to sound, but she doubted she'd be able to get the hang of it right away.

Juliet sat with her legs crossed and rested her hands, palms open, on her knees. She took a deep breath and closed her eyes, but it took her longer than usual to center and silence her mind. Still, she stayed at it.

When she finally felt at ease, she probed for her fire, shivering from the warm comfort she found there. She made it flow from her chest to her fingertips. When she heard the familiar sizzle, she opened her eyes.

"Good. Now, release one of your hands, keeping the fire in one hand while you try to summon your ice in the other. It sounds harder than it is—not that I've ever been able to try, but from the research I've done, it shouldn't be too difficult."

"Oh yeah? What did you find?" Juliet asked, curiosity getting the better of her.

"Some old books and stuff—not important, though. You need to focus."

Juliet nodded. He was right. They didn't have time to waste. Maybe he'd tell her more about it later.

Closing one of her hands, she drew its fire back into her body. She shut her eyes again and searched for the cold that now roamed inside. Just like the fire, the moment she found it, a satisfying comfort filled her—only this one made her feel valiant and powerful, unlike the fire, which made her feel safe and protected. She hooked onto the coldness and guided it through her shoulder and to her waiting fingertips.

She opened her eyes, not wanting to miss this next part. With another deep breath, Juliet willed the cold out. Frost escaped her fingertips. She let it fill her palm, cupping it in her hand while she stared at her father with wide eyes.

Malachai gave a nod, a gleam in his eyes, though he was still all business. "Incredible. Morph them both into spheres and we'll decide which one to use."

It was surreal. She couldn't believe how easy it was for her to work with both her powers at the same time. Her fire and ice were like magnets, pulling at each other even as she sought to keep them apart. She was curious to see what would happen when they collided. *One step at a time.*

Juliet wiggled her fingers and played with the fire and the frost until they both took round shapes. One of fire. One of ice. The frost ball gained weight as it slowly got colder. The frost cleared, the thick, heavy ball of ice in her hand looking like glass. Her fireball sat in her other hand, looking just like it did the last time she'd done this.

Remembering the next step, she handed the ball of fire to her father so she could begin to hollow out the balls. She knew the fire would come easily, since she'd done it before, but she didn't know how the ice would react. She studied the cold ball in her hand. With a tap of her finger on the top, a perfect hole appeared. She closed her eyes and focused, and when she turned it upside down, snow flowed out of the hole until all she held was a thin, hollow, sphere of ice. Afraid her dad would ruin it with his fire, she carefully placed it on the floor next to her feet.

She reached for the ball of fire and expertly made another hole, summoning the embers inside to fall out of it as ash.

Setting the fire ball on her other side, she took a handful of ash and thought of the picture she wanted to make. Juliet was still heartbroken over the scene in the Grand Hall, so she decided to bring back the breaking heart—this time it would be intentional. With the image of a heart splitting in half, Juliet picked up the ball of ice and filled it with the ash. After she closed the hole on the top, she set it back down.

Next, Juliet took a handful from the pile of snow and gave it the same image she'd just given the ash. She filled the hollow ball of fire with snow and closed the hole on the top.

She handed the ball of fire to her dad and took hold of the ice one. They were about to shake when the door clicked locked.

Nik was trying to warn them.

Malachai took Juliet's hand and ran to the door to listen to what was happening on the other side.

"I– I– I was just patrolling this hall," Nik said, stuttering, his voice muffled. "The door was unlocked, so I fixed it."

"Under whose orders?"

"Um…"

"This is a penalty for you, private." The guard cut him off before he could answer. "Just because you're the general's assistant, doesn't give you a pass. Report to him immediately."

Their footsteps faded down the hall.

Juliet wiped away a tear. "What are they going to do to him? This is all my fault."

"Nothing he can't handle, hon. He'll be okay." Malachai sounded guilty as he guided Juliet away from the door. "Let's take a look at these, but then we should get going."

Juliet nodded, unable to form words. She wanted to go after Nik, but it didn't make sense for her to get caught, too. It wasn't like she could do anything about it, anyway.

In her misery, she took the ball of ice and shook it. Behind the shiny surface, a broken heart bloomed from the ash and grew into flames. When it broke in half, snow fell from the cracks.

"Whoa," she whispered, momentarily forgetting everything else.

Malachai shook his head, apparently speechless.

He shook the shiny orange globe in his hands next, and out of the snow, a heart made of ice materialized and split in half leaking thick, red lava.

"Whoa is right. This has to stay between us." Malachai looked dazed as he studied one ball, then the other. "Aside from... Well, at least this was a successful lesson. Good job. Let's meet in the morning to discuss a safer way to do this. You always make me proud, Juliet."

Juliet hung her head to hide the warmth in her cheeks. It had been so long since he'd said those words to her.

"I'll take these for safe-keeping," Malachai said as he gently pried the ice sphere from Juliet's hands. "Before we go, is there anything else you'd like to tell me? Something about being manipulated?"

"It's just that..." Juliet hesitated, unsure if she could tell her father everything. Their relationship was by no means repaired, and she still wasn't sure she trusted him not to go all *Dracul Lackey* on her again, but maybe he could help. "It's just that the general at least *has* the ability to influence others, if he wanted to. You don't think anyone is acting... out of character, do you?"

The blank stare on Malachai's face was answer enough.

"Never mind. It's stupid."

"No. Not stupid. Just, don't mention this to anyone else, okay? I'll keep my eyes peeled."

"Thanks."

Juliet's memory of the fire and ice globes was the only thing that helped distract her enough to get her back to her room in one piece—well, that and her father's proud words.

She told her heavy heart that she would find Nik tomorrow. She just hoped he'd be okay until then.

CHAPTER 32

Kenzie

Kenzie sat in her Vampire History class, her leg jiggling, her eyes glued to the ebook in front of her, yet seeing nothing. The teacher, Wilhelm Klotz, was going on again about how they'd defeated shifters, how they'd won against shifters, how the shifters were beneath them. Kenzie wanted to gag. Or leave. But she held her spot, trying to keep up appearances. Chances were, this would be her last day here, anyway.

At least the vampire teaching the class still retained much of his German accent. His voice always sounded so soothing. It kind of made her want to sleep—which would be severely unwise, considering he was of the Klotz sire line. It seemed Draven kept the retired sires content by employing them. Smart.

All the sires except the Beaulieus, apparently. They chose to keep a lower profile. But Kenzie wanted to put that line right out of her mind.

Instead, she glanced at the watch on her wrist. Five more

minutes. She could last, right?

"And that's how La Framboise Island was defeated," Mr. Klotz said, while several Initiates studiously took notes. Kenzie chewed on her lip, glancing again at her watch.

"Ms. MacLugh, do you have somewhere to be?" the teacher asked, and Kenzie's head shot up, her eyes wide.

"No, sir." She looked down at her bouncing leg and stilled it, then smiled at Mr. Klotz. "I'm sorry. I seem to have a bit of excess energy today."

"Perhaps you would like to take some time to burn it off in the Combat Training Room?"

Kenzie snorted, but at the look Mr. Klotz was giving her, she wiped the smirk off her face. "Thank you, sir. I'll consider it."

Mr. Klotz's eyebrows raised, his lips tight, his eyes narrowed.

Kenzie looked around the room; all eyes pointed at her. She gave them a nervous smile, then, as best she could, she buried her crimson face in the ebook.

The bell rang, and Kenzie let out a sigh of relief. She threw the tablet in her bookbag and shouldered it, joining the crowd as they headed for the door.

"Ms. MacLugh. A moment, if you will," Mr. Klotz said.

Kenzie stilled, pivoting on the balls of her feet to give Mr. Klotz her full attention. "Yes, sir."

"Ms. Morton is requesting you see her before you retire for the afternoon."

"Oh. Okay, thanks." Kenzie turned to leave.

"One more thing, Ms. MacLugh."

"Yes?" Kenzie pasted on a smile, but only turned her head to acknowledge him.

"Let her know I'd be particularly interested in her current creation." The way he smiled at Kenzie, like a snake who'd found its meal—made her skin crawl. To be honest, a lot of the vampires looked at her like that. But she smiled back and gave him a curt nod before leaving his class—for what she hoped was the last time.

She took the stairs two at a time to the Combat Training Room, where she knew Ms. Morton would be, as that was her area of expertise. One of the few instructors who were not of the sire lines, Ms. Morton was more than skilled at combat. She'd sparred with other vampires during training sessions, and the results were always mind-numbing. No one could beat the woman, not the burliest man or the slyest woman. Old or newly turned, she could trounce them all. Kenzie had a feeling only the sires could best Ms. Morton, and even then, it would probably be a close contest.

Kenzie walked into the Combat Training Room, looking around warily. Only a few dedicated students remained, and some of them regarded her with disdain. Kenzie was pretty sure she was failing this class, but her magic made her valuable enough for it not to matter much. Not to mention she was assigned to a vampire. That's what all these people wanted—the chance to show themselves worthy of joining the ranks of the bloodsuckers.

On some level, Kenzie got it. This was the only supernatural existence that earned a person immortality. But she couldn't get past the fact that it turned them into monsters.

Well, most of them.

Kenzie's gaze found Ms. Morton, and she took a step her way, but the combat instructor was by her side in an instant.

"Kenzie. Let's talk in my office." Ms. Morton put a hand to Kenzie's back and guided her out of the training room.

Kenzie nodded, more than happy to leave, but her heartrate

kicked up a notch at the thought of facing Ms. Morton alone. Kenzie had the sudden, awful idea that Ms. Morton had found out she'd gone to visit Leif yesterday. Would Kenzie be punished for that? Thrown in the dungeons? Tortured and beaten?

"There's no need to be so nervous. You're not in trouble." Ms. Morton guided her into a room down the hall and shut the door behind them—which did nothing to put Kenzie at ease.

Ms. Morton sat behind a mahogany desk, motioning that Kenzie should sit in one of the leather-clad seats opposite her. Kenzie gulped as she perched on the edge of one of the seats, letting her bookbag fall to the floor but keeping the straps in her hands. "What did you need?"

Ms. Morton laughed. "Seriously, it's going to be fine. I'm sorry to keep you in suspense, but bloodmixes are highly sought after in this place."

Kenzie nodded as she stifled a gag. She waved her hand at her face, trying to get herself under control, throwing Ms. Morton an apologetic smile. "Sorry. I'm hemophobic," she said, once she felt able to do so.

Ms. Morton smiled, her head cocked to the side. "And yet you chose to associate with vampires." Loose white curls spilled around her face, her features positively radiant. Kenzie wondered how much of her beauty came from being a vampire, and how much she'd been born with.

Kenzie shrugged. "What can I say? I like to live on the edge."

"I can see," Ms. Morton said, eyeing Kenzie's perch.

Kenzie chuckled and scooted back, though she still didn't bother to lean fully on the chair.

"Anyway, I was hoping to get a sample from you. It wouldn't be much, since I know most of your resources are required by Adam, but a little would go a long way toward making this batch special. Leif and I have a lot to celebrate."

Kenzie's ears perked at this, and she slid forward again. Right now, she'd do just about anything for Leif. The thought that she might be able to help him, even just a small amount, made her willing, almost eager, to donate to the mix. She nodded, though she had a feeling Ms. Morton already knew— and that she'd have gotten what she was after whether Kenzie agreed to it or not.

"How do we...?" Kenzie spun her finger in the air, then lifted her hands into a shrug.

"I'll be extracting it the human way." Kenzie paled, and Ms. Morton rushed to add, "If you'd like, I might be able to influence you to make this situation a little more comfortable."

"You want to bite me first?" Kenzie asked.

Ms. Morton laughed. "No. I was planning on hypnotizing you. I'm surprised that hasn't already been done, considering you're a *contributing* Initiate."

Kenzie adjusted in her seat. "Oh. I hadn't even considered that." And she wasn't sure she wanted to. A vampire messing with her mind? "That's all you would do, right? Make sure I don't gag or something?"

Ms. Morton chuckled. "A cautious one. But yes, that's all I would do."

"If you'll allow me to verify?" Kenzie waited for Ms. Morton to nod, then lifted her palm toward the woman and said, "Fírrineth." Green light shot from her palm into Ms. Morton's chest, rippling outward from where it hit.

Ms. Morton looked down, rubbing where the magic had disappeared. "Interesting. What exactly did you do?"

"It's a truth spell. You won't be able to lie for the next half hour or so."

"Good to know. As I'm sure you'll want to hear again, then, I'll only alleviate your hemophobia while I have you under my influence. Unfortunately, the effects are only temporary. I don't have Draven's powers."

Kenzie nodded. Maybe it was stupid to trust the vampire, but she figured it couldn't hurt. And Ms. Morton *was* telling the truth.

"That's a neat little spell. What would happen if I changed my intent?"

Kenzie shrugged. "I don't know how it works, but I trust it." Mostly. Though now she couldn't get the thought out of her head that Ms. Morton was going to mess with her.

"Go ahead and sit back."

Kenzie took a deep breath and settled in. "Okay. Fire away."

Ms. Morton began speaking, but the words flew past Kenzie's understanding, creating a comforting lull. A prick in her arm made her start, but as she looked down at the vial filling with blood, there was no uncomfortable sensation. It looked like liquid rubies, or a strawberry glaze. Kenzie smiled, then looked up into the face of the angelic woman hovering over her. She reached out her hand to touch one of the delicate white curls, but the woman vanished. Kenzie stared at the void a moment longer before her world snapped back into focus.

"There, that's done." Ms. Morton was sealing the spot with liquid bandage, and Kenzie hissed at the accompanying burning sensation. "You're welcome to pick up some juice and snacks from the kitchen if you're feeling hungry. We wouldn't want our star selkie passing out." She winked at Kenzie, who ducked her head. "You know, Adam speaks very highly of you."

"Does he?" Kenzie was surprised. Adam always seemed so selfish in his intentions. To think he thought of anyone other than himself was shocking, not to mention that he'd spoken of her to others. Although, maybe that was to brag?

"You have to know. I mean, he wanted you as his Initiate."

Kenzie felt her face heat, and all the urgency to leave came rushing back. She didn't want to think of Adam as anything other than the snake she knew him to be. The physical attraction was too hard to ignore if she didn't. "If that's all," she said as she stood, heaving her bag onto her shoulder.

"Yes. I'll see you tomorrow, Kenzie."

Kenzie nodded, but left before her body had a chance to betray her. She didn't want to hear anything else about blood or Initiates or Adam. She wanted out—needed it, really—and she had a date with the one woman who could help make that a reality.

***

Kenzie sat in Myreen's room, checking out the lush, red-and-black decor. The room looked like something from a magazine, a canopy bed and a large flat screen television the most notable pieces.

Kenzie pointed to the television. "You ever watch that thing?"

Myreen let out an amused huff. "I guess, if you can really call turning it on and ignoring the thing 'watching television'." She pushed a piece of hair behind her ear. "Let's focus. If we can get Kol and Char to the roof and healed, they can carry Leif and Ty and you back."

"What about you?" Kenzie asked, pulling out the apple she'd grabbed from the kitchen and taking a bite. Her appetite had definitely ramped up since being assigned to Adam, though to be honest, she hadn't noticed until Myreen said she was leaving.

"I'm a harpy, too, remember?"

"Oh, duh. Wait, didn't I hear you're a bear, too?"

"Ursa, and yes."

"How's that going for you?" Kenzie was thinking of Wes again, wondering how he was holding up. Had he gotten used to being a mao? Where had he gone? Had he found someone else to fall for? Kenzie dismissed the thought. Yeah, Myreen was right. She needed to focus.

Myreen ran her fingers along her neckline. "Actually, that's been one of the good things that's come out of all this. Draven gave me a turquoise necklace, and it's really helped. I don't feel so out of control anymore."

Kenzie's brows shot up. Turquoise. She'd have to remember that.

"So the question is, how do we get everyone on the roof? And when?" Myreen asked, flipping through her tablet for anything useful. There was nothing, of course. Kenzie had already looked. The vampire school info was focused more on their dominance over the shifters than anything else.

"Well, Leif and Ty are relatively easy, since they're practically *on* the roof already," Kenzie said.

"Maybe I should leave you with collecting them, then. I've got an idea for Kol and Char."

"Does Ty know he's coming?" Kenzie asked, leaning back in the plush red chair.

Myreen sighed. "Not yet. I was going to wait until the last minute and just use my siren voice on him if he resisted."

"You don't want to give him a choice?"

"Kenzie, I can't leave him here."

"But you said he really likes you, right? It should be easy." Kenzie took another bite of her apple.

"It's not that simple. He's been told shifters killed his mom, though I'm not entirely certain that's true. But he's been groomed by Draven for a long time. And Draven is really good to Ty—at least, from what I've seen."

"Doesn't mean Ty wouldn't want out."

Myreen eyed the apple. Kenzie pulled another one out of her bag and offered it to Myreen, who shook her head.

"Ty might be okay with leaving, but I don't want him telling Draven of our plans if he's not."

"Okay, so we wait until the last minute. But maybe give the kid a choice?"

"He's ten, Kenzie." Myreen's head rolled back, and she ran her hands over her face.

"And a smart kid, if everything you say is right."

"I don't want to leave him here."

"And maybe you won't have to." Kenzie spotted a trash bin by the dresser and tossed the apple core in like it was a basketball.

Myreen gave a noncommittal grunt. "What are we going to do about Leif? Is he going to be in any condition to travel?"

"I don't know. I'm going to suggest he feeds off me. His vampire abilities should start working again once I get him free of those shackles."

Myreen's brows furrowed.

"What?"

"It's just... how much blood have you given Adam?"

Kenzie shrugged. "Dunno. And Ms. Morton took some more from me today, though not much. But it'll be okay. It'll have to be."

Myreen's brows shot up. "Not cool. I don't want you bleeding yourself dry for anyone."

Kenzie shook her head. "Leif wouldn't do that."

"Have you *seen* him lately? Kenzie, he's not himself."

"I know," Kenzie snapped. "I'm trying to fix that."

Myreen sighed. "Give me your hand."

Kenzie held out her hand. Myreen took it, her smooth skin reminding Kenzie that she didn't have to try to be so tough in front of her best friend. Even after all Myreen had been through, her touch was still so delicate, so comforting.

A warm tingle started in the hand that Myreen still held, traveling up her arm and through her whole being. Strands of light pulled from the lit candle on the dresser and wrapped around Kenzie's body in a brilliant dance. Kenzie's mouth fell open, and when Myreen opened her eyes again, there was a smile on her lips.

Kenzie felt stronger, less drained, and when she brought her fingers to her neck, the scabs where Adam had bitten her were gone, leaving smooth skin. She couldn't remember the last time she'd felt so... awake? Alive? It felt as if Adam *hadn't* been trying to suck her dry for a week. Kenzie gave Myreen a mystified smirk.

"Pretty cool, huh?"

"The best! Do it again?" Kenzie leaned forward, and Myreen laughed, the sound still so sweet and endearing.

"I think that's enough for now. I'll need my strength for recovering Kol and Char." Myreen closed her eyes and ran her hands over her face again. Come to think of it, she did look awfully tired.

"Okay. So maybe I should go scout out the path for Leif and Ty. The best time to leave in order to avoid Ms. Morton will be during school. You might want to find out when Draven will be occupied."

Myreen's shoulders slumped, the light dying from her eyes. "You're probably right."

"Unless you want *me* to do that. I'm sure you're probably tired of dealing with dear old daddy."

Myreen shook her head. "No. It should be me. I can ask questions you can't because I'm his daughter and I have what he wants."

"And what's that?"

"My blood."

Kenzie wrinkled her nose, but didn't feel like gagging. She kind of like not being so grossed out by the stuff, and wondered how long the effects would last. Too bad it wasn't permanent.

Myreen wrinkled her nose, too. "Yeah, I know. It's the last piece in his plan to become a hybrid."

"Good thing you haven't given him that yet."

"Yeah. Weird, right? He said he wanted my permission and seemed pretty determined he'd earn it. But so far..." Myreen shrugged.

Kenzie breathed a sigh of relief. "At least you've been able to keep him from getting *some*thing he wants. I practically served him daywalking on a silver platter."

"Kenzie—"

Kenzie shook her head. "No. I've been stupid. That's on me."

"You know, one of my teachers told me that living in the past is useless. We can feel guilty over it, but it won't change anything. And it will probably keep you from doing what you're meant to do to make things better. Or something like that."

Kenzie nodded. "Sounds like good advice. I'm not sure I'm there yet, though."

Myreen nodded. "I understand. Just try not to beat yourself up too much. I'd hate for you to do something stupid right as we're about to get out of this place."

Kenzie laughed. "Sounds like something I'd do. Okay. I'll try."

***

Kenzie stalked the halls of the upper towers, pulling her sweater tighter across her chest. On one level, she knew vampires didn't need the heat, but it still seemed weird that any place occupied by a living being would be kept so cold. Although, vampires weren't technically alive.

Still, she'd already performed her heat spell once, so she wasn't too bad off, though the chill was trying to seep back in.

So she was surprised when she rounded a bend and ran into another student—another flesh-and-blood creature—roaming the Elite halls.

Kenzie flashed a panicked smile at the girl, who looked vaguely familiar. Large spectacles made her wide eyes look even wider, and her thin frame was trembling in the freezing cold of the tower.

"Are you okay?" Kenzie asked without thinking. She should be leaving, but something kept her rooted to the spot. Maybe it was that memory trying to push to the surface.

"F– f– fine," the girl chattered. "Hey, ar– aren't you that s– selkie girl?"

Kenzie stood for a moment with her mouth open, but decided it wasn't worth hiding. Everyone at this place knew who she was, thanks to Draven. Probably in the shifter world, too.

"Cheás," Kenzie said, pointing her palm at the girl.

"Oh!" The girl lifted her coat off her shoulders, looking at herself in amazement. The chattering had stopped, and she looked a little flushed.

"Sorry. Too warm?"

The girl laughed. "Never. I can't stand the cold. Thanks, by the way."

"Yeah, sure. I should probably be..." Kenzie hitched a thumb over her shoulder, then turned to leave.

"Wait!"

Kenzie stopped and pivoted back.

"I'm sorry, but you knew Leif before... well, before. Am I right?"

Kenzie gave a quick nod, then looked at her feet. She didn't want to deny it, but she didn't know this girl or what she wanted. Her first thought was that Ms. Morton had sent her to spy on Kenzie, for whatever reason. But then, why would anyone suspect she was up here in the first place?

"I just... I'm Piper. I was Leif's Initiate until... well, you know." She held out her hand, and Kenzie took it and they pumped in an awkward shake.

So this was the girl Kenzie had gotten so jealous over. She took another appraising look at Piper, and felt a small sense of satisfaction that she wasn't some busty babe. "You look a bit thin to be donating."

Piper laughed. "I've got just as much blood as any other girl, but Leif never drank from me." There was a note of regret in her voice, but Kenzie detected something else, something she couldn't quite identify.

"So you're looking forward to becoming a vampire someday?"

Piper cast a nervous glance around the hall, but they were alone. "Not exactly. But don't tell anyone I said that."

"Our secret." Kenzie smiled, but then she had an idea, one that made her itch with nerves, but she had to ask. And they were alone. She could always erase the girl's memory if something went wrong. "Do you want to...? I mean, would you ever consider leaving without becoming a... you know?"

Piper bit her lip, but nodded. "But I don't have a chance. It's kind of like the mafia here—once in, you can never leave."

"Oh. What if I told you we were executing a brilliant escape plan and you could come with?"

"Really?" Piper's eyes widened, then narrowed at Kenzie.

"Why would you do that? You have everything an Initiate could dream of."

Kenzie leaned forward and whispered conspiratorially. "I never wanted to be an Initiate in the first place. I came for Leif... and some others. You're welcome to come, if you can keep from spilling the beans and come to the roof when I say."

Piper nodded enthusiastically. "Oh, yes. Please! Do you need me to run any calculations? Or help you plot escape routes or anything?"

Kenzie smiled. "I think we've got it covered. Give me your info and I'll message you when we know more. It'll all be coded, though, to sound like school stuff."

Piper laughed. "Piece of cake. Half the school would probably be able to decipher anything you could come up with. We're all brilliant."

"Brilliant idiots," Kenzie said under her breath. But she smiled at Piper. "Sounds good."

They exchanged info, and Kenzie sent Myreen a message, which earned her an unamused emoji in return. But she'd get Myreen on board. The girl was too much of a bleeding heart to leave someone like Piper behind.

"What are you doing up here, anyway?" Kenzie asked.

"I heard... Have you seen Leif lately?"

Kenzie nodded. "Yeah, but I wouldn't recommend a visit. He's in bad shape, and the stuff they're injecting him with is messing with his mind."

Piper nodded. "Copper. All the vampires are weak to the stuff."

"Really? They'd inject one of their own with copper?"

"Apparently."

Kenzie frowned. She didn't know why she was so surprised,

but it just seemed so cruel—too cruel even for Draven. But then she remembered the last spell she'd found, and an idea blossomed. "Okay. But I really should be going now."

"Yeah. Me too, if I'm not going to visit Leif. Do you want to—?" Piper pointed down the hall toward the way out.

Kenzie nodded. "Sure."

They nearly made it to the elevator when Kenzie remembered where she'd seen Piper before. "You were the one who sealed my wounds that first day I got here, weren't you?"

Piper nodded. "I'm kind of surprised you remember that."

"Thanks, by the way."

"No thanks needed. When you're around a bunch of vampires long enough, you come up with some precautions."

Kenzie smiled to herself. She kind of liked this girl. And yeah, getting out another body might be a pain in the butt, but at least this one was healthy—and smart. They'd make it work. Besides Piper was so skinny, she and Ty combined probably still wouldn't be the same weight as a regular adult.

Kenzie felt like their team was complete. Now she just needed to prep Leif for their great escape.

Leif

Sitting on Leif's lap, Rainbow purred his perfect middle C sound. Leif's mind played with the sound, as if following the notes on sheet music. His fingers tapped along his knees, and he could almost hear himself playing Mozart's *Sonata in C.* It was soothing, playing the happy melody, even through the minor transitions. They always returned to the happy major themes, anyway.

He was brought out of his momentary trance as he felt a tugging at his shackles. Rainbow was biting at the mechanism that dumped copper shavings directly into his wrists, hissing in the process. Leif wondered if the cat detected the copper and was attempting to help rid Leif of the poison.

Smiling lazily, he held his shaking arms up so the cat had easier access to the cuffs.

"If you can rid me of these bonds, I'll make sure you are the happiest kitty in the world," Leif mumbled. He hoped the encouragement would motivate Rainbow, although he wasn't entirely sure the cat truly understood. But the fantastic feline had successfully torn away a heavy piece of metal covering from the window—the shackles binding Leif's arms couldn't be that much stronger.

But the cat's attempt was in vain. Either the metal was resistant to his teeth and claws, or Rainbow was losing his touch.

Rainbow's ears poked up, and he gazed at the doorway.

Leif was more coherent at the moment, which meant he was likely due for another injection of copper soon. "What is it?"

Rainbow looked at him with red eyes, then leapt down from his lap and bolted out the door. Leif knew a visitor was approaching, and sure enough, a few moments later, in walked Beatrice.

She wasn't wearing her typical black hoodie and pants, but a sleeveless forest green dress that hugged her waist, then trailed down to her ankles. Beatrice stood taller than he was used to, wearing a pair of golden high heels. Her hair was styled, her makeup done in such a way that brightened her features. Leif couldn't deny just how beautiful she looked.

Beatrice twirled, her green dress twisting from the movement. "What do you think?" she asked.

He found himself unable to look away. She looked angelic, as if she was no longer a vampire at all.

"You look..." the word slipped away from him. This wasn't right. Beatrice in any form wasn't right. Finally, he settled on saying, "Different."

Her warm features clouded. "That's not was I was hoping to hear." She continued to move closer, and Leif kept his eyes on hers to avoid her swaying hips.

Get a grip, he told himself.

"It appears I haven't taken you down memory lane enough," Beatrice said, and she held an arm toward him. At this point, he noticed she was holding a glass of dark red blood, its contents sloshing back and forth as she approached.

A moment of clarity allowed him to determine how Beatrice had manipulated him. Whatever was in the drinks she brought to him induced his visions of the past—visions Beatrice had meddled with. At least, he was pretty sure they weren't real. They were always about Gemma. But the Gemma of those visions were unlike the Gemma he knew from memory. And he'd been through so many of them that things were beginning to blur. But the visions *always* came after he'd consumed Beatrice's bloodmixes.

"I'm not thirsty," he said, eyeing the cup with distrust. It was difficult to say. Blood was one of the few things that still brought him comfort. And he *was* getting thirsty.

"I'm afraid that doesn't matter," replied Beatrice. "I have you on a schedule, and today marks another feeding rotation. So drink up."

He held out his shackled arms. "Let's make a deal, then. Take these things off me and I'll drink."

She ran her free hand through her hair and laughed. The sound of it reminded him of how she used to laugh back at the boarding house. Carefree and happy, rather than the dark and sinister version that accompanied her vampire-ness.

Beatrice walked to him and sat on the couch, her shoulders brushing against his. She gently placed the glass on the end table next to her. "How about a counter-offer? I remove your bonds and you hold me in your embrace for the next few hours."

Eliminate one kind of torture for another, he thought with a smirk. Still, it was a tempting offer. He was so tired of the coppery mist his mind was always in. If he could be free of that for a couple of hours...

Her thin fingers slipped into his weak hands, and she squeezed softly. "I try so hard, Leif Villers. I tried to move on after what happened at the boarding house. I rose to greatness among the vampires, and Draven saw it. Through him, I've achieved what every vampire dreams of. But you know what? I'd trade it all if it meant I could receive your love. I've loved you since I met you, walking up the dirt road carrying a knapsack with your meager belongings. Time has moved on, but my love for you hasn't. And it never will."

Her sincerity touched him. She wore her true feelings like her dress, and it did mean a lot to Leif. But his clarity was still there, and he knew that Beatrice was responsible for the conflicting thoughts about Gemma now pervading his mind. She was trying to turn him against his fiancé.

"I don't know what I did to gain your interest," he said softly. "Back then, there might have been something. And while that might feel like a blazing bonfire in your soul, that little spark in my heart went out long ago."

"Let me reignite it, then," she pleaded. "Let me in so I can *show* you my love. What I feel for you... it can't be explained with words."

Burning at his wrists indicated that more copper was being pushed into his body, and he grimaced. To say he was used to the pain at this point would be a lie, but he at least knew what to expect.

His head lolled and his body loosened on the couch. Leif could still feel Beatrice's hands in his, but he held them limply.

"It hurts," Beatrice said. Leif barely heard her through the burning, but he nodded his affirmation. She continued. "No, it pains me to see you hurting like this. I want to take those torture bands off. I want you to make a commitment to me."

Leif nearly agreed to her terms, just to get some relief. But through the foggy haze his mind was swimming in, he knew he couldn't just say what she wanted to hear. If there was one quality he truly valued about himself, it was his loyalty. He'd been loyal to the Frosts, and had managed their orchard for ten years because of it. He'd been loyal to Camilla, loving her like she was a sister. He'd even been loyal to Draven before the destruction of the previous shifter school in South Dakota. More recently, Leif had been loyal to Oberon and the shifter cause.

But always, he'd been loyal to Gemma. Through life and death. And despite his conflicting thoughts about her, she was still his guiding light.

Beatrice would *never* replace her.

"No," he mumbled. "If you care for me"—Leif raised his quaking arms, the metal rattling at the effort—"even a little bit... Remove these and let me go." He lifted his chin and looked into her brown eyes. "Please."

Sorrow spread across Beatrice's face. "Why? The woman you loved has been gone for so long, while the woman who loves you is standing right in front of you. Why can't you see that? You act as if the torture you feel is only caused by your bonds, but you can't even tell that the real torture you're experiencing is caused by your mind. You desire that which you can't have, and it tears you up inside." She tapped her chest. "*I* can fix that. Just let me."

Leif wagged his head back and forth. "There's... nothing to fix. Please let me go."

Beatrice stared at him for a long moment, her eyes blazing with... anger? Hatred? No, those weren't the right emotions. Jealousy.

"I can't let you go, Leif," she said. "I've tried to be reasonable with you, and it hasn't worked. That leaves me only one other option. I must continue breaking you into submission. I'd prefer your affection to come willingly, but it's clear to me that such a wish is impossible. But I *will* have it, even if it kills me."

Leif looked away from her, but made no reply. It wasn't worth the effort to tell her the same things he'd told her before.

Beatrice grabbed him by the chin and forced him to look at her. She looked down at his mouth, and he was sure she was going to kiss him. Instead, she squeezed a little harder, forcing his mouth open, then with her other hand, she grabbed the cup of bloodmix and began pouring it into his mouth.

Leif didn't fight back, but swallowed the small flow of the drink as it tickled his taste buds. It was sweet and soothing, and while it didn't cast away the fog in his mind, the blood at least made it more bearable. He closed his eyes and fell into the intoxicating effects of the drink.

"At first, you didn't want to drink this," Beatrice said as he gulped away. "But see? You've tried it, and you just keep drinking. The same will happen if you try me."

He barely heard her words, too caught up in the blast of flavor bombarding his mouth.

"How do I explain my desire to break off our engagement?"

It was Gemma. Leif's eyes focused on her, just over Beatrice's shoulder.

They were no longer in Beatrice's quarters, but back in the boarding house. Upstairs, in Gemma's room. It was just as he'd remembered it: meticulously well-kept and clean. The familiar scent of fresh herbs spiced the room.

Next came Camilla's voice. "The better question is, why did you agree to marriage in the first place?" Their cruel laughs followed.

"What was I supposed to say?" Gemma said. "Leif is tough, but had I rejected him outright, that would have broken him entirely. And I could not do that to him."

"Your plan is to lead him on, then?" Camilla asked. "That seems more cruel than a rejection."

"At least this way I can let him down slowly," Gemma replied.

"I have learned how to maintain the orchards," Camilla said. "Perhaps I can persuade my father to evict Leif from the premises. The boarding house could use somebody more worthwhile."

Camilla looked tangibly real. Her voice and mannerisms were spot on. The scene playing before Leif seemed authentic.

Except it wasn't.

Bringing his eyes back to Beatrice's, he said, "Stop this."

She lifted an eyebrow. "Stop what?"

"These games you keep playing with me," he replied. "These false memories."

"How do you know they're false?" Beatrice asked. "Camilla and Gemma were close. Surely they had conversations about you in private."

Leif gritted his teeth. "Not *these* conversations."

"You weren't there for them," Beatrice countered. "You don't know what they discussed."

"Neither do you," Leif said. "So stop twisting the personalities of the people I love the most. Making a mockery of them will not break me, but will only increase my resolve to resist you."

"We have eternity to work through these charades," Beatrice said. "Eventually, you will break."

He was already physically broken, but his mind was a protected fort of determination. Willing control over the substance that clouded his brain, he cast the images of Gemma, Camilla, and the boarding house away, leaving him once again in Beatrice's room. For a brief moment, he recalled how he used to have frequent flashbacks where he experienced his memories—

the good and the bad. Draven had seen to their end back when Leif first joined the vampires. There were days he wished he could get lost in those memories again.

Staring Beatrice in her eyes, Leif said, "My eternal love is for Gemma MacLugh, and for her only. Whatever you do to me will only make me resent you further. So keep it up, and let's see whose resoluteness wins."

Beatrice got to her feet, throwing the empty cup to the ground. The force with which she cast the glass caused it to shatter into hundreds of pieces, sounding like hail pattering against a window.

"I am your only door to freedom," she said. "And you should know by now that I don't give up until I get what I want. You will submit."

She turned to walk away, but stopped short, turning her head and peering at him from the side. "One of the greatest experiences of my life was drinking the blood of the one I loved. *Your* blood."

Leif recalled the hypnotic moment as if it were yesterday. She'd bit him, lulling him into a stupor. He'd felt his blood drain and the pleasure her sweet venom brought on before turning him into a vampire.

"Did Gemma ever let you taste her blood?" she asked.

Leif shook his head. "I would *never* have asked her."

Beatrice snorted. "So honorable. Now you can say that you've tried her relative." She pointed at the broken glass. "Half of that bloodmix came from Kenzie. And you seemed to really enjoy it." Beatrice shrugged. "Maybe it had a *hint* of Gemma, seeing as they're both MacLughs. And she gave it so willingly."

Leif looked down at the broken glass, panic striking his heart. Kenzie had given up her blood for a bloodmix?

Knowingly? The panic streaming through his body turned to shame and guilt. He'd never intended on drinking her blood. Never. Surely Beatrice had purposely done it.

Anger and resentment blotted out the rest of his feelings, like two black storm clouds slamming into each other and encompassing the sky. But as he brought his attention back to where Beatrice had been standing, he found himself alone.

"Beatrice!" Leif yelled. At least, he thought it was a yell. In his weakened state, it came out as a half-hearted grumble.

His shoulders dropped, and so did his gaze. In the candlelight, Leif saw a single red drop dangling from a jagged shard of glass. He stared at it for some time, waiting to see if it would drip to the polished floor. It held onto the glass resolutely, defying the gravity trying to bring it down. He tried to place an analogy to it, but Kenzie's betrayals blocked his attempt.

Kenzie. Leif had placed so much hope in the selkie girl, but she'd ended up doing the unthinkable to him.

Movement at the doorway caught his view, and he looked up to find her standing there, looking so much like Gemma. She had the red hair—albeit far too short—and the facial features, but her eyes were wrong. They weren't the emerald green of his betrothed. They were hazel—tinged with a little more brown. And they were filled with pity.

Taking a quick look behind her, she entered quietly. "Can I come in?"

He shrugged weakly. "It looks like you already have."

As Kenzie drew nearer, she sucked in a breath. "You're still not healed?"

He looked down, observing the wounds still peppering his arms. They'd come a long way, but he wasn't entirely healed yet, thanks to the copper injected in his body.

"Yeah, thanks for that," he mumbled. "You've really made things better for me, Kenzie. A fine rescue operation."

"I know you hate me right about now, but you have to listen. Please?" She appeared to be considering turning around and walking out the door, depending on his reaction.

Sighing, he nodded his head.

Kenzie looked over her shoulder once more, then muttered, "Aonrúgh." Leif recognized it. Gemma had used the spell several times as she'd attempted to make him a daywalker. It placed a soundproof bubble around the spell weaver and whoever she was talking to—in this case, himself.

She looked back at him, the pity still solemnly hanging there. "I'm really sorry. For everything. I know I messed up."

Leif looked away. The look in her eyes revealed that she was speaking the truth, but it was hard for him to swallow. "Yeah, well, an apology doesn't make the pain stop."

Looking back at her, he saw Kenzie nod as she brushed her fingers along fresh bite marks in her neck. "I know."

Leif's eyes widened. "Kenzie? Are you...?" He couldn't bring himself to finish the question. She wouldn't have gone so far, would she?

"A vampire?" she said with a laugh. "No, my magic is far too valuable to Draven for him to allow that. But I'm an Initiate to a brand-new vampire who's as thirsty as the Sahara." She rubbed at her arm. "Beatrice took some of my blood, too. For you."

Leif looked down at the broken glass. "I'm sorry she did that to you. I know blood puts you on edge."

She swatted a hand through the air. "It wasn't so bad. Beatrice made it tolerable. Did you drink it?"

Leif nodded, unable to hide the guilt. "I didn't know it was yours until after, though."

"I wanted you to have it," she said. "Okay, so it's kind of weird. But I wanted you to... I was hoping it would help...." She waved a hand in his direction, encompassing all of him.

He didn't know how to properly respond to that, so he went with, "Thanks." It seemed like such a small repayment for the terrible things she'd done.

"Look, I don't have much time, but I talked to Myreen," she said. "We're planning an escape."

He laughed weakly. "You've had your fill, too, huh?"

"I didn't come for laughs and giggles," Kenzie snapped. "But being here has still been an eye-opener."

"To what?" he asked.

She stepped closer, avoiding the broken shards of glass on the floor. "Just how bad things can be. Just how bad *vampires* can be. I feel like I've been falling down the black hole of evil with them. It's a miracle you're so... you."

Leif chuckled. "I'm glad I've finally proven that point. What's your grand plan for escaping Heritage Prep?"

Kenzie sat next to him on the couch and tucked her legs under herself. "It'll probably happen within the next twenty-four hours or so. We've got to verify a few things first. But it'll be a lot harder to do anything if you're dead weight... Get it?" She laughed, but quickly sobered. "Never mind. Sorry." She swung her bag around and placed it on her lap. She muttered something under her breath—Leif couldn't quite make it out—and suddenly, Gemma's grimoire appeared.

"Nice trick," he said.

"I've come a long way since getting this thing." She flashed a warm smile, wearing a confidence that surprised him. She used to be so timid when it came to her abilities.

"Is that so? I hope you have something that can remove

these shackles from my wrists."

"I'll do you one better." Kenzie eagerly flipped the old pages of the grimoire and ultimately came to a stop on one of them. She held the book up to show him. "See this spell? Recognize the handwriting?"

Like a magnet, Leif reached his bound hands to the book, brushing his fingertips along the strange words he couldn't understand. Long ago, Gemma had touched this same page with her hands, and for a brief moment, Leif felt as if he'd touched his fiancé.

"Gemma," he whispered.

Kenzie held the old book steady for a few more seconds, then pulled it away and placed it on her lap. "I thought you'd like that. Okay. From what I've been able to decipher, she was working on a spell designed specifically for you."

Leif furrowed his brow. "What spell?"

"It's an immunity spell," she said. "Immunity to copper."

His mouth widened, threatening to drop to the floor like the empty glass had. "Gemma was working on the spell?"

"Yep. She wasn't able to finish it, but I think I've been able to fill in the gaps. Thanks in part to Adam."

Leif raised an eyebrow. "You *think*?"

"Well, I haven't exactly been able to test it out," she said. "It won't work on anybody but you."

"That sounds extremely specific," replied Leif.

"This spell is different," Kenzie explained. "There's one component I'm not sure how to integrate." She paused a beat and met Leif's eyes. "Love."

Love. He was too scared to ask whose love the spell must be infused with—Kenzie's or Gemma's?

"I think Gemma really loved you, Leif," she said, looking back at the book. "And I know how much you loved her." There was a wistful note to her words, maybe even hopeful?

Leif bit his lip. Kenzie made it seem like that love was gone now, that it'd only existed while Gemma had been alive.

"I still love her," he said. "And always will." He wished he could feel the weight of Gemma's brooch in his pocket.

"Right. Of course," Kenzie said, keeping her eyes on the spell and clearing her throat. "Should we give this a shot?"

Leif breathed in deeply, then exhaled. "Let's do it."

"Okay, here we go," she said with a nod, clearing her throat once more and placing a finger on Gemma's handwriting. "Chumachtah co'parm, asfaíl-day..." Kenzie trailed off and narrowed her eyes at the grimoire.

A small light was radiating from her body as she spoke, and Leif found himself squinting.

"Well, that could've ended badly." She scratched her forehead, then said, "Scrioságha." Immediately, the gentle light around her disappeared.

"What is it?" he asked.

Kenzie looked at him and gave a nervous laugh, her cheeks reddening. "I messed up the spell—the light's not very good in here."

"I'd offer to open the window, but I really don't want my skin to burn to a crisp again."

"Right," she said, her cheeks flushing further. She took a deep breath, then said, "Let me try again. Ready?"

Leif nodded. "As ready as I'll ever be."

This time, he closed his eyes and pictured Gemma as the one reading from the grimoire, trying to feel her love. To his joy, it worked. It was her voice, and he could feel her love pounding in his heart.

Her voice was rich as she spoke in a chant. "Chumachtah

co'parm, ascaíl'do nímah. Consúilé le'bainech mácharth, a thibhairn ach'saole." Gemma—or Kenzie—paused, and he heard a sob of emotion, which caused him to open his eyes. He found Kenzie looking at him, tears pooling. The glow about her increased, but didn't cause him to squint this time. His heart swelled—Leif could see the love in her eyes, could feel it mingling with that of Gemma's within him. With a sniff, Kenzie continued. "Cheanghail le'moghránsh, le'mochroísh, Leif."

The glow around her pulled away, slipping through the air, then enveloped him and he could *feel* Gemma. Like she was embracing him, causing his skin to tingle all over. He closed his eyes again, getting lost in the moment. The fogginess of his head cleared entirely. The painful burns that hadn't yet healed all the way subsided, and as he looked back up, Kenzie was staring at him with wonder.

She rubbed her nose, her cheeks wet with tears. "Leif?"

Strength returned to his limbs, and he sat up straight, his eyes widening. Looking at his arms, his skin had returned to normal. There was no blemish or wound marking his time in the sun.

"It worked," he mumbled, hardly believing it was true. "Bless you, Kenzie, it worked!" Without even thinking about it, he swung his arms outward, snapping the metallic bonds in half, then pulled Kenzie into a hug, and she hugged him back, her body trembling against his as more tears fell from her eyes.

Gratitude for the girl swelled within him. He hadn't received such a gift since Gemma had made him a daywalker.

Next thing he knew, Rainbow jumped onto his lap and nuzzled him and then Kenzie, humming away in his middle C purr.

"Rainbow?" Kenzie said, pulling away from Leif and running a hand along the cat's gray fur.

"He came after me," Leif said. "After I was caught, I

thought he was the only creature left in all the world that cared about me."

Kenzie playfully slugged him in the shoulder. "That's not true. Some of us just... take a little longer."

They sat there on the couch, petting a very happy Rainbow, like a little family enjoying an evening together. But they were in the most dangerous place in all the world, and after some time, Leif placed a hand on Kenzie's. "You've done a wonderful thing for me today, and I'll never forget it. But the longer you stay here, the more dangerous things will be. If what you say is true, and you and Myreen plan to escape the citadel, do your best to keep me informed. I will do what I can to help."

Kenzie hesitated a moment before getting to her feet, as if she wanted to stay with him. She took the watch off her wrist and handed it to him. "Here. So we can contact you."

Leif took it and nodded to the door. "I'll see you soon."

Kenzie flashed him a half-smile. "You better believe it."

CHAPTER 34

Myreen

Myreen's fingertips roamed Ty's ribs like spider legs, digging in every now and then to throw him into a fit of helpless giggles. His laughter rang like windchimes. It was fast becoming her favorite sound in the world, and she had no intention of relenting any time soon.

Agnus, who had just entered Ty's room and now stood in the doorway, cleared her throat loudly. Myreen was sure that if she looked up, she'd see a disapproving frown wrinkling the woman's shrew face. God forbid Ty should have any fun.

"Myreen, your father wants to see you in the Conference Room," Agnus said when Myreen didn't acknowledge her presence.

Myreen's fingers stopped their siege on Ty's abdomen, her eyes staring blankly at his black tufts of hair that had been disheveled by his rolling on the floor.

Draven never called for her. When he wanted to talk with

her, he always came to her in person. This couldn't be good. Something was up. Did he know about her and Kenzie's plans?

"Best not keep him waiting," Agnus said, snapping Myreen out of her pause. "And Ty, you have a chess game in ten minutes."

Myreen stood and pulled Ty to his feet. "I'll see you at dinner," she told him, hoping it was true. Then, before she left the room, she called back, "Have fun playing *chess*." She made a funny face as she said the last word.

Ty smirked and waved goodbye, and she left the room, her blood a crescendo in her ears as she headed for the main floor with her guards in tow. A million paranoid *what ifs* flitted through her mind as she traipsed down the stairs, her guards following close behind. For all her former arrogance over being Draven's daughter, she suddenly wasn't so sure that she mattered any more to him than a fly on the wall. If he knew she betrayed him, or that she was planning to, she wouldn't be safe from his wrath.

But she couldn't let herself get too worked up. This meeting could be about something completely innocent, and if she came to him with a racing pulse, he'd get suspicious—if he wasn't already. No, she had to be calm. She had to behave as if there was no reason for suspicion.

She took a deep, soothing breath as she approached the Conference Room so that by the time she reached the door, her heart rate had returned to normal.

She opened the door and entered. Draven sat in the same seat as yesterday when she'd come to beseech him on Kol's behalf, and when he saw her, he smiled and opened his hand toward her former seat. She came forward and lowered herself into the chair, all the while analyzing his blank expression as he looked at her.

"I noticed you weren't at Kenzie's Initiation ceremony

yesterday," he said, leaning forward and steepling his hands in front of him. "You missed my transformation into a daywalker. And here I thought we were growing close."

Of course he'd notice that she wasn't there. Not that she particularly wanted to watch her best friend making her father even more lethal, but he definitely expected her to be there— he'd even sent a fancy e-vite, though she had a feeling one of his underlings did that for him. And had she not been preoccupied, she would've been there, right alongside Ty.

"What else was so important that you had to miss such a momentous historical event?" One of his perfectly arched eyebrows raised, and she could hear the edge of imminent accusation in his tone.

"I was upset over your decision about Kol," she said with a smooth voice. "I needed time to process." She chose her words carefully. None of what she said was a lie, and if she didn't lie, her pulse wouldn't jump.

He pursed his lips and nodded. "Do you think I'm an idiot?"

Myreen's breath caught in her throat. "What?" she managed to ask without stuttering.

"Answer the question, Myreen. Do you think I'm an idiot?"

I think you're a lot of things, but you're definitely not an idiot. She shook her head.

"I thought I smelled you down there, but I told myself it was just your scent clinging to my clothes."

Her mind flashed back to that moment in the dungeon when Draven stopped right next to where she was hiding. He had known she was there. *Crap!*

"You went to see him right after I gave you my decision. For what purpose, Myreen?"

His eyes began to glow red, and she couldn't bear to look at them. He was terrifying.

"For what purpose?" he yelled, making her jump. She'd never heard him raise his voice before—he was scary enough without needing to.

"I needed to warn him that worse punishment was coming," she confessed. "I needed him to know that I had at least tried." Again, not a lie. She hadn't gone down to the dungeon with the intention of getting Kol out and going with him. No, she'd made that decision after.

"You love him, don't you?" Draven accused.

Her eyes darted to his, the question catching her off guard. She didn't know how to answer that. Not to Draven, or to herself.

"You're a fool," he sneered. "Have you not seen the way he clings to that dragon girl that came with him? He's obviously gotten over you, the little hatchling." His words were meant to cut her, to slice her up, and she couldn't deny the sting they inflicted. Even with what she now knew about the curse, it wasn't easy to see another girl so close to Kol. "You're a Denholm. You're *my daughter*. You don't pine over someone who clearly doesn't want you."

"Why not? You pined over my mother for sixteen years after she left you," Myreen shot back, anger at his degradation clouding her fear. "Or was your love for her just a lie?"

Not a second after the words left her lips, something struck her hard across the face. Her hand instinctively rushed to cover her throbbing cheek, and she saw the blur of his white hand still raised from his slap.

"You will not talk back to me," he hissed in a dangerously soft voice. "I am your father, and you will speak to me with the respect that title deserves."

She pressed her hand against her cheek, refusing to look at

him and fighting back tears.

"Yes, I continued to love your mother after she ran away, and I will love her until the end of time," he continued. "But she didn't reject me. She ran away out of fear and confusion. This boy clearly doesn't see that you are superior to him in every way, and that he should worship the ground you walk on. He is an arrogant dragon brat, just like the rest of his filthy bloodline. Even if he did love you and wanted to join our cause, I wouldn't let you be with him. He's beneath you. If you must consort with a shifter and not an appropriate suitor of noble vampire blood, then give your affections to Kendall. He is a mer, and a noble at that. He's not worthy of my daughter, but at least he comes close."

Every vile word that came out of Draven's mouth boiled her blood hotter and hotter. If the moon wasn't currently waxing, her ursa might have rampaged out of her then and there, despite the soothing influence of the turquoise. That Draven thought he could control her in matters of the heart made her furious. And what was worse was that he wanted her to be with Kendall.

"There will be no more dungeon rendezvous for you," he said with finality.

Again, her eyes shot to him.

"Clearly, your guards aren't doing their job, or you would never have made it to the dungeon in the first place." Suddenly, Draven vanished from the seat in front of her, and the horrifying sounds of snapping bones and squishing liquid preceded two short-lived, agonized screams. Myreen spun in her chair to see Draven standing over the corpses of her guards, their oozing hearts in both of his hands. She didn't want to, she told herself not to, but she couldn't help but look at the bodies of the vampires that been her shadows since she arrived. The image of their shattered chests burned into her memory. She fought the urge to throw up.

Draven tossed down their hearts and stepped over their legs, taking a red handkerchief out of his breast pocket and wiping his hands with it as he returned to his seat.

"I don't enjoy hurting people," he said as he continued to wipe the blood from his fingers.

Liar! she hissed in her mind, the rest of her body frozen in shock and horror.

"You will be given four new guards. Please, be a good girl and don't make me hurt them, too. If I have even a suspicion that you've been to see the dragon again, I'll kill him and make you watch."

Then he rose from his seat, leaned over her shoulder and planted a kiss on her forehead. "See you at dinner," he whispered, then left her in the room with the guards whose hearts she might as well have ripped out herself. Their deaths were on her hands as surely as they were on his.

***

Myreen didn't go back to her room. She knew she could be too easily found there, and she didn't want to be found. She wanted time to think. So she went to the only place where she could be truly alone, where even her guards couldn't follow her: the girls' bathroom in the Initiate quarters. She went inside and curled up in one of the stalls, so that even if one of the Initiates came in, they wouldn't bother her, especially with her four new guards standing watch just outside the door.

Draven really was a monster. He murdered his own guards right in front of her, and they hadn't done anything wrong, save for not reporting all the times she slipped away from them. There was no need, since she always came back. But she wasn't going to dwell on the guilt over their deaths. She wasn't the one who killed them. Draven was. He really was heartless.

She sat in her stall for at least an hour, trying to shake off the shock of his brutality. She needed to have a clear head for what was to come. The escape needed to happen tomorrow at noon, when the sun was at its highest and the vamps couldn't come after them if they caught on. She needed to be ready.

When she was finally calm and all the tears had dried, she left her stall and looked in the mirror. Her reflection was not the same girl it used to be. The mildly rebellious blue streaks of her over-sheltered youth were still there, but the face looking back at her was the face of a woman who had seen suffering and pain and death—and was stronger for it.

Just before she was about to turn away, she noticed something. On her arm. There was a strange little red dot. She looked at her upper left arm, only then noticing the slight itch. Had she been bitten by a bug? With how cold it always was here, she didn't think mosquitos could survive, much less compete with all the other bloodsuckers.

She rubbed at it, and the skin beneath hurt. Odd for a mosquito bite. Whatever. She had more serious things to worry about than a minor irritation. She left the bathroom and went straight to Ty's room. Her guards were good little dogs and didn't follow her in.

"Hi, Myreen. Wanna play?" he asked with that innocent smile she adored, and she knew she was doing the right thing.

She knelt to his level and grabbed his shoulders, then, using her siren voice, said, "Tomorrow at noon, you will follow Kenzie wherever she takes you. You will not argue or make a sound, and you will forget this conversation."

The glazed look came and went, and then she said, "I'll play later. Right now, I need to use your servants' access. Don't tell anyone, okay?" She put her finger to her lips.

Ty gave her a mischievous smile. "Okay."

"Thanks, kiddo." She ruffled his hair and hurried to the hidden door in the wall.

Thankfully, they were back in their original quarters, the vampires making quick work of the repairs needed after the shifter attack. She'd never opened the hidden door before, too afraid a servant might be coming out and catch her, but tonight she had no such fear because she knew she would handle it if she had to.

Luckily, there was no one in the narrow, dark corridor, just an empty winding staircase. Myreen securely closed the door behind her and practically flew down the steps, descending as quickly and quietly as she could. At the bottom of those steps was an elevator, and she rode it to the bottom. When the door opened, she found herself in a short corridor. Another hidden door stood at the end. She cracked it open and peered through it. The bright kitchen on the other side was empty, so she pushed through. She hurried through the Grand Hall, descending to Kenzie's room, trying to be invisible so no one could place her.

She knocked on Kenzie's door, and when she answered, Myreen handed her a note that read: Tomorrow at noon. Destroy after reading.

Kenzie briefly looked at the note, then nodded and muttered something, and the paper was instantly consumed by flames. Myreen nodded back and Kenzie closed the door.

"Myreen. Pleasure seeing you down here."

Ugh, not now.

She turned around and cast narrowed eyes on Kendall.

"And no guards?" he asked, wearing a friendly smile.

"Didn't you hear? Draven killed them," she said flatly.

"What?" His expression instantly changed from playful to concerned. "Did they hurt you?"

She laughed dryly. "They didn't do anything wrong, except give me an ounce of freedom. Apparently, that's worth getting your heart ripped out, so maybe you should keep your distance." She spun and walked away.

"Hey, wait." He raced ahead and stopped in front of her. "What's going on? Something's wrong."

"Oh, and you didn't see it coming? I thought you were Draven's pet seer."

He held up his hands defensively. "The visions don't work that way. I can't control what I see."

"So you didn't see Kol getting tortured and nearly killed down in the dungeon? Well, I did. That's why Draven killed my guards."

"You went down there? After I warned you not to?"

She scowled at him even more dramatically. "I had to. Kol was down there. I know you guys had it out for each other at the Dome, but he's one of us. I couldn't just let him suffer."

"So, what? You thought you'd break him out?" Kendall looked exasperated. "Myreen, when are you going to get it through your head that he's no good for you?"

"And you are?" she snapped. He must have known that Draven wanted her to be with him. Even more reason for him to want Kol out of the way.

His brows puckered and his shoulders slacked. "You know how I feel about you. I thought—I hoped—that if I gave you space, you'd come around, and you'd see that we were meant to end up here. Then Kol swooped in and dragged you right back under his toxic wings. You have to let him go, Myreen. Not because I want you to choose me, but because he's going to get you killed if you keep trying to save him. Draven will never let him leave, and the longer you hold onto that hope, the longer you'll suffer."

She was angry at Kendall for what he'd done, but she could see the depth of his feeling for her reflecting in his beachy eyes. As much as she wanted to hate him, she didn't. They'd been so close, once. He made bad choices—siding with Draven being the worst of them. But she'd experienced first-hand how persuasive and charming Draven could be; she'd almost fallen for his nice-guy routine. Looking at Kendall, she almost wished she could take him with them. If he stayed, they would be enemies from this day forward, and that thought hurt.

She looked around, making sure they were alone. "Do you really care for me?"

"More than you could ever know," he professed, intensity blazing in his eyes.

She took his hand in both of hers and pleaded at him with her eyes. "Then come with me. I'm leaving this place tomorrow and I'm never coming back."

"You're leaving? How?" he asked, taking a step toward her.

"Never mind the how for now. Just say you'll come with me. You don't belong here."

"And go where? Back to the Dome to pretend we're not all sitting ducks?" He shook his head and withdrew his hand. "I understand you and Draven are struggling to connect, but this is where you belong, Myreen. Draven is your dad, and Ty is your brother. They're the only family you have left. There's nothing for you at the Dome but hollow friendships and death."

She was losing him. He was going to say no and expose her plan. She had to say whatever she could to bring him with her, anything to get him out of this place.

"Fine. Then we won't go to the Dome. Draven told me my mom was a princess of a still-submerged mer colony. That she came to land to convince her people they needed to move topside, but she never went back. Let's go find them, together. Please."

"Of course I'll help you find your colony." His pitch was high with excitement, and it filled her with hope. "I'm sure if you talk to Draven about it, he'll fund the whole expedition. He'd probably even offer to support their migration." And her hopes fizzled out like day-old soda.

"There's nothing I can say to make you leave here, is there?" she said, her tone heavy.

"No," he said, putting his hands on her shoulders and rubbing her skin with his thumbs. "This is where I'm meant to be, and so are you. Stay with me. Forget about the dragon who doesn't see how amazing you are. Forget about the people at the Dome who shunned you. Forget about whatever allegiances you feel obligated to keep with people who never appreciated you. And just... stay. I know you'll understand that I can't let you leave."

She sighed. "And I can't let you ruin my plans. I'm sorry, Kendall." Then she broadened her throat and, in her musical siren song, said, "You never saw me tonight. We never had this conversation. You are now very tired and need to go to your room."

Kendall yawned loudly, turned around and walked away, disappearing down the hall. She could've done to him what she did to Ty. She could've forced him to come with her. But she hated doing that to Ty as it was. No one should be forced to do anything against their will. Kendall was old enough to make his own choices, and he chose to stay with Draven.

She wondered how things might have been different if he hadn't made that choice. They might have grown closer as Kol played ping pong with her heart. She might have chosen him over Kol eventually. Kendall wasn't a bad guy. He was just misguided. So much for his visions of being with her. She felt sorry for him.

There was one more stop on her agenda before returning to Ty's room. Ever since Leif had mentioned Draven's trophy room, she was curious. She suspected his office was the trophy room, though he never called it that—at least, not in her presence. She had to see whatever it was he was trying to hide from her. She couldn't leave here without knowing.

Myreen peeked out the entrance of the Initiate quarters into the Grand Hall. There were always a few vampires loitering about, but she saw no one of consequence who would care that she was here.

She crossed the Grand Hall as inconspicuously as she could, then hovered in front of the door to Draven's office. Draven always made his rounds with his new recruits in the evenings, so she knew his office would be empty right now, but for how long, she couldn't be sure. She had to move quickly.

She tried the handle, but of course it was locked. She doubted her keycard would work, and she didn't want to leave behind any kind of technological trace, if that was even how it worked. There had to be another way to get into that room that wouldn't leave evidence.

Draven had taught her that ursas could move objects with their minds. She'd only tried it that one time he'd forced her to shift, but maybe she could access her telekinesis in human form to unlatch a simple lock.

She was already here; she might as well try.

She reached for the necklace around her neck and caressed the center turquoise stone as she stared at the doorknob and focused. She envisioned the bolt clearly in her mind, imagined it sliding out of its socket, felt her will pushing on the smooth little metal piece.

And then a small click sounded within the door.

She grabbed the knob and turned, and... it opened. She was thrilled at her success for an instant.

Until she saw what was on the other side of the door.

All four walls were adorned with plaques and racks of various, well-preserved shifter body parts. A pair of harpy wings, a naga tail, dragon claws. This was worse than she could've ever imagined!

Draven was diabolical. These were pieces of actual people, and Draven had stuffed them and lacquered them like they were kills from hunts. She could practically see the ghost of the person still attached to every appendage. A sweet young harpy girl, hanging dead from her racked wings. The dragon claws conjured images of Kol's face. Is this what Draven planned to do with him when he was done torturing him?

Her heart swelled with sorrow, slitting in a million places and seeping blood for the pain these poor creatures must have suffered. What kind of monster could not only do something so horrible, but then enjoy sitting amongst these reminders of those acts every day? It was beyond deplorable.

She'd seen enough. She closed the door and made for the kitchen.

But the sound of Draven's voice around the corner made her alarm bells go off, and she darted to one of the couches, grabbing a magazine from the coffee table and shoving it in front of her face, hoping against hope that he didn't discover she was there. If he found her roaming about without her guards again, she didn't know what he would do, and she didn't want to find out.

"Begin working on this right away," Draven said to someone behind her.

"Yes sir." She recognized Adam's voice. "I'm surprised she gave it to you so quickly. I really thought it would've taken her more time to come around to our way of thinking."

Draven sighed. "In fact, she did not give it willingly. Despite all the goodwill I've showered upon her, she remains loyal to the shifters. She's very strong-willed, just like her mother. She needs to be broken, but that will take time—too much time. I took it from her this afternoon after she confessed to visiting the Dracul boy without my consent. She doesn't even know I did it. How long until you can create a serum from her blood?"

"Give my team a day. Maybe two. But you'll have it, I promise. And you'll be the world's first hybrid."

"I made the right choice turning you, Adam. You're invaluable to our cause."

"Thank you, sir."

Draven's door closed and Adam swaggered away like a dog who'd just been given a bone for being a good boy.

Myreen sat on the couch, wide eyes staring unseeing at the well-dressed celebrities on the pages in front of her, the feeling of violation sinking into every inch of her skin like muck into a sponge.

Draven took her blood. Without asking her or warning her. He'd done it without her even knowing. But how? And when? She didn't even feel... *the bug bite.* She looked at the dot on her upper arm. Now that she knew better, she saw it for what it was. There was no puffy mound or irritated pink skin, just a small, red puncture, the exact size of a needle tip.

Her stomach twisted with disgust and fury and panic. Draven had the one thing he wanted most: her blood. And once Adam converted it into a serum, Draven would become a hybrid. He wouldn't need her anymore.

The escape had to go perfectly tomorrow. If it didn't—and maybe even if they did—they were all doomed.

Juliet

For the first time since Myreen left, Juliet finally slept through the night.

It was as if the moment she connected her fire with her ice, something clicked, like a final puzzle piece pressing into place. The balance she felt was a wonderful change.

Still, the lingering guilt over everything stopped her from truly embracing this new feeling.

How could she be happy when the Dome was falling to pieces? How could she walk around with a smile on her face when Myreen was gone? When Kol was imprisoned? When she hadn't heard from Kenzie for what felt like ages? Each time contentment tried to settle, her stomach would twist as her reality came back into focus.

She needed a distraction.

She decided to attend her classes today—*all* of them. Even

though no fun ones remained. She desperately missed music and art.

But what she looked forward to most was her one-on-one time with her dad. It was the only time that she could really explore her new gifts.

Malachai lied to Dracul when he requested that their sessions be restored. They were supposed to be working on defense and tactics, only. But not once since they started up again had they trained for that. Juliet always broke a sweat, but not from physical exertion.

Juliet kept her head down as she made her way to her dad's office. Even with her headphones on, she could still hear the soldier's yells. They tried so hard to make the students synchronized, and they didn't care how they sounded doing it. She made sure to be in sync with everyone else so she didn't draw any unwanted attention. It was easy for her to fall into step with the other students, because it was like a dance. Especially with her music blaring through her headphones.

"Remove the device. I don't want to see it out in these halls again." The nasty guard—the one who seemed intent on getting her in trouble—looked down at her as he pulled her from the group.

"You mean my headphones?" She snickered, but knew as soon as she did that she would regret it.

"Excuse me?" He initiated an intense stare-off—one she wouldn't be trying to win.

Juliet cleared her throat as she stuffed her headphones in her bag. "I apologize. It won't happen again." She saluted him with precise movement. On the outside it looked like she was calm and collected, but on the inside, she was a mess. She wanted nothing more than to show him just how good she was at defense. The thought of a few bruises on his face brought calmness to her mind.

If only I could act on it.

The soldier gave her a wary look, but returned the salute. She turned away and finished walking to her dad's. The soldier followed her, though. She could hear the clacking of his heavy boots hitting the floor behind her. It was as if he wanted her to know he was there—that really worried her.

When she finally made it to her dad's door, she entered as quickly as she could, not daring to look back.

"Is everything okay?" Malachai asked, concern lining his eyes.

"Yeah. That guard that keeps taking my name down just made me take my headphones off." She tried to downplay it with a casual tone. "I didn't entertain him by overreacting, so I think it upset him 'cause he followed me here." It probably wasn't something to stress over. If it were serious, he would've entered behind her.

Still, Malachai warily looked toward the door. "We should still be careful."

"You know, it's not fair. You helped General Dracul kick the last director out, but his little lackey won't even give me a break," she said, her frustration beginning to spill out.

"Juliet Quinn, lower your voice," Malachai said, his words coming out barely above a whisper. "Lord Dracul only cares about keeping the shifters safe, not keeping scores or diverting high school drama. I highly recommend you stop thinking that if you get caught he'll go easy on you."

Juliet opened her mouth to tell her dad she *didn't* think the general would go easy on her, but a knock sounded at the door.

Malachai gently pushed Juliet behind him. Her heart stammered as she hooked onto her dad's arm. It was sad that this was their reaction to a visitor. What had the general done?

"Who is it?" her dad's deep and authoritative voice rumbled.

"Open the door, under the general's orders. I'm here to escort Ms. Quinn to his office."

Malachai spun, gently grabbing Juliet's shoulders.

"Deny anything and everything he accuses you of," he quietly urged. "Show no fear but don't fight back. And whatever you do, promise me you'll keep your fire and ice inside."

He shook her when she didn't respond, staring at him with wide and fearful eyes. "I promise," she whispered.

"Come find me as soon as you step foot out of there."

Another thunderous knock echoed throughout the room.

Her dad pulled her in for a hug, then straightened his back and walked to the door. As soon as he opened it, Juliet recognized the soldier. He was the one who had followed her. The one who had it in for her. And his beady eyes were focused on Juliet, carrying a bright glee despite his stoic expression. *What is this guy's problem?*

The soldier took one step toward her, but Malachai blocked his way.

"Major Peters, if even one hair on her head is out of place when her meeting is over, it'll be *me* that *you'll* have to deal with." He stepped aside, his hands behind his back, his head raised.

Major Peters narrowed his eyes, then circled Juliet until he stood behind her. "This doesn't look like a defense training session," came the major's sour voice.

"I don't have to explain myself to *anyone,* least of all, you," Malachai said, his hands balling into fists.

"Actually, you do." Major Peters' cocky tone made Juliet want to hit something. "But that will be a conversation for a later time."

"Then get on with it or get out."

Juliet hadn't seen Malachai this enraged. Ever. She knew he

was trying to stay calm for both their sakes. She certainly hadn't inherited her dad's self-control.

"Miss Quinn, General Dracul would like to speak with you in his office. Follow me or face the consequences."

He *almost* made it sound like she had a choice in the matter.

Juliet didn't think she could hold back her temper if they pushed her, but she would do her best. She squared her shoulders. "I'll go."

Major Peters gave her the side-eye, then marched out of the room.

She quickly followed him, purposely leaving her bag in her dad's office so she'd have an excuse to go back. And she stayed close on his heels, knowing he was probably looking for any and every reason to snitch on her.

"So, what does he want to talk to me about?" She didn't like the major, and she didn't care for small talk, but the silence and their destination was working up her nerves. Besides, she didn't like to be surprised. Especially by someone like *Lord Dracul.*

"You're about to find out." Major Peters sounded amused. He probably enjoyed seeing her shake in her boots.

They approached the door that used to be Oberon's, and Juliet took a deep breath, reminding herself to stay calm, focused, and as balanced as possible. She didn't need her uncontrollable fire to make an impromptu appearance—or her ice. Especially not in front of the general.

The major knocked on the door in a special pattern, then entered. Juliet thought of her dad and how he would assess the situation if he were in her shoes. A push of courage followed. She straightened her back and held her head high as the major announced her name.

Oberon's old office, once filled with the feeling of safety

and comfort, seemed a completely different place. Lord Dracul's cold displeasure was everywhere, from the furniture to the décor, even emanating from the floor and walls.

Juliet stood in front of the desk and bravely kept her eyes trained on the new director.

"Please, take a seat," General Dracul said, the corners of his lips turning up in a small but sinister sneer.

She knew not to be stubborn or difficult, so she looked down, but only to take her seat. Perched on the edge, Juliet tried to subtly size him up.

Lord Dracul looked like Kol—or rather, Kol looked like his dad—but the director had a much more ancient and powerful air to him. Aside from their looks, father and son couldn't be more different. Although he was serious, Kol seemed to have more depth, and an openness to possibilities—especially after Myreen arrived. General Dracul, on the other hand, was the definition of rigid force and intimidation. It seeped out of his pores and lasered through his gaze. He sat straight, his hands folded on the desk in front of him—even seated, he towered over her. Everything about the man screamed dark, and for just a moment, she felt sorry for Kol. This was his father, the man who'd raised him.

Juliet took a deep breath. "You wanted to see me?" she said, taking the lead so the general would know she had a backbone. "I was training with my father."

"Hardly," Major Peters chimed from behind her.

"If I may," Juliet said, stuffing her hands under her legs to keep them from balling into fists, "I don't feel comfortable with Nanny McPhee, here, breathing down my neck. I'd only just walked into my father's office when I was ambushed—not that I have to explain myself to *you* Mr. Peters." She knew she was treading a thin line. It was a line she definitely *wouldn't* be crossing with the general, but his officers were a different matter.

The general's laugh was deep and menacing, the stuff of nightmares. "Major, step outside. I'll let you know when your services are required again." He sounded amused—which couldn't be good. But this would go better without the pipings of the major, so she was satisfied.

Juliet gave the general her full attention.

"I see here in your records that you're quite the warrior. Your stats in defense are off the charts. And for a newbie like you, that's impressive."

Was that a compliment or an insult? Was this an interrogation or some kind of recruitment? Juliet didn't like either choice. She stayed quiet, letting him finish.

"Yet, there's an entire page of red marks due to 'uncontrollable habits.' But let's pin it on the fact that you were recently thrown into this world. Still, you helped defeat an entire vampire ambush during your first transformation." He clapped three times, and it made Juliet want to cringe. "So, with a record like this, why haven't you looked into joining our ranks? It's in your blood, isn't it? Being a Quinn ties you to the protection of the school, correct? So if we provide the best protection, why aren't you on our side? Isn't Myreen your friend? Does her return mean anything to you?"

He paused for a second. She didn't know if she should answer him or if he'd consider it an interruption.

"Is it that you're occupied with other things? Of course it could be. I know you're my assistant's precious *Juliet.*" Another sinister snicker. "But I also know that I keep him busy, so that couldn't be taking up all of your time. What else could you be so engaged in?" Another pause.

Should she answer? "I've had to take time to... reassess

myself," she said. "After what happened with Myreen, I became unbalanced again."

He lifted two fingers to shut her up. Apparently she wasn't supposed to answer him.

"No, I don't think it's that, either," he argued. "You see, when there are groups of kids together, it's inevitable that a rumor mill is created. It's a school; that's normal, I get it. Now, I don't usually regard anything that comes out of a teenager's mouth, but when it comes out of several, that's when we choose to monitor the mill. Make sense?" The rhetorical questions unsettled her. She wished this conversation would end.

"Would you like to know the juicy story of the week? I'm sure you would, since you're the star. Apparently you, Miss Quinn, have been holding secret meetings with some of the students here." He paused again, and Juliet had to fight the warmth itching to escape her fingertips. "At first, I thought that nobody in their right mind would be that stupid. But then as Major Peters continued to brief me, it made a little more sense. So here we are. What do you think of the latest gossip?"

"It's false. This isn't the first time I've been at the center of a rumor. And like you said, I wouldn't be *stupid* enough to do something that... well, stupid."

General Dracul's gaze bored into her as he studied her. And she let him. *Show no fear.*

"Is that your final answer?"

"Yes. My dad would kill me if I did something like that, and I wouldn't dare betray you, sir. I have enough on my plate. And I know you don't care, but I just got Nik back. I wouldn't risk losing him again." If this shifter thing didn't work out for her, acting might be her calling. She was proud of that performance.

General Dracul fisted his hands below his chin and stared

several minutes too long.

"Major Peters, reenter."

The major entered with a sour face as he took his place behind Juliet.

"Let me be clear, I do not tolerate dishonesty, Miss Quinn. If we discover these rumors are indeed factual, you will be sorry. Consider this your warning." He glanced at his officer. "Major, return Miss Quinn to her father. I'm sure she has so much to tell him." And it was over. With a wave of his hand, they were dismissed.

The walk back to her dad's office was awkwardly silent—although, silence was preferable to speaking with the major. When they finally reached the door, Major Peters gave her a long, stern look, then spun and marched away.

Juliet entered the office without knocking, plastering her back on the closed door. Malachai rushed over and wrapped his arms around her. She trembled against her father, soaking in his warmth.

"We *have* to get him out of here," she whispered. It seemed impossible, but now more than ever the risk was worth it. She needed to be smarter than General Dracul, or he *would* catch her and her friends.

"Shhhh." Malachai's breath caught Juliet's curls as he gently rocked her. "It'll be okay."

Juliet nodded, pulling back and taking a deep breath.

"About your question regarding the general and his abilities..." Malachai said.

He had Juliet's attention. "Yeah?"

"If he's abused that ability in the past, there doesn't seem to be any evidence of it."

"No? Not even Delphine?" Juliet wanted to swallow her words as soon as they came out, but she couldn't take it back, even if she tried.

Malachai shook his head. "She's a seer, Jules. Acting out of character doesn't necessarily mean she's being influenced—at least not by another shifter."

Juliet stared at her hands. She hated to even think it, but part of her had hoped to catch the general in some evil deed so she could get *him* thrown out. That's how he'd gotten rid of Oberon, after all.

"But hey, good news. At least the man's still playing fair."

"But that means Delphine turned her back on us."

"You don't know that. The woman has mad intuition. I'm sure she's just doing what she thinks is best."

"You're probably right." And at the very least, it gave her hope that her dad would help her set everything right again. He'd already come this far. Maybe once her group got somewhere, she'd bring Malachai in on the plot to get Oberon back.

Myreen

Myreen used the same method of escaping her guards as last time, letting them think she was eating lunch with Ty only to escape through the servants' access. She only had to use her siren voice on one servant in the hidden stairwell, as the woman was heading up to find out what Ty wanted for lunch just as Myreen was coming down.

Once safely through the kitchen, Myreen walked past the dining hall door without looking, hoping Kenzie saw her. She'd already sent a text to Kenzie—only to get a reply from Leif. That girl had a funny way of trying to help. Giving her smartwatch to Leif just before trying to execute an escape plan? Myreen shook her head and smiled.

Myreen made her way to the Grand Hall and sat in a chair to wait, pulling out her tablet so she didn't look lost. The area was fairly vacant. A few bodies wandered around, patrolling the grounds, but they payed more attention to what was outside than what was within.

A few minutes later, there were footsteps on the stairs, and then Kenzie's shock of copper hair came into view. The two exchanged a look, and then Kenzie headed down toward the Initiate quarters. Myreen took her time, getting up, putting her tablet away, and stretching, before following Kenzie.

Kenzie grabbed Myreen's hand as she descended into the first common room, which was empty, thanks to it being lunchtime on a school day.

Kenzie gave Myreen a knowing smile. "Is it time?"

Myreen nodded, excitement and nerves roiling through her. She just wanted this to be over, to be back in the safety of the Dome, back in some semblance of normalcy. Not that she thought anything would be entirely normal ever again.

"Okay, I'll get Piper and Ty and Leif. We'll meet you at the rendezvous point." Kenzie nodded and turned to leave, but Myreen grabbed her arm.

"Wait. Do you have any magic for... I don't know, luck? Or to calm my nerves."

Kenzie laughed. "Sorry. Not that I know of. But you're gonna do great. You're the big bad siren, remember?"

Myreen sighed, but she smiled, giving Kenzie a nod. *I can do this.* "I'll keep that in mind."

"One more thing. Do you mind sending Leif a message to let him know I'm on my way? Just send it to me. I gave him my smartwatch."

Myreen rolled her eyes. "Yeah. I'll do that. And I figured out what happened to your smartwatch when I tried to message *you* earlier."

"Whoops. Can't blame a girl for trying, can you?" Kenzie

gave Myreen a cheesy smile.

Myreen chuckled and shook her head.

Kenzie threw a final wink as she headed upstairs. Myreen went the opposite way, into the bowels of the citadel, her heart hammering against her ribs. The guards were the same, making her job easy. Her siren abilities still worked their magic, allowing her to come and go unnoticed.

She kept her eyes averted as she walked past other prisoners. She couldn't afford to add anyone else to their plan. As it was, she still had doubts about bringing Piper with them. But Kenzie said she'd take care of it, so it was out of Myreen's hands.

Kol and Char threw off their feigned fatigue and injuries when Myreen walked in, rising with an eager expectancy.

"You have a plan?" Kol asked, his eyes bright and hopeful.

Myreen smiled. "We're leaving now."

Kol blinked and Char's mouth hung open. Char glanced around the room. "Are you sure?"

Myreen nodded. "Kenzie's gathering a few more people. They'll meet us on the roof. We're going to fly out of here."

Kol smirked. "Because flying is better than swimming?"

Myreen laughed, Char looking between the two.

"Okay. First things first; let's get you out of that cage." She went to the guard at the front of the dungeon, summoning her melodic voice and said, "Unlock the dragons' cell and release their bonds. You will not see them leave, or notice once they're gone."

The guard nodded, a vacant look in his eyes as he set about doing her bidding. Kol and Char pulled the fake bandages off while they waited, then carefully stepped out as the door popped open.

Kol threw Myreen a smile once he was free. "It feels good to get out of that cage."

Myreen nodded. "How do you feel?"

Kol shrugged, but Char stepped forward. "We're okay, but if we've got time, a little more healing would go a long way."

Myreen nodded. "Any chance either of you can summon your fire?"

"Maybe." Kol held out a hand, sparks and puffs of smoke appearing, but not enough for her purposes.

Myreen shook her head. "No worries. I brought backup." She fished the lighter she'd brought with her from her pocket and handed it to Kol, who lit it. Myreen called on her healing powers, pulling the light from the flickering flame and sending it to Kol and then to Char. Color warmed their cheeks, the dark circles under their eyes lessening. If it weren't for the grime, tattered clothes, and messy hair still marring their appearance, they'd probably look like themselves again. Myreen nodded, and Kol let the lighter snuff.

"What's next?" Kol asked.

"Any chance that brought your powers back?"

Kol looked to Char with a smile. "Shall we?"

Char nodded, and they both held out their hands. Their eyes glowed a luminous blue as they used their powers to summon blazes that burned bright.

Myreen clapped, then looked around the room. "Okay, maybe that's enough for now. I don't know if they have a fire alarm system down here."

Both fires extinguished, but both Kol and Char had a gleam in their eyes. Jealousy reared its ugly head, and Myreen turned away, putting a hand to her chin to try to make it look like she was just thinking. Even after everything she'd heard—and what Kol had directly told her—part of her wondered what that relationship held. They obviously had history. But now wasn't the time to sort out feelings. They'd talk once this was all over.

Myreen took a deep breath. "Here's what I'm thinking. I know Kol can make himself invisible as a dragon, which I know isn't common, but I'm hoping you can too, Char?"

Char shook her head, her eyes wide-eyed like the question was ludicrous. "No. Not possible."

Kol piped up, the smirk on his face making Myreen's heart catch. "Actually, now I can make myself invisible as a human, too. I don't have to be shifted to access it."

Myreen's brows shot up. "Okay, well that makes sneaking you around a little easier." She turned to Char. "But we'll have to take you to Kenzie's room and clean you up. If you blend in, it'll be easier to try to sneak you out. We'll just have to stay away from vampires. But we'll have to do that anyway, since I don't think invisibility includes your scent."

"Wait," Kol said, his face advertising deep concentration. "Maybe I can make Char invisible, too? I discovered by accident that I can disappear in human form. I've never tried making anyone else invisible before—shielding them, sure, but not making them disappear—but it's worth a shot."

Myreen nodded. "Okay. Give it a try. If that doesn't work, then we'll go with a disguise for Char."

Kol walked to Char and placed a hand on her shoulder, then closed his eyes. After a few moments, Kol disappeared, and like slow motion, invisibility enveloped Char.

Myreen's mouth fell open as she stared at the emptiness. Not even a glimmer of their forms gave their location away. If she hadn't just seen them disappear, she would think that space was empty. As it was, it was still difficult to convince herself they hadn't moved. "That's amazing! Do you think you can keep that up? We just need to get you two to one of the elevators."

"Yeah, I think so," Kol said.

His disembodied voice floated from where she'd last seen him, and she felt goosebumps prickle her arms. *So weird.* Myreen wrapped her arms around herself, suddenly aware of just how cold it was down here. "What happens if you let go of each other?"

Char materialized, stepping away from where Myreen had last seen her as if walking through a portal.

"And touch her again?" Myreen said.

Part of Char's hand disappeared as Kol took it, and after a few tense moments, Char disappeared too.

"I can touch her while invisible, but it doesn't pass on unless I push the invisibility on her," Kol said.

Myreen felt the little green monster flaring to life again, but she stamped it down. He wasn't holding Char's hand out of want, but out of need. Whether he liked it or not could be sorted out—later.

"Ready when you are," came Kol's voice again.

Myreen gave a nervous giggle. "That's going to take some getting used to. Okay. Let's go."

Nodding to the guards, she left, assuming Kol and Char were following. Not like she could see them. They moved quietly, but every now and again she could hear shuffling against the cold concrete. She cringed as she thought about their bare feet having to walk across the freezing floor, but there was nothing she could do about it right now. They'd be out of here soon. They'd worry about shoes then.

At least their fire had been restored. Hopefully that would keep them warm. They'd need it, especially once they got outside. She was glad her smart clothes had survived everything, otherwise she'd be freezing for sure.

It felt like the dungeon had tripled in length, so Myreen was relieved when they finally reached the stairs leading out.

But one of the guards standing there was different, and he looked at the other vampires with his brows creased. "Does anybody else smell that?"

"What is that?" said another vampire, whose name Myreen had never bothered to learn.

She had a sickening sensation as she realized these vampires might all be dead by this time tomorrow. But she couldn't let that stop her. As far as she knew, they willingly followed Draven. And he was a monster.

Myreen closed her eyes and summoned her siren voice, focusing on the vampires. "No one here has seen or sensed anyone or anything unusual. Your orders are to stay in this room until your shift ends."

She opened her eyes to see the vampires as their gazes unglazed, and they all stared past her as if she wasn't there. Myreen let out a pent-up breath and marched up the stairs, keeping her pace steady and unhurried. Just a few more floors and they'd be home free.

"You two still with me?" Myreen whispered as they came into the common room. She sighed with relief as warmth flooded over her. Thank goodness the human quarters were heated.

"Yeah, we're still here," came Kol's voice from the space next to her. It was so strange having him right there, but not being able to see him. He was so tall, it almost seemed like his voice was coming from the ceiling. If she wasn't so nervous, she'd probably be giggling.

"Okay, there are three more levels of human quarters, then the Grand Hall. From there we'll either need to go to the main elevator in the Grand Hall, the next stop above the two school levels, or we'll need to head through the kitchen to take the servants' access. I'd rather take the kitchen route, but we're going to have to see."

"Way to plan this out," came Char's voice, followed by an *oof.* "Not cool, Kol."

Myreen stifled a smile. "I'm sorry it's not better planned out, but we've got a lot of people we're trying to rescue."

"Wait. Who else is coming with us?" Kol asked.

"My little brother, for one. And Kenzie found an Initiate who wants out. Plus, we're rescuing the vampire who's been helping protect the Dome. His name is Leif."

"Wait. Hold that thought about a little brother. So Oberon really *was* dealing with a vampire?" Was that anger lacing Kol's words?

Myreen sighed. She'd forgotten this was all news to them. "Yeah. But he's one of the good guys. Kenzie knows him, too."

"I'm still not entirely sure I trust the selkie, either," he grumbled.

"Well I do. She's sacrificed a lot to try to get us all out." *Maybe too much.* But Myreen didn't want to think about that, either.

"And you have a little brother?" Kol asked, concern in his voice.

"Yeah. Half-brother, really." She looked down at the floor, not bothering to offer any more information. She didn't know how Kol would react to bringing Ty with them, especially knowing he was Draven's son, but it wasn't his decision to make. She could feel his eyes still on her. "Come on. We don't want to waste any time."

"Right."

They started up the stairs again, this time a little faster. Myreen's pulse raced, and she started taking the steps two at a time, just so they could get to the top more quickly. The need to be out of there was building, becoming almost impossible to ignore.

"Maybe not so fast," Kol whispered. "Char and I can't keep up while we're linked like this, and I don't want to drop my concentration and expose us."

"Right." Myreen slowed back down, but it gave her more time to think, more time to worry. She wondered how Kenzie was faring, if she'd gotten everyone to the roof yet.

Finally, they made it to the Grand Hall. Myreen held a hand up as she peeked around the corner. There were more people there than normal, and Myreen looked at her watch. *Shoot.* Lunch break was over. That meant both the kitchen and the way to the elevator would be busy. And to make matters worse—

"Myreen!"

Myreen stiffened as a familiar guy came over. It took her a moment, but then she recognized the vampire who'd been feeding on Kenzie—Adam. Myreen took a few steps forward, waving a hand at Kol and Char in the hopes they'd take the hint and back up a bit. She felt a welcome flare of anger as she looked at the guy who'd helped make her friend's life miserable. Maybe that would help mask the fear lacing every move. "Hey."

"Have you seen Kenzie?" He ran a hand through his hair, his stance casual.

Myreen crossed her arms, her foot beginning to tap. "Not today."

"Oh. I saw you coming out of the human quarters and thought..."

Myreen shrugged. "Draven made a suggestion. I decided to check it out." She didn't know if Adam knew that Draven thought she should date Kendall, but he'd been forthcoming with plenty of *other* information about her.

"Oh. Okay. Well, thanks." Adam turned to leave, then turned back. "Aren't you supposed to have some guards?"

Myreen gave a nervous chuckle. "Oh, they're right— Wait. I think I see Kenzie."

"Where?" Adam's head swung around.

"It looked like she was going to class."

"Thanks." Adam sped away.

Myreen leaned back into the stairwell and hissed, curling a beckoning finger. She was herding invisible dragons. If it wasn't so dire, it would be hilarious. She headed for the kitchen. Carefully looking around, she noticed a few people wore confused looks. She hurried her steps. There were too many people around, but she couldn't afford to wait for things to clear back up.

She was almost to the kitchen when a hand on her arm spun her around. "Hey!"

It was Adam again. "She's not there. Never was. I'd know her scent anywhere and it's not there. What's going on?"

"Nothing."

"Do I smell shifters?" Adam nosed the air. "Based on the burnt smell, I'd guess dragons." He leered at Myreen. "Couldn't stay away, could you?"

Myreen gave him a smile. "You caught me." She placed a hand on his, pulling on her siren abilities once more, though she kept her voice near a whisper. "You never saw me, and you already found Kenzie. You've got some free time. I suggest you spend it wisely."

Adam nodded and turned to leave. Myreen slipped into the conference room, holding the door open so Kol and Char could follow.

"Whew. That was close. Who was that guy?"

Kol released the invisibility, and he and Char popped back into view. Myreen locked the door, glancing around the room.

She wouldn't put it past Draven to have cameras in here, but hopefully no one would be watching. "Adam. Kenzie was assigned to him... so he could feed off her."

"What?" Kol and Char said at the same time, disgust clear on their faces.

"I told you she's sacrificed a lot. The guy's a real jerk, too." With a final glance at the room she asked, "Do you think you can make me invisible, too?"

Kol shrugged. "I don't see why not."

Myreen took Char's hand, deciding she needed a buffer between her and Kol. Sure, it wasn't easy watching him hold Char's hand, but she wouldn't have to for much longer. Kol looked at Myreen for a long minute, pain and confusion flashing for an instant, and she knew she'd made the right decision. As painful as it might be, now was not the time to get swept up in relationship drama. They'd talk later. They had to.

Char took Kol's hand, and Kol closed his eyes to concentrate again. This time Myreen watched them disappear with a little more curiosity, and similar to his scales, it seemed that their skin flipped over. She looked down at herself, and saw nothing. Apparently she was invisible even to herself.

"Perfect. Okay, we're going to the kitchen. Follow my lead."

Myreen unlocked the door and left the conference room behind, angling toward the kitchen. When they arrived, the room was abuzz with activity, the staff hurrying to clean lunch up. She had to wait a few minutes before their chain of three could slip in without being detected. Once in, she guided them around the edges of the room. One of the staff knocked into her, shaking their head and blinking at the blank space before moving on. Myreen let out a long breath, then tugged on the chain as they made their way to the secret door and slipped in.

SUMMONED

Once they confirmed the elevator was empty, they all climbed in and dropped their chain. Myreen sank to the floor as the metal box carried them upward.

"How much more?" Char asked, sitting next to Myreen.

Kol shrugged as he joined them on the floor.

"Not much more now. We've just got to get past the guards standing outside Ty's room and then head down to the roof access. But the Elite quarters are usually pretty empty, so it's only the guards we'll have to worry about."

Char nodded, wrapping her arms around herself. Kol gave her a pitiful look, but kept his distance.

"So, how do you two know each other?" Myreen asked, hugging her knees closer to her chest.

"Friends since childhood," Kol said.

Char stared at the floor.

Myreen searched Kol's face, but it appeared he was telling the truth. She wanted to pursue the conversation, but there wasn't any more time. The elevator gave a ding, the upward momentum stopping, then settling.

Myreen stood and dusted off her bottom, as did Kol and Char, though there was little reason to do so given the state of their smart clothing.

They headed up the final steps, Myreen in the lead. She didn't think anyone would be there, not since Kenzie was supposed to grab Ty and go. She hoped Kenzie hadn't had any problems with the guards Myreen had left behind.

But when Myreen cracked the secret door open, she realized she'd made a critical error. She'd forgotten about Agnus.

Ty's nanny had the door to the hall open, and all four of Myreen's guards were inside, some of them with freshly-healing wounds. The woman yelled at them, demanding to know what had happened to Ty. They all looked at each other, worry and confusion on their faces. Well, at least Ty had gotten out of there.

Myreen held a hand up, signaling that Kol and Char should stay out of sight. Then she went into the room, not waiting for the guards to leave. She didn't know how far Kenzie had gotten, and didn't wan to risk them coming after her.

One of the guards noticed Myreen first, and Agnus swung around, her eyes widening. She marched to Myreen, hands on her hips. "What have you done with him? Do you have any idea what the Master will do when he discovers his son is missing?"

Myreen set her chin. "Ty is a child, but you want to treat him like he's an adult. You people have robbed him of his childhood, and I won't allow it to continue."

"That's not your call to make, young lady. I don't care who you are, Ty is my charge and I will make sure he measures up to the Master's expectations."

"I'm his sister," Myreen ground out, as Agnus turned to the guards. Myreen summoned her siren voice once more, putting everything she had into it. "Ty is no longer your responsibility. You all will leave and go straight to the elevator, not stopping until you are far from this room. Find something to do that doesn't include me or Ty or Draven. In fact, I suggest you leave the citadel as soon as you can, while you still can." Her voice, so familiar yet so foreign, bathed Agnus and the guards with her will. They shuffled out the door, the glaze in their eyes still not cleared.

Myreen despised Agnus. Not quite as much as Draven, but enough. She'd been so instrumental in keeping Ty repressed. Myreen wouldn't let anyone do that to him ever again.

But that still didn't mean she wanted to see the woman killed. Myreen only hoped Agnus took her suggestion and left, rather than sticking around and paying for her actions. Myreen didn't want any more blood on her hands, if she could help it.

After a few moments, she opened the door to the servant's access. A woman lay at Kol's feet, unconscious. Myreen's eyes widened. "What happened?"

Kol sighed. "She came up while you were talking. Don't worry, we didn't kill her. She'll wake up soon, though."

Myreen swallowed, but nodded. "Sorry."

Kol shrugged.

"Let's get out of here," Char said, brushing past Myreen.

Myreen couldn't agree more.

Leif

Leif jingled his new pair of shackles. Not long after he'd been granted Kenzie's gift of copper immunity, Beatrice had come back and saw the bonds he'd mutilated. When she'd asked about what happened, he claimed he'd had a fit of sorts, and in the process, a moment of vampire strength had returned. Through the copper-induced spasms, he'd broken the shackles. It was the best explanation he could come up with, and Beatrice hadn't been entirely convinced. He'd kept his new cuffs in perfect shape, and in the times she'd come back to check on him, he acted as if the copper was weakening him.

Beatrice was gone, and thankfully, since Kenzie's smart-watch—which he'd hidden under the cushions of the couch—had received a message from Myreen. They had begun executing the plan, which meant Kenzie was on her way.

Leif resisted the urge to break the new shackles. He'd do that once Kenzie arrived. It wasn't worth risking their destruction, just in case Beatrice made an impromptu visit.

Nearby, Rainbow was sharpening his fangs on the base of Beatrice's desk.

"Good cat," Leif said, urging on his feline friend on. "Mark up that furniture as much as you can." He still had no idea how Rainbow had survived this long without being caught. His food source was probably outside, unless he was secretly making his rounds down in the Initiate dorms. The very thought of a vampire cat jumping on sleeping Initiates made him chuckle.

Suddenly, Rainbow froze, his ears standing high and his red eyes opening wide. Leif heard light footsteps approaching, and before the cat could prance away, Leif sped to him and scooped him up. If it was Beatrice, he'd be in trouble.

Please be Kenzie. Please be Kenzie.

It seemed an awfully long time went by before he decided to bolt to the door. Leif had to check for himself. Upon reaching the threshold, he nearly slammed into Kenzie. Rainbow let out an odd sing-song meow and tried to jump away, but Leif held him close.

"Whoa there, turbo," Kenzie said, putting her hands out to stop the near-collision, though it would've done little good had he not been able to stop.

"I had to be sure it was you," he said.

"Right," Kenzie replied. She tapped him on the shoulder, then held her hand out. "My watch. Now."

Leif bobbed his head back. "It's inside, on the couch." He stepped back, allowing enough room for Kenzie to pop in and run across the room. Slipping on the watch, she tapped at it madly.

"What are you doing?" he asked.

"Playing Minesweeper," she replied. "What does it look like I'm doing? Sending a message."

"To Myreen?" Leif hated that he didn't know more about Kenzie's escape plan.

"No, to Piper. We're breaking her out, too."

Leif gave her an incredulous look. "Piper? I mean, she's a nice girl, but why are we breaking her out?"

Kenzie let her arm drop, then bounded toward him. "Turns out she doesn't want to be a vampire. Come on, we need to go."

Leif looked off to the side. Softly, he said, "One soul saved. I *actually* got through to her."

"Yeah. Great job, Gandhi. When we get back to Chicago, I'll give you a gold star or something. Speaking of Chicago, we need to go. Now."

Leif gathered himself as Kenzie moved past him. "Right. I'm bringing Rainbow along."

"I figured," she said, tiptoeing into the hallway—as if it would stop vampires from hearing her. "I hope your pet likes flying."

Leif moved after her. "Flying?"

"Yep," she said without turning around, keeping a brisk pace toward the tower stairs. "On a dragon, no less."

His brows furrowed. "So, what exactly *is* your plan?"

They made it to the stairs and began descending. Kenzie took two at a time. "Just follow my lead. I've got this."

"I think I should mention right about now that I have serious issues with dragons," he whispered, hearing his hushed voice bouncing off the stairwell walls. *I hope nobody hears us.*

"Don't be such a worry-wart," she puffed. Her rapid pace was taking a toll on her. "One of them is Myreen's boyfriend, Kol—at least, I think they're together. Maybe not. It's complicated."

Leif hesitated. "Kol, as in Malkolm *Dracul?* You can't expect me to ride with a Dracul."

"Then ride with his dragon friend," she said, huffing loudly, pausing at the floor that connected all the towers together and catching her breath. "I really don't care. But that will only happen if Myreen can break them out without getting caught."

"Malkolm Dracul is here at Heritage Prep?" Leif could hardly believe what he was hearing. Had she told him all this before? Had Beatrice? His memory wasn't so great.

"Yep, and I'm sure he'll be happy to tell you all about his time here. You guys might even have an epic bonding moment over it, being vampire prisoners and all. But we need to get to Myreen's brother..." She looked at her smartwatch, then continued, "...two minutes ago." She turned around and speed-walked to another stairwell.

"How many people are we breaking out?" he asked, more and more concern building. Back when he'd first been imprisoned, he'd been the only one who'd needed rescue. That had dramatically changed.

"You, Myreen, Ty, Kol, Char, and Piper. Oh, and Rainbow."

"Six of us total," he mumbled. "And your plan is to have four of us fly away on the backs of two dragons?"

"Myreen has her own wings," Kenzie said breathlessly. "Ty is ten and weighs about as much as a toothpick. And Piper *is* a toothpick."

The stairwell. Leif's eyes widened.

Kenzie began climbing. "Why?" Kenzie said, huffing and puffing now. "Why do there have to be so many stairs? Draven lives and breathes technology. Why aren't these all escalators?"

Leif smiled. "Because he believes that his underlings should have to work to climb to the top—in all aspects of life."

Leif could hardly believe they hadn't run into anybody, but it was the middle of the day. Vampires were busy studying or practicing within the darkness the citadel provided them... which reminded him of one massive flaw in her plan.

"Kenzie," he said in a panic. "The sun's out!"

"Yeah," she wheezed. "Bright. Noonday. Sun. It's kind of what makes our escape possible. No vampires can catch us once we're outside. Well, except for Draven, but I have a plan for that."

"I can't daywalk anymore," he said. "Remember?"

Kenzie stopped, drawing in a few breaths. "I forgot about that little detail," she said, and Leif didn't have to see her face to know she was grimacing. "We'll think of something."

"Unless you have sunflower seeds and moonflower petals and roots, how am I getting out of here?"

"The reversal spell was supposed to be temporary. I don't know why that didn't work," Kenzie mumbled. "I dunno. Maybe Myreen can bend the light so it doesn't hit you or something?"

"All the way back to Chicago?"

The black stairs dumped them out into a wide corridor. The black walls were more distanced from each other than the ones that made up Beatrice's tower, which meant this was the tallest tower in the citadel. Draven's tower.

"Kenzie, why are we up here?"

"We're getting Ty," Kenzie replied.

"Ty as in—?" But Leif stopped himself as they approached a corner, and he grabbed Kenzie's arm, nearly dropping Rainbow in the process. She stopped, turning to look at him. He quickly drew his finger to his lips. Hushed voices were coming down the next hallway. Leif drew closer to the corner, putting himself between Kenzie and the others to listen in on the conversation.

"I think Draven's got something big planned."

"Of course he does. He's always got something big planned. I was here when he conquered the citadel thirty or forty years ago. He dreams big, but no dream is too big."

Kenzie tapped Leif's shoulder, and he looked back at her to find her gesturing to him to come close.

He angled his head down so she could reach his ear easily.

"Those are Myreen's guards," she whispered. "We have to get past them. Ty—her brother—is in the room they're guarding."

Leif looked back at Kenzie and mouthed the words *I've got this*. He turned to leave, but she grabbed his arm. She gave him a stern look and mouthed *Be careful*.

Nodding, Leif twisted around the corner, instantly drawing the attention of the other vampires.

"Hey!" one of them shouted. "You're Leif Villers—the traitor. What are you doing up here?"

"I'm a bit... lost," he said, acting as spacey as he remembered being just a day ago. It was a good thing he hadn't bothered to break his shackles yet. "I found this cat... did you know there are cats here? It's a nice cat." He walked over to them, not exactly knowing how this was going to play out.

"Where did you find it?" one of them asked, looking warily at Rainbow.

"Actually, he found me," he said. "I think."

"Those eyes are weird," said another vampire. "Why are they all red?"

"It shouldn't be here. How did it even get in the school?" The vampire on the right reached for Rainbow, who sprang from Leif's bound arms. In less than a second, the cat was latched onto the bald vampire's head, scratching with quick blows, raking skin and flesh. The guard screamed, and the other vampires lunged as the first guard reached up to tear Rainbow off.

But rainbow quickly jumped away and ran down the corridor.

The three unharmed vampires took chase, and as the bald vampire's wounds healed, he gathered himself and went after the cat in a screaming rage.

"That was remarkably easy," Kenzie said, creeping up to Leif.

"I just hope Rainbow will be okay," Leif replied. "If they catch him..."

She placed a kind hand on his shoulder. "Hey, he'll be okay." She moved past him and knocked on the door. "Okay, let's get Ty, then head to the roof."

A few moments passed, then the door opened. Standing before them was a boy—the same boy he'd seen leaving Draven's trophy room on a few occasions.

"Hey Ty," Kenzie said sweetly. "Are you coming with us?"

Ty was the spitting image of his father, and Leif wondered why he'd never made the connection before. He also wondered just how wise it was that they were kidnapping the vampire leader's son.

Ty shrugged. "Yeah, I guess. I was just eating some lunch. Agnus was getting me some hot chocolate. But Myreen told me to go with you."

Kenzie placed a hand on his shoulder. "Thanks for listening. You wanna go and meet her?"

He nodded, then looked at Leif and pointed. "Hey, I know him. He's the vampire who tried to stab my dad in the back."

Kenzie let loose a nervous laugh. "He and your dad have a long history. But Leif has been trying so hard to protect your sister, and that makes him one of our friends."

Ty eyed him for a few more moments, then shrugged again. "Okay. Where are we going?"

Kenzie glanced at her smartwatch. "To the roof. Have you ever been to the roof before?"

Bouncing on his toes, Ty said, "It's one of my favorite places in the citadel."

"Well, we're going to play a game up there," Kenzie said, beaming. "Hide and seek."

Ty's eyes widened. "Ooh, that sounds fun."

It was a partial-truth, and Leif wondered if maybe Kenzie was taking things a bit too far with the boy.

"Let's go," she said, taking Ty's hand. They shut his door, then went back for the stairs, heading down to the level that would allow them roof access.

Leif looked down at his bound arms. The shackles had come in handy, but he probably wouldn't need them anymore. Yanking his wrists away from each other, Leif snapped the metal he'd pretended had been enough to keep him subdued. The device embedded in it sparked, and Leif remembered that it contained a GPS unit. He wouldn't be tracked any more. One by one, he crumpled the clasps and freed his wrists entirely. They clinked to the floor, and Leif reveled in his freedom.

Miraculously, as they bound down the stairs, Rainbow came into view. Leif looked past the cat, expecting to see the vampires hot on the cat's tracks. But there wasn't even a sound. Rainbow must've lost them somehow. The cat jumped up, and Leif caught him gently. Without his shackles, he didn't look like a complete fool holding Rainbow. Then again, he was probably quite the sight. *A Cat and His Vampire* sounded like a great title for a book.

They pressed on, and Ty kept turning and looking at him with his big, blue eyes. At last, the boy asked, "Why do you have a cat?"

Leif chuckled. "I don't know. Maybe Kenzie could help us out on that one?"

"It's *not* story time," Kenzie quipped. "Less talking, more running. We're almost there."

They came to a blank landing, and Leif's brows crumpled.

Kenzie stared at the wall, her hands on her hips.

"It's locked," a voice said from below said. "I think from the outside."

Leif whirled about defensively. "Piper!" he exclaimed. She stepped up the stairs and approached him timidly, shoving her glasses higher on her nose.

"Hey Leif," she said, a pitying look in her eyes. "I heard about what's happened to you. I'm *really* sorry."

Leif stepped the rest of the way to her and wrapped his free arm around her, bringing her into a side-hug while holding Rainbow in the other.

"You have nothing to apologize for," he said. "I'm glad you're coming with us."

Off to the side, Kenzie looked up the stairs nervously. "I hate to break up the happy reunion, but we've got to get through this door."

"It's a special lock," Ty said, stepping forward. He placed his hand on bits of the stone, and a grinding sound came from the faintly-outlined doorway, but it didn't budge. Ty's brows creased. "That's never happened before."

Leif ran a finger along the dark material and discovered the issue.

"The door is welded shut," he said, glancing at Kenzie. He didn't mean for it to be an accusatory gaze, but she took it that way.

"How was I supposed to know that? Who welds a door shut? Why even have a door at all?"

Several footsteps could be heard coming from around the black-walled corner.

"They've found us," Leif hissed.

"We're trapped," Piper chirped, her voice barely audible.

"Why, oh why did I ever get involved with vampires?"

"Get behind me," Leif said, dropping the hissing Rainbow and reaching his arms out protectively. He felt Kenzie place her hands on his sides while placing her head against his shoulder to get a good look at their attackers.

But the guards and the woman who came into view didn't even look at the group assembled there. They walked past as if in a daze. Piper whimpered, and Kenzie's hand clung tighter to Leif's shoulder.

Ty cocked his head. "Agnus?" he said, and everyone's eyes widened.

But the group of five didn't stop or respond, and the woman—Agnus—mumbled something about an elevator. Leif looked at the others, who looked as confused and incredulous as he felt. What was going on?

And then Myreen came into view, along with the Dracul boy and another young woman Leif didn't recognize.

"Myreen!" Kenzie shouted—a little too loudly for Leif's comfort. They weren't away from the vampire school yet, and the zombie-like group that had just passed them had him unnerved. The selkie stepped away from him and waited to meet the others joining them. Ty went running to his sister with his arms extended. It warmed Leif's heart to see their reunion. It was so odd to think that these loving, peaceable people were related to Draven Denholm, lord of all vampires.

"What's going on?" Ty asked Myreen.

Kol met Leif's eyes and nodded his head in acknowledgement. Leif reminded himself that this boy might be related to Aline Dracul, but he was not his ancestor. Nor did he bear her offenses.

Leif was about to say something, but a noise like fingernails on chalkboard—magnified by one hundred—sounded from the door.

"Rainbow!" Piper said. "Leif, your crazy cat is going to draw the attention of every vampire in Heritage Prep!"

Rainbow was crawling *up* the door, his claws poking into the thick metal. With one of his front paws, a single hooked claw was lodged into the welding. A line of sunlight spilled its way into the corridor. Right onto Leif.

"Watch out, Leif!" Kenzie yelled, jumping into him and tackling him to the ground. It was too late. The light had already struck him.

But no pain came.

The scorching of Draven's sunroom was vividly on his mind, but he felt none of that same burning.

Kenzie was still on top of him, and their eyes met.

"Are you okay?" she asked, running a hand along his face, checking for fresh wounds.

He smiled up at her. "It didn't burn me. You were right—it was just a temporary spell." Gratitude for the girl flooded his soul, and he drew her in close for an embrace. "Thank you. Thank you so much, Kenzie."

Kenzie's eyes widened. "Wait, the cancelling spell..."

The loud scraping of Rainbow's claws stopped, and then more sunlight poured in as the door teetered, then fell out, slamming on the roof of the citadel and revealing their exit.

Kenzie got to her feet and held out a hand to Leif. He didn't necessarily need her help, but he gladly accepted it and stood up.

"The gate's open," he said, looking past the others to make sure a stream of vampires wasn't coming. Not a soul in sight. They'd lucked out. Kenzie's plan worked. "Let's get out of here."

Kenzie

Kenzie slipped her bag to the floor and broke away from the group as they began preparing for flight.

"Where are you going?" Myreen asked as she attempted to help Ty climb onto Kol's back.

"Where are *we* going?" Ty asked, stubbornly planting his feet. "When are we gonna get back?"

Leif and Piper were exchanging misgiving glances, and the dragons looked to be in about the same condition. Piper took a step away from Leif as she eyed Rainbow, sitting comfortably in the vampire's arms.

Kenzie laughed at the odd scene. "A little magical cleanup. It should only take a moment. Nobody do anything stupid while I'm gone."

"Okay, but if you're not back in five minutes, I'm coming after you," Myreen said, then turned back to Ty. "Don't you want to fly on the back of a dragon?"

Ty had his hands on his hips. "They're shifters! Shifters killed my mom, in case you forgot."

Kenzie stopped, her hand on the empty doorframe. "If I'm not back in five minutes, go on without me." She didn't wait for a response, stepping over the door as she cast a barrier spell on the open space. The hunk of metal righted itself and sealed under the influence of her magic. Now the others couldn't follow her in, and no one else could get out.

Maybe it was stupid, coming back in, but they'd made a clean getaway. She wanted to make sure their luck held out. Hopefully Myreen would have everyone straightened out by the time Kenzie finished.

"Sweeph an bolladhá, sweeph an bolladhá, camdach, diúltidhá, sweeph an bolladhá." Kenzie repeated the chant a few times, using her hands to direct her magic as far as she could manage. She wanted to make sure the vampires didn't track them here. If the trail ended at the elevator, then they'd have to speculate what happened.

Every little bit helped.

Now for phase two. Kenzie rubbed her hands together, then crouched and placed her palms against the floor on either side of herself. She had no idea if this would work, but it was worth a shot.

"Ta'inthreachá," she said, and the air seemed to charge with electricity around her. Kenzie channeled it through both her hands, then brought them together and back to the floor. She repeated the process again, and then a third time.

Her science was a little spotty, but she hoped the lightning spell would create an electrostatic discharge that would work as an EMP, killing everything electronic within the citadel. Hopefully that would take care of all the vehicles parked in the hangar that might try to take them down.

Kenzie stood and jogged back to the door, but before she could reach it, a hand grabbed her arm, stopping her as it swung her around.

"Adam?" Kenzie's jaw dropped, her heart taking a long pause before it attempted to gallop out of her chest. "What are you doing here?"

"I got a whiff of you before it disappeared." He licked his lips and sucked them in, then let them go with a pop. "I should be asking you the same thing." He leaned in, drawing a deep breath. "Man, you smell so good."

Kenzie gave a nervous laugh, trying to edge closer to the door. If she could just get there and cast the unlock spell, she could have that door open in a jiffy—and Adam would be unable to follow her into the sunlight waiting on the other side.

But maybe Adam caught her movements, because his eyes narrowed. "Kenzie, what are you doing?"

She flashed a nervous smile. "Would you believe me if I told you I've been working on making you a daywalker, too?"

Adam shook his head. "You know I'd love that, but no, I don't believe it." His hand shot past her head and he leaned forward, boxing her in against the wall. "You'd need moonflowers for that spell. And Draven's permission, I assume."

"Maybe. Or maybe I embellished the spell to delay giving Draven his powers."

Adam tsked. "You know, you're kinda cute when you lie."

Kenzie's heart beat an erratic rhythm. "Who says I'm lying?"

Adam leered. "You do. The way your eyes cast to the side, the smoky scent of adrenaline mixing with the fruity brightness of your magic..." He leaned in, taking a deep breath by Kenzie's neck.

Kenzie held still, digging in her mind for a spell that would help. But the ones that were the most effective would take too long to cast, and terror at what Adam might do to her locked her brain as well as her body.

"The way your heart beats faster, your blood singing a siren song."

Kenzie gasped as his tongue licked the spot he'd last bit her, the fang holes fully healed again thanks to Myreen. Kenzie shivered, fear twisting with desire. He'd fed on her enough that she was coming to crave his bite, the surge of good feelings that accompanied a feeding were almost like a high.

"What I don't understand, though, is why. With your magic and my intelligence and vampire powers, we could be unstoppable together. And when you grew old, I'd still be there, waiting for that final bite, waiting to take you with me through eternity. Isn't that what every girl wants? Love that lasts forever?"

Kenzie looked at him with pleading eyes. "No, Adam. I'm not just any girl. And you don't love me, not really."

"I forgave you when you betrayed me the first time. And I took care of you when you came here. You wouldn't have gotten this far at Heritage Prep without me. If that's not love, then I don't know what love is."

"That's the problem. You *don't* know what love is. Not like—" Kenzie stopped herself, not wanting to give anything else away.

Adam's brows furrowed as he stared deep into Kenzie's eyes. "There's someone else, isn't there?"

Kenzie shook her head. "Adam, you have to let me go."

"No," he breathed.

The familiar sting of his teeth was on her neck, and her body pleaded with her to relent. It would be so easy. She'd done it so many times before.

The door jiggled, and then there was banging on it. Someone's voice was shouting, but Kenzie couldn't quite understand, between the muffling of the door and the haze grasping at her mind.

Kenzie wouldn't relent to the venom this time. Not if she could help it.

Her body was beginning to cave to Adam's will. She had to do something. Now "Chovlún sollaís," she said, the first spell that came to mind. A bright light flashed, and Adam staggered back, shielding his face.

"What the—? Bitc—"

"Leich ín dhaermandah," Kenzie threw at him next, though she had no intention of making him forget anything. It seemed no matter how many times she magically wiped his mind, his memories kept coming back. But the spell would stop him long enough to complete another.

Adam stood there, looking a little unsteady, his guylined eyes fogged over as he awaited her instructions. It was a pity his heart wasn't as attractive as his face.

Kenzie shook her head to clear it, then walked slowly toward Adam, her hand outstretched. "Fiáscha na olch. Tóggo boggé na folía. Diúltódha darshada."

Adam backed up until he hit the wall, his whole body pressed against the cool stone, bound by her magic.

"I'm done being your toy. I'm done giving you what you want." She put two fingers to the bite on her neck, still seeping blood. "Leasheth'asa," she said, and the wounds closed. Wiping the remaining blood off her skin, she put her fingers to Adam's mouth. "Enjoy, because that's the last taste of me you'll ever get." He was still too dazed to respond.

"Díghlisál," Kenzie said as she neared the door to the roof, releasing the magic that held it in place. The banging stopped as Ty tumbled in.

Adam groaned from behind her, and she considered finishing off the forget spell. But to be honest, she wanted him to hurt. So she left it open, trusting fate to do what was right. Either Adam would be fine, or he'd have brain damage. Either way, he'd be hurting from what little bit of sunlight could reach him. She could already smell the sizzle of his flesh.

Ty regarded Kenzie with wide eyes.

Myreen stepped in behind him. "Ty, are you—? What the heck?" Myreen sent a worried glance past Kenzie to the vampire stuck to the wall.

Kenzie waved dismissively at him. "Don't mind him." She bent over so she was eye-level with Ty. "Ready to go?"

Ty shook his head. "You're all monsters. Dad!" He took off running down the stairs, faster than Kenzie could even react.

"Ty!" Myreen called, starting after him, but Kenzie caught her around the waist.

There were more footsteps out there than Ty's.

"Come on," Kenzie said. "We have to go. Now!"

"But Ty..." Myreen looked so forlorn, but they didn't have time to deal with it.

Kenzie pulled Myreen into the sunlight just as the first few pale faces came into view. With a flourish of her hand, she cast the sealing spell, and the door fitted itself back into the empty space. She jumped as loud bangs came from behind the door, the metal denting where the vampires attempted to ram it through.

"What happened in there?" Char asked, Piper seated on her back.

Kenzie shook her head. "Wait. Where did Kol go? And Leif?"

Kol swept back up at that moment. "The vampire wanted to run for it. Something about cats not being meant to fly or something."

Kenzie's heart sunk. Did Leif still harbor hate toward her?

He'd been through so much.

Another loud bang sounded, followed by screeching as the lead vampire felt the first fruits of his success—fresh burns from the midday sun.

"Hop on Kol," Myreen urged Kenzie.

Kenzie complied, bringing her bag with her. She only took half a second to admire her friend in harpy form. Myreen's wings were out, her feet talons. Kenzie hadn't even seen her kick off her shoes, but there didn't seem to be any tatters or shreds around. Myreen really was an angel, in her own way. And right now, she was a very sad angel.

"You'll want to find some handholds between my scales," Kol instructed Kenzie. Piper was already hanging on for dear life, her pale skin looking almost sickly—and the ride hadn't even started yet.

"Ready?" Myreen asked, casting a worried glance at the battered door.

Kenzie started to nod when the door finally caved. Kol, Char, and Myreen shot into the air like a bullet, and Kenzie hung onto her dragon as best she could, squeezing her legs and gripping her chosen scales with all her might. Warmth seeped through his flesh and into her. Good. At least that would help with the freezing air, which seemed to get even colder as it whipped past her.

Looking back at the roof of the citadel, Kenzie saw the only other vampire who could followed them. He had his arms crossed and was shaking his head, Ty standing by his side looking angry and betrayed. Kenzie glanced at Myreen, who looked like she might swoop back down. But they all knew it was too dangerous.

A sound erupted from the west and stole their attention—a keening wail wrapped in a monstrous screech that rumbled through Kenzie's body. Her eyes wide, she looked at Myreen.

"What. The. Crap. Was. *That?*"

Myreen shook her head. "I don't know, but I'm not sticking around to find out."

Kenzie nodded.

Draven's laughter floated behind them, sending chills down Kenzie's spine.

She cast another worried glance at Myreen, but her face was forward, all her concentration on flying.

"Let's fall into a line," Char instructed. "I'll lead." Piper's eyes widened, and Kenzie thought she detected a faint chatter.

Kenzie released one hand from Kol for a moment to send some warming magic to Piper, who gave her a grateful smile, her chattering ceasing.

"No, I'll lead," Kol said, swooping to the front.

Kenzie pulled her bookbag more firmly onto her shoulders, then released the latch on her smartwatch and let it fall away, then found her handhold again. The bag held her grimoire, hidden via spell, and so light as a result that the bag felt empty. She wouldn't lose it, if she could help it. That grimoire had come too far for her to lose it again.

Another monstrous cry filled the air, the sound approaching the citadel as they flew away. The sound terrified Kenzie. What new hell awaited them?

Kenzie scanned the ground below, but couldn't see Leif through the foliage—assuming he was below them and not on a different course.

Worry wormed through the fiber of Kenzie's being until the amazement of being in flight—on a dragon, no less—faded into background noise. A shiver ran through her, and she wasn't sure if it was from the whipping wind or from the giant question mark that still seemed to hang over them all.

Juliet

Fear followed Juliet to every secret meeting, but General Dracul's threat turned her into a nervous wreck. Even Nik suggested they cut down on having them. So they did. But they couldn't stop. Not if they wanted to achieve their goal to get Oberon back.

When Juliet was confident everyone was in their rooms for the night, she cracked her door open. She peeked through, then snuck out. She quietly closed the door behind her and tiptoed across the hallway to the supply closet. Again, she looked around to make sure nobody was there, then squeezed into the closet.

With her heart pounding too fast, Juliet leaned against the wall to steady herself. As she tried to regulate her anxiety, she looked around the small room. Most of the usuals were there— Leya and Alessandra, Nik and Brett, though not Jesse this time, as his attempts to stay under the radar had earned him extra training—but Katya was there, too, the kitsune girl Brett often talked about. *Why is Katya here?* Her already hammering heart notched up a beat.

Brett snickered. "Don't look so surprised," he said to Juliet.

"It's okay, Jules," Nik said, giving her a reassuring nod. "She's with us."

"I asked her to help with security, and when she figured out why, she offered to help," Brett said, playing with the corners of the paper he held.

"And in addition to keeping eyes on this place, I'm working on tracking down Oberon's location," Katya volunteered, not bothering to look up from her screen. The light glowed eerily off her face.

"How exactly did she 'figure out' about these meetings?" Juliet asked Nik, trying to steady the tremble in her voice. She went next to him, sliding down the wall until she was seated.

Katya shrugged. "Everyone's talking about it. It was just a good guess."

Juliet leaned toward Nik. "I thought we weren't inviting anyone new with everything going on." Like the general's threat.

Brett shook his head. "What? Nik can bring a chick, but I can't?" he said, but he cut his eyes at Leya.

Juliet really hoped he was joking.

Nik grabbed Juliet's hand and squeezed it. "Brett thinks he's funny, though we all keep telling him he's not."

Brett rolled his eyes and shook his head.

Nik gave her hand another squeeze. "I was about to run to my room to get this map that I took from the General's desk. It could point us in the right direction. I'll be right back, okay?"

Juliet nodded, not trusting her voice.

"Okay, you guys play nice." Nik's stern gaze drilled holes into Brett. "Am I good?" Juliet realized he was directing the question at Katya.

"One sec..." Her hurried tapping continued. Juliet didn't think anyone could type that fast. "Yep. All clear."

Nik nodded, then left.

Juliet would be lying if she said she wasn't nervous to speak with Brett without Nik or Kol there. He was just so cocky and blunt, and it intimidated her more than she liked to admit. Brett must have known. He laughed under his breath a few times, speaking to Katya occasionally, but he didn't say anything more to Juliet. Leya and Alessandra were across the room having their own conversation, and Juliet thought about joining them, but she had no idea what she'd say. So she sat in silence, waiting anxiously for Nik to return.

When the doorknob finally rattled, Juliet let out the breath she was holding. But then there was a knock. Alessandra and Leya let out some startled squeaks. Juliet's eyes bulged, and her hands began to shake.

Nik wouldn't be knocking.

Katya's eyes widened as she stared at the screen, then she phased, seeming to melt into the wall, throwing an apologetic glance at the rest as she and her computer disappeared.

Juliet frantically looked around the closet to see if there was somewhere to hide, but nothing was big enough. And even if they could hide, they were still sitting ducks. She looked over at the others and they mirrored the same panic she felt.

The door opened and in marched Major Peters. "Well, well, what do we have here?" He stared at Juliet with a mocking grin. He didn't even try to hide it. "Let's go. The four of you, follow me."

The one and only silver lining was that Nik wasn't there to get caught with them. He'd just gotten out of one of Dracul's punishments, and didn't need to relive any of it. She only hoped the others knew to keep their mouths shut. Although, the general had a way of making people talk—sometimes with just one look, if rumors were to be believed.

Juliet felt like she was walking the plank as they made their way to the director's office. General Dracul had warned her, and she got caught. He didn't care who her father was, and she had absolutely no leverage.

Juliet's hands shook and it became difficult to breathe. This was not good... especially for the ice she had to keep hidden.

They got to the general's door and Major Peters opened it, revealing a dark room—no one was there. The major entered and turned the lights on, then gestured for them to line up in front of the desk.

"Wait here. I suggest you don't sit down."

Meany. The soldier left, shutting the door behind him.

"What should we—?" Brett started, but Juliet shushed him. Who knew if there was some kind of recording device in there to spy on them? Not to mention she didn't think she had the courage to speak.

The door swung open and Juliet had to force herself to look. It was Malachai. He seemed just as nervous as Juliet, his skin flushed, his posture rigid. He wouldn't be able push much against the director or his position would be at risk, but she hoped her dad's presence would at least help.

"I came as soon as I heard the major had found you all." Malachai gave Juliet's shoulder a squeeze as he stood tall behind her, the rest of the students beside her still rigidly facing forward. "Whatever *any* of you do, *do not* confess to or agree with anything he accuses you of. No matter how scary he might act or sound, none of you are obligated to participate in an interrogation without your parents or lawyers present."

The door opened again, this time delivering the general and

his grinning soldier.

General Dracul looked expectantly at Malachai. "Lieutenant General Quinn. I must admit, I'm not surprised. My only wonder is how you found out so quickly. The only logical answer here is that someone was able to send you the warning."

"I went to check on my daughter and when I didn't find her in her room, I came straight here, sir."

"Or, you knew she was orchestrating these secretive gatherings all along," the general said.

"No, sir. Neither of those statements are factual."

"Ah, I beg to differ. But right now, I have more pressing things to address. I would appreciate it if you took a step back and kept your thoughts to yourself. Technically, you weren't invited to this meeting, but I'll let it slide. I'd want to be present if it were my child getting penalized. Then again, my son wouldn't put himself in a situation like this." With a flick of the general's hand, Malachai took a step back.

"So what I have is a prissy mer, a mousy harpy, a phoenix who has held my son back for years, and another, rather unruly phoenix who I recently sent a warning to. Am I missing something... or some*one*? What about my assistant? Have any of you seen Private Candida tonight?" He looked at them expectantly.

Juliet would never tell, but she wasn't so sure she could count on the others. Thankfully, they stayed silent, no one so much as twitching—which would probably get them in more trouble. Still, Juliet was proud that nobody wanted to rat out Nik.

"I hope you're all being honest. If I find out he knew about this, you won't like what I do to him." General Dracul stared at Juliet, and she had to stop herself from rubbing her arms. "You other three, go to your rooms. You'll report back here first thing tomorrow. Enjoy your last night of freedom." He stroked his chin as he stared down at Juliet.

Brett, Leya, and Alessandra scurried out of the room, throwing Juliet worried glances as they left. They were gone several moments before the general spoke again.

"Do you know what irritates me the most about this situation?" He paused, but she knew not to respond. "The fact that I had the decency to give you a warning. I could've punished you right then and there. But I gave you the benefit of the doubt. Now the joke's on me, and I don't like to be the butt of *any* joke. So here's what's going to happen."

This was it, the moment Juliet was dreading. General Dracul walked around his desk, then leaned against the front.

"Judging by your records and stats, you're more than qualified to receive the same type of reprimand that any of my Privates would receive. So I'm going to give you the same punishment Private Candida had—consider it a gift for your budding relationship."

Malachai stepped forward. "Sir, please."

The general shot her dad a sharp glare. "And why waste time? Let's begin now. Under normal circumstances, I'd let one of my majors get the ball rolling. But this is a special case, isn't it? So I'll do it. Let's go." He led the way out of his office.

Juliet dared to look at her father as the general's ominous presence left the room—she wasn't quite ready to follow. Fear shone through his eyes, and the dread that had been building hit a crescendo. She felt like a prisoner, like she'd just committed a crime and the judge had passed her sentence. She shouldn't feel this way, not in the school that promised to protect her.

"You're not even going to ask me why?" Juliet said at the retreating form of the general. She wanted to sound strong and brave, but her voice came out meek and fragile instead.

General Dracul stopped in his tracks and spun to face her.

"Juliet," Malachai said with a warning in his voice.

The general held out his hand to silence Juliet's father. "No, I would love to hear this. I didn't ask because I don't care, but since Miss Quin thinks it's so important, I'd like to hear what she has to say."

Juliet took a deep breath, but kept her gaze on the floor. "We were attacked, then had our director thrown away like he was garbage. Then you marched in and—"

"Juliet," Malachai tried again.

But the general lifted his hand again. "Continue," he pressed.

Juliet swallowed. This would probably get her in more trouble, but she'd had enough. The words burned in her throat, longing to be free. "Then *you* marched in and expected us to skip the part where we got over our trauma. And you replaced it with combat. It was too much—for *everyone*. Some of us just needed a reprieve. If that's what I'm being punished for, then fine. I'll take it." She was proud of herself, despite the hole she'd dug for herself.

The corners of Lord Dracul's mouth twitched. "You're being punished for disobeying and betraying your director *after* receiving a formal warning. The rest is none of my concern." He spun, motioning for Juliet and her father to join him and the major, who hardly seemed to leave the general's side.

Juliet pulled on her stubborn will to try to convince herself that she'd be okay, despite the fear trying to overtake her. She just hoped he didn't make her do anything with her powers.

They arrived at the Avian Training Room. It was odd seeing it so bright and yet so empty.

General Dracul clapped once, letting it echo through the room. "The others will be joining you at six a.m. sharp, and you four will spend the day doing drills. But you, Miss Quinn, will begin drills in just a moment. Major Peters will stay with you until you complete every single set on this list." Out of nowhere, Dracul flashed a printed paper and handed it to Juliet.

She glanced at the long list, her eyes bulging. "I'll be here all night! How do you expect me to do all this without any rest?"

"Where is that fierce Quinn spirit? It's written all over your record. And you obviously didn't think sleep was very important when you met after hours with your foolish group of *friends*. You'll get it done, I'm certain, one way or another." He gave her a curt sneer, then turned his head to look her father in the eyes.

Juliet hated seeing the general disrespect her father like that. It made her want to loose her fire. She knew she couldn't, but that didn't mean she wasn't at least on the verge of it. If Lord Dracul said anything more, Juliet swore she would explode. But she refused to give him what he wanted: a reaction. So as the general spun on his fancy heels and left, Juliet didn't say a word.

Even though she wanted to scream.

But Major Peters was still there, and he wouldn't let her forget it. "Are you going to stand there all night, or would you like to start now?"

Juliet sniffed, but she wouldn't let her temper get the best of her. More than ever, she wished she had her headphones with her. It would be easier to ignore him with her #GirlBoss playlist blasting in her ears.

Malachai cleared his throat. "Major, my offer still stands. Harm one hair on my daughter's head, and these drills you're feeding her will look like child's play." He sent Juliet an apologetic grimace, but she understood. It wouldn't do for both of them to be exhausted tomorrow, though she wasn't sure how well he'd be able to sleep.

She gave him a firm nod, then looked again at the list in her hands. What would be easiest? Laps. That shouldn't be too bad.

Somehow, they were worse. And they took way longer than she'd expected.

Halfway through the list, she thought she might break down in tears. But she didn't. She *wouldn't*. No matter how much pain she was in, no matter how tired she was, and no matter how numb she felt, she refused to let any of it show.

Dracul wanted to know where the Quinn spirit was? Well, he would get it.

***

Two and a half hours.

That was all the sleep Juliet got before she had to wake up and do it all over again. She thought her limbs would fall off. She barely had the energy to get out of bed. But if she was late, more drills would be added to her list. She was *not* letting that happen.

She dragged herself out of bed early enough to get a small breakfast before she had to see to the rest of her "detention." She even threw her hair up into a high ponytail and put on her best workout clothes on. She might have been tired, sore, and numb, but she wouldn't let them see that.

As she walked into the training room, she nearly laughed at the sight of Major Peters. The bags under his eyes were deep and dark, and it looked like he didn't have enough time to run a comb through his usually gelled-back hair. His uniform was meticulously pressed, but he probably had them ready ahead of time. He stifled a yawn, the whistle nearly falling out of his mouth. She mentally gave herself a pat on the back for at least *looking* like she had it together.

When he caught sight of Juliet, Major Peters squinted his already droopy eyes. She kept her mouth closed as her lips lifted into a grin. Only when she raised her eyebrows did she look away. She gave a nod to her fellow detainees and lunged into a stretch.

Major Peters blew his whistle and pointed to the door, his way of telling them that their first order of business was going to be laps around the Dome. Lucky for her, it was exactly what she wanted to start with.

She gave Major Peters one last look before she took the lead. She hoped the rest of the day would be exactly like that—silent and right to the drill.

By the looks of it, she wasn't the only one who couldn't wait for the day to be over. *Good luck Major Peters.*

Oberon

Oberon stretched his tired wings, then tucked them close to his body. His heart pounded in his chest like a racing drum. His claws gripped the cold snow beneath him, and nearby, Ren was catching his breath. The kitsune shifted back to human form, his black hair long and unkempt. Oberon smiled. His Japanese-American friend was in dire need of a haircut.

Pulling the large bag off his shoulders, Ren withdrew his personal dehumidifier and turned on the heat.

Oberon shifted to his human form, too, stepping close to the dehumidifier. It wasn't the best method of survival in the freezing Canadian Rockies, but it was the most economical.

"Nothing?" Ren asked, running a hand through his messy hair. It shot in multiple directions, reminding Oberon of some random anime character.

Oberon shook his head, then looked around at the un-

393

touched snow-covered surroundings. "Nothing. Not even the slightest scent on the wind."

Ren removed a tablet from his bag, powering it on and accessing a map that had altogether too many red *X*'s on it. Ren made another criss-cross on the name *Mount Ovington*.

"We've been at this for over two weeks, Oberon," Ren said. "We've checked every mountain between Mount Joffre and here. I'm calling it. Either Delphine's succeeded in executing the world's cruelest practical joke, or you've forgotten what your own kind smell like."

Ren was still looking at the tablet while Oberon scooped up a handful of snow and packed it together. After the snowball had been formed, Oberon threw it with perfect accuracy, smacking Ren right in the cheek.

"Ow!" cried Ren, nearly dropping the tablet in the snow. With a free hand, he rubbed the snow away, revealing a red welt surrounding his cheekbone. "What was that for?"

"Delphine's never wrong," Oberon said nonchalantly. Then, taking on a darker tone, he said, "I don't know how it works for kitsunes, but I could never forget the scent of gryphons."

Ren looked like he was about to reply, but must've thought better of it and went back to looking at the map on his tablet. "Maybe we went the wrong way," he said, zooming out and scrolling down. Oberon moved behind the kitsune to get a good view of the map. "There are... just so many mountains up here. We're not even in Alberta anymore. This part of the Rocky Mountains is considered British Columbia. And we've angled our way northwest, stopping at each peak. But our search hasn't included these few mountains just south of Mount Joffre."

"High winds," Oberon marveled. "We've probably set a record on reaching each of these peaks in such a short amount of time."

Ren laughed. "Between how long my hair is getting, as well as your beard, we'll look like regular mountain men before too long."

Oberon found himself stroking at his brown beard as his friend spoke. Based on what was showing on the map, they needed to make a decision.

"We can keep traveling northwest," Ren said, dragging his finger up and circling a different area. "The Northern Rocky Mountains."

Zooming out, Oberon marveled. "That's about halfway between where we started looking and Whitehorse. Mount Logan. My gut tells me that heading that way is taking us away from Delphine's lead."

Ren nodded. "I'm exhausted. I'm sure you're exhausted. I'm sure gryphons are more cut out for mountain living than kitsunes. And the concept of backtracking..."

"You're right," Oberon said, reaching his chilled fingertips closer to the warmth of the dehumidifier. "Ren, my friend, I thank you for your devotion, but you don't belong in the mountains." And they were running low on supplies. One of them would have to head for a city soon, anyway.

Ren snorted. "What, after all we've been through, you're just going to send me away?"

Oberon placed a hand on his friend's shoulder. "I'm going to send you back to Calgary to rest."

"And what? You're going to fly all the way down to Mount Joffre in one go? That trip has taken us *weeks*."

Oberon pointed up with a single finger. "The wind will obey my command. Up there, I'll summon a current so strong that it'll literally carry me down the mountain range faster than an airplane."

Ren started laughing, softly at first, growing steadily louder.

"What?" Oberon said, standing awkwardly, wondering if

he'd missed a joke. "You don't think I can do it?"

Ren wiped at his damp eyes—he was laughing that hard. Once he managed to sputter out the last few chuckles, he said, "Oh, I know you can do it. What's hilarious is that you think I'd miss the opportunity to be a part of it."

One corner of Oberon's mouth raised, forming a half-smile. "Last time I checked, kitsunes didn't have wings. And as awesome as your tail-spinning can be, I'd love to see you try to helicopter yourself into the air."

"*I'm* not going to fly, buddy," Ren said, pointing to himself. He jabbed a finger into Oberon's chest. "You are. And you're going to carry me."

"Ho!" Oberon said with mock-surprise. "Is that so? A fine lot we'll look." He jabbed his finger back into the sky, staring up with fake-wonder. "*Look mommy, a bird and a fox are hugging in the air!*"

Ren straightened his stance and tugged at the base of his smart shirt. "A magical moment for anybody to witness, to be sure."

It wasn't a bad idea.

"So, how long will it take you to kick up that windstorm?" Ren asked.

A broad grin crept along Oberon's face. He closed his eyes and inhaled, tapping into his gryphon powers. He knew his eyes were glowing purple at this point, hidden beneath his eyelids.

A sudden, brisk wind gusted through the air, blowing his hair to the side. He squinted at Ren, who was madly packing up the dehumidifier. Once he had the bag slung over his back, red fur began to sprout along his body, and in no time at all, Ren was standing in kitsune form.

Oberon followed suit, sprouting his brown feathers while his nose and mouth formed into a beak.

Ren stood on his back legs and held his front paws out. "Okay, Obie, my sweet," he said, batting his fox eyes. "Take me for a ride."

Oberon pushed off the ground and flung his wings to the side, catching the current and flapping mightily. He zipped ahead, then angled back, fighting against the wind he'd summoned, climbing high. The goal was to cause Ren to think he was being abandoned on an inhospitable Canadian mountain in the middle of winter.

After reaching a high altitude, Oberon's piercing eyes spotted the kitsune trying to shield his eyes from the increasing wind. And Oberon went into a breakneck, speeding dive. Before crashing into the snow-capped mountain, he swung his wings out, giving him just enough of an angle to grab Ren with his claws.

The strangest noise erupted from the kitsune upon impact. It was high-pitched, like the sound of a microphone too close to the speaker screaming with feedback. It was less electronic though, and more like a wounded animal.

"That's for calling me Obie," Oberon said, catching the wind currents with his wings and following the diagonal run of the Rocky Mountains.

"You know," Ren said, his voice nearly stripped away by the air. "I thought the wind was going to do it, but nope. It was you. *You* blew me away."

Oberon released a shrill call as he flew faster than he'd ever gone before. If Ren wanted to be blown away, he'd give the kitsune an experience he wouldn't forget.

***

The mountains passed quickly below, like an old film strip spinning still pictures.

The best part was that it didn't take long for Ren to pass

out. Oberon assumed it was due to a mixture of velocity and altitude. But the quietness provided by the kitsune's unconsciousness was welcome. Ren had been more sarcastic as of late, and that was due to their so-far unsuccessful journey through the Rockies. At least he was getting some rest.

"Foxes weren't meant to fly," Oberon muttered, slowing the wind down as he passed over Mount Joffre. The familiar peak brought his attention back to Delphine. He'd been out of cellphone range—and therefore out of contact with her—for a while. He had no idea what was going on with the school, as well as Myreen's status.

Myreen. Was she still alive? Had she been rescued? If not, what kind of torture was she enduring at Draven's hands? What evil purposes was he using her for?

A scent on the air halted his thinking. A familiar scent that shocked his system so much, he nearly let go of Ren.

It smelled almost identical to Serilda. It was a variation, but extremely similar.

Oberon's heart thudded against his chest, and he looked around to gain his bearings. His wings had moved him farther south as his mind was reeling. He wasn't quite sure where he was.

"Mount Lancaster," Ren mumbled beneath him, as if reading his mind. Oberon barely heard him, but was grateful his friend was coming around to navigate. "We're approaching Mount Lancaster."

"Sleep well?" Oberon asked.

"I think so, yes," replied Ren. "How long was I out?"

"That doesn't matter," Oberon said quickly. "What does matter is that I smell them, Ren! The scent of gryphons is in the air!"

Ren sniffed a few times. "Are you sure? All I smell is... you. By my ninth tail, Oberon, you need a bath."

Oberon laughed. "Trust me, you don't smell so great yourself."

"I'm offended," Ren said. "Kitsunes have a natural internal cleansing process that circulates itself constantly. We can never put off a stink."

"Really?" said Oberon. "I never knew that about kitsunes."

"That's because it's not true," Ren said, nudging Oberon in the ribs. "But I had you going for a few seconds, didn't I?"

"You know, I could still drop you into the snow below like a cookie in milk."

"But you won't," said Ren.

"How do you know that?" Oberon asked with a snort.

"Because you never dunk your cookies in milk. You're lactose intolerant. Really, if you're going to use analogies, you should at least make them realistic. By the way, you just passed Mount Lancaster."

"That's because they're not there," Oberon said. The scent was getting stronger, and he was determined to follow his nose to wherever it led.

And then his rapid heartbeat stopped entirely, as if somebody had a remote and had pushed the *pause* button. With his eagle eyes, he saw the outline of three gryphons up ahead. Cocking his head to the side, he observed them as he slowed his flying. The wind had calmed, no longer urged on by his powers.

"What's up?" Ren asked.

"I see them," he replied breathlessly. "Up ahead."

The larger of the three had a solid body entirely wrapped in white feathers, just as Seri did. The other two were golden brown—a lighter shade of Oberon's. The smallest was apparently new to flying—he or she was flapping in an awkward way, completely out of sync.

"All my life, I've wondered if I was truly the last gryphon

alive," he said distantly, unable to keep his eyes off his flying kin ahead. "I'm not alone."

"I see them!" Ren said. "There's three?"

"Yep. And we're about to meet them." Letting loose a call, he gave it his all. This was a momentous occasion—one of the most important in Oberon's life.

The three stopped whatever aerial exercises they were doing and looked his way. After a few moments, the two golden-brown gryphons flew down, toward the snowy mountains. The large white gryphon's wings flapped hard, and Oberon saw that in moments, they'd reach each other. The other gryphon released a piercing call in return, and Oberon didn't know his kin well enough to tell whether it was a welcome or a warning. He erred on the side of a welcome.

Swinging his wings out like two parachutes, Oberon caught the draft and slowed his momentum, descending ever so slightly.

The other gryphon drew near, slowing down as well.

"A gryphon I don't recognize," the white shifter yelled. "Identify yourself and your purpose."

Only a few feet separated them now. Oberon detected no malice in the other bird's eyes and tone, but cautious curiosity.

"My name is Oberon Rex, and I have come seeking my kin rumored to be in the mountains of Canada."

"Rumored?" the other gryphon said. Of course he'd feel concern about such a rumor. Gryphons had been hunted down and killed throughout the centuries. Rumors of gryphons rarely ended well.

"Forgive me. My words were inaccurate." Oberon hesitated, wondering just how much information he should give up. "A close friend of mine is a seer, and she had a vision of a flock of gryphons up here. I've been searching for you for more than two weeks."

The other gryphon mulled Oberon's information over for a bit, then said, "Does anybody else know of such a rumor?" He looked down where the other gryphons had landed. "My family and I have had to run from enemies before. We're only getting settled here—to uproot ourselves again is something we don't want to have to do."

"If anybody else knows about your location, it's not because of us," Oberon said. The other gryphon dropped his gaze down to Ren.

"What is that?" the gryphon asked. "Some feral pet you keep?"

"I beg your pardon?" Ren said incredulously. "Did you say feral? Dear noble creature, my name is Ren Suzuki, and I happen to be a Master Tinkerer."

The gryphon eyed him with interest. "I don't know what that means. But I'm unfamiliar with most other shifters and their... titles."

"I'm a kitsune," Ren said. "And as for my *title,* it means I'm extremely savvy with technology. Savvy?"

"Forgive my friend," Oberon said, squeezing Ren a little tighter. "He can be a bit socially awkward at times. May I ask your name?"

The other gryphon paused for a moment before replying. "Perhaps it would be better if you came down and met the entire family."

"I'd love that," said Oberon.

"Follow me." The gryphon tucked his wings and dove. Oberon did the same, although he wasn't quite as graceful while holding the additional weight that was Ren.

The air upon his feathers brought added joy as he realized he was flying with another gryphon again. As they drew nearer to the mountains below, Oberon's ears popped—at least, that's what he initially thought. But at the same time, suddenly three log cabins, with chimneys puffing smoke, appeared below him. They hadn't been there before. Oberon would've seen them with his enhanced eyes, no problem. Did these gryphons have some type of cloaking technology? That would also mean that they were somewhat tech *savvy*.

The white gryphon landed, and Oberon slowed his descent, gently placing Ren between the three houses. To the side, there was another smaller wooden structure that Oberon figured must be an outhouse or something.

"Welcome," the gryphon said, "to our home. We call it the Sanctum."

The door of the smaller building opened, and a woman bundled in sky-blue winter gear came out. A girl in a lavender coat and royal purple snow pants followed close behind.

"Oberon Rex," the gryphon said, still in his feathered form. "This is my life-mate, Gwendolyn. Behind her is our daughter, who has just recently come of age, Juniper."

"June," the girl said. "I go by June."

"Like a tree in the wild," the white gryphon started, "my daughter is a bit stubborn. Her name is quite fitting."

"But we wouldn't have her any other way," Gwendolyn said, placing a hand on her husband's feathered side.

Oberon shifted back to human form, and both Gwendolyn and June covered their eyes.

"That's what the shifting room is for!" June said, pointing her free hand to the place she'd just come from.

"Fascinating," the white gryphon said, eyeing Oberon with one of his big blue eyes. "Clothing that doesn't tear when shifting? How is that possible?"

"A product of my tinkering," Ren said. He'd also shifted

back, hands on his hips and chest puffed out. "But smart clothing does much more than let you shift back and forth without ruining your wardrobe. It regulates body temperature and—"

"That's quite enough for now, Ren," Oberon said. He didn't come all this way to have Ren give a lecture on how his inventions worked. "Why don't you get the dehumidifier running again. It's a bit cold out here, even with this *temperature regulator.*" Turning his attention back to the gryphon, he said, "It's been a pleasure meeting your wife and daughter. May I ask for your name?"

The white gryphon bowed. "Of course. My name is Tobias. Tobias Vogel."

Vogel.

It was as if Oberon had been slapped in the face. He found it hard to breathe as his mind reeled. A wave of lightheadedness hit him, and he slouched over, placing his hands on his exposed knees.

Gwendolyn was at his side in moments, placing supporting hands under his arm.

"Are you alright?" she asked. "You went as pale as Tobias's feathers."

"V– Vogel," Oberon stammered "Your last name is Vogel?" He had to verify, just in case he'd heard Tobias wrong.

"Yes," the gryphon replied. "Are you familiar with that name?"

Oberon looked at Tobias. "Do you have any relation to a Serilda Vogel?"

The gryphon's expression was impossible to decipher. Time seemed to slow down. Oberon bit his lip.

At last, Tobias spoke. "Serilda was my sister."

CHAPTER 41

Kenzie

The journey was long and exhausting. Even with all their speed, it took all day to get from Washington back to Chicago. Kenzie had looked on with wonder for a while, but soon the rolling hills and passing forests all started looking the same. And they had to stop in the middle for a break. Kenzie and Myreen used their abilities to help ease the aches of travel, but by the time they reached the outskirts of Chicago, everyone was beat.

Kol wanted to go further into the city to land, saying that the cover of night would keep them concealed, but Char forbade it. Apparently the chick had some authority, because Kol didn't fight her on it. Or maybe the exhaustion was enough to persuade him to ride the L.

Leif was able to run into town ahead of them, grabbing funds for their travel through the city and some trench coats for Kol and Char, to help keep their disheveled appearances concealed.

The evening lighting didn't hurt in that respect, either.

And meanwhile, Rainbow had taken to himself again, escaping into the streets of Chicago when he tired of riding in Leif's arms. Kenzie asked Leif about it, but he assured her the cat would be fine. If he had taken care himself, tracking Leif across the country and surviving in the citadel, then certainly he could handle himself in Chicago. Kenzie hoped Leif was right. No one needed a vampire cat on the rampage right now.

Everyone agreed the best thing to do was to head straight to the Dome. It wasn't going to be easy, convincing staff to let in their rag-tag group, but there wasn't anywhere else safe for them.

A vampire, a selkie, and a human walk into a school for shifters... There had to be a punchline in there somewhere. She just hoped security found it entertaining. *Right.*

And with Oberon out of the picture, Kenzie wasn't sure *what* they were walking into. From the little time they'd had to speculate, she learned that Kol's father was in charge of the school now. Basic prognosis: not good. But there was nowhere else to go.

So with weary bodies and heavy hearts, they made it to the secret platform. Kenzie had to use her magic on the door, since no one had a keycard on them. The shifter train sped through the tunnel, the occupants quiet and thoughtful.

Kenzie turned to watch out the glass-covered tunnel. Lights from within the Dome shone through the dark water, beckoning them closer, promising warmth and safety. Kenzie hoped those promises were true. She needed time.

Her actions while at Heritage Prep weighed on her as heavily as if the lake had come crashing on their heads. What she'd done—what she'd *had* to do—was beyond words. She hadn't given herself space to even think about it, but in the icy silence that accompanied their flight, and now approaching the one place she wanted to be more than anywhere else in the world, those memories assaulted her with vigor. And it wasn't like she could rely on Adam's venom to wash them away.

Not that she wanted to be in biting distance of that leech.

Still.

The Dome was lost from view as they rounded the final bend, and Kenzie straightened in her seat, pulling the strap on her seemingly empty bag higher on her shoulder. This was it. This was the moment of truth.

This was—

"Freeze!"

The train had come to a stop, the doors hissing open, but nobody moved. Several security personnel—though they looked more hardened and organized than the ones Kenzie had run into last time—stood outside the doors, weapons drawn, faces grim.

Kenzie's eyes widened as she realized who their gazes were trained on. *Leif.*

Kenzie stepped in front of him, realizing too late that probably wasn't the smartest move. She was a hated selkie, after all. What would prevent them from shooting her, too? Two birds, and all that.

But Myreen stepped in front of Kenzie a moment later. Kol tensed like he was about to do the same, but Myreen threw out an arm to signal him to stop, and Kol stilled on the edge of his seat, looking tense.

"Put your guns down," Myreen said, her voice carrying authority despite the weariness that seeped through the edges.

The guards stared at her for a long moment. "But you have a vampire with you."

"And a selkie and a human. Yes. But we're all on the same

side, here. So put your guns down. Don't make me use my siren voice on you."

The guards exchanged a look, then slowly lowered their guns.

"General Dracul has been alerted to your presence," the same guard said, running a hand over his short-cropped hair.

In fact, they all wore about the same haircut. *What's going on around here?*

The guards escorted them in, still eying Leif warily, when the leader stopped, holding up a hand. "What do we do with the bloodsucker?"

"Don't call him that," Kenzie huffed, folding her arms.

Leif shrugged. "I don't need much. A room with a piano would be my first choice, but other than that, I don't require more than a space to exist in. Preferably in peace."

"Damn creepy," muttered another guard, and Kenzie bristled. "How did he get past the copper, anyway?"

Kenzie thought about volunteering her involvement in Leif's copper immunity, but another guard turned to her, his eyes narrowed.

"You're that selkie that made Draven a daywalker."

It wasn't a question, so Kenzie held her tongue. She didn't really trust her voice at the moment, either.

"We all made sacrifices to be here, soldiers," Char said. "We're hungry and weary. We can answer all your questions once we've had some time to recover."

"Of course," the leader said, though the faces of all the guards remained tight and their eyes alert. "Does anyone need medical attention?" The group began walking again, this time a little more slowly.

Myreen looked the group over. "It might be good to have Ms. Heather check everyone. I used my harpy powers and Kenzie used her magic to heal them all the best we could, but I wouldn't mind getting a second opinion."

"I'm fine," Kol said.

Char nodded. "Yeah. I think I'd rather take a shower than get probed by the school nurse."

"How does everyone else feel?" Myreen asked.

"Some food and a bed would be divine," Piper said.

Kenzie shrugged. "Whatever." She was too numb with amazement to care what they did. There were shifters everywhere, though none of them students—probably due to the late hour. Dragons climbed the vaulted ceilings, while weres of every stripe stood in mid-howls and growls. Mermaids propped up doorways, gryphons stood sentinel, and phoenixes blazed in frozen pyres. It was majestic and unsettling in every way.

A mao caught her eye and Kenzie reached out to touch it, but a sharp look from one of the guards made her pull her hand back.

And then there was a bleary-eyed student coming down the stairs, but one wide-eyed look at the group and they turned around.

The lead guard scowled. "Great. Let's get the bloodsucker somewhere secure before we start a riot."

Kenzie rolled her eyes, but Leif still seemed unphased. He was a better man than she could ever hope to have. And in that moment, something clicked inside of her. She loved Leif with every fiber of her being, but maybe not in the way she thought. Sure, she'd still like to feel those perfect lips against hers, if only to make her determination final, but she didn't imagine it would ignite her. Not really. Not like...

"Jensen and Hanks, take him to the old Tinkerer's office." The lead officer pointed to two of the guards and then to Leif.

Jensen and Hanks nodded and flanked Leif, leading him away from the group. Kenzie hoped it was really to the safety of an empty office and not somewhere more sinister. Did the Dome have a dungeon? Kenzie shook her head. This wasn't Heritage Prep. Hopefully the similarities ended at the word "school."

Char and Kol trudged up the stairs, and Myreen and Piper began walking another direction. Kenzie followed Myreen, not knowing where else to go. The lead guard eyed them, then turned back toward the entrance.

This was it. Kenzie was really here.

And suddenly she felt about three inches tall.

After everything she'd done, did she really deserve to be in these halls? She was here now, after all her striving and begging, but she felt like an imposter, an outsider. She'd made the most deadly vampire even more unstoppable. She'd let Adam feed off her, even enjoying it on some sick level. She was the scum of the earth.

She almost turned back, almost insisted on walking out and never coming back. But she was hungry and tired and just wanted to be done for the day.

Myreen led them into the kitchen, opening the huge double-door refrigerator and rummaging through the contents while Kenzie and Piper seated themselves at the counter.

"Need help?" Kenzie asked, and Piper nodded.

Myreen shook her head. "Nah. You two just sit tight. Ooh, score."

She pulled out some trays of food, one with a variety of fruit, one with roasted chicken, and one with mashed potatoes. The girls all made themselves plates, then sat quietly eating their food. No one bothered to warm anything up.

Kenzie only finished about half the plate before she pushed it away, fatigue tugging at her lids. But she needed a moment to give Gram a magical ring and let her know they were back.

Maybe a quick call to Wes, too. Maybe.

Myreen pushed the plate back toward Kenzie. "You should finish."

"Tomorrow." Kenzie gave Myreen a weary smile. "Any chance I can get a moment to make some calls? It's not that I'm trying to get away from everyone, it's just..."

"You need a moment to yourself. I get it." Myreen nodded, as did Piper.

"Yeah," Kenzie said, then stifled a yawn. "I should probably call Gram, too."

"You have your phone?" Myreen asked.

Kenzie snorted. "Nope. And I tossed the smartwatch as soon as we left the citadel. But selkies have their ways." She gave the girls a sly look.

Piper cracked a smile, and Myreen laughed.

"Okay. I'll take care of it. You two sit tight. Kenzie, behave yourself." Myreen left as Kenzie saluted her.

The girls sat and scraped at the contents of their plates, the air heavy once more.

"What do you have in that bag, anyway?" Piper asked, pointing to the backpack still firmly slung over Kenzie's shoulders. "You haven't taken it off once since leaving Heritage Prep, but it looks empty."

"Magic," Kenzie said, smiling.

"Really?" Piper pushed her glasses up her nose. How the girl managed to keep them on the whole flight here, Kenzie had no idea.

"In a way, yes."

"Can you show me?"

Kenzie shook her head. "If I did, I'd have to kill you. Or send you back to Heritage Prep." She smiled, but as soon as the words left her mouth, she wished she hadn't said them.

Piper stared at her half-eaten food, then sighed and put her fork down. "How long do you think we'll be safe down here?"

Kenzie shrugged. "Draven will come for us sooner or later. Probably sooner."

"Definitely sooner," Myreen said as she came back in. "He has my blood now. I overheard him telling..."—she cut her gaze at Kenzie for a moment—"saying that he took my blood without my knowledge. He'll be a hybrid before we know it."

Kenzie's shoulders sagged. "That sucks."

Myreen shrugged. "We'll figure it out later. You two can stay in the avian wing with me and Juliet. They've got some empty rooms up there."

"Empty?" Kenzie asked, lifting a brow.

"Yeah. I don't know the story, but if *Lord Dracul* is any bit as accommodating as I remember, they probably left."

"That doesn't sound encouraging," Piper said.

"I'm sure shifters at their worst are still better than Draven at his best," Kenzie said, giving her best smirk.

Myreen didn't deny it, but she didn't look entirely convinced, either. Kenzie wondered what Myreen could've gone through at the hands of *Lord Dracul* to make her feel that way.

"Are you two done?" Myreen asked, casting a worried glance at the half-eaten plates.

Piper nodded. "Yeah, I could use some sleep."

Kenzie raised her hand. "I am. Any way I can wrap this up for later? I hate to waste food." She turned to Piper. "You want your leftovers?"

Piper shook her head.

"More for me." Kenzie combined and wrapped up hers and Piper's food while Myreen and Piper put everything away, leaving the kitchen like they'd found it.

The three trudged up the stairs to the avian common room.

The dim lighting and lack of movement was kind of eerie. Kenzie wondered how things would look in the morning—if she woke up in time to see. Part of her was convinced that once she hit the sack, she'd be there for days.

"This room's mine," Myreen said, pointing at a door. "And the one next to it is Juliet's. Assuming she's still here." She added the last part with a low voice. Kenzie wanted to go check on Juliet immediately, but decided it could wait.

"You two are in these two rooms," Myreen said, indicating the doors they'd come to stand in front of. "Take your pick. Bathrooms are down the hall," she said, and Kenzie looked where she was pointing to see a sign. "And you've already been to the kitchen, though technically it's after hours and students are supposed to be in their bedrooms."

"Good thing we're not students," Piper said, offering a half-hearted smile.

Kenzie snorted. *Yet.* But there was always a chance it wouldn't happen, if the shifters hated her enough for what she'd done.

"Goodnight," Kenzie said when no one moved. Then she headed for one of the doors Myreen had indicated, sending one last glance at Myreen and Piper, who were heading for their own rooms.

The bedroom she stepped into was simple and utilitarian, but it definitely had a lighter feel than the rooms at Heritage Prep. For one, the walls weren't black. But there was something else in the simplicity of it all, a blank slate waiting to be filled with art and knowledge and life.

Kenzie stared at those walls for several moments before she slung the bag off her shoulder and dropped it on the floor. There were some simple outfits in the closet, and Kenzie selected one. As she was putting it on, she muttered the magical words of the contact spell, focusing her mind on Gram.

"Gram? Are you there?"

There was some grunting, and Kenzie had the faint feeling of confusion.

"Gram. It's me, Kenzie."

"Kenzie?"

Kenzie smiled, imagining Gram fumbling for the lamp at her bedside. "Yeah. It's me."

"I was wondering when you'd call. I'm sorry I fell asleep."

"Pfft. No worries. It's late. I just wanted to let you know we reached the shifter school."

"Everyone make it out okay?"

"Mostly. Myreen has a little brother at Heritage Prep she wanted to bring with us. Apparently, he didn't feel the same way."

"Oh, I'm sorry to hear that. Are you on your way home?"

"Not tonight. They've got us set up at the school with rooms for now." *And hopefully for the foreseeable future.* "I'll let you know more when I do."

"Okay. Glad you're back safe and sound."

Mostly. Kenzie wanted to dump every deplorable thing that had been eating at her, but she was yawning again, her eyes barely able to stay open. Still, she did have one more question.

"How's Wes?"

Gram laughed. *"Fine, last we saw him. He's a good kid. He's gonna be just fine."*

"Cool." Kind of. She wanted more, but Gram didn't hold the answers she was looking for. "M'kay. I'm gonna hit the sack. I'm beat."

"Okay. Sleep well, Kitten."

Kenzie snuggled into bed, the crisp blankets cradling her, the fluffy pillow like a cloud beneath her head.

"Kenzie?"

Kenzie's eyes shot open, the haze of sleep still clinging to the edges of her vision. "Yeah?"

"The grimoire... you still have it, right?"

Kenzie smiled. "Yes Gram. Safe and sound."

"Good. Now goodnight."

"'Night Gram."

Kenzie let the connection drop and closed her eyes, sleep quickly taking her.

Everything would be better tomorrow. She could feel it in her bones.

Kol

The enormity of the events from the past several weeks pressed into Kol's bare shoulders with the weight of the snowy mountains he wished he could escape to.

He sat on the edge of his bed. He was finally back at the Dome, finally safe within its walls, and finally showered. He counted the beats of his pulse. The steady rhythm soothed him. Counting and numbers. Concrete facts and truths always soothed him.

Someone knocked.

"Come in," he said, not bothering to pull his shirt over his head just yet. He was decent in his new smart clothing and jeans.

A clean-faced Char entered hesitantly. Her blonde hair was pulled into a tight bun at the back of her head, her military uniform pressed and tidy. If not for the haunted look in her eyes, she could've been the same Char who appeared in the sim a little more than three weeks ago.

"Hey," she said, pushing the door slowly closed until it clicked, then folded her hands in front of her. "How are you holding up?"

Kol answered with a bitter smile. "We could've died in there, Char," he said, but was glad to see she wasn't completely broken. There were times in that cell he thought she might be.

"I know," she said softly, then moved to sit next to him on the bed.

"Harpy magic is pretty thorough," Kol said, gesturing to his shoulder.

She glanced at the skin, unblemished and smooth. Not just healed, but as if the wounds from having scales ripped from it never happened.

Harpy magic didn't replace scales, though. In dragon form, both he and Char would forever have weak spots in their armor, on Kol's left side and Char's right. Fortunately, the larger weak spot on Kol—his shoulder, where two were taken—didn't house anything vital.

"I almost wish she'd left a scar," he said, shrugging. "You know, a reminder?"

"I know a skilled naga tattoo artist," Char said. "I know a lot of officers who have her immortalize their former wounds. She mixes the ink with some of her venom. Not enough to inebriate, but harpies can't always help with the mental scars. Touching a tattoo mixed with naga venom eases the PTSD."

"Are you?" he asked, pointing at her side.

She nodded. "I can give you her number."

"Please." He touched his shoulder. He might've imagined it, but the pressure of his fingertips seemed to help already, even though there wasn't a tattoo yet.

A handful of breaths passed.

Then Char asked, "Have you seen her? Since we've been back?"

Kol pulled his t-shirt over his head to hide the frown. "Not yet."

She patted his knee with her hand—it was friendly gesture. "I'm sure you will."

But they both knew she wouldn't. The curse was effective.

"C'mon," Char said, rising from the bed. "Let's go get some food."

Kol's stomach rumbled in response and he stood to follow her out the door.

***

With plates piled high with various cuts of meat—the kitchen staff prepared several dragon favorites when Kol and Char returned—Kol and Char found a table toward the back of the dining hall. They muttered hellos to the various shifters who greeted them, nodding their heads toward them. The students all looked morose and Kol wondered if it was because they knew he and Char had been tortured at the hands of Draven and didn't know how else to react. It was different than the way they used to treat him like royalty, but it still wasn't preferable.

But when he finally opened his eyes to the other students, the ones who didn't even seem to notice his and Char's presence, they *all* had that look.

Depression. Exhaustion. Beaten down.

More than a few even looked like they had literally been *beaten down*, because they were sporting black eyes and split lips.

"What's happened here?" Char whispered, noticing the same strange behavior.

The familiar blond surfer-cut and swagger—with maybe a little less swagger—walked toward their table. Kol rose to clasp the hand of his friend, who then uncharacteristically pulled him into a hug.

"Thought you were a goner, man," Brett said, snatching a piece of bacon from Kol's plate when they'd seated again. "That video Draven broadcasted..." He trailed off, eyes widened, and he let out a low whistle.

The corner of Kol's lips rose. He recognized Brett's deflecting. But his friend wasn't wrong, and the smile dropped again. Kol was grateful Draven hadn't broadcasted everything.

Brett and Char exchanged pleasantries while Kol downed half a plate of brisket. When Nik and Juliet joined them with identical expressions of fatigue and matching circles around their eyes, Kol worried something was seriously wrong. He didn't know Juliet as well, but Brett had always been better at hiding stress than Nik.

Kol drank half a glass of water, then leaned forward, keeping his tone low. "What is going on?" he asked.

Juliet averted her eyes and Nik stared at the table, suddenly silent. Brett looked at the pair of them, then rolled his eyes.

"Your dad is quite the drill sergeant," Brett said. The words sounded joking, but his tone was serious. "The general, *Lord Dracul*, has turned the school into a military training zone."

Nik shot Brett a look.

"What?" Brett asked, shrugging. "He should know."

"What do you mean, *a military training zone?*" Kol asked, his eyebrows knit.

Nik sighed. "Offensive classes, increased training, mandatory sim exercises."

"And he's taken away all of the fun classes," Juliet added, using her hands to illustrate. "Art, music, anything but military history and math... *gone!* Plus a few new winners, like tactical training. Ugh."

"People are getting hurt," Nik said. "Kids are fainting from exhaustion. Miss Heather and the harpies in the medical wing are being overworked just trying to keep the students standing."

"That's... not right," Kol said, no other words accessing themselves.

"He wants us to be ready for the imminent attack," Nik said, as if it was an excuse.

Kol's newly-revived fire churned at his core, overflowing until it rushed through his limbs. He clenched his fists to avoid accidentally conjuring a fireball. "The students at the Dome are not the military!" he shouted. "They're just kids!"

"Tell us about it," Juliet said wryly, a smirk playing at her lips.

As if hearing his name called, Eduard entered the dining hall, flanked by two officers Kol didn't recognize. They walked straight for Kol and his friends' table.

"Malkolm," his father said, his booming tone filling the hall with more joviality than merited. "And Charlotte. I see that you've had a chance to clean up and get some food."

Kol pushed his plate away. He was mostly finished anyway, but his appetite fled soon after learning what his father was doing to Oberon's school. To *his* school.

"Your escape was remarkable." Eduard beamed. "How you managed to get *all* six—including the bloody vampire stuffed in Mr. Suzuki's office—out of that fortress is truly remarkable."

Kol didn't correct him. There had been seven to begin with. They weren't able to get *all* out. Char remained still, but Nik, Brett, and Juliet all shifted in their seats.

"And speaking of the vampire, how did he manage to get past the copper?"

Kol shrugged. "I don't know."

"Perhaps it's in need of some thickening," Eduard said,

turning to look at the officer on his right.

"I can't take the credit for the escape, Dad," he said. "It was Myreen and Kenzie's plan. Myreen broke myself and Char from that cell." Kol's chest tightened when he said Myreen's name.

"*Selkie's plan,*" Eduard scoffed. "Yes. Well, their plan wouldn't have worked without two dragons to fly everyone out on their backs like common mules."

"Except Myreen," he said quietly. The pressure in his chest increased.

"Yes, Myreen certainly is an impressive creature," Eduard mused.

Kol wasn't sure how he felt about his father being *impressed* by the girl he was in love with, but he didn't say anything.

"It's good to have you back, son," Eduard said, his professional smile plastered on his face.

Kol felt several pairs of eyes trained on him, but he didn't need the prompting. "What's going on here, Dad?" he asked before Eduard could walk away.

"Don't mumble, Malkolm. I'm not sure of your meaning."

"I didn't *mumble,*" Kol said through gritted teeth. "What have you done to our school?" He kept his eyes trained on Eduard, but gestured to the room full of students and to his friends.

Brett rose to leave, but from Kol's peripheral he saw Char shoot him a look that sunk him back into his seat.

"They're telling me that you're treating the Dome like a military school?" Kol heard the accusatory tone flip up in his voice, which was good because his heart rate was slowly increasing.

Eduard's expression didn't change, but Kol knew him well enough to see the faint twitch of his mouth. Though rare.

"They're kids, Dad."

"You might be right, but they must be prepared. Especially in light of your escape. I'm certain Draven will soon be at our door."

"They're *kids*, Dad," Kol repeated. "They're not soldiers and no matter what you do, they won't be ready. You're torturing them."

"Nonsense!" he snapped, walking forward and jabbing a finger in Kol's direction. "I've seen how capable you are. I saw how you handled yourself in that simulation. With discipline and training—"

"They're not me!" Kol shouted, getting several stares from students who were suddenly paying attention.

"Perhaps we should move this conversation elsewhere?" Eduard took a step back and lowered his tone, gesturing that his officers should move away from the conversation.

"Here is fine," Kol said as the soldiers stationed themselves at the exit. He sensed more uncomfortable shifting of his friends at the table. They wanted him to *move the conversation elsewhere.*

But Eduard didn't object.

"Yes, I've been trained all my life, but they haven't," Kol continued. "Many just recently shifted for the first time. Some only recently *became* or *found out* they're shifters." Kol shot a look at Juliet, who gave him a small smile. "I'm seventeen, Dad, but some of these kids just started puberty."

"There are plenty of other seventeen-year-olds and eighteen-year-olds here at the Dome," Eduard countered, gesturing a hand at Kol's table.

"But none of them are *Draculs*! You can't hold them to the same standards you hold me to." Kol stood, strengthened by a full stomach. "Do you know how quickly Char and I were captured?" Kol lowered his tone. "It was pathetically easy for Draven." He didn't add the part about Kenzie's hand in their capture. "Whatever you do to these kids not only won't be enough, but you're *torturing* them." His voice hitched on the word.

Eduard's expression still didn't change, but Kol could tell something struck him. "Please do not use that word. What happened to you and Charlotte was abhorrent." His voice was even. "I'm not the monster Draven is. I'm not a psychopathic vampire."

"And about that, too," Kol said. "Why didn't you come for us?" He gestured to Char. "Why didn't you send a team? *Hell*, why didn't you come rescue us yourself?" He crossed his arms over his chest. "Was running your military school too damned important? More important than your own flesh and blood?"

That struck a nerve. He would never admit it, but it looked as if Eduard finally realized he'd been in the wrong. He should've done something to save them. "I knew you'd make it out," he said quietly. "You're a *Dracul.*"

"I'm a seventeen-year-old kid, Dad."

Eduard nodded. "Your mother is on her way," he said, his voice suddenly more chipper. "She'll be here by tonight, I suspect, and she wishes to see you. She's been worried sick."

"Is that wise?" Kol asked, but then realized that his father might not worry about his mom's safety the way he did. "Aren't we prepping for Draven's attack?"

"I couldn't convince her to stay." Something about Eduard's eyebrows and the way his mouth slackened slightly was strange. "When that woman gets it into her head that she wants something..." He trailed off, shaking his head and... *smiling?* "Let's just say that nothing I could've said or done would've made her stay away. Even the likelihood of another vampire attack."

Kol kept his stance and expression the same. This was not the Eduard Dracul he was used to. This was not the father he remembered. Sure, he'd been furious with his dad moments ago in their little stand-off, but this was not the general—the *Lord*

Dracul—he knew.

And he didn't know quite how to react.

Eduard sobered after a few seconds and shook his head. "And you're right, Malkolm. Victoria, *your mother*, pleaded with me to come to you or send another team. And I should've. You and Charlotte could've died, and it would've been on my head."

Kol resisted the urge to allow his jaw to slacken, to scrape the floor with this sudden change in his rigid and stern parent.

"I can't imagine what it would've done to your mother if things had turned out differently. And it would've been my fault." Eduard took a step toward Kol, placing a hand on each of his shoulders. "It would've broken me to see that sort of pain on her face."

Kol stood as stone when his father turned and left the way he'd come. Had Draven's torture techniques messed with his head? He doubted his words miraculously changed his father's heart. But what had? He couldn't believe that turn of conversation had actually happened.

But when he finally thawed and looked at the faces of his friends—Nik and Brett, Char and Juliet—he knew he hadn't imagined it.

Kol lifted his shoulders before saying, "Hopefully that helped?"

Nik and Brett began talking at once, marveling at the scene they'd witnessed. Even Juliet was in awe, proving that she'd had enough run-ins with Eduard to know he'd somehow changed.

"Do you think he'll bring back the art and music classes?" she asked.

CHAPTER 43

Myreen

Morning—or was it after noon, now?—brought fresh sorrow.

They'd all escaped... all except Ty.

Myreen blamed herself. She'd tried to use her siren powers, rather than explaining things to Ty, like Kenzie had said. He'd been confused and upset when he realized they were traveling with shifters. And understandably so, since he thought shifters had killed his mom. Myreen doubted the truth of that story, since it had come from Draven, but it didn't make Ty's pain any less real.

And so they'd argued, and he escaped. Myreen couldn't blame him, but her heart still hurt to think of him under Draven's care, still preparing to become the new Denholm Heir and leader of the vampires.

Myreen pulled on some jeans and a soft shirt, then went looking for food. Her stomach rumbled—apparently it was more awake than she was. She thought about seeing if Kenzie was still in her room, but she didn't want to wake her friend. Food first. She'd catch up with Kenzie later.

The lunch buffet was almost through by the time she arrived, and she gladly got her food in peace. She found an out-of-the-way spot to sit, avoiding the dwindling number of students who seemed to watch her with weary expressions. If anything, things had grown more awkward since her return to the Dome.

She stared at her food as she ate, eavesdropping on nearby conversations. Some of the students were talking about some confrontation between Kol and his father over the treatment of students. Myreen wasn't sure she believed it. At least there was no talk about her destroying school property or being the daughter of Draven.

Suddenly, Myreen was flanked by two bodies. Hopeful it was Juliet or someone else she knew, she was surprised when she looked up to see Trish and Alessandra sitting on either side of her. A moment later, Joanna was seated across from Myreen.

"If you're looking for trouble, you've come to the wrong place," Myreen said, sticking her fork in her cooling lunch.

"Chill," Alessandra said, rolling her eyes. "We didn't come over here to pummel you, if that's what you're thinking."

Trish let out a humorless laugh. "Yeah, I don't know what you did to me, little miss mer-out-of-water, but I can't even *think* of looking at someone cross-eyed without putting myself in their shoes."

"Sucks for you," Myreen mumbled.

Joanna let out an amused chuckle. "To be honest, we're here to apologize."

"For what, exactly?" Myreen hoped they hadn't gone in her room and trashed it while she was eating.

Joanna looked at the table. "For telling you that you should go with Draven."

"And for the teasing when you first came, though I'm sure you deserved *some* of it," Trish added, sincerity lacing her attempt at humor.

"I finally convinced these two that you didn't have me attacked by those stupid vampires," Alessandra said, a haunted look in her gray eyes.

Myreen's brows rose. "Seriously?"

Trish and Joanna nodded.

"You surrendered yourself to Draven for us. For all of us. And we saw those videos with Kol... So, sorry."

Myreen gave them a half-smile. "Thanks." She looked around at the thinning crowd. "You know, I'm kind of surprised you're still here, with General Dracul turning this into a military school, and all."

Alessandra shrugged and Joanna smiled, but it was Trish who spoke. "You think that man can drive out the mer? This is *our* school, after all."

Myreen laughed, shaking her head. Same girls, different day.

"So, you wanna come back to the mer dorms?" Trish asked, pushing a strand of her perfectly-styled strawberry blond hair behind her ear.

Myreen took a deep breath. "I think I'm good where I'm at."

Alessandra nodded. "That's fine, too. But if Headphones ever ticks you off, you're welcome to hang with us."

Joanna smirked. "Or maybe bring Headphones with you."

Myreen laughed. "Thanks. That means a lot. To both of us."

The trio stood and turned to leave.

"Where are you all going?" Myreen asked.

"Class," Trish said, turning back with a smirk. "*Some* of us still have work to do. And instructors to piss off."

Myreen chuckled, shaking her head as the trio left. She

ducked her head and finished her food. As she polished off the rest of her plate, another person dropped into the seat next to hers. *Kol.* Her heart gave a stutter

"I see you've surfaced."

Myreen swallowed and set her fork down, pushing her empty plate away. "It was a long flight. I'm surprised we were able to do all that in one day."

Kol nodded, his mouth set in a grim line. "You didn't have to fly the whole way. I could've carried you."

Heat rose in Myreen's cheeks, and she waved Kol away. "You were already carrying Kenzie."

"I could've handled two," Kol said. The words hung between them, full of promises and regrets. "Do you...? Do you still want to talk?"

Myreen nodded. "But let's go somewhere else." She looked around at the few remaining students, many of whom ducked their heads when her gaze came their way.

"Yeah. That's probably a good idea." Kol stood and held out his hand, a question in his golden eyes.

Myreen looked at his outstretched hand for a long moment, chewing on her lower lip. She finally took it, needing to feel the warmth of another, desperately hoping it wouldn't lead her to ruin.

As his hand enveloped hers, a certain giddiness returned. The feeling was nothing like what she'd felt before—before she felt the sting of his betrayal, before she lost faith that the robot he pretended to be was all for show, before she'd come to doubt everything they had between them. But it was something, and she was glad to know she wasn't completely broken by everything that had transpired.

Her heart hammering against her chest like a bird trying to escape its cage, she followed Kol through the Grand Hall and then up to the avian wing. She cast a glance behind her as they headed toward his room, wondering if there was a better place to go. But no, his room would be private. They could talk freely.

And if things went poorly, she could always head to the girl's side and see if she could find Kenzie or Juliet. Though, Juliet was probably attending classes. It was strange to think it was still mid-week. It had been so long since Myreen had attended a class that she'd lost track of time.

As the door clicked closed behind them, Kol let out a deep breath. He let go of her hand as he sat on the edge of the bed, offering her the spot next to him.

Myreen remained standing and folded her arms. "So there was a curse."

Kol bowed his head, looking at his hands. "Yes."

"That if you fell in love with someone, then they'd hate you."

"Yes." His voice was small, and she felt herself softening.

But dread pooled in her stomach. "Why didn't you tell me?"

"It's not exactly something we Draculs talk about." He let out a bitter laugh. "In fact, I spent most of my life trying to avoid it."

"And how did that work out for you?"

"Oh, it worked. Until you."

Myreen drew in a breath. "But your dad said—"

"What my dad said was all true." He lowered his head more and grabbed a fistful of his hair. She wasn't sure why he did that. But then he let go and lifted his head to look at her. "I was supposed to befriend you. He wouldn't say it out loud, but he wanted me to... seduce you. I tried to resist, but you were so..."

"Fragile?"

"No. Persistent? Strong? But more than anything, you demanded my respect. And you earned it. Every scrap."

Did his voice catch there at the end?

"And then he told you to break up with me."

"Yes. But I couldn't do it. I couldn't lose you. And then I realized that your selkie friend might be able to help me. And she did. But when I got back to the Dome, you hated me. I thought for sure I triggered the curse."

"But now you're not so sure?" Myreen's arms had fallen to her sides, and she sat next to Kol, feeling the warmth of his arm pressed against hers.

"I think... I think the curse has been lifted. The way you..." he paused. "You have to understand, I watched my mom for years—her loving my dad and him despising her. There was respect, but not love. Never love. It killed me to see her like that. I didn't want that for you. For me." He took a breath. "But you aren't looking at me the way my dad has always looked at Mom."

Myreen nodded, letting her fingers weave through Kol's. "And Char?"

"To keep the Dracul line going, we had to arrange marriages. She was my *arrangement*. I'll always care for Char as a friend, but I don't love her. Not like that. Not like..." Kol's amber eyes searched hers, the depths reflecting more emotion than words alone could convey. "Myreen Fairchild, I fought my love for you until I could stand it no more. And then I fought to love you until I thought I would break. I don't expect you to love me in return, not after everything that's happened—"

Myreen put a finger to his lips—those soft lips she'd tasted more times than she could count, the lips that had set her on fire with their cinnamon fervor, the lips that confessed his love for her. She stared at those lips as she spoke. "I thought I'd severed this connection when I left. I thought I'd left behind every shred of my heart that still cared for you. But when I thought Draven was going to..." She stopped, looking into his eyes, reliving the anguish and terror of those awful moments. "Malkolm Dracul, you have frustrated me more times than I can count. And somehow, you still set me on fire." She dropped her voice to a whisper, as if the moment would somehow shatter and float away if she spoke too loudly. "I love you, too."

Kol lifted a hand to her face, his thumb caressing her cheek. He brought his face close to hers, their breath mingling, their foreheads touching. And then softly, reverently, Kol lifted his lips to hers.

The instant their mouths touched, it ripped open every shred of hesitation, leaving a gaping hole. Everything poured out as the searing flames of passion ignited—every ache and pain and shattered dream. Their kisses turned to *sorry's*, to *I miss you's*, to *I never want to lose you again's*. They kissed until their lips burned, until their breath had run out, until everything left unsaid had been laid bare.

And then they kissed some more.

When they finally emerged, chests heaving for breath, Kol wrapped her in an embrace that closed the gulfing distance the lack of kissing had left behind. Myreen wiped the tears from her cheeks, then held onto the arms encircling her, the arms she hoped would never let her go.

"What happened with your dad?" Myreen asked when her heart had once more found a steady rhythm.

"He's... different. I think I got through to him. He's going to put the school back the way it used to be."

Myreen sat up and turned to look at him. "And *you* did that?"

"I guess? I dunno. Without the curse... I have a feeling we're all in for a few surprises."

Myreen gave Kol a hopeful smile, and he matched it, planting another soft kiss on her lips.

"I could do this all day, you know," Kol said, his voice husky.

If she was drowning, she never wanted to resurface. "I could do this all day, too."

CHAPTER 44

Juliet

Juliet was still recovering from Dracul's drills when Nik dragged her out of bed to grab breakfast. She was annoyed that he wanted her to get out of bed so early, but he promised it was for a good reason. He waited outside her door while she got ready, but when she opened her door, she was surprised to find the rumor mill on full-blast. Not because the rumor mill was buzzing, but because of what they were saying.

Usually she tried to ignore the gossip, but what was odd was that they were all saying the same thing—for perhaps the first time since she'd been at that school.

Nik took her hand and led her to the dining room with no explanation. Not that he had to—everyone else said it for him.

Juliet's stomach tied in knots, hoping they were right. Nik's silence seemed to confirm the rumors. Juliet no longer cared about sore bones and annoying drill instructors.

She wanted to see her friends.

Brett was already seated with Kol and Char when Nik and Juliet arrived. She kept looking around for Myreen, but she wasn't anywhere in sight. She practically bounced through the food line, but as they approached Kol and Char, still looking so beaten and bruised from their time in captivity, all of Juliet's enthusiasm drained. She had no idea what to say to them, so she clammed up.

Kol took a deep drink, then leaned forward, as if exchanging some secret. "What's going on?" he asked, his stare penetrating. She could almost feel him studying the bags under her eyes, and she dropped her gaze to her plate. She didn't want to be the one to tell him the horrible things his dad had done as director of the Dome.

Brett didn't seem to have the same misgivings.

"Your dad is quite the drill sergeant. The general, *Lord Dracul*, has turned the school into a military training zone."

Nik's head snapped up, his hand tightening around Juliet's.

Brett shrugged. "What? He should know."

"What do you mean, a military training zone?" Kol asked, his brows knit, his voice holding an edge of darkness.

Nik sighed, and Juliet wanted to hug him. "Offensive classes, increased training, mandatory sim exercises."

"And he's taken away all of the fun classes," Juliet added, finally finding her tongue. "Art, music, anything but military history and math... *gone!* Plus a few new winners like tactical training. Ugh." Once she started, it all poured out.

Nik went on, but Juliet's mind wandered. Where was Myreen? She wanted to ask, but what Nik was telling Kol was important. Maybe Kol could even do something about it.

"The students at the Dome are not the military!" Kol suddenly shouted, pulling Juliet's attention back to the conversation. "They're just kids!"

"Tell us about it," Juliet said as she fought off a grin. It sounded like Kol wanted to help. After all he'd been through, she could see the fire in him—even stronger than before.

And then general Dracul himself walked in.

Juliet's stomach sank. She was already on the general's radar, and he was headed toward their table.

But then it hit her: Kol was here. It gave her hope that she might be protected from further attacks. In fact, Kol's arrival might just make the general more open to leniency. Not even Major Peters' presence could dissuade her that she was in the clear. For now, anyway.

And then Kol. Blew. Up.

He spoke up for the students and for the Dome, and her heart soared with him. She held her breath as she waited to see what the general would do. Her mouth fell open to see how *agreeable* Lord Dracul was being. Was this the same man who made her do drills through the night not even forty-eight hours ago?

But more than that, Kol's reference to Myreen and Kenzie brought her hopes high again. Where were they? Were they at the Dome, or were they hiding out somewhere else? Juliet's leg began to bounce, and she itched to go find them.

And then it was over. General Dracul and his lackeys left, the general's admissions that he'd done things wrong still ringing in Juliet's ears. Nik and Brett began to talk excitedly, but Juliet's gaze bounced between Kol and his father's retreating form, trying to wrap her head around what had just happened.

"Do you think he'll bring back the art and music classes?" Juliet asked, hope surging hot and cold through her.

She finished her breakfast and kissed Nik goodbye so she could go look for Myreen—there was no way she'd be able to concentrate in a class.

Juliet walked around the halls at such a rapid pace that she worried she might get a violation from one of the soldiers on patrol. She didn't care, though. She stuck her head in and out of classrooms, she knocked on Myreen's door, she even threw herself into the rumor mill and asked the other students if they'd seen her. The responses made her dizzy, so she flattened her back against the wall and tried to gather her bearings. She took a few deep breaths, then steeled herself to continue her search.

With a slower pace, Juliet walked the halls again, hoping to see Myreen's face in the crowd. When she ended up back at the Dining Hall just after lunch—*was the Dome really that big?*—she wanted to give up. But a group of girls walked out, gushing about seeing Myreen with the mer-trio. Juliet pushed through the girls, ignoring their groans as she scanned every face there—and came up empty.

She went back to the halls and spotted Trish and her mer-squad disappearing around a corner. A new desperation kicked in, giving her the courage to chase after them.

"Trish, have you seen Myreen?" Juliet asked, her sore muscles complaining at being pushed again so soon. Hopefully, getting right to the point would speed up the conversation.

"Of course. She left with Kol after we squashed our beef. Looks like you just missed her." Trish still held a sense of superiority, but there was something about her and the way she responded that was softer, more approachable. Maybe Alessandra had been talking to her?

"Uh, thanks. See ya." Juliet didn't stop to think about the difference in Trish and her goons. That would have to wait until later. Juliet still had a best friend to find.

But as she headed toward the dorms to look for Myreen,

she realized she couldn't barge in on whatever was happening with her and Kol. As much as she needed her friend, she could only imagine those two needed space more. And she wasn't about to put a time limit on it.

So she turned toward the library instead. It seemed like the perfect distraction, and when she spotted a map there—she was certain it was the one Nik had stolen from Dracul—it seemed luck was finally on her side. Finding Oberon was the last thing on her to-do list. It would be the perfect way to cap-off what was turning out to be a pretty incredible day.

***

Hours later and ready to crawl out of her skin, Juliet folded up the map and put it back where she'd found it. Kol and Myreen had had enough time. It was her turn now—if she could actually find Myreen.

No. Not if, *when*. She *would* find Myreen, even if it meant breaking into Dracul's office to use the electronic PA system.

Juliet headed straight to Myreen's room with a determined stride. She knocked three times, then silently counted to five. She was about to knock once more when the door opened.

"Myreen," Juliet whispered.

"J." Myreen's lips curled into a grin.

They fell into each other's arms and tears exploded. Juliet didn't even care that they were out in the open, or that they were loud, and she certainly didn't care that this would likely be recounted in the rumor mill.

Myreen pulled away first, grabbing Juliet's hand to lead her inside. "I'm *so* happy to see you." She closed the door, but didn't let go of Juliet's hand.

"I'm happy to see you, too. I missed you so much."

"You have *no* idea... but you look... terrible." Myreen gave a nervous laugh, but there was concern in her blue eyes.

"Gee, thanks. I could say the same to you." Juliet playfully nudged Myreen's arm.

"Yeah, well I'm sure you pretty much know what I went through. But why do *you* look like an ursa who missed hibernation? Has Nik been keeping you up?" Myreen giggled and wiggled her eyebrows as she wiped away her tears.

"Um, no. Actually, the general thought the Dome was his new military camp. I got on his radar. You know—the norm?" Juliet shrugged, trying to downplay her experience over the last few weeks. It wasn't anything compared to the horrible things Myreen must have gone through with Draven.

"I feel like so much has happened since I last saw you." Myreen looked down at her hands, and Juliet felt her own tears trying to resurface.

"I know. Are you... okay?" Juliet asked. Myreen had been through so much at the hands of Draven. Hopefully she understood what Juliet was trying to ask.

"That's a hard question to answer." Myreen hesitated, and Juliet wasn't sure if she was going to continue. "I'm okay because I'm back here. With you guys. But some things just stick with you..." Myreen's tears began to flow again.

Juliet pulled her in for another hug. "I'm so sorry you went through that. I hate that it happened, and I wish I could take it back for you." Juliet's tears mixed with Myreen's, as if their hearts hurt in sync.

"But you can't go back and change things, and neither can I." Myreen sniffled, once more trying to dry her face. "But I think we'll be okay. If we stick together, we'll be okay."

"And now that I have your permission, I'm never leaving your side." Juliet couldn't take any more of their somber mood.

The girls laughed as they dried their eyes.

They laid on Myreen's bed and stared at the ceiling, enjoying a comfortable silence for a while. Then Myreen turned onto her side to face Juliet, and Juliet followed suit, bring flushed face to flushed face, blotchy eyes to blotchy eyes.

"So, what do I have to look forward to at the new Dome?" Myreen asked, her voice low.

Juliet rolled her eyes and snorted. "You really don't want to know. But I feel obliged to prepare you. All the fun classes are gone. The common rooms aren't for hanging out anymore. If you step foot in the Defense Room, you'll have an entire set of drills to do—including a trip to the sim room. And the general's favorite form of punishment is a very special list of drills. They're *brutal*, trust me."

"This is so wrong. What would Oberon think?"

"If he were dead, he'd be rolling over in his grave," Juliet said with a snicker, then sobered, hoping that Oberon wasn't dead somewhere. It had been so long since anyone had heard from him... "Do you think with Kol back, the general will be different? You should've seen the way Kol stood up to his dad. And how apologetic Lord Dracul was. Maybe he could be persuaded to put things back the way they were?" Juliet's hope seeped through her words.

"I don't know. I hope so, but J, is that really what you want? Lord Dracul staying, I mean."

Juliet slowly shook her head. The Dome would never be the same without Oberon as director. And that reminded Juliet of what she'd found.

Juliet abruptly sat up. "You're right. Before I came here, I was in the library."

"Surprise, surprise," Myreen said, rolling her eyes.

Juliet gave her another playful nudge. "Whatever. Anyway... Nik left a map in there that he took from Dracul's office and it had some pretty classified information on it. Information about Oberon."

Myreen sat up, too, a spark in her eyes. "What did you find? Can I see it?"

"Of course you can see it. We'll have to go to the library, because it's there—I don't think Nik's had the chance to retrieve it yet. I should warn you, though, finding Oberon isn't going to be easy—it took me hours just to get the coordinates—but I think we can find him with this new information." Juliet was cautiously proud of her discovery—they still needed a plan.

"Ha. Nothing is ever easy, it seems. Especially when it comes to shifters. But we can do this. Together." Myreen's confident smile was contagious.

"You're right." Juliet nodded, then stood.

"Okay, let's go see this map. We'll need the guys, and Kenzie, too." Myreen stood and slipped on her shoes, throwing her hair into a bun.

"Kenzie's here, too?" Juliet asked. Apparently she was the new girl everyone was talking about.

"Yup. But maybe let's just you and I go for now. I still haven't gotten my fill of Juliet, yet." Myreen gave Juliet a quick wink.

Juliet followed Myreen out, giving her another quick hug. "It's so good to have you back."

Leif

Gadgets were everywhere. On the metal desk Leif stood next to, several of the devices glowed, illuminating a thin layer of dust. Whoever used this as an office hadn't been here for some time.

At random, one of the cylindrical devices began flashing a red light. An accompanying alarm sounded, and it sounded like a chirping bird. A chirping bird being tortured, that is.

Only tolerating a few seconds of it, Leif reached over and slammed a sturdy fist down on it, smashing it as thin as a CD. Only this particular CD would never make another sound.

Without even looking, Leif could feel a set of eyes on him from the doorway. Looking over his shoulder, he found that it wasn't one of his guards, but the shifter military general. Malkolm's father. Eduard Dracul.

The general's eyes stared at the smashed device, and his mouth formed an amused grin.

"I see you care for Mr. Suzuki's contraptions about as much as I do," he said.

Leif didn't reply, but kept his eyes glued to the dragon shifter. Upon being brought to the shifter school—a place he'd never actually seen before—he'd been thrown into this room with two guards posted just outside. He'd gone from one prison to another. But this one he was at least a little grateful for. It kept out those shifters who might see him as an enemy, despite all he'd been through to help the Dome.

The general walked over to the desk, picking up the flattened device, giving it a studious look. He then brought his gaze back to Leif.

"I've been doing some digging," he said. "Your name is Leif Villers, a vampire who also happens to be a shifter sympathizer. But what I can't seem to understand is *why*? I've been fighting vampires my whole life. What makes you so different than the rest of your kind?"

Leif chuckled, his eyes going distant for a moment as he recollected his past—his hand in the destruction of The Island which resulted in the deaths of hundreds of shifters. The same event that caused Gemma's voice to disappear like a cloud in the wind.

"Pardon the pun, but I guess you could say that I still have a heart," Leif replied, his eyes refocusing on the general. "Believe me, I tried to live like them. I didn't belong. I *never* belonged."

The general's eyes narrowed. "And you think you belong here, among shifters?"

Leif shrugged. "What *I* think is that I don't belong anywhere. I have only ever fit in one place, and that was a long time ago. And your ancestor put an end to that particular place."

The general cocked his head to the side and studied him. "I'm afraid I'm not entirely sure to whom and what you're referring."

"I'll help you out. I'm talking about Aline Dracul and the first shifter school—the Frost Boarding House in Vancouver, Washington."

The general scoffed. "If my knowledge of history is accurate, it wasn't Aline's fault that the school was destroyed, but an army of vampires."

Leif set his jaw, forcing back the retort he wanted to throw. This was Aline's descendant, not Aline herself. Controlling himself, he said, "I was there, over one hundred years ago. Like a pebble being dropped into a puddle, I witnessed the ripples of her actions."

"So, you have magnified anger toward shifters," Lord Dracul said. "But that still doesn't answer my question. Why sympathize with us? Why aid Oberon and the shifter cause?"

The flurry of emotions threatened to overwhelm Leif. Guilt. Anger. Frustration.

He breathed in deeply, then released the air. "Because in a short amount of time, I did terrible things to shifters. I was the reason for *so* many deaths. I played the part of Draven's good little pet, and I've had to live with that despairing guilt ever since." He pointed a finger at the general. "But protecting shifters like you? I've gained back some self-respect. I could've run away from it all—stowed myself away in a small township in the middle of nowhere, ignoring the travesties going on. The travesties I was a part of."

The general nodded, accepting Leif's answer. "You've suffered for aiding the shifters I've worked hard to protect throughout my career. For that, I thank you." Lord Dracul laughed for a moment, shaking his head. "Never in all my life did I expect to thank a vampire for anything."

"I understand," Leif said. "I, too, had not expected to join forces with the shifters. Most of my life has been solitary. You asked where my place is, and that's it. There's no one else like me, which makes me an outcast. My place is wherever I can find myself alone."

The general studied him for a few moments, then slowly reached a hand out toward Leif. "I think Oberon was right. You belong with us."

Leif gazed at the dragon shifter's hand with surprise.

"Your being here has caused quite a stir," Lord Dracul said. "By now, the parents of many of the students here are aware that there's a vampire living among their children. That fact will scare many."

"That certainly puts you in a difficult position," Leif said.

"I'm no Oberon Rex. But take comfort in the fact that I have officers stationed at your door. They aren't there to confine you, but to regulate who comes and goes. No doubt, you could protect yourself if one of the shifters here decided to pay you a nasty visit. I don't want that to happen."

"Neither do I," Leif replied.

"I also realize that you're a wasted resource being cooped up in here," Lord Dracul continued. "I have other matters to attend to, but if you have any idea what Draven and his legion are planning, I would very much appreciate any information you can provide."

Leif ran a hand through his long, black hair. It felt greasy against his fingers, and he suddenly wished he could wash it. He couldn't remember the last time he'd had such a luxury.

"The past few weeks have been... a blur," Leif said. "He had me under some heavy drugs. Anything I heard—or thought I heard—probably can't be trusted. But I'm a strategist. And I know how Draven thinks, probably better than anyone else."

"I'll take your educated guess over simply planning for the worst," the general said.

"Planning for the worst would be the wisest course of action," Leif said. "But I can shed some light on how he thinks, because Draven is a strategist like me."

"Shoot."

"First thing?" said Leif, pointing toward the ceiling. "If you think you're safe within the walls and glass of the Dome, you're wrong."

Lord Dracul nodded. "Right. Not enough copper. I've noticed you haven't been suffering from it."

Leif shook his head, not willing to divulge information about the enchantment Kenzie had performed on him, freeing him from the effects of the red metal. Such secrets were better left unknown, particularly by people in places of power.

"I don't think that's your problem," Leif said. "Draven is a dreamer, and he doesn't limit himself with small stepping stones. He goes big, and he goes hard. The Dome is an obstacle. And he will crush it."

Pride encircled the general's countenance. "Impossible. He already tried to crush us once, and we stopped him."

"He had different purposes then," Leif said, remembering what Beatrice had told him. Draven only ended his barrage once Myreen gave herself up. "Draven won't stop this time until the Dome is destroyed and everyone is dead."

Like a balloon losing its air, Lord Dracul shrunk at his words.

"I've seen it before," Leif said. "I was there when he toppled the shifter school at La Framboise Island. And trust me when I say that you don't want the blood of every last shifter here on your hands."

The general went back to studying the flattened device he still held. After a few moments, he flung it back on the desk, and the chinking sound of metal on wood reverberated in Leif's ears.

"So what do you suggest we do?" he asked.

Leif blinked. "Evacuate every last person from the premises of the school and get as far away from here as possible."

"Run?" the general asked incredulously. "That's your advice? Mr. Villers, I'm general of the shifter military. We will not run from the Dome. We will stand and fight, or at least die in the process. Besides, we don't know who's on the other side of the school's exit. Evacuating the students would be like sending lambs to the slaughter. Many of them are unskilled with their abilities—they wouldn't be able to protect themselves."

Of course. Leif knew the general's answer before he even said it. Still, he'd offered the same counsel he would've given Oberon.

"Then I will stand and fight by your side," he said.

Lord Dracul's eyes widened. Leif took momentary satisfaction in the wonder he'd caused, especially in a Dracul.

The general placed a hand on his shoulder. "These are mad times. To think I will be fighting alongside a vampire..." He shook his head, unable to finish his thought.

Leif half-smiled. "How about fighting alongside a friend?" He extended his hand this time, and slowly, Lord Dracul took it, squeezing firmly while shaking.

"I can do that," said the general.

Leif nodded, releasing his hold. "Draven will attack soon. If you haven't already, I highly recommend calling in all the military reserves you've got, as well as any shifters who are willing to fight for the school."

Lord Dracul nodded. "We're already working on it." He cleared his throat, then started walking for the door. Before exiting, he turned around and gazed at Leif. "Mr. Villers, on behalf of all shifters, I want to thank you for the services you've rendered on our behalves. Perhaps someday we can discuss a potential career serving in the military."

Chuckling at such a notion, Leif said, "If we survive, perhaps we can have such a discussion."

The general looked at him for a few more moments, then turned and walked out of sight.

Leif sat on the metal desk, mindlessly poking at a white orb lying nearby. *That didn't go exactly as I had anticipated,* he thought.

"Can I see him?"

Leif swiveled his head back to the doorway when he heard the words. It was Kenzie's voice.

"Yes, you're one of the few General Dracul authorized to visit the vampire," came the guard's response. "Go on ahead."

"Thanks," she said. Leif could envision her giving a mock salute to them.

Kenzie walked through the threshold, bag in tow as usual, and a skip to her step.

Leif got back to his feet as she entered, and he gave her a warm smile. She'd become a close friend, and he found himself happy to see her.

"Hey, Kenzie," he said, combing his hair with his fingers and realizing for the second time just how nasty it felt.

"I was waiting for Kol's dad to leave," she said, throwing her thumb over her shoulder. "He wasn't a jerk to you, was he?"

Leif chuckled and shook his head. "Quite the opposite, actually. He just wanted to know if I knew any of Draven's plans, which I don't. But I did clue him in on how Draven's mind works."

Kenzie's expression dropped as she made her way around the desk and sat in the nice chair behind it. She spun on it a few times before coming to a stop. "He's coming, isn't he? Draven, I mean."

Leif nodded morosely. "It won't be long, now. And it

won't be pleasant."

Her frowning drooped even more. "I *finally* get into the shifter school just in time for it to get attacked by vampires."

"At least you finally made it," Leif consoled, giving her a warm smile. "It's what you've always wanted, right?"

She bobbed her head ever so slightly. "Now we just have to protect it so I can actually attend."

Leif chuckled and looked around the room. "A fine pair we make, here in this school for shifters. We stick out like dragons with feathers."

Kenzie snorted. "Oh, they'd accept us in a heartbeat if that's how we looked."

"Probably so," he replied, chuckling some more.

A quiet silence followed, and while it wasn't awkward, it was as if something hung in the air—something they needed to discuss.

"I've been meaning to tell you," he started, "how very proud I am of you."

Kenzie's face lit up, and she sat up straight, as if his words had cast away the doomsday feeling. "Really?" she asked.

"Yep. When I first met you, you were almost terrified of your selkie magic. Now, it seems that nothing can stop you. I've witnessed you doing some incredible things. You're not the same girl I discovered on the streets of Chicago just months ago. What you've done for me..." He looked down at his hands, rubbing his wrists where Beatrice's shackles used to hold him bound. "You amaze me. I can't thank you enough."

Kenzie burst from the chair and stepped quickly to Leif, wrapping her arms around him. At first, he marveled at the sudden affection. But he drew her in and hugged back, feeling her heart beating so close to him.

They stood there silently for some time, just the two of them.

Leif closed his eyes, allowing himself to feel her warmth. He pulled away just slightly, so he could see her face, and as Kenzie looked up into his eyes, something about her appearance tapped into his memory, and he found himself experiencing a déjà vu-like moment. That wasn't quite the right expression, but it was close enough. It was so reminiscent of his precious nights with Gemma, when they'd held each other close, as if each embrace might be their last.

But Kenzie was not Gemma, and Leif could still see a bit of that spark of hope in the young selkie's eyes. Hope for something he could never give her.

Clearing his throat, he pulled away, letting her hands drop into his. "Kenzie, I must apologize."

She bit her lip, as if anticipating a slap to the face. It caused Leif to hesitate, but only for a moment. He needed to address this, if not for her, then for himself.

"I've put you at a disadvantage, and it's no fault of your own." He brought one hand up and ran the back of his fingers along the skin of her soft, warm cheek. She closed her eyes and sucked in a breath. "Sometimes when I look at you, all I see is Gemma. And it's that projection I apologize for. You're a brilliant, beautiful young woman with a potential I admire greatly. And someday, you will be a dream come true for somebody."

She released her lip and it trembled. Her glistening eyes told him she was waiting for him to continue.

Leif sighed. "That somebody can't be me."

He saw her throat move as she thickly swallowed. But she nodded, and there wasn't pain in her eyes, which Leif was glad to see.

"Gemma must've been quite the woman," Kenzie said with a soft laugh as she looked down. "But I understand. And you're right. I can't be Gemma. She's lucky to have somebody so loyal. An eternal being with eternal love." She brought her hazel eyes back up to his. "That's kind of epic."

Was that true? Mortals held such fleeting lives. Was their capacity for love diminished because of their expiration dates?

Answering his own question, Leif shook his head. "I think that one day, you'll find somebody who'll develop that same kind of love for you. And it'll be completely and entirely just for you. And you'll be able to return it."

Kenzie hugged him again, and this time, Leif felt the love of friendship in the expression.

While embracing, she said, "Well, good news. I already have your replacement lined up. He happens to be a cat now, go figure."

Leif blinked. "You better not be talking about Rainbow..."

Kenzie huffed a laugh. "Nah, I think I'm done with vampires for now." She took a step back, looking him in the eyes. It was perhaps the most direct and sincere look she'd ever given him. "Except you. And Rainbow, of course. You're always welcome." She lifted a finger in his face. "And you better not drop me like a bad habit now that you're not 'projecting' and all that."

Leif laughed, then pulled her into another embrace. "Never."

"Good. Now that we've got that straightened out, you should probably know... I think I figured out how to bring Gemma back."

Time froze. Leif still loved Gemma with all his heart, but the memories Beatrice had planted in his mind were poisonous seeds. He didn't want to believe any of them were true, but he couldn't help but wonder what Gemma and Camilla had talked about when he wasn't around. Be that as it may, he'd do anything to have her back.

Kenzie's brows creased ever so slightly. "What? Cat got your tongue?"

"Have you been able to perfect your resurrecting spell?" he asked. "Because as much as I love Rainbow, I wouldn't want to place Gemma in a similar situation."

Kenzie snorted, sliding away from him and slipping her bag from her shoulders. "You sure about that? A musical vampire cat woman sounds like just your thing." She mumbled under her breath and Gemma's family grimoire suddenly emerged from the bag. "I found something else in the sealed portion." Placing it gently on the desk, she gingerly turned the ancient pages.

Leif found himself clenching his hands with anticipation. Had she figured it out? Was the spell intricate? It had to be.

His mind continued to race like the flitting pages of the grimoire. And then the page turning stopped, and Leif gasped. Kenzie pointed at a rough drawing of a five-pointed leaf with a face in the middle. It was far from a perfect replica of Gemma's brooch, but there was no doubt about what it represented. Above the sketch were the words *Life Essence Encasement Spell*. Below the image were a few lines of text he couldn't read.

"You know that pin you've been carrying around for the past century?" Kenzie asked. "I think that's where Gemma is."

Leif's mind was racing before, but now it was reeling. He slipped his hand into his pocket and found it empty, and the blooming hope that was building within him fizzled out like hot coals doused with water.

Gemma's brooch was at Heritage Prep.

He cringed and placed a hand on his face. "It's in Beatrice's possession."

Kenzie's shoulders plunged, as well as her expression. "You've *got* to be kidding me. Please, tell me this is some sick, twisted joke of yours."

"All this time," he said. "I've had it on me *all this time*! And when I finally really need it, it's hundreds of miles away." He looked at Kenzie and shook his head. "And here I was, thinking I was done with Beatrice once and for all."

CHAPTER 46

Kenzie

Kenzie felt different, changed. The talk with Leif cemented her resolve. He would forever be an important part of her life, and she knew she'd see him again, once he got that pin back, but the ache of longing she got when she was around him had disappeared.

Kenzie made a quick magical call to Gram, though she still didn't bother with the gory details of her time at Heritage Prep. That was probably a conversation best had in person, anyway. But her heart felt buoyed. For now, that was enough.

Kenzie headed to the avian common room, concerned for how Myreen was faring. But she caught sight of her disappearing down the other end of the hall, hand-in-hand with Kol, a healthy flush in her cheeks. Kenzie smirked. Yeah, Myreen was fine.

Inspired, Kenzie decided to make one more magical call. She grabbed one of the bowls of salad the kitchen staff were getting ready to put up and made herself comfy in the empty cafeteria.

"Claoigha," Kenzie said, not bothering to hide what she was

doing. She didn't have to here. At least, she hoped not. She focused her attentions on Wes—his spiced chai eyes, his caramel hair, his honeyed lips...

"Wes?"

"What the—?"

Kenzie snickered. "It's your inner woman calling."

"Kenzie?" Wes's confusion was palpable, and Kenzie laughed again.

"Yeah, it's me."

"How?"

"Selkie. Remember? Magic and crud?"

"Oh yeah. Dang, so you can get in my head?"

"Think of it more like a magical phone call. You still have to talk for it to work, but you get impressions of stuff, too."

"Is that why I'm getting a warm, fuzzy feeling?"

Kenzie laughed again. "That's probably just you." Maybe.

"Wait. Are you okay? Are you back? What happened?"

"Whoa, whoa, whoa. One question at a time. Yes, I'm fine. Yes, I'm back. I'm in Chicago, actually. And it's a long story."

"You're in Chicago? Can I see you?"

Kenzie hesitated a moment. She wanted to see Wes, but after everything that had happened between her and Adam, she didn't know if she could face him. Still...

"Please. I've... I've missed you. And I've been worried sick about you. There are... some things I should tell you."

Kenzie sighed. "Yeah, we should talk, I guess. Do you know where the shifter school is?"

"Sort of. But Kenzie, I can't go in there."

"Why not?" He wasn't talking about just physically coming in. Part of her understood, but Wes needed these people. He was still a new shifter. It wasn't like he could go back to the hunters. Could he?

"I just can't. Is there any place nearby we can meet?"

Kenzie wracked her brain, but there was only one place she could think of. "Mack's Diner? But I don't have any money."

"No worries. See you there."

Kenzie let her magical connection drop, then took her salad bowl to her dorm room and threw it in the mini fridge. Yeah, she couldn't bear to waste even that.

She went to the bathroom next. One look in the mirror and she knew she'd made the right decision. She still hadn't taken the time to really clean up. There wasn't much she could do in a rush, but at least she could make herself a little more presentable.

Kenzie snorted when she realized seeing Leif hadn't elicited that response. Though, he was in about the same condition as her. Still, even covered in grime, he was deliciously handsome. And still just her friend.

She splashed some water on her face and ran her wet hands through her hair to try to tame the pieces still sticking up from sleep. Had she really been walking around like this? With a shake of her head, she ran back to her room and grabbed her jacket.

Her stomach rumbled, and she hoped Wes was planning on getting some food at Mack's. Her mouth watered as she remembered the chili cheese fries she'd shared with Kol last time she'd been there. The salad could wait. She hoped.

She practically flew to the entrance of the Dome, but stopped cold when she reached security. She approached one of the guards, who gave her a wary look.

"Any chance I can get an access badge so I don't have to use my magic to break back in?" she asked.

"You're planning on returning?" he asked, regarding her warily.

Kenzie snorted. "You're not getting rid of me that easy. So, what'll it be?" She held out her hand, looking at the guard expectantly.

The man sighed, then turned and rummaged in a drawer. He handed her a card, and she flashed him a smug smile. "This is a guest badge. You won't get a permanent one unless it's cleared by the director."

Kenzie gave a curt nod. "Understood. Thank you, soldier." She saluted, then turned on her heel and headed for the train. Although she couldn't see the man anymore, she had a feeling he was shaking his head. She smiled. Yeah, this place definitely needed a rogue selkie. Maybe she could get one immortalized in stone.

She watched out the windows as the train slid through the tunnel, heading back for land. She didn't want to leave the Dome behind just yet, but this wasn't for good. She had a guest badge, after all.

When she finally reached the cold streets of Chicago, she zipped her jacket and folded her arms across her chest. She made her way toward Mack's, but stopped when she heard feet running her way. Her breath caught in her throat as she turned to see Wes coming for her. Granola had never looked so good.

Wes caught her in his arms and swung her around, then set her down, meeting her gaze, his eyes asking for permission. Her lips parted in response, and she gave the barest of nods.

And then Wes's warm lips were against hers, and she forgot how to think, how to breathe. For all that she'd missed Wes while at Heritage Prep, she hadn't realized just how empty she'd felt without him. His kiss seemed to fill her until she thought she'd explode into a million fireworks.

They pulled apart, breathless, and Wes took her hand as they continued down the street.

"Hello to you, too," Kenzie said, a soft smile on her still buzzing lips as she looked sideways at Wes.

Wes snickered. "Sorry. I just... I missed you."

Kenzie squeezed his hand, and Wes beamed. "So, how's the cat life going?"

Wes threw back his head and laughed. "That *would* be your first question."

Kenzie shrugged. "Hey, it's not *my* fault you picked a cat person. Take it or leave it."

"I'll take it. Any day, anywhere."

He looked at her again, but Kenzie's eyes were trained on the ground. She took a deep breath. Better she tell him now, than wait for him to find out some other way. Unless he already knew, thanks to Draven's little broadcast... "You should know, I did some stupid stuff at Heritage Prep."

"You were going undercover. I understand."

Kenzie shook her head. "There was this guy that I met before I went. We only got together a couple of times before I found out he was an Initiate. He was... he was spying on a vampire I was helping, and he was using me to get information. Among other things." She mumbled the last sentence, hoping she wouldn't have to repeat herself, hoping he didn't catch her meaning.

Wes's shoulders slumped. "How bad was it?"

Kenzie took a steadying breath and closed her eyes, glad that Wes hadn't retracted his hand. Yet. "He was at Heritage Prep. He asked to have me assigned to him when they turned him. He fed off me. More than I care to admit." She shivered, and Wes's fingers tightened around hers, giving her strength. "And... well, he wanted to pick up our relationship where we left off."

"And you had to. To keep up your cover." He supplied the words, a hopeful note in his tone. He was giving her a way out, a way to sweep everything that had happened under the rug. And while she wanted to do that, she knew she couldn't lie to him. If he really wanted a relationship with her, then he needed to know just how flawed she was.

Mack's came into view, but they stopped, neither looking at each other.

"Maybe? I don't know what would've happened if I refused, but as guilty as I feel for indulging, a part of me wanted it. Especially when he became a vampire. When he fed on me..." She swallowed, the bittersweet pleasure of Adam still fresh in her memory. She put a hand to her neck. "But that's no excuse. And all the while, I couldn't help but think that I was betraying you. I didn't know if I'd make it out alive, let alone see you again..."

"Kenzie," Wes said, tugging on her hand.

She stopped and looked at him for the first time since she'd started her story. Once more, he surprised her with the depth of understanding—and feeling—in those caramel eyes.

"You don't have to explain yourself to me. Believe me when I say that I know what it feels like to sacrifice for the greater good."

Kenzie searched his eyes. "What happened with you?"

Wes's lips wrenched into a half-smile. "I was forced to switch sides."

Kenzie nodded. "And how's that going?"

Wes sighed, running his free hand through his hair. "I'm making progress. It's not easy having to change your whole belief system overnight."

"What will you do?"

"What I've *been* doing. Taking things one day at a time. Work. Train. Try to keep myself from going nutso." He smiled at her, and the sight sent a shot of warmth through Kenzie.

"Come to the shifter school with me? They could probably teach you a thing or two about your inner cougar."

Wes lifted his free hand in a playful claw and swiped it at her. "Rawr."

Kenzie snorted.

"And I prefer Puma. But I don't know. Would they really take an ex-hunter under their wings?"

Kenzie shrugged. "Not sure, but they were against a selkie enrolling. That didn't stop me."

"I don't think there's a force in the world that could stop you, Kenzie MacLugh." Wes caught her up in another kiss, and she let go of his hands to better wrap them around his neck and never let go.

Kenzie's stomach grumbled, and she could feel Wes's smile against her lips.

"I should probably feed that wild beast before it gets out," Wes said, pulling back enough so she could see his face.

"I never turn down good food."

***

The food at Mack's was just as good as Kenzie remembered, maybe even better. They long overstayed their welcome, talking about everything. Kenzie finally got the chance to spill all her regrets, and Wes confessed he'd been in contact with the hunters, trying to figure out a way to make sure Kenzie was okay.

Kenzie couldn't help but remember her conversation with Leif just a few hours ago. He said she'd find a love like he had with Gemma. Looking into Wes's face, beaming at her, her own cheeks sore from steady smiling, she wondered if this was it. Could it really be this easy? She hoped so. Wes was an incredible guy. Even if they weren't really meant for forever, she felt lucky he'd noticed her all those long weeks ago on the L.

Kenzie's eyes grew wide when she realized just how much time had passed. The sky was filling with sherbet hues.

"I should get back to the Dome before it gets dark."

"Yeah. I should probably get back to my place," Wes said, his countenance losing some of its sparkle. He got the bill and paid, and they headed toward the subway entrance, their hands entwining again.

They lingered on the sidewalk, neither saying anything, though Kenzie felt like her heart might crack if she let Wes go. "Come with me?" she asked once more.

Wes shook his head. "I want to, Kenzie, but only because I don't want to let you go again."

"Then don't let me go. I'm a selkie, after all. You never know when we're going to disappear in a puff of smoke."

Wes laughed. "You're a magic user, not an illusionist. Wait, you can't do that for real, can you?"

Kenzie lifted a brow. "I wouldn't test me if I were you."

He leaned toward her, his nose touching hers, his lips tantalizingly close. "Then I'll have to find a way to keep you coming back for more."

His breath tickled her nose, and Kenzie inhaled the delicious scent. "Chili cheese fries. Mmmm. That'll do it, sir."

Wes's lips brushed hers, but a rumble traveled through the city, followed by monstrous roar. Kenzie and Wes broke apart, staring at each other with wide eyes.

"What the hell was that?" Wes asked.

Kenzie shook her head. "Nothing good. I've only heard that sound once before—as we were escaping Heritage Prep." She'd nearly forgotten about that awful sound, and fear shot through her like lightning.

A panicked scream came from down the street, the direction they'd heard the sound coming from. Wes grabbed Kenzie's hand as they ran toward it. When Lake Michigan came into view, Kenzie let out a gasp. Long, tentacled arms were disappearing below the surface, suckers the size of Kenzie's body lining each snake-like arm.

"Is that—?" Wes started.

"A kraken," Kenzie finished. "And it's headed for the school."

Kol

Kol clicked the door behind himself and Myreen and met her smile. Life was uncertain. It was inevitable that Draven would retaliate for their escape, but that didn't matter much to Kol.

The curse was *broken*.

He loved Myreen and she loved him back, and now that she was finished having her moment with Juliet, it was his turn to have a moment.

Through her dark eyelashes, her twinkling blue eyes lifted to his. A coy smile played as she grabbed both of his hands and drew him nearer.

He wrapped both arms around her before kissing her again. She twined her arms around his neck and ran her fingers through his hair. He broke their kiss with his giddy smile.

"Alone. Finally," he said. Kol lifted his hands to brush the hair from her face and twisted a lock of her silky blue-black hair around one of his fingers.

"Yes, finally." She giggled, then backed away toward his bed, pulling him with her, until she sat on the edge.

Kol sat beside her—but needed to be touching her now that they were finally together—and hooked an arm around her shoulder, pulling her tight against his chest.

"What do you think will happen now?" she whispered, her words laced with worry and trepidation.

Kol blew a breath upward, throwing the hair from his eyes—he was in need of a haircut—then fell backward on the bed with his arms crossed over his face. "I don't want to think about that right now," he said. A fight was coming. That was certain. Whether Draven attacked now or in a year was all a matter of Draven's chosen strategy and the level of his patience.

Kol ventured to guess it would happen sooner rather than later. But either way, Draven wasn't attacking at the moment, and Kol didn't want to discuss *what will happen* just yet.

He felt the weight of Myreen press into his chest and the softness of her lips on his before he moved his arms to return to where they belonged—wrapped around the girl he loved.

"Then let's not think about it right now," she said, breaking away only long enough to say the words before kissing him again.

Kol reveled at the insane reality that he was somehow experiencing what generations of Dracul's never knew: reciprocal love. He had a hard time wrapping his head around the notion. A small part of him even waited to wake up and realize it was all just a dream. They broke apart and she laid against his chest for several minutes.

"What's this?" Myreen shot up and took a book from the shelf before plopping back down on the bed. "Frost Boarding House?"

It was the heavy history book Kol borrowed from the

library to learn more about Aline Dracul. Part of him wished he'd spent more time at the possible location of the property when he and Char scouted it out, but he'd been bitter and broken-hearted. Still, he felt a little guilty for cursing his ancestor. She lived her entire life with unreciprocated love, and now he didn't have to. No Dracul would ever have to again.

"I was researching." Kol tried to sound bored about it, like it was for some history assignment. He remained lying on the bed to sell it.

She pointed an eyebrow at him. "*Researching?*" Myreen was no fool.

Kol sat up and gave her a quick peck on the lips before removing the book from her lap and flipping through it. "Can't put anything past you," he teased, flipping to the page with the picture of Aline and pointing to her. " *That* is my ancestor."

Myreen looked at him with confusion right as his tablet pinged. He lifted it to see a message from his mom.

"What is it?" Myreen asked.

"My mom's here," he said. "She wants to see me."

She pulled at him. "Then we should go."

"Not yet. She's with my dad. She said to come down in five minutes."

Myreen turned back to the book.

"The curse," Kol continued like it was explanation enough, but could tell it wasn't. "Aline was the reason for it."

"Why?"

Kol shrugged. "I dunno. No one is really sure why, but some selkies—Kenzie's relatives actually—"

"Right, she mentioned something about that," she mused.

"Yes. Kenzie's relatives were the ones who placed it, but I didn't know that until later..." he paused, thinking about the day he'd gone to her and the stark contrast he'd felt in a matter of seconds when he thought the curse was broken—and then *not.* "Knowing Kenzie was a selkie," he continued. "I went to her, hoping she could remove it." He smiled. Now he knew the curse had been broken this entire time. Myreen was just hurt and angry at him for some things Eduard said.

"And she did," Myreen said.

"And she did," Kol repeated.

Myreen flipped to another page. The one with the picture of the Frosts and their daughter, Camilla.

"That's Leif!" Myreen shouted, pointing at the other man on the page. The man beside Jane Frost who looked like he was in his twenties.

Kol narrowed his eyes and looked closer. Sure enough, it was the very vampire who had escaped from Heritage Prep with them. "*Huh...*" he mused. His academic mind reeled with the implications—the possible knowledge a vampire as old as Leif Villers would know. He might have to interview the man someday.

"The stories he could tell..." Myreen said, as if reading Kol's mind, then looked at the clock on Kol's tablet. "It's been five minutes. We should go down to see your mom."

Kol smiled at his beautiful girlfriend and leaned forward to kiss her quickly. "Yes, we should," he said, loving that she'd said *we.*

***

Victoria held Kol in a crushing embrace the instant he walked into Oberon's office—his father's office, at the moment.

"I saw the video," she said, a sob choking her words. "I thought he was going to—" She buried her face into his side, gripping him with white knuckles.

"I'm okay, Mom," he said, wrapping his arms around her.

461

Kol glanced over her head at Myreen, expecting a smile, but her expression was sober. Maybe she was thinking about the video too. "I'm okay," he said again to both women.

Victoria Dracul pulled away to look up at Kol. "I heard they ripped off some of your scales?"

Kol swallowed and nodded. He hoped there wasn't a video of that, but it was practically common knowledge. Dragons didn't lose their scales easily. Every dragon he knew—save himself and Char—still had all of theirs. Including Eduard.

Draven had taken three from Kol.

"Why are you here, Mom?" he asked. "Draven might attack any day. You should've stayed home."

"While two of the men I love are here?"

Eduard walked in when she said it, and her eyes shot to him and followed his movement until he stood beside her.

"Besides, you're only seventeen, Malkolm," she added. "And you were t– tortured." Her voice caught with a new sob.

Eduard lifted an arm to wrap around the shoulder of his wife of twenty-five years. She leaned against him as she wiped away the tears. It took all Kol's power not to react to this strange interaction between his parents. But he couldn't help the small smile he offered his mom when only she was looking at him.

"Which is why you're leaving with me," she said, straightening.

Kol turned to Eduard. "Who, me?"

Eduard met Kol's gaze. "Yes. You'll leave with your mother."

"But you'll need me!" Kol said. "I'm more experienced and capable than most of the students here!" he argued. "You can't expect the shifter army to just defeat Draven and his vampires, can you?"

Kol could see the struggle in Eduard's eyes. He *did* want Kol to stay and help with the fight. He agreed with what Kol said.

"It's what your mother wants."

Kol's jaw nearly scraped the floor.

A loud boom reverberated the walls, and everyone flinched. It took two seconds for Kol to glance at his father before the two of them bounded toward the commotion. When Myreen let out a frustrated noise, Kol grabbed her hand and dragged her with him. He could hear the clack of his mother's heels close behind them as they raced from the office and down the hallway.

Students and soldiers stood as still as statues. Whatever the noise was, they'd heard it too. Which meant it was even larger than Kol assumed.

They made their way through the main building, Eduard stopping to speak with different officers along the way.

"Kol!" It was Nik with Juliet in tow—mirroring Kol and Myreen.

"What happened?" Kol asked.

Nik shrugged. "Everyone's panicked. We came to find you to see if you knew."

"We heard the noise," Myreen said.

Kol noticed an interchange between her and Juliet after the phoenix looked down at their interlocked fingers. He had an inkling what it meant, but couldn't think about that at the moment. He looked to where Eduard had been. But he was gone. And so was Victoria.

"Should we see if something...?" Myreen paused, like she didn't want to continue. Kol squeezed her hand, prompting her to look up at him. She did, but her expression didn't change. She looked back at Nik and Juliet. "If something is attacking from the lake?"

Kol wanted to smack himself in the head. He hadn't

thought of that. In all the years he'd attended the Dome, nothing had ever attacked from the lake until Draven took Myreen. Hell, nothing had attacked the Dome from *anywhere* until recently. Thinking back to the moment they heard the loud boom, there was nowhere else he could think that could be the source, except the glass that kept the lake out.

Another boom shook the walls, and four shifters—the same four who first encountered Draven's vampires and nearly lost—raced down the stairs and made their way out of the building. It was difficult because hordes of students were pouring *into* the building on their way to the subway entrance. The four had to swim upstream to get out.

It was darker than usual outside. The screen that so often simulated sunlight, instead of Lake Michigan, was turned off so that all that could be seen was the dark depths of the lake.

But the three thick, long appendages that draped themselves across the outside of the glass were unmistakable. Even if Kol hadn't experienced one in the sim, even if he didn't notice the round suction cups pressed against the glass, the sheer size of the tentacles were proof enough.

Myreen squeezed Kol's hand tightly and reached for Juliet's free one.

Someone screamed.

The Dome was being attacked by a kraken.

Juliet

Juliet sat in her room with Nik, Brett, Jesse, Leya, and Alessandra. Well, Katya was there, too, but Juliet hadn't quite forgiven her yet—or dismissed the idea that Katya had been the one to rat them out. After all, Major Peters only found them the same night Katya made her first attendance. But Katya swore she hadn't told, and Brett backed her up. So Juliet let it slide.

Myreen left to go spend some more time with Kol, and Juliet couldn't quite blame her. Those two love-birds deserved all the time they could manage to snag. And Kenzie had disappeared to who-knew-where, and she didn't have a phone on her, so that reunion would have to wait.

Juliet looked at the gathered group. All of them—well, aside from Katya—had gotten a taste of Dracul's wrath, and it showed. They were in no position to get caught again, but with Oberon's search coming to a head, no one wanted to quit. They were all willing to take any risk necessary to bring him home.

Besides, with Kol's return and that strange confrontation with his father that morning, everyone was hopeful things would be different. Maybe the general would even welcome the return of Oberon.

Katya typed away like a madwoman on her laptop, Brett and Nik hovering over her shoulders as she worked her magic. Juliet was too on edge to sit still, so she paced between her bed and desk.

The coordinates Juliet found had led them to some remote area in Canada, but they couldn't risk sending someone to check. Katya had volunteered to track them digitally, but as of yet, they hadn't been able to confirm anything.

To add to Juliet's anxiety, every noise she heard made her jump. Would General Dracul or one of his soldiers try to catch them again? She hoped Kol's presence would continue to soften the general, but that didn't mean her body had forgotten the punishment it had endured. And there was no sense getting comfortable, either. Even the best version of General Dracul couldn't compare to having Oberon as director.

"I just don't understand why we can't find him," Brett said, beginning to show signs of cabin fever.

"Because he's in the middle of nowhere," Katya spat back.

Brett sucked his teeth, then went to stand by the door, his arms folded. "I'll go get some grub for everyone. I'm sure I won't be missing anything." Brett slipped out the door.

Katya slammed her laptop shut, letting her head fall back to stare at the ceiling. "He's right. We're getting nowhere."

Jesse, Alessandra, and Leya shot worried glances at Nik.

"Let's just take a few, deep breaths," Nik said in his calm, soothing voice. Usually that worked to ease Juliet's nerves, but not this time.

Juliet couldn't believe she was siding with Brett. "We need more information."

"Come on," Nik said. "We have a map we aren't supposed to have, coordinates that took *you* all day to find, and a kitsune who rules the cyber world."

"Pfft. I wish. I'm nothing like Ren," Katya said, then added in a low tone, "But thanks."

"Ren..." Juliet said.

The group's eyes darted to Juliet, their faces reflecting the same look of confusion—well, except Jesse, who was grinning like a fool.

"What are the chances that Ren could be with Oberon?" Juliet began.

"And if he is..." Jesse added.

"Then he'd be working with something that gave off a signal," Nik finished, shooting Juliet a look of pride.

Katya reopened her laptop and began clacking at the keyboard. Juliet popped into the empty seat next to Katya, looking over one shoulder as Nik looked over the other. Jesse, Alessandra, and Leya stood nervously nearby, looking like they wanted to squeeze behind Katya, too.

Within two minutes, Katya was done. She removed her fingers from the laptop and stared at the screen. "Now we wait. Ren's tech is pretty distinctive, so I set parameters to scan for his signature, but I have a dual scan for any technology in that area, to anywhere within a five-hundred-mile radius of those coordinates. If we see any red waves, it's them. Blue waves could be them, but it's a little less sure. If it's a cluster of blue waves, then it's probably a town or something that isn't on the internet maps."

Juliet was thankful Brett wasn't there. He probably

wouldn't be able to sit through more waiting.

A crash sounded outside of Juliet's door. Juliet and Nik stood right away, Katya still glued to her laptop. Jesse, Leya, and Alessandra's head whipped toward the sound, their eyes wide.

A scream ripped Nik from his stupor, but before he could get to the door, it swung open to reveal a pale, panic-stricken Brett.

Katya's startled gaze went back to her laptop when it started beeping. "I found them! But that's weird... Not enough blue for a town or city, but there's definitely something else there... I can just connect to whatever Ren is streaming off of..." Katya seemed to be speaking more to herself as she started typing again.

"Brett, what's going on?" Nik asked, casting an anxious glance at Katya. Juliet could hear chaos in the hallways, but Brett had already shut the door, looking like he might never leave Juliet's room again.

"Everyone's going crazy. The rumor mill... The things they're saying... We're under attack. We're all gonna... Ugh, I don't feel so good." Brett sunk to the floor, his hands pulling at his hair like Kol often did.

Juliet held a hand in front of her mouth, stunned. "Who..? What..?"

Jesse took a quick glance around the room, then bolted, his eyes glowing an eerie red.

"Okay, Brett, get it together. We're going to need you," Nik said, springing to action. "Katya can you get through to Oberon or Ren?"

Katya shook her head. "I can't pinpoint the signal. There's some sort of interference I can't get around."

"Okay. Keep working on that. Juliet, you and I will rally the students and try to calm them down. We need to get the younger ones to safety, if possible. Brett, I want you to figure out exactly what's going on and let us know what you find. Leya, you'll probably be needed in the medical wing. Alessandra—"

"Don't worry about me," Alessandra said, whipping her hair over her shoulder and sauntering out the door.

Juliet shook her head, a wry grin on her face.

"Okay, Brett and Katya, join us in getting the younger students out as soon as you can." It seemed that Nik had everything under control—at least within the walls of her bedroom. Juliet couldn't be more grateful for her boyfriend than in that moment. From the way it sounded outside, they had a lot of work to do, but she felt ready for it.

"Let's go." Nik grabbed Juliet's hand as they took off to start gathering students, Brett jetting out behind them and heading downstairs.

Like a scene in a horror movie, students ran in every direction, some screaming, most crying. Nik let go of Juliet and with a single nod, he went left while Juliet went to the right. She spotted a group of girls crying and decided to start there. Hopefully she could get their cluster to break up and start moving.

"Guys, I know this is scary, but sitting here will only put you in more danger. If we move to the exit, we can work on escaping. If we work together, we can get through this. I promise. Follow me." It took her longer than she liked to get the girls moving, but once they were on their feet, Juliet led the terror-stricken girls to the exit platform. She stopped along the way to pick up others who were too afraid to move, the group getting stronger as they banded together.

"We got this, guys. We have to turn our fear into courage, our doubt into hope, and our innocence into strength. We can do this!"

Juliet and her group met up with Nik and his group and

they started ushering students onto the train, Nik checking with some of the older and more able to see if they truly wanted to flee or if they were willing to stay and fight.

Katya and Brett caught up to them as the first load of students sped away to what Juliet hoped was safety. They'd been instructed not to leave the secret platform before checking to see if the coast was clear.

"I can't be sure that Ren or Oberon will even see the messages, but I did my best," Katya said, bracing her hands on her knees.

Juliet high-fived Katya.

"Brett?" Nik asked.

Brett shrugged. "The Dome's projection screen is still lit, so I couldn't see what was going on, but the attack is definitely coming from the lake. My guess is it's vampires again, but it sounds... bigger than before. Maybe some sort of machinery?"

Nik nodded. "That's okay. Let's try and get as many students out as we can, and rally anyone who's willing to stay and fight. Katya, do you think you could turn off the projection screen so we can see what's out there?"

Katya nodded, then took off down the hallway.

Nik was still calling the shots, but Juliet could sense his calm starting to fade. She felt her own worry turn into determination. She'd be there for Nik, whatever he needed. They'd come through this together. Just like all the other times.

"We know how to fight," Juliet said, looking around at their small group. "Let's show these vamps! If General Dracul taught us anything, it's how to defend ourselves and our Dome."

There were murmurs and nods. Another tremor shook the school, screams and cries coming from everywhere.

Nik raised his hands, shooting Juliet a grateful glance.

"Alright, any of you who are willing to stay, we need your help gathering students. Anyone who wants to leave should be brought here and sent to the secret platform." Just then a fresh car arrived, the doors hissing open, as if eager to take more frightened students away. "You two," Nik said, pointing at a pair of students Juliet couldn't remember the names of, "stay here and help students onto the trains. We don't want to overload the cars and cause more harm than good."

The two students nodded and started directing waiting shifters onto the train. More students filtered in by the second, and Juliet briefly wondered how many would be left to help defend the Dome.

"The rest of you, let's get to work," Nik said, then clapped his hands. "We need to find Myreen and Kol," he said to Juliet as he took her hand, and she nodded.

Nik and Juliet took off running, through the Grand Hall and toward the training rooms.

"Kol!" Nik said just as Juliet spotted Kol and Myreen standing near General Dracul.

"What happened?" Kol asked.

Nik shrugged. "Everyone's panicked. We came to find you to see if you knew."

"We heard the noise," Myreen said.

Juliet looked at Mryeen's hand, interlocked with Kol's, and she exchanged a knowing look. The two were obviously back together. Too bad the timing sucked.

"Should we see if something...?" Myreen paused. She looked at Kol, worry etched on her face, then she looked back at Nik and Juliet. "If something's attacking from the lake?"

Another boom shook the walls. Juliet looked up, noticing for the first time that the simulated sunlight was off, the murky depths of the lake the only thing that could be seen. Katya must have figured it out.

Juliet wanted to smile, but three thick arms covered in suction cups pressed against the glass. Juliet could hardly breathe, and she almost didn't feel Myreen taking her free hand. Someone screamed, and Juliet shuddered.

"What the heck is that?" Juliet asked.

"A kraken," Kol replied, his soft voice and matter-of-fact tone so opposite of what Juliet was feeling.

Myreen's concerned face matched Juliet's.

Nik looked to Katya as she and Brett caught back up with the group. "Get all the kitsunes together. We need to try to get rid of that thing."

Katya nodded, then left on her new mission. Juliet gripped Nik's hand, the eerie silence of the Dome unsettling her. It made Juliet feel like something was going to explode at any moment.

Juliet, are you there?

Juliet squealed as she heard a voice not her own sounding in her mind. Had fear driven her mad? Everyone looked at Juliet as her squeal echo through the silent halls.

"Are you alright?" Nik whispered.

Letting go of Nik and Myreen's hands, Juliet shook her head and tapped by her ear, trying shake out the voice. But just when she thought she'd gotten her bearings back, the voice returned.

"Oh, duh, I should probably mention it's Kenzie in your head. And Juliet, if you're there, I'm going to need you to answer me out loud 'cause I can't hear that pretty head of yours rattle. It's magic, not a crystal ball. Okay, so I'm officially freaking out. Are you guys okay? Talk. To. Me!"

Juliet sighed in relief, glad her sanity wasn't failing her.

"Juliet?" Nik stared at her wide-eyed.

"Um, Kenzie... she's talking to me... in my head?" Juliet felt like she needed to sit. Instead, she walked to the wall and reached out her hand to hold her balance against it.

"What?" Nik and Brett said at the same time.

"Yes! It's me. In your head. Sort of. Is everyone okay?"

"Kenzie?" Juliet spoke to herself. She didn't understand how to communicate this way, and she couldn't quite remember what Kenzie had told her. Hopefully it was as easy as that.

"Are guys you safe? Who are you with?"

Juliet closed her eyes, as if it would make it easier to stay connected with Kenzie. "We're safe. I'm with Nik and Brett and Myreen and Kol and a bunch of other students. They're scared, but we're prepared to fight if we have to. Nik wants to try and get most everyone out. Where are you? Are you okay?"

"Yes, I'm fine. I'm outside the Dome. Long story. Sorry, I would've tried to contact Myreen first because she knows about this spell, but honestly my brain's fried and you're the first person that popped in when I cast it. Sorry if I freaked you out." Kenzie couldn't hide the worry in her tone, and Juliet's heart throbbed at her friend's panic.

"It's because she's a selkie, isn't it?" Nik asked, bringing up Juliet's chin so she would look at him. "Jules, do you think you can ask her if she could contact Oberon?"

She wanted to praise him for being a genius, but she felt she needed to concentrate. Instead, she spun away, burying her head and plugging her ears. "Kenz, we need a favor."

"Anything."

"We need Oberon. Do you think you can speak to him like this? Just to tell him that we're in danger and that we need him." Juliet's voice laced with desperation.

"Yes. Shouldn't be a problem. I'm going to try to get in

there as soon as I can. You all stay safe, you hear? Oh crap. Wes? What's this w—?" It was Kenzie's last message before she mentally hung up. Juliet felt it end, like a heaviness that lifted off her head.

She turned and faced Nik and the others. "She's doing it."

"Good," Nik said, and it seemed hope spread like a wildfire between the students.

Katya ran back at that moment, followed by a group of kitsunes. Juliet didn't know half of them, but she was grateful, nonetheless.

She looked around for General Dracul, for the first time noticing that he'd disappeared. Had the general of the shifter army really deserted them? She prayed Kenzie could get through to Oberon before it was too late.

Oberon

Family.

Oberon was with family again, and although they weren't his blood-relatives, they were his in-laws. That was close enough for him.

He and Ren had stayed overnight and all throughout the next day, getting acquainted with the Vogels. The group had just finished a hearty dinner, and the sun was on the verge of setting. The jovial feeling that had surrounded their becoming acquainted was beginning to wear off as conversations became more serious.

Oberon sat in a recliner inside the warm cabin living room, the nearby fireplace crackling with burning wood. On the couch across the way, Tobias—who, in human form, looked like a masculine form of Seri—sat next to his life-mate Gwendolyn. Their daughter, June, sat cross-legged in front of the fireplace, staring into the depths of the orange-red coals, lost in her own thoughts.

"All this time, we thought she'd died." It was Seri's father, Gabriel Vogel, who was sitting on the arm of another couch nearby. He was holding the hand of his wife—Seri's mother. Oberon loved her name—Savannah—it seemed to suit her well. She looked like an older version of Seri, with wrinkles and white hair that hinted at being blonde in her early years. The biggest difference between them were their eyes. Oberon's mother-in-law's were a dark brown. Seri inherited her father's blue eyes.

Sitting on the other side of Savannah was Seri's grand-mother.

Seri had very few memories of her family. She'd been "orphaned" as a five-year-old, and had only ever told Oberon small details she remembered—a camping trip, lullabies, and other such things.

Gabriel continued. "We were in Maine when we lost her. Savannah was pregnant with Tobias, although we didn't know it at the time. The vampires struck fast and hard. My father was killed in the attack, and after the vamps leveled our house, little Seri was nowhere to be found. We wanted to go back and search for her, but it was too dangerous. Vamps stayed close by, watching and waiting to see if we'd return. And little Seri... We always assumed the worst."

Oberon set his jaw as he stared at the dancing flames in the rock fireplace. "Somehow, she got away. But the vampires got her in the end." A lump formed in his throat as he said it, and the image of her lifeless body lying in a pool of blood flashed through his mind.

"But she found her life-mate," Savannah said. "At least she was able to experience the joy of gryphon love."

Oberon nodded, tears stinging his eyes. "Yes. I fell in love with her the day we met. We were quite inseparable after my father found Seri and brought her to The Island."

"The Island?" Tobias said. "What's that?"

Oberon chuckled, managing to tear his gaze from the flames. "The Island was a school for shifters that stood for fifty years. We had students from all over. Within its walls, we felt protected and safe to study and learn how to best use our abilities."

"That sounds like a place of paradise," Gwendolyn said.

"It sounds like a huge target for the vampires," Gabriel corrected.

Oberon shrugged. "It was well hidden. It took the vampires half a century to find it."

Savannah sniffed, and Oberon found her crying. "That's when you lost Seri, isn't it?"

Oberon didn't have it in his heart to tell them about the baby. His eyes marked June, and he could almost imagine a child of his own, not much older than she, sitting in front of the fire.

"That's when I lost everything," Oberon said distantly.

"Except for me," Ren said from the corner of the room. Oberon had almost forgotten the kitsune was present, he'd been so unusually quiet. But Ren was smart enough to know that this was an important moment, and Oberon was grateful for it.

"Yes, Ren has been my closest friend through thick and thin," Oberon said. "I lost Seri that terrible day, but I also lost my parents. A lot of shifters died that day. I thought..." The lump in his throat grew, and his voice threatened to fail him. "For a long time, I thought I was the last gryphon in the world."

"We're still around," Gabriel said. "But there are so few of us left."

"What happened to the school?"

Oberon glanced at June, surprised that the young lady chimed into the conversation.

"It was destroyed," he said. "But I helped start another one. It's hidden from the vampires and is the safest place for shifters. Students are guided by teachers and are taught how to master their abilities. History, biology, and mathematics are among a few of the classes we provide, and—" He stopped himself, smiling as he dropped his eyes to the cabin floor. "Forgive me. That was turning into a recruitment pitch."

"I want to go," June said.

"That's out of the question," Tobias countered as soon as June spoke, as if he'd known she'd say it. "Did you not just hear the story about The Island? An assembly of shifters is just asking for a vampire massacre."

"They can't reach us," Oberon said. "The school is at the bottom of a lake. The entire structure is built with copper alloys running throughout. Entering the school would bring death to any vampire."

The group fell silent, and the crackling flames in the fireplace seemed to grow louder. It was Seri's grandmother who spoke, her voice aged and soft.

"Juniper is no longer a child. A school of shifters sounds like the right place for her. She has nobody here she can relate to."

"We're not tearing this family apart," Tobias argued. "School or no school, June's place is here with her own kind."

Oberon nodded. He didn't come searching for gryphons to cause family disputes. "Just know that the door will always remain open. June will always be welcome."

Tobias sat back, noticeably relaxing.

Savannah cleared her throat. "Did you and Seri consider having any children?"

There it is, he thought. It was hard enough to bring Seri up, let alone their unborn child.

He sucked in his lower lip for a moment before answering. "She was pregnant when The Island fell. When she—"

A loud chirp sounded, and Oberon nearly fell out of his chair. "What's that?" he asked, casting his eyes about to find the source of the noise.

The Vogels were already on their feet, panic lacing each of their faces.

"Proximity alert," Gabriel hissed. "Someone tripped the Sanctum sensors."

Ren suddenly disappeared, phasing into the wall.

"Preen my feathers," Savannah gasped. "Your friend just walked through the wall."

Oberon didn't respond, running to the nearest window. The sun had already set, and he couldn't see much. His breath steamed the glass, which didn't help with visibility.

"Did anybody know you were coming here?" Gabriel asked.

Oberon shook his head. "The seer who sent us this way was the only one."

"Would your seer have told anybody else where you were going?"

Oberon considered the question for a moment. Would Delphine sell him out? Even if she'd informed Eduard about his quest, he highly doubted the general would get involved. He had bigger issues to see to. "She knows just how important finding gryphons is to me. Whoever these visitors are, I don't think they came from her."

Ren rematerialized in the living room, his eyes wide. "Vampires. They're ransacking one of the other cabins right now."

Tobias threw Oberon an accusing glare. "They followed you here."

Oberon tasted the terror in the room. It was thick and

growing thicker.

"That's impossible," he said. "The vampires wouldn't know about my quest."

"They have Myreen," Ren reminded. "Draven could've discovered from her that you're no longer the director. He wouldn't pass up the opportunity to hunt down a gryphon."

Oberon set his jaw. "If that's the case, he just struck gold." He looked at the scared Vogels surrounding him. They were looking to him for help. They were looking to him as a leader.

And Oberon realized that this was his second chance. This was the opportunity he'd missed at La Framboise Island. He wouldn't let the vampires hurt Seri's family. *His* family. He would protect them. Or die trying.

"You all need to shift. Right now. Shift into your gryphon forms and take to the skies."

"What about you?" Tobias asked.

Oberon looked at Ren. "We've got some payback to take care of, don't we?"

Red fur sprouted along Ren's skin, bursting through the clothing the Vogels lent to him. His nose elongated, and his ears rose farther up his head, coming to black points. With a swish, nine tails blossomed like a budding rose behind him, already crackling with electricity.

"I'm ready to rock and roll," Ren said. Without another word, the kitsune phased through the wall once again.

Turning his gaze back to the Vogels—who were now all clustered together in terror—Oberon pointed to the safest exit and said, "Out the back door. Don't worry about your clothes. Just get outside, shift, and fly away."

They didn't need more prodding. Savannah led the way, holding Grandma Vogel's hand. Once they'd filed out, Oberon ran for the main entrance, leaving the comfortable cabin and stepping into the harsh chill of the Canadian Rockies.

Crashing noises were coming from one of the other cabins. It enraged Oberon to know they were desecrating his family's sanctuary.

"Hey! Draven's little pets!" he called out, still in human form. "Looking for someone?"

The door peeled from its hinges and was tossed aside. A dark mist hovered at the doorway, then slowly faded into a person. No, a vampire. Two more appeared behind him.

"Oberon Rex, the infamous gryphon," he jeered, taking small steps forward. He was in no hurry to start a fight.

Oberon extended his arms out to the sides. "I'm afraid I don't know you. Where's Draven? Too busy to come himself?"

Two other vampires emerged from the cabin. Five in total. Oberon wondered how many more were hiding within.

The five began to fan out, slowly closing in on his position.

The lead vampire snickered. "It's mighty big of you to think you're worth Draven's time. But he's got bigger fish to fry, so to speak. You're just a minor detail. Like a little dust bunny on a great tapestry that needs some cleaning."

Oberon popped his knuckles, as if preparing for a fist fight. Of course, he'd never try such a foolish thing with a vampire. "Actually, I think he's scared of me. The last time we fought, he barely stepped away alive."

A chorus of laughter erupted from the vampires now surrounding him, and he took the moment of distraction to call upon the sky above. In an instant, black storm clouds blotted out the starry sky like a jar of ink spilling over.

"I think you underestimate us, pal," the lead vampire said. "And Draven."

Thunder boomed overhead, and Oberon began to shift. His brown feathers grew like thick hairs, and his form increased. Taloned claws tore through his shoes. Lighting flashed nearby just as he finished the transformation, causing the converging vampires to stop.

"And you underestimate a gryphon protecting his family."

With his powerful wings, he launched himself into the air, then summoned a mighty wind to blow. The vampires toppled over from the monstrous gust, uselessly trying to grab at the snowy ground that continually gave way before them.

"Turn back now," he yelled, sending his voice on the wind. "If you don't, your doom awaits you."

Oberon knew that Ren was useless as long as the wind kept up—he'd be blown away just as quickly as the vampires. But he only summoned the wind to disorient the attackers. He willed it to subdue again, letting it peter out with one final breeze.

The vampires got to their feet, looking at each other, communicating with their expressions. For a moment, Oberon wondered if they were going to retreat. And then the hulking vampire held a finger to his ear. Even from how far away Oberon was, he heard the vampire say, "Shoot him down, Brody."

From behind, there was a resounding clap, and Oberon felt a slight displacement in his right wing. Flying higher, he angled to get a look at whoever and whatever had shot at him.

To the west stood Ren, his lightning tails sizzling with electricity. Next to him, a beheaded vampire body crumpled to the ground, his head off to the side a foot or so.

Ren raised a paw and gave him a lazy salute. "Just like the good old days," the kitsune yelled up to him. "I've *still* got your back." He swirled his tails about as he analyzed the other vampires.

"He killed Brody!" the front vampire said, pointing a pale

finger at Ren. "He killed our brother! Kill the fox!"

The five charged forward faster than sight, but Oberon didn't need to see the oncoming enemy to strike them with bolts of lightning. Electricity had a way of finding conductors just fine on its own.

From the sky, five individual bolts plummeted like spears, forking and angling until they struck their targets.

In an instant the vampires were blown back, thrown farther than what the wind had done. And the lightning didn't stop raining down on them. Fluttering down to the leader, Oberon watched him convulse as unharnessed energy immobilized him. The vampire's eyes were wide, and Oberon wondered if he was even capable of hearing. It didn't matter much, though.

"I learned my lesson over twenty years ago," he said. "A vampire can never be struck with too much lightning."

Releasing his hold on the single bolt, Oberon pounced on top of the large vampire, who was still quaking on the snowy ground as if the bolt was still striking him.

With a quick snap of his beak, Oberon popped the vampire's head off like a bottle cap, then flung it away.

"Ren, let's make quick work of the rest," Oberon called out, releasing his hold on the four remaining vampires.

"I thought you'd never ask," Ren replied. Like a shade in the night, the kitsune ran from vampire to vampire, ending their miserable existences with crackling blows.

Oberon looked into the sky, dispelling the storm clouds and revealing the pale moon and blinking stars. Even night could not contain light.

High above him, he could see the Vogels circling like vultures over carrion. But these were more than vultures waiting for an easy meal. These were gryphons. They were family.

"I just did a perimeter sweep," Ren said, coming to Oberon's side. "I think we're in the clear."

"Thank you, my friend," Oberon said. "I'll gather the Vogels."

Launching himself back into the night sky, he pumped his wings as hard as he could, climbing toward his family. In no time, he was among them. June still struggled, but Tobias and Gwendolyn were doing a good job keeping her wings steady. It was the gray-feathered Grandma Vogel that surprised Oberon the most. Like the gracefulness of a ballerina, she danced through the sky, seemingly a youth enjoying her freedom. He watched her with marvel.

"That was quite a sight, Oberon," Gabriel said, flying close to him. "You must have a lot of experience fighting vampires."

"More than I should," he replied. "But come, let's return to the Sanctum and get you all back inside the warmth. It's been a tough night."

***

The cabin the vampires had attacked from was a complete mess. They hadn't just overturned furniture—they'd destroyed it beyond repair.

"We'll have to build new furniture," Tobias said picking up part of a headboard and shaking his head.

"You all have the choice to remain," Oberon started, "but I'd highly advise against staying here. It's likely the vampires notified Draven about our location before they attacked. No doubt, there'll be more who come."

Tobias sighed heavily, throwing the mangled wood to the floor.

"Where would we go?" Gabriel asked. "With you? Back to the shifter school you spoke of?"

Oberon looked him in the eye. "The Dome could house

you all, at least temporarily. But it *is* a school. If any of you are willing to teach,"—he glanced at June—"or be taught, there's always room."

"*Oberon?*"

He frowned at the voice in his head. He'd never experienced anything quite like it. It was a girl's voice, emerging like a hand from a wall.

"*Oberon, can you hear me?*"

"Am I going mad? What's going on?" he mumbled, then felt the eyes of all the Vogels look in his direction.

"*Whoops! No time to explain. This is Kenzie MacLugh, the selkie. We've met before. I'm Myreen's friend.*"

"What are you doing in my head?" he said, shoving his fingers through his brown hair. It had been a long time since he'd felt so unsettled.

"*No time! The Dome is under attack. Maybe even all of Chicago. We need you.* Right. Now!"

Myreen

Myreen stared at the Dome as the pressure from the kraken began to cause the glass to groan and crack. But there was something else just beyond the massive body of the kraken, something that turned her blood cold.

She could see the deep red sunset through the water.

The warm hues cast an eerie glow, one that shouldn't even be possible considering how deep the Dome was beneath the surface of the lake. Which meant that either the Dome was being ripped from its place along the bed of the lake, or the water was ebbing. Based on the fact that she could see Draven walking along the bottom of the lake, a gleeful smile on his devilish face, the sides of his neck moving with an unnatural flow, Myreen was certain that the water was receding.

Draven had done it. He was a hybrid. And her blood had given him this power.

Myreen closed her eyes and tried to reach out to the

disappearing lake, but it was no use. Water manipulation had always been her weakest ability.

A group of kitsune students gathered around the edges of the Dome, under the direction of Nik and Juliet. They sent bolts of electricity through the glass and toward the kraken's tentacles, hoping to shake him free.

The kraken gave a monstrous roar, lifting arm after arm away, only to relatch onto the glass moments later.

Myreen thought she could see Draven laughing, though the water along the bed had grown murky from all the activity. He must have the kraken under his control. Myreen wondered where such a beast could have come from. But another roar reminded Myreen of the hideous screech they'd heard when leaving the citadel.

Myreen's eyes widened as she saw mer heading into the water. The mer trio were among them, and Alessandra looked Myreen's way, giving her a nod before ducking into the secret exit. Going out there was suicide.

"I have to join them," Myreen said, but Kol's hand on her arm steadied her even as it held her back.

"And do what? You've said it yourself, your mer powers aren't your biggest strength."

"I can't just let everyone around here die for me! I have to do something. This has to end."

"And what are you going to do? Surrender to Draven again? Myreen, he's not here for you. Not this time. He won't stop until we're destroyed."

Myreen swallowed as she surveyed the mounting destruction. Red hair caught her eye as Delphine's slender form ducked into the secret exit, but not before giving Myreen a knowing wink.

The prophecy.

But what could she do? She was no more prepared now than when she first learned of it. And then the murk in the water outside cleared, just for a moment, and Myreen caught a glimpse of Draven, confident in his new powers. It sickened her what he'd done...

And in that moment, she knew what she had to do.

Draven was far too powerful. It was time he met his match.

Myreen scanned the faces of the crowd, not resting until she found what she was looking for. Leif's pale skin and dark hair stood in stark contrast to the bustle of shifters scrambling to defend their home. But he was wearing a shifter army-issued uniform, and he was walking alongside the last person she ever expected: General Dracul.

Myreen slipped away from Kol as he tried to help some others, pushing through the crowd until she reached her target. She laid a hand on Leif's arm, and he turned to look at her, concern in his blue eyes. She was struck by how unchanged he was, the photo of him in Kol's history book, though aged, could've easily been taken yesterday.

"I need your help. Come with me."

Leif's brows creased, but he nodded. He turned his head to address the general. "Eduard, I'll be back in a moment."

Lord Dracul nodded, his lips pulled into a tight line.

Myreen found the first empty room she could and pulled Leif in. "I need you to change me."

Confusion flitted across his face, slowly replaced by horror as he realized what she was asking. "No," he said, shaking his head emphatically.

"Please. This is our only chance to defeat Draven." There was the hint of a whine in her voice, but she needed him to change her. If he didn't, there was no one else who could.

"There's got to be another way," Leif said, running a hand through his long, dark hair.

The Dome shook again, and a horrific creaking echoed throughout. Hissing followed, and the unmistakable patter of water on stone drove Myreen's point home better than words ever could.

"Don't you see? There *is* no other way. I'm the only person capable of becoming a hybrid, but I can't do it without you."

"What if my bite kills you?" Leif asked, pacing the length of the room. "You won't be able to help anyone if you're dead."

Myreen straightened her spine. "It *will* work. It has to."

The prophecy she so dreaded now gave her strength. With every fiber of her being, she knew this was what was supposed to happen, what *needed* to happen if the shifters were going to survive and Draven was going to be defeated once and for all. Her stomach still churned at the thought of having to kill him, but this was so much bigger than her. Her friends were putting their lives on the line. This had to stop before she lost everything she loved.

She wouldn't get another chance.

"I've never turned anyone before," Leif said, his voice quiet and thick with emotion. "I never wanted to subject anyone else to this abhorrent life. Now you're asking me to throw all that aside on a gamble."

Myreen bit her lip. She understood this was a gamble, but it was a gamble she had to take. "I was made for this. Draven thought he was creating the means to power, but he was creating his own undoing."

"You should know that it took me three days to go from bite to fully-formed vampire. We don't know how long this will take. You could be incapacitated for hours or even days."

Myreen shook her head, the movements becoming more vigorous the more Leif talked. "We can't think like that. This has to be done. Please."

Leif stared at her for a long moment, a pained look on his grave face.

There was another roar and a groaning creak, followed by an increase in the sound of leaking water, which bore the echo of many locations and the steady rush of a waterfall. Shrieks followed. Myreen gave Leif another pleading look.

Leif swallowed, then gave an almost imperceptible nod.

Myreen lifted the hair from her neck, focusing on the other wall, unable to face what was coming. The moments ticked by and she worried that Leif had changed his mind. But a moment later, cool hands gripped her arms.

"The most effective way to do this is to drain your whole body of blood. The venom will begin to take effect before that, and I'm not sure if the sedative venom will be enough to counter the effects of turning you. I'll try to be as efficient and gentle as possible, but I can give you no guarantees." He paused, letting out a long breath that tickled her neck. "Last chance to back out."

"No. Do it." Myreen had no idea what would happen, but she had faith this would all work out. She clung to that belief with every fiber of her being, silently praying that she wasn't making the worst mistake of her life.

Pain lanced her neck, followed almost instantaneously by a sense of comfort and goodwill like she'd never experienced.

A sigh escaped her lips. This was a good feeling, one she never wanted to end. Her eyes became heavy, her body going limp as she sank into the bliss enveloping her. She could almost hear her mother's voice calling to her, almost feel those soft arms encompassing her as her mind slid further and further away.

And then her body seized, snapping Myreen out of her happy memories. She cried out, and the pressure on her neck ceased, but the fire in her blood raged on. It felt almost like when the ursa in her had activated, but worse.

So. Much. Worse.

She barely felt the cold arms around her, keeping her from crashing to the floor. Her body convulsed, her teeth chattering so hard she thought she might chip a tooth. The burn flowing through her veins alternated between fire and ice, pricking and poking like thousands of tiny needles.

Myreen wanted to die, to end the pain once and for all. There was a rumble and a quake, and Myreen couldn't tell if it came from her or the Dome.

She was falling apart.

She was ruined.

Despair blinked through the encroaching blackness, and Myreen reached for those edges, hoping to pull them close, to succumb to the nothingness that would end her suffering.

Just as suddenly as it had begun, it stopped. Myreen thought she must be dead. She swirled through the blissful blackness, quiet solitude blanketing her like an old friend.

But there was a creaking groan, and a fresh wave of screams.

Myreen willed her eyes to open, and they obeyed in a blink. The brightness of... well, everything, caused her to squint, but her eyes quickly adjusted. The world was in technicolor, clearer and more brilliant than she'd ever seen. Myreen bolted upright, and the arms holding her let go, Leif's body stumbling backwards.

"Are you all right?" Myreen asked, speeding to Leif's side as fast as she could think.

Leif reared away from her. "Whoa! You might need to slow

down."

Myreen shook her head. "I'm sorry. I didn't realize..."

She looked down at her hands, their porcelain features more perfect than she ever remembered. On a whim, she flicked a finger, and a long harpy talon emerged, making Leif flinch again.

"Sorry." She retracted her talon, feeling for her ursa and mermaid as well. They were all still inside her.

Finally, she put a tentative hand to her mouth. Her teeth felt no different... until she willed them to come out, and her canines grew into wicked fangs.

"Are *you* all right?" Leif asked, scrutinizing her.

Myreen shook her head. "Yes? I think so." Power surged through every muscle, her body zinging with energy. She could fly for days, climb peaks in mere minutes, destroy any obstacle in her path. Myreen looked at Leif with an awed smile. "It worked."

Leif breathed a sigh of relief. "That looked painful."

Myreen laughed. "It was worse. But it was worth it. I'm a hybrid now. I'm actually surprised it happened so quickly."

Leif shrugged. "I've known Draven a long time, and he doesn't do things in halves. I'm sure he did everything he could to make the hybrid process as quick and painless as possible."

Myreen giggled with a lightheaded sort of giddiness. "Or maybe just quick. I can't imagine anything could be worse than what I just went through."

The Dome rocked again, and Myreen threw out a hand to stabilize herself.

"We're running out of time," Leif said, meeting Myreen's wide-eyed gaze. "It's up to you now."

Myreen took a steadying breath. "Thank you. For everything you've done for the shifters. For *me*."

Leif nodded. "Now if you'll excuse me, I'm sure others

could use my help."

"Of course." Myreen swallowed as Leif left, then followed him into the chaos.

The kitsunes still held their positions on the edge, but the rising water inside the Dome made it difficult to send electricity anywhere without accidentally zapping anyone nearby. And their efforts were hindered by the mer outside, who were doing their best to dislodge the kraken, though the enormous tentacles were nearly immovable. Even as she watched, one arm swiped at a mer, pinning her to the Dome.

Myreen's eyes widened, a gasp escaping her lips as she realized it was Trish pinned to the glass. Joanna and Alessandra rushed to her aid, but they weren't enough. Trish's eyes bulged, her face and body pressed awkwardly against the Dome.

Anger bubbled within Myreen, and she focused every ounce of it on the monster outside.

"Stop," she commanded, the mellifluous tones of her voice rising above the din. The panic in the Dome ceased, but it was the kraken outside that caught her attention. The arms were disconnecting from the Dome. "You will no longer attack this place or these people," she sang further, unwilling for any misunderstanding to hinder the kraken's retreat.

A smile formed on Myreen's lips. She was winning.

A cheer went up from the crowd, but it was another noise that caught her attention. The kraken reacted to the noise, slamming tentacles back to the glass, though it hesitated, turning its head as if looking for assurances as to what to do.

Confused, Myreen commanded the kraken again, and he began to relent. But the opposing sound came once more, the tug-of-war of wills evident in the jerking motions of the fluid creature.

This time she recognized the voice, despite the melodious

chords that bolstered it. Chills erupted on her arms and went zinging down her spine.

It was a sound so much like her own voice.

It was a chilling song that bore no melody.

It was the voice of her father.

Draven had inherited her siren powers.

CHAPTER 51

Kenzie

Her magical call to Oberon over, Kenzie's panic rose fast. Water seeped through the streets of Chicago as if someone was running a hose through a slip-and-slide, except there was no quick ride to the other end.

"Where's it coming from?" Kenzie asked Wes.

"Looks to me like the lake is emptying out." He stood a short ways in front of her, squinting over the expanse of water.

"Into Chicago?" Kenzie asked in utter disbelief. How could this happen? Was the kraken displacing that much water? Sure, it was huge, but not quite huge enough for this. Right?

"That's not natural. Look." Wes pointed at the shore—or at least, where it had been just minutes before. Water lapped over the edge, looking like fingers raking at the land.

"Holy crap! How in the world—?"

"Mermaids can manipulate water like that, but I've never

495

heard of it happening on such a large scale like this."

Kenzie wrinkled her nose. "Do you think the kraken is doing it?"

Wes shrugged. "All I know is if this keeps up, Chicago will be underwater in no time."

It was true. Already the water had risen from her ankles to her knees. Debris began to sweep by in the current, the contents of the lake bed mixing with the trash of the city.

Kenzie slung her bag off her back, careful to keep it above water and said, "Nochtann a coinnasha." She opened the instantly-heavier bag and took out the now-revealed book, saying the MacLugh name and opening it. There were tons of spells in there, and some were even for use with water, but nothing was quite what she needed—something that would stop the flow and keep all of Chicago safe. She knew without looking, but hope drove her forward, praying that she'd missed something, that she'd overlooked something—anything—helpful.

As the water reached her waist, Kenzie slammed the book shut and dropped it in her bag. The sun had sunk below the horizon, the twilight hues turning the dusky rose of sunset to blues and grays.

A noise caught Kenzie's ears, a sloshing in the water. Most of the people had fled, seeking shelter from the unnatural flood, though a few stood around staring, while even fewer seemed to be trying to go about their lives as normal—one such man was hitting the hood of his car, cursing it and bemoaning the fact that he was going to be late to a meeting.

The sloshing noise didn't come from any of them. Kenzie peered into the growing dim, her heart beating in her throat. What new hell awaited them?

As the first pale face zipped past, Kenzie screamed. Her

panic was taken up by the humans still around, and Wes was by her side a moment later, his wet arms encircling her.

Another vampire ran past, and then another and another. None of them seemed to notice her and Wes, huddled in the middle of the street. They obviously had other goals.

Kenzie had to do something before all of Chicago was underwater, but the vampires were headed for the school. She wanted to warn someone, but she didn't think she had time. A muffled roar rose from the waters, and then there was a sound, so similar to the siren voice Myreen had used, yet distinctly male.

"No," Kenzie whispered, despair taking hold. "No, no, no." She shook her head, her teeth beginning to chatter as the water and the wind and the cold winter day finally began to take its toll. "Cheás," she said, directing the warmth at both her and Wes. That siren sound couldn't be Draven. But even as she denied it, she knew it must be the truth. He'd used Myreen's blood, and had inherited her powers. Would anyone ever be able to stop him?

But the water was nearly covering her stomach. She couldn't think about what might be; she had to do something. Now!

Kenzie closed her eyes, thinking back on all the spells she knew. Barriers and warmth and moving things came to mind. None of the spells were perfect, but if she could just bring their essence into something cohesive...

"Kenzie, we have to get out of here," Wes said by her side, but she shushed him.

An idea was forming, something terrifying: an experiment in magic. She knew what it did to her father, but if she didn't try something, the damage would be too great. She sent a quick prayer that her efforts wouldn't cause more harm than good.

First she'd go simple. Maybe if she could put on the water,

like she did the seal skin, she'd have a shot at bending it to her will. It was stupid, but easier and less dangerous than trying to make up her own spell.

"Aon," Kenzie commanded her magic, focusing on the water. But her body refused to take the mantle. Just as well. She had no idea what would happen if she turned herself into water.

"Fiáscha na... Fiáscha na ulsché," Kenzie said, trying to bolster her confidence. Her father's story played in her mind over and over. She didn't want to kill herself with a stupid spell—or Wes, for that matter. Kenzie swallowed, and repeated the beginning of her cobbled spell. "Fiáscha na ulsché. Aonrúgh, cheás— Ow!" Heat lanced her temples, her fingers seemingly on fire. Behind her, Wes roared, his fingers clawing into her arms. "Scrioságham" she cried. The burning sensation stopped.

Wes's grip eased. "What the—? Kenzie, you can't—"

"I have to!"

"Let's get to higher ground first," Wes argued, and she could hear the panic and desperation lacing his voice.

"We don't have time." Already the water was up to her chin, and Wes had to hold onto her to keep them from being pushed through the streets. Kenzie turned to face Wes. "I love you," she said, then pressed her lips to his, the desperate need for him to know the depth of her feeling driving her momentary indulgence. Just in case...

But Kenzie couldn't think of that. She pulled away from Wes, though he still held onto her, then turned her head to the sky and hoped she had enough breath to finish the spell. "Fiáscha na ulsché, thobh thriarah de'thaobha. Aonrúgh, cheás, camdach e diúltidhá!" Kenzie focused all her magic, willing every ounce into the water—which was slowly beginning to pull them into its sweeping current—into protecting her and Wes and all of

Chicago. Just as the water began to crest her upturned chin, it fell away. Both Kenzie and Wes stumbled, though Wes was able to keep them from falling. Kenzie opened her eyes to see what had happened. A bubble surrounded her and Wes, warm enough that they wouldn't freeze from the damp and wind. The water flowed around the bubble, leaving the protected area dry.

She'd done it.

But it needed to be bigger. So much bigger.

Kenzie let go of Wes and turned her hands toward the lake. "Wes, cover me."

There was no way the incoming vampires would ignore her now, though she hadn't seen any recently. Maybe they were all past? Maybe Draven didn't have so large an army as they'd feared. Maybe—

A splash behind her made Kenzie turn around. Adam leapt through the bubble she'd created, landing in a crouch before Wes. Kenzie lost her breath, her every ability to move. *No.*

"Kenzie! Do your thing. I've got you," Wes said, throwing a protective arm in front of her while not taking his eyes off Adam.

Kenzie took a stuttering breath, tears forming in her eyes as she focused once more on the lake. "Fiáscha na ulsché thobh thriarah de'thaobha. Fiáscha na ulsché thobh thriarah de'thaobha." Kenzie intoned the first half of the spell over and over, focusing on enlarging the bubble around her and Wes— and now Adam.

A fierce growl sounded behind her, and then a pained screech. Kenzie felt as if she'd been punched in the gut. She turned to peek, but couldn't tear her gaze away once she saw. Wes and a polar bear—an ursa—faced off. Where had the ursa come from? But the ursa felt familiar, and Adam was nowhere in sight... Did Draven make Adam a hybrid?

Wes lunged at the ursa. "Kenzie! Your magic. Focus!"

Kenzie nodded, turning her back on the scene. Already the bubble was beginning to shrink. She couldn't afford to waste any more magic. A screech sounded, and Kenzie wanted to turn, but held onto her hope that Wes was alive, winning, keeping her safe. She had to believe, though the pain racking her body made her doubt.

"You sure know how to pick 'em, Kenzie," Adam said.

Kenzie squeezed her eyes shut and focused. She didn' want the bubble protecting them to shrink—or worse, collapse. With fresh moisture on her cheeks and a tremble to her voice, she continued the spell. It was working. She'd seen the bubble expanding, and could feel it even now as she continued her chant, but it still wasn't large enough, and it wasn't growing as fast as she needed it to.

And Wes was in pain. She could feel it in every fiber of her being.

Kenzie put all her fears and frustrations into the spell, bidding it to grow beyond herself, beyond the city. Every once in a while, she'd add the second line, reinforcing the bubble and lending a little warmth. And she did her best to ignore the jabs of pain that struck her, and the cries of the cougar she loved behind her as he dueled with the vampire who had done nothing but use her.

And so she didn't notice when two new figures came to stand by her side, lending their magic to her own, until the effects began to bolster, began to push the water further up and out. It was as if it was caught between two walls, though the wall Kenzie created grew larger and firmer with every breath.

Kenzie felt the first pinprick of hope as she realized the voices beside her were that of Mom and Gram. How they'd gotten here so fast, she had no idea. She'd have to ask them later. For now, they needed to keep fueling the bubble of protection.

A warm and wrinkled hand on her face made Kenzie's eyes fling open. Gram was looking her in the eye, not breaking her own utterance of the spell as she broke eye contact and her gaze hit something behind Kenzie. Kenzie's eyes widened, and her lips stuttered. Gram gave her a nod and a nudge toward it. Apparently Gram thought they could handle things without Kenzie for a moment.

Kenzie held her breath as she turned to see what Gram was indicating, her chest growing tight, her feet like lead. She couldn't look, and yet curiosity drove her onward.

When her gaze locked onto the two figures there, a sharp intake of air cut off the cry trying to burst from her.

The eerie twilight boasted an even deeper shade, thanks to the watery dome working to protect the city, and it cast a chilling hue on the scene before her. Wes, still in cougar form, lay on the ground, panting and bleeding. Standing over Wes was the polar bear ursa—Adam—the bones of his face and nose snapping back into place with a sickening pop and the white fur receding into his skin. Kenzie held a hand over her mouth as bile threatened to overwhelm her.

Adam's gaze sped to hers, and she had the fleeting thought that she must look as pale as him. He sneered, taking a step over Wes's now-prone form. "You left me for *that*?" he spat. He spread his arms wide. "What do you think of me now? I'm a cuddly shifter, too. You can have it all, Kenzie." But Kenzie couldn't find her tongue. Adam wiped some blood off his face and licked his fingers, then scowled. "Tainted by that mangy thing. You, however, will sate me nicely."

"No," Kenzie breathed, a gag doubling her over. Wes

groaned behind Adam. She had to help him. "Fiáscha na olch," she ground out the first part of the vampire binding spell, thrusting her hand toward him, praying it would work despite his hybrid status. He was on her in a second, but as the last word came tumbling out, he froze, his extended canines grazing the skin of her neck.

Kenzie spit out the bile in her mouth, then cleared her throat. "Tóggo boggé na folía," she continued, her magic binding tighter around the vampire-shifter hybrid. She straightened just enough to look Adam in the eyes, her confidence bolstering. "You will *never* use me again."

A moment later, Adam's eyes widened with horror, his mouth opening as blood poured out. He fell forward, and Kenzie saw Wes just behind, holding an arm around his own middle, his other hand letting go of the knife sticking out of Adam's back.

Wes gave Kenzie a weak smile, then crumpled to the ground next to Adam. Kenzie went down with Wes, biting back a fresh wave of nausea and pain. He was naked, so she pulled off her coat and draped it over him, though for his sake, not for hers. All she wanted now was to know that he was okay, but she could feel the life draining from him. It leached from her as well, binding them in a morbid downward spiral. She wanted to ask him about the knife that clattered to the ground behind her, pushed out by gravity, but didn't think she had the time.

"I have to let go... of you," Wes rasped, his hand finding hers. Horror lanced her as she realized what he was saying. Their connection, the one that formed as a result of him marking her as his mate, connected them physically. Every jab, every ounce of pain she'd felt while Adam and Wes fought mirrored Wes's wounds, laid bare by his nakedness. She could feel his life ebbing, even as it pulled on hers. Wes was dying.

A sob escaped as Kenzie's fingers curled around his, their warmth so quickly fading. "No. You assume I'll let *you* go." Her lips found his, still coated in his blood. Sorrow helped her push her revulsion aside. Their kiss tasted of metal and salt, of sorrows and could-have-beens. This *couldn't* be their last one, but Kenzie put her all into the kiss anyway, unwilling to leave things any other way.

She broke away with a sniffle, then wiped her nose. "You can't die on me. I just got you back."

Wes groaned again. "I won't... take you down... with me."

"Leasheth'asa," Kenzie breathed, directing all her magic into him, willing it to make him whole again. She was tired, so tired, but she needed Wes to live. None of this would be worth it without him there. "Leasheth'asa!" she shouted at him, demanding that he heal, that he be okay.

Gram was by her side a moment later, silently directing Kenzie's attention above, even as she continued to chant the spell of protection holding the bubble of magic up. Kenzie tore her eyes from Wes's ashen face only to see the magic dome was shrinking. They needed her to keep the magic going. Kenzie bit back a sob as she cast one last glance at Wes. He lay still, and she couldn't tell if he was breathing or even alive. The connection between them felt so hollow. She swallowed thickly, then took Gram's hand and took her place between Mom and Gram.

As she gave herself to her magic, joining their incantation to protect the city, she sent a silent prayer that Wes would be okay. Then she squeezed her eyes shut and lost herself to the rhythmic chanting, pouring every ounce into keeping the city safe.

CHAPTER 52

Juliet

Nik, coordinated with Katya and the other kitsunes, using their power to electrocute the kraken. For the most part it worked, but as the water rose, it became more difficult for them to control where the electricity went. And then the mer started attacking from the lake, making the kitsunes' electricity too dangerous to use.

The pounding in Juliet's chest felt louder than the chaos erupting around them. Her hands shook and nausea overcame her, but she couldn't have a panic attack in the middle of a kraken attack. It was time to come together and fight.

Or in their current case, survive.

The battle of melodies stalled the kraken for a few precious moments, but then Myreen's siren voice ceased, and the kraken began his attack anew. Juliet glanced at her friend, who stared outside the Dome. Juliet's eyes widened when she noticed the mer trio fighting with one tentacle that had Trish pinned to the glass.

An enormous crack stole Juliet's attention, starting at the top of the Dome and traveling like lightning down the middle. Juliet guessed they were lucky it didn't split all the way—it would've opened like Pac-Man, dumping the weight of the lake on the remaining shifters. Instead, water poured through the gaps, but didn't flow too rapidly.

They had enough time to get to a safer, less flooded area of the Dome. But they really needed to get out before the Dome filled entirely.

The kraken shook the Dome, and Juliet held out her arms to balance herself. The rumble reverberated through the glass, causing the fracture to grow. The loud screech of grinding glass forced everyone to cover their ears. Water filled faster around their ankles.

Something else had to be done, but they didn't have the luxury to stop and plan. Juliet's anxiety grew, and she nearly lost control and shifted, but seeing Malachai run through the group of soldiers steadied her.

"Dad!"

Water splashed around his feet as he hurtled toward her, his eyes wide. He embraced Juliet the moment he got there.

"I'm so glad you're safe. We're trying to evacuate everyone now, but we need to stop that water flow." Malachai looked at the crack, then back at Juliet.

"What can we do to help?" she asked.

They took a silent moment, but Juliet was coming up with nothing. Malachai's eyes grew, and it was as if Juliet could see the light bulb above his head flicker on.

"You, Juliet. You have to use your new gift. You can slow down the flow of water." Juliet couldn't believe his words. Nik looked like he couldn't either as he joined them.

Juliet didn't think she had enough control of her ice to use it in such a dire situation. And... "What about Dracul?"

"I have to agree with your dad, Jules," Nik said. "It could help. The water's already up to our knees. If the kraken shakes us again, the Dome will break. We need to do something."

"I won't let the general do a thing to you, hon. You can do this," Malachai said, desperation fueling his words.

That won Juliet over.

With a nod and a deep breath, Juliet lugged herself through the now waist-high water until she reached the waterfall pouring from the crack. She looked back at Nik and Malachai, who watched her with pride and what felt like an urgent expectancy. Everyone else looked confused.

Juliet returned her gaze to the water and closed her eyes. It was easy for her to find her fire. But she didn't need her fire; she needed her ice.

She focused on the cold and called to it. Unlike the familiar, soothing warmth, a voltaic chill ran over her like icy tendrils, freezing her to the bones. But like her fire, the ice carried a satisfying comfort with it. The cold wrapped around her insides at a dizzying speed. Her fire tried to latch onto it, tried to snuff it out. Juliet squeezed her eyes shut as she fought for the control to keep them separated.

When her fingertips began to spit out flurries of ice, Juliet knew it had worked. She focused on what she wanted: a piece of ice to fill the crack. It had to be thick enough to keep it from melting right away but not so thick that it would put weight on the crack and deepen it. The math of it made Juliet hesitate, but there was no time to waste.

She raised her hands above her head, aiming at the opening.

The coldness left her body like an avalanche and connected with the pouring water. Pieces of ice flew everywhere in what felt like a hail storm, plinking off the Dome's glass like rocks. Juliet wanted to stop, but the water was still coming in. She groaned against the pressure as the water tried to break through her ice.

With one last shout, Juliet pushed against the heaviness she felt until the water stopped pouring through. Reluctantly, she opened her eyes. A ball of spikes hung in the crack, frightening in its size and deadliness. Juliet's arms hung weighty and numb at her sides. In fact, if she wasn't standing in water, she probably would've crumbled to the ground. It was kinda lucky that she could float until she got the feeling back in her arms and legs.

Splashes neared her, and she spun to see who was coming.

"Yes! You did it!" Nik hugged her tight, then let go, staring at the ominous iceberg.

Juliet shyly looked around the room until she spotted Myreen. Was the look on her face pride or shock? It wasn't the time to ask, but it was most likely both. And something seemed odd, though Juliet couldn't quite put her finger on it.

She didn't dare examine anyone else's reaction. She knew what they were probably thinking: *Where the heck did that come from?*

Malachai reached Juliet a couple moments after Nik, and he pulled her close to his side, gripping her shoulder. Pride shone in his eyes; he didn't even need to say the words. They figured out how to delay the flooding, but they were still trapped inside with an angry kraken at their door.

Juliet had no idea where her father pulled the tablet from, but the screen filled with a blueprint of the Dome. He and Nik were trying to figure out what to do next.

Juliet spaced out, the amount of water inside the Dome

stealing her attention. She couldn't believe the destruction it caused. She finally felt at home somewhere and vampires were trying to take that away. Again.

Rage ran through her. That level of emotion wasn't safe for her or anyone around her. The call of a shift was hard to ignore. Maybe if she was outside with Kenzie, she could use her phoenix to fight, but here in the Dome it was far too dangerous—especially with the ice hanging above their heads, the only thing standing between them and drowning.

One of the kraken's tentacles slammed against the Dome, shaking Juliet from her thoughts. It tightened its hold and tugged, and the Dome rumbled and groaned against the pressure. The water around their waists sloshed to one side, and Juliet was pulled in. She fell back, becoming completely submerged. Fighting to resurface, she finally was able to pull in a breath.

Something had changed.

Several mer floated around the perimeter of the Dome—Joanna among them—hands outstretched, the water inside settling like a trained pup. Yes! That's what they needed. Shifters working together, using their abilities to their full potential. Juliet smiled at Joanna, who gave her a curt nod, her face twisted in what looked like a suppressed smile.

Juliet heard a strange noise, and looked up just as some pieces broke off her iceberg, splashing in the water nearby.

Some students screamed—Juliet was grateful that there were at least fewer screams this time—but all voices silenced as a striking popping sound came from the plugged crack.

Water shot from between the cracks like a geyser, spewing into the Dome. Juliet looked at the iceberg with dismay. She hadn't stopped anything, just delayed the inevitable. While the thought of giving up made her teeth grind and her hands fist, this looked hopeless.

But then the kraken backed away.

The sun setting behind it gave off a gloomy color, filling the Dome with its murky orange and red glow. But they shouldn't be able to see the colors of sundown so deep in the lake. There was only one explanation. The *lake* was draining.

An uncertain hush settled over the Dome as people watched the kraken retreat. A tentative cheer went up, then fell back away. The water still poured in, but Juliet didn't think that would be a problem too much longer. If the ice would just hold...

The water was now up to their necks and Juliet had to keep her feet moving to stay afloat.

Nik—who she'd nearly forgotten was there—spun Juliet around and took her face in his hands. With a crazed look in his eyes, he leaned in and placed a deep, passionate kiss on her lips. "I love you, Jules."

And then he was gone.

Juliet didn't even have a chance to argue or ask what he was doing, but that didn't stop her from trying to swim after Nik. But Malachai's large hand gripped her arm, holding her back. He shook his head, wordlessly telling her to let Nik go.

Juliet looked away from her father. Nik had climbed so that he was mostly out of the water. He seemed to be standing on something—maybe a bench or something else bolted to the ground.

He jumped, and she thought he was just going to fall back into the water. Instead, beautiful, enormous, deep-red wings caught him mid-shift. He flew above the water as he finished transforming.

All Juliet could do was stare, heat rising to her cheeks.

Nik flew to the far side of the Dome and pulsed his wings

to hover. He looked down at Juliet one last time, then lowered his head and dove at a dizzying speed.

She watched in horror, a scream clawing at her throat, but finding no escape.

The screech of breaking glass filled her ears as the red blur of Nik disappeared. Water funneled after him, and Juliet realized he must've made a hole in the glass near the base of the Dome. Had the lake really drained so much?

She had to make sure Nik was okay.

Juliet let the water carry her with it, and thankfully this time her father let her go. She found something to grab onto when she got closer to the hole so she wouldn't drain out. Still, she kicked against the current to keep herself steady, but she almost lost it when she finally caught sight of Nik.

Still in dragon form, Nik wobbled as he tried to remain standing, situated just beyond the splash of water pouring from the Dome like an open tap. He was hurt. Was the impact of making the hole too much? He shook his head and tried to lift off the ground. He needed help.

Juliet tore her eyes from Nik. Brett was still helping the kitsunes, and Kol and Myreen were preoccupied. Malachai was trying to keep students from getting swept up in the current, though the water was draining fast.

Juliet looked back at Nik, feeling helpless. But she couldn't help but notice the strange way the water seemed to scurry away from where it fell. Maybe the mer were doing something to help? She'd have to solve that mystery later.

Juliet conjured her fire and shot it at the top edge of the hole Nik had made, widening it. Between that and the decreasing water flow, Nik was able to lunge back into the Dome.

He splashed and skidded across the water. Juliet hauled

herself to her feet and sloshed toward him, thankful the water had dropped back down to knee-level. She fell at Nik's side, putting her arm under him to keep his head from falling below the water. The trauma must've been too much, because he was back in human form.

Juliet helped him to his feet as Brett came splashing their way. He smacked Nik on the back as a way of praise. Nik winced, and Brett paled, his brows drawn.

Juliet wanted to throw her arms around Nik and repeat their kiss, but the sound of cracking glass stole her attention again.

Everyone looked at the glacier, backing away as chunks began to fall again. Several students scrambled for cover.

Juliet's eyes traveled below the berg, and fear choked her. Kol and a few other soldiers were still trying to get students out of the way.

They were cutting it close.

Juliet couldn't look away, the sense of dread building with each second that passed. Her heart beat faster and faster as she watched everyone scramble to get out of the way. She wanted to scream, to shout, to make them hurry, even though it looked like they were going as fast as they could.

She stood up instinctively, knowing their time was up. Kol didn't seem to notice in his rush to help.

"Oh no," Juliet whispered.

"What? What is it?" Nik groaned as he tried to get a look at what she stared at. When his eyes locked on Kol, he darted from under their cover with a speed she didn't think possible given his condition.

Juliet reached out a hand as time seemed to slow. Somehow Malachai was by her side, keeping her from chasing after Nik—again.

"No!" her father shouted, filling his voice with a fierce authority. He knew what she didn't want to accept. It was a suicide mission.

Juliet twisted in her dad's grip, screaming at Nik to stop.

He didn't, even seeming to run faster. She wanted to close her eyes. Maybe if she didn't see it, it wouldn't really happen. But her eyes stayed steadfastly open, watching as the rest of the glacier swayed, shuddered, and finally fell.

Kol registered surprise as Nik threw him out of the way.

The ice made an explosive boom as it hit the thin layer of water on the ground and shook the floor beneath their feet. Malachai threw his body over Juliet's, protecting from most of the ice shards thrown in every direction as the iceberg broke into a million pieces.

Juliet numbly waited for it to be over. She needed to find Nik.

When the rumbling finally stopped, Malachai lifted himself off Juliet and helped her to her feet. Ice littered everything, bobbing in the water, coating the backside of her father like he'd been frosted.

Juliet looked to the pile of rubble in the center—where she feared Nik must be. She had to find Nik, though she wasn't sure she was ready for what she would find.

The vampires chose that moment to pour into the Dome like the water had what seemed like just seconds—and simultaneously a lifetime—ago. She wasn't quite sure what had happened to the kraken, but that mattered little to her.

Juliet saw red. She was going to get to Nik, one way or another.

Malachai raced toward a vampire and got right to kicking butt, so Juliet jumped over some debris and dodged around clumps of ice. She couldn't see Nik, but she knew where to look.

Three vampires tried to block her, unaware she'd been

holding in her anger for far too long. She found her fire and ice eagerly waiting. With a violent push, Juliet spread her arms, fire blazing from one hand while an icy chill shot from the other.

Thrusting her ice toward her enemies' feet, she encased their ankles, fusing them to the ground. She raised her fire, aiming at their heads, and put all her rage into. Like a flamethrower, Juliet lit up the vampires until all that was left was their feet, still frozen to the ground.

She raced again toward where she'd last seen Nik. Tears filled her eyes as she began turning over ice and furniture, looking frantically for the man she loved, but coming up empty.

Then she saw his feet.

They weren't moving.

With a lump in her throat, Juliet threw herself next to his body, barely registering that Kol was already there. She might have told Kol to leave, or screamed, or... well, something, but Kol left, releasing his own distressed roar as he shifted and took to the air.

Nik's still, lifeless body—with a gaping hole in the center— told her he was gone even before she touched him. Her hands shook, and she clutched at her stomach. This was her fault. Her ice had killed him. And all because of *them.*

She couldn't breathe.

She couldn't see straight.

She couldn't keep from exploding.

Juliet slammed her fists on the ground, sizzling as her fire met what little remained of the water. She swallowed around a lump as her heartbeat slowed. It was coming—her shift. She couldn't stop it, and she didn't want to. She choked on a sob, then fell on her back as she accepted the darkness. If *he* was gone, she wanted to be gone with him. And for a second, she could let herself believe that the death that came with shifting was permanent. She put her hand on Nik's, letting her heart thrum its final beat.

There was a click in her chest when fire reignited her.

She was the phoenix.

Talons clacked against the floor, long silky wings beat against the air. Her enhanced vision darted to the limp body beside her. She opened her beak to let out a grief-stricken shriek. To her surprise, ice misted the air in front of her, creating a frozen wall.

Now to get this over with so I can sulk in peace.

Juliet didn't leave that spot. She kept the ice wall too her back, hovering above Nik's body as the vampires attacked. She swore to herself she wouldn't let Nik out of her sight, no matter how tough the fight got. She couldn't protect him when he was alive, but she *would* protect him in death.

Tears sizzled down her beak, her heart breaking like the shattered iceberg all around. She would avenge the only boy she'd ever loved. There was enough fury in her, and enough fire and ice, to blast them all into oblivion.

Kol

"Damn you Nik!" Kol roared as he flew through the crack in the Dome. In the chaos of the strange ice shards that nearly impaled him—and did impale Nik—he'd lost sight of Myreen.

Kol knew why he'd done it. It was Nik's stupid notion that Kol Dracul, the dragon prince, just *had* to be saved. To hell if he was killed in the process. It was probably payback for Kol saving Nik's life months ago during that first vampire attack. The vampire attack that *nearly* killed Kol... *but didn't.* Kol survived it.

But now Nik was dead.

Kol knew Nik was gone the moment the ice pierced his friend's chest. If he'd stayed in his dragon form, he would still be alive, but Kol watched the clear shard pierce Nik's very human flesh, and saw the light leave his eyes. He watched as Nik's fiery girlfriend stumbled over to them and the look on her face—the contorted, gut-wrenching look of agony—confirmed he was looking at reality.

That her boyfriend, and his best friend, was dead.

Nik's words after Kol saved him in the alley shouted in his memory:

"Do you have any idea what it would've done to me if you'd died?" Nik had said. *"That my best friend not only took lead shrapnel for me, but died doing it?"*

Kol shook his head of the memory. "Do you have any idea what you've done to me, Nikolai Candida?" he roared. "My best friend took a dagger of ice for me, and *died* doing it!"

The world was fuzzy and Kol was losing focus of his task. He couldn't lose it now. His pain would be a hundred-fold if Myreen also ended up dead because Kol's grief over losing Nik blinded him too much. He scanned the muddied lake bed. Even in the waning moonlight, Kol could see the small black dots running straight into the lake and right toward the small gathering of shifters as the water receded further.

The vampires were coming in force. Some poured into the Dome and others headed toward a huddled, scared pack of students who had managed to make it out. They were like sitting ducks, ready to be plucked off.

Kol veered to the right and dove toward them, scorching two vampires, with his fire before reaching the group. The vampires twitched and jerked on the ground, their skin charred black, but Kol didn't think they were dead.

Only a handful of the students had shifted.

"Shift! Now!" he shouted at those still huddling in fear when he was closer. "Protect yourselves!" He'd donned his usual dark-gray scales in hopes that the majority of them would recognize him better, but when several dazed expressions seemed to look right past him, he flipped his color to camouflage, then gold. It did the trick. Immediately dozens of his classmates snapped to attention and shifted into their various animal forms.

But Myreen wasn't among them.

A phoenix lifted from the group, zoomed past him and screeched.

It was Brett. He circled around to flank Kol.

"Where's Nik and Char?" he asked, a little breathless and probably chagrined since he'd been among the huddled students. Kol wondered if Brett was one of the ones who were paralyzed in their fear. After all, Brett had only battled vampires and other threats in the sim. "I think the four of us could do some damage against that approaching group of blood-suckers."

Kol was glad his friend had snapped out of it. His phoenix skills were on par with his and Nik's dragon ones.

If Nik had been in dragon form when that ice fell, he would've been fine. He would've barely felt it shatter against his scales.

"I don't know where Char is," Kol said, hoping it would deflect from the Nik question. "She's probably already out there attacking. She's shifter military, after all."

The two of them looked at the melee that had begun. Maos and hounds were racing at full speed toward the vampires. With the various shipwrecks and garbage that littered the lake bed, it was a maze-like labyrinth for both groups. Still, they would meet in minutes, and the shifters could definitely use some air—and fire—support. A blue dragon appeared as a tiny dot near what was once the short end of Lake Michigan. Kol knew instinctively it was Char. He briefly wondered where his parents were, but needed to focus on finding Myreen first.

"Have you seen Myreen?" Kol asked.

Brett turned his head toward a second group of vampires

coming from a different direction. Her dark blue-black hair was easy to spot among the harpies, kitsunes, and nagas attacking the new arrivals. Especially because she hadn't shifted. She fought in human form.

Kol pivoted mid-air, aiming right for her. He had to get her away from the danger, but his vision was suddenly filled with red-orange flames and he had to dodge.

"Wait, you didn't say where Nik is," Brett said, blocking his way again. "I'll find him while you go for Myreen."

Kol paused, the two of them drifting in the sky as if time had stopped, as if for this brief moment a raging battle wasn't happening below. As if his friend hadn't died only minutes ago. And he needed to get to the girl he loved before the same happened to her.

Kol envied Brett for that moment of ignorance.

Piercing pain shot through his tail. It was from Brett's beak.

"Ow!" he screeched and snapped his jaw at his fire-bird friend, but only caught a mouthful of air.

"Where. Is. Nik?"

"Nik's dead!" Kol roared.

Brett nearly fell from the sky, tripping over an air current.

"Some stupid ice fell from the Dome and was supposed to kill me, but Nik pushed me out of the way." Kol took a ragged breath. "It stabbed him. It killed him. Nik is dead."

"Ice?" Brett's stunned tone pierced Kol's insides. "Where did ice come from?"

"I have no idea..." Kol said, but didn't have time to think about it too hard. "Now please, let me go grab my girlfriend before she gets killed by more mysterious ice or a not-mysterious vampire."

Wordlessly, Brett veered up and out of Kol's way. "I'm gonna see if I can help Char," he said, his voice low and very un-

Brett-like. "Catch up when Myreen's safe?"

"Yes, of course," Kol muttered, but wasn't listening intently.

"And don't get yourself killed." Brett's tone was flat. "It won't be fun killing zombies by myself."

"Hey, you be careful too," Kol said, snapping back to the moment. "I'm not losing both my best friends in one day. I promise I'll catch up soon."

Brett nodded. "Your girlfriend is pretty capable, you know."

Kol knew, but that didn't change the fact that she could still die. He wasn't letting that happen.

"Mer, harpy, ursa—she's made of some pretty intense stuff. She might be more deadly than you, Dracul."

"I'm not losing her."

When Brett flew off toward where they'd seen Char in the distance, he let out an anguished cry that echoed what Kol felt in his core. Nik was dead. Their friend was dead, and it was likely that he wouldn't be the only casualty in this bloody battle. Kol roared an identical response before diving toward the battle below.

Myreen—still human—kicked a blonde vampire in the jaw, sending it reeling back. Kol landed behind her and clamped his teeth around the one lunging at her back, hearing a sickening snap as he broke the spine. It still scratched and clawed at his nose even though its bottom half didn't seem to work, so Kol blew out a fiery breath, engulfing the vampire entirely in his flames. When the barbecued creature finally went limp, he tossed it into another group heading toward them, knocking several momentarily off their feet.

He raced toward her, ready to open his claws to grab her and take flight, but caught sight of a shirtless vampire hacking at a dead naga's tail using a pocket-knife. They were partly hidden near a broken canoe, and Kol whipped his own tail at the vampire with enough force to shatter the fiberglass of the canoe. He heard the pop of the vampire's neck, then scorched that one too.

Myreen, stopped her kick-boxing exercise for a split-second and looked at Kol with her head cocked to the side. "Here to join us?" she asked, no amusement in her tone. "I like the gold, by the way."

Kol didn't answer and roughly gripped her in his claws before pushing himself high again.

"Kol!" she screamed, pounding her hands into his claws. She was strong, and he nearly lost his grip. She pounded again, and dropped like a rock before split-shifting into her harpy.

Pumping her wings with force, she reached his height within seconds. "What are you doing?" she shouted.

"Making sure my girlfriend doesn't get killed!" he shouted back, then clamped one of her talons between his teeth and pulled her higher.

"Let go!" she screeched and clawed at his eye.

He released her, but kicked his legs up to grip both of her wings with his claws, holding them firmly without damaging them. "No," he said, racing east, toward the shore. He attention was momentarily diverted as he spotted something that looked remarkably like the Dome sitting above the city of Chicago—sparkling?

But Myreen wouldn't stop resisting. She jerked to the right, then a blinding light flashed in his face and the split-second of disorientation caused him to lose his left claw's hold on her wing. It was enough that she broke free and moved out of his reach.

Kol was faster in the air, and quickly gained on her and blocked her way.

"Drop. Now," he said.

She did, but probably because he sounded more pleading than commanding.

He dropped next to her on the lake bed near a ship-wrecked fishing boat named the *Amanda*, shifting the second his feet touched ground. Immediately he conjured an orange fireball to see. His human eyes weren't as sharp in the darkness as his dragon ones. She shifted back a little bit slower. The glow of the fire revealed the fury etched in every feature of her face.

"What the *hell* was that, Kol?" she screamed, lunging forward to shove him in the chest. Her quick movement startled him more than he felt the blow. He quickly moved the fireball away from her to avoid burning her.

Kol's eyebrows pinched, but he felt his face fall. "I'm not losing you, Myreen Fairchild."

Her face softened. He wondered if she heard the hitch in his voice.

"Losing me?" she gripped his arm firmly, but it felt like her anger was gone. "Wait. What happened?"

Kol shrugged to mask the tremble in his lips. He drew them into a thin, hard line to keep them from shaking. "When you left," he said. "Right after you got out of the Dome... some ice fell."

"Ice?" Myreen's brows scrunched, then lifted in surprise. He wasn't sure what was going through her head, but he had to get this out before he lost his nerve.

Kol looked at the ground, running his fingers through his hair and gripping a fist-full. When he released his grip, he lifted his eyes back to her. "It would've killed me," he continued. "But Nik..."

Myreen's eyes widened. "What happened to Nik, Kol?" she asked, her beautiful features glowing in the fire-light.

Kol shrugged again as his eyes burned. He closed them tightly, along with his fists at his sides. "The ice fell... and Nik pushed me out of the way. "

He felt Myreen's grip tighten. Painfully. "Nik's hurt?

Where's Juliet?"

When Kol opened his eyes, resisting the urge to wince at Myreen's painful grip, a tear escaped. With his free hand, he hastily wiped it away. "Nik's dead. Last I saw, Juliet was fighting off the vampires around his body."

"Nik's dead?" she whispered, then threw her arms around his neck. "Oh Kol, I'm so sorry." She sobbed against his throat. "And poor Juliet," she whispered.

Kol tried to pry her arms away from his neck as she slowly cut off his air. "M– Myreen," he choked.

She let go before he got the word out. Her speed was... inhuman. He looked at her pale face, at her smooth skin. Even in the lower light, she looked *different.* And her touch had been so cold.

"What?" Kol didn't even know what to ask. Was this the result of *another* shifter gene? The strength certainly came from her ursa nature, the blinding light was definitely her harpy, but the speed? The paleness? Neither of those were mer qualities—or *any* shifter qualities, at least none that he could think of.

"Okay, so I know you probably have questions, but we don't really have time for guessing games." Even her words seemed to come out at super-speed. "When Draven *created* me, he was experimenting to create hybrids."

"Hybrids." Kol folded his arms, directing the fireball to hover above them. "No, not possible. Shifters would never survive the change."

"Yes, shifter-vampire hybrids." She waved her hands as she spoke—the movement made them look more like helicopter blades than human appendages at her speed. "When I realized Draven had become the first hybrid, I decided that there was only way to beat him and that—"

"You didn't." Kol backed away, unfolding his arms and

holding them up as if surrendering. "You didn't," he said much quieter.

"I had to," she said, walking closer, faster. She held his arm again. "It's the only way. The prophecy says that a siren—"

"Yes, a *siren*! Not a *vampire*, Myreen." Kol raked his fingers through his hair again. His heart hammered against his chest. When did it happen? When did she change? But he heard the creak of the wood behind him too late.

It was a blur of teeth and speed and ear-splitting growls. Kol barely felt the sharp points at his throat before they were ripped away again and the severed head of a pale-faced, shaved-head vampire rolled against his bare toes.

He kicked it away, resisting the urge to gag.

"Draven is a hybrid," Myreen said, not even slightly breathless from the effort.

Kol's jaw hung ajar.

"If we... if *I* have a chance of beating him..." She paused, her face crumpling. "I didn't have another choice."

He stared at her. There were no words, only a million questions and an intense paradigm shift.

Myreen is a vampire, he thought. The mere thought should disgust him, he should shirk back in fear, or shift into attack mode. Shifters were supposed to die if a vampire attempted to turn them. There was no such thing as a vampire-shifter hybrid. It just didn't happen. And because it didn't happen, Kol never had the opportunity to even entertain the idea that someone he loved—a shifter he loved—could become a vampire. The worst thing a vampire could do to a loved one was kidnap or kill them.

Never turn them.

"D– do you still love me?" she asked, her voice a low hiss. Barely a whisper.

"Do I still love you?" he repeated. Of course he loved her. But becoming a vampire was no small thing. Instead of answering, he pulled her into his arms and kissed her roughly. Even her lips felt different, no longer the soft, warm ones he'd enjoyed just hours ago, so he quickly pushed her away.

Her expression looked as though she'd been slapped, but he couldn't fix that now. Not while their friends were fighting for their lives. Kol needed to find Brett and Char. He needed to see if his parents were in the fight—he assumed they were. He worried about his mom. Kol walked a few steps, bending his knees in preparation to shift again.

"Why did you pull me out of there?" Myreen blurted, her hand on his arm again.

Kol looked at her with a neutral expression. "I just saw my best friend get impaled," he said. "I was coming to get you out of the fight. I didn't want to lose you, too."

Myreen's eyebrows furrowed above her glistening blue eyes. "You know," her mouth twisted and Kol wondered if she was trying not to cry. "Since I'm a mer, harpy, and an ursa, I could've defended myself, even without…"

"Yes, I know. I was reminded of that." Kol heard the irritation in his voice, but didn't correct it or apologize.

"But you were coming to save me anyway?"

He nodded.

"And now?" Her voice caught.

"And now I know you're a hybrid, bent on killing Draven."

She reached up and planted a kiss on his lips. His response was minimal.

"And you're leaving now because you know I'm a hybrid and can defend myself?" Her eyes pleaded with him.

The bellow of the kraken shook the ground, the rotted

SUMMONED

boards of the boat behind him creaking. The beast was attacking
again. Kol briefly wondered where the squid-octopi—*whatever*—
had been up until that point. He bent his knees again and
extinguished the fire.

"Something like that," he said.

"Come with me?" she asked, now a disembodied voice as his
eyes tried to adjust again to the darkness. "Fight alongside me?"

"I need to get to Brett and Char," he said.

She paused, then sighed before saying, "Okay."

He jumped and shifted mid-air, choosing his camouflage
scales so he vanished immediately.

***

Leaving his vampire girlfriend behind, Kol headed toward the
southern shore, the direction Brett had gone. But the ones
holding the line had lost serious ground. Their line had been
bleeding drastically since before Kol left the Dome—vampires
were already attacking inside the Dome before he left—but now
the bulk of the fighting was very near the Dome.

Kol remained camouflaged as he assessed the scene. He
glided on a warm air pocket as he took a breath. Forcing his eyes
to roll over the mess of blood and broken bodies, he focused on
the shifters who still moved, scanning them for his friends and
parents. A jet-black dragon fought in the midst of the battle.
Eduard's maneuvers and attacks—not to mention his fire—were
almost instantly lethal to the vampires. It seemed that one flick
of his claw, one well-aimed fire blast, and his target fell to the
ground, forever unmoving. It wasn't something to smile about,
seeing his father as a killing machine, but at least Kol didn't need
to be worried if the general would make it out alive.

Kol couldn't spot the pearly white of his mom's dragon and
hoped that she'd flown high above the clouds and away from the

danger. He'd never heard her speak of battle or fighting, but Kol suspected the extent of his mother's combat experience were the spars she learned at the academy—long before the school even had sim technology.

He doubted she had any real-life battle experience.

A thick, blue tentacle slid over the side of the cracked Dome and into it, looking very much like a gigantic slug with the absence of water. The Dome was ruined, cracked like an egg crushed by a spoon. It would never protect anyone again—the vampires still trickling inside proved that.

A different shade of blue caught Kol's eye, and he snapped his head toward it. Char. He raced to her, flipping his scales to match hers, and called to her.

"Kol!" she shouted back, a little breathless.

"Where's Brett?" he asked, a lurching panic threatening to gut him.

"He's inside," she said, motioning to the broken Dome. "That feisty girl, Juliet? He went inside to help her. He said something about phoenix's banding together and not letting Nik's girlfriend get killed."

Kol nodded.

"I heard about Nik," she said softly.

Kol didn't respond, only locking eyes with her.

"Remember that thing you did in your final sim?" Char asked after a beat. "With the kraken? How you flew up high and dropped it?"

"Yeah," he said, grateful she'd changed the subject and wasn't dwelling on Nik's death. If they survived, they had the rest of their lives to mourn their friend. "But this kraken is at least three times the size of that one. The thought crossed my mind, but I struggled even getting that one high enough. And besides, it was a *sim.*"

"Well, I think the two of us might be able to do it." It was clear she'd put a lot of thought into it.

Kol glanced down at the black dragon. It would be easier with three, but he had his hands full. When the kraken pulled out a tentacle wrapped around a student, kicking and screaming, the decision was made.

"Let's do it." He said. "Let me take care of that first."

Char made a yipping sound of excitement and took off after the kraken before Kol did.

He flipped his scales invisible again before diving toward the tentacle squeezing his classmate. Building the fire within to an intense heat and pressure, he released it, blowing it out like a torch on the appendage nearer to the body, causing a sizzling sound as the slimy skin scorched. Then, opening his jaws wide, he bit down on the freshly burned spot, hacking at it until it fell away from the creature. The kraken screamed and the tentacle flip-flopped on the ground for several seconds, wriggling and squeezing the girl tighter, before finally slowing and relaxing.

The girl pushed the tentacle away from her and shifted into her naga form. She was okay.

The momentary distraction nearly cost Kol, though, as another tentacle reached for him. Its suckers were wide and ready to snatch him in the air, but Kol was quicker and shot up higher than it could reach. It was a close miss. Despite Kol's invisibility, the kraken's aim was good. If Charlotte—

It was too late. She roared as another tentacle wrapped itself around her. Kol raced for her as the translucent blue tentacle pinned Char's wings painfully against her body. It didn't seem to matter that she was much larger in her dragon form than the naga girl, Char was just as effectively immobilized.

Kol prepped his fire again, but the tentacle lowered Char quickly into the broken Dome, disappearing from his sight. He couldn't risk hurting anyone below with his blast, and so he followed it into the Dome. He hoped his invisibility would prevent himself from being grabbed by one of the six tentacles still left.

Char screamed again right as Kol re-entered the Dome, giving him a clear view of the four vampires clamoring to kill her. One had located her vulnerability—the spot in her side where the scale had been ripped off—and bit down in an attempt to drain her.

"Char!" Kol shouted.

"I've got this!" a fire-bird yelled at the same time. It was Brett. He sounded much better than he had the last time Kol had seen him, almost excited.

Another fire-bird joined him with a shriek of her own. Juliet.

A fire-rope appeared and wrapped itself around the tentacle as Brett sent a cannon-ball sized fire orb at one of the vampires. It blasted away, crashing into the broken fountain. Kol shifted his scales to dark gray for his friend's sakes as he went for the vampire who drank from Char.

The vampire was efficient. Charlotte looked slightly pale when he finally reached her. He clamped his teeth around the center of the vampire and ripped her away, bringing another scream from Char as her flesh tore.

Another dragon roar came from above and slammed into the tentacle holding Charlotte. The impact stunned the appendage enough for Charlotte to break free. Kol snapped his head to the dragon, whose speed was much quicker than his own *or* his father's.

The iridescent, mother-of-pearl coloring of her scales was

unmistakable.

"Mom?" Kol said, following her up and out. He was impressed by her speed. Brett and Juliet continued dispatching the vampires below with fire waves and ropes. The tentacle retreated from the opening again.

"Hi, sweetheart," Victoria said, slowing as she gained a safe altitude. "Charlotte."

"Thank you, Mrs. Dracul," Char said, a little sheepishly. "I think we can try it now, Kol. If your mom helps..." She trailed off.

"Helps with what?" Kol could hear the eagerness in her voice. She might be his mother and *Lady Dracul*, but that was the dragon in her speaking.

"In my final sim test, there was a kraken," Kol explained. "It wasn't nearly this big, but I lifted it high enough that when I dropped it—"

"Let's do it!" his mom interrupted. She scanned the kraken draped against the Dome, then dove a second later.

Kol and Char exchanged a glance and followed her— arriving more seconds after her than he thought possible. He knew he was fast. He had no idea his mom was faster.

Kol located a spot at the back of the kraken's head near the base of two tentacles and sunk his claws in. Victoria had the top of the head, and Char was around the other side in a similar spot as Kol.

"Lift!" Victoria commanded. "And watch for the tentacles!"

"Yes, but there are only seven," Kol informed.

They lifted in unison and managed to get the entire creature several feet above the ground, which was quite the feat, especially when they realized how long it was stretched out from head to the tip of its tentacles. It took great effort, but between the three of them, it was possible.

But the kraken was only stunned for a few seconds before the tentacles came to life and wriggled up, reaching for each of them.

"Go higher!" Charlotte screamed. "Before he gets ahold of one of us!"

Kol flashed to his camouflage right before one of the tentacles brushed against his back. His invisibility probably wouldn't help in the situation, but it might buy him some time. He turned his head and blasted the tentacle with his fire, causing it to sizzle and fold on itself to get away. He couldn't see Charlotte, but he hoped she did the same to any tentacle that came her way. He hoped his mother was out of the octopus's reach.

Someone lost their grip and gave gravity the upper hand, the kraken jerking toward the ground.

"Got him!" Char shouted, and the kraken became lighter again.

Above him, Kol heard his mother snap her jaws and roar, the rushing sound and heat wave indicating that she blasted her fire. He took a split-second to look up at her right as a flash of white was snatched away by *two* of the tentacles.

"Mom!"

Kol nearly lost his grip as the kraken rushed toward the earth again. Without his mother's help, gravity was winning the tug-o-war. But Char must've lost hers, because the kraken slipped through his hold when another hard jerk tore it from his claws.

Without thinking, he took a nose-dive as it crashed toward the lake-bed, the white form of his mother clutched in two of its tentacles. It was getting smarter. Two would be harder.

Kol bit down on one of them, again and again, hoping to sever it like he had the first one, but he felt more frantic than he had before. This was his mom. He couldn't lose his mom, too. Not like he'd lost Nik.

Kol could see Char's blue in his peripheral trying to do the same, biting frantically. The flesh felt tougher than before. He felt like he wasn't making quick enough progress. Maybe it was because he'd cooked the other one before chomping down? Maybe it was because he was trying to save his mother now and not a nameless naga girl? Char's form jerked away and out of sight, as if swatted away like a pesky fly. Kol's head jerked up to see if she was okay as she crashed into the glass of the Dome. When she lay limp, lifeless, against the side, his heart tore inside him and he released his grip.

He didn't see the same tentacle that swatted her away wrap around him. He could feel the slimy mucus slide over his scales and get caught in his own vulnerable places at his side and shoulder. The suckers licked over him, pulling him tight. As the appendage situated itself around him, squeezing until his wings were immobile, his fore-claws dug between a few of his scales and pierced his skin.

"Kol!" Brett popped up and over the jagged Dome with Juliet at his heels. "Mrs. Dracul?" His bafflement didn't last long and the two of them headed toward them.

A slithering tentacle writhed along the ground toward the unmoving blue form of Char.

"Get Char out!" Kol shouted at them. He could swear she was still breathing, even as his vision blurred with the severely reduced reserve of oxygen—the kraken was squeezing his lungs tightly.

Brett and Juliet didn't hesitate and quickly got to Char's side, blasting the creeping tentacle enough for it to curl away. Kol hoped they could get Charlotte to safety. He craned his neck and tried to look at his mom, to see if she was still conscious, but all he could see was her tail hanging limply next to him.

He wriggled, trying to break himself free, but his energy was sapped as his airway was further constricted. It was all he could to do keep his eyes open as he felt himself losing consciousness.

"Malkolm!" a deep voice cried. "Victoria!" The second cry was laced with deep pain.

Though the second part confused him, Kol knew the voice as well as his own. It was Eduard. It was his father.

Air rushed into his lungs as the tentacle holding him hung limply, an oozing gash ripped through the side—a bite mark. Kol flew up and out of its grip, though his wings felt heavy from the oxygen deprivation. Spots floated in front of his vision as he strained to stay airborne. *Fly higher*, he ordered himself, and he forced more air into his body, gulping huge breaths. *Get up to safety until your head clears.*

Kol forced himself to keep his gaze on the horizon and not the chaos below. *A few more seconds.* He counted down from ten.

Ten... nine... eight...

If he raced back, prematurely, he'd be useless to help his dad get his mom free. But if he waited too long...

Seven... six... five...

Roars sounded below. Kol closed his eyes tightly. His head felt less fuzzy, a few more seconds.

Four... three... two...

One.

He opened his eyes before diving. Eduard managed to rip apart one of the tentacles to free Victoria, but they had done their work. She was unconscious. Still, the kraken seemed more determined to keep squeezing.

Kol went to work, gripping the tentacle with his hind claws and pulling up, forcing it away from her.

"Victoria!" Eduard sobbed, then hurled himself into the kraken's head, maybe hoping the shock would wrench her free. "Pull harder Kol!"

Kol obeyed, feeling his own sobs work its way up his throat as he pulled with everything he had. "C'mon mom!" he said, but knew it was useless. "Use your strength, break free!" Kol could *not* lose his mom. She was kind and gentle. She was strong, and apparently very fast. She needed to know the curse was broken. She needed to feel the joy of being loved back.

Myreen's face briefly rushed through his head. Myreen *did* lose her mom. Not to a kraken, but violently to vampires. His heart ached for her as he put himself in her place, as he contemplated how he could possibly survive losing his mom.

Kol didn't know what Eduard was doing, but whatever his tactic, it seemed to be working. Kol pulled again and the tentacle slipped further away from the white dragon.

"Again!" Eduard shouted. Determined.

Kol pulled again, using all the strength he had, and hoped it was enough.

It was enough.

Victoria rolled to the lake bed in a slump.

"Get her to safety!" Eduard shouted, then snapped at the tentacle aiming for him. He bit off the tip and spit it to the side.

Kol looked at the space where Char had been. She was gone, but so was Brett and Juliet. He'd hoped they would come back to help. With no time to waste, Kol gripped his mother's body behind the shoulders and lifted. He felt immediate relief when her chest rose and fell.

She was alive.

Kol would not lose his mother.

Eduard roared behind him and Kol nearly lost his grip. *He can handle it*, Kol told himself. Lord Eduard Dracul, the general of the shifter army, *his father*, could handle himself. He would get out alive.

But when he roared again, Kol couldn't help but look behind him. The kraken had rolled on its side and lifted its tentacles to reveal its massive, hard black beak. The jet-black dragon was struggling in two of the tentacles and was slowly nearing the crushing jaws.

Kol gently placed his mom on the ground and thankfully saw two flashes of red-orange rise up and over the Dome.

"Help her!" he shouted without looking, and hoped that wherever they'd taken Charlotte, that his mom could be brought to safety, too. He desperately hoped they'd both make it.

But he also couldn't allow a kraken to eat his dad.

He rushed forward, shooting fire as fast and furious as he could, snapping—but missing—the tentacles that neared him.

Eduard fought violently, charring the flesh near the base of several of the tentacles, but the kraken was on a mission.

Kol flew harder. Faster.

But he wasn't fast enough.

The black beak opened into a gaping maw and, in a flash, crushed down right into the center of his father's dragon.

Kol flinched at the gut-wrenching crunch and snap. A few seconds later he forced himself to look, to see if there was any possible way his dad survived.

But Eduard was gone.

Leif

Chaos was everywhere. The school Leif had tried so hard to protect for the past fifteen years was in ruin. The thick glass that gave the Dome its nickname was shattered. Like a turtle that had its shell ripped off by bloodthirsty predators, the school now lay exposed. And Draven's forces were inside, fighting the shifters still trapped there.

Leif was in the thick of it, and it terrified him. The ferocity of the shifters was alarming. The last battle at a shifter school had been a massacre. It was very apparent that Oberon had taken the loss of The Island seriously. If only he were still around to see the fruits of his labors.

Still, both sides were taking losses. Leif was cautious, for although he was wearing a shifter military uniform given to him by General Dracul, he was afraid an enraged shifter would still see him as a vampire and attack. He doubted word had gotten out that a lone vampire was on their side.

Nearby, the biggest ursa Leif had ever seen was wrestling a vampire. His roaring sounded like thunder, but as strong as he was, he wasn't fast enough to contain the vampire. The werebear tumbled as the vampire struck its knee, causing the ursa to rumble in pain.

The vampire laughed at the huge form now lying in front of him, snout raised defiantly with teeth bared. Leif remembered the helplessness he'd felt at the battle in La Framboise, but that was no longer a part of him. He could help these shifters face their enemies. And he could save this ursa—a person he didn't know, but one he knew deserved to live.

Charging the vampire, Leif threw one solid punch, connecting with the vampire's cheek and sending him sprawling from the ursa. Leif gave the werebear a nod, seeing the surprise in his face, then went after the stunned vampire.

"The daywalker who ran," the vampire spat, rubbing at his cheek. "Leif Villers. I learned all about you in vampire history. Besides Draven, no other vampire has ever climbed in status so quickly. But you went soft and ran."

Leif knew the vampire was talking just to get into his head, but it was alarming to hear that Draven had his history teachers telling his story. He wondered how much of it was true.

The vampire spat after getting to his feet. "Look at you now. Dressed in a shifter military uniform and everything." He shook his head, looking him up and down with disgust. "To think you fell so far after achieving so much."

"I've been around long enough to know that Draven's followers are too deep into his vision," Leif said. He pointed at the injured ursa who had transformed back into a man—likely one of the teachers. "These shifters have done nothing to deserve your malice. Turn away and contemplate your superiority complex. Your existence is no greater than theirs."

"I think I'll kill you and as many shifters as I can," the vampire said. His resoluteness caused Leif to take a defensive stand. Risking a quick glance at the ursa behind him, Leif saw he was being helped away by another shifter.

When he turned back around, he saw the eyes of the attacking vampire wide in shock. He tried to say something, but it came out a struggled gurgle. Then he fell forward, straight on his face. Protruding from his back was a knife, and standing directly behind him was Leif's former Initiate.

"Piper!" he cried out with excitement.

The tall, thin woman adjusted her glasses, saluted him, then bent over and pulled the knife from the fallen vampire.

"Hey Leif," she said, wiping the blade along her torn pants. "Copper knives are extremely effective. I think I've found my future career."

Leif snorted. "Piper Adams, vampire hunter."

"A far cry from molecular biology," she said. "Somehow, this is much more invigorating."

"Forgive me," Leif said. "Never in a million years would I have guessed at what you've become."

"I had a pretty good teacher," she said, smiling brightly.

Behind her, a wolf-like hound with ashy-brown fur growled.

"What is it, Jesse?" Piper asked, whirling around.

Leif wondered at their relationship for a moment. Piper hadn't been at the Dome for too long...

The hound sniffed at the air. "More vampires coming down the corridor. I can smell them."

"You both need to get to safety," Leif said, filling the commanding role he felt within his military garb.

"Take a look around," Jesse said. "There's no safety to run to. And no offense, but I don't answer to vampires."

A trio of vampires rounded the corner. Leif recognized one of them—Rory the Dungeon Master. Apparently, Draven had really scraped the bottom of the bowl to assemble his army of vampires.

"Well, well, well," Rory said as he came to a stop, his gelled, spiky white hair shooting off in every direction. "If it isn't Leif Villers, himself." He wagged a finger at Leif. "You may have had the boss fooled with your little drowning charade, but I knew your true intents ever since you came back to Heritage Prep. In fact, I've been promoted for my discerning intellect."

The two vampires behind him laughed evilly, and Leif wondered what Rory might be referring to. Whatever it was, it couldn't be good, but he didn't plan on Rory living long enough for it to matter.

Jesse's teeth were bared, and Piper took a defensive stance, holding her copper knife horizontally in front of her.

"Three against three, boys!" Rory cried, charging forward.

Leif, Piper and Jesse held their positions, but the wings growing from Rory's back and the talons bursting from his boots nearly caused Leif to stumble.

But before the attackers made it more than a few steps, the kraken high above boomed like a jet engine firing up, causing the vampires to freeze, Rory looking like a greasy angel of death. A second later, a massive, wriggling pillar of blue came crashing down, shaking the ground and squashing the vampires like a rolling pin dropped on dough.

The huge tentacle writhed like a worm, as if it were its own living, breathing entity. The suction cups on the side facing them pulsed in and out, a thick translucent goo spilling from them.

Piper's knife clattered to the wet ground. "That's... disgusting."

There was a groan from beneath the tentacle, and Leif saw black feathers before he saw the rest of the vampire squirming out. Leif grabbed Piper's knife and stabbed Rory clean through the heart before he could pull himself clear, then ripped his head off to be certain the abomination he'd become didn't continue. How many more hybrids had Draven created? This could be disastrous to their fight. Nothing else appeared to be emerging, and Leif turned back to Piper to hand her the knife.

But Piper was staring at the ceiling. Leif looked overhead to see what had her attention. The kraken was shrinking like a sponge drying out. As it grew smaller, it plummeted to the wet ground in front of them, landing with a splat next to his still-writhing tentacle.

Kneeling on one knee was the human form of the kraken—with no smart clothing to cover his body.

The kraken was a shifter.

"Oh my!" Piper squealed, throwing her hands to her mouth, staring on at the well-toned man. His every possible muscle was flexed, and Leif wondered what the shifter had to do to keep up such an incredibly toned and fit body. At the top of his head sat a mass of blue dreadlocks, the same color of his kraken tentacles. Leif swore they were moving all on their own. The shifter also sported a blue beard that looked like blue algae crawling down the sides of his face and surrounding his lips.

His eyes had been closed during his landing, but they flashed open and stared directly at Leif.

The shifter looked back at the tentacle behind him. "That hurt," he said, with a deep voice that sounded so unnatural—almost as if he were speaking through a bubble. He turned back around and analyzed Leif. "The siren commanded me not to kill vampires. So why do you stand defensively in front of shifters?"

"Because he's not one of *our* vampires."

Leif's eyes left the kraken shifter and rested on the new threat stepping into the fray.

"Beatrice," Leif hissed.

She casually walked over to the naked shifter, and he stood as she approached. She traced her finger down one of his shoulders, over his bulging bicep, then intertwined her fingers with his. His golden eyes glared at Leif, his teeth gritted with rage.

"Octavius, meet Leif," Beatrice said. "The last man to hold my heart." She slid a hand into the pocket pouch at the front of her soaked hoodie, then withdrew the object Leif valued the most in the world—the thing he'd do just about anything for. Holding it up, she said, "And I hold *his* heart."

"Give that back," Leif demanded, taking a single step forward and staring at Beatrice, pleading for her to do as he said. "Please."

"He's so attractive when he begs," she said, as if narrating a story to the kraken. "But he doesn't know that I've found a better eternal being. He doesn't know that you've been commanded to be my love by Draven's siren voice."

The kraken's features softened as he looked down at Beatrice, standing nearly twice her size. "If you ask it of me, my sweet water, I will crush him for his insolence."

She gave Octavius an endearing look. "I think not, Octavius. That duty is mine." She handed Gemma's brooch over to the massive shifter. "But why don't you hold on to this while I take care of him."

Octavius nodded, removing his large hand from hers to take the pin. Raising it above him, his blue dreadlocks opened, and he placed the emerald brooch within. The snaking hair swirled back into place, hiding the precious piece of jewelry.

Anger blossomed within Leif. He needed Gemma's brooch. It was his only chance at bringing her back. If he had to, he'd tear Octavius's head off to get it. But it looked like he'd have to get through Beatrice first.

"You make everything so much harder!" he yelled. "You *always* have!"

She moved away from Octavius, who stood watching with his arms crossed, and faced Leif. "It didn't have to be this way, Leif. We could've lived out a normal life together, petty humans in a world meant for vampires. But you gave me no choice. And as far as choices go, I've given you countless chances to come with me, to run away and live our lives the way we were meant to all those years ago."

"I'd rather die than ever be at your side," he hissed.

Beatrice smirked, cocking an eyebrow. "And *that* is your last choice."

"Piper, Jesse, run," he muttered, readying himself for Beatrice's oncoming storm. "This fight isn't for you."

"What about the kraken?" Jesse said.

"Run!" Leif growled.

He heard their footsteps splash away.

With mockery, Beatrice said, "The great Shifter Protector. What a waste."

"Their cause is greater than Draven's," Leif replied. "You're misguided."

She stepped closer, laughing cruelly. "At least I dream bigger than a tiny selkie trinket."

Gemma. Leif's entire existence was for her. And as small as her brooch was, the love he had for her was grander than anything in the world. Not even the size of the kraken could compare. On top of everything, Kenzie had told him the pin was his only chance of getting Gemma back.

Leif closed his eyes. *For you, Gemma.*

He heard Beatrice before opening his eyes, and by the time he did, he sidestepped, sending her crashing right on by. Breathing in, Leif used the very thought and memory of Gemma to fuel him, rather than his hatred for his enemy.

Beatrice was back up, throwing jabs at a rate he'd only encountered a handful of times. He managed to block most of them, but she connected with several blows that felt like a hammer striking his body. Still, he kept his focus.

"You've been practicing," she said, gritting her teeth.

"I've actually been imprisoned," he replied, ricocheting more fierce strokes away. *Left, right, left, right, jump, sidestep, lunge.*

With the ball of his hand, he slammed her forehead, causing her to get out of her rhythmic jabbing. Jumping forward, he kicked her in the chest, sending her sprawling in the shallow water.

His mind held onto the day he'd asked Gemma to marry him, held onto her sincere, resounding acceptance.

Beatrice got to her feet, trying a kick of her own. But Leif caught her attack with his hands and twisted, a jarring crack sounding from the movement. Beatrice screamed, nearly pulling Leif out of his thoughts of Gemma, but he forced himself to remember a shady summer day when his love had surprised him with a picnic in the orchard.

Leif cut the distance between them, not wasting any time to allow for Beatrice's broken ankle to heal. Pulling her out of the water, her blonde hair framed her harrowed features.

"Please, Leif, have mercy," she begged.

"You'll just keep coming back for me," he said. "Over and over and over. It stops. Now."

She punched him, but they were half-hearted strikes that

didn't hurt enough to bruise. Tears mingled with the water she was soaked with from the lake. "You already killed me," she sobbed. "All those years ago when you let me go, you killed me. I tried so hard to come back, but my every vampiric moment was spent hoping you'd come back to me." She wept bitterly, and Leif realized for the first time that what heartache he'd suffered in losing Gemma, as well as his attempts at bringing her back—Beatrice had experienced the same with him. "Even now, I still want you. I even gave up the chance to become a hybrid in the hopes that you would see the truth and come back to me."

Leif loosened his grasp on her wet clothing, staring into her haunted, sad eyes. He'd broken her long ago. And Beatrice had returned the favor.

She must have seen the resolve in his gaze, because her expression changed from cold sadness to fiery anger, and with a speed he couldn't deflect, she grabbed him by the head.

Tears streamed down her pale cheeks as she gritted her teeth. "You should've killed me, because I can no longer keep living knowing you're alive and not mine to have."

Leif grabbed her arms and pulled, trying to escape her vice grip. But he couldn't. Her determination was too much, and he felt his neck begin to pop, the pressure building—promising a quick death.

And then he heard Gemma's voice, so clear it was as if she were there by his side. *I love you. Now end this, once and for all.*

The words rejuvenated his body and cleared his head. Her voice returned Leif's resolve, and he grabbed Beatrice by the waist, then tripped her legs out from beneath her. Together, they toppled to the ground.

Out of the corner of his eye, just next to him, he saw red resting in the shallow water—like the color of Gemma's hair. In one quick movement, he grabbed the copper knife—something that would have scalded his hand before Kenzie's brilliant enchantment had brought on his immunity. With both hands high above, he plunged the blade into Beatrice's chest, right through her heart.

She didn't scream. She made no sound. But her brown eyes revealed a beautiful agony that stabbed back at Leif. And then they went lifeless.

He sat next to her, breathing hard. He wasn't tired, not physically, anyway, but the ordeal had been exhausting.

And then he heard running behind him.

The kraken. How could he have forgotten? Turning to spot the massive shifter, he found Octavius running the opposite way. He was escaping from the fight, and he still had Gemma's brooch.

"No!" he said, jumping to his feet, bolting through the watery mess of the Dome. Leif didn't get far before he heard a scream nearby.

"Leif! Help!"

It was Piper. Leif skidded to a stop, turning back the way he'd come. He didn't even have to think about it. Piper needed him, though his heart threw a regretful thought toward the retreating kraken. Maybe he could make this quick.

She called out to him again, although her tone was weaker. Turning the corner Jesse and Piper had taken before Beatrice attacked, he slipped inside a training room of sorts. Sparks were flying from electronics, spraying the watery floor and causing a series of hisses. In the darkness, Leif could see Jesse in his shifted form, unmoving. He hoped the hound was still alive. Several feet away, a female vampire was hunched over Piper, who had stopped calling for help. The vampire was slurping loudly, and Leif could see her fangs embedded in Piper's neck.

Briefly, the vampire pulled away. "There we go, nice and quiet-like."

Piper was reacting to the venom, its soothing serenade drawing her into a dreamlike state.

"That's it," the vampire cooed. "You won't even realize your death has come as I drink you dry."

Fortunately for Leif, the vampire hadn't noticed him yet, and he couldn't just stand and watch his friend die. He bolted over the slick, watery floor and grabbed the vampire by the shoulders, tearing her away from Piper and throwing her directly at one of the sparking electronics.

The vampire screamed with surprise until she impacted the broken device, at which point the electricity stole her voice. As she fell to the ground, she spasmed, steam rising from her body. Leif didn't hesitate. In one swift bound, he was at her seizing form, and in one precise movement, he tore her head from her shoulders.

It made him sick—he was no killer. But he couldn't let anyone suck Piper dry.

Looking away, he tossed the vampire's head and ran back to his former Initiate. Piper's sandy-blonde hair was swimming in the pooled-up water on the floor, her pupils dilated.

"Leif," she said dreamily, drugged by the venom swimming in her veins. She slowly raised her hand to the side of his face, her skin hardly holding any warmth. "You're here." She brought her hand back to her neck where the fresh fang marks were. "I think I got bit."

Leif chuckled. "Yeah, you did. But you're safe now."

He held Piper close, and movement to the side ripped his attention away. Jesse was shifting back to human form, and after he was done, he groaned as he slowly got to his feet.

The shifter's eyes landed on him, then looked over at the

beheaded vampire.

"She was waiting for us," he said, rubbing the top of his head. "I took a pretty bad blow." Jesse's eyes landed on Piper and he seemed to forget his own pain as he ran over. "Oh, no! Is Piper okay?"

It warmed Leif to see the boy's concern for his former Initiate.

"I'm fine," she said, swinging a hand lazily in Jesse's direction. "Have I ever told you how hot you are?"

Leif grimaced and looked at Jesse. "She might be a little bit under the influence of vampire venom. But she'll be okay."

Jesse seemed to take her compliment well.

Leif looked back at Piper and realized that the kraken must have gotten away with Gemma's brooch. Leif had chosen to save a friend over chasing after Octavius. And further, the shifters still needed him.

Though his heart ached at the thought of losing her again, Gemma would have to wait a little while longer.

Myreen

Myreen continued to attempt to hold off the vampires, alongside Ms. Dinu in her dragon form and Mr. Coltar who had gone full ursa and was demolishing vampires left and right. But she felt hollow after Kol's abrupt departure.

She hadn't put much thought into her decision to become a hybrid—not that she'd had much time to think about it anyway. It was literally what she was created for, and she felt in her heart that it was the right move. It was the only way she could be equal to Draven and more capable of defeating him.

But she never considered how her friends—Kol especially— would feel about it. Of course Kol would have issues with her being a vampire. His family had a long-standing hatred for vampires, and Kol had been tortured for days by the most powerful vampire of all. Now, after everything they'd been through, she faced losing him again for a sacrifice she had to make.

Leif's venom had definitely made her far more powerful. She could fight off the attacking vampires with her eyes closed if she wanted to. Ripping off a head was as easy as plucking an unsuspecting flower from a garden bed, which in itself was a little terrifying. She'd had to try quite hard not to hurt Kol when he struggled to whisk her away from the fight.

She'd almost wondered if her shifter abilities would be somehow nullified, overwritten by the vampire blood flowing through her veins. Instead, they'd been amplified tenfold. She could *feel* the water that dammed all around the battlefield like it was a second skin, could sense the powerful light of the rising half-moon on the horizon behind her. Everything was so much more intense.

Including the pain of Kol's dismissal.

The storm of emotions inside her made it difficult to keep her ursa contained, even with her harpy wings out. She considered letting it out, going berserk on the vampires just like Mr. Coltar was. But her mind was foggy as a bear, to say the least, and she needed to have a clear head for the battle to come.

After dispatching a twig of a vampire girl, Myreen looked over the horde of vampires to where Draven stood in the background. She needed to get to him. She needed to end this. She could figure out her relationship with Kol later.

If there was a later.

Suddenly, the battle shifted. The near-constant earthquake from the kraken's movements ceased, and the vampires in front of her stopped charging and fell back. The abrupt halt of action made Myreen, Ms. Dinu, and Mr. Coltar hover in battle stance, waiting for whatever the vampires had in store for them next.

Myreen stole a quick glance behind her at the Dome and froze in confusion. The kraken was nowhere in sight. Had the shifters defeated it? Was that why the vampires were falling back—were they actually retreating? Perhaps the shifters at the Dome had gotten an advantage over the vampires to win the battle.

Her internal quandary was soon answered.

Like some dark fallen angel, Draven flew over their heads with a magnificent pair or raven-black wings, shimmering in the moonlight as if they'd been dipped in oil. When she saw who was in his arms, her heart thudded, threatening to plummet straight to the ground.

Kendall!

Had Kendall defected? Was Draven going to kill him to make an example?! Despite their differences, she didn't want to see Kendall die. A very real part of her still cared for him, even if not in the same way he professed to care for her. She turned her back to the vampire army and bent her knees, ready to leap for Kendall at the first sign of abuse.

Draven and Kendall landed on a swirling disk of water that manifested at the top of the Dome where the glass had been smashed. Somewhere in the back of her mind, she noticed that the fighting had also stopped inside the Dome, and that the vampires within had converged to one side, leaving the shifters there just as confused and cautious as those outside.

"Attention, shifters of the Dome." It was Draven's voice, reverberating throughout the air, loud and clear. "For millennia, our kind have been at war. Countless lives have been lost on both sides. This doesn't need to continue any longer, for I have a solution that has never before been possible. We're at a precipice, where two can now become one. I am the first vampire-shifter hybrid, and I have the power to give this gift to anyone I choose." He held his hand out to Kendall, who was still standing beside him. "Kendall is one of you, a mer. He saw the future I wanted to create for both our species and decided to join us. As a reward for his allegiance, I will turn him into a hybrid right here, right now, for all of you to witness."

Kendall stepped in front of Draven with his back to him so that everyone below could see his face, could see that he was a willing participant. Draven wrapped his arms around Kendall, who extended his neck to one side, and Draven sunk his teeth in. Kendall swooned, his eyes fluttering, and for an instant, the two looked like lovers in an embrace. The scene wasn't violent to watch. In fact, it was almost sensual. Draven appeared to take great care in the way he handled Myreen's former suitor.

The bite didn't take long, and when Draven released Kendall, the mer collapsed onto the thin water layer beneath him. As the venom set in, he curled into a ball, releasing an agonized scream.

Several shifters inside the Dome cursed and threw their fists, assuming that what was happening to Kendall was what usually happened when a vampire injected their venom into a shifter. They thought he was dying. Myreen knew better, and shuddered at the memory of the pain her own transformation had brought.

"Fear not," Draven's voice boomed. "The transformation is incredibly painful, yet mercifully brief. Rather than lasting days as from a human to a vampire, the hybrid process takes only minutes. Watch."

After the longest minute Myreen had ever endured, Kendall's screaming stopped. With her new, vampiricly-enhanced vision, even from this great distance and in the dim light of the evening, she could see the pale shine to his skin as he rose and stood tall before his audience.

Myreen didn't even realize she'd been holding her breath until she exhaled at seeing Kendall rise. As scared as she was that he would've died from the venom, seeing the new, marble-white skin that covered his chiseled face made her heart ache. There was no going back for him now.

"How do you feel, Kendall, my boy?" Draven asked, patting him on the back.

Kendall's face was painted with awe, like that of a child seeing his presents under the tree on Christmas morning. "Incredible," Kendall gasped, staring as he blurrily twisted his hands backward and forward, like he was seeing them for the first time.

"Why don't you flash them a smile," Draven invited.

Kendall grinned wide, flashing his new fangs for all to see. The crowd collectively gasped, and Myreen absentmindedly ran her tongue over her own long canines, which she hadn't noticed had come back out until just then.

"Do you see?" Draven announced. "We can end this war tonight. If you surrender now and swear fealty to me, Draven Denholm, leader of the vampires and future ruler of this world, I'll forgive all previous transgressions and welcome you into my coven as hybrid vampires, just as I have for Kendall. No more shifter blood need be spilled. So, what will it be? Eternal life on the winning side, or a meaningless and merciless death? The choice is yours."

Myreen looked around. All the shifters—students and teachers and parents, alike—stood silent, passing questioning, panicked glances between one another. And all the vampires stood like statues, waiting.

She had no idea if Draven's offer was genuine. Adding hybrids to his army would make him infinitely more powerful, but his hatred for shifters was deep. She feared he would gather any who surrendered into a small confined space and simply slaughter them all.

She watched everyone closely, scared for anyone that might be foolish enough to defect to the vampires. If they joined Draven, they were likely in even more danger than if they stayed in the fight.

To her relief, no one stepped forward. The uncertainty and fear that she saw on every face slowly turned to resolve, postures straightening to battle stances.

Delphine emerged from the crowd of shifters on the grass inside the Dome, standing firm in front of the vampire militia. "For the Dome!" she shouted, thrusting her fist into the air and charging at the vampires.

The shifters behind her immediately followed suit, and the two opposing armies crashed like angry waves, blood splashing into the air with the tide.

"Death it is," Draven's voice echoed. "No one is to touch the siren. She's mine."

And like a river flowing around a rock, the vampires zoomed past her, no one daring to so much as graze her as they passed. They flooded into the crack in the Dome, despite Mr. Coltar's rampage form trying to keep them out. She wanted to turn around and fight the vampires, to protect her fellow students, friends and mentors. But Draven leapt from his perch above the Dome and landed several yards away from her at the base of his water wall. He was waiting for her.

She hated him. Everything he had said to her about not wanting to hurt shifters, about wanting to form a lasting peace—that had all been a lie. If his so-called trophy room hadn't been proof of that fact, there was no denying it now. Draven wouldn't stop until every last shifter was dead.

She had to end this. Draven had to die. And she had to be

the one to kill him.

This was the moment the prophecy spoke of. She held onto it like a prayer as she trekked forward.

"It didn't have to be this way, Myreen," he said as she squared her stance. "You could've joined my side. Been the daughter you were meant to be. The attack didn't have to happen like this."

"So if I'd stayed, you wouldn't have come here and killed every last shifter?" she threw at him.

He shrugged. "Not exactly. I would've offered clemency to those who surrendered, but yes, those who opposed would've inevitably been executed. Shifters are an unnatural disease of humanity."

"So are vampires," she said. "At least shifters don't have to kill to survive."

"No, but they kill anyway. Do you have any idea how many innocent humans have fallen to out-of-control weres? Or lost their lives fighting for the dragon causes? At least when we kill, we kill with purpose. Vampires are the superior species. We have unmatched intellect and powers that could steer humanity into the future. We are the rightful rulers of this earth. And you could've reigned by my side as the princess you were born to be. But you chose to die with the shifters who tossed you aside."

"Only one of us will die tonight," she promised. "And it won't be me."

He chuckled dismissively. "You know, it broke poor Tyberius' heart when you abandoned him for the dragons. He's been inconsolable. He loved you, and now he sees you for the traitorous disgrace you are. He hates you."

That stung. She loved Ty more than she ever expected to. She wanted what was best for him, and the life Draven had groomed him for was so far from that. She tried to tell herself that it was okay, that Draven had brainwashed him so deeply that he couldn't see past that, but still, knowing he hated her hurt all the same.

"I'll do right by him one day," she said, more to herself than to Draven.

"Yes, your death will serve him well," Draven said with a laugh. "As it will the rest of my followers. Once you're dead, I'll drain your body of every last drop of blood and create the perfect army of unstoppable hybrids. Then, finally, the world will see us vampires for the kings we were created to be."

Kendall froze behind Draven like a deer in the headlights, a conflicted look twisting his boyishly handsome face, only made more beautiful by vampire venom. He passed cautious eyes between Myreen and Draven.

"More like monsters," Myreen spat, aiming her words at Draven. "Enough talking." She arched her wings behind her and flung out the talons on her hands. "This ends now."

Draven crossed his arms and smiled. "Kendall, my boy. It's time to prove your loyalty."

At this, Myreen's eyes shot to Kendall, who stood a few feet behind Draven, his eyes nearly bugging out of his head. *Not like this*, she thought, fearing what was to come.

"Kill her," Draven commanded.

Myreen's mouth went completely dry, and her heart galloped like a spooked unicorn.

Kendall shook his head and stepped forward. "That was never part of the deal. You promised she would remain unharmed." He cast pleading eyes on Myreen, begging her to understand this was not what he wanted.

"She has chosen her side, therefore she has chosen to die,"

Draven said. "And if you would like to stay on the winning side, you must obey my orders. Kill the siren."

Kendall shook his head even more desperately. "No, I won't."

A breath of relief rushed shakily out of Myreen's nostrils. Kendall wasn't completely lost after all.

Draven looked sideways at Kendall with a mildly bored expression. "Love has made you weak. But you will obey me, whether you want to or not." Myreen knew what was coming, and she was powerless to stop it. In his devastatingly melodic siren voice, Draven said, "Kill Myreen, or die trying."

A glaze came over Kendall's eyes, his lids closing for a moment as the command set in. When his eyes opened again, his expression was deadly. True fear shot through Myreen's chest.

Before she had time to prepare herself, Kendall flung out his hand and a spear of water shot from the liquid wall behind Draven and slammed right into Myreen's chest, knocking the wind out of her.

She crumpled to the ground, clutching her abdomen and gasping for breath. "Kendall," she choked. "Kendall, snap out of it. You... don't want... to do this."

But Kendall kept coming at her, throwing more water arrows at her, which she was able to sloppily dodge. She caught her breath and got to her feet, using her wings to absorb the blows that kept coming.

In this moment, she felt like the helpless damsel she used to be—like she didn't have the power of three different shifters enhanced by vampire venom. Like she didn't have any physical training at all. Because she didn't want to use any of that against Kendall. Traitor or not, he was still a good guy.

"Kendall, stop!" she yelled. "I don't want to fight you!"

Her cries fell on deaf ears. It was as if he didn't know her at all. She was merely a target to him, and she was sure he'd stop at nothing to kill her. She didn't want to kill him, but she needed to make him stop, even if it wounded him.

She arched her right wing and flung it at him, sending feather-daggers shooting toward him. He lifted his hand and a water shield manifested in front of his torso, blocking the feathers. But one pierced straight through his foot, pinning him to the ground.

He didn't react—no cries of pain or even so much as a flinch. When he realized he couldn't keep walking, he looked down at the feather with slight irritation. Then he bent down, gripped the razor-sharp feather and yanked it out, blood spilling down his hand as it cut through his flesh. Again, no reaction to the pain. He just threw down the feather and continued to stalk toward her as the gash in his palm and hole in his foot healed.

She summoned her siren voice and issued a command of her own. "Kendall, stop!"

Kendall paused, blinking several times, and sentience returned to his eyes for a split second.

"Myreen," he grunted through clenched teeth, barely audible. "...R– run... I. Can't."

"Finish this," Draven commanded in his siren voice.

At that, Kendall sprinted at her like a cheetah on the prowl.

She had no choice but to flee. If she let him get ahold of her, she'd have to kill him. But if she could outrun—or out*fly* him—she could spare him and focus on Draven. Draven was her true enemy, and she hated him even more for turning her friend against her.

She sprung into the air, her wings adopting her vampire speed and making her a bullet in the sky. But something cold and wet latched onto her foot seconds after she leapt. It quickly swirled up her body, and she soon found herself fully engulfed by floating water.

Myreen choked at the water that invaded her lungs and faltered, the seemingly living pool that surrounded her dragging her down to the water of the lake. She slammed against the water like smacking into glass, the impact momentarily rocking her.

Struggling to regain her wits as the water intentionally drowned her, as soon as she could reason once again, she split-shifted into a mermaid, her harpy wings still out. Her gills opened on her neck, the skin there stinging for a moment at the speed of her transformation, as if the flesh had been sliced by a knife. But the relief at being able to breathe again far outweighed the pain. She inhaled deeply, the rapacious water forcing its way down her throat no longer bothering her.

Kendall entered the water not far behind her, and she felt it like he was entering a part of her. Angling her wings like daggers, she shot through the water, desperate to get away. Her wings gave her speed, allowing her to cut through the lake like a torpedo. But Kendall was a far more skilled swimmer, having been raised in water from birth. And with the enhancement of vampiric speed, he caught up quickly.

Frustrated panic sizzled through her. She wouldn't be able to outswim him, and apparently flying wasn't going to work. She had to try her siren voice one more time.

With frazzled uncertainty, she scooped her wings, spinning in the water to face Kendall. Calling on water was easier now than it had ever been, and she had no problem using it like a large fist to grasp Kendall, seizing his swim. He flailed, squirming against the chainlike currents that held him in place. She could feel him willing the water to let him free, but her will was stronger, fueled by desperation.

Closing her eyes, she centered herself and summoned her siren voice with all the force she could muster. The strength of it vibrated through her bones, and when her voice left her lips, the timber of it sent ripples through the water around them.

"You will no longer abide the commands of Draven Denholm. You are free from his influence from this day forward."

Like a rope snapping, she felt Draven's hold over Kendall sever. The fog left his eyes completely, and he was himself again. He was her Kendall. *Yes!* she cried inwardly.

"Now get as far away from this place as you possibly can, as fast as you can," she ordered, knowing this could be the last time she ever saw him. But he had to get away. That was the only way he'd be safe.

The command set in, and now free of her water bonds, Kendall dove forward, slicing through the lake.

Her relief was overwhelming.

Kendall hadn't gotten far before water wrapped around his and Myreen's waists and yanked them angrily out, throwing them on the ground like a whip snapping.

Myreen floundered like a fish out of water, coughing at the dry air and forcing her gills to close and her tail to split. Kendall had shifted back to human form faster than she could, and he was quickly at her side, helping her to her feet.

"Myreen, are you alright?" he practically begged.

Too late, she heard the telltale whip of something shooting through the air, and Kendall's eyes widened, his breath caught in his throat.

"Kendall?" she asked in a shrill pitch.

Kendall made a strange gurgling sound, then looked down at his chest. Terrified, Myreen's eyes followed his to see a long, black dagger-like feather protruding from his smartsuit, right through his heart. Over Kendall's shoulder, she could see Draven standing sideways with his wing aimed pointedly at them, and she knew what must've happened.

"No one betrays me," Draven said softly.

Kendall's knees buckled, and Myreen followed him to the ground, feeling useless as death dug its clutches into Kendall's soul. He looked up at her, and a strange spark of understanding lit his beach-blue eyes.

"This was my vision," he said, his voice cracking and weak. "All this time..." He shook his head.

Myreen forced a dry swallow. "It– it's okay," she stammered nervously. "I'll just pull it out and you'll be fine." Her head nodded so vigorously that it made her neck hurt. But it should work. Kendall was a hybrid now; his flesh would seal as soon as she removed the feather. And if it didn't, she could heal him with her harpy magic. *He'll be fine*, she repeated in her mind to convince herself.

She wrapped all ten fingers around the feather, not caring that it cut into her flesh, blood spilling down her arms. She wrenched it out. Keeping her eyes glued to the puncture in his chest, she could see the skin slowly begin to close.

"See?" she said.

But just as Kendall looked back up at her, his chest jerked forward at the same time that she heard a disgusting, bone-crunching sound.

He gripped her arms so tightly that it should've hurt. "Myreen... uh... love you." His voice faded before the last syllable left his lips, the light leaving his eyes completely. He fell limp to the ground. Dead.

Completely baffled at what just happened, she caught him in

her arms, cradling him like he was something frail and precious.

A shadow loomed over her, and she looked up with frantic, questioning eyes. Draven stood over them, and in his hand was Kendall's oozing heart.

All the blood drained from Myreen's face. It might as well have been her heart that Draven ripped out.

"He was weak," Draven said as he took a step toward her. "What a waste of my venom he turned out to be."

Tears spilled down her cheeks as she took one last longing look at Kendall's empty face. Despite everything, she still truly cared for him. And now he was gone.

A thousand thoughts sped through her mind. She was a harpy. If she could somehow put his heart back inside his chest, she could heal him. Right?! Kendall couldn't be dead, he just couldn't!

But she knew the truth. Even for a vampire, this kind of death was final.

Anger coursed through her veins like a poison, making every inch of her seethe and burn. Storm clouds appeared overhead, swirling and rumbling, mimicking the way she felt inside. She gently lay Kendall down and rose to her feet, narrowing her eyes at her father as a rogue wind whooshed through the empty lake bed and whipped at her hair.

"Let's finish this."

Oberon

As a child, roiling storm clouds, booming thunder, and rushing wind terrified Oberon. His younger self knew that someday he'd be able to control the elements—that they'd follow his instructions as a horse follows its master's bridle and reins.

Tonight, the elements listened to him. But the wind that pushed him and Serilda's family through the night sky was not the force of one gryphon, but many. Oberon had never flown so fast in all his life. And, like when he was a child, it was terrifying.

He kept it together, but Ren—who happened to be in a full-body hold by Oberon—was currently freaking out. He'd been in and out of consciousness during the rapid journey, and Oberon kind of wished he'd have remained unconscious for the duration.

"This is not normal!" Ren screamed. "There's too much air, but it seems like it's going past me faster than I can breathe it!"

"It probably is," Oberon yelled back so he could be heard.

Somehow, he managed to keep his own voice steady.

Craning his neck, he checked on his niece, June, who was still technically learning to fly. She seemed to have no problems keeping herself perfectly balanced on the racing wind, and looked to be enjoying the freedom of the air without her parents having to interfere. The eyes of the other zooming gryphons glowed a brilliant purple. Chills ran through Oberon's body, and not from the wintery air. He liked to think that this was how his species used to charge into battle as great warriors, working together.

Bringing his attention to the ground far below, Oberon spotted a series of large lakes approaching.

"That's Lake Superior," Oberon said. "And Lake Michigan is—"

The sight of the empty lake caused Oberon to release his hold on the wind, and a decrease in velocity came as a result. Which was okay. They needed to slow down, anyway.

"Floating in the air?" Ren finished. "It looks like a giant wall of water hovering over Chicago!"

That was alarming, but Oberon was more disturbed by where the water *should* be. From this distance, it seemed like ants were pouring into a hole at the top of the exposed school, but Oberon knew very well what they were.

"Look at the Dome," Oberon said, not entirely sure Ren could see what was going on in the darkness of night.

"Vampires," Ren hissed, confirming that the moonlight was enough for his eyes. "How did they drill a hole into it? And look at all the cracks!"

It pained Oberon to see his home and life's work in such disarray.

The wind suddenly died down, indicating that others had stopped using their elemental abilities as well. Oberon flapped his large wings, circling back so he could communicate with the other gryphons.

They followed his lead until their bodies formed a perfect circle.

"We might be too late," Oberon said. "The vampires are already within the school. Our time to aid them is now."

"We're ready," Gabriel said. "What's your plan?"

Oberon had been considering this the entire flight from Alberta, but was unfamiliar with strategy among a team of gryphons. But their combined abilities got them to Lake Michigan in record time...

"We combine our powers again," Oberon concluded. "If we can summon enough thunderclouds, perhaps we can chain our lightning to stop the vampires from entering the school."

The gryphons' glowing purple eyes returned, and together they summoned one giant black cloud that crackled with unbridled electricity.

"Think the vampires are ready for a light show?" Ren asked.

"Ready or not," Oberon said, "here we come! Gryphons! This is your time for payback for the wrongs the vampires have committed against you! Now, fly with me!"

He dove, causing Ren to scream out loud again, and Oberon chuckled. Hearing the fox's frightened squeal never got old.

Oberon found Gabriel at his left, and with a quick look to his right, he spotted Tobias matching his speed. Savannah lined up next to her husband, as did Gwendolyn. Even Grandma Vogel and June arranged themselves on the ends, preparing to take on the foes that had kept them on the run over the years. Oberon would do whatever it took to protect them.

Inhaling deeply, Oberon released a piercing call louder than any that had ever escaped his beak, and he was shocked to hear a chorus of equally-loud gryphon calls surrounding him.

The seemingly endless vampire forces stopped their charging and looked to the sky.

Reaching a safe enough distance from the lake bed, Oberon released Ren, whose nine-tails charged with electricity mid-air. The kitsune landed elegantly and began his fluid attacks against the surprised vampires.

Oberon and the others pulled up from their dive, and Oberon yelled, "Summon your lightning and chain your bolts with one another!"

Looking up, he called upon the dark clouds that blotted out the stars and moon. Gladly releasing its barely-contained power, multiple lightning bolts streaked out of the sky. Like static manipulation, Oberon felt his feathers pull at the energy plummeting to the empty lake.

Fearful shouts came from the vampires, and as the bolts struck them at random, Oberon made sure to tether his bolt to the next closest—one summoned by Savannah. The connection shot through a dozen vampires, holding them in place and causing them to seize up. Tobias's bolt bridged with Oberon's on the other side, and soon, the sizzling electric current was holding at least forty vampires pinned in place.

Oberon swooped higher, taking a glance at the linked lightning that was now making a rough, uneven circle straight through countless vampires. So many more were trapped within.

"Fill in the gap!" Oberon called.

Summoning more lightning from the cloud in the sky, they each pulled on the electricity, then pushed outward, connecting one side of the ever-changing circle to the other. Their combination of lightning looked like a wagon wheel of light.

But Oberon knew the lightning would only freeze these vampires in place. No amount of electricity could kill them.

And then heads began to roll.

Ren Suzuki phased in and out of the gryphons' lightning bolts, whipping his electrically-charged nine tails in a blur. The kitsune made short work in such a quick time, but things got even better as a new wave of shifter military began to arrive, a portion of them breaking off to assist Ren's attack. Dragons, harpies, weres, phoenixes—it was a sight to behold, all shifter-kind working together, prepared to defend themselves and each other. But the fight wasn't over yet.

A familiar, dark-gray-scaled dragon swooped close to him. "It's good to have you back, Oberon."

"Malkolm Dracul," Oberon replied. So even the students were defending the school. *Just how it should've been at La Framboise Island,* he thought. "I'm happy to fight at your side."

"Me too," Kol said. "I just wish it would've been sooner." The young dragon hovered for another couple of moments, then shot away, his scales flipping invisible as he angled toward the fight. But Oberon wondered at Kol's words.

It was almost unfair how easy the battle was. But this was only one part of the battle, and more of the Dome was damaged than he'd originally thought. Metal bracing helped keep the structure's shape, but a good portion of the glass was either cracked or completely shattered. He'd have to find out what exactly happened to cause such destruction.

Off toward the middle of the broken Dome, lances of water and light caught Oberon's attention, and he gasped. Draven was elevated on a disc of water. The vampire leader must've stolen thruster technology or something—unless...

Months ago, Leif had told him that Draven's goal was to make vampire-shifter hybrids. Had the vampire leader figured it out?

Oberon's train of thought was shattered as he saw who

Draven was fighting against.

"Myreen!" he cried out. The girl was holding her own against Draven—moving as fast as a vampire. She weaved light, and so did he. Their attacks clashed against each other like swords. Lances of water flung at Myreen, and with unseen rapidity, she dashed the water away, turning it into falling rain.

They seemed to be at an impasse—father and daughter tangled up in a dangerous dance.

This was the moment—the culmination of Delphine's vision. Myreen was the prophesied siren.

And she needed help to tip the scales in her favor.

Oberon nearly let go of his bolt of lightning, but a swirling sphere of water—big enough to contain a person—stopped next to him. Narrowing his eyes, he could see Delphine, illuminated by the bright lightning still flickering below. She was in mermaid form, protected in her cocoon of water, her fiery red hair floating every-which way.

Poking her head out of the water, she said, "I'm glad you made it." She nodded toward the other gryphons. "And I'm glad my vision held true for you. Seeing your team of gryphons come diving in to save the day was indescribable. And your timing was none too early."

"I was afraid we were too late," Oberon said. "After we win this battle, we'll have plenty of time to catch up. But we have a siren who could use our help."

Delphine smiled, pushing her water carriage away. "I'm already on it. Keep mopping these vampires up, will you?"

Oberon nodded. "We'll stop their attack here, but it will all be in vain if Draven gets away."

"Then we'll make sure he doesn't," replied Delphine. She slipped her head back into her watery transport and sloshed toward the fight raging between Draven and Myreen.

Quickly analyzing the lightning-circle-of-death he was still linked to, Oberon saw that the majority of vampires in the area had been killed. They needed to move on to other areas.

"Spread out!" he called to his family. "Spread out and divide by twos! The other shifters will take care of the vampires if you can pin them with lightning. But be mindful to keep out of range of the vampires' weaponry."

The breathtaking electricity fizzled away, and the gryphons did as Oberon suggested. Even June was right there with her dad. Oberon suspected she'd had training with her weather manipulation abilities, at least a little.

Gwendolyn and Savannah set out together, leaving Gabriel and Grandma Vogel as the final gryphon duo.

He looked about for other recognizable shifters in the battle. He'd spotted Kol, but where was Eduard's distinctive black dragon? He should've been out among his forces, leading them, but Oberon didn't see him anywhere. Sure, there were other black dragons flying about, but they were smaller and didn't have Eduard's spread of black spikes on the sides of their jaws.

Fortunately, Paskal Candida was picking up the slack, leading the dragon's fight. It had been a long time since he'd seen Nikolai's father. Their last communication had been over the phone, when he'd demanded his son be taken out of the school and made Eduard's personal assistant.

Malachai's bright phoenix could be seen leading a group of his kind. A few weres followed them from the ground, clawing and taking bites out of vampires as they went. He recognized a few other shifter military officers stepping up.

At least there's some organization going on, he thought.

Getting his head back into the game, Oberon's first instinct was to work with Ren—just like the old days. But a pained scream ripped his attention away, and Oberon's eyes focused on the fight between Draven and Myreen.

Myreen had been thrown to the side and was trying to regain her bearings, but the scream hadn't come from her. Draven was rising on his watery platform. Above him was Delphine in human form, her watery shield stripped away. Two spears of light held her tacked to the air by the shoulders, and blood dripped like tears from the wounds.

Harpy abilities? Draven could manipulate light? *And* water?

"No," Oberon stammered, keeping the steady beat of his wings going. He seemed frozen in place, unable to move in to help.

Delphine wriggled uselessly in the air, her chest heaving in a mix of panic and shock. The platform of water Draven was standing on suddenly submerged him entirely—Delphine's attack. It broke Oberon out of his helpless trance. He flapped his wings hard. Perhaps if Draven could be contained in the water for long enough, he'd drown.

To his horror, Oberon watched as Draven's shadowy legs formed into a long, black tail. Which also meant he had gills. The vampire leader couldn't drown. He was a chimera hybrid.

With even more resolve flowing through him, Oberon flew as hard as he could, calling upon the lightning stewing in the clouds overhead.

Faster than he could bring a bolt down, a single hand jutted from the watery pod containing Draven and grabbed a hold of Delphine's neck.

"No!" yelled Oberon, directing the crackling electricity he'd summoned straight at Draven. Before the bolt struck the water, Draven's hand twisted. Delphine's head instantly jutted off at an odd angle, and Oberon could hear the audible crack that accompanied the movement. Delphine's struggling legs went limp.

Oberon's lightning struck its mark, but too late. The staves of light pinning her to the air disappeared, and she fell, tumbling from the sky until her body slammed into the floor of the exposed Dome.

"Delphine!" cried Oberon. But there was nothing he could do for her. Not now. His heart felt as if it would burst. With the rage of having lost so much to this monster, he pummeled the water Draven had regained control of with as much electricity as he could pull from the thundercloud above.

He let loose a piercing call. Myreen got to her feet close to where Delphine's still, broken body lay. Tears were in her eyes as she looked up. The water at Draven's feet peeled back, causing him to fall from the air, too—obviously Myreen had gained some skill with her water manipulation.

Oberon kept Draven pinned to the ground, recalling the eerily similar scene following his wife and parents' deaths at the hands of the monstrous vampire leader. But he wouldn't let go this time, not until Draven was dead.

"You killed my wife!" Oberon growled. He had no idea if Draven could hear him, but he didn't care. "You killed my parents. You killed my unborn child. And that's just the tip of the feather on how much blood is on your hands." He edged closer to the hybrid creature, pouring enough energy into him to power the city of Chicago.

He looked at Myreen, who was hunched over Delphine's body, heavy sobs causing her petite form to quake. This was too much for the girl. She wasn't ready. Whatever Eduard had tried to teach her, it wasn't enough to deal with what had happened tonight.

Suddenly, Oberon's electricity jumped away from Draven by a foot, as if an invisible field were deflecting it. Oberon gritted his teeth and pushed harder, but his bolt veered off to the side. Just beyond, he saw Draven stand up and throw him an evil smile.

"Oberon Rex—gryphon of legend—has returned," mocked Draven. A sudden movement revealed that the hybrid was using the light of Oberon's lightning to bend the destination of his lightning bolt. Slowly, Draven bent it in such a way that it reflected the electricity right back at Oberon.

It felt as if a million burning, freezing needles slammed into him from beak to tail. He was flung backward from the force of his bolt. He tried to force his wings out, but they wouldn't respond—the electricity in his body stripped his ability to control himself. Fortunately, losing control of his body also severed his connection to the lightning, and it ceased its assault as his body plowed into the ground.

When Oberon could think again, the first thing he detected was the smell of charred feathers. He hurt all over. But he wasn't dead.

"How does it feel?" Draven said, suddenly at his side, bent over him like a big game hunter watching his catch in its final moments. The vampire leader pulled on one of his wings—none too gently—and *tsk*ed. "For so long I've wanted these wings hanging in my trophy room. I suppose the fact that they're singed will remind future generations of vampires and hybrids of what happened today." Then in a whisper, Draven said, "Don't worry. You'll be with your precious wife in a few moments."

Draven craned Oberon's head to the side, bringing it to its very limits.

"Do you hear her voice calling to you?" Draven teased as Oberon's neck creaked from the pressure, ready to snap at any moment. "Do you hear her beckoning for you to join her in death?"

Oberon tried to resist the hybrid's strength, but to no avail. It was over. He closed his eyes in preparation for the end.

And then, in an out-of-this-world voice, Myreen spoke. It

was a melody that carried a power beyond description—but the words were distinct, and they were targeted at Draven.

"Release him!"

The grip on his head relaxed, and Oberon shook it back and forth, then watched Myreen in all her glory. She hovered in the air in harpy form, like an angel casting out darkness. Her eyes glowed white, something Oberon had never seen before among any shifter. But something told him that Myreen wasn't just a shifter anymore.

Draven was under the spell of her words, and he stared at her, as if waiting for further commands.

His posture changed suddenly, like that of a predator waking up from a brief slumber, only to find his prey standing nearby.

"Your siren voice won't work on me, Myreen," he growled. "It's my will against yours."

It seemed he'd forgotten about Oberon for the time being, but the gryphon cared little for his safety now.

Myreen took several hesitant steps backward, fear splashing across her face.

And then Draven's siren voice—like a thousand tympanies—boomed across the sky, rivaling the still-thundering cloud. The hybrid's determination was forged into his words, and all hope within Oberon seemed to blow away.

"You will do my bidding and take your place at my side, Myreen."

The terror on her face subsided, and for a moment Oberon thought Draven was successful in commanding Myreen. But the white glow of her eyes shifted from her father to Oberon, and he saw something else there.

And then she looked back at Draven, the glow in her eyes disappearing. "I might be your daughter," she said stepping toward him. "But you aren't my father."

Pouring more malice into his voice, Draven spat, "Succumb to me!"

"Never," she replied, unaffected by his powerful voice. Oberon watched with wonder. These two beings were the most powerful in the world. Myreen's eyes began to glow white once more. "But *you* will submit to me!"

Oberon couldn't see Draven's face, but the back of the hybrid's body quaked.

"No!" Draven called back.

"Submit!" Myreen yelled again.

Draven fell to one knee, still quaking under her voice. "No!" The determination in his voice was gone, now replaced with sheer terror.

"Submit!" Myreen called, and Oberon thought the world was on the verge of rending itself under the force of her will.

Draven dropped to both knees, his head angled up, waiting on Myreen's next command.

"Put your hands on your head," she said in that same haunting tune. Draven did as he was commanded. "Now, tear that monstrous head away from your neck and rid the world of your venomous, toxic existence."

It seemed as if Draven hesitated, fighting against the voice of the siren. But it only lasted a few moments.

The vampire leader—the vampire-shifter hybrid—removed his head from his shoulders with one thunderous *snap*.

The corpse knelt there, frozen in time, until at last, he toppled, collapsing to the lakebed floor.

The sound of rushing water broke the silent moment like a hurricane. Released from Draven's manipulation, the wall of water crashed back down the side of the empty lake.

"Oh, no," Oberon muttered. The shifters from the Dome weren't going to die at the hands of Draven, but instead from the freezing, drowning waters of Lake Michigan.

Miraculously, the water stopped flowing before he could finish his anxious thought. Peering across the broken school and lakebed, he saw countless merfolk raising their hands, manipulating the water together, stopping it from crashing back down where it belonged.

Looking back at Myreen, she nodded in approval, then boomed her siren voice loudly across the empty lake, magnified for all to hear. "Draven's followers, you are now leaderless. I send you away from this area, and place in you a desire to never return. Leave now!"

Oberon wondered if a siren voice could work in such a way, commanding hundreds—or even thousands—at once.

But the vampires—at least, what remained of them—began to run. They spilled from the broken parts of the Dome. They ran up the sides of the empty lake, some climbing over each other to get away. The shifters protecting their home and school stopped and watched the mass retreat.

Oberon shifted back to his human form and—with difficulty—got to his feet. Staring with wonder at Myreen, he said, "I knew it. All along, I knew you would fulfill the prophecy."

The white glow in her eyes dissipated, and she looked at Oberon. And then she ran to him and gave him a hug, her strength nearly throwing him back to the ground. He embraced her back.

"*We* fulfilled the prophecy," she said, fresh tears streaming from her eyes and landing on Oberon's smart clothing. "All the shifters. Together. We stopped Draven."

"Together," Oberon agreed.

The battle was over.

Kol

Kol stared after the retreating vampires with his mouth agape, his scales shifting from camouflage to gold.

"What happened?" Char asked, landing next to him. She'd recovered enough to rejoin the fight. But Kol didn't want to dwell on that, because it conjured up other concerns—his mom... his dad... Nik...

He stared at her, then again at the fleeing enemy. "I don't know," he said. His entire body felt like lead, glued to the spot. It had been a long night.

Char looked over their shoulders at the Dome, then back again at Kol. "Do you think it's over? That felt too... easy."

"Unless Draven's dead," Kol said, his voice flat. "But that seems impossible."

"But the water..." Char looked at the perimeter of the dry area, warily eyeing the unnatural walls that had threatened to drown them just moments ago. "And what was that sound? I swear it sounded like a voice telling them to leave."

That also seemed impossible, but he would know that siren voice anywhere. "I think it was Myreen." He looked into the cloudless sky. The storm had vanished, leaving a dark-blue palette filled with brilliant stars. Even the purple color of the milky way was visible with the lights of Chicago dampened. The waning moon hung low, and Kol wondered if the night was almost over.

"It's close to dawn," Char said with her human voice, confirming his suspicion. Kol hadn't noticed her shift back. She held a small phone in her hand and was looking at the bright screen. "Maybe they're just running off to hide out until dark?" She held up a finger. "Cover for me a minute? I'll make a quick call."

Kol didn't answer, but stayed in his dragon form, keeping his enhanced eyes peeled for danger. He felt useless though, since it was clear the danger had fled. Three dragons touched down near them. Kol's prior dragon mastery teacher and relative, Miss Dinu, Corporal Modder with his mud-brown scales, and Mr.—er... *Colonel* Candida, Nik's dad. As a new addition to the shifter military, Kol would need to get used to using his title, instead of *Mr.* Candida.

All three had the same questioning looks on their faces.

He motioned at Charlotte. "Sergeant Stern is finding out."

Charlotte's back was turned, and she had one hand on her hip as she spoke in low tones. With Kol's dragon ears, he could hear her side of the conversation, but the *yes, sir's* and *no, sir's* and *we'll be right there, sir,* gave nothing away.

It wasn't until she turned and a grin appeared on her face that Kol knew. He explode-shifted and closed the gap between them with a *well?* written on his face. He heard shifting behind him, and the three others formed a small circle.

"It's over," Char said, weariness and relief etched on her face. "Oberon Rex and the other gryphons—"

"Gryphons?" Miss Dinu said. "As in plural? I thought Oberon was the last—"

"Me too," Char interrupted.

"So..." *Colonel* Candida said, crossing his arms. "Oberon Rex ended the battle? What about Draven?"

Charlotte's eyes flitted to Kol. "Myreen Fairchild, the siren, killed him," she said. "And that *was* her voice we heard. She used her siren voice to make the surviving vampires leave."

Kol's insides twisted. Part of him wanted to shift and fly to her. The other part remembered that she'd become a vampire to kill Draven. To her credit, it sounded like she'd succeeded.

Instead, he mimicked the Colonel's stance with his arms crossed.

Without a word, Miss Dinu shifted and lifted off in the direction of the Dome. Corporal Modder looked to the Colonel and Char for orders. When Nik's dad made a move to follow Miss Dinu, motioning for Corporal Modder to do the same, Kol stopped him.

"Colonel Candida," Kol said, but shook his head and closed his eyes like he regretted speaking. His mouth felt like cotton. But he felt a hand on his shoulder before he could say more. He opened his eyes.

"I know about Nik," he said, his voice gravelly. "Don't blame yourself."

Kol set his teeth and nodded.

Nik's dad and Corporal Modder walked a few paces and shifted, then pushed off the ground. Char took a step to follow, but Kol stopped her with a hand on her arm.

"Wait? A second?" he pleaded.

Her eyebrows furrowed, but she stopped.

After a moment of silence, she broke it with a smile and said, "Your girl ended it. It's over. It's time to get back and repair."

"I know, I just..." Kol ran a hand through his hair. "I just need a minute." Now his voice was raspy.

Another pause.

"Don't you want to get back to her?" she asked. "Don't you want to get back to your mom? Especially after your dad—"

"Could I borrow that phone?" he interrupted.

Her eyes narrowed.

"Tatiana needs to know," he said. "She needs to know about dad and I'm not about to make my mom do it."

Char handed him the phone and he dialed.

"Hello?" his sister answered.

"Tat?"

"Kol!" she cried. "What the *hell*? First, you get captured by a psychopathic vampire and *tortured*, and as soon as I get word that you've escaped and are okay, I get this stupid military blanket email from dad about a vampire attack and then *radio silence*? I got a freaking *email* Kol!" She didn't even stop to take a breath as she rambled. "You have no idea what I've been through the last few hours. I've been sick, Kol. Absolutely *sick!* And did you know mom was coming to see you? Please tell me she didn't make it before the attack. *Please* tell me she's okay and is holed away at the condo in Manhattan?"

"She was here."

"*Was?* As in *past-tense?*" Tatiana's voice cracked.

"Mom's fine," he said quickly. "The kraken—"

"There's a freaking *kraken?*" she shouted. "I'm hanging up, I'm catching a flight—"

"Don't hang up Tatiana!" he shouted back. "The battle's

over. Draven's dead. The vampires are gone."

His sister let out an audible breath on the other line.

"Did you know that mom is insanely fast?" he asked, simultaneously lightening the mood and stalling. Char shot him a look to get on with it.

"Yeah. She broke a few dragon speed records when she was younger."

Kol ran a hand through his hair, feeling his heart speed as he braced himself for what he was about to say. He had to tell her about their dad. "Look... Tatiana."

"*Uh oh,*" she said. "Don't you use that voice on me, *Malkolm Dracul.* Spit it out. What happened?"

How could he possibly phrase it? Kol had never been very good with emotion. It was why he was often accused of being a robot. It was only recently, with Myreen, that he'd improved. But nothing prepared him for this conversation. Maybe he should've left it to his mom. Kol took a deep breath. "The kraken had mom—"

"You said she's okay!" she cried. "You said—"

"The kraken killed dad!" he blurted, and felt instant remorse for the way it came out. He took another breath. She was silent on the other end, but he managed to lower his voice to get out the rest. "The kraken had mom, it was crushing her—it was *killing* her—and dad... died saving her."

"He... *sacrificed* himself for her?" Tatiana's voice was barely a whisper. "You're saying that our dad, *Eduard Dracul,* saved our mother, *Victoria Dracul...* from a kraken?"

"Yes." Kol hardly believed it himself, and he'd witnessed it.

"Why?"

Kol cleared his throat and finally had something to smile about. "There's something you should know about the family curse," he said, allowing the giddiness of that fact to overwhelm the apprehension of the recent complication in his and Myreen's relationship. "I got some selkies to break it. It worked."

"He loved her," Tatiana breathed.

Kol nodded, even though he knew his sister couldn't see it.

Char shot him a guilty *wrap it up* look. They needed to get back to the Dome.

"Hey uh, Tat, I've gotta go."

"Yeah, of course. I'm in Paris," she said, her voice suddenly vacant and far away. "I'll get there as soon as I can and I'll uh... call Adam and Alex." *Right.* Kol often forgot about his half-brothers. They weren't exactly close, but they should know about their dad's death.

"You should probably call their mom too," Kol said.

"Yes. You go... oh, but wait? Kol?"

"Hmm?"

"Delete the voice messages I left on your phone."

"Why?"

"Just do it. Don't listen to them. It can wait."

The fact she asked ensured that Kol would do exactly that—listen to them. But for now, he had other things to worry about.

He ended the call and handed the phone to Char, who tucked it in a pouch in her smart uniform.

"Don't you need to call your parents?" he asked.

"I messaged them to tell them I was okay and that I'll call them later," she said, then added when she caught Kol's expression, "Look, I wasn't telling them that a family member died in the battle. I can call them later. They're probably already on their way, anyway."

Kol nodded.

"You ready?" Char asked. She could always read Kol better

than most.

He shrugged. He didn't think he'd ever be ready to face his grieving mother, dead best friend or his now vampire girlfriend. "Do I have a choice?" he asked.

But she didn't answer, and they took off toward the school.

***

Kol didn't know the plans for repairing—if the school would be shut down indefinitely, or even re-located. But it wasn't his decision to make or his problem to fix. Still, it was strange *flying* into the broken roof from the air, and not entering the school by subway. When he touched down near the main building, he felt a sort of vulnerability he'd never felt at the school before. The cracked-open Dome with the starry sky above felt vastly different than the glass bubble hidden from the world below the waves.

Char rushed off to find whoever was taking control of the military after Eduard's death. She wanted orders. She needed to be busy. Kol offered to go with her, since he was also shifter military, but she ordered him to face his personal tragedies first.

Personal tragedies. Kol stood outside the main building, as frozen in place as he'd been moments after the battle ended, without a clue about what to do. Who should he look for first? His mother? Nik's family? Myreen?

"Malkolm," Oberon said, exiting the building.

"Oberon," Kol said, looking to the former director, to the gryphon he respected and looked up to.

Oberon clapped a hand on his shoulder. "We've experienced many losses today."

It frustrated him that Oberon felt the need to state the obvious. "Yes, and maybe if you hadn't left, things would've turned out differently." Kol was surprised by the anger he didn't know he'd harbored. "Maybe if you'd fought harder and insisted on staying and keeping the school safe... Maybe my dad wouldn't be dead. Maybe Nik wouldn't be dead." Maybe Myreen wouldn't have felt the need to turn into a vampire-shifter hybrid— *whatever.*

"I wasn't aware Nikolai was among the casualties," he said, his voice lowered. "But it was not my choice to leave."

"I know, I know." Kol gripped a fistful of his hair and sunk to the ground, leaning his back against some rubble with his long legs close to his chest. "You were kicked out. It's my dad's fault—" His voice caught, and he put his forehead on his knees to hide his face. "It was his fault."

"It was no one's fault," Oberon said, his voice close, as if he crouched to Kol's level. "Draven was an evil vampire, and I don't doubt he would've attacked no matter who was in charge of the school."

Kol didn't move or respond, keeping his head buried.

"And who knows? Maybe things would've ended up worse if I'd still been here?" Kol felt Oberon slump next to him against the rubble. "Eduard prepared the older students to fight better than I did, and the younger ones escaped to safety because of his leadership. For all we know, we might've lost more."

Kol lifted his head.

"Look, I don't know why things happen the way they do," Oberon continued. "But we can learn from what has happened, look for the good, and find ways to move forward."

"Look for the good?" Kol couldn't think of a single thing that could be described that way.

"I found my family," Oberon said. "By being sent away, I found my dear Serilda's family."

"The gryphons."

Oberon nodded. "I'm sorry we didn't arrive sooner. And it may feel like a small thing to you that I found my family, because of your father's actions, but I'll be forever grateful to him for it."

"Look for the good," Kol said, but didn't feel it. He couldn't see how Oberon finding his long-lost family justified what happened tonight.

"Exactly." Oberon paused. "I'm truly sorry for the loss of your father, and your friend."

"Thank you," he muttered, but didn't feel the sincerity in his own words.

They sat in silence for several moments.

"Look, we're grieving as a people," Oberon said, as if something occurred to him. "We've lost some teachers and students today, and I know you've recently joined the shifter military, but under the circumstances I wonder if your superiors would allow you to come back to the school for a few years as a sort of instructor?"

"You want me to teach? Does that mean you're the director again?"

"The battle just ended, Kol. It hasn't been decided who will lead the school, but I think it would help if you returned to the place you're familiar with—to your home—as we all heal. It would also help the other students if you could teach your exceptional skills." A small smile lifted the corner of Oberon's mouth. "As a teacher's assistant."

Teacher's assistant. He was only seventeen and had really only joined the military early to save Myreen. It would be good to return to the walls he was familiar with—to the people, the teachers and students, he'd spent the past several years with. Char would be disappointed, but it wouldn't be forever. And though he still didn't have answers about Myreen, he'd be near her, too.

Kol nodded. "Look for the good."

Oberon clapped a hand on Kol's shoulder and stood, then helped Kol to his feet.

Kol offered a small smile. "I'd better find my mom."

"She was in one of the greenhouses, last I heard."

"Thanks," Kol said, and rounded the main building, navigating through the rubble to head toward the greenhouses.

Several students, teachers and military nodded at Kol as he passed, but he hardly acknowledged any of them.

One of the greenhouses was smashed, but Kol didn't know if that was left over from Myreen's ursa rampage or a result of the battle. He found his mom tending to some orchids, of all things, in the back corner of the furthest greenhouse—the only one that looked fully intact. Why they felt the need to grow orchids in the Dome was beyond him, but they were his mother's favorite, so he mouthed *thanks* to whoever decided they were worth the space.

"Mom," he said, his steps slowing as he neared her.

"Kol," she said. *Smiling.* And he knew it was a real smile, because it reached her eyes.

Kol's mouth hung open. Those smiles were the rare kind, and he never thought he'd see one ever again. Especially after losing Eduard. He clamped his mouth shut again. "I called Tatiana," he said, but paused and wondered if she knew about Dad.

"How?" she asked. "I have your phone here." She handed it to him.

He noticed several missed calls and messages from his sister. Tatiana told him to delete them. He'd listen to them first, but they could wait.

"Char had a phone," he explained and pocketed his.

"Oh good. Did you tell her about your father?"

He nodded and walked closer to her, taking both of her hands in his and looked down at her amber eyes—eyes that matched his. The only physical feature he inherited from her. "Are you okay?" he asked, noting the redness around her eyes. She'd been crying, she just wasn't now. "You don't have to be brave for me."

She reached up to touch his cheek with her hand. "I'm not." Her eyes welled with tears, proving her words. "But you have no idea how things have been these past few weeks."

Kol immediately went into defensive mode. "He didn't hurt you—?"

"No, no!" She interrupted, putting the other hand on his opposite cheek so she held his face between them. "I think he somehow..." Now her smile was giddy. She removed her hands and placed a palm on her forehead.

"What? What did he do?"

"Malkolm, he somehow... *I don't know...* was stubborn enough that he broke through the curse?" Her laugh was incredulous. "Like it didn't affect him anymore."

Kol's eyes widened. Not because he was surprised—he knew the curse was broken—but because he never thought he'd ever see his mother so happy. Especially hours after his father's passing.

"Yes!" She laugh-sobbed. "Your father has been more loving, more kind, these past few weeks—" Her voice caught as a tear rolled down her cheek. "I'm sad that he's gone. I really am. But if I had to choose, I would take those few precious weeks and lose him like we did, rather than live the rest of my life with a man who didn't love me."

Kol wrapped his arms around his mom and rested his chin on the top of her head. His mother was happy. It was everything he'd ever wanted for her—to be happy, and to be loved by the man she loved. She thought that in Eduard's stubbornness and overbearing personality, he'd somehow given a big middle finger to the curse and said *to hell with it, I'm not abiding by it* and decided to love her anyway.

She didn't know the curse was actually broken for *all* the Draculs, not just her and Eduard. Kol almost opened his mouth to correct her, but he liked her version better. He'd let her believe her version, and tell her the truth in a few days so she could continue to believe it. Kenzie's family probably wouldn't mind if they fudged the date in the event anyone cared to ask.

"How about you?" Victoria asked, pushing him away to look at him. "How are you doing?"

He attempted a shrug and smile, but it failed as tears welled. "I'm sad about dad, of course," he said. "But glad you had that time with him."

"And he saved you, too," she added.

"Yes, and for that—for sacrificing himself for you and for me—I'm beyond proud to be a Dracul." He stood straighter as he spoke.

"But...?"

"But... Nik *died* to save me, too," he said, his voice cracking.

She pulled him into her arms again, briefly, before aiming a stoic face his way. "Let's go offer our condolences to the Candidas."

Kol nodded, and they walked toward the exit arm in arm.

"How are things with Myreen?" she asked.

"She turned into a hybrid to defeat Draven."

"I know. And how do you feel about that?"

"Like I don't want to think about it right now."

She nodded. "Can I say one thing?"

"Of course."

"That girl's a keeper. I hope that you can get past the sacrifice she had to make."

Kol didn't answer. He wasn't so sure he could. It felt like he would be betraying his dad if he even entertained the idea.

"And if it's the curse you're worried about," she continued. "I've only talked with her a handful of times, but she seems like the type to say *to hell* with the curse, too."

"Thanks, Mom," he said, but didn't say anything else as they pushed the door open to leave the greenhouse.

***

Kol was nowhere near ready to face the Candidas. Or Brett. Or Juliet. But he was more ready for that than he was for the conversation he needed to have with Myreen, and so welcomed his mom's suggestion to find them.

They entered the Grand Hall, where the still-alive-but-injured were congregated en masse, some lying on the floor, others propped against the walls. More blood than he'd ever seen. Harpies flitted up and down rows, looking bedraggled from using so much of their energy to heal. The room was dark, but it only took a split-second for Kol to figure out why. He'd seen enough harpy magic lately.

He conjured a fireball, growing it to the size of the chandelier that hung in the center and pushed it to hover next to it. Ms. Heather shot him a grateful look, and pulled light from it to heal a large gash in the arm of a small mer.

Victoria created an identical orb of flame and hovered it next to Kol's. It was enough for several more healings at least. She approached the harpy teacher. "We'll send more dragons and phoenixes to bring you more light," Victoria said quietly. "Where have they taken the dead?"

Ms. Heather pushed a lock of hair from her face, covering

an emotion close to the surface. "To the Defense Room. Away from young, sensitive eyes."

Victoria nodded. "We're looking for Nikolai Candida."

Ms. Heather looked at Kol. He lowered his eyes and didn't see her face when she said, "I believe they took Nik to Malachai Quinn's office."

"Thank you." Victoria linked arms with Kol again as they walked to Juliet's dad's office.

Kol took a ragged breath before entering the crammed office. Nik's body was laid on the desk. If it weren't for the grayness of his coloring, it almost looked as if Nik was asleep. But then Mrs. Candida and the Lieutenant General moved to greet Kol and his mother, and Kol saw the gaping wound where Nik's heart should've been.

The damned ice didn't even have the decency to stick around and admire its work, Kol thought bitterly. It was the perfect killing weapon. He still had no clue where it had come from.

Brett approached from the right and slapped a hand on Kol's back. Kol returned the gesture, but when they broke apart, Brett wouldn't meet his eyes and moved back to the wall he'd been holding up.

Kol didn't have to look at the two figures clutching each other on the left side to know who they were. Small. Female. Juliet, the fiery phoenix who'd helped save Char and his mother along with Brett. *And Myreen.*

Kol resisted looking at her with as much self-control as he could muster, but he was tired. He couldn't help but give in. Their eyes locked. She asked a silent question. He looked away.

But not quickly enough to see the tear-stained cheeks of both her and Juliet.

Another person entered the room and cleared her throat.

"Myreen?" Ms. Heather asked quietly. "I hate to ask, but we could use the help—"

"Of course. I'm coming," Myreen interrupted, squeezing Juliet tightly before meeting Ms. Heather near the doorway.

When she brushed past Kol, he gripped Myreen's arm to stop her. She looked up at his eyes. He closed them and let go, then turned back toward Nik.

When Myreen and Ms. Heather didn't leave right away, everyone in the room looked at them. Ms. Heather's face was a mixture of determination and excitement. Of magic and concentration. Victoria and Kol moved out of her way as she approached Nik's body.

"What—?" Brett started, but Juliet shushed him sharply from across the room. All eyes trained on the harpy teacher as she hovered her hands over Nik's body.

There's no way, Kol thought. *It's impossible. Nik's dead, not injured. Even a harpy—*

"Fire? Please?" Miss Heather asked the room.

Five fireballs of varying colors simultaneously appeared above Nik. Brett's was a deep orange, Victoria's near-blinding white, Nik's dad's was a brilliant green, and Juliet's was pink. Kol conjured one that looked almost gold and positioned it between Juliet's and the colonel's before they began to spin slowly in a circle.

Myreen walked to Ms. Candida, wrapping one arm around her and holding her hand with the other.

The room collectively held their breath. Juliet silently sobbed, but her fire didn't waver or become destructive, and took the shape of a heart.

The distraction of Juliet's heart hovering for all to see momentarily peeled Kol's eyes away from the light Ms. Heather weaved. But when he looked back, he watched her pull bright strands from each ball of fire and twisted it together. Then, she positioned it downward into Nik's mortal wound. It glowed brightly in the sickening cavity, blinding all who looked at it, but also shielding everyone from being able to see what it was doing.

Ms. Heather pulled and pulled from the fire balls until they slowly unraveled and shrunk in size. Kol moved to make another one, to fuel the light for Miss Heather, but Victoria placed a hand on his.

He looked at Nik's face. His eyes were still closed, he still looked asleep. Or dead. But his face was a healthy pink. It was no longer gray.

Ms. Heather collapsed, Myreen's strong arms keeping her from hitting the floor. Victoria rushed to her aid, but Kol remained watching his friend's face. Willing Nik's eyes to open. Willing his chest—now whole—to rise in breath.

Kol felt like he had in battle—right after the kraken had crushed his lungs and spots invaded his vision and he was unable to catch his breath. He looked up at the ceiling. Ten seconds. Just ten seconds and he'd get the oxygen he needed to return to the battle. To reality.

Ten... nine... eight...

Juliet choked out another sob.

Seven... six... five...

"Miss Heather!" Myreen cried, quietly, but an edge of panic in her voice. "Miss Heather!"

Four... three... two...

"Let's get Miss Heather to the other harpies," Victoria said.

One.

Kol lowered his gaze, ready to face reality, but fully expecting to see his still-dead best friend lying on the desk.

Nik's eyes were open.

Kol smiled. No one else looked at him in their concern for Ms. Heather. "Do you have *any* idea what it would've done to me, Nik?" he teased. "That my best friend not only took a dagger of ice for me, but *died* doing it?"

Nik matched his smirk. "Then we're even," he croaked.

Several of the women gasped. Juliet threw herself into Nik's arms and sobbed harder. The entire room converged on the now-alive Nikolai Candida. Back from the dead.

Kol's mom, Nik's dad and Myreen rushed Ms. Heather to get help. Myreen said the harpy-nurse hadn't regained consciousness when she returned.

The next half hour was chaos, but the good sort of chaos that only happens when a loved one magically returns to life.

When everyone settled, and Mrs. Candida was convinced that her son was okay, she left to check on Ms. Heather, leaving the five teenagers to stare at each other in a strange sense of awe.

Juliet sat on the desk next to a now-sitting Nik. One of his arms wrapped around her and she nestled with her head leaning against him. Myreen sat on the other side of Juliet and clutched her hand tightly. Kol leaned against the wall next to Brett and stared at the floor with a smile on his face that was mostly genuine.

"Alright, guys," Nik said. "Spill."

All eyes turned to him.

"The battle must be over? And at least some of the Dome is still intact?" he gestured at the small office.

Brett cleared his throat. "Yeah, that siren chick over there ripped Draven's head off." He chuckled. "Like literally. The battle is over."

Kol expected to see Myreen's face color, but figured it was her vampire nature that prevented it.

"Okay..." Nik said when the room fell silent again. "What

else did I miss?"

Myreen jumped from the desk. "I should go see if I can help," she said. "With Miss Heather unconscious, they could probably use another harpy."

Juliet shot Kol a look, like he should follow her. He kept his expression neutral. He wasn't ready.

When she put her hand on the door handle, Myreen paused and turned to him. "Could we talk for a minute, Kol?" she asked, inclining her head toward the door. Indicating that she wanted to speak alone.

Kol gestured at Nik, as if it wasn't a good time to talk privately.

"Lord Dracul was eaten by the kraken," Brett said, siding with Kol that they weren't finished filling Nik in. At least Brett had the decency to cringe after the words so tactlessly left his mouth.

"Kol... I'm sorry," Nik said. "Do you think—?"

"I don't think any harpy could bring him back," Kol interrupted. "Not even Miss Heather."

"Delphine and Kendall died, too," Myreen said softly. "But the other harpies said they can't risk falling unconscious to bring back the dead. They don't think they could do it, even if they weren't needed to help the injured. What Miss Heather did was... *incredible.*"

Nik didn't seem to have any more questions, and leaned his cheek against the top of Juliet's head with his eyes closed.

"Please, Kol?" Myreen whispered.

Kol pushed from the wall and slowly followed her.

"Well, I'm out," Brett said following him. "I'm not about to be the third wheel in here." He pointed at Juliet and Nik. "But I do take credit for you two."

Everyone turned to look at Brett.

His face was one of astonishment. "What? Don't you

remember, Nik? I *told* you to ask Juliet out months ago."

Kol laughed and crossed his arms.

"You did not," Nik said. "Why would you tell me to ask her out?"

"No, he's right, Nik," Kol said. "But he didn't tell you, he *dared* you to ask her out."

Juliet pulled away from Nik with a hurt look. "Why would Brett dare you to ask me out?"

"Because you're a phoenix," Kol said. "And Nik's a dragon."

"So what?" Juliet argued. "You're a dragon, and Myreen is a mer-harpy-ursa-vampire-hybrid-*whatever*." She smiled and rolled her eyes as she said it.

Kol didn't look at her face, but could feel Myreen stiffen next to him.

"Exactly," Nik said, pulling Juliet close to him and kissing her. "After what we've been through. It doesn't matter that you're a phoenix and I'm a dragon."

Juliet smiled and kissed him again.

"See you guys later," Brett said as he pushed past Myreen and Kol.

"Wait... did you say Myreen was a *vampire-hybrid?*" Nik said as Myreen and Kol followed Brett.

They stopped partway down the hall and watched Brett's saunter disappear around the corner.

The light tone followed Brett, and a heaviness fell over Kol and Myreen. Kol leaned against the wall, his eyes glued to the floor again. He couldn't bring himself to look at her.

"It does matter," she guessed. "That I'm a mer-harpy-ursa—" She blew out a breath. "That I'm a hybrid."

Kol didn't have the words. He shuffled his feet in an

awkward response.

"I *had* to do it, Kol," she said, rushing toward him. Willing him to look at her.

He refused.

"Draven was too strong. I had to do it! To end it."

Several painful moments passed.

"Kol..." she prodded. "Please talk to me?"

He finally looked at her. At those brilliant, beautiful eyes. But they were different. They were sharper. They weren't the beautiful blue eyes he fell in love with all those months ago. They weren't the ones he met in the kitchen as she mourned her mom. They weren't the ones he watched breathlessly as she opened her Christmas present. They weren't the ones that told him she loved him when he finally realized the curse was broken only yesterday.

They were the eyes of a vampire.

"Did Draven do it?" he blurted. "Tell me it was another one of his cruel tricks. That he coerced you to become like him as part of his sick little plan?"

"Why would Draven do it?" she asked, tears gathering in her eyes. "He wouldn't turn me so that I could kill him. No, it was Leif." A tear slipped down her cheek.

"Was it your idea?" he asked.

"What?"

He set his teeth, willing himself to remain in control. "Was it your idea or did someone force it on you?" Because if she'd been forced, then it wasn't her fault. It might be more easily overlooked.

She sighed. "It was my idea."

"*Damn it,* Myreen!" Kol ran both hands through his hair. "You have no idea how impossible you've made our situation.

You know that, right? Now you're a cold, hard, immortal *being*. You're the enemy! You've become the number one enemy of all shifters, including me."

"I'm not your enemy—"

Kol walked away.

"Kol!" she cried.

"I just can't talk to you right now," he said, and stormed off. Kol was grateful she didn't follow. He needed time.

He pulled out his phone, hoping that whatever his sister had to say in her messages would distract him from the churning, fire-maelstrom of emotions he was feeling.

He listened to the first message and smiled. Tatiana had good news.

Kol listened to the next. And the next. They were increasing in panic—about the email she'd received from Eduard, about the attack wondering what was going on, and *Are you alive? Or do I need to kill you myself for ignoring my messages?*

When he'd listened to them all, he briefly wondered why she wanted them deleted without listening to them, and figured it was probably because of the first one. Her good news.

Being the sensitive person she was, she wanted her good news to wait.

He wanted her to wait, too, but for a different reason.

Dialing her number, Kol got Tatiana's voicemail. She was probably already on her flight from Paris.

"You told me not to listen to your messages, but I did anyway," he said after the beep. "I'm happy for you, but for mom's sake, could you not tell her for a few weeks? In fact, could you say that it happened long after the attack on the school? I'll explain later, but trust me. It's for mom. See you when you get here."

Kol hung up.

Before deleting the messages, he listened to the first one once more.

"Kol, it's Tatiana," she said. *"I'm engaged! You know I've been in love with William Stern like, forever right?"*

Kol smiled. Will was Char's older brother. And he did know she'd held a flame for him.

"Well he loves me, too! I think the curse is fading or something, because he said he loves me back and wants to marry me! We're getting married!"

Look for the good.

At least his mom and sister had their happily ever afters.

Kenzie

The jostling of her shoulder shook Kenzie from her spell-haze, the words of the chant still spilling from her mouth. Her throat was dry and her lips cracked, but her magic still flowed through every word. She briefly wondered how much longer her body would hold out under the stress. But her eyes focused on the face of the person who had drawn her attention.

Myreen.

Kenzie's words faltered, the magic fizzling as she lost her concentration. Blackness crept into her vision and her knees buckled, but Myreen's arms shot out at a dizzying speed and caught Kenzie with incredible strength. The waning moonlight and twilight blush sparkled off Myreen's pale skin, the water suspended above them casting a faint, blue hue.

Myreen looked different, but Kenzie couldn't quite figure out why. She blushed as her insides did an ecstatic dance. *What the heck is going on?*

"Do you think you could seal the Dome with your magic, like you did that door back at Heritage Prep when we were escaping?" Myreen asked.

Kenzie blinked twice, her lashes fluttering. "Maybe? How bad is the Dome?" She looked around for what felt like the first time after awaking from a deep sleep. She was still in the streets of Chicago, probably still within view of the lake shore—if all the water wasn't currently suspended above them. Gram and Mom stood nearby, faithfully holding up the water with their magic.

Myreen shook her head. "It's... just come try? Please?"

Kenzie nodded. Her breath caught as she looked to where she last remembered seeing Wes. He was still there, looking far too pale, but she thought she detected the faint rise and fall of his chest. It could be a trick of the light, though. Kenzie's vision blurred.

Myreen followed Kenzie's gaze, then looked to the moon. She pulled a perfect strand of golden light from the pale orb, then split it between Kenzie and Wes.

Kenzie's chest filled with warmth, and she heard a sharp intake of breath coming from Wes's direction before Myreen whisked her away. Kenzie noticed for the first time that several people stood in a loose perimeter around where she'd been, arms crossed. Some waved as Kenzie and Myreen sped off. And Adam... She didn't see his body, only the blood-covered knife glinting in the dim light, but she was quickly moving away. Maybe Adam had been moved while she'd been under the influence of her magic?

"I'm sorry I couldn't do more, but we're running out of time," Myreen said, then paused. "Okay, deep breath. I'll keep an air pocket around your head as we go through the wall of water, but after that it gets pretty windy."

Kenzie nodded just as they passed through the wall. It was strange, almost like she was buried in the water, though none of it touched her face. Then they shot out the other side, and the force of the wind pulled her breath away.

Kenzie momentarily wondered at Myreen's ability to navigate so smoothly through the gale, but the Dome stole her attention.

It looked as if someone had taken a giant hammer to the top. Funeral pyres—maybe for the vampires?—burned at the edges of the water, just barely kept alive in the wind by dragons and phoenixes. Old wreckage added bones to the graveyard. A few precious shifter bodies—presumably dead—were being toted inside by different weres. A couple dragon bodies were piled on top of each other, being given the cremation treatment.

Several people stood around the perimeter of the wall of water, their hands raised. Kenzie realized they must be mer, keeping the water at bay for a little longer, though bits and pieces slid through, soaking the bloodied ground further.

Everyone looked exhausted, and as the first pinks of dawn began to rim the horizon, Kenzie realized just how long the battle must have lasted.

Kenzie looked up to Myreen as she brought them inside the Dome and out of the wind.

"Did...?" Words failed her as she considered the answer, but she had to know. The wreckage had been so absolute, so devastating. It seemed unlikely that everyone she cared about had come out unscathed. "Kol? Char? Juliet?"

Myreen bit her bottom lip as it began to tremble. She lowered Kenzie to the debris-strewn floor before alighting and retracting her wings, shaking her head.

Kenzie's eyes widened. "No," she whispered.

Myreen shook her head again, this time more emphatically.

"It's not... not them, but still so many..." Myreen cleared her throat. "The Dome? We can talk later."

Kenzie nodded. She still just wanted to crash, as she was certain everyone else did, but Myreen's light-magic had helped.

Kenzie focused all her power as she recited the spell that had sealed the door back at Heritage Prep. How long and how short that time seemed. Flashes of Wes seared her memory, laying in the street, unmoving, but she pushed it aside. She had to focus.

The howl of wind skimming the Dome died down, and the waters outside began to rise. Pieces of broken glass slid back into place, locked and sealed by her magic. A yawn cut through yet another recitation, but Kenzie swallowed it so she could continue.

She saved the top of the Dome for last, but this largest portion seemed far too large and shattered for her waning power. Kenzie looked to Myreen with pleading eyes, but it was Mom coming toward her that gave her new hope.

She raised a brow at Mom, sending a silent question as to how she'd gotten here so fast and what state Gram and Chicago and Wes were in. But the water was rising fast. Mer bodies swam past the walls of the Dome, working bubbles around any spots that sprang leaks. And several were above the top, keeping the water from spilling into the Dome.

Mom's voice joined Kenzie's, giving the magic enough strength to finish its task. Shards of glass, big and small, rose into the air like diamonds, taking their rightful places, filling the gaps.

The postures of the mer visibly relaxed as the last of the water slid into place, leaving Lake Michigan whole again—or at least, Kenzie assumed so.

The magic complete, Kenzie's shoulders slumped, and she buried her head in her mom's shoulder as they embraced. "Thank you," Kenzie whispered, while Mom's nimble hands stroked her hair.

"Yes, thank you," Myreen repeated from behind them. Kenzie's head shot up, guilt coloring her cheeks. Myreen didn't have her mom for comfort. But Mom held out her arm and beckoned Myreen to join them. Myreen did, and the three stood in a tender embrace.

The women broke apart, and Myreen cleared her throat. "Sorry, but I should get back to helping the harpies. I only left because Oberon wanted me to find you," she said, directing her last statement at Kenzie.

"Me?" Kenzie asked, her brows shooting upward.

"Yeah," Myreen gave Kenzie a knowing smile. "You know, your magic didn't only protect all of Chicago, but it kept the evacuated shifters safe—some of the youngest at the school. I would think a heroic deed like that might just earn you something special."

Kenzie's jaw dropped open as she watched Myreen walk away. Had the people surrounding the area she'd left Wes and Mom and Gram in been shifters, there to protect her and her family as they protected the city and everyone in it? Kenzie wanted to follow Myreen, to ask her if she meant what Kenzie thought she meant and if she knew for sure, but a man of orient heritage approached, his features kind and playful, as if they hadn't all just been through hell and back.

"Well, grow me a tenth tail, that was amazing! Any idea how long the magic will last?"

Mom cleared her throat, pushing her hair behind one ear. "I'm not sure, but you'll want to get that permanently fixed as soon as possible."

"Oh, we can rebuild it. We have the technology." The man winked, then held out his hand toward Kenzie's mom. "The name's Ren. I hope you lovely ladies will stay with us until the repairs are finished? You know, just in case the magic needs a little more zing."

Kenzie's mom shook Ren's hand, her face reddening. "Of course. We'd be happy to help."

Oberon approached at that moment, his regal features looking haggard, but hopeful. "Ren, I trust you're not bothering anyone."

"Who, me? I'm a constant delight. You know this."

Oberon chuckled and shook his head.

Kenzie bit her lower lip. "Oberon, sir, I was wondering if...?"

Oberon nodded. "I'm not sure what the future holds, but I'll do everything in my power to make sure you're welcomed into this school."

"Thanks." Kenzie shuffled her feet. "Did you get the Christmas basket?"

Oberon gave her a half-smile. "Yes. It was delicious."

"Oh, is that the one with the KitKat? The one you wouldn't give me a break of?" Ren asked, a mischievous gleam in his eye.

"If memory serves, I couldn't give you a piece of it because you ate the whole thing before I had the chance."

A peal of throaty laughter made the group turn, and Kenzie saw Gram coming in, Wes limping along on the arm of someone else she didn't recognize. It warmed her heart to see how thoroughly and quickly the surviving shifters were moving as they worked to recover.

Oberon cast a worried eye on Wes. "Jesse, if you'll get this young man to the Grand Hall so the harpies can have a look at him."

The young man supporting Wes nodded, and the two turned to leave, Wes casting a backward glance at Kenzie as they shuffled away.

Kenzie's heart constricted.

"Who's that?" Oberon asked.

"My cougar. And one of the best things to ever happen to me," Kenzie whispered, then bit her lower lip. She cast a worried gaze on her mom, but Mom had taken up conversation with Ren again, laughing just a little too hard at his jokes. Gram was paying attention, though, and she winked at Kenzie.

***

After Myreen's help was no longer needed, and Kenzie had had a short nap, she and Myreen caught up on the details of the battle in the comfort of Myreen's room, comparing accounts from opposite sides of the wall of water. It was strange, hearing that Draven was dead. The vampire threat was over. For good.

It was also kind of strange that the dorm room was still intact, but Kenzie would take what wins she could get.

"But I had to become a hybrid to do it, and now I think Kol hates me," Myreen finished, lifting a hand to wipe away yet another tear. It seemed as if there would be no end of them—for every good thing, there was something to mourn. So many lives had been lost, so many injured.

And *Nik*. Kenzie still couldn't quite wrap her head around that one—back from the dead. It's too bad Leif couldn't have gotten a harpy back in the day to get Gemma back. But then, Kenzie probably wouldn't have met Leif.

But even as she thought of Leif's pale, handsome face, she was reminded of Wes. Kenzie knew she wanted to go see her *were* before too long, but the thought of all the injured—all the *blood*—made her hesitate.

Besides, Myreen needed her, and for once, Kenzie was there for her.

"There's no way Kol can hate you," Kenzie said, though she worried for Myreen. She'd lost so much already. Although, if Kol broke her heart over something so stupid as being a hybrid, Kenzie would find a way to break him for it. Her threat still stood.

"I don't know, Kenzie. You didn't see the way he looked at me. Or won't look at me. It's like I'm some sort of monster now."

"Then he's crazy. You're not a monster, you're amazing! And your skin—good gravy, you're gorgeous. If I weren't with Wes, I'd totally date you." Kenzie lifted the side of her mouth in a smirk.

"Ooh, tell me more about your guy."

Kenzie laughed. "If you're not too tired of listening to me talk..." She looked down at her hands. It didn't seem fair, her going to talk to Wes when the rift between Myreen and Kol was so deep. Maybe she'd do something about that, too, before she finally crashed. Maybe.

Myreen made a face and waved Kenzie off. "I'm part vampire now, remember? I'm not sure I ever get tired—*that's* going to take some getting used to. So? Dish!"

"Okay. Short version—Wes was a hunter, but he got bit and now he's a mao. You should *see* him in kitty form." She sighed. "Powerful, majestic... cuddly."

Myreen and Kenzie giggled.

"I should probably go check on him at some point," Kenzie said, looking at her hands again.

"Yeah. Of course you want to see him. I'm sorry. I shouldn't have—"

Kenzie held up a hand. "Don't apologize. You're my number one girl, and I'm more than happy to be here for you. *Finally.* I can't imagine he misses me too bad—he's probably swooning under the touch of some harpy, anyway."

Myreen laughed, shaking her head. "I'm not sure it's like that."

Kenzie raised a brow. "I don't know that many harpies, but so far, you're all gorgeous. I'm going to have to keep a tight leash on that cougar—if he decides to join the school."

"Do you think he will?"

Kenzie shrugged. "I think he needs this place. Almost as much as I do."

Myreen smiled, then gave Kenzie another hug. "It's going to be so good having you here."

"Duh! Why do you think I wanted to be here so bad? For everyone else's sake, of course." She winked at Myreen, then stood.

"Oh, you'll probably need a little of my magic, now that you're part vampire," Kenzie said, hanging onto the doorknob. "You know, so you don't have to worry about pesky things like sunlight and copper."

Myreen shrugged. "Probably. But we've got some time. Get some rest and we'll work out the details later."

Kenzie nodded, but she still didn't let go of the knob. "You remember that rose I gave you for Christmas?"

Myreen nodded, casting a nervous glance at the obviously wilted plant.

Kenzie laughed. "It's okay. I just... I was working with Leif to try to figure out how to raise his beloved from the grave. And I was thinking... that maybe... you know..."

Myreen gave Kenzie a sad smile. "I love my mom more than anything in the world, and I would love to have her back, but I'm not so sure it's the best idea. I... I've kind of come to terms with her death, but I can't imagine what she'd think of me, now that I'm not only a chimera, but a hybrid."

"For what it's worth, I think she'd be proud."

Myreen flashed a grateful smile, and Kenzie gave a single nod as she finally left the room.

Kenzie went to the Great Hall, taking a deep breath as she entered. It was dark, though fireballs were lit from time to time, warming the air and lending light to the harpies, who bent it in a dizzying array of colors to heal the wounded.

It took a few moments for Kenzie's eyes to adjust, and even longer for her to find Wes. She had to look past the dark spots marring nearly every surface, the metallic tang filling the air. Blood. She shuddered, but her life had changed a lot since going to Heritage Prep, and the familiar repulsion at the mere mention of blood had slowed to a dull roar.

She finally spotted Wes on one end, where several shifters sat, slept, or stood, the lot looking better than anyone else in the place. Kenzie made her way to Wes, and he caught her in a tight embrace as she reached him.

His lips crashed into hers, and Kenzie colored to think that everyone was staring, but she couldn't be happier to be embarrassed than she was at that moment.

"You're alive," she breathed when they finally broke apart. There were some calls of encouragement from some of the guys in the crowd around them, and Kenzie blushed further.

"Thanks to you," Wes said, bringing his forehead to hers.

"I couldn't—"

"You didn't lose me. I'm right here."

Kenzie nodded.

"The guy who attacked me, was that...?"

Kenzie couldn't meet Wes's eyes. She bit her lip and nodded again.

"Do you know what happened to him? I thought we'd left him for dead, but I didn't see him when I left."

Kenzie shrugged. "I'm not sure. Maybe ask one of the shifters that helped to guard us?"

"Do you know any of them?"

Kenzie shook her head. "Wes, if he's still out there—"

"We'll take care of him." Wes wrapped his arms around her, holding her tight. To think that Adam might still be out there, so powerful, so cunning...

But there was one question that she needed an answer to first.

"Are we...?" Kenzie started, then had to stop to swallow the emotion bubbling in her throat. She wasn't sure what had happened up in the streets of Chicago, whether Wes had died or severed the bond between them or just been too weak for her to really feel him. She couldn't identify the part of herself tied to him—if she still was—though she'd gone the entire time at Heritage Prep not realizing the depth of link they shared.

"Are we still bound?" Wes finished for her, his eyes searching hers.

Kenzie blinked, pulling in her lips.

Wes's warm hands encompassed her face, and he gave her another kiss, this one softer, searching. When he pulled away, there was a hint of relief in his eyes. "I tried to sever our bond, but it appears, Ms. MacLugh, that our bond is too strong to fight. Even if it *is* for your own good."

Kenzie slapped his chest playfully, a relieved chuckle on her lips. "Never do that to me again. It's *us*. Now and forever. You got me?"

Wes smiled, then pulled her in for another kiss, warming her with a hug. His chin rested on the top of her head. With Kenzie's ear to his chest, she could hear his heartbeat, and she knew instinctively that her own heart beat to the same rhythm.

"There's something you should know," Wes said.

Kenzie didn't bother to lift her head, just closing her eyes and nodding as she held on like she'd never let go.

"There's something else I should tell you. I started to before..." Wes took a deep breath, gently forcing Kenzie to look at him. "When I contacted the hunters, I told them about that vampire school. I was going crazy, thinking what you might be going through there."

"Really? Are you sure contacting them was such a great idea?"

Wes shrugged. "It probably didn't do much good, seeing how the vampires chased you lot here. The school was probably empty by the time they arrived."

Kenzie smirked. "I'm sure they still had their hands full. There were a lot of Initiates there, and probably at least a few vampires. Who knows? Maybe they were able to clean up the rest of this mess by being over there while the majority of the vampires were over here."

"We can only hope. It's not like I can contact them again."

"Speaking of... it looks like I'm in. Here, I mean. I'm gonna be going to school here."

Wes looked around the room skeptically. "I'm not sure anyone is gonna be going to school here any time soon."

"Are you kidding? This place'll be up and running in no time. Especially with a hybrid and a selkie to help clean things up." Kenzie smiled broadly at Wes. "Any chance there's an incredibly attractive cougar were that would like to help, too? It sure would make the work easier to have a little eye-candy hanging around."

"Rawr," Wes said, bringing his forehead to hers again. "It's puma, and if it'll keep you out of trouble..."

Kenzie spit out a laugh. "I don't think there's anything in the world that can keep me out of trouble."

"I'll spend my life trying."

"Then you'll never get bored."

Kenzie yawned, her eyes drooping involuntarily. The nap had helped, but it hadn't been nearly enough.

"Come on. Let's get you someplace so you can rest."

Kenzie nodded, following Wes as he brought her into the Dining Hall where cots and cushions had been laid out for shifters to sleep.

Wes found a spot, and laid down with Kenzie, holding her tight. She fell asleep with her head against his warm chest, feeling for all the world like she was in the safest place she could possibly be.

***

Kenzie's eyes fluttered, sleepily wondering where she was. And then she remembered everything. She lifted her head, noticing a dark stain on Wes's shirt where her mouth had been. Kenzie wiped self-consciously at her chin, then tried to tame the little pieces of hair that always wanted to stick up when she slept.

Wes's eyes opened, and when he saw Kenzie, he smiled. "That's a good look for you."

"Oh, man. How bad is it?"

Wes put a hand to her hair, patting it a few times before laughing. "It's perfect."

"Ugh."

A throat cleared behind her, and Kenzie whipped around. Her mom stood there, arms crossed, foot tapping.

"Mom!" Kenzie said, scrambling off the cot and landing on her rear.

"Mrs. MacLugh, I'm sorry—"

Mom held up a hand, stopping Wes's apology. "I don't suppose there's any stopping you two, anyway."

Ren came up behind her, a smile on his handsome face. "I can always give him a jolt, if you need." He let a slip of electricity arc between his thumb and forefinger, winking at Wes.

Mom laughed, fuller and heartier and more real than anything Kenzie had heard from the woman since they'd lost Dad. "Save it." She turned back to Wes. "Are you planning on attending here?"

Wes's forehead crinkled. "Uh, I've been considering it."

Ren smiled. "Lita, here, tells me you're in need of some training. We've got plenty of toy mice and feathers, if you're interested."

Kenzie laughed along with her mom this time.

Wes gave a nervous chuckle, rubbing the back of his neck with his hand. "I don't suppose she told you about my previous profession?"

Ren gave Mom a questioning look.

Oberon walked up behind the two, placing a hand on each of their shoulders. "The hunter has become the hunted. I was the one who sent you the acceptance letter. And yes, we know of your history. Our seer is—was—quite gifted."

"My history's complicated." Wes sighed.

"Isn't it always?" Oberon said, letting his arms fall to his sides.

Wes shrugged. "I suppose."

"So you're in, too?" Kenzie asked him, hope soaring.

Wes nodded.

"Good," Ren said, giving Mom a conspiratorial grin. "Just remember to behave yourself. I'll be watching. And I'm *everywhere*." He phased from solid to a ghost-like state and then back, and Kenzie and Wes's eyes both widened.

"Come on," Oberon said. "We have a lot of work to do. Breakfast is being served in the gymnasium, and they're coordinating everything from there, too."

Kenzie and Wes nodded. Wes got up first, helping Kenzie to her feet. As they left the room, Kenzie noticed more shifters sleeping on the makeshift beds than before, most of them she recognized as being harpies who had been healing the injured.

It was still a bit dark in the Grand Hall as they tiptoed through, but so much had changed while she'd slept. There were a few injured still lying around, but no one looked near death anymore. Even the blood had been mopped up.

Wes's fingers threaded through hers, and she pulled her eyes away from the room. He gave her a kiss on the forehead, then tugged her along.

She was sure there would be more tears before everything was done, but they'd made it. The threat was over. Now it was time to rebuild and heal.

And Kenzie was right where she needed to be.

Leif

Repairs were well underway, and Leif was impressed with how efficient Ren Suzuki and his team of kitsunes were at utilizing technology to fix the broken Dome. The giant hole at the top had been blocked with Kenzie's skillful selkie magic as a temporary fix. It held firmly as the water of Lake Michigan had returned to where it belonged, the magic bolstered by mer water manipulation that kept pressure off the cracks.

The interior was also undergoing repairs, and Leif imagined that before long, the school would be functioning just as it used to—before Draven's attack.

Draven. The vampire leader was gone. The first hybrid was killed—at his own hands, no less. But at least one hybrid remained. Leif still questioned whether or not turning Myreen was the right decision. But without her, the shifters would've lost.

Leif stood in Oberon's office—previously occupied by Eduard Dracul. Regrettably, the shifter military leader had died, but he'd returned honor back to the Dracul name before doing so. All these long years, that name had brought nothing but violent anger to Leif's soul. Not anymore.

Oberon instructed Leif to "sit tight" while he oversaw the clean-up affairs of the school. Apparently, sight of a vampire within the walls of the school—even a *good* vampire—was still unsettling to some of the residents of the Dome.

A knock came at the door, which Leif found odd. Oberon wouldn't knock at his own door.

"Come in," Leif said, placing his hands behind his back as he gripped them together tightly.

The door creaked open and Kol Dracul slipped in. Closing it quickly behind him, the amber eyes of Eduard's son rested on Leif.

Leif bowed slightly. "Hello, Malkolm."

Kol nodded his acknowledgement. "Can we talk?"

Smiling, Leif said, "I really don't have much else to do at the moment. Honestly, I would appreciate the company."

The boy looked to be in a bit of turmoil, as if his mind had been raging its own battle recently. It seemed as if a verbal flood was dammed within him, on the verge of surging out.

"My condolences about your father," Leif said. "I didn't know him very well, but in the end, he put his faith in me—which wasn't an easy thing for him, I think. And he was invested in protecting the school and the shifters here."

Casting his eyes to the ground, Kol muttered, "Thanks."

That was it. Kol didn't elaborate, which told Leif that something else was the matter.

"Is everything all right?" Leif asked.

Kol crossed his arms. "You turned Myreen."

Leif detected bitterness in Kol's accusatory tone, but he nodded. "Per her request, I did. To be frank, though, had I declined, she probably would've forced me to do the deed by use of her siren voice."

Kol cast his eyes to the ground. There was no way the boy could argue that point. Leif half-expected him to blow up. Instead, Kol's arms unwound and fell to his sides, and his shoulders drooped.

"What should I do?" he asked. "My whole life, I've been trained to hate vampires. I've been trained to *kill* vampires."

Chuckling, Leif stepped over to Kol. Placing a hand on his shoulder, he said, "And yet, here you are, confiding in one."

Kol met his gaze. "Well, you're different than other vampires."

Raising an eyebrow, Leif said, "On the contrary, from a biological standpoint, I'm the same as all vampires. My differences lie in the enchantments that have been placed on me. And technically, I didn't make Myreen a vampire. She's a hybrid."

Kol shrugged. "Same difference."

Leif patted him lightly on the back. "I'm approaching one hundred and fifty years of living on this earth, and you know what I've discovered? It doesn't matter if you're a shifter, a selkie, a human, or a vampire." He patted his chest. "What we choose to become is what matters most." Flashes of the destruction he caused at La Framboise Island twenty years ago bombarded his mind—motionless shifter bodies on the riverside, stone blasted to rubble making up a massive grave for countless others. In a whisper, he said, "I've done some terrible things."

"But you changed," Kol said.

Leif nodded. "Yes, I changed. My place was not with Draven. And one day, I had an opportunity to not only escape from his clutches, but to reach a helping hand to Oberon. Ever since, my place has been among the shifters."

"But when I see Myreen, I can't help but see the changes

she's been through," Kol said. "I can't help but *feel* the vampire coursing through her veins."

"Do you still love her?" Leif asked.

Kol thought for a moment. "I love who she was."

Leif sighed. "Long ago, I was turned against my will. I was madly in love with a selkie—one of Kenzie's relatives, actually."

"Really?" Kol said.

Again, Leif nodded. "Her name was Gemma. I had plans to ask her hand in marriage, but before I could, I was turned. When she found out, she had every right to shut me out, to see me for the monster I'd become. But she didn't. Instead, she looked for ways to spend *more* time with me. Because of Gemma's enchantment, I can walk in sunlight without being harmed."

Kol slowly shook his head. "How did she do it? How could she see beyond you being a vampire?"

Leif smiled, the memory of their engagement trickling back into his mind. "Because to Gemma, I was still Leif. And I still loved her more than anything." He cast his eyes to the ground. "I still do."

"What happened to her?" Kol asked.

The last thing Leif wanted was to bring more pain to Kol. Sharing the story about one of his ancestors murdering Gemma didn't seem like a good idea. "That," he said, holding up a finger, "is a story for another time. What I'm telling you is that Myreen might be different physically, but inside, she's the same. Love sees no difference in such changes. I know you still love her, otherwise you wouldn't have come to me to talk about it. And the greatest thing about a strong love connection? You won't focus so much on what you both are, but on what you can become—together."

Kol looked him in the eyes. "You really believe that,

don't you?"

Leif bobbed his head. "I do."

Another knock sounded at the door. From the other side came a voice. "Leif, it's Kenzie. Can I come in?"

Leif gave Kol a questioning look.

Kol nodded. "You've given me a lot to think about. I should probably get going, anyway."

Leif smiled, then raised his voice. "Come on in, Kenzie."

The door opened and in walked Kenzie. There seemed to be a lightness about her—a happiness he'd never seen on her before.

"Oh, Kol," she said, her hazel eyes first looking at him. "I'm not interrupting, am I?"

"We were just finishing," Kol said, redness forming on his cheeks. He looked at Leif. "Thanks for talking."

"Of course," he said with a nod. As the young dragon shifter headed for the door, Leif quickly said, "One last thing, Kol. Battles can make or break us. They can turn warm hearts cold. You've been through a lot. Right about now, you could use what Myreen has to offer you. And she could use what you have to offer her, too."

Kol didn't say anything, but nodded before he left, closing the door behind him.

Kenzie threw a thumb over her shoulder. "What did *he* want?"

"He's working through some issues and needed some advice," Leif said.

"I know he lost his dad. And things are rough with..." Kenzie pushed a few loose strands of hair out of her face. "I'm just surprised he turned to *you*. You know, being a vampire and all."

Leif smirked. "I think that's precisely why he came. But enough about Kol. How are you holding up, Kenzie?"

A sly smile crossed her face. "Apparently I'm pretty good at holding up Lake Michigan. Who'd have guessed?"

Leif laughed. "Oberon told me about your heroic actions." He turned serious. "Look, I know I've told you before, but I'm really proud of you."

She beamed at his words.

"I think Gemma would be proud of you, too," he said, his face dropping as an image of Octavius formed in his mind—the scene of him placing her brooch within the confines of his strange, blue dreadlocks.

"You know, the idea of bumping into my great-great-great-great-whatever the heck we are to each other *should* be really crazy." Kenzie sat in one of Oberon's chairs and pulled her knees to her chest. "But honestly, after hearing you talk about her, and knowing what she's added to the family grimoire—I almost feel like I know her. I'd love to meet her."

Leif grimaced. "Bringing Gemma back got a lot more difficult after the kraken ran away."

Kenzie's brow furrowed in confusion. "What does the kraken have to do with bringing Gemma back?"

He set his jaw. "Before I fought Beatrice, she gave him the brooch, and he took off with it."

"She was able to communicate with that giant, slimy thing?"

"He was human at the time."

"Wait, you saw the kraken in human form?" she said incredulously. "Is he a shifter?" She gave a low whistle. "Talk about shift happening."

"That's not important," Leif replied, shaking his head in amusement. "The fact is, he has Gemma's brooch. I would've gone after him, but Piper was in trouble. I couldn't leave her behind to die. And there were so many vampires within the Dome. I had to help the shifter military hold them off."

Kenzie chuckled. "I hear you. Adam threw me a for a loop when he showed up while I was protecting Chicago from drowning. Turns out he's an ursa now, too. I thought he was dead, but his body disappeared. No one knows what happened to him."

Leif let out a long breath. He'd thought their hybrid problem had been nearly resolved, but now? "Does Oberon know?"

Kenzie nodded. "I told him. The shifters are on it."

She looked down, her mood growing even more somber. She brought her hazel eyes back to Leif after a few moments. "You've said you're proud of me. For what it's worth, I'm proud of you, too. Knowing what you've gone through—what you've overcome..." She trailed off, as if seeking the right words to speak. "You're just, like, freaking awesome. I don't think anything in the world could keep Gemma's brooch from you for long. Not even a kraken shifter."

Her words were kind and hopeful, and Leif walked over and sat in the chair next to her. "You're a good friend," he said.

"And you're sure you want to keep it that way?"

Leif raised a brow.

"Just kidding. I got my own true-love story. I think." Kenzie's cheeks colored. "You keep loving my great-great-great-great-*whatever*. Dang, I hope Gemma comes back as she was and not as an extremely old lady."

Leif chuckled. "I'm sure it'll be fine. You're an amazing girl, Kenzie. Your guy's a lucky one. You know what you've taught me?"

"To like cats?" she answered with a smirk.

Chuckling, Leif held up a finger. "One cat. But in all seriousness, you've taught me that some people are worth trusting. You and I—we've been through a lot together."

Kenzie reached out and gave him a hug, and he welcomed it.

They sat there for some time, and at last she pulled away. "So that's the plan, then? You're going to slam that kraken back where he came from and get the brooch?"

"It's all I can do," he said. "With the vampire threat abated, there isn't a whole lot I can do here at the shifter school."

Kenzie's sly grin reappeared. "I think you'll find that people are more accepting here than they used to be. You won't believe this, but I'm in! *Finally*, I get to go to this school. At least, what's left of it."

"That's great news!" Leif exclaimed. "You've earned it. And the shifter world should open their arms to you and your family for all the help you've given. I can't imagine the prejudice against your kind will linger for too long. Perhaps Oberon will invite other selkies to the school."

Their conversation came to an abrupt end as the door swung open. Oberon entered quickly, then spotted the duo sitting next to each other.

"Oh, Ms. MacLugh, pardon me," Oberon said. "I was just coming to retrieve Leif."

"No problem," Kenzie said, hopping to her feet. "I wanted to tell him the good news—after all, he promised he'd help me get in here." She winked at Leif. "It looks like he kept that promise."

"Indeed," Oberon said. "But if you'll excuse us, Leif's presence has been requested for a meeting that's about to start."

Kenzie nodded, then looked at Leif. "If I don't see you before you go off on your kraken hunt..." She trailed off and her face grew serious. "Just... take care of yourself, okay?"

Leif gave her a smile of gratitude. "You too. And when I return—"

"Ha! I'm already ready," she said, then turned around and took several lively steps out the door. "Bring her home, baby!"

she threw over her shoulder.

Oberon watched Kenzie prance away, then brought his brown, studious eyes to Leif.

"Kraken hunt?" the gryphon shifter asked.

"It's a long story," Leif replied. "But suffice it to say, Kenzie discovered how to bring Gemma back. In order to perform the resurrection spell, she needs Gemma's brooch. Unfortunately, the kraken is in possession of it."

Oberon gave him a confused look. "How did the kraken obtain such an object?"

Leif sighed, standing up and walking over to the shifter. "Oberon, there's much to catch up on, but something tells me this meeting I've been summoned to is of special importance. It's not every day a vampire gets an invitation to a shifter meeting."

Oberon clapped him on the shoulder. "The first of many, I'm sure. Shall we?"

"Lead the way," Leif said, gesturing toward the door. He followed Oberon out of the office, and they began weaving in and out of debris that was still being removed.

"I heard you got kicked out of the school," Leif said as they walked the new hallways being constructed.

"I got called back—by Ms. MacLugh, no less," Oberon replied. "But my time away was well rewarded. I found my life-mate's family and brought them back here. My niece, June, has been admitted to the school. I think she'll thrive here."

"I'm glad to hear you're not the last of your species," Leif remarked. "And that you discovered your wife's family, no less."

"Yes, but it would never have happened without Delphine's guidance." Oberon paused his speech, but increased his walking speed. Leif was well aware of the seer's death. It had left a shadow on the school, one that might never completely go away.

Delphine was one of the school's originators.

Feeling the need to change the subject, Leif asked, "What's this meeting about?"

It took a few moments for Oberon to respond. "So much has happened over the past few months, it remains clear that we need to make some changes as a group of shifters. As such, it's time for the shifter world to adapt."

"So this meeting is about adaptation? How does a vampire play into the mix?"

"We're about to find out. Here's the simulation room. It's typically used for combat training, but we've modified it as a conference room."

They approached a large wall with a control panel next to a large door. It opened as they neared it and as Leif entered, he saw a nice, homey room. A fireplace stood off to the side, burning brightly, and in the center was a long, light-wooded table. Surrounding it were several shifters—none of whom Leif recognized.

Most of them appeared to be quite uneasy about his presence, but he couldn't blame them. He didn't exactly feel comfortable being among people who looked at him as an extreme threat.

"Everyone, this is Leif Villers, one of our greatest allies," Oberon introduced. "He's been aiding us for the past fifteen years—at great personal expense, I might add."

A few of the shifters' postures relaxed. Leif could see the trust they had in Oberon, and he was grateful for it.

"I know you never thought you'd be sitting around a table with a vampire," Leif said, sliding into one of the free chairs nearby. Oberon sat next to him. "Nor did I ever expect to be sitting among shifters. But perhaps, someday, I'll have earned your trust as an ally."

Nods of approval swung about the table, and Leif was appreciative of it. *Smooth*, he thought.

"Well said." Oberon brought his hands forward to address the group. "Introductions are in order as we discuss the future of the shifter world. Here on the other side of me is Malachai Quinn, a phoenix and lieutenant general of the shifter military."

Leif stared at the man in uniform, wondering if he had any relation to Evandrus Quinn from the Frost boarding house. Before he could ask, Oberon continued.

"Next to him is Victoria Dracul, a dragon shifter and wife of the late Eduard Dracul." Oberon's cadence lost its formality for a moment. "Once again, you have our condolences Victoria."

She had bags under her eyes—as if she hadn't slept for a very long time—but she held herself resolute and nodded. "Thank you, Oberon."

Oberon smiled, then continued. "Next is Henry Coltar and his wife, Jane. Both are teachers here at the Dome. Henry is an ursa, and his wife is a human. And finally, there's the rascally Ren, a kitsune and master technology buff."

Leif recognized the kitsune, although he looked quite older than the last time they'd met. Ren had used his electric tails to send him flying into a fixture full of candy at the store near La Framboise Island—back when The Island was destroyed. Leif found himself touching his chest at the memory.

"Still feeling that tail blast?" Ren asked with a half-smile.

Leif snorted. "The memory of it, yes."

Ren's smile broadened. "I'm glad I left a mark."

"That's quite enough, Ren," Oberon said. "I didn't bring Leif here so you could boomerang your ego around the room. We have pressing matters to discuss."

All eyes turned to the gryphon, whose very demeanor and words screamed ultimate leadership. Yes, this was a man of authority Leif could look up to without hesitation. He didn't flaunt his status like Draven had.

Oberon cleared his throat. "I've gathered you all here to discuss a need to organize an official Shifter Council. This would be an organization that governs the affairs of both The School for the Shifted and the shifter military, as well as all other related shifter business. We've caused quite a stir in Chicago with non-shifters, and will have to face those consequences. But life must go on. Classes must continue. The protection of our people is still imperative: the vampires won't be happy with the loss of Draven. Countless other affairs need to be tended to. Are you all in agreement that such a council should exist?"

Small conversations happened among the group, and Leif sat secluded next to Oberon, wondering how his opinion on the matter would apply. Still, nobody was speaking their mind, so he took the opportunity.

"I know most of you probably wouldn't look to a vampire for his thoughts. I'd say that the more organized your people can become, the better off you'll be. It's my understanding that Oberon was ousted from his position by the military. It begs the question: why did the military have such control over a school?" Out of the corner of his eye, he saw Victoria shift uncomfortably, and he wondered if he shouldn't have indirectly made a reference to her husband. To recover, he decided to indirectly point a finger at Draven. "Above all, I've experienced just how terrible one person in a place of power can become. I think having a council to look to and consult with will make all the difference for your people."

The room had grown silent during his spiel. His words

elicited several nods from the people surrounding the table, which brought him some much-needed relief.

"I agree with Leif, as I believe most of you do," Oberon said. "As such, it's been proposed—and I agree—that we should organize the council with members from each species." He held up a tablet. "I have a list of names of those who I trust would serve well." He handed the tablet to Leif. "Would you read the names off?"

The action surprised Leif, and he wondered if it was Oberon's way of trying to include him in the meeting. Still, a quick glance revealed he was not being considered to join the council.

"Of course," Leif replied, then began reading down the list. "Henry and Jane Coltar. Nadia Candida. Victoria Dracul. Malachai Quinn. Maya Heather. Milo Slegr. Lorenzo Santoni. Queen Anali. Jonathan Barnes. Oberon Rex. And finally, Ren Suzuki."

Ren burst out laughing. "You want *me* on the council? I'd be about as helpful as smart clothing without battery cells."

"Nonsense," Oberon replied. "You're our most experienced kitsune, and you'd be a valued member of the council—as long as you could learn to use your quips when appropriate."

"Impossible," Ren said, crossing his arms. "My quips are part of the package. I can't very well just flip a switch and be boring. That would take too much effort. Besides, I don't want it. My place isn't in political decision-making but in inventing and creating."

Oberon looked ready to force the issue, but Malachai spoke up before the gryphon could.

"If I might interject, one of our specialists in the military might be better suited. His ingenuity played an integral part on the mission at the vampire school. He thinks objectively, and I trust him with my life."

"Who?" Oberon asked.

"Haru Torisei," answered Malachai.

"I second that," Ren said. "Mostly because it gets me out of a slum of a job. But Haru is a great guy. One of my brighter students over the years, although not nearly as funny as me."

"Sounds like he's the right choice, then," Oberon said, smiling at Ren.

"Don't make me reconsider," Ren threatened.

Oberon chuckled. "What do you think, Victoria. Are you in?"

She nodded solemnly. "I'll do whatever I can to help represent all dragon shifters."

Henry and Jane were holding hands, displayed on the table. "We will gladly join the council," Henry said. "Me as an ursa representative and my wife as a mediator between humans and shifters."

"Wonderful," Oberon said. "What do you say, Malachai?"

"I'll represent both the military and every phoenix," the lieutenant general stated boldly. "We'll aid the council as they request."

Oberon nodded. "And I'll represent the gryphons, which has particular meaning now that there are a few more among us. Maya is still recovering, but I'll extend a personal invitation once she's ready. Milo Slegr still lives near Lubbock, Texas, but I knew his sister Zabrina quite well. I believe he'll be a good fit to represent the werecats. Lorenzo Santoni is a naga, and I got to know him through one of my best friends at The Island. He's older, but will bring great wisdom to the council, if he accepts."

"He's a great guy," Ren said. Leif half-expected a pun to roll off the kitsune's tongue, but he kept himself serious. "I wish his daughter, Jade, was still alive to fill the role."

"Me too," Oberon said, his eyes going distant.

Leif wondered what happened to her, and if she was one of the many shifters that had died when Draven toppled the school in South Dakota.

Oberon shook his head. "Who's next on the list, Leif?"

"Queen Anali?" Leif said. He didn't recognize the name.

"Right," Oberon said, his melancholy tone holding. "Delphine would've been my first choice to represent the merfolk. Her death is a major blow to us. But if you all concur, I believe Queen Anali of Zardani would be an excellent choice for representation. I've had dealings with her in the past in terms of recruitment, and she's always shown concern for the Dome. She was also very close to Delphine."

"She's a good choice," Victoria agreed.

Malachai nodded. "I'm on board."

"I'll reach out to Anali, then," Oberon said. "To represent the hounds, Jonathan Barnes has been suggested. His son, Jesse, attends school here, but he's lived and worked among humans his whole life. I think his experience would help our cause."

Murmurs of agreement abounded from around the table.

"It sounds like we have our shifter council, pending the selected members agree to joining," Oberon announced. "And as a council, we have three decisions to make right now. The council needs a head, the school needs a director, and the military needs a general. As for the military, I believe the choice is obvious."

All eyes made their way to Malachai.

"If this is the will of the council," Malachai said, "then I humbly accept the position."

Oberon smiled. "Let it be known that as of today, by the authority of this new shifter council, Malachai Quinn has been promoted to the rank of General of the shifter military."

Malachai nodded. "What will become of my classes?"

"We'll find replacements," Oberon said. "I believe Charlotte Stern would be a good option for teaching Shifter Politics. We'll find somebody else to teach Phoenix Mastery."

Malachai nodded again. "I think you should be the head of the shifter council, Oberon. Your diplomacy skills are unmatched."

Ren laughed out loud, and everybody turned to see what was so funny.

"Oberon becoming the head of the shifter council?" The kitsune's laughing increased until tears streamed out of his eyes. "Woohoo, that's too good, Malachai. I mean, that was the funniest thing I've heard in a long time. Somebody give the new general a medal!" Ren laughed some more, wiping at his eyes. Leif couldn't help but laugh along, for some reason.

"You don't think Oberon would make a good council head?" Victoria asked, annoyance in her voice. Leif could tell she didn't think much of Ren, and he wondered if most people had a tough time getting along with the humorous kitsune.

"No, no, no," Ren replied. "I'm not saying that at all. Oberon would do a terrific job in such a role. But tell me. Can any of you look at him outside of his role as director of the school? Who would replace him there?"

Leif looked at the others, and saw they were taken aback. Technically, Ren had no say in what the council chose, because he'd kicked himself off the member roster.

"He's right," Victoria said. "Everyone who has ever studied or taught at the Dome has loved Director Rex. And while my husband had his disagreements with Oberon from time to time, he always respected him."

Oberon cleared his voice. "My niece is a student here at the Dome, and I'd love to be a part of her growth. I know it's not exactly my say, but if I had the choice, I would remain director of the academy. And I helped create this school. I'm a part of it as much as it's a part of me."

Henry got to his feet and pounded a fist on the table, like a judge declaring a sentence. "I vote for Oberon's reinstatement as director."

"Me too," Jane agreed.

"So do I," Victoria added.

"So let it be done," Malachai said. "Welcome back, old friend. The school wasn't the same without you, and I think the students will be excited for your return."

"We'll see about that," Oberon said with a laugh. "But I appreciate your words. It's good to be back."

Leif looked at the remaining present council members and couldn't guess who'd end up as the head. He doubted Jane Coltar would, based on the fact that she was human. That left Henry and Victoria, unless they decided on someone who wasn't present.

It was as if Henry was of the same mindset, though, as he spoke next. "I love my job, and I love how I can hold the same schedule as my wife. While I'm happy to participate on the council, I vote for Victoria to be the head of the council. Having been married to Lord Dracul, she already has a good idea of what the military is all about. She's also a mother, and I've had her children in my General History class. I know she has a big heart, and a capacity for love few of us will probably ever understand."

Married to a Dracul, Leif could imagine. But he couldn't give Eduard too hard of a time. He wasn't like Aline.

"What do you think, Victoria?" Oberon asked.

Her cheeks puffed wide as she blew out slowly. "I think you're too kind. But as long as I have you all here to help me, I believe this is something I can do."

"We're here to support you, however we can," Malachai said.

Oberon laughed. "And in the meantime, you'll be able to help keep our heads on straight."

The room fell silent as everybody soaked in what had just happened. Leif shifted uncomfortably in his seat. He felt out of place, and didn't quite understand why Oberon had brought him to this meeting.

The director must have noticed. "One last thing before we adjourn," Oberon said. "Months ago, I made a promise to Leif. I told him if he aided us with the impossible task of overthrowing Draven, then I'd help him in his quest to find his lost love." He looked at Victoria. "We owe it to him."

Victoria gave him a pensive look that seemed to go on for several minutes. "Then we'll hold true to that promise. We'll help him in his quest."

Surprise flooded Leif's body like a drug, freezing him in place. He felt his jaw drop—all on its own. Who'd have thought the promise he'd made with Oberon in a restaurant months ago would expand to getting help from the entire shifter world?

He stammered for a moment, then finally found the words to speak. "I'll accept any help I can get."

Victoria smiled and nodded. "Let us know what you need, and we'll do our best to give it to you."

Leif looked at Oberon, as if he needed further approval. But Victoria was in charge. This was really happening.

Taking a deep breath, he said, "I need to find the kraken. If you all have a way to locate him, I can handle the rest."

"Wait," Ren said, rubbing at his temples as if his mind had just been blown. "Let me get this straight. The kraken is your lost love?"

The room erupted with laughter, and Leif joined in.

"The kraken is in possession of an object that belongs to my lost love," Leif explained. "If I can get that item back..." He paused, wondering just how odd it would be to tell them about his desire to bring someone back from the dead. "...then finding her will be easy."

The room quieted, and Victoria stared hard at Leif. "Attracting the kraken's attention back to the Dome is the last thing I want to do. It's far too dangerous. That being said..." She rubbed her chin thoughtfully. Her face brightened, and she looked at the kitsune. "Ren, what are the chances you've got the gear to locate the shifter remotely?"

Ren perked up. "Do we still have chunks of that nasty tentacle?"

Oberon nodded. "I believe it's been cut up and frozen. The plan is to throw portions into Lake Michigan over time and give the fish a steady, safe source of food."

"Mind if I dig my hands into some of it?" Ren said. "A DNA analysis should allow us to track his location."

"You can have as much as you want," Oberon said. "I'm sure the kitchen staff will approve of having more space back."

Ren looked at Leif. "I'll whip something up for you. Shouldn't take me too long to develop."

"How long are we talking?" Leif asked.

The kitsune shrugged. "A week at most. I should be able to tweak some of the gear we already have that searches for vampires. Leave your number and I'll call you as soon as it's ready."

It was more than Leif could ask for.

"Thank you," he said. "Thank you all so much. This means the world to me, and to my fiancé."

"We'll make sure you find her," Victoria said.

He nodded, unable to say anymore as his emotions gushed within.

"This has been a productive meeting," Oberon said. "Shall

we conclude?"

Everyone surrounding the table concurred.

Leif was the first to his feet. As happy and grateful as he was, he had one last thing to take care of.

"Leaving so soon?" Oberon asked as the simulation fizzled away, leaving the room as nothing but an empty, white box.

"I've got a friend I have to check on," Leif replied. "I'm hoping at my apartment in Chicago."

Oberon reached into his pocket and handed Leif a card. "You're officially a shifter friend, which means you get an official key to the Dome. Ren will get a retinal scan on you as well. Feel free to come and go as you please. But please... don't lose that keycard."

"Don't worry," Leif said, pocketing the card. "Consider it glued to me. Can you point me toward the exit?"

Oberon extended his arm, pointing down one of the hallways under repair. "Follow it all the way down and you'll walk straight to the door that leads to the subway. I must warn you, though, the train cars are lined with copper."

Leif shrugged. "Shouldn't be a problem."

Oberon gave him a confused look.

"Another long story for another time," Leif said with a grin. "Goodbye, Oberon."

"See you around," the gryphon replied.

Leif nodded and walked away, feeling the school director's eyes on him. But Leif got lost in thought, barely noticing as he exited the Dome and entered the train. The shifters were helping him. All the suffering he'd been through at Draven's and Beatrice's hands was going to pay off. He'd do it all again if it meant he'd get this kind of aid.

The ride was smooth, and before he knew it, he was walking off the L and up the stairs that led to the location he'd been assigned to wait for Myreen and her friends to appear. And to his surprise, something was waiting for him.

Rainbow sat on his hind legs, his gray tail whipping back and forth.

"Rainbow!" Leif said, and as he spoke the vampire cat's name, it leaped off the ground and landed precisely in his arms. "My friend, I have some good news."

And he told Rainbow everything, sensing no urgency to hurry back to his apartment, feeling truly free for the first time in a very long time.

CHAPTER 60

Myreen

It was such a nice day. The sky projected at the top of the newly-repaired Dome was sunny and bright, and Myreen could even feel the sun's heat on her skin. The ingenuity of the kitsunes—namely Mr. Suzuki—never ceased to amaze her. Now that she was a vampire—a hybrid—this manufactured sunlight would be the only kind she'd ever get to enjoy again, at least until Kenzie used her magic to make Myreen a daywalker. With her vampirically-enhanced vision, it was almost too bright, but Myreen savored it, nonetheless.

Yes, it was a beautiful day, even if it was for a mass memorial ceremony.

The Dome was more packed with people than she'd ever seen. Parents and relatives—both of students who died in battle and of students who survived—were here en masse. The whole of the shifter military was in attendance as well. All to say their final goodbyes to the friends, teachers, children and soldiers that lost their lives to Draven's forces.

A week had passed since that bloody day, and it felt both like a lifetime and a blink. The glass of the Dome had been repaired, as well as the buildings that had been crushed by the kraken's temper tantrum. Everyone had worked tirelessly to pitch in.

Classes were scheduled to resume after the memorial, but Myreen didn't think life at the Dome would ever be the same. There were so many faces she'd grown accustomed to seeing that she never would again. Delphine's loss would be especially hard to deal with. Myreen had never enjoyed Mer Training or Water Manipulation before, and she was expecting to find both unbearable without Delphine's vibrant attitude to brighten the room. She didn't know the mer they'd found to replace her, but no one could ever really hold a candle to Delphine. She was truly one in a million.

"Are you ready?" Juliet came up beside her in the Grand Hall, looking very natural dressed in all black.

"Yep," Myreen said, even though she would never really be ready to say goodbye. "Where's Nik?"

The two had been inseparable since Nik's resurrection, and they were almost disgusting to watch. Holding hands like they were joined at the fingertips. Kissing in shaded corners every stolen moment. Getting as much of each other as they could before he left the school to take up his new position as assistant to the Head of the Council, Mrs. Dracul. Myreen was happy for them. They were finally getting their happily ever after.

It was just that whenever things were going well for Juliet and Nik, things between Myreen and Kol were rocky, and that had never been more true than it was now.

"He's getting ready with Kol," Juliet said. "They'll be down in a minute."

Myreen nodded, though she did flinch at the mention of Kol.

"He still hasn't talked you, huh?" Juliet guessed with a frown.

Myreen shook her head. Not that there had been much time to talk. Myreen had been kept quite occupied the last few days, tending to injured shifters with the harpies, while Kol attended to whatever duties were required of the Dracul prince upon the death of his father. Whenever they were both in the avian common room at the same time, he didn't avoid her, but he didn't seek her out either, didn't give her any kind of closure from the relationship-ending talk they'd had outside the training room all those days ago.

She hoped he just needed time. He was dealing with so much. She knew from experience how soul-crushing it was to lose a parent. And he'd almost lost his best friend, too. She kept hoping that if she just gave him some space, he'd come around. They'd been through so much together. After escaping Heritage Prep, she really thought they were done with this hot-and-cold nonsense.

She had lost just as much as he had. Kendall. Delphine. And killing her own father had been no easy task, either, despite how much she hated what he'd done to her and her friends. She didn't know if she'd ever truly accept that it was necessary to take a life—his life—for the good of the world.

There was plenty of pain to work through, but it would've been easier if she'd had Kol to lean on, to cry with, to hold her and tell her everything would be okay.

"Don't worry, I know you guys will get through this," Juliet said. "You guys have that epic, star-crossed thing happening. An *Edward and Bella* kind of bond, only in this case I guess you'd be Edward, fangs and all." She laughed, and Myreen gave her a flat look. "Too soon? Okay, but you know what I mean. Just give him time, and he'll figure out that you're still the most kick-butt girl in the world and that he's being stupid."

Myreen shrugged and looked at her feet. "We should get to the field before it's too crowded. It's going to start soon."

"Right."

Juliet looped her arm through Myreen's. Myreen didn't realize how starved for physical touch she was until then, because that little show of solidarity felt so good. They joined the flow of bodies exiting the Grand Hall, heading toward the large field where the memorial was being held.

The crowd congregated around the human-sized, newly-added headstone, inscribed with the names of everyone who died defending the school. Myreen hadn't seen it up close yet, hadn't counted the names carved on it. Part of her didn't want to know exactly how many died for a war she was partially responsible for. It was her father who started it, after all.

Myreen spotted Kenzie standing between the hunter-turned-mao, Wes, and her grandmother and mom. Myreen pushed through the crowd to join her, tugging Juliet along. Despite the black dress that covered her curvy figured, Kenzie was positively glowing. Myreen couldn't think of a time she'd ever seen her selkie best friend looking so deeply content. Maybe it was her acceptance into the school, or the new guy, but she appeared to want for nothing. That made Myreen smile.

"Hey Myreen," Kenzie greeted in a hushed tone when Myreen and Juliet fell in behind them. "Why don't you stop by my room tonight and I'll perform the daywalker spell for you? It would sure be nice not to have wait till nightfall to go out with my bestie." Kenzie winked.

"Sure, thanks Kenz," Myreen whispered back. Kenzie had

been given Myreen's old room in the Mer wing. Since selkies had never been admitted before, finding the prime they best fit into was a bit of an argument for the school leaders. It was ultimately decided that oceanid was the most appropriate, as selkies could shift into a marine creature. It would be strange entering the Mer wing on a regular basis again. At least she didn't have to worry about the mer trio bothering her anymore.

"We'll do the copper spell, too, so you can actually leave the property." She snickered, and Myreen managed a smirk.

Wes whispered something to Kenzie and took her attention off Myreen, so Myreen took that as a chance to look behind her in search of Kol and Nik. The crowd was filling in thicker and thicker, and if Myreen were any shorter, she wouldn't have been able to see over the heads to know that Kol's overstretched figure wasn't among them.

When Nik appeared next to Juliet a few minutes later, sans Kol, Myreen really got confused.

"Where's Kol?" she whispered to Nik.

"Up front with his mom." Nik pointed to the upper left corner closest to the headstone, where there were chairs for the new Council members. There, Myreen saw Mrs. Dracul with her son's unmistakable head of thick, black hair beside her. While it made sense for Kol to be with his mom during the ceremony, Myreen couldn't help but feel, in the hidden corners of her heart, that he was doing it to avoid having to be around her.

The crowd fell silent as Oberon rose from his seat and stood in the open area next to the headstone. "We've gathered here today to remember the colleagues, friends, students and family that fell during the Battle of the Dome." His voice was smooth and steady, yet echoed in the courtyard as if he was using a microphone—probably more of Mr. Suzuki's technology. "We've all lost someone precious—many of us, more than one. But we must remember that they didn't fall in vain. Thanks to their bravery and unbreakable spirits, the battle was won, and the rest of us will live to fight another day..."

Oberon's speech continued, but Myreen's mind was on those she had lost.

Kendall. His spirit was unbreakable. She wouldn't exactly call him brave, but he had a conviction about him that was admirable. He really thought he was doing what was best. She remembered how he allowed Draven to turn him into a hybrid in front of the entire school. He had believed that joining the vampires was the only way to survive, to end the war, just as Draven had promised. He no doubt hoped that others would find hope in his transformation and follow his example. He was only trying to prevent the bloody battle he had foreseen all his life. He made plenty of mistakes, but his heart had been in the right place. And even through Draven's siren command, he fought to resist. For her.

And then there was Delphine. Myreen remembered watching her die. It felt like her mother had died all over again. They would've gotten along well, Delphine and her mom. They were both fiery and strong-willed. And Myreen had failed Delphine so many times—first as a student, and then after her death.

Once Myreen saw how Ms. Heather had been able to resurrect Nik, she snuck off to find Delphine's body to do the same. Ms. Heather was only a harpy, after all, and Myreen was a hybrid chimera, acclaimed by many after her defeat of Draven as the most powerful being in the world. If Ms. Heather could do it, why couldn't she?

Myreen had brought a lighter with her and lit some paper on fire. Then she focused on Delphine's lifeless body as hard as she could, syphoning the light so forcefully that the fire went out. She released so much of her energy that, even though she no longer needed to sleep, she felt like was going to pass out and sleep for days.

But life didn't return to Delphine. Her skin remained cold and blue.

Myreen refused to give up. She relit the paper, her hands shaking and her fingers slipping against the flint of the lighter several times before it ignited. But as she placed her hands on Delphine's chest once more, her energy was so drained that she couldn't even pull light from the dying flames of the mostly-charred cinders.

All the hope that Nik's revival had inspired snuffed out like a candle in a rogue breeze. Myreen broke down and cried. She hadn't been able to save Kendall, and she couldn't save Delphine. She may have killed Draven, but she was the one who was defeated.

"I'd like to offer this moment for anyone who would like to come up and share a fond memory of someone we lost," Oberon invited as Myreen came back to the moment.

For the next hour, mourners stood before the crowd and shared stories of fallen students, teachers, and soldiers. Some of the stories made Myreen laugh and some made her cry. Especially when Princess Reya of Zardani, Kendall's mother, shared a story from Kendall's youth. The princess broke down in tears before she could finish the story and fled from the spotlight. Kendall was her only child. Myreen couldn't help but blame herself for the princess's pain.

Eventually, no one else wished to speak, and Oberon ended the ceremony, welcoming everyone into the Dining Hall for the reception.

Myreen hung back as people funneled toward the main building. She wanted to pay her respects to Kendall's mom.

Once the area had cleared enough for her to navigate through, she found Princess Reya wiping her eyes beside Queen Anali. Both women were stunning beauties, even for mermaids. Princess Reya had the same sandy-brown hair as Kendall, yet it floated about her in a way that reminded Myreen of her mom. She remembered that Kendall had told her the two princesses had met years ago and become friends. Myreen could easily imagine the two young women talking and laughing together.

"Princess Reya?" Myreen began as she approached. "I'm Myreen, Zaia's daughter." She extended a hand of introduction.

Nostalgia sparked in the princess's eyes, for a moment taking her away from her sorrow. "You're Zaia's daughter? Yes, I can see her eyes on your pretty face. How is she? Is she here? I'd love to see her again. It's been ages."

Myreen's heart dropped. "Umm, no, she... passed away a few months ago."

"Oh, dear, I'm so sorry." Her brows pinched in sincere pity. "To lose a mother at such a young age."

Myreen nodded, momentarily choking on the loss of her mother. She swallowed. "I knew your son. Kendall was a good person."

Princess Reya laughed pitifully. "You don't have to sugarcoat it for me, dear. I know all about his desertion. He disgraced the royal family when he sided with the vampires. But... he was still my son." She bit her lip as it puckered in sadness.

"He may have made some bad choices, but I wanted you to know that in the end, he fought bravely. In the end, he made the right decision, and Draven killed him for it. Your son died redeemed."

Princess Reya smiled and really started weeping. "Thank you, Myreen. Someday, when the wound isn't so fresh, I'd love to hear your side of the story. It would be nice for our people to remember him as a hero and not a traitor."

"Of course," Myreen said. "I'd be happy to preserve Kendall's memory in any way I can." She smiled and rubbed the princess's shoulder, then quickly withdrew her hand remembering that she was touching *royalty*.

Queen Anali excused the two of them and they adjourned to the main building with everyone else. Myreen felt a little lost as they left, like she was floating alone in an empty sea.

A tap on her shoulder made her jump. She spun around.

Kol stood in front of her with his hands shoved awkwardly in the pockets of his black dress pants. His expression looked conflicted, yet surprisingly vulnerable.

"Can we talk?" he asked.

Yes, yes, YES!!! she screamed in her head, but shrugged and nodded.

He began to walk toward the garden, gesturing for her to follow him. They strolled leisurely until they reached the pavement between the flower beds, the tension between them tighter than a tightrope. Kol sat down on the nearest bench, and Myreen sat beside him, waiting for whatever he had to say. Was this the end for them, or was it an apology? Or perhaps they would talk about something completely unrelated while they swept their issues under the rug. All three were possible with Kol.

"I've had a lot of time to think about things," he began. "I wanted to apologize for keeping my distance. You've been grieving, as we all have, and I wasn't there to support you. As I *should* have. For that, I'm sorry. I know you and Delphine were close."

Her heart was doing cartwheels of joy in her chest at his

acknowledgement of this, but she didn't let it show. "It's okay. You've been grieving, too. And I'm so sorry about your dad. If I could've..." She stopped. Even if she'd been successful in bringing Delphine back, Kol's dad was beyond recovery. The kraken had *eaten* him. There wasn't a magic on earth that could reverse such a thing.

Kol nodded, looking distant for a moment.

"The real reason I wanted to talk..." he said, after what looked like an internal debate. "Look, I'm *not* okay with you... being a vampire. Hybrid—whatever. I've been raised from birth to hate vampires. You becoming one feels like the cruelest joke the universe could ever play on me."

"I really am sorry, Kol," she pleaded. "It wasn't like I was some Twilight fanatic who desperately wanted to be a vampire. I never wanted that. But I *had* to make that choice, or Draven would've killed me. Killed all of us."

"I know," Kol said, with a tone of acceptance that surprised her. "I said I'm not okay with it, but I'm *trying* to be. I've recently come to see that maybe it doesn't matter *what* you are. Human, shifter, selkie... vampire. What matters is *who* you are, and what you do with *what* you are. And you, Myreen,"—he took her hand into both of his—"you're the sweetest, most driven and willful girl I've ever met. You wear your heart on your sleeve and fight with your entire soul for the things and people you care about. You amaze me over and over again. I love you—the you underneath that pale, flawless vampire skin—more than I ever thought I could love someone. And if you'll still have me, I'll spend every day for the rest of my life giving you the happily ever after you deserve."

Tears dripped off Myreen's chin, and for the first time in a week, they were tears of joy. She laugh-cried as she threw her arms around Kol's neck and pressed salty, wet lips on his. He stiffened at first, then closed his arms around her and kissed her back.

"Just be gentle with me," he said when their lips parted. "You're a lot stronger than me now."

She giggled. "And don't you ever forget it. And if you *ever* go cold on me again, Malkolm Dracul, I swear..."

He chuckled. "I promise to only be warm to you from this day forward." He pulled her close, his warm breath caressing her face, and whispered, "And sometimes, even a little hot." His lips grazed hers teasingly, and her whole body heated from the top of her scalp to the tips of her toes, which curled inside her shoes.

"Sounds good to me," she said breathily against his lips before getting lost in them.

***

"Okay, this is it. The final round of zombie killing that will decide who wins the crown," Brett said as he plopped on the couch, controller in hand.

"My bet's on the sexy mao," Kenzie said from beside Myreen, digging into the bucket of popcorn she made for this event.

"You better believe it," Wes said, perched on the edge of a cushion on the other side of Nik.

"Don't hold your breath," Brett said. "You may be good with a gun in real life, but in the world of video games, I reign supreme."

"Oh? Is that why Kol's record of kills is longer than yours?" Nik retorted with a smirk.

"And you play a lot more than he does," Juliet added.

"Hey, no one asked the peanut gallery," Brett complained. "Prince Dracul, would you hurry up and turn the game on so we can end this debate?"

Kol arched an eyebrow at Brett as he started the system and took his seat next to him.

"Or would it be King Dracul now?" Brett wondered out loud. "Now that your dad is out of the way. Just saying."

"Shut up and play," Kol dismissed, and instantly the thumbs of all the boys were speedily tapping away at their controllers, threatening to crush them into useless plastic.

"Well, it's not exactly the same as going to the movies, but it's fun to watch our guys go head-to-head in something so pointless," Kenzie said, popping a handful of fluffy snack into her mouth.

"And it's really funny to watch them argue over said pointless thing," Myreen said, curling against Kenzie and indulging in the popcorn as well.

"In my opinion, this is way better than a movie," Juliet said. "Because you can't change the outcome of a movie. But I know that if I, say..." She scooped a handful of popcorn out of the bucket. "...throw a popcorn at Brett..." And she threw it so it rained down all over Brett. "...he's gonna lose."

"Hey!" Brett snapped, shaking off the popcorn, and in so doing, blowing himself up with his own grenade. He groaned. "No fair! Nik, your girlfriend cheated!"

"Not my problem," Nik laughed without looking away from the screen. "She does what she wants. It just so happens to work in my favor right now." He stuck his tongue out.

"You know what we need to do?" Kenzie asked. "We need to find Brett a girlfriend. Maybe then he won't play as much."

"Not likely," Brett said as his first-person shooter respawned. "No girl could ever come between me and my video games."

"What about Leya?" Myreen teased. "I've seen the way you look at her."

Brett paused, blushing furiously.

"Careful, Myreen, I think you hit a nerve." Kol flashed her a wink.

"You know what, Brett," Nik said, a giddy look coming over his face. "I *dare* you to ask her out."

Kol and Nik laughed wholeheartedly, and Brett frowned, muttering to himself.

Myreen leaned back on the couch and smiled from ear to ear as she watched the boys—*their* boys—taunt each other. Life hadn't just gone back to normal after the memorial. Somehow, it had gotten even better.

Everything was as it should be. *Finally.* Myreen could wait to see what else life had in store—for all of them.

About the Shifter Academy Authors

This series is the brain child of 5 award-winning and *USA Today* best-selling paranormal romance and urban fantasy authors. For the Siren Prophecy Series, each character was brought to life by a different author. For the remainder of the ongoing Shifter Academy series, a new book will release every six weeks by one or more of the authors, as there are just too many stories to tell in this amazing shifter world. Engage more with the Shifter Academy world at: www.theShifterAcademy.com

Myreen was written by Tricia Barr. Follow Tricia's work here: www.tricia-barr.com

Oberon & Leif were written by Jesse Booth. Follow Jesse's work here: http://www.authorjessebooth.com

Kol was written by Joanna Reeder. Follow Joanna's work here: http://www.joannareeder.com

Kenzie was written by Angel Leya. Follow Angel's work here: http://www.angeleya.com

Juliet was written by Alessandra Jay. Follow Alessandra's work here: http://www.facebook.com/AuthorAlessandraJay/

www.ingramcontent.com/pod-product-compliance
Lightning Source LLC
Chambersburg PA
CBHW071727110726
47908CB00006B/1524